Ernest Hemingway Super Pack

The *Ernest Hemingway Super Pack* is a work of fiction. Names, characters, businesses, organizations, places, events and incidents are either the products of the author's imagination or are used fictitiously. Any resemblance to actual persons, living or dead, events, locales or institutions is entirely coincidental.

Trade Paper Back ISBN: 978-1-5154-6308-5
Hard Cover ISBN: 978-1-5154-6309-2
E-book ISBN: 978-1-5154-6310-8

Ernest Hemingway Super Pack

by Ernest Hemingway

Three Short Stories & Ten Poems
in our time
The Torrents of Spring
The Sun Also Rises
Men Without Women
A Farewell to Arms

Three Short Stories & Ten Poems

Stories

Poems

UP IN MICHIGAN

Jim Gilmore came to Hortons Bay from Canada. He bought the blacksmith shop from old man Horton. Jim was short and dark with big mustaches and big hands. He was a good horseshoer and did not look much like a blacksmith even with his leather apron on. He lived upstairs above the blacksmith shop and took his meals at A. J. Smith's.

Liz Coates worked for Smith's. Mrs. Smith, who was a very large clean woman, said Liz Coates was the neatest girl she'd ever seen. Liz had good legs and always wore clean gingham aprons and Jim noticed that her hair was always neat behind. He liked her face because it was so jolly but he never thought about her.

Liz liked Jim very much. She liked the way he walked over from the shop and often went to the kitchen door to watch for him to start down the road. She liked it about his mustache. She liked it about how white his teeth were when he smiled. She liked it very much that he didn't look like a blacksmith. She liked it how much A. J. Smith and Mrs. Smith liked Jim. One day she found that she liked it the way the hair was black on his arms and how white they were above the tanned line when he washed up in the washbasin outside the house. Liking that made her feel funny.

Hortons Bay, the town, was only five houses on the main road between Boyne City and Charlevoix. There was the general store and post office with a high false front and maybe a wagon hitched out in front, Smith's house, Stroud's house, Fox's house, Horton's house and Van Hoosen's house. The houses were in a big grove of elm trees and the road was very sandy. There was farming country and timber each way up the road. Up the road a ways was the Methodist church and down the road the other direction was the township school. The blacksmith shop was painted red and faced the school.

A steep sandy road ran down the hill to the bay through the timber. From Smith's back door you could look out across the woods that ran down to the lake and across the bay. It was very beautiful in the spring and summer, the sky blue and bright and usually whitecaps on the lake beyond the point from the breeze blowing in from Charlevoix and Lake Michigan. From Smith's back door Liz could see ore barges way out in the lake going toward Boyne City. When she looked at them they didn't seem to be moving at all but if she went in and dried some more dishes and then came out again they would be out of sight beyond the point.

All the time now Liz was thinking about Jim Gilmore. He didn't seem to notice her very much. He talked about the shop to A.J. Smith and about the Republican Party and about James G. Blaine. In the evenings he read The Toledo Blade and the Grand Rapids paper by the lamp in the front room or went out spearing fish in the bay with a jacklight with A.J. Smith. In the fall he and Smith and Charley Wyman took a wagon and tent, grubs, axes, their rifles and two dogs and went on a trip to the pine plains beyond Vanderbilt deer hunting. Liz and Mrs. Smith were cooking for four days for them before they started. Liz wanted to make something special for Jim to take but she didn't finally because she was afraid to ask Mrs. Smith for the eggs and flour and afraid if she bought them Mrs. Smith would catch her cooking. It would have been all right with Mrs. Smith but Liz was afraid.

All the time Jim was gone on the deer hunting trip Liz thought about him. It was awful while he was gone. She couldn't sleep well from thinking about him but she discovered it was fun to think about him too. If she let herself go it was better. The night before they were to come back she didn't sleep at all because it was all mixed up in a dream about not sleeping and really not sleeping. When she saw the wagon coming down the she felt weak and sick sort of inside. She couldn't wait till she saw Jim and it seemed as though everything would be all right when he came. The wagon stopped outside under the big elm and Mrs. Smith and Liz went out. All the men had beards and there were three deer in the back of the wagon, their thin legs sticking stiff over the edge of the wagon box. Mrs. Smith kissed Alonzo and he hugged her. Jim said "Hello, Liz," and grinned. Liz hadn't known just what would happen when Jim got back but she was sure it would be something. Nothing had happened. The men were just home, that was all. Jim pulled the burlap sacks off the deer and Liz looked at them. One was a big buck. It was stiff and hard to lift out of the wagon.

"Did you shoot it, Jim?" Liz asked.

"Yeah. Ain't it a beauty?" Jim got it onto his back to carry it to the smokehouse.

That night Charley Wyman stayed to supper at Smith's. It was too late to get back to Charlevoix. The men washed up and waited in the front room for supper.

"Ain't there something left in that crock, Jimmy?" A.J. Smith asked, and Jim went out to the wagon in the barn and fetched in the jug of whiskey the men had taken hunting with them. It was a four gallon jug and there was quite a little slopped back and forth in the bottom. Jim took a long pull on his way back to the house. It was hard to lift such a big jug up to drink out of it. Some of the whiskey ran down on his shirt front. The two men smiled when Jim came in with the jug. A.J. Smith sent for glasses and Liz brought them. A.J. poured out three big shots.

"Well, here's looking at you, A.J.," said Charley Wyman.

"That damn big buck, Jimmy," said A.J.

"Here's all the ones we missed, A.J.," said Jim, and downed his liquor.

"Tastes good to a man."

"Nothing like it this time of year for what ails you."

"How about another, boys?"

"Here's how, A.J."

"Down the creek, boys."

"Here's to next year."

Jim began to feel great. He loved the taste and the feel of whiskey. He was glad to be back to a comfortable bed and warm food and the shop. He had another drink. The men came in to supper feeling hilarious but acting very respectable. Liz sat at the table after she put on the food and ate with the family. It was a good dinner. The men ate seriously. After supper they went into the front room again and Liz cleaned up with Mrs. Smith. Then Mrs. Smith went upstairs and pretty soon Smith came out and went upstairs too. Jim and Charley were still in the front room. Liz was sitting in the kitchen next to the stove pretending to read a book and thinking about Jim. She didn't want to go to bed yet because she knew Jim would be coming out and she wanted to see him as he went out so she could take the way he looked up to bed with her.

She was thinking about him hard and then Jim came out. His eyes were shining and his hair was a little rumpled. Liz looked down at her book. Jim came over back of her chair and stood there and she could feel him breathing and then he put his arms around her. Her breasts felt plump and firm and the nipples were erect under his hands. Liz was terribly frightened, no one had ever touched her, but she thought, "He's come to me finally. He's really come."

She held herself stiff because she was so frightened and did not know anything else to do and then Jim held her tight against the chair and kissed her. It was such a sharp, aching, hurting feeling that she thought she couldn't stand it. She felt Jim right through the back of the chair and she couldn't stand it and then something clicked inside of her and the feeling was warmer and softer. Jim held her tight hard against the chair and she wanted it now and Jim whispered, "Come on for a walk."

Liz took her coat off the peg on the kitchen wall and they went out the door. Jim had his arm around her and every little way they stopped and pressed against each other and Jim kissed her. There was no moon and they walked ankle-deep in the sandy road through the trees down to the dock and the warehouse on the bay. The water was lapping in the piles and the point was dark across the bay. It was cold but Liz was hot all over from being with Jim. They sat down in the shelter of the warehouse and Jim pulled Liz close to him. She was frightened. One of Jim's hands went inside her dress and stroked over her breast and the other hand was in her lap. She was very frightened and didn't know how he was going to go about things but she snuggled close to him. Then the hand that felt so big in her lap went away and was on her leg and started to move up it.

"Don't, Jim," Liz said. Jim slid the hand further up.

"You musn't, Jim. You musn't." Neither Jim nor Jim's big hand paid any attention to her.

The boards were hard. Jim had her dress up and was trying to do something to her. She was frightened but she wanted it. She had to have it but it frightened her.

"You musn't do it, Jim. You musn't."

"I got to. I'm going to. You know we got to."

"No we haven't, Jim. We ain't got to. Oh, it isn't right. Oh, it's so big and it hurts so. You can't. Oh, Jim. Jim. Oh."

The hemlock planks of the dock were hard and splintery and cold and Jim was heavy on her and he had hurt her. Liz pushed him, she was so uncomfortable and cramped. Jim was asleep. He wouldn't move. She worked out from under him and sat up and straightened her skirt and coat and tried to do something with her hair. Jim was sleeping with his mouth a little open. Liz leaned over and kissed him on the cheek. He was still asleep. She lifted his head a little and shook it. He rolled his head over and swallowed. Liz started to cry. She walked over to the edge of the dock and looked down to the water. There was a mist coming up from the bay. She was cold and miserable and everything felt gone. She walked back to where Jim was lying and shook him once more to make sure. She was crying.

"Jim," she said. "Jim. Please, Jim."

Jim stirred and curled a little tighter. Liz took off her coat and leaned over and covered him with it. She tucked it around him neatly and carefully. Then she walked across the dock and up the steep sandy road to go to bed. A cold mist was coming up through the woods from the bay.

OUT OF SEASON

On the four lira he had earned by spading the hotel garden he got quite drunk. He saw the young gentleman coming down the path and spoke to him mysteriously. The young gentleman said he had not eaten but would be ready to go as soon as lunch was finished. Forty minutes or an hour.

At the cantina near the bridge they trusted him for three more grappas because he was so confident and mysterious about his job for the afternoon. It was a windy day with the sun coming out from behind clouds and then going under in sprinkles of rain. A wonderful day for trout fishing.

The young gentleman came out of the hotel and asked him about the rods. Should his wife come behind with the rods? Yes, said Peduzzi, let her follow us. The young gentleman went back into the hotel and spoke to his wife. He and Peduzzi started down the road. The young gentleman had a musette over his shoulder. Peduzzi saw the wife, who looked as young as the young gentleman, and was wearing mountain boots and a blue beret, start out to follow them down the road, carrying the fishing rods, unjointed, one in each hand. Peduzzi didn't like her to be way back there. Signorina, he called, winking at the young gentleman, come up here and walk with us. Signora, come up here. Let us all walk together. Peduzzi wanted them all three to walk down the street of Cortina together.

The wife stayed behind, following rather sullenly. Signorina, Peduzzi called tenderly, come up here with us. The young gentleman looked back and shouted something. The wife stopped lagging behind and walked up.

Everyone they met walking through the main street of the town Peduzzi greeted elaborately. Buon' dì, Arturo' Tipping his hat. The bank clerk stared at him from the door of the Fascist café. Groups of three and four people standing in front of the shops stared at the three. The workmen in their stone-powdered jackets working on the foundations of the new hotel looked up as they passed. Nobody spoke or gave any sign to them except the town beggar, lean and old, with a spittle-thickened beard, who lifted his hat as they passed.

Peduzzi stopped in front of a store with the window full of bottles and brought his empty grappa bottle from an inside pocket of his old military coat. A little to drink, some marsala for the Signora, something, something to drink. He gestured with the bottle. It was a wonderful day. Marsala, you like marsala, Signorina? A little marsala?

The wife stood sullenly. You'll have to play up to this, she said. I can't understand a word he says. He's drunk, isn't he?

The young gentleman appeared not to hear Peduzzi. He was thinking, what in hell makes him say marsala? That's what Max Beerbohm drinks.

Geld, Peduzzi said finally, taking hold of the young gentleman's sleeve. Lire. He smiled, reluctant to press the subject but needing to bring the young gentleman into action.

The young gentleman took out his pocket book and gave him a ten lire note. Peduzzi went up the steps to the door of the Specialty of Domestic and Foreign Wines shop. It was locked.

It is closed until two, someone passing in the street said scornfully. Peduzzi came down the steps. He felt hurt. Never mind, he said, we can get it at the Concordia.

They walked down the road to the Concordia three abreast. On the porch of the Concordia, where the rusty bobsleds were stacked the young gentleman said, Was wollen Sie? Peduzzi handed him the ten lira note folded over and over. Nothing, he said, Anything. He was embarrassed. Marsala, maybe. I don't know. Marsala?

The door of the Concordia shut on the young gentleman and the wife. Three marsalas, said the y. g. to the girl behind the pastry counter. Two, you mean? she asked. No, he said, one for avecchio. Oh, she said, a vecchio, and laughed, getting down the bottle. She poured out the three muddy looking drinks into three glasses. The wife was sitting at a table under the line of newspapers on sticks. The y. g. put one of the marsalas in front of her. You might as well drink it, he said, maybe it'll make you feel better. She sat and looked at the glass. The y. g. went outside the door with a glass for Peduzzi but could not see him.

I don't know where he is, he said, coming back into the pastry room carrying the glass.

He wanted a quart of it, said the wife.

How much is a quarter litre? the y. g. asked the girl.

Of the bianco? One lira.

No, of the marsala. Put these two in, too, he said, giving her his own glass and the one poured for Peduzzi. She filled the quarter litre wine measure with a funnel. A bottle to carry it, said the y. g.

She went to hunt for a bottle. It all amused her.

I'm sorry you feel so rotten, Tiny, he said. I'm sorry I talked the way I did at lunch. We were both getting at the same thing from different angles.

It doesn't make any difference, she said. None of it makes any difference.

Are you too cold? he asked. I wish you'd worn another sweater.

I've got on three sweaters.

The girl came in with a very slim brown bottle and poured the marsala into it. The y. g. paid five lire more. They went out the door. The girl was amused. Peduzzi was walking up and down at the other end out of the wind and holding the rods.

Come on he said, I will carry the rods. What difference does it make if anybody sees them? No one will trouble us. No one will make any trouble for me in Cortina. I know them at the municipio. I have been a soldier. Everybody in this town likes me. I sell frogs. What if it is forbidden to fish? Not a thing. Nothing. No trouble. Big trout, I tell you. Lots of them.

They were walking down the hill toward the river. The town was in back of them. The sun had gone under and it was sprinkling rain. There, said Peduzzi, pointing to a girl in the doorway of a house they passed. My daughter.

His doctor, the wife said, has he got to show us his doctor?

He said his daughter, said the y. g.

The girl went into the house as Peduzzi pointed.

he girl went into the house as Peduzzi pointed.

They walked down the hill across the fields and then turned to follow the river bank. Peduzzi talked rapidly with much winking and knowingness. As they walked three abreast the wife caught his breath across the wind. Once he nudged her in the ribs. Part of the time he talked in D'Ampezzo dialect and and sometimes in Tyroler German dialect. He could not make out which the young gentleman and his wife understood the best so he was being bilingual. But as the young gentleman said Ja Ja Peduzzi decided to talk altogether in Tyroler. The young gentleman and the wife understood nothing.

Everybody in the town saw us going through with these rods. We're probably being followed by the game police now. I wish we weren't in on this damn thing. This damned old fool is so drunk, too.

Of course you haven't got the guts to just go back, said the wife. Of course you have to go on.

Why don't you go back? Go on back Tiny.

I'm going to stay with you. If you go to jail we might as well both go.

They turned sharp down the bank and Peduzzi stood his coat blowing in the wind gesturing at the river. It was brown and muddy. Off on the right there was a dump heap.

Say it to me in Italian, said the young gentleman.

Un' mezz'ora. Piu d'un' mezz'ora.

He says it's at least a half hour more. Go on back. Tiny. You're cold in this wind anyway. It's a rotten day and we aren't going to have any fun, anyway.

All right, she said, and climbed up the grassy bank.

Peduzzi was down at the river and did not notice her till she was almost out of sight over the crest. Frau! he shouted. Frau! Fraulein! You're not going? She went on over the crest of the hill.

She's gone! said Peduzzi. It shocked him.

He took off the rubber bands that held the rod segments together and commenced to joint up one of the rods.

But you said it was half an hour further.

Oh, yes. It is good half an hour down. It is good here, too.

Really?

Of course. It is good here and good there too.

The y.g sat down on the bank and jointed up a rod, put on the reel and threaded the line through the guides. He felt uncomfortable and afraid that any minute a gamekeeper or a posse of citizens would come over the bank from the town. He could see the houses of the town and the campanile over the edge of the hill. He opened his leader box. Peduzzi leaned over and dug his flat, hard thumb and forefinger in and tangled the moistened leaders.

Have you some lead?

No.

You must have some lead. Peduzzi was excited. You must have piombo. Piombo. A little piombo. Just here. Just above the hook or your bait will float on the water. You must have it. Just a little piombo.

Have you got some?

No. He looked through his pockets desperately. Sifting through the cloth dirt in the linings of his inside military pockets. I haven't any. We must have piombo.

We can't fish then, said the y. g. and unjointed the rod, reeling the line back through the guides. We'll get some piombo and fish tomorrow.

But listen caro, you must have piombo. The line will lie flat on the water.

Peduzzi's day was going to pieces before his eyes. You must have piombo. A little is enough. Your stuff is all clean and new but you have no lead. I would have brought some. You said you had everything.

The y. g. looked at the stream discolored by the melting snow. I know, he said, we'll get some piombo and fish tomorrow.

At what hour in the morning? Tell me that.

At seven.

The sun came out. It was warm and pleasant. The young gentleman felt relieved. He was no longer breaking the law. Sitting on the bank he took the bottle of marsala out of his pocket and passed it to Peduzzi. Peduzzi passed it back. The y. g. took a drink of it and passed it to Peduzzi again. Peduzzi passed it back again. Drink, he said, drink. It's your marsala. After another short drink the y. g. handed the bottle over. Peduzzi had been watching it closely. He took the bottle very hurriedly and tipped it up. The gray hairs in the folds of his neck oscillated as he drank, his eyes fixed on the end of the narrow brown bottle. He drank it all. The sun shone while he drank. It was wonderful. This was a great day after all. A wonderful day.

Senta caro! In the morning at seven. He had called the young gentleman caro several times and nothing had happened. It was good marsala. His eyes glistened. Days like this stretched out ahead. It would begin at seven in the morning.

They started to walk up the hill toward the town. The young gentleman went on ahead. He was quite a way up the hill. Peduzzi called to him.

Listen caro can you let me take five lira for a favor?

For today? asked the young gentleman frowning.

No, not today. Give it to me today for tomorrow. I will provide everything for tomorrow. Pane, salami, formaggio, good stuff for all of us. You and I and the signora. Bait for fishing, minnows, not worms only. Perhaps I can get some marsala. All for five lira. Five lira for a favor.

The young gentleman looked through his pocketbook and took out a two-lira note and two ones.

Thank you caro. Thank you, said Peduzzi, in the tone of one member of the Carleton Club accepting the Morning Post from another. This was living. He was through with the hotel garden, breaking up frozen manure with a dung fork. Life was opening out.

Until seven o'clock then caro he said, slapping the y. g. on the back. Promptly at seven.

I may not be going, said the young gentleman putting his purse back in his pocket.

What, said Peduzzi, I will have minnows Signor. Salami, everything. You and I and the Signora. The three of us.

I may not be going, said the y. g., very probably not. I will leave word with the padrone at the hotel office.

MY OLD MAN

I guess looking at it now my old man was cut out for a fat guy, one of those regular little roly fat guys you see around, but he sure never got that way, except a little toward the last, and then it wasn't his fault, he was riding over the jumps only and he could afford to carry plenty of weight then. I remember the way he'd pull on a rubber shirt over a couple of jerseys and a big sweat shirt over that, and get me to run with him in the forenoon in the hot sun. He'd have, maybe, taken a trial trip with one of Razzo's skins early in the morning after just getting in from Torino at four o'clock in the morning and beating it out to the stables in a cab and then with the dew all over everything and the sun just starting to get going, I'd help him pull off his boots and he'd get into a pair of sneakers and all these sweaters and we'd start out.

"Come on, kid," he'd say, stepping up and down on his toes in front of the jock's dressing room, "let's get moving".

Then we'd start off jogging around the infield once maybe with him ahead running nice and then turn out the gate and along one of those roads with all the trees along both sides of them that run out from San Siro. I'd go ahead of him when we hit the road and I could run pretty stout and I'd look around and he'd be jogging easy just behind me and after a little while I'd look around again and he'd begun to sweat. Sweating heavy and he'd just he clogging it along with his eyes on my back, but when he'd catch me looking at him he'd grin and say, "Sweating plenty?" When my old man grinned nobody could help but grin too. We'd keep right on running out toward the mountains and then my old man would yell "Hey Joe!" and I'd look back and he'd he sitting under a tree with a towel he'd had around his waist wrapped around his neck.

I'd come back and sit down beside him and he'd pull a rope out of his pocket and start skipping rope out in the sun with the sweat pouring off his face and him skipping rope out in the white dust with the rope going cloppetty cloppety clop clop clop and the sun hotter and him working harder up and down a patch of the road. Say it was a treat to see my old man skip rope too. He could whirr it fast or lop it slow and fancy. Say you ought to have seen wops look at us sometimes when they'd come by going into town walking along with big white steers hauling the cart. They sure looked as though they thought the old man was nuts. He'd start the rope whirring till they'd stop dead still and watch him, then give the steers a cluck and a poke with the goad and get going again.

When I'd sit watching him working out in the hot sun I sure felt fond of him. He sure was fun and he done his work so hard and he'd finish up with a regular whirring that'd drive the sweat out on his face like water and then sling the rope at the tree and come over and sit down with me and lean hack against the tree with the towel and a sweater wrapped around his neck.

"Sure is hell keeping it down, Joe" he'd say and lean back and shut his eyes and breath long and deep, "it aint like when you're a kid". Then he'd get up before he started to cool and we'd jog along back to the stables. That's the way it was keeping down to weight. He was worried all the time. Most jocks can just about ride off all they want to. A jock loses about a kilo every time he rides, but my old man was sort of dried out and he couldn't keep down his kilos without all that running.

I remember once at San Siro, Regoli, a little wop that was riding for Buzoni came out across the paddock going to the bar for something cool and flicking his bouts with his whip, after he'd just weighed in and my old man had just weighed in too and came out with the saddle under his arm looking red faced and tired and too big for his silks and he stood there looking at young Regoli standing up to the outdoors bar cool and kid looking and I says, "What's the matter Dad?" cause I thought maybe Regoli had bumped him or something and he just looked at Regoli and said, "Oh to hell with it" and went on to the dressing room.

Well it would have been all right maybe if we'd stayed in Milan and ridden at Milan and Torino cause if there ever were any easy courses its those two. "Pianola, Joe". My old man said when he dismounted in the winning stall after what the wops thought was a hell of a steeplechase. I asked him once, "This course rides its-self. It's the pace you're going at that makes riding the jumps dangerous Joe. We aint going any pace here, and they aint any really bad jumps either. But it's the pace always—not the jumps that makes the trouble".

San Siro was the swellest course I'd ever seen but the old man said it was a dog's life. Going back and forth between Mirafiore and San Siro and riding just about every day in the week with a train ride every other night.

I was nuts about the horses too. There's something about it when they come out and go up the track to the post. Sort of dancy and tight looking with the jock keeping a tight hold on them and maybe easing off a little and letting them run a little going up. Then once they were at the barrier it got me worse than anything. Especially at San Siro with that big green infield and the mountains way off and the fat wop starter with his big whip and the jocks fiddling them around and then the barrier snapping up and that bell going off and them all getting off in a bunch and then commencing to string out. You know the way a bunch of skins gets off. If you're up in the stand with a pair of glasses all you see is them plunging off and then that bell goes off and it seems like it rings for a thousand years and then they come sweeping round the turn. There wasn't ever anything like it for me.

But my old man said one day in the dressing room when he was getting into his street clothes, "None of these things are horses Joe. They'd kill that bunch of skates for their hides and hoofs up at Paris". That was the day he'd won the Premio Commercio with Lantorna shooting her out of the field the last hundred meters like pulling a cork out of a bottle.

It was right after the Premio Commercio that we pulled out and left Italy. My old man and Holbrook and a fat wop in a straw hat that kept wiping his face with a handkerchief were having an argument at a table in the Galleria. They were all talking French and the two of them were after my old man about something.

Finally he didn't say anything any more but just sat there and looked at Holbrook and the two of them kept after him, first one talking and then the other and the fat wop always butting in on Holbrook.

"You go out and buy me a Sportsman, will you Joe?" my old man said and handed me a couple of soldi without looking away from Holbrook.

So I went out of the Galleria and walked over to in front of the Scala and bought a paper and came back and stood a little way away because I didn't want to butt in and my old man was sitting back in his chair looking down at his coffee and fooling with a spoon and Holbrook and the big wop were standing and the big wop was wiping his face and shaking his head. And I came up and my old man acted just as though the two of them weren't standing there and said, "Want an ice Joe?" Holbrook looked down at my old man and said slow and careful, "You son of a bitch" and he and the fat wop went out through the tables.

My old man sat there and sort of smiled at me but his face was white and he looked sick as hell and I was scared and felt sick inside because I knew something had happened and I didn't see how anybody could call my old man a son of a bitch and get away with it. My old man opened up the Sportsman and studied the handicaps for a while and then he said, "You got to take a lot of things in this world

Joe". And three days later we left Milan for good on the Turin train for Paris after an auction sale out in front of Turner's stables of everything we couldn't get into a trunk and a suit case.

We got into Paris early in the morning in a long dirty station the old man told me was the Gare de Lyon. Paris was an awful big town after Milan. Seems like in Milan everybody is going somewhere and all the trams run somewhere and there aint any sort of a mixup, but Paris is all balled up and they never do straighten it out. I got to like it though, part of it anyway, and say it's got the best race courses in the world. Seems as though that were the thing that keeps it all going and about the only thing you can figure on is that every day the buses will be going out to whatever track they're running at going right out through everything to the track. I never really got to know Paris well because I just came in about once or twice a week with the old man from Maisons and he always sat at the Cafe de la Paix on the Opera side with the rest of the gang from Maisons and I guess that's one of the busiest parts of the town. But say it is funny that a big town like Paris wouldn't have a Galleria isn't it?

Well, we went out to live at Maisons-Lafitte, where just about everybody lives except the gang at Chantilly, with a Mrs. Meyers that runs a boarding house. Maisons is about the swellest place to live I've ever seen in all my life. The town aint so much, but there's a lake and a swell forest that we used to go off humming in all day, a couple of us kids, and my old man made me a sling shot and we got a lot of things with it but the best one was a magpie. Young Dick Atkinson shot a rabbit with it one day and we put it under a tree and were all sitting around and Dick had some cigarettes and all of a sudden the rabbit jumped up and beat it into the brush and we chased it but we couldn't find it. Gee we had fun at Maisons. Mrs. Meyers used to give me lunch in the morning and I'd he gone all day. I learned to talk French quick. It's an easy language.

As soon as we got to Maisons my old man wrote to Milan for his license and he was pretty worried till it came. He used to sit around the Cafe de Paris in Maisons with the gang there, there were lots of guys he'd known when he rode up at Paris before the war lived at Maisons, and there's a lot of time to sit around because the work around a racing stable for the jocks that is, is all cleaned up by nine o'clock in the morning. They take the first batch of skins out to gallop them at 5.30 in the morning and they work the second lot at 8 o'clock. That means getting up early all right and going to bed early too. If a jock's riding for somebody too he can't go boozing around because the trainer always has an eye on him if he's a kid and if he aint t kid he's always got an eye on himself. So mostly if a jock aint working he sits around the Café de Paris with the gang and they can all sit around about two or three hours in front of some drink like a vermouth and seltz and they talk and tell stories and shoot pool and it's sort of like a club or the Galleria in Milan. Only it aint really like the Galleria because there everybody is going by all the time and there's everybody around at the tables.

Well my old man got his license all right. They sent it through to him without a word and he rode a couple of times. Amiens, up country and that sort of thing, but he didn't seem to get any engagement. Everybody liked him and whenever I'd come in to the Café in the forenoon I'd find somebody drinking with him because my old man wasn't tight like most of these jockey's that have got the first dollar they made riding at the World's Fair in St. Louis in Nineteen ought four. That's what my old man would say when he'd kid George Burns. But it seemed like everybody steered clear of giving my old man any mounts.

We went out to wherever they were running every clay with the car from Maisons and that was the most fun of all. I was glad when the horses came back from Deauville and the summer. Even though it meant no more humming in the woods, cause then we'd ride to Enghien or Tremblay or St. Cloud and watch them from the trainers' and jockeys' stand. I sure learned about racing from going out with that gang and the fun of it was going every day.

I remember once out at St. Cloud. It was a big two hundred thousand franc race with seven entries and Kzar a big favourite. I went around to the paddock to see the horses with my old man and you never saw such horses. This Kzar is a great big yellow horse that looks like just nothing but run. I never saw such a horse. He was being led around the paddock with his head down and when he went by me I felt all hollow inside he was so beautiful. There never was such a wonderful, lean, running built horse. And he went around the paddock putting his feet just so and quiet and careful and moving easy like he knew just what he had to do and not jerking and standing up on his legs and getting wild eyed like you see these selling platers with a shot of dope in them. The crowd was so thick I couldn't see him again except just his legs going by and some yellow and my old man started out through the crowd and I followed him over to the jock's dressing room hack in the trees and there was a big crowd around there too but the man at the door in a derby nodded to my old man and we got in and everybody was sitting around and getting dressed and pulling shirts over their heads and pulling boots on and it all smelled hot and sweaty and linimenty and outside was the crowd looking in.

The old man went over and sat down beside George Gardner that was getting into his pants and said, "What`s the dope George?" just in an ordinary tone of voice cause there aint any use him feeling around because George either can tell him or he can't tell him.

"He won't win" George says very low, leaning over and buttoning the bottoms of his pants.

"Who will" my old man says leaning over close so nobody can hear.

"Kircubbin" George says, "And if he does, save me a couple of tickets".

My old man says something in a regular voice to George and George says, "Don't ever bet on anything I tell you" kidding like and we beat it out and through all the crowd that was looking in over to the 100 franc mutuel machine. But I knew something big was up because George is Kzar's jockey. On the way he gets one of the yellow odds sheets with the starting prices on and Kzar is only paying 5 for 10, Cefisidote is next at 3 to 1 and fifth down the list this Kircubbin at 8 to 1. My old man bets five thousand on Kircubbin to win and puts on a thousand to place and we went around back of the grandstand to go up the stairs and get a place to watch the race.

We were jammed in tight and first a man in a long coat with a grey tall hat and a whip folded up in his hand came out and then one after another the horses, with the jocks up and a stable boy holding the bridle on each side and walking along, followed the old guy. That big yellow horse Kzar came first. He didn't look so big when you first looked at him until you saw the length of his legs and the whole way he's built and the way he moves. Gosh I never saw such a horse. George Gardner was riding him and they moved along slow, back of the old guy in the gray tall hat that walked along like he was the ring master in a circus. Back of Kzar, moving along smooth and yellow in the sun, was a good looking black with a nice head with Tommy Archibald riding him and after the black was a string of five more horses all moving along slow in a procession past the grandstand and the pesage. My old man said the black was Kircubbin and I took a good look at him and he was a nice looking horse all right but nothing like Kzar.

Everybody cheered Kzar when he went by and he sure was one swell looking horse. The procession of them went around on the other side past the pelouse and then back up to the near end of the course and the circus master had the stable boys turn them loose one after another so they could gallop by the stands on their way up to the post and let everybody have a good look at them. They weren't at the post hardly any time at all when the gong started and you could see them way off across the infield all in a bunch starting on the first swing like a lot of little toy horses. I was watching them through the glasses and Kzar was running well back with one of the bays making the pace. They swept down and around and came pounding past and Kzar was way back when they passed us and this Kircubbin horse in front and going smooth. Gee it's awful when they go by you and then you have to watch them go farther away and get smaller and smaller and then all bunched up on the turns and then come around towards into the stretch and you feel like swearing and goddaming worse and worse. Finally they made the last turn and came into the straightaway with this Kircubbin horse way out in front. Everybody was looking funny and saying "Kzar" in sort of a sick way and they pounding nearer down the stretch, and then something came out of the pack right into my glasses like a horse-headed yellow streak and everybody began to yell "Kzar" as though they were crazy. Kzar came on faster than I'd ever seen anything in my life and pulled up on Kircubbin that was going fast as any black horse could go with the jock flogging hell out of him with the gad and they were right dead neck and neck for a second but Kzar seemed going about twice as fast with those great jumps and that head out–but it was while they were neck and neck that they passed the winning post and when the numbers went up in the slots the first one was 2 and that meant Kircubbin had won.

I felt all trembly and funny inside, and then we were all jammed in with the people going down stairs to stand in front of the board where they'd post what Kircubbin paid. Honest watching the race I'd forgot how much my old man had bet on Kircubbin. I'd wanted Kzar to win so damned had. But now it was all over it was swell to know we had the winner.

"Wasn't it a swell race Dad?" I said to him.

He looked at me sort of funny with his derby on the back of his head, "George Gardner's a swell jockey all right", he said, "It sure took a great jock to keep that Kzar horse from winning".

Of course I knew it was funny all the time. But my old man saying that right out like that sure took the kick all out of it for me and I didn't get the real kick back again ever, even when they posted the numbers up on the board and the hell rang to pay off and we saw that Kircubbin paid 67.50 for 10. All around people were saying "Poor Kzar. Poor Kzar!" And I thought, I wish I were a jockey and could have rode him instead of that son of a bitch. And that was funny, thinking of George Gardner as a son of a bitch because I'd always liked him and besides he'd given us the winner, but I guess that's what he is all right.

My old man had a big lot of money after that race and he took to coming into Paris oftener. If they raced at Tremblay he'd have them drop him in town on their way hack to Maisons and he and I'd sit out in front of the Café de la Paix and watch the people go by. It's funny sitting there. There's streams of people going by and all sorts of guys come up and want to sell you things and I loved to sit there with my old man. That was when we'd have the most fun. Guys would come by selling funny rabbits that jumped if you squeezed a bulb and they'd come up to us and my old man would kid with them. He could talk French just like English and all those kind of guys knew him cause you can always tell a jockey and then we always sat at the same table and they got used to seeing us there. There were guys selling matrimonial papers and girls selling rubber eggs that when you squeezed them a rooster came out of them and one old wormy looking guy that went by with post cards of Paris showing them to everybody, and of course nobody ever bought any and then he would come back and show the under side of the pack and they would all be smutty post cards and lots of people would dig down and buy them.

Gee I remember the funny people that used to go by. Girls around supper time looking for somebody to take them out to eat and they'd speak to my old man and he'd make some joke at them in French and they'd pat me on the head and go on. Once there was an American woman sitting with her kid daughter at the next table to us and they were both eating ices and I kept looking at the girl and she was awfully good looking and I smiled at her and she smiled at me but that was all that ever came of it because I looked for her mother and her every day and I made up ways that I was going to speak to her and I wondered if I get to know her if her mother would let me take her out to Auteuil or Tremblay but I never saw either of them again. Anyway I guess it wouldn't have been any good anyway because looking back on it I remember the way I thought out would be best to speak to her was to say, "Pardon me, but perhaps I can give you a winner at Enghien today?" and after all maybe she would have thought I was a tout instead of really trying to give her a winner.

We'd sit at the Café de la Paix, my old man and me, and we had a big drag with the waiter because my old man drank whisky and it cost five francs and that meant a good tip when the saucers were counted up. My old man was drinking more than I'd ever seen him, but he wasn't riding at all now and besides he said that whiskey kept his weight down. But I noticed he was putting it on all right just the same. He'd busted away from his old gang out at Maisons and seemed to like just sitting around on the boulevard with me. But he was dropping money every day at the track. He'd feel sort of doleful after the last race, if he'd lost on the day, until we'd get to our table and he'd have his first whiskey and then he'd be fine.

He'd be reading the Paris-Sport and he'd look over at me and say, "Where's your girl Joe?" to kid me on account I had told him about the girl that day at the next table. And I'd get red but I liked being kidded about her. It gave me a good feeling. "Keep your eye peeled for her Joe." he'd say, "She'll be back."

He'd ask me questions about things and some of the things I'd say he'd laugh. And then he'd get started talking about things. About riding down in Egypt, or at St. Moritz on the ice before my mother died, and about during the war when they had regular races down in the south of France without any purses, or betting or crowd or anything just to keep the breed up. Regular races with the jocks riding hell out of the horses. Gee I could listen to my old man talk by the hour, especially when he'd had a couple or so of drinks. He'd tell me about when he was a boy in Kentucky and going soon hunting and the old days in the states before everything went on the bum there. And he'd say, "Joe, when we've get a decent stake, you're going back there to the States and go to school."

"What've I get to go back there to go to school for when everything's on the bum there?" I'd ask him.

"That's different." he'd say and get the waiter over and pay the pile of saucers and we'd get a taxi to the Gare St. Lazare and get on the train out to Maisons.

One day at Auteuil after a selling steeplechase my old man bought in the winner for 30.000 francs. He had to bid a little to get him but the stable let the horse go finally and my old man had his permit and his colors in a week. Gee I felt proud when my old man was an owner. He fixed it up for stable space with Charles Drake and cut out coming in to Paris and started his running and sweating out again and him and I were the whole stable gang. Our horse's name was Gillford, he was Irish bred and a nice sweet jumper. My old man figured that training him and riding him himself he was a good investment. I was proud of everything and I thought Gillford was as good a horse as Kzar. He was a good solid jumper a bay, with plenty of speed on the flat if you asked him for it and he was a nice looking horse too.

Gee I was fond of him. The first time he started with my old man up he finished third in a 2.500 meter hurdle race and when my old man got off him, all sweating and happy in the place stall and went in to weigh I felt as proud of him as though it was the first race he'd ever placed in. You see when a guy aint been riding for a long time you can't make yourself really believe that he has ever rode. The whole thing was different now cause down in Milan even big races never seemed to make any difference to my old man, if he won he wasn't ever excited or anything, and now it was so I couldn't hardly sleep the night before a race and I knew my old man was excited too even if he didn't show it. Riding for yourself makes an awful difference.

Second time Gillford and my old man started was a rainy Sunday at Auteuil in the Prix du Marat, a 4.500 meter steeplechase. As soon as he'd gone out I beat it up in the stand with the new glasses my old man had bought for me to watch them. They started way over at the far end of the course and there was some trouble at the barrier. Something with goggle blinders on was making a great fuss and roaring around and busted the barrier once but I could see my old man in our black jacket with a white cross and a black cap sitting up on Gillford and patting him with his hand. Then they were off in a jump and out of sight behind the trees and the gong going for dear life and the pari mutuel wickets rattling down. Gosh I was so excited I was afraid to look at them but I fixed the glasses on the place where they would come out back of the trees and then out they came with the old black jacket going third and they all sailing over the jump like birds. Then they went out of sight again and then they came pounding out and down the hill and all going nice and sweet and easy and taking the fence smooth in a bunch and moving away from us all solid. Looked as though you could walk across on their backs they were all so hunched and going so smooth, Then they bellied over the big double Bullfinch and something came down. I couldn't see who it was but in a minute the horse was up an galloping free and the field, all bunched still, sweeping around the long left turn into the straightaway. They jumped the stone wall and came jammed down the stretch toward the big water jump right in front of the stands. I saw them coming and hollered at my old man as he went by and he was leading by about a length and riding way out over and light as a monkey and they were racing for the water jump. They took off over the big hedge of the water jump in a pack and then there was a crash and two horses pulled sideways out off it and kept on going and three others were piled up. I couldn't see my old man anywhere. One horse knee-ed himself up and the jock had hold of the bridle and mounted and went slamming on after the place money. The other horse was up and away by himself, jerking his head and galloping with the bridle rein hanging and the jock staggered over to one side of the track against the fence. Then Gillford rolled over to one side off my old man and got up and started to run on three legs with his off hoof dangling and there was my old man lying there on the grass flat out with his face up and blood all over the side of his head. I ran down the stand and bumped into a jam of people and got to the rail and a cop grabbed me and held me and two big stretcher bearers were going out after my old man and around on the other side of the course I saw three horses, strung way out, coming out of the trees and taking the jump.

My old man was dead when they brought him in and while a doctor was listening to his heart with a thing plugged in his ears I heard a shot up the track that meant they'd killed Gillford. I lay down beside my old man when they carried the stretcher into the hospital room and hung onto the stretcher and cried and cried and he looked so white and gone and so awfully dead and I couldn't help feeling that if my old man was dead maybe they didn't need to have shot Gillford. His hoof might have got well. I don't know. I loved my old man so much.

Then a couple of guys came in and one of them patted me on the back and then went over and looked at my old man and then pulled a sheet off the cot and and spread it over him; and the other was telephoning in French for them to send the ambulance to take him out to Maisons. And I couldn't stop crying, crying and choking, sort of, and George Gardner came in and sat down beside me on the floor and put his arm around me and says, "Come on Joe old boy. Get up and we'll go out and wait for the ambulance."

George and I went out to the gate and I was trying to stop bawling and George wiped off my face with his handkerchief and we were standing back a little ways while the crowd was going out of the gate and a couple of guys stopped near us while we were waiting for the crowd to get through the gate and one of them was counting a bunch of mutuel tickets and he said, "Well Butler got his all right."

The other guy said, "I don't give a good goddam if he did, the crook. He had it coming to him on the stuff he's pulled."

"I'll say he had," said the other guy and tore the bunch of tickets in two.

And George Gardner looked at me to see if I'd heard and I had all right and he said, "Don't you listen to what those bums said, Joe. Your old man was one swell guy."

But I don't know. Seems like when they get started they don't leave a guy nothing.

MITRAIGLIATRICE

The mills of the gods grind slowly;
But this mill
Chatters in mechanical staccato.
Ugly short infantry of the mind,
Advancing over difficult terrain,
Make this Corona
Their mitrailleuse.

OKLAHOMA

All of the Indians are dead
(A good Indian is a dead Indian)
Or riding in motor cars–
(the oil lands, you know, they're all rich)
Smoke smarts my eyes,
Cottonwood twigs and buffalo dung
Smoke grey in the teepee–
(Or is it myopic trachoma)
The prairies are long,
The moon rises,
Ponies
Drag at their pickets.
The grass has gone brown in the summer–
(or is the hay crop failing)
Pull an arrow out:
If you break it
The wound closes.
Salt is good too
And wood ashes.
Pounding it throbs in the night–
(or is it the gonorrhea)

OILY WEATHER

The sea desires deep hulls–
It swells and rolls.
The screw churns a throb–
Driving, throbbing, progressing.
The sea rolls with love
Surging, caressing,
Undulating its great loving belly.
The sea is big and old–
Throbbing ships scorn it.

ROOSEVELT

Workingmen believed
He busted trusts,
And put his picture in their windows.
"What he'd have done in France!"
They said.
Perhaps he would–
He could have died
Perhaps,
Though generals rarely die except in bed,
As he did finally.
And all the legends that he started in his life
Live on and prosper,
Unhampered now by his existence.

CAPTIVES

Some came in chains
Unrepentent but tired.
Too tired but to stumble.
Thinking and hating were finished
Thinking and fighting were finished
Retreated and hoping were finished.
Cures thus a long campaign,
Making death easy.

CHAMPS D'HONNEUR

Soldiers never do die well;
Crosses mark the places,
Wooden crosses where they fell,
Stuck above their faces.
Soldiers pitch and cough and twitch—
All the world roars red and black;
Soldiers smother in a ditch,
Choking through the whole attack.

RIPARTO D'ASSALTO

Drummed their boots on the camion floor,
Hob-nailed boots on the camion floor.
Sergeants stiff,
Corporals sore.
Lieutenants thought of a Mestre whore—
Warm and soft and sleep whore,
Cozy, warm and lovely whore;
Damned cold, bitter, rotten ride,
Winding road up the Grappa side.
Arditi on benches stiff and cold,
Pride of their country stiff and cold,
Bristly faces, dirty hides—
Infantry marches, Arditi rides.
Grey, cold, bitter, sullen ride—
To splintered pines on the Grappa side
At Asalone, where the truck-load died.

MONTPARNASSE

There are never any suicides in the quarter among people one knows
No successful suicides.
A Chinese boy kills himself and is dead.
(they continue to place his mail in the letter rack at the Dome)
A Norwegian boy kills himself and is dead.
(no one knows where the other Norwegian boy has gone)
They find a model dead
alone in bed and very dead.
(it made almost unbearable trouble for the concierge)
Sweet oil, the white of eggs, mustard and water, soap suds
and stomach pumps rescue the people one knows.
Every afternoon the people one knows can he found at the café.

ALONG WITH YOUTH

A porcupine skin,
Stiff with bad tanning,
It must have ended somewhere.
Stuffed horned owl
Pompous
Yellow eyed;
Chuck-wills-widow on a biased twig
Sooted with dust.
Piles of old magazines,
Drawers of boy's letters
And the line of love
They must have ended somewhere.
Yesterday's Tribune is gone
Along with youth
And the canoe that went to pieces on the beach
The year of the big storm
When the hotel burned down
At Seney. Michigan.

CHAPTER HEADING

For we have thought the longer thoughts
And gone the shorter way.
And we have danced to devils' tunes,
Shivering home to pray;
To serve one master in the night,
Another in the day.

IN OUR TIME

CHAPTER 1

Everybody was drunk. The whole battery was drunk going along the road in the dark. We were going to the Champagne. The lieutenant kept riding his horse out into the fields and saying to him, "I'm drunk, I tell you, mon vieux. Oh, I am so soused." We went along the road all night in the dark and the adjutant kept riding up alongside my kitchen and saying, "You must put it out. It is dangerous. It will be observed." We were fifty kilometers from the front but the adjutant worried about the fire in my kitchen. It was funny going along that road. That was when I was a kitchen corporal.

CHAPTER 2

The first matador got the horn through his sword hand and the crowd hooted him out. The second matador slipped and the bull caught him through the belly and he hung on to the horn with one hand and held the other tight against the place, and the bull rammed him wham against the wall and the horn came out, and he lay in the sand, and then got up like crazy drunk and tried to slug the men carrying him away and yelled for his sword but he fainted. The kid came out and had to kill five bulls because you can't have more than three matadors, and the last bull he was so tired he couldn't get the sword in. He couldn't hardly lift his arm. He tried five times and the crowd was quiet because it was a good bull and it looked like him or the bull and then he finally made it. He sat down in the sand and puked and they held a cape over him while the crowd hollered and threw things down into the bull ring.

CHAPTER 3

Minarets stuck up in the rain out of Adrianople across the mud flats. The carts were jammed for thirty miles along the Karagatch road. Water buffalo and cattle were hauling carts through the mud. No end and no beginning. Just carts loaded with everything they owned. The old men and women, soaked through, walked along keeping the cattle moving. The Maritza was running yellow almost up to the bridge. Carts were jammed solid on the bridge with camels bobbing along through them. Greek cavalry herded along the procession. Women and kids were in the carts crouched with mattresses, mirrors, sewing machines, bundles. There was a woman having a kid with a young girl holding a blanket over her and crying. Scared sick looking at it. It rained all through the evacuation.

CHAPTER 4

We were in a garden at Mons. Young Buckley came in with his patrol from across the river. The first German I saw climbed up over the garden wall. We waited till he got one leg over and then potted him. He had so much equipment on and looked awfully surprised and fell down into the garden. Then three more came over further down the wall. We shot them. They all came just like that.

CHAPTER 5

It was a frightfully hot day. We'd jammed an absolutely perfect barricade across the bridge. It was simply priceless. A big old wrought iron grating from the front of a house. Too heavy to lift and you could shoot through it and they would have to climb over it. It was absolutely topping. They tried to get over it, and we potted them from forty yards. They rushed it, and officers came out alone and worked on it. It was an absolutely perfect obstacle. Their officers were very fine. We were frightfully put out when we heard the flank had gone, and we had to fall back.

CHAPTER 6

They shot the six cabinet ministers at half-past six in the morning against the wall of a hospital. There were pools of water in the courtyard. There were wet dead leaves on the paving of the courtyard. It rained hard. All the shutters of the hospital were nailed shut. One of the ministers was sick with typhoid. Two soldiers carried him downstairs and out into the rain. They tried to hold him up against the wall but he sat down in a puddle of water. The other five stood very quietly against the wall. Finally the officer told the soldiers it was no good trying to make him stand up. When they fired the first volley he was sitting down in the water with his head on his knees.

CHAPTER 7

Nick sat against the wall of the church where they had dragged him to be clear of machine gun fire in the street. Both legs stuck out awkwardly. He had been hit in the spine. His face was sweaty and dirty. The sun shone on his face. The day was very hot. Rinaldi, big backed, his equipment sprawling, lay face downward against the wall. Nick looked straight ahead brilliantly. The pink wall of the house opposite had fallen out from the roof, and an iron bedstead hung twisted toward the street. Two Austrian dead lay in the rubble in the shade of the house. Up the street were other dead. Things were getting forward in the town. It was going well. Stretcher bearers would be along any time now. Nick turned his head carefully and looked down at Rinaldi. "Senta Rinaldi. Senta. You and me we've made a separate peace." Rinaldi lay still in the sun breathing with difficulty. "Not patriots." Nick turned his head carefully away smiling sweatily. Rinaldi was a disappointing audience.

CHAPTER 8

While the bombardment was knocking the trench to pieces at Fossalta, he lay very flat and sweated and prayed oh jesus christ get me out of here. Dear jesus please get me out. Christ please please please christ. If you'll only keep me from getting killed I'll do anything you say. I believe in you and I'll tell everyone in the world that you are the only thing that matters. Please please dear jesus. The shelling moved further up the line. We went to work on the trench and in the morning the sun came up and the day was hot and muggy and cheerful and quiet. The next night back at Mestre he did not tell the girl he went upstairs with at the Villa Rossa about Jesus. And he never told anybody.

CHAPTER 9

At two o'clock in the morning two Hungarians got into a cigar store at Fifteenth Street and Grand Avenue. Drevitts and Boyle drove up from the Fifteenth Street police station in a Ford. The Hungarians were backing their wagon out of an alley. Boyle shot one off the seat of the wagon and one out of the wagon box. Drevetts got frightened when he found they were both dead. Hell Jimmy, he said, you oughtn't to have done it. There's liable to be a hell of a lot of trouble.

—They're crooks ain't they? said Boyle. They're wops ain't they? Who the hell is going to make any trouble?

—That's all right maybe this time, said Drevitts, but how did you know they were wops when you bumped them?

Wops, said Boyle, I can tell wops a mile off.

CHAPTER 10

One hot evening in Milan they carried him up onto the roof and he could look out over the top of the town. There were chimney swifts in the sky. After a while it got dark and the searchlights came out. The others went down and took the bottles with them. He and Ag could hear them below on the balcony. Ag sat on the bed. She was cool and fresh in the hot night.

Ag stayed on night duty for three months. They were glad to let her. When they operated on him she prepared him for the operating table, and they had a joke about friend or enema. He went under the anæsthetic holding tight on to himself so that he would not blab about anything during the silly, talky time. After he got on crutches he used to take the temperature so Ag would not have to get up from the bed. There were only a few patients, and they all knew about it. They all liked Ag. As he walked back along the halls he thought of Ag in his bed.

Before he went back to the front they went into the Duomo and prayed. It was dim and quiet, and there were other people praying. They wanted to get married, but there was not enough time for the banns, and neither of them had birth certificates. They felt as though they were married, but they wanted everyone to knew about it, and to make it so they could not lose it.

Ag wrote him many letters that he never got until after the armistice. Fifteen came in a bunch and he sorted them by the dates and read them all straight through. They were about the hospital, and how much she loved him and how it was impossible to get along without him and how terrible it was missing him at night.

After the armistice they agreed he should go home to get a job so they might be married. Ag would not come home until he had a good job and could come to New York to meet her. It was understood he would not drink, and he did not want to see his friends or anyone in the States. Only to get a job and be married. On the train from Padova to Milan they quarrelled about her not being willing to come home at once. When they had to say good-bye in the station at Padova they kissed good-bye, but were not finished with the quarrel. He felt sick about saying good-bye like that.

He went to America on a boat from Genoa. Ag went back to Torre di Mosta to open a hospital. It was lonely and rainy there, and there was a battalion of arditi quartered in the town. Living in the muddy, rainy town in the winter the major of the battalion made love to Ag, and she had never known Italians before, and finally wrote a letter to the States that theirs had been only a boy and girl affair. She was sorry, and she knew he would probably not be able to understand, but might some day forgive her, and be grateful to her, and she expected, absolutely unexpectedly, to be married in the spring. She loved him as always, but she realized now it was only a boy and girl love. She hoped he would have a great career, and believed in him absolutely. She knew it was for the best.

The Major did not marry her in the spring, or any other time. Ag never got an answer to her letter to Chicago about it. A short time after he contracted gonorrhea from a sales girl from The Fair riding in a taxicab through Lincoln Park.

CHAPTER 11

In 1919 he was travelling on the railroads in Italy carrying a square of oilcloth from the headquarters of the party written in indelible pencil and saying here was a comrade who had suffered very much under the whites in Budapest and requesting comrades to aid him in any way. He used this instead of a ticket. He was very shy and quite young and the train men passed him on from one crew to another. He had no money, and they fed him behind the counter in railway eating houses.

He was delighted with Italy. It was a beautiful country he said. The people were all kind. He had been in many towns, walked much and seen many pictures. Giotto, Masaccio, and Piero della Francesca he bought reproductions of and carried them wrapped in a copy of Avanti. Mantegna he did not like.

He reported at Bologna, and I took him with me up into the Romagna where it was necessary I go to see a man. We had a good trip together. It was early September and the country was pleasant. He was a Magyar, a very nice boy and very shy. Horthy's men had done some bad things to him. He talked about it a little. In spite of Italy, he believed altogether in the world revolution.

—But how is the movement going in Italy? he asked.

—Very badly, I said.

—But it will go better, he said. You have everything here. It is the one country that everyone is sure of. It will be the starting point of everything.

At Bologna he said good-bye to us to go on the train to Milano and then to Aosta to walk over the pass into Switzerland. I spoke to him about the Mantegnas in Milano. No, he said, very shyly, he did not like Mantegna. I wrote out for him where to eat in Milano and the addresses of comrades. He thanked me very much, but his mind was already looking forward to walking over the pass. He was very eager to walk over the pass while the weather held good. The last I heard of him the Swiss had him in jail near Sion.

CHAPTER 12

They whack whacked the white horse on the legs and he knee-ed himself up. The picador twisted the stirrups straight and pulled and hauled up into the saddle. The horse's entrails hung down in a blue bunch and swung backward and forward as he began to canter, the monos whacking him on the back of his legs with the rods. He cantered jerkily along the barrera. He stopped stiff and one of the monos held his bridle and walked him forward. The picador kicked in his spurs, leaned forward and shook his lance at the bull. Blood pumped regularly from between the horse's front legs. He was nervously wobbly. The bull could not make up his mind to charge.

CHAPTER 13

The crowd shouted all the time and threw pieces of bread down into the ring, then cushions and leather wine bottles, keeping up whistling and yelling. Finally the bull was too tired from so much bad sticking and folded his knees and lay down and one of the cuadrilla leaned out over his neck and killed him with the puntillo. The crowd came over the barrera and around the torero and two men grabbed him and held him and some one cut off his pigtail and was waving it and a kid grabbed it and ran away with it. Afterwards I saw him at the café. He was very short with a brown face and quite drunk and he said after all it has happened before like that. I am not really a good bull fighter.

CHAPTER 14

If it happened right down close in front of you, you could see Villalta snarl at the bull and curse him, and when the bull charged he swung back firmly like an oak when the wind hits it, his legs tight together, the muleta trailing and the sword following the curve behind. Then he cursed the bull, flopped the muleta at him, and swung back from the charge his feet firm, the muleta curving and each swing the crowd roaring.

When he started to kill it was all in the same rush. The bull looking at him straight in front, hating. He drew out the sword from the folds of the muleta and sighted with the same movement and called to the bull, Toro! Toro! and the bull charged and Villalta charged and just for a moment they became one. Villalta became one with the bull and then it was over. Villalta standing straight and the red kilt of the sword sticking out dully between the bull's shoulders. Villalta, his hand up at the crowd and the bull roaring blood, looking straight at Villalta and his legs caving.

CHAPTER 15

I heard the drums coming down the street and then the fifes and the pipes and then they came around the corner, all dancing. The street full of them. Maera saw him and then I saw him. When they stopped the music for the crouch he hunched down in the street with them all and when they started it again he jumped up and went dancing down the street with them. He was drunk all right.

You go down after him, said Maera, he hates me.

So I went down and caught up with them and grabbed him while he was crouched down waiting for the music to break loose and said, Come on Luis. For Christ sake you've got bulls this afternoon. He didn't listen to me, he was listening so hard for the music to start.

I said, Don't be a damn fool Luis. Come on back to the hotel.

Then the music started up again and he jumped up and twisted away from me and started dancing. I grabbed his arm and he pulled loose and said, Oh leave me alone. You're not my father.

I went back to the hotel and Maera was on the balcony looking out to see if I'd be bringing him back. He went inside when he saw me and came downstairs disgusted.

Well, I said, after all he's just an ignorant Mexican savage.

Yes, Maera said, and who will kill his bulls after he gets a cogida?

We, I suppose, I said.

Yes, we, said Maera. We kills the savages' bulls, and the drunkards' bulls, and the riau-riau dancers' bulls. Yes. We kill them. We kill them all right. Yes. Yes. Yes.

CHAPTER 16

Maera lay still, his head on his arms, his face in the sand. He felt warm and sticky from the bleeding. Each time he felt the horn coming. Sometimes the bull only bumped him with his head. Once the horn went all the way through him and he felt it go into the sand. Someone had the bull by the tail. They were swearing at him and flopping the cape in his face. Then the bull was gone. Some men picked Maera up and started to run with him toward the barriers through the gate out the passage way around under the grand stand to the infirmary. They laid Maera down on a cot and one of the men went out for the doctor. The others stood around. The doctor came running from the corral where he had been sewing up picador horses. He had to stop and wash his hands. There was a great shouting going on in the grandstand overhead. Maera wanted to say something and found he could not talk. Maera felt everything getting larger and larger and then smaller and smaller. Then it got larger and larger and larger and then smaller and smaller. Then everything commenced to run faster and faster as when they speed up a cinematograph film. Then he was dead.

CHAPTER 17

They hanged Sam Cardinella at six o'clock in the morning in the corridor of the county jail. The corridor was high and narrow with tiers of cells on either side. All the cells were occupied. The men had been brought in for the hanging. Five men sentenced to be hanged were in the five top cells. Three of the men to be hanged were negroes. They were very frightened. One of the white men sat on his cot with his head in his hands. The other lay flat on his cot with a blanket wrapped around his head.

They came out onto the gallows through a door in the wall. There were six or seven of them including two priests. They were carrying Sam Cardinella. He had been like that since about four o'clock in the morning.

While they were strapping his legs together two guards held him up and the two priests were whispering to him. "Be a man, my son," said one priest. When they came toward him with the cap to go over his head Sam Cardinella lost control of his sphincter muscle. The guards who had been holding him up dropped him. They were both disgusted. "How about a chair, Will?" asked one of the guards, "Better get one," said a man in a derby hat.

When they all stepped back on the scaffolding back of the drop, which was very heavy, built of oak and steel and swung on ball bearings, Sam Cardinella was left sitting there strapped tight, the younger of the two priests kneeling beside the chair. The priest skipped back onto the scaffolding just before the drop fell.

CHAPTER 18

The king was working in the garden. He seemed very glad to see me. We walked through the garden. This is the queen, he said. She was clipping a rose bush. Oh how do you do, she said. We sat down at a table under a big tree and the king ordered whiskey and soda. We have good whiskey anyway, he said. The revolutionary committee, he told me, would not allow him to go outside the palace grounds. Plastiras is a very good man I believe, he said, but frightfully difficult. I think he did right though shooting those chaps. If Kerensky had shot a few men things might have been altogether different. Of course the great thing in this sort of an affair is not to be shot oneself!

It was very jolly. We talked for a long time. Like all Greeks he wanted to go to America.

THE TORRENTS OF SPRING

PART ONE

RED AND BLACK LAUGHTER

The only source of the true Ridiculous (as it appears to me) is affectation.

HENRY FIELDING

CHAPTER 1

Yogi Johnson stood looking out of the window of a big pump-factory in Michigan. Spring would soon be here. Could it be that what this writing fellow Hutchinson had said, "If winter comes can spring be far behind?" would be true again this year? Yogi Johnson wondered. Near Yogi at the next window but one stood Scripps O'Neil, a tall, lean man with a tall, lean face. Both stood and looked out at the empty yard of the pump-factory. Snow covered the crated pumps that would soon be shipped away. Once the spring should come and the snow melt, workmen from the factory would break out the pumps from piles where they were snowed in and haul them down to the G. R. & I. station, where they would be loaded on flat-cars and shipped away. Yogi Johnson looked out of the window at the snowed-in pumps, and his breath made little fairy tracings on the cold windowpane. Yogi Johnson thought of Paris. Perhaps it was the little fairy tracings that reminded him of the gay city where he had once spent two weeks. Two weeks that were to have been the happiest weeks of his life. That was all behind him now. That and everything else.

Scripps O'Neil had two wives. As he looked out of the window, standing tall and lean and resilient with his own tenuous hardness, he thought of both of them. One lived in Mancelona and the other lived in Petoskey. He had not seen the wife who lived in Mancelona since last spring. He looked out at the snow-covered pump-yards and thought what spring would mean. With his wife in Mancelona Scripps often got drunk. When he was drunk he and his wife were happy. They would go down together to the railway station and walk out along the tracks, and then sit together and drink and watch the trains go by. They would sit under a pine-tree on a little hill that overlooked the railway and drink. Sometimes they drank all night. Sometimes they drank for a week at a time. It did them good. It made Scripps strong.

Scripps had a daughter whom he playfully called Lousy O'Neil. Her real name was Lucy O'Neil. One night, after Scripps and his old woman had been out drinking on the railroad line for three or four days, he lost his wife. He didn't know where she was. When he came to himself everything was dark. He walked along the railroad track toward town. The ties were stiff and hard under his feet. He tried walking on the rails. He couldn't do it. He had the dope on that all right. He went back to walking along the ties. It was a long way into town. Finally he came to where he could see the lights of the switch-yard. He cut away from the tracks and passed the Mancelona High School. It was a yellow-brick building. There was nothing rococo about it, like the buildings he had seen in Paris. No, he had never been in Paris. That was not he. That was his friend Yogi Johnson.

Yogi Johnson looked out of the window. Soon it would be time to shut the pump-factory for the night. He opened the window carefully, just a crack. Just a crack, but that was enough. Outside in the yard the snow had begun to melt. A warm breeze was blowing. A chinook wind the pump fellows called it. The warm chinook wind came in through the window into the pump-factory. All the workmen laid down their tools. Many of them were Indians.

The foreman was a short, iron-jawed man. He had once made a trip as far as Duluth. Duluth was far across the blue waters of the lake in the hills of Minnesota. A wonderful thing had happened to him there.

The foreman put his finger in his mouth to moisten it and held it up in the air. He felt the warm breeze on his finger. He shook his head ruefully and smiled at the men, a little grimly perhaps.

"Well, it's a regular chinook, boys," he said.

Silently for the most part, the workmen hung up their tools. The half-completed pumps were put away in their racks. The workmen filed, some of them talking, others silent, a few muttering, to the washroom to wash up.

Outside through the window came the sound of an Indian war-whoop.

CHAPTER 2

Scripps O'Neil stood outside the Mancelona High School looking up at the lighted windows. It was dark and the snow was falling. It had been falling ever since Scripps could remember. A passer-by stopped and stared at Scripps. After all, what was this man to him? He went on.

Scripps stood in the snow and stared up at the lighted windows of the High School. Inside there people were learning things. Far into the night they worked, the boys vying with the girls in their search for knowledge, this urge for the learning of things that was sweeping America. His girl, little Lousy, a girl that had cost him a cool seventy-five dollars in doctors' bills, was in there learning. Scripps was proud. It was too late for him to learn, but there, day after day and night after night, Lousy was learning. She had the stuff in her, that girl.

Scripps went on up to his house. It was not a big house, but it wasn't size that mattered to Scripps's old woman.

"Scripps," she often said when they were drinking together, "I don't want a palace. All I want is a place to keep the wind out." Scripps had taken her at her word. Now, as he walked in the late evening through the snow and saw the lights of his own home, he felt glad that he had taken her at her word. It was better this way than if he were coming home to a palace. He, Scripps, was not the sort of chap that wanted a palace.

He opened the door of his house and went in. Something kept going through his head. He tried to get it out, but it was no good. What was it that poet chap his friend Harry Parker had met once in Detroit had written? Harry used to recite it: "Through pleasures and palaces though I may roam. When you something something something there's no place like home." He could not remember the words. Not all of them. He had written a simple tune to it and taught Lucy to sing it. That was when they first were married. Scripps might have been a composer, one of these chaps that write the stuff the Chicago Symphony Orchestra plays, if he had had a chance to go on. He would get Lucy to sing that song tonight. He would never drink again. Drinking robbed him of his ear for music. Times when he was drunk the sound of the whistles of the trains at night pulling up the Boyne Falls grade seemed more lovely than anything this chap Stravinsky had ever written. Drinking had done that. It was wrong. He would get away to Paris. Like this chap Albert Spalding that played the violin.

Scripps opened the door. He went in. "Lucy," he called, "it is I, Scripps." He would never drink again. No more nights out on the railroad. Perhaps Lucy needed a new fur coat. Perhaps, after all, she had wanted a palace instead of this place. You never knew how you were treating a woman. Perhaps, after all, this place was not keeping out the wind. Fantastic. He lit a match. "Lucy!" he called, and there was a note of dumb terror in his mouth. His friend Walt Simmons had heard just such a cry from a stallion that had once been run over by a passing autobus in the Place Vendôme in Paris. In Paris there were no geldings. All the horses were stallions. They did not breed mares. Not since the war. The war changed all that.

"Lucy!" he called, and again "Lucy!" There was no answer. The house was empty. Through the snow-filled air, as he stood there alone in his tall leanness, in his own deserted house, there came to Scripps's ears the distant sound of an Indian war-whoop.

CHAPTER 3

Scripps left Mancelona. He was through with that place. What had a town like that to give him? There was nothing to it. You worked all your life and then a thing like that happened. The savings of years wiped out. Everything gone. He started to Chicago to get a job. Chicago was the place. Look at its geographical situation, right at the end of Lake Michigan. Chicago would do big things. Any fool could see that. He would buy land in what is now the Loop, the big shopping and manufacturing district. He would buy the land at a low price and then hang onto it. Let them try and get it away from him. He knew a thing or two now.

Alone, bareheaded, the snow blowing in his hair, he walked down the G. R. & I. railway tracks. It was the coldest night he had ever known. He picked up a dead bird that had frozen and fallen onto the railroad tracks and put it inside his shirt to warm it. The bird nestled close to his warm body and pecked at his chest gratefully.

"Poor little chap," Scripps said. "You feel the cold too."

Tears came into his eyes.

"Drat that wind," Scripps said and once again faced into the blowing snow. The wind was blowing straight down from Lake Superior. The telegraph wires above Scripps's head sang in the wind. Through the dark, Scripps saw a great yellow eye coming toward him. The giant locomotive came nearer through the snow-storm. Scripps stepped to one side of the track to let it go by. What is it that old writing fellow Shakespeare says: "Might makes right"? Scripps thought of that quotation as the train went past him in the snowing darkness. First the engine passed. He saw the fireman bending to fling great shovelfuls of coal into the open furnace door. The engineer wore goggles. His face was lit up by the light from the open door of the engine. He was the engineer. It was he who had his hand on the throttle.

Scripps thought of the Chicago anarchists who, when they were hanged, said: "Though you throttle us today, still you cannot something something our souls." There was a monument where they were buried in Waldheim Cemetery, right beside the Forest Park Amusement Park, in Chicago. His father used to take Scripps out there on Sundays. The monument was all black and there was a black angel. That was when Scripps had been a little boy. He used often to ask his father: "Father, why if we come to look at the anarchists on Sunday why can't we ride on the shoot the chutes?" He had never been satisfied with his father's answer. He had been a little boy in knee pants then. His father had been a great composer. His mother was an Italian woman from the north of Italy. They are strange people, these north Italians.

Scripps stood beside the track, and the long black segments of the train clicked by him in the snow. All the cars were Pullmans. The blinds were down. Light came in thin slits from the bottom of the dark windows as the cars went by. The train did not roar by as it might have if it had been going in the other direction, because it was climbing the Boyne Falls grade. It went slower than if it had been going down. Still it went too fast for Scripps to hitch on. He thought how he had been an expert at hitching on grocery wagons when he was a young boy in knee pants.

The long black train of Pullman cars passed Scripps as he stood beside the tracks. Who were in those cars? Were they Americans, piling up money while they slept? Were they mothers? Were they fathers? Were there lovers among them? Or were they Europeans, members of a worn-out civilization world-weary from the war? Scripps wondered.

The last car passed him and the train went on up the track. Scripps watched the red light at its stern disappearing into the blackness through which the snowflakes now came softly. The bird fluttered inside his shirt. Scripps started along the ties. He wanted to get to Chicago that night, if possible, to start work in the morning. The bird fluttered again. It was not so feeble now. Scripps put his hand on it to still its little bird flutterings. The bird was calmed. Scripps strode on up the track.

After all, he did not need to go as far as Chicago. There were other places. What if that critic fellow Henry Mencken had called Chicago the Literary Capital of America? There was Grand Rapids. Once in Grand Rapids, he could start in in the furniture business. Fortunes had been made that way. Grand Rapids furniture was famous wherever young couples walked in the evening to talk of home-making. He remembered a sign he had seen in Chicago as a little boy. His mother had pointed it out to him as together they walked barefoot through what now is probably the Loop, begging from door to door. His mother loved the bright flashing of the electric lights in the sign.

"They are like San Miniato in my native Florence," she told Scripps. "Look at them, my son," she said, "for some day your music will be played there by the Firenze Symphony Orchestra."

Scripps had often watched the sign for hours while his mother slept wrapped in an old shawl on what is now probably the Blackstone Hotel. The sign had made a great impression on him.

LET HARTMAN FEATHER YOUR NEST

it had said. It flashed in many different colors. First a pure, dazzling white. That was what Scripps loved best. Then it flashed a lovely green. Then it flashed red. One night as he lay crouched against his mother's body warmth and watched the sign flash, a policeman came up. "You'll have to move along," he said.

Ah, yes, there was big money to be made in the furniture business if you knew how to go about it. He, Scripps, knew all the wrinkles of that game. In his own mind it was settled. He would stop at Grand Rapids. The little bird fluttered, happily now.

"Ah, what a beautiful gilded cage I'll build for you, my pretty one," Scripps said exultantly. The little bird pecked him confidently. Scripps strode on in the storm. The snow was beginning to drift across the track. Borne on the wind, there came to Scripps's ears the sound of a far-off Indian war-whoop.

CHAPTER 4

Where was Scripps now? Walking in the night in the storm, he had become confused. He had started for Chicago after that dreadful night when he had found that his home was a home no longer. Why had Lucy left? What had become of Lousy? He, Scripps, did not know. Not that he cared. That was all behind him. There was none of that now. He was standing knee-deep in snow in front of a railway station. On the railway station was written in big letters:

PETOSKEY

There were a pile of deer shipped down by hunters from the Upper Peninsula of Michigan, lying piled the one on the other, dead and stiff and drifted half over with snow on the station platform. Scripps read the sign again. Could this be Petoskey?

A man was inside the station, tapping something back of a wicketed window. He looked out at Scripps. Could he be a telegrapher? Something told Scripps that he was.

He stepped out of the snow-drift and approached the window. Behind the window the man worked busily away at his telegrapher's key.

"Are you a telegrapher?" asked Scripps.

"Yes, sir," said the man. "I'm a telegrapher."

"How wonderful!"

The telegrapher eyed him suspiciously. After all, what was this man to him?

"Is it hard to be a telegrapher?" Scripps asked. He wanted to ask the man outright if this was Petoskey. He did not know this great northern section of America, though, and he wished to be polite.

The telegrapher looked at him curiously.

"Say," he asked, "are you a fairy?"

"No," Scripps said. "I don't know what being a fairy means."

"Well," said the telegrapher, "what do you carry a bird around for?"

"Bird?" asked Scripps. "What bird?"

"That bird that's sticking out of your shirt." Scripps was at a loss. What sort of chap was this telegrapher? What sort of men went in for telegraphy? Were they like composers? Were they like artists? Were they like writers? Were they like the advertising men who write the ads in our national weeklies? Or were they like Europeans, drawn and wasted by the war, their best years behind them? Could he tell this telegrapher the whole story? Would he understand?

"I started home," he began. "I passed the Mancelona High School—"

"I knew a girl in Mancelona," the telegrapher said. "Maybe you knew her. Ethel Enright."

It was no good going on. He would cut the story short. He would give the bare essentials. Besides, it was beastly cold. It was cold standing there on the wind-swept station platform. Something told him it was useless to go on. He looked over at the deer lying there in a pile, stiff and cold. Perhaps they, too, had been lovers. Some were bucks and some were does. The bucks had horns. That was how you could tell. With cats it is more difficult. In France they geld the cats and do not geld the horses. France was a long way off.

"My wife left me," Scripps said abruptly.

"I don't wonder if you go around with a damn bird sticking out of your shirt," the telegrapher said.

"What town is this?" Scripps asked. The single moment of spiritual communion they had had, had been dissipated. They had never really had it. But they might have. It was no use now. It was no use trying to capture what had gone. What had fled.

"Petoskey," the telegrapher replied.

"Thank you," Scripps said. He turned and walked into the silent, deserted Northern town. Luckily, he had four hundred and fifty dollars in his pocket. He had sold a story to George Horace Lorimer just before he had started out with his old woman on that drinking trip. Why had he gone at all? What was it all about, anyway?

Coming toward him down the street came two Indians. They looked at him, but their faces did not change. Their faces remained the same. They went into McCarthy's barber shop.

CHAPTER 5

Scripps O'Neil stood irresolutely before the barber shop. Inside there men were being shaved. Other men, no different, were having their hair cut. Other men sat against the wall in tall chairs and smoked, awaiting their turn in the barber chairs, admiring the paintings hung on the wall, or admiring their own reflections in the long mirror. Should he, Scripps, go in there? After all, he had four hundred and fifty dollars in his pocket. He could go where he wanted. He looked, once again, irresolutely. It was an inviting prospect, the society of men, the warm room, the white jackets of the barbers skillfully snipping away with their scissors or drawing their blades diagonally through the lather that covered the face of some man who was getting a shave. They could use their tools, these barbers. Somehow, it wasn't what he wanted. He wanted something different. He wanted to eat. Besides, there was his bird to look after.

Scripps O'Neil turned his back on the barber shop and strode away up the street of the silently frozen Northern town. On his right, as he walked, the weeping birches, their branches bare of leaves, hung down to the ground, heavy with snow. To his ears came the sound of sleigh bells. Perhaps it was Christmas. In the South little children would be shooting off firecrackers and crying "Christmas Gift! Christmas Gift!" to one another. His father came from the South. He had been a soldier in the rebel army. 'Way back in Civil War days. Sherman had burned their house down on his March to the Sea. "War is hell," Sherman had said. "But you see how it is, Mrs. O'Neil. I've got to do it." He had touched a match to the white-pillared old house.

"If General O'Neil were here, you dastard!" his mother had said, speaking in her broken English, "you'd never have touched a match to that house."

Smoke curled up from the old house. The fire was mounting. The white pillars were obscured in the rising smoke-wreaths. Scripps had held close to his mother's linsey-woolsey dress.

General Sherman climbed back onto his horse and made a low bow. "Mrs. O'Neil," he said, and Scripps's mother always said there were tears in his eyes, even if he was a damned Yank. The man had a heart, sir, even if he did not follow its dictates. "Mrs. O'Neil, if the general were here, we could have it out as man to man. As it is, ma'am, war being what it is, I must burn your house."

He motioned to one of his soldiers, who ran forward and threw a bucket of kerosene on the flames. The flames rose and a great column of smoke went up in the still evening air.

"At least, General Sherman," Scripps's mother said triumphantly, "that column of smoke will warn the other loyal daughters of the Confederacy that you are coming."

Sherman bowed. "That is the risk we must take, ma'am." He clapped spurs to his horse and rode away, his long white hair floating on the wind. Neither Scripps nor his mother ever saw him again. Odd that he should think of that incident now. He looked up. Facing him was a sign:

BROWN'S BEANERY THE BEST BY TEST

He would go in and eat. This was what he wanted. He would go in and eat. That sign:

THE BEST BY TEST

Ah, these big beanery owners were wise fellows. They knew how to get the customers. No ads in *The Saturday Evening Post* for them. THE BEST BY TEST. That was the stuff. He went in.

Inside the door of the beanery Scripps O'Neil looked around him. There was a long counter. There was a clock. There was a door led into the kitchen. There were a couple of tables. There were a pile of doughnuts under a glass cover. There were signs put about on the wall advertising things one might eat. Was this, after all, Brown's Beanery?

"I wonder," Scripps asked an elderly waitress who came in through the swinging door from the kitchen, "if you could tell me if this is Brown's Beanery?"

"Yes, sir," answered the waitress. "The best by test."

"Thank you," Scripps said. He sat down at the counter. "I would like to have some beans for myself and some for my bird here."

He opened his shirt and placed the bird on the counter. The bird ruffled his feathers and shook himself. He pecked inquiringly at the catsup bottle. The elderly waitress put out a hand and stroked him. "Isn't he a manly little fellow?" she remarked. "By the way," she asked, a little shamefacedly, "what was it you ordered, sir?"

"Beans," Scripps said, "for my bird and myself."

The waitress shoved up a little wicket that led into the kitchen. Scripps had a glimpse of a warm, steam-filled room, with big pots and kettles, and many shining cans on the wall.

"A pig and the noisy ones," the waitress called in a matter-of-fact voice into the open wicket. "One for a bird!"

"On the fire!" a voice answered from the kitchen.

"How old is your bird?" the elderly waitress asked.

"I don't know," Scripps said. "I never saw him before last night. I was walking on the railroad track from Mancelona. My wife left me."

"Poor little chap," the waitress said. She poured a little catsup on her finger and the bird pecked at it gratefully.

"My wife left me," Scripps said. "We'd been out drinking on the railroad track. We used to go out evenings and watch the trains pass. I write stories. I had a story in *The Post* and two in *The Dial*. Mencken's trying to get ahold of me. I'm too wise for that sort of thing. No *politzei* for mine. They give me the *katzenjammers*."

What was he saying? He was talking wildly. This would never do. He must pull himself together.

"Scofield Thayer was my best man," he said. "I'm a Harvard man. All I want is for them to give me and my bird a square deal. No more *weltpolitik*. Take Dr. Coolidge away."

His mind was wandering. He knew what it was. He was faint with hunger. This Northern air was too sharp, too keen for him.

"I say," he said. "Could you let me have just a few of those beans. I don't like to rush things. I know when to let well enough alone."

The wicket came up, and a large plate of beans and a small plate of beans, both steaming, appeared.

"Here they are," the waitress said.

Scripps fell to on the large plate of beans. There was a little pork, too. The bird was eating happily, raising its head after each swallow to let the beans go down.

"He does that to thank God for those beans," the elderly waitress explained.

"They're mighty fine beans, too," Scripps agreed. Under the influence of the beans his head was clearing. What was this rot he had been talking about that man Henry Mencken? Was Mencken really after him? It wasn't a pretty prospect to face. He had four hundred and fifty dollars in his pocket. When that was gone he could always put an end to things. If they pressed him too far they would get a big surprise. He wasn't the man to be taken alive. Just let them try it.

After eating his beans the bird had fallen asleep. He was sleeping on one leg, the other leg tucked up into his feathers.

"When he gets tired of sleeping on that leg he will change legs and rest," the waitress remarked. "We had an old osprey at home that was like that."

"Where was your home?" Scripps asked.

"In England. In the Lake District." The waitress smiled a bit wistfully. "Wordsworth's country, you know."

Ah, these English. They travelled all over the face of the globe. They were not content to remain in their little island. Strange Nordics, obsessed with their dream of empire.

"I was not always a waitress," the elderly waitress remarked.

"I'm sure you weren't."

"Not half," the waitress went on. "It's rather a strange story. Perhaps it would bore you?"

"Not at all," Scripps said. "You wouldn't mind if I used the story sometime?"

"Not if you find it interesting," the waitress smiled. "You wouldn't use my name, of course."

"Not if you'd rather not," Scripps said. "By the way, could I have another order of beans?"

"Best by test," the waitress smiled. Her face was lined and gray. She looks a little like that actress that died in Pittsburgh. What was her name? Lenore Ulric. In *Peter Pan*. That was it. They say she always went about veiled, Scripps thought. There was an interesting woman. Was it Lenore Ulric? Perhaps not. No matter.

"You really want some more beans?" asked the waitress.

"Yes," Scripps answered simply.

"Once again on the loud ones," the waitress called into the wicket. "Lay off the bird."

"On the fire," came the response.

"Please go on with your story," Scripps said kindly.

"It was the year of the Paris Exposition," she began. "I was a young girl at the time, a *jeune fille*, and I came over from England with my mother. We were going to be present at the opening of the exposition. On our way from the Gare du Nord to the hotel in the Place Vendôme where we lodged, we stopped at a coiffeur's shop and made some trifling purchase. My mother, as I recall, purchased an additional bottle of 'smelling salts,' as you call them here in America."

She smiled.

"Yes, go on. Smelling salts," Scripps said.

"We registered, as is customary, in the hotel, and were given the adjoining rooms we had reserved. My mother felt a bit done in by the trip, and we dined in our rooms. I was full of excitement about seeing the exposition on the morrow. But I was tired after the journey—we had had a rather nasty crossing—and slept soundly. In the morning I awoke and called for my mother. There was no answer, and I went into the room to waken Mummy. Instead of Mummy there was a French general in the bed."

"Mon Dieu!" Scripps said.

"I was terribly frightened," the waitress went on, "and rang the bell for the management. The concierge came up, and I demanded to know where my mother was.

"'But, mademoiselle,' the concierge explained, 'we know nothing about your mother. You came here with General So-and-so'—I cannot remember the general's name."

"Call him General Joffre," Scripps suggested.

"It was a name very like that," the waitress said. "I was fearfully frightened and sent for the police, and demanded to see the guest-register. 'You'll find there that I am registered with my mother,' I said. The police came and the concierge brought up the register. 'See, madame,' he said. 'You are registered with the general with whom you came to our hotel last night.'

"I was desperate. Finally, I remembered where the coiffeur's shop was. The police sent for the coiffeur. An agent of police brought him in.

"'I stopped at your shop with my mother,' I said to the coiffeur, 'and my mother bought a bottle of aromatic salts.'

"'I remember mademoiselle perfectly,' the coiffeur said. 'But you were not with your mother. You were with an elderly French general. He purchased, I believe, a pair of mustache tongs. My books, at any rate, will show the purchase.'

"I was in despair. In the meantime the police had brought in the cab driver who had brought us from the gare to the hotel. He swore that I had never been with my mother. Tell me, does this story bore you?"

"Go on," said Scripps. "If you had ever been as hard up for plots as I have been!"

"Well," the waitress said. "That's all there is to the tale. I never saw my mother again. I communicated with the embassy, but they could do nothing. It was finally established by them that I had crossed the channel with my mother, but they could do nothing beyond that." Tears came into the elderly waitress's eyes. "I never saw Mummy again. Never again. Not even once."

"What about the general?"

"He finally loaned me one hundred francs – not a great sum even in those days – and I came to America and became a waitress. That's all there is to the story."

"There's more than that," Scripps said. "I'd stake my life there's more than that."

"Sometimes, you know, I feel there is," the waitress said. "I feel there must be more than that. Somewhere, somehow, there must be an explanation. I don't know what brought the subject into my mind this morning."

"It was a good thing to get it off your mind," Scripps said.

"Yes," the waitress smiled, the lines in her face not quite so deep now. "I feel better now."

"Tell me," Scripps asked the waitress. "Is there any work in this town for me and my bird?"

"Honest work?" asked the waitress. "I only know of honest work."

"Yes, honest work," Scripps said.

"They do say they're hiring hands at the new pump-factory," the waitress said. Why shouldn't he work with his hands? Rodin had done it. Cézanne had been a butcher. Renoir a carpenter. Picasso had worked in a cigarette-factory in his boyhood. Gilbert Stuart, who painted those famous portraits of Washington that are reproduced all over this America of ours and hang in every schoolroom – Gilbert Stuart had been a blacksmith. Then there was Emerson. Emerson had been a hod-carrier. James Russell Lowell had been, he had heard, a telegraph operator in his youth. Like that chap down at the station. Perhaps even now that telegrapher at the station was working on his "Thanatopsis" or his "To a Waterfowl." Why shouldn't he, Scripps O'Neil, work in a pump-factory?

"You'll come back again?" the waitress asked.

"If I may," Scripps said.

"And bring your bird."

"Yes," Scripps said. "The little chap's rather tired now. After all, it was a hard night for him."

"I should say it was," agreed the waitress.

Scripps went out again into the town. He felt clearheaded and ready to face life. A pump-factory would be interesting. Pumps were big things now. Fortunes were made and lost in pumps every day in New York in Wall Street. He knew of a chap who'd cleaned up a cool half-million on pumps in less than half an hour. They knew what they were about, these big Wall Street operators.

Outside on the street he looked up at the sign. BEST BY TEST, he read. They had the dope all right, he said. Was it true, though, that there had been a Negro cook? Just once, just for one moment, when the wicket went up, he thought he had caught a glimpse of something black. Perhaps the chap was only sooty from the stove.

PART TWO

THE STRUGGLE FOR LIFE

And here I solemnly protest I have no intention to vilify or asperse any one; for though everything is copied from the book of nature, and scarce a character or action produced which I have not taken from my own observations or experience; yet I have used the utmost care to obscure the persons by such different circumstances, degrees, and colors, that it will be impossible to guess at them with any degree of certainty; and if it ever happens otherwise, it is only where the failure characterized is so minute, that it is a foible only which the party himself may laugh at as well as any other.

HENRY FIELDING

CHAPTER 6

Scripps O'Neil was looking for employment. It would be good to work with his hands. He walked down the street away from the beanery and past McCarthy's barber shop. He did not go into the barber shop. It looked as inviting as ever, but it was employment Scripps wanted. He turned sharply around the corner of the barber shop and onto the Main Street of Petoskey. It was a handsome, broad street, lined on either side with brick and pressed-stone buildings. Scripps walked along it toward the part of town where the pump-factory stood. At the door of the pump-factory he was embarrassed. Could this really be the pump-factory? True, a stream of pumps were being carried out and set up in the snow, and workmen were throwing pails of water over them to encase them in a coating of ice that would protect them from the winter winds as well as any paint would. But were they really pumps? It might all be a trick. These pump men were clever fellows.

"I say!" Scripps beckoned to one of the workmen who was sloshing water over a new, raw-looking pump that had just been carried out and stood protestingly in the snow. "Are they pumps?"

"They will be in time," the workman said.

Scripps knew it was the factory. They weren't going to fool him on that. He walked up to the door. There was a sign on it:

KEEP OUT. THIS MEANS YOU

Can that mean me? Scripps wondered. He knocked on the door and went in.

"I'd like to speak to the manager," he said, standing quietly in the half-light.

Workmen were passing him, carrying the new raw pumps on their shoulders. They hummed snatches of songs as they passed. The handles of the pumps flopped stiffly in dumb protest. Some pumps had no handles. They perhaps, after all, are the lucky ones, Scripps thought. A little man came up to him. He was well-built, short, with wide shoulders and a grim face.

"You were asking for the manager?"

"Yes, sir."

"I'm the foreman here. What I say goes."

"Can you hire and fire?" Scripps asked.

"I can do one as easily as the other," the foreman said.

"I want a job."

"Any experience?"

"Not in pumps."

"All right," the foreman said. "We'll put you on piece-work. Here, Yogi," he called to one of the men, who was standing looking out of the window of the factory, "show this new chum where to stow his swag and how to find his way around these diggings." The foreman looked Scripps up and down. "I'm an Australian," he said. "Hope you'll like the lay here." He walked off.

The man called Yogi Johnson came over from the window. "Glad to meet you," he said. He was a chunky, well-built fellow. One of the sort you see around almost anywhere. He looked as though he had been through things.

"Your foreman's the first Australian I've ever met," Scripps said.

"Oh, he's not an Australian," Yogi said. "He was just with the Australians once during the war, and it made a big impression on him."

"Were you in the war?" Scripps asked.

"Yes," Yogi Johnson said. "I was the first man to go from Cadillac."

"It must have been quite an experience."

"It's meant a lot to me," Yogi answered. "Come on and I'll show you around the works."

Scripps followed this man, who showed him through the pump-factory. It was dark but warm inside the pump-factory. Men naked to the waist took the pumps in huge tongs as they came trundling by on an endless chain, culling out the misfits and placing the perfect pumps on another endless chain that carried them up into the cooling room. Other men, Indians for the most part, wearing only breech-clouts, broke up the misfit pumps with huge hammers and adzes and rapidly recast them into axe heads, wagon springs, trombone slides, bullet moulds, all the by-products of a big pump-factory. There was nothing wasted, Yogi pointed out. A group of Indian boys, humming to themselves one of the old tribal chantries, squatted in a corner of the big forging room shaping the little fragments that were chipped from the pumps in casting, into safety razor blades.

"They work naked," Yogi said. "They're searched as they go out. Sometimes they try and conceal the razor blades and take them out with them to bootleg."

"There must be quite a loss that way," Scripps said.

"Oh, no," Yogi answered. "The inspectors get most of them."

Upstairs, apart in a separate room, two old men were working. Yogi opened the door. One of the old men looked over his steel spectacles and frowned.

"You make a draft," he said.

"Shut the door," the other old man said, in the high, complaining voice of the very old.

"They're our two hand-workers," Yogi said. "They make all the pumps the manufactory sends out to the big international pump races. You remember our Peerless Pounder that won the pump race in Italy, where Franky Dawson was killed?"

"I read about it in the paper," Scripps answered.

"Mr. Borrow, over there in the corner, made the Peerless Pounder all himself by hand," Yogi said.

"I carved it direct from the steel with this knife." Mr. Borrow held up a short-bladed, razorlike-looking knife. "Took me eighteen months to get it right."

"The Peerless Pounder was quite a pump all right," the high-voiced little old man said. "But we're working on one now that will show its heels to any of them foreign pumps, aren't we, Henry?"

"That's Mr. Shaw," Yogi said in an undertone. "He's probably the greatest living pump-maker."

"You boys get along and leave us alone," Mr. Borrow said. He was carving away steadily, his infirm old hands shaking a little between strokes.

"Let the boys watch," Mr. Shaw said. "Where you from, young feller?"

"I've just come from Mancelona," Scripps answered. "My wife left me."

"Well, you won't have no difficulty finding another one," Mr. Shaw said. "You're a likely-looking young feller. But take my advice and take your time. A poor wife ain't much better than no wife at all."

"I wouldn't say that, Henry," Mr. Borrow remarked in his high voice. "Any wife at all's a pretty good wife the way things are going now."

"You take my advice, young feller, and go slow. Get yourself a good one this time."

"Henry knows a thing or two," Mr. Borrow said. "He knows what he's talking about there." He laughed a high, cackling laugh. Mr. Shaw, the old pump-maker, blushed.

"You boys get along and leave us get on with our pump-making," he said. "Henry and me here, we got a sight of work to do."

"I'm very glad to have met you," Scripps said.

"Come on," Yogi said. "I better get you started or the foreman will be on my tail."

He put Scripps to work collaring pistons in the piston-collaring room. There Scripps worked for almost a year. In some ways it was the happiest year of his life. In other ways it was a nightmare. A hideous nightmare. In the end he grew to like it. In other ways he hated it. Before he knew it, a year had passed. He was still collaring pistons. But what strange things had happened in that year. Often he wondered about them. As he wondered, collaring a piston now almost automatically, he listened to the laughter that came up from below, where the little Indian lads were shaping what were to be razor blades. As he listened something rose in his throat and almost choked him.

CHAPTER 7

That night, after his first day in the pump-factory, the first day in what was or were to become an endless succession of days of dull piston-collaring, Scripps went again to the beanery to eat. All day he had kept his bird concealed. Something told him that the pump-factory was not the place to bring his bird out in. During the day the bird had several times made him uncomfortable, but he had adjusted his clothes to it and even cut a little slit the bird could poke his beak out through in search of fresh air. Now the day's work was over. It was finished. Scripps on his way to the beanery. Scripps happy that he was working with his hands. Scripps thinking of the old pump-makers. Scripps going to the society of the friendly waitress. Who was that waitress, anyway? What was it had happened to her in Paris? He must find out more about this Paris. Yogi Johnson had been there. He would quiz Yogi. Get him to talk.

Draw him out. Make him tell what he knew. He knew a trick or two about that.

Watching the sunset out over the Petoskey Harbor, the lake now frozen and great blocks of ice jutting up over the breakwater, Scripps strode down the streets of Petoskey to the beanery. He would have liked to ask Yogi Johnson to eat with him, but he didn't dare. Not yet. That would come later. All in good time. No need to rush matters with a man like Yogi. Who was Yogi, anyway? Had he really been in the war? What had the war meant to him? Was he really the first man to enlist from Cadillac? Where was Cadillac, anyway? Time would tell.

Scripps O'Neil opened the door and went into the beanery. The elderly waitress got up from the chair where she had been reading the overseas edition of *The Manchester Guardian*, and put the paper and her steel-rimmed spectacles on top of the cash register.

"Good evening," she said simply. "It's good to have *you* back."

Something stirred inside Scripps O'Neil. A feeling that he could not define came within him.

"I've been working all day long" – he looked at the elderly waitress– "for *you*," he added.

"How lovely!" she said. And then smiled shyly. "And I have been working all day long – for *you*."

Tears came into Scripps's eyes. Something stirred inside him again. He reached forward to take the elderly waitress's hand, and with quiet dignity she laid it within his own. "You are my woman," he said. Tears came into her eyes, too.

"You are my man," she said.

"Once again I say: you are my woman." Scripps pronounced the words solemnly. Something had broken inside him again. He felt he could not keep from crying.

"Let this be our wedding ceremony," the elderly waitress said. Scripps pressed her hand. "You are my woman," he said simply.

"You are my man and more than my man." She looked into his eyes. "You are all of America to me."

"Let us go," Scripps said.

"Have you your bird?" asked the waitress, laying aside her apron and folding the copy of *The Manchester Guardian Weekly*. "I'll bring *The Guardian*, if you don't mind," she said, wrapping the paper in her apron. "It's a new paper and I've not read it yet."

"I'm very fond of *The Guardian*," Scripps said. "My family have taken it ever since

I can remember. My father was a great admirer of Gladstone."

"My father went to Eton with Gladstone," the elderly waitress said. "And now I am ready."

She had donned a coat and stood ready, her apron, her steel-rimmed spectacles in their worn black morocco case, her copy of *The Manchester Guardian* held in her hand.

"Have you no hat?" asked Scripps.

"No."

"Then I will buy you one," Scripps said tenderly.

"It will be your wedding gift," the elderly waitress said. Again there were tears shone in her eyes.

"And now let us go," Scripps said.

The elderly waitress came out from behind the counter, and together, hand in hand, they strode out into the night.

Inside the beanery the black cook pushed up the wicket and looked through from the kitchen. "Dey've gone off," he chuckled. "Gone off into de night. Well, well, well." He closed the wicket softly. Even he was a little impressed.

CHAPTER 8

Half an hour later Scripps O'Neil and the elderly waitress returned to the beanery as man and wife. The beanery looked much the same. There was the long counter, the salt cellars, the sugar containers, the catsup bottle, the Worcestershire Sauce bottle. There was the wicket that led into the kitchen. Behind the counter was the relief waitress. She was a buxom, jolly-looking girl, and she wore a white apron. At the counter, reading a Detroit paper, sat a drummer. The drummer was eating a T-bone steak and hashed-brown potatoes. Something very beautiful had happened to Scripps and the elderly waitress. Now they were hungry. They wished to eat.

The elderly waitress looking at Scripps. Scripps looking at the elderly waitress. The drummer reading his paper and occasionally putting a little catsup on his hashed-brown potatoes. The other waitress, Mandy, back of the counter in her freshly starched white apron. The frost on the windows. The warmth inside. The cold outside. Scripps's bird, rather rumpled now, sitting on the counter and preening his feathers.

"So you've come back," Mandy the waitress said. "The cook said you had gone out into the night."

The elderly waitress looked at Mandy, her eyes brightened, her voice calm and now of a deeper, richer timbre.

"We are man and wife now," she said kindly. "We have just been married. What would you like to eat for supper, Scripps, dear?"

"I don't know," Scripps said. He felt vaguely uneasy. Something was stirring within him.

"Perhaps you have eaten enough of the beans, dear Scripps," the elderly waitress, now his wife, said. The drummer looked up from his paper. Scripps noticed that it was the *Detroit News*. There was a fine paper.

"That's a fine paper you're reading," Scripps said to the drummer.

"It's a good paper, the *News*," the drummer said. "You two on your honeymoon?"

"Yes," Mrs. Scripps said; "we are man and wife now."

"Well," said the drummer, "that's a mighty fine thing to be. I'm a married man myself."

"Are you?" said Scripps. "My wife left me. It was in Mancelona."

"Don't let's talk of that any more, Scripps, dear," Mrs. Scripps said. "You've told that story so many times."

"Yes, dear," Scripps agreed. He felt vaguely mistrustful of himself. Something, somewhere was stirring inside of him. He looked at the waitress called Mandy, standing robust and vigorously lovely in her newly starched white apron. He watched her hands, healthy, calm, capable hands, doing the duties of her waitress-hood.

"Try one of these T-bones with hashed-brown potatoes," the drummer suggested. "They got a nice T-bone here."

"Would you like one, dear?" Scripps asked his wife.

"I'll just take a bowl of milk and crackers," the elderly Mrs. Scripps said. "You have whatever you want, dear."

"Here's your crackers and milk, Diana," Mandy said, placing them on the counter. "Do you want a T-bone, sir?"

"Yes," Scripps said. Something stirred again within him.

"Well done or rare?"

"Rare, please."

The waitress turned and called into the wicket: "Tea for one. Let it go raw!"

"Thank you," Scripps said. He eyed the waitress Mandy. She had a gift for the picturesque in speech, that girl. It had been that very picturesque quality in her speech that had first drawn him to his present wife. That and her strange background. England, the Lake Country. Scripps striding through the Lake

Country with Wordsworth. A field of golden daffodils. The wind blowing at Windermere. Far off, perhaps, a stag at bay. Ah, that was farther north, in Scotland. They were a hardy race, those Scots, deep in their mountain fastnesses. Harry Lauder and his pipe. The Highlanders in the Great War. Why had not he, Scripps, been in the war? That was where that chap Yogi Johnson had it on him. The war would have meant much to him, Scripps. Why hadn't he been in it? Why hadn't he heard of it in time? Perhaps he was too old. Look at that old French General Joffre, though. Surely he was a younger man than that old general. General Foch praying for victory. The French troops kneeling along the Chemin des Dames, praying for victory. The Germans with their "*Gott mit uns.*" What a mockery. Surely he was no older than that French General Foch. He wondered.

Mandy, the waitress, placed his T-bone steak and hashed-brown potatoes on the counter before him. As she laid the plate down, just for an instant, her hand touched his. Scripps felt a strange thrill go through him. Life was before him. He was not an old man. Why were there no wars now? Perhaps there were. Men were fighting in China, Chinamen, Chinamen killing one another. What for? Scripps wondered. What was it all about, anyway?

Mandy, the buxom waitress, leaned forward. "Say," she said, "did I ever tell you about the last words of Henry James?"

"Really, dear Mandy," Mrs. Scripps said, "you've told that story rather often."

"Let's hear it," Scripps said. "I'm very interested in Henry James." Henry James, Henry James. That chap who had gone away from his own land to live in England among Englishmen. Why had he done it? For what had he left America? Weren't his roots here? His brother William. Boston. Pragmatism. Harvard University. Old John Harvard with silver buckles on his shoes. Charley Brickley. Eddie Mahan. Where were they now?

"Well," Mandy began, "Henry James became a British subject on his death-bed. At once, as soon as the king heard Henry James had become a British subject he sent around the highest decoration in his power to bestow – the Order of Merit."

"The O. M.," the elderly Mrs. Scripps explained.

"That was it," the waitress said. "Professors Gosse and Saintsbury came with the man who brought the decoration. Henry James was lying on his death-bed, and his eyes were shut. There was a single candle on a table beside the bed. The nurse allowed them to come near the bed, and they put the ribbon of the decoration around James's neck, and the decoration lay on the sheet over Henry James's chest.

Professors Gosse and Saintsbury leaned forward and smoothed the ribbon of the decoration. Henry James never opened his eyes. The nurse told them they all must go out of the room, and they all went out of the room. When they were all gone, Henry James spoke to the nurse. He never opened his eyes. 'Nurse,' Henry James said, 'put out the candle, nurse, and spare my blushes.' Those were the last words he ever spoke."

"James was quite a writer," Scripps O'Neil said. He was strangely moved by the story.

"You don't always tell it the same way, dear," Mrs. Scripps remarked to Mandy. There were tears in Mandy's eyes. "I feel very strongly about Henry James," she said.

"What was the matter with James?" asked the drummer. "Wasn't America good enough for him?"

Scripps O'Neil was thinking about Mandy, the waitress. What a background she must have, that girl! What a fund of anecdotes! A chap could go far with a woman like that to help him! He stroked the little bird that sat on the lunch-counter before him. The bird pecked at his finger. Was the little bird a hawk? A falcon, perhaps, from one of the big Michigan falconries. Was it perhaps a robin? Pulling and tugging at the early worm on some green lawn somewhere? He wondered.

"What do you call your bird?" the drummer asked.

"I haven't named him yet. What would you call him?"

"Why not call him Ariel?" Mandy asked.

"Or Puck," Mrs. Scripps put in.

"What's it mean?" asked the drummer.

"It's a character out of Shakespeare," Mandy explained.

"Oh, give the bird a chance."

"What would you call him?" Scripps turned to the drummer.

"He ain't a parrot, is he?" asked the drummer. "If he was a parrot you could call him Polly."

"There's a character in 'The Beggar's Opera' called Polly," Mandy explained.

Scripps wondered. Perhaps the bird was a parrot. A parrot strayed from some comfortable home with some old maid. The untilled soil of some New England spinster.

"Better wait till you see how he turns out," the drummer advised. "You got plenty of time to name him."

This drummer had sound ideas. He, Scripps, did not even know what sex the bird was. Whether he was a boy bird or a girl bird.

"Wait till you see if he lays eggs," the drummer suggested. Scripps looked into the drummer's eyes. The fellow had voiced his own unspoken thought.

"You know a thing or two, drummer," he said.

"Well," the drummer admitted modestly, "I ain't drummed all these years for nothing."

"You're right there, pal," Scripps said.

"That's a nice bird you got there, brother," the drummer said. "You want to hang onto that bird."

Scripps knew it. Ah, these drummers know a thing or two. Going up and down over the face of this great America of ours. These drummers kept their eyes open. They were no fools.

"Listen," the drummer said. He pushed his derby hat off his brow and, leaning forward, spat into the tall brass cuspidor that stood beside his stool. "I want to tell you about a pretty beautiful thing that happened to me once in Bay City."

Mandy, the waitress, leaned forward. Mrs. Scripps leaned toward the drummer to hear better. The drummer looked apologetically at Scripps and stroked the bird with his forefinger.

"Tell you about it some other time, brother," he said. Scripps understood. From out of the kitchen, through the wicket in the hall, came a high-pitched, haunting laugh. Scripps listened. Could that be the laughter of the Negro? He wondered.

CHAPTER 9

Scripps going slowly to work in the pump-factory in the mornings. Mrs. Scripps looking out of the window and watching him go up the street. Not much time for reading *The Guardian* now. Not much time for reading about English politics. Not much time for worrying about the cabinet crises over there in France. The French were a strange people. Joan of Arc. Eva le Gallienne. Clemenceau. Georges Carpentier. Sacha Guitry. Yvonne Printemps. Grock. Les Fratellinis. Gilbert Seldes. *The Dial*. *The Dial* Prize. Marianne Moore. E. E. Cummings. *The Enormous Room*. *Vanity Fair*. Frank Crowninshield. What was it all about? Where was it taking her?

She had a man now. A man of her own. For her own. Could she keep him? Could she hold him for her own? She wondered.

Mrs. Scripps, formerly an elderly waitress, now the wife of Scripps O'Neil, with a good job in the pump-factory. Diana Scripps. Diana was her own name. It had been her mother's, too. Diana Scripps looking into the mirror and wondering could she hold him. It was getting to be a question. Why had he ever met Mandy? Would she have the courage to break off going to the restaurant with Scripps to eat? She couldn't do that. He would go alone. She knew that. It was no use trying to pull wool over her own eyes. He would go alone and he would talk with Mandy. Diana looked into the mirror. Could she hold him? Could she hold him? That thought never left her now.

Every night at the restaurant, she couldn't call it a beanery now – that made a lump come in her throat and made her throat feel hard and choky. Every night at the restaurant now Scripps and Mandy talked together. The girl was trying to take him away. Him, her Scripps. Trying to take him away. Take him away. Could she, Diana, hold him?

She was no better than a slut, that Mandy. Was that the way to do? Was that the thing to do? Go after another woman's man? Come between man and wife? Break up a home? And all with these interminable literary reminiscences. These endless anecdotes. Scripps was fascinated by Mandy. Diana admitted that to herself. But she might hold him. That was all that mattered now. To hold him. To hold him. Not to let him go. Make him stay. She looked into the mirror.

Diana subscribing for *The Forum*. Diana reading *The Mentor*. Diana reading William Lyon Phelps in *Scribner's*. Diana walking through the frozen streets of the silent Northern town to the Public Library, to read *The Literary Digest* "Book Review." Diana waiting for the postman to come, bringing *The Bookman*. Diana, in the snow, waiting for the postman to bring *The Saturday Review of Literature*. Diana, bareheaded now, standing in the mounting snow-drifts, waiting for the postman to bring her the *New York Times* "Literary Section." Was it doing any good? Was it holding him?

At first it seemed to be. Diana learned editorials by John Farrar by heart. Scripps brightened. A little of the old light shining in Scripps's eyes now. Then it died. Some little mistake in the wording, some slip in her understanding of a phrase, some divergence in her attitude, made it all ring false. She would go on. She was not beaten. He was her man and she would hold him. She looked away from the window and slit open the covering of the magazine that lay on her table. It was *Harper's Magazine*. *Harper's Magazine* in a new format. *Harper's Magazine* completely changed and revised. Perhaps that would do the trick. She wondered.

CHAPTER 10

Spring was coming. Spring was in the air. (Author's Note – This is the same day on which the story starts, back on page three.) A chinook wind was blowing. Workmen were coming home from the factory. Scripps's bird singing in its cage. Diana looking out of the open window. Diana watching for her Scripps to come up the street. Could she hold him? Could she hold him? If she couldn't hold him, would he leave her his bird? She had felt lately that she couldn't hold him. In the nights, now, when she touched Scripps he rolled away, not toward her. It was a little sign, but life was made up of little signs. She felt she couldn't hold him. As she looked out of the window, a copy of *The Century Magazine* dropped from her nerveless hand. *The Century* had a new editor. There were more woodcuts. Glenn Frank had gone to head some great university somewhere. There were more Van Dorens on the magazine. Diana felt that might turn the trick. Happily she had opened *The Century* and read all morning. Then the wind, the warm chinook wind, had started to blow, and she knew Scripps would soon be home. Men were coming down the street in increasing numbers. Was Scripps among them? She did not like to put on her spectacles to look. She wanted Scripps's first glimpse of her to be of her at her best. As she felt him drawing nearer, the confidence she had had in *The Century* grew fainter. She had so hoped that would give her the something which would hold him. She wasn't sure now.

Scripps coming down the street with a crowd of excited workmen. Men stirred by the spring. Scripps swinging his lunch-bucket. Scripps waving good-by to the workmen, who trooped one by one into what had formerly been a saloon. Scripps not looking up at the window. Scripps coming up the stairs. Scripps coming nearer. Scripps coming nearer. Scripps here.

"Good afternoon, dear Scripps," she said. "I've been reading a story by Ruth Suckow."

"Hello, Diana," Scripps answered. He set down his lunch-pail. She looked worn and old. He could afford to be polite.

"What was the story about, Diana?" he asked.

"It was about a little girl in Iowa," Diana said. She moved toward him. "It was about people on the land. It reminded me a little of my own Lake Country."

"That so?" asked Scripps. In some ways the pump-factory had hardened him. His speech had become more clipped. More like these hardy Northern workers'. But his mind was the same.

"Would you like me to read a little of it out loud?" Diana asked. "They're some lovely woodcuts."

"How about going down to the beanery?" Scripps said.

"As you wish, dear," Diana said. Then her voice broke. "I wish – oh, I wish you'd never seen that place!" She wiped away her tears. Scripps had not even seen them. "I'll bring the bird, dear," Diana said. "He hasn't been out all day."

Together they went down the street to the beanery. They did not walk hand in hand now. They walked like what are called old married people. Mrs. Scripps carried the bird-cage. The bird was happy in the warm wind. Men lurching along, drunk with the spring, passed them. Many spoke to Scripps. He was well known and well liked in the town now. Some, as they lurched by, raised their hats to Mrs. Scripps. She responded vaguely. If I can only hold him, she was thinking. If I can only hold him. As they walked along the slushy snow of the narrow sidewalk of the Northern town, something began to beat in her head. Perhaps it was the rhythm of their walking together. I can't hold him. I can't hold him. I can't hold him.

Scripps took her arm as they crossed the street. When his hand touched her arm Diana knew it was true. She would never hold him. A group of Indians passed them on the street. Were they laughing at her or was it some tribal jest? Diana didn't know. All she knew was that rhythm that beat into her brain. I can't hold him. I can't hold him.

AUTHOR'S NOTE:

For the reader, not the printer. What difference does it make to the printer? Who is the printer, anyway? Gutenberg. The Gutenberg Bible. Caxton. Twelve-point open-face Caslon. The linotype machine. The author as a little boy being sent to look for type lice. The author as a young man being sent for the key to the forms. Ah, they knew a trick or two, these printers.

(In case the reader is becoming confused, we are now up to where the story opened with Yogi Johnson and Scripps O'Neil in the pump-factory itself, with the chinook wind blowing. As you see, Scripps O'Neil has now come out of the pump-factory and is on his way to the beanery with his wife, who is afraid she cannot hold him. Personally, we don't believe she can, but the reader will see for himself. We will now leave the couple on their way to the beanery and go back and take up Yogi Johnson. We want the reader to like Yogi Johnson. The story will move a little faster from now on, in case any of the readers are tiring. We will also try and work in a number of good anecdotes. Would it be any violation of confidence if we told the reader that we get the best of these anecdotes from Mr. Ford Madox Ford? We owe him our thanks, and we hope the reader does, too. At any rate, we will now go on with Yogi Johnson. Yogi Johnson, the reader may remember, is the chap who was in the war. As the story opens, he is just coming out of the pump-factory. (See page three.)

It is very hard to write this way, beginning things backward, and the author hopes the reader will realize this and not grudge this little word of explanation. I know I would be very glad to read anything the reader ever wrote, and I hope the reader will make the same sort of allowances. If any of the readers would care to send me anything they ever wrote, for criticism or advice, I am always at the Café du Dôme any afternoon, talking about Art with Harold Stearns and Sinclair Lewis, and the reader can bring his stuff along with him, or he can send it to me care of my bank, if I have a bank. Now, if the reader is ready – and understand, I don't want to rush the reader any – we will go back to Yogi Johnson. But please remember that, while we have gone back to Yogi Johnson, Scripps O'Neil and his wife are on their way to the beanery. What will happen to them there I don't know. I only wish the reader could help me.)

PART THREE

MEN IN WAR AND THE DEATH OF SOCIETY

It may be likewise noted that affectation does not imply an absolute negation of those qualities which are affected; and therefore, though, when it proceeds from hypocrisy, it be nearly allied to deceit; yet when it comes from vanity only, it partakes of the nature of ostentation: for instance, the affectation of liberality in a vain man differs visibly from the same affectation in the avaricious, for though the vain man is not what he would appear, or hath not the virtue he affects, to the degree he would be thought to have it; yet it sits less awkwardly on him than on the avaricious man, who is the very reverse of what he would seem to be.

HENRY FIELDING

CHAPTER 11

Yogi Johnson walked out of the workmen's entrance of the pump-factory and down the street. Spring was in the air. The snow was melting, and the gutters were running with snow-water. Yogi Johnson walked down the middle of the street, keeping on the as yet unmelted ice. He turned to the left and crossed the bridge over Bear River. The ice had already melted in the river and he watched the swirling brown current. Below, beside the stream, buds on the willow brush were coming out green.

It's a real chinook wind, Yogi thought. The foreman did right to let the men go. It wouldn't be safe keeping them in a day like this. Anything might happen. The owner of the factory knew a thing or two. When the chinook blew, the thing to do was to get the men out of the factory. Then, if any of them were injured, it was not on him. He didn't get caught under the Employer's Liability Act. They knew a thing or two, these big pump-manufacturers. They were smart, all right.

Yogi was worried. There was something on his mind. It was spring, there was no doubt of that now, and he did not want a woman. He had worried about it a lot lately. There was no question about it. He did not want a woman. He couldn't explain it to himself. He had gone to the Public Library and asked for a book the night before. He looked at the librarian. He did not want her. Somehow, she meant nothing to him. At the restaurant where he had a meal ticket he looked hard at the waitress who brought him his meals. He did not want her, either. He passed a group of girls on their way home from high school. He looked carefully at all of them. He did not want a single one. Decidedly something was wrong. Was he going to pieces? Was this the end?

Well, Yogi thought, women are gone, perhaps, though I hope not; but I still have my love of horses. He was walking up the steep hill that leads up from the Bear River out onto the Charlevoix road. The road was not really so steep, but it felt steep to Yogi, his legs heavy with the spring. In front of him was a grain and feed store. A team of beautiful horses were hitched in front of the feed store. Yogi went up to them. He wanted to touch them. To reassure himself that there was something left. The nigh horse looked at him as he came near. Yogi put his hand in his pocket for a lump of sugar. He had no sugar. The horse put its ears back and showed its teeth. The other horse jerked its head away. Was this all that his love of horses had brought him? After all, perhaps there was something wrong with these horses. Perhaps they had glanders or spavin. Perhaps something had been caught in the tender frog of their hoof. Perhaps they were lovers.

Yogi walked on up the hill and turned to the left onto the Charlevoix road. He passed the last houses of the outskirts of Petoskey and came out onto the open country road. On his right was a field that stretched to Little Traverse Bay. The blue of the bay opening out into the big Lake Michigan. Across the bay the pine hills behind Harbor Springs. Beyond, where you could not see it, Cross Village, where the Indians lived. Even further beyond, the Straits of Mackinac with St. Ignace, where a strange and beautiful thing had once happened to Oscar Gardner, who worked beside Yogi in the pump-factory. Further beyond, the Soo, both Canadian and American. There the wilder spirits of Petoskey sometimes went to drink beer. They were happy then. 'Way, 'way beyond, and, in the other direction, at the foot of the lake was Chicago, where Scripps O'Neil had started for on that eventful night when his first marriage had become a marriage no longer. Near there Gary, Indiana, where were the great steel mills. Near there Hammond, Indiana. Near there Michigan City, Indiana. Further beyond, there would be Indianapolis, Indiana, where Booth Tarkington lived. He had the wrong dope, that fellow. Further down there would be Cincinnati, Ohio. Beyond that, Vicksburg, Mississippi. Beyond that, Waco, Texas. Ah! there was grand sweep to this America of ours.

Yogi walked across the road and sat down on a pile of logs, where he could look out over the lake. After all, the war was over and he was still alive.

There was a chap in that fellow Anderson's book that the librarian had given him at the library last night. Why hadn't he wanted the librarian, anyway? Could it be because he thought she might have false teeth? Could it be something else? Would a little child ever tell her? He didn't know. What was the librarian to him, anyway?

This chap in the book by Anderson. He had been a soldier, too. He had been at the front two years, Anderson said. What was his name? Fred Something. This Fred had thoughts dancing in his brain – horror. One night, in the time of the fighting, he went out on parade – no, it was patrol – in No Man's Land, and saw another man stumbling along in the darkness and shot him. The man pitched forward dead. It had been the only time Fred consciously killed a man. You don't kill men in war much, the book said. The hell you don't, Yogi thought, if you're two years in the infantry at the front. They just die. Indeed they do, Yogi thought. Anderson said the act was rather hysterical on Fred's part. He and the men with him might have made the fellow surrender. They had all got the jimjams. After it happened they all ran away together. Where the hell did they run to? Yogi wondered. Paris?

Afterward, killing this man haunted Fred. It's got to be sweet and true. That was the way the soldiers thought, Anderson said. The hell it was. This Fred was supposed to have been two years in an infantry regiment at the front.

A couple of Indians were passing along the road, grunting to themselves and to each other. Yogi called to them. The Indians came over.

"Big white chief got chew of tobacco?" asked the first Indian.

"White chief carry liquor?" the second Indian asked.

Yogi handed them a package of Peerless and his pocket flask.

"White chief heap big medicine," the Indians grunted.

"Listen," Yogi Johnson said. "I am about to address to you a few remarks about the war. A subject on which I feel very deeply." The Indians sat down on the logs. One of the Indians pointed at the sky. "Up there gitchy Manitou the Mighty," he said.

The other Indian winked at Yogi. "White chief no believe every goddam thing he hear," he grunted.

"Listen," Yogi Johnson said. And he told them about the war.

War hadn't been that way to Yogi, he told the Indians. War had been to him like football. American football. What they play at the colleges. Carlisle Indian School. Both the Indians nodded. They had been to Carlisle.

Yogi had played centre at football and war had been much the same thing, intensely unpleasant. When you played football and had the ball, you were down with your legs spread out and the ball held out in front of you on the ground; you had to listen for the signal, decode it, and make the proper pass. You had to think about it all the time. While your hands were on the ball the opposing centre stood in front of you, and when you passed the ball he brought his hand up smash into your face and grabbed you with the other hand under the chin or under your armpit, and tried to pull you forward or shove you back to make a hole he could go through and break up the play. You were supposed to charge forward so hard you banged him out of the play with your body and put you both on the ground. He had all the advantage. It was not what you would call fun. When you had the ball he had all the advantage. The only good thing was that when he had the ball you could rough-house *him*. In this way things evened up and sometimes even a certain tolerance was achieved. Football, like the war, was unpleasant; stimulating and exciting after you had attained a certain hardness, and the chief difficulty had been that of remembering the signals. Yogi was thinking about the war, not the army. He meant combat. The army was something different. You could take it and ride with it or you could buck the tiger and let it smash you. The army was a silly business, but the war was different.

Yogi was not haunted by men he had killed. He knew he had killed five men. Probably he had killed more. He didn't believe men you killed haunted you. Not if you had been two years at the front. Most of the men he had known had been excited as hell when they had first killed. The trouble was to keep them from killing too much. It was hard to get prisoners back to the people that wanted them for identification. You sent a man back with two prisoners; maybe you sent two men back with four prisoners. What happened? The men came back and said the prisoners were knocked out by the barrage. They would give the prisoner a poke in the seat of the pants with a bayonet, and when the prisoner jumped they would say, "You would run, you son of a bitch," and let their gun off in the back of his head. They wanted to be sure they had killed. Also they didn't want to go back through any damn barrage. No, sir. They learned those kind of manners from the Australians. After all, what were those Jerries? A bunch of goddam Huns. "Huns" sounded like a funny word now. All this sweetness and truth. Not if you were in there two years. In the end they would have softened. Got sorry for excesses and begun to store up good deeds against getting killed themselves. But that was the fourth phase of soldiering, the gentling down.

In a good soldier in the war it went like this: First, you were brave because you didn't think anything could hit you, because you yourself were something special, and you knew that you could never die. Then you found out different. You were really scared then, but if you were a good soldier you functioned the same as before. Then after you were wounded and not killed, with new men coming on, and going through your old processes, you hardened and became a good hard-boiled soldier. Then came the second crack, which is much worse than the first, and then you began doing good deeds, and being the boy Sir Philip Sidney, and storing up treasures in heaven. At the same time, of course, functioning always the same as before. As if it were a football game.

Nobody had any damn business to write about it, though, that didn't at least know about it from hearsay. Literature has too strong an effect on people's minds. Like this American writer Willa Cather, who wrote a book about the war where all the last part of it was taken from the action in the *Birth of a Nation*, and ex-servicemen wrote to her from all over America to tell her how much they liked it.

One of the Indians was asleep. He had been chewing tobacco, and his mouth was pursed up in sleep. He was leaning on the other Indian's shoulder. The Indian who was awake pointed at the other Indian, who was asleep, and shook his head.

"Well, how did you like the speech?" Yogi asked the Indian who was awake.

"White chief have heap much sound ideas," the Indian said. "White chief educated like hell."

"Thank you," Yogi said. He felt touched. Here among the simple aborigines, the only real Americans, he had found that true communion. The Indian looked at him, holding the sleeping Indian carefully that his head might not fall back upon the snow-covered logs.

"Was white chief in the war?" the Indian asked.

"I landed in France in May, 1917," Yogi began.

"I thought maybe white chief was in the war from the way he talked," the Indian said. "Him," he raised the head of his sleeping companion up so the last rays of the sunset shone on the sleeping Indian's face, "he got V.C. Me I got D.S.O. and M.C. with bar. I was major in the Fourth C.M.R.'s."

"I'm glad to meet you," Yogi said. He felt strangely humiliated. It was growing dark. There was a single line of sunset where the sky and the water met way out on Lake Michigan. Yogi watched the narrow line of the sunset grow darker red, thin to a mere slit, and then fade. The sun was down behind the lake. Yogi stood up from the pile of logs. The Indian stood up too. He awakened his companion, and the Indian who had been sleeping stood up and looked at Yogi Johnson.

"We go to Petoskey to join Salvation Army," the larger and more wakeful Indian said.

"White chief come too," said the smaller Indian, who had been asleep.

"I'll walk in with you," Yogi replied. Who were these Indians? What did they mean to him?

With the sun down, the slushy road was stiffening. It was freezing again. After all, maybe spring was not coming. Maybe it did not make a difference that he did not want a woman. Now that the spring was perhaps not coming there was a question about that. He would walk into town with the Indians and look for a beautiful woman and try and want her. He turned down the now frozen road. The two Indians walked by his side. They were all bound in the same direction.

CHAPTER 12

Through the night down the frozen road the three walked into Petoskey. They had been silent walking along the frozen road. Their shoes broke the new-formed crusts of ice. Sometimes Yogi Johnson stepped through a thin film of ice into a pool of water. The Indians avoided the pools of water.

They came down the hill past the feed store, crossed the bridge over the Bear River, their boots ringing hollowly on the frozen planks of the bridge, and climbed the hill that led past Dr. Rumsey's house and the Home Tea-Room up to the pool-room. In front of the pool-room the two Indians stopped.

"White chief shoot pool?" the big Indian asked.

"No," Yogi Johnson said. "My right arm was crippled in the war."

"White chief have hard luck," the small Indian said. "Shoot one game Kelly pool."

"He got both arms and both legs shot off at Ypres," the big Indian said in an aside to Yogi. "Him very sensitive."

"All right," Yogi Johnson said. "I'll shoot one game."

They went into the hot, smoke-filled warmth of the pool-room. They obtained a table and took down cues from the wall. As the little Indian reached up to take down his cue Yogi noticed that he had two artificial arms. They were brown leather and were both buckled on at the elbow. On the smooth green cloth, under the bright electric lights, they played pool. At the end of an hour and a half, Yogi Johnson found that he owed the little Indian four dollars and thirty cents.

"You shoot a pretty nice stick," he remarked to the small Indian.

"Me not shoot so good since the war," the small Indian replied.

"White chief like to drink a little?" asked the larger Indian.

"Where do you get it?" asked Yogi. "I have to go to Cheboygan for mine."

"White chief come with red brothers," the big Indian said.

They left the pool-table, placed their cues in the rack on the wall, paid at the counter, and went out into the night.

Along the dark streets men were sneaking home. The frost had come and frozen everything stiff and cold. The chinook had not been a real chinook, after all. Spring had not yet come, and the men who had commenced their orgies were halted by the chill in the air that told them the chinook wind had been a fake. That foreman, Yogi thought, he'll catch hell to-morrow. Perhaps it had all been engineered by the pump-manufacturers to get the foreman out of his job. Such things were done. Through the dark of the night men were sneaking home in little groups.

The two Indians walked on either side of Yogi. They turned down a side street, and all three halted before a building that looked something like a stable. It was a stable. The two Indians opened the door and Yogi followed them inside. A ladder led upstairs to the floor above. It was dark inside the stable, but one of the Indians lit a match to show Yogi the ladder. The little Indian climbed up first, the metal hinges of his artificial limbs squeaking as he climbed. Yogi followed him, and the other Indian climbed last, lighting Yogi's way with matches. The little Indian knocked on the roof where the ladder stopped against the wall. There was an answering knock. The little Indian knocked in answer, three sharp knocks on the roof above his head. A trap-door in the roof was raised, and they climbed up through into the lighted room.

In one corner of the room there was a bar with a brass rail and tall spittoons. Behind the bar was a mirror. Easy-chairs were all around the room. There was a pool-table. Magazines on sticks hung in a line on the wall. There was a framed autographed portrait of Henry Wadsworth Longfellow on the wall draped in the American flag. Several Indians were sitting in the easy-chairs reading. A little group stood at the bar.

"Nice little club, eh?" An Indian came up and shook hands with Yogi. "I see you almost every day at the pump-factory."

He was a man who worked at one of the machines near Yogi in the factory. Another Indian came up and shook hands with Yogi. He also worked in the pump-factory.

"Rotten luck about the chinook," he said.

"Yes," Yogi said. "Just a false alarm."

"Come and have a drink," the first Indian said.

"I'm with a party," Yogi answered. Who were these Indians, anyway?

"Bring them along too," the first Indian said. "Always room for one more."

Yogi looked around him. The two Indians who had brought him were gone. Where were they? Then he saw them. They were over at the pool-table. The tall refined Indian to whom Yogi was talking followed his glance. He nodded his head in understanding.

"They're woods Indians," he explained apologetically. "We're most of us town Indians here."

"Yes, of course," Yogi agreed.

"The little chap has a very good war record," the tall refined Indian remarked. "The other chap was a major too, I believe."

Yogi was guided over to the bar by the tall refined Indian. Behind the bar was the bartender. He was a Negro.

"How would some Dog's Head ale go?" asked the Indian.

"Fine," Yogi said.

"Two Dog's Heads, Bruce," the Indian remarked to the bartender. The bartender broke into a chuckle.

"What are you laughing at, Bruce?" the Indian asked.

The Negro broke into a shrill haunting laugh.

"I knowed it, Massa Red Dog," he said. "I knowed you'd ordah dat Dog's Head all the time."

"He's a merry fellow," the Indian remarked to Yogi. "I must introduce myself. Red Dog's the name."

"Johnson's the name," Yogi said. "Yogi Johnson."

"Oh, we are all quite familiar with your name, Mr. Johnson," Red Dog smiled. "I would like you to meet my friends Mr. Sitting Bull, Mr. Poisoned Buffalo, and Chief Running Skunk-Backwards."

"Sitting Bull's a name I know," Yogi remarked, shaking hands.

"Oh, I'm not one of those Sitting Bulls," Mr. Sitting Bull said.

"Chief Running Skunk-Backwards's great-grandfather once sold the entire Island of Manhattan for a few strings of wampum," Red Dog explained.

"How very interesting," Yogi said.

"That was a costly bit of wampum for our family," Chief Running Skunk-Backwards smiled ruefully.

"Chief Running Skunk-Backwards has some of that wampum. Would you like to see it?" Red Dog asked.

"Indeed, I would."

"It's really no different from any other wampum," Skunk-Backwards explained deprecatingly. He pulled a chain of wampum out of his pocket, and handed it to Yogi Johnson. Yogi looked at it curiously. What a part that string of wampum had played in this America of ours.

"Would you like to have one or two wampums for a keep-sake?" Skunk-Backwards asked.

"I wouldn't like to take your wampum," Yogi demurred.

"They have no intrinsic value really," Skunk-Backwards explained, detaching one or two wampums from the string.

"Their value is really a sentimental one to Skunk-Backwards's family," Red Dog said.

"It's damned decent of you, Mr. Skunk-Backwards," Yogi said.

"It's nothing," Skunk-Backwards said. "You'd do the same for me in a moment."

"It's decent of you."

Behind the bar, Bruce, the Negro bartender, had been leaning forward and watching the wampums pass from hand to hand. His dark face shone. Sharply, without explanation, he broke into high-pitched uncontrolled laughter. The dark laughter of the Negro.

Red Dog looked at him sharply. "I say, Bruce," he spoke sharply; "your mirth is a little ill-timed."

Bruce stopped laughing and wiped his face on a towel. He rolled his eyes apologetically.

"Ah can't help it, Massa Red Dog. When I seen Mistah Skunk-Backhouse passin' dem wampums around I jess couldn't stand it no longa. Whad he wan sell a big town like New Yawk foh dem wampums for? Wampums! Take away yoah wampums!"

"Bruce is an eccentric," Red Dog explained, "but he's a corking bartender and a good-hearted chap."

"Youah right theah, Massa Red Dog," the bartender leaned forward. "I'se got a heart of puah gold."

"He is an eccentric, though," Red Dog apologized. "The house committee are always after me to get another bartender, but I like the chap, oddly enough."

"I'm all right, boss," Bruce said. "It's just that when I see something funny I just have to laff. You know I don' mean no harm, boss."

"Right enough, Bruce," Red Dog agreed. "You are an honest chap."

Yogi Johnson looked about the room. The other Indians had gone away from the bar, and Skunk-Backwards was showing the wampum to a little group of Indians in dinner dress who had just come in. At the pool-table the two woods Indians were still playing. They had removed their coats, and the light above the pool-table glinted on the metal joints in the little woods Indian's artificial arms. He had just run the table for the eleventh consecutive time.

"That little chap would have made a pool-player if he hadn't had a bit of hard luck in the war," Red Dog remarked. "Would you like to have a look about the club?" He took the check from Bruce, signed it, and Yogi followed him into the next room.

"Our committee room," Red Dog said. On the walls were framed autographed photographs of Chief Bender, Francis Park-man, D. H. Lawrence, Chief Meyers, Stewart Edward White, Mary Austin, Jim Thorpe, General Custer, Glenn Warner, Mabel Dodge, and a full-length oil painting of Henry Wadsworth Longfellow.

Beyond the committee room was a locker room with a small plunge bath or swimming-pool. "It's really ridiculously small for a club," Red Dog said. "But it makes a comfortable little hole to pop into when the evenings are dull." He smiled. "We call it the wigwam, you know. That's a little conceit of my own."

"It's a damned nice club," Yogi said enthusiastically.

"Put you up if you like," Red Dog offered. "What's your tribe?"

"What do you mean?"

"Your tribe. What are you – Sac and Fox? Jibway? Cree, I imagine."

"Oh," said Yogi. "My parents came from Sweden."

Red Dog looked at him closely. His eyes narrowed.

"You're not having me on?"

"No. They either came from Sweden or Norway," Yogi said.

"I'd have sworn you looked a bit on the white side," Red Dog said. "Damned good thing this came out in time. There'd have been no end of scandal." He put his hand to his head and pursed his lips. "Here, you," he turned suddenly and gripped Yogi by the vest. Yogi felt the barrel of an automatic pushed hard against his stomach.

"You'll go quietly through the club-room, get your coat and hat and leave as though nothing had happened. Say polite good-by to anyone who happens to speak to you. And never come back. Get that, you Swede."

"Yes," said Yogi. "Put up your gun. I'm not afraid of your gun."

"Do as I say," Red Dog ordered. "As for those two pool-players that brought you here, I'll soon have them out of this."

Yogi went into the bright room, looked at the bar, where Bruce, the bartender, was regarding him, got his hat and coat, said good-night to Skunk-Backwards, who asked him why he was leaving so early, and the outside trap-door was swung up by Bruce. As Yogi started down the ladder the Negro burst out laughing. "I knowed it," he laughed. "I knowed it all de time. No Swede gwine to fool ole Bruce."

Yogi looked back and saw the laughing black face of the Negro framed in the oblong square of light that came through the raised trap-door. Once on the stable floor, Yogi looked around him. He was alone. The straw of the old stable was stiff and frozen under his feet. Where had he been? Had he been in an Indian club? What was it all about? Was this the end?

Above him a slit of light came in the roof. Then it was blocked by two black figures, there was the sound of a kick, a blow, a series of thuds, some dull, some sharp, and two human forms came crashing down the ladder. From above floated the dark, haunting sound of black Negro laughter.

The two woods Indians picked themselves up from the straw and limped toward the door. One of them, the little one, was crying. Yogi followed them out into the cold night. It was cold. The night was clear. The stars were out.

"Club no damn good," the big Indian said. "Club heap no damn good."

The little Indian was crying. Yogi, in the starlight, saw that he had lost one of his artificial arms.

"Me no play pool no more," the little Indian sobbed. He shook his one arm at the window of the club, from which a thin slit of light came. "Club heap goddam hell no good."

"Never mind," Yogi said. "I'll get you a job in the pump-factory."

"Pump-factory, hell," the big Indian said. "We all go join Salvation Army."

"Don't cry," Yogi said to the little Indian. "I'll buy you a new arm."

The little Indian went on crying. He sat down in the snowy road. "No can play pool me no care about nothing," he said.

From above them, out of the window of the club came the haunting sound of a Negro laughing.

AUTHOR'S NOTE TO THE READER

In case it may have any historical value, I am glad to state that I wrote the foregoing chapter in two hours directly on the typewriter, and then went out to lunch with John Dos Passos, whom I consider a very forceful writer, and an exceedingly pleasant fellow besides. This is what is known in the provinces as log-rolling. We lunched on rollmops, Sole Meunière, Civet de Lièvre à la Chez Cocotte, marmelade de pommes, and washed it all down, as we used to say (eh, reader?) with a bottle of Montrachet 1919, with the sole, and a bottle of Hospice de Beaune 1919 apiece with the jugged hare. Mr. Dos Passos, I believe, shared a bottle of Chambertin with me over the marmelade de pommes (Eng., apple sauce). We drank two vieux marcs, and after deciding not to go to the Café du Dôme and talk about Art we both went to our respective homes and I wrote the following chapter. I would like the reader to particularly remark the way the complicated threads of the lives of the various characters in the book are gathered together, and then held there in that memorable scene in the beanery. It was when I read this chapter aloud to him that Mr. Dos Passos exclaimed, "Hemingway, you have wrought a masterpiece."

P. S. – FROM THE AUTHOR TO THE READER

It is at this point, reader, that I am going to try and get that sweep and movement into the book that shows that the book is really a great book. I know you hope just as much as I do, reader, that I will get this sweep and movement because think what it will mean to both of us. Mr. H. G. Wells, who has been visiting at our home (we're getting along in the literary game, eh, reader?) asked us the other day if perhaps our reader, that's you, reader – just think of it, H. G. Wells talking about you right in our home. Anyway, H. G. Wells asked us if perhaps our reader would not think too much of this story was autobiographical. Please, reader, just get that idea out of your head. We have lived in Petoskey, Mich., it is true, and naturally many of the characters are drawn from life as we lived it then. But they are other people, not the author. The author only comes into the story in these little notes. It is true that before starting this story we spent twelve years studying the various Indian dialects of the North, and there is still preserved in the museum at Cross Village our translation of the New Testament into Ojibway. But you would have done the same thing in our place, reader, and I think if you think it over you will agree with us on this. Now to get back to the story. It is meant in the best spirit of friendship when I say that you have no idea, reader, what a hard chapter this is going to be to write. As a matter of fact, and I try to be frank about these things, we will not even try and write it until tomorrow.

PART FOUR. THE PASSING OF A GREAT RACE AND THE MAKING AND MARRING OF AMERICANS

But perhaps it may be objected to me, that I have against my own rules introduced vices, and of a very black kind, into this work. To which I shall answer: first, that it is very difficult to pursue a series of human actions, and keep clear from them. Secondly, that the vices to be found here are rather the accidental consequences of some human frailty or foible, than causes habitually existing in the mind. Thirdly, that they are never set forth as the objects of ridicule, but detestation. Fourthly, that they are never the principal figure at that time on the scene: and lastly, they never produce the intended evil.

HENRY FIELDING

CHAPTER 13

Yogi Johnson walking down the silent street with his arm around the little Indian's shoulder. The big Indian walking along beside them. The cold night. The shuttered houses of the town. The little Indian, who has lost his artificial arm. The big Indian, who was also in the war. Yogi Johnson, who was in the war too. The three of them walking, walking, walking. Where were they going? Where could they go? What was there left?

Suddenly under a street light that swung on its drooping wire above a street corner, casting its light down on the snow, the big Indian stopped. "Walking no get us nowhere," he grunted. "Walking no good. Let white chief speak. Where we go, white chief?"

Yogi Johnson did not know. Obviously, walking was not the solution of their problem. Walking was all right in its way. Coxey's Army. A horde of men, seeking work, pressing on toward Washington. Marching men, Yogi thought. Marching on and on and where were they getting? Nowhere. Yogi knew it only too well. Nowhere. No damn where at all.

"White chief speak up," the big Indian said.

"I don't know," Yogi said. "I don't know at all." Was this what they had fought the war for? Was this what it was all about? It looked like it. Yogi standing under the street light. Yogi thinking and wondering. The two Indians in their mackinaw coats. One of the Indians with an empty sleeve. All of them wondering.

"White chief no speak?" the big Indian asked.

"No." What could Yogi say? What was there to say?

"Red brother speak?" asked the Indian.

"Speak out," Yogi said. He looked down at the snow. "One man's as good as another now."

"White chief ever go to Brown's Beanery?" asked the big Indian, looking into Yogi's face under the arc light.

"No." Yogi felt all in. Was this the end? A beanery. Well, a beanery as well as any other place. But a beanery. Well, why not? These Indians knew the town. They were ex-service men. They both had splendid war records. He knew that himself. But a beanery.

"White chief come with red brothers." The tall Indian put his arm under Yogi's arm. The little Indian fell into step. "Forward to the beanery." Yogi spoke quietly. He was a white man, but he knew when he had enough. After all, the white race might not always be supreme. This Moslem revolt. Unrest in the East. Trouble in the West. Things looked black in the South. Now this condition of things in the North. Where was it taking him? Where did it all lead? Would it help him to want a woman? Would spring ever come? Was it worth while after all? He wondered.

The three of them striding along the frozen streets of Petoskey. Going somewhere now. En route. Huysmans wrote that. It would be interesting to read French. He must try it sometime. There was a street in Paris named after Huysmans. Right around the corner from where Gertrude Stein lived. Ah, there was a woman! Where were her experiments in words leading her? What was at the bottom of it? All that in Paris. Ah, Paris. How far it was to Paris now. Paris in the morning. Paris in the evening. Paris at night. Paris in the morning again. Paris at noon, perhaps. Why not? Yogi Johnson striding on. His mind never still.

All three of them striding on together. The arms of those that had arms linked through each other's arms. Red men and white men walking together. Something had brought them together. Was it the war? Was it fate? Was it accident? Or was it just chance? These questions struggled with each other in Yogi Johnson's brain. His brain was tired. He had been thinking too much lately. On still they strode. Then, abruptly, they stopped.

The little Indian looked up at the sign. It shone in the night outside the frosted windows of the beanery.

BEST BY TEST.

"Makeum heap big test," the little Indian grunted.

"White man's beanery got heap fine T-bone steak," the tall Indian grunted. "Take it from red brother." The Indians stood a little uncertainly outside the door. The tall Indian turned to Yogi. "White chief got dollars?"

"Yes, I've got money," Yogi answered. He was prepared to go the route. It was no time to turn back now. "The feed's on me, boys."

"White chief nature's nobleman," the tall Indian grunted.

"White chief rough diamond," the little Indian agreed.

"You'd do the same for me," Yogi deprecated. After all, perhaps it was true. It was a chance he was taking. He had taken a chance in Paris once. Steve Brodie had taken a chance. Or so they said. Chances were taken all over the world every day. In China, Chinamen were taking chances. In Africa, Africans. In Egypt, Egyptians. In Poland, Poles. In Russia, Russians. In Ireland, Irish. In Armenia – -

"Armenians no take chances," the tall Indian grunted quietly. He had voiced Yogi's unspoken doubt. They were a canny folk these red men.

"Not even in the rug game?"

"Red brother think not," the Indian said. His tones carried conviction to Yogi. Who were these Indians? There was something back of all this. They went into the beanery.

AUTHOR'S NOTE TO READER

It was at this point in the story, reader, that Mr. F. Scott Fitzgerald came to our home one afternoon, and after remaining for quite a while suddenly sat down in the fireplace and would not (or was it could not, reader?) get up and let the fire burn something else so as to keep the room warm. I know, reader, that these things sometimes do not show in a story, but, just the same, they are happening, and think what they mean to chaps like you and me in the literary game. If you should think this part of the story is not as good as it might have been remember, reader, that day in and day out all over the world things like this are happening. Need I add, reader, that I have the utmost respect for Mr. Fitzgerald, and let anybody else attack him and I would be the first to spring to his defense! And that includes you too, reader, though I hate to speak out bluntly like this, and take the risk of breaking up a friendship of the sort that ours has gotten to be.

P. S. – TO THE READER

As I read that chapter over, reader, it doesn't seem so bad. You may like it. I hope you will. And if you do like it, reader, and the rest of the book as well, will you tell your friends about it, and try and get them to buy the book just as you have done? I only get twenty cents on each book that is sold, and while twenty cents is not much nowadays still it will mount up to a lot if two or three hundred thousand copies of the book are sold. They will be, too, if every one likes the book as much as you and I do, reader. And listen, reader. I meant it when I said I would be glad to read anything you wrote. That wasn't just talk. Bring it along and we will go over it together. If you like, I'll re-write bits of it for you. I don't mean that in any critical sort of way either. If there is anything you do not like in this book just write to Mr. Scribner's Sons at the home office. They'll change it for you. Or, if you would rather, I will change it myself. You know what I think of you, reader. And you're not angry or upset about what I said about Scott Fitzgerald either, are you? I hope not. Now I am going to write the next chapter. Mr. Fitzgerald is gone and Mr. Dos Passos had gone to England, and I think I can promise you that it will be a bully chapter. At least, it will be just as good as I can write it. We both know how good that can be, if we read the blurbs, eh, reader?

CHAPTER 14

Inside the beanery. They are all inside the beanery. Some do not see the others. Each are intent on themselves. Red men are intent on red men. White men are intent on white men or on white women. There are no red women. Are there no squaws any more? What has become of the squaws? Have we lost our squaws in America? Silently, through the door which she had opened, a squaw came into the room. She was clad only in a pair of worn moccasins. On her back was a papoose. Beside her walked a husky dog.

"Don't look!" the drummer shouted to the women at the counter.

"Here! Get her out of here!" the owner of the beanery shouted. The squaw was forcibly ejected by the Negro cook. They heard her thrashing around in the snow outside. Her husky dog was barking.

"My God! What that might have led to!" Scripps O'Neil mopped his forehead with a napkin.

The Indians had watched with impassive faces. Yogi Johnson had been unable to move. The waitresses had covered their faces with napkins or whatever was handy. Mrs. Scripps had covered her eyes with *The American Mercury*. Scripps O'Neil was feeling faint and shaken. Something had stirred inside him, some vague primordial feeling, as the squaw had come into the room.

"Wonder where that squaw came from?" the drummer asked.

"Her my squaw," the little Indian said.

"Good God, man! Can't you clothe her?" Scripps O'Neil said in a dumb voice. There was a note of terror in his words.

"Her no like clothes," the little Indian explained. "Her woods Indian."

Yogi Johnson was not listening. Something had broken inside of him. Something had snapped as the squaw came into the room. He had a new feeling. A feeling he thought had been lost for ever. Lost for always. Lost. Gone permanently. He knew now it was a mistake. He was all right now. By the merest chance he had found it out. What might he not have thought if that squaw had never come into the beanery? What black thoughts he had been thinking! He had been on the verge of suicide. Self-destruction. Killing himself. Here in this beanery. What a mistake that would have been. He knew now. What a botch he might have made of life. Killing himself. Let spring come now. Let it come. It couldn't come fast enough. Let spring come. He was ready for it.

"Listen," he said to the two Indians. "I want to tell you about something that happened to me in Paris."

The two Indians leaned forward. "White chief got the floor," the tall Indian remarked.

"What I thought was a very beautiful thing happened to me in Paris," Yogi began. "You Indians know Paris? Good. Well, it turned out to be the ugliest thing that ever happened to me."

The Indians grunted. They knew their Paris.

"It was the first day of my leave. I was walking along the Boulevard Malesherbes. A car passed me and a beautiful woman leaned out. She called to me and I came. She took me to a house, a mansion rather, in a distant part of Paris, and there a very beautiful thing happened to me. Afterward someone took me out a different door than I had come in by. The beautiful woman had told me that she would never, that she could never, see me again. I tried to get the number of the mansion but it was one of a block of mansions all looking the same.

"From then on all through my leave I tried to see that beautiful lady. Once I thought I saw her in the theatre. It wasn't her. Another time I caught a glimpse of what I thought was her in a passing taxi and leaped into another taxi and followed. I lost the taxi. I was desperate. Finally on the next to the last night of my leave I was so desperate and dull that I went with one of those guides that guarantee to show you all of Paris. We started out and visited various places. 'Is this all you've got?' I asked the guide.

"'There is a real place, but it's very expensive,' the guide said. We compromised on a price finally, and the guide took me. It was in an old mansion. You looked through a slit in the wall. All around the wall were people looking through slits. There, looking through slits could be seen the uniforms of men of all the Allied countries, and many handsome South Americans in evening dress. I looked through a slit myself. For a while nothing happened. Then a beautiful woman came into the room with a young British officer. She took off her long fur coat and her hat and threw them into a chair. The officer was taking off his Sam Browne belt. I recognized her. It was the lady whom I had been with when the beautiful thing happened to me." Yogi Johnson looked at his empty plate of beans. "Since then," he said, "I have never wanted a woman. How I have suffered I cannot tell. But I've suffered, boys, I've suffered. I blamed it on the war. I blamed it on France. I blamed it on the decay of morality in general. I blamed it on the younger generation. I blamed it here. I blamed it there. Now I am cured. Here's five dollars for you, boys." His eyes were shining. "Get some more to eat. Take a trip somewhere. This is the happiest day of my life."

He stood up from his stool before the counter, shook the one Indian impulsively by the hand, rested his hand for a minute on the other Indian's shoulder, opened the door of the beanery, and strode out into the night.

The two Indians looked at one another. "White chief heap nice fella," observed the big Indian.

"Think him was in the war?" asked the little Indian.

"Me wonder," the big Indian said.

"White chief said he buy me new artificial arm," the little Indian grumbled.

"Maybe you get more than that," the big Indian said.

"Me wonder," the little Indian said. They went on eating.

At the other end of the counter of the beanery a marriage was coming to an end. Scripps O'Neil and his wife sat side by side. Mrs. Scripps knew now. She couldn't hold him. She had tried and failed. She had lost. She knew it was a losing game. There was no holding him now. Mandy was talking again. Talking. Talking. Always talking. That interminable stream of literary gossip that was bringing her, Diana's, marriage to an end. She couldn't hold him. He was going. Going. Going away from her. Diana sitting there in misery. Scripps listening to Mandy talking. Mandy talking. Talking. Talking. The drummer, an old friend now, the drummer, sitting reading his *Detroit News*. She couldn't hold him. She couldn't hold him. She couldn't hold him.

The little Indian got up from his stool at the beanery counter, and went over to the window. The glass on the window was covered with thick rimy frost. The little Indian breathed on the frozen windowpane, rubbed the spot bare with the empty sleeve of his mackinaw coat and looked out into the night. Suddenly he turned from the window and rushed out into the night. The tall Indian watched him go, leisurely finished his meal, took a toothpick, placed it between his teeth, and then he too followed his friend out into the night.

CHAPTER 15

They were alone in the beanery now. Scripps and Mandy and Diana. Only the drummer was with them. He was an old friend now. But his nerves were on edge tonight. He folded his paper abruptly and started for the door.

"See you all later," he said. He went out into the night. It seemed the only thing to do. He did it.

Only three of them in the beanery now. Scripps and Mandy and Diana. Only those three. Mandy was talking. Leaning on the counter and talking. Scripps with his eyes fixed on Mandy. Diana made no pretense of listening now. She knew it was over. It was all over now. But she would make one more attempt. One more last gallant try. Perhaps she still could hold him. Perhaps it had all been just a dream. She steadied her voice and then she spoke.

"Scripps, dear," she said. Her voice shook a little. She steadied it.

"What's on your mind?" Scripps asked abruptly. Ah, there it was. That horrid clipped speech again.

"Scripps, dear, wouldn't you like to come home?" Diana's voice quavered. "There's a new *Mercury*." She had changed from the London *Mercury* to The American *Mercury* just to please Scripps. "It just came. I wish you felt like coming home, normale's a splendid thing in this *Mercury*. Do come home, Scripps, I've never asked anything of you before. Come home, Scripps! Oh, won't you come home?"

Scripps looked up. Diana's heart beat faster. Perhaps he was coming. Perhaps she was holding him. Holding him. Holding him.

"Do come, Scripps, dear," Diana said softly. "There's a wonderful editorial in it by Mencken about chiropractors."

Scripps looked away.

"Won't you come, Scripps?" Diana pleaded.

"No," Scripps said. "I don't give a damn about Mencken any more."

Diana dropped her head. "Oh, Scripps," she said. "Oh, Scripps." This was the end. She had her answer now. She had lost him. Lost him. Lost him. It was over. Finished. Done for. She sat crying silently. Mandy was talking again.

Suddenly Diana straightened up. She had one last request to make. One thing she would ask him. Only one. He might refuse her. He might not grant it. But she would ask him.

"Scripps," she said.

"What's the trouble?" Scripps turned in irritation. Perhaps, after all, he was sorry for her. He wondered.

"Can I take the bird, Scripps?" Diana's voice broke.

"Sure," said Scripps. "Why not?"

Diana picked up the bird-cage. The bird was asleep. Perched on one leg as on that night when they had first met. What was it he was like? Ah, yes. Like an old osprey. An old, old osprey from her own Lake Country. She held the cage to her tightly.

"Thank you, Scripps," she said. "Thank you for this bird." Her voice broke. "And now I must be going."

Quietly, silently, gathering her shawl around her, clutching the cage with the sleeping bird and the copy of *The Mercury* to her breast, with only a backward glance, a last glance at him who had been her Scripps, she opened the door of the beanery, and went out into the night. Scripps did not even see her go. He was intent on what Mandy was saying. Mandy was talking again.

"That bird she just took out," Mandy was saying.

"Oh, did she take a bird out?" Scripps asked. "Go on with the story."

"You used to wonder about what sort of bird that was," Mandy went on.

"That's right," Scripps agreed.

"Well that reminds me of a story about Gosse and the Marquis of Buque," Mandy went on.

"Tell it, Mandy. Tell it," Scripps urged.

"It seems a great friend of mine, Ford, you've heard me speak of him before, was in the marquis's castle during the war. His regiment was billeted there and the marquis, one of the richest if not the richest man in England, was serving in Ford's regiment as a private. Ford was sitting in the library one evening. The library was a most extraordinary place. The walls were made of bricks of gold set into tiles or something. I forget exactly how it was."

"Go on," Scripps urged. "It doesn't matter."

"Anyhow, in the middle of the wall of the library was a stuffed flamingo in a glass case."

"They understand interior decorating, these English," Scripps said.

"Your wife was English, wasn't she?" asked Mandy.

"From the Lake Country," Scripps answered. "Go on with the story."

"Well, anyway," Mandy went on, "Ford was sitting there in the library one evening after mess when the butler came in and said: 'The Marquis of Buque's compliments and might he show the library to a group of friends with whom he has been dining?' They used to let him dine out and sometimes they let him sleep in the castle. Ford said, 'Quite,' and in came the marquis in his private's uniform followed by Sir Edmund Gosse and Professor Whatsisname, I forget it for the moment, from Oxford. Gosse stopped in front of the stuffed flamingo in the glass case and said, 'What have we here, Buque?'

"'It's a flamingo, Sir Edmund,' the marquis answered.

"'That's not my idea of a flamingo,' Gosse remarked.

"'No, Gosse. That's God's idea of a flamingo,' Professor Whatsisname said. I wish I could remember his name."

"Don't bother," Scripps said. His eyes were bright. He leaned forward. Something was pounding inside of him. Something he could not control. "I love you, Mandy," he said. "I love you. You are my woman." The thing was pounding away inside of him. It would not stop.

"That's all right," Mandy answered. "I've known you were my man for a long time. Would you like to hear another story? Speaking of woman."

"Go on," Scripps said. "You must never stop, Mandy. You are my woman now."

"Sure," Mandy agreed. "This story is about when Knut Hamsun was a streetcar conductor in Chicago."

"Go on," Scripps said. "You are my woman now, Mandy."

He repeated the phrase to himself. My woman. My woman. You are my woman. She is my woman. It is my woman. My woman. But, somehow, he was not satisfied. Somewhere, somehow, there must be something else. Something else. My woman. The words were a little hollow now. Into his mind, though he tried to thrust it out, there came again the monstrous picture of the squaw as she strode silently into the room. That squaw. She did not wear clothes, because she did not like them. Hardy, braving the winter nights. What might not the spring bring? Mandy was talking. Mandy talking on in the beanery. Mandy telling her stories. It grows late in the beanery. Mandy talks on. She is his woman now. He is her man. But is he her man? In Scripps's brain that vision of the squaw. The squaw that strode unannounced into the beanery. The squaw who had been thrown out into the snow. Mandy talking on. Telling literary reminiscences. Authentic incidents. They had the ring of truth. But were they enough? Scripps wondered. She was his woman. But for how long? Scripps wondered. Mandy talking on in the beanery. Scripps listening. But his mind straying away. Straying away. Straying away. Where was it straying? Out into the night. Out into the night.

CHAPTER 16

Night in Petoskey. Long past midnight. Inside the beanery a light burning. The town asleep under the Northern moon. To the North the tracks of the G. R. & I. Railroad running far into the North. Cold tracks, stretching North toward Mackinaw City and St. Ignace. Cold tracks to be walking on at this time of night.

North of the frozen little Northern town a couple walking side by side on the tracks. It is Yogi Johnson walking with the squaw. As they walk Yogi Johnson silently strips off his garments. One by one he strips off his garments, and casts them beside the track. In the end he is clad only in a worn pair of pump-maker shoes. Yogi Johnson, naked in the moonlight, walking North beside the squaw. The squaw striding along beside him. She carries the papoose on her back in his bark cradle. Yogi attempts to take the papoose from her. He would carry the papoose. The husky dog whines and licks at Yogi Johnson's ankles. No, the squaw would carry the papoose herself. On they stride. Into the North. Into the Northern night.

Behind them come two figures. Sharply etched in the moonlight. It is the two Indians. The two woods Indians. They stoop and gather up the garments Yogi Johnson has cast away. Occasionally, they grunt to one another. Striding softly along in the moonlight. Their keen eyes not missing a single cast-off garment. When the last garment has been cast off they look and see far ahead of them the two figures in the moonlight. The two Indians straighten up. They examine the garments.

"White chief snappy dresser," the tall Indian remarks, holding up an initialled shirt.

"White chief going get pretty cold," the small Indian remarks. He hands a vest to the tall Indian. The tall Indian rolls all the clothing, all the cast-off garments, into a bundle, and they start back along the tracks to the town.

"Better keep clothes for white chief or sellem Salvation Army?" asks the short Indian.

"Better sellem Salvation Army," the tall Indian grunts.

"White chief maybe never come back."

"White chief come back all right," grunted the little Indian.

"Better sellem Salvation Army, anyway," grunts the tall Indian. "White chief need new clothes, anyhow, when spring comes."

As they walked down the tracks toward town, the air seemed to soften. The Indians walk uneasily now. Through the tamaracks and cedars beside the railway tracks a warm wind is blowing. The snow-drifts are melting now beside the tracks. Something stirs inside the two Indians. Some urge. Some strange pagan disturbance. The warm wind is blowing. The tall Indian stops, moistens his finger and holds it up in the air. The little Indian watches. "Chinook?" he asks.

"Heap chinook," the tall Indian says. They hurry on toward town. The moon is blurred now by clouds carried by the warm chinook wind that is blowing.

"Want to get in town before rush," the tall Indian grunts.

"Red brothers want be well up in line," the little Indian grunts anxiously.

"Nobody work in factory now," the tall Indian grunted.

"Better hurry."

The warm wind blows. Inside the Indians strange longings were stirring. They knew what they wanted. Spring at last was coming to the frozen little Northern town. The two Indians hurried along the track.

AUTHOR'S FINAL NOTE TO THE READER

Well, reader, how did you like it? It took me ten days to write it. Has it been worth it? There is just one place I would like to clear up. You remember back in the story where the elderly waitress, Diana, tells about how she lost her mother in Paris, and woke up to find herself with a French general in the next room? I thought perhaps you might be interested to know the real explanation of that. What actually happened was that her mother was taken violently ill with the bubonic plague in the night, and the doctor who was called diagnosed the case and warned the authorities. It was the day the great exposition was to be opened, and think what a case of bubonic plague would have done for the exposition as publicity. So the French authorities simply had the woman disappear. She died toward morning. The general who was summoned and who then got into bed in the same room where the mother had been, always seemed to us like a pretty brave man. He was one of the big stockholders in the exposition, though, I believe. Anyway, reader, as a piece of secret history it always seemed to me like an awfully good story, and I know you would rather have me explain it here than drag an explanation into the novel, where really, after all, it has no place. It is interesting to observe, though, how the French police hushed the whole matter up, and how quickly they got ahold of the coiffeur and the cab-driver. Of course, what it shows is that when you're travelling abroad alone, or even with your mother, you simply cannot be too careful. I hope it is all right about bringing this in here, but I just felt I owed it to you, reader, to give some explanation. I do not believe in these protracted good-bys any more than I do in long engagements, so I will just say a simple farewell and Godspeed, reader, and leave you now to your own devices.

The Sun Also Rises

BOOK ONE

CHAPTER 1

IN THE LATE SUMMER of that year we lived in a house in a village that looked across the river and the plain to the mountains. In the bed of the river there were pebbles and boulders, dry and white in the sun, and the water was clear and swiftly moving and blue in the channels. Troops went by the house and down the road and the dust they raised powdered the leaves of the trees. The trunks of the trees too were dusty and the leaves fell early that year and we saw the troops marching along the road and the dust rising and leaves, stirred by the breeze, falling and the soldiers marching and afterward the road bare and white except for the leaves.

The plain was rich with crops; there were many orchards of fruit trees and beyond the plain the mountains were brown and bare. There was fighting in the mountains and at night we could see the flashes from the artillery. In the dark it was like summer lightning, but the nights were cool and there was not the feeling of a storm coming.

Sometimes in the dark we heard the troops marching under the window and guns going past pulled by motor-tractors. There was much traffic at night and many mules on the roads with boxes of ammunition on each side of their pack-saddles and gray motor trucks that carried men, and other trucks with loads covered with canvas that moved slower in the traffic. There were big guns too that passed in the day drawn by tractors, the long barrels of the guns covered with green branches and green leafy branches and vines laid over the tractors. To the north we could look across a valley and see a forest of chestnut trees and behind it another mountain on this side of the river. There was fighting for that mountain too, but it was not successful, and in the fall when the rains came the leaves all fell from the chestnut trees and the branches were bare and the trunks black with rain. The vineyards were thin and bare-branched too and all the country wet and brown and dead with the autumn. There were mists over the river and clouds on the mountain and the trucks splashed mud on the road and the troops were muddy and wet in their capes; their rifles were wet and under their capes the two leather cartridge-boxes on the front of the belts, gray leather boxes heavy with the packs of clips of thin, long 6.5 mm. cartridges, bulged forward under the capes so that the men, passing on the road, marched as though they were six months gone with child.

There were small gray motor cars that passed going very fast; usually there was an officer on the seat with the driver and more officers in the back seat. They splashed more mud than the camions even and if one of the officers in the back was very small and sitting between two generals, he himself so small that you could not see his face but only the top of his cap and his narrow back, and if the car went especially fast it was probably the King. He lived in Udine and came out in this way nearly every day to see how things were going, and things went very badly.

At the start of the winter came the permanent rain and with the rain came the cholera. But it was checked and in the end only seven thousand died of it in the army.

CHAPTER 2

THE NEXT YEAR there were many victories. The mountain that was beyond the valley and the hillside where the chestnut forest grew was captured and there were victories beyond the plain on the plateau to the south and we crossed the river in August and lived in a house in Gorizia that had a fountain and many thick shady trees in a walled garden and a wistaria vine purple on the side of the house. Now the fighting was in the next mountains beyond and was not a mile away. The town was very nice and our house was very fine. The river ran behind us and the town had been captured very handsomely but the mountains beyond it could not be taken and I was very glad the Austrians seemed to want to come back to the town some time, if the war should end, because they did not bombard it to destroy it but only a little in a military way. People lived on in it and there were hospitals and cafés and artillery up side streets and two bawdy houses, one for troops and one for officers, and with the end of the summer, the cool nights, the fighting in the mountains beyond the town, the shell-marked iron of the railway bridge, the smashed tunnel by the river where the fighting had been, the trees around the square and the long avenue of trees that led to the square; these with there being girls in the town, the King passing in his motor car, sometimes now seeing his face and little long necked body and gray beard like a goat's chin tuft; all these with the sudden interiors of houses that had lost a wall through shelling, with plaster and rubble in their gardens and sometimes in the street, and the whole thing going well on the Carso made the fall very different from the last fall when we had been in the country. The war was changed too.

The forest of oak trees on the mountain beyond the town was gone. The forest had been green in the summer when we had come into the town but now there were the stumps and the broken trunks and the ground torn up, and one day at the end of the fall when I was out where the oak forest had been I saw a cloud coming over the mountain. It came very fast and the sun went a dull yellow and then everything was gray and the sky was covered and the cloud came on down the mountain and suddenly we were in it and it was snow. The snow slanted across the wind, the bare ground was covered, the stumps of trees projected, there was snow on the guns and there were paths in the snow going back to the latrines behind trenches.

Later, below in the town, I watched the snow falling, looking out of the window of the bawdy house, the house for officers, where I sat with a friend and two glasses drinking a bottle of Asti, and, looking out at the snow falling slowly and heavily, we knew it was all over for that year. Up the river the mountains had not been taken; none of the mountains beyond the river had been taken. That was all left for next year. My friend saw the priest from our mess going by in the street, walking carefully in the slush, and pounded on the window to attract his attention. The priest looked up. He saw us and smiled. My friend motioned for him to come in. The priest shook his head and went on. That night in the mess after the spaghetti course, which every one ate very quickly and seriously, lifting the spaghetti on the fork until the loose strands hung clear then lowering it into the mouth, or else using a continuous lift and sucking into the mouth, helping ourselves to wine from the grass-covered gallon flask; it swung in a metal cradle and you pulled the neck of the flask down with the forefinger and the wine, clear red, tannic and lovely, poured out into the glass held with the same hand; after this course, the captain commenced picking on the priest.

The priest was young and blushed easily and wore a uniform like the rest of us but with a cross in dark red velvet above the left breast pocket of his gray tunic. The captain spoke pidgin Italian for my doubtful benefit, in order that I might understand perfectly, that nothing should be lost.

"Priest to-day with girls," the captain said looking at the priest and at me. The priest smiled and blushed and shook his head. This captain baited him often.

"Not true?" asked the captain. "To-day I see priest with girls."

"No," said the priest. The other officers were amused at the baiting.

"Priest not with girls," went on the captain. "Priest never with girls," he explained to me. He took my glass and filled it, looking at my eyes all the time, but not losing sight of the priest.

"Priest every night five against one." Every one at the table laughed. "You understand? Priest every night five against one." He made a gesture and laughed loudly. The priest accepted it as a joke.

"The Pope wants the Austrians to win the war," the major said. "He loves Franz Joseph. That's where the money comes from. I am an atheist."

"Did you ever read the 'Black Pig'?" asked the lieutenant. "I will get you a copy. It was that which shook my faith."

"It is a filthy and vile book," said the priest. "You do not really like it."

"It is very valuable," said the lieutenant. "It tells you about those priests. You will like it," he said to me. I smiled at the priest and he smiled back across the candle-light. "Don't you read it," he said.

"I will get it for you," said the lieutenant.

"All thinking men are atheists," the major said. "I do not believe in the Free Masons however."

"I believe in the Free Masons," the lieutenant said. "It is a noble organization." Some one came in and as the door opened I could see the snow falling.

"There will be no more offensive now that the snow has come," I said.

"Certainly not," said the major. "You should go on leave. You should go to Rome, Naples, Sicily—"

"He should visit Amalfi," said the lieutenant. "I will write you cards to my family in Amalfi. They will love you like a son."

"He should go to Palermo."

"He ought to go to Capri."

"I would like you to see Abruzzi and visit my family at Capracotta," said the priest.

"Listen to him talk about the Abruzzi. There's more snow there than here. He doesn't want to see peasants. Let him go to centres of culture and civilization."

"He should have fine girls. I will give you the addresses of places in Naples. Beautiful young girls—accompanied by their mothers. Ha! Ha! Ha!" The captain spread his hand open, the thumb up and fingers outspread as when you make shadow pictures. There was a shadow from his hand on the wall. He spoke again in pidgin Italian. "You go away like this," he pointed to the thumb, "and come back like this," he touched the little finger. Every one laughed.

"Look," said the captain. He spread the hand again. Again the candle-light made its shadows on the wall. He started with the upright thumb and named in their order the thumb and four fingers, "soto-tenente (the thumb), tenente (first finger), capitano (next finger), maggiore (next to the little finger), and tenente-colonello (the little finger). You go away soto-tenente! You come back sotocolonello!" They all laughed. The captain was having a great success with finger games. He looked at the priest and shouted, "Every night priest five against one!" They all laughed again.

"You must go on leave at once," the major said.

"I would like to go with you and show you things," the lieutenant said.

"When you come back bring a phonograph."

"Bring good opera disks."

"Bring Caruso."

"Don't bring Caruso. He bellows."

"Don't you wish you could bellow like him?"

"He bellows. I say he bellows!"

"I would like you to go to Abruzzi," the priest said. The others were shouting. "There is good hunting. You would like the people and though it is cold it is clear and dry. You could stay with my family. My father is a famous hunter."

"Come on," said the captain. "We go whorehouse before it shuts."

"Good-night," I said to the priest.

"Good-night," he said.

CHAPTER 3

WHEN I CAME BACK to the front we still lived in that town. There were many more guns in the country around and the spring had come. The fields were green and there were small green shoots on the vines, the trees along the road had small leaves and a breeze came from the sea. I saw the town with the hill and the old castle above it in a cup in the hills with the mountains beyond, brown mountains with a little green on their slopes. In the town there were more guns, there were some new hospitals, you met British men and sometimes women, on the street, and a few more houses had been hit by shell fire. It was warm and like the spring and I walked down the alleyway of trees, warmed from the sun on the wall, and found we still lived in the same house and that it all looked the same as when I had left it. The door was open, there was a soldier sitting on a bench outside in the sun, an ambulance was waiting by the side door and inside the door, as I went in, there was the smell of marble floors and hospital. It was all as I had left it except that now it was spring. I looked in the door of the big room and saw the major sitting at his desk, the window open and the sunlight coming into the room. He did not see me and I did not know whether to go in and report or go upstairs first and clean up. I decided to go on upstairs.

The room I shared with the lieutenant Rinaldi looked out on the courtyard. The window was open, my bed was made up with blankets and my things hung on the wall, the gas mask in an oblong tin can, the steel helmet on the same peg. At the foot of the bed was my flat trunk, and my winter boots, the leather shiny with oil, were on the trunk. My Austrian sniper's rifle with its blued octagon barrel and the lovely dark walnut, cheek-fitted, schutzen stock, hung over the two beds. The telescope that fitted it was, I remembered, locked in the trunk. The lieutenant, Rinaldi, lay asleep on the other bed. He woke when he heard me in the room and sat up.

"Ciaou!" he said. "What kind of time did you have?"

"Magnificent."

We shook hands and he put his arm around my neck and kissed me.

"Oughf," I said.

"You're dirty," he said. "You ought to wash. Where did you go and what did you do? Tell me everything at once."

"I went everywhere. Milan, Florence, Rome, Naples, Villa San Giovanni, Messina, Taormina–"

"You talk like a time-table. Did you have any beautiful adventures?"

"Yes."

"Where?"

"Milano, Firenze, Roma, Napoli–"

"That's enough. Tell me really what was the best."

"In Milano."

"That was because it was first. Where did you meet her? In the Cova? Where did you go? How did you feel? Tell me everything at once. Did you stay all night?"

"Yes."

"That's nothing. Here now we have beautiful girls. New girls never been to the front before."

"Wonderful."

"You don't believe me? We will go now this afternoon and see. And in the town we have beautiful English girls. I am now in love with Miss Barkley. I will take you to call. I will probably marry Miss Barkley."

"I have to get washed and report. Doesn't anybody work now?"

"Since you are gone we have nothing but frostbites, chilblains, jaundice, gonorrhea, self-inflicted wounds, pneumonia and hard and soft chancres. Every week some one gets wounded by rock fragments. There are a few real wounded. Next week the war starts again. Perhaps it start again. They say so. Do you think I would do right to marry Miss Barkley—after the war of course?"

"Absolutely," I said and poured the basin full of water.

"To-night you will tell me everything," said Rinaldi. "Now I must go back to sleep to be fresh and beautiful for Miss Barkley."

I took off my tunic and shirt and washed in the cold water in the basin. While I rubbed myself with a towel I looked around the room and out the window and at Rinaldi lying with his eyes closed on the bed. He was good-looking, was my age, and he came from Amalfi. He loved being a surgeon and we were great friends. While I was looking at him he opened his eyes.

"Have you any money?"

"Yes."

"Loan me fifty lire."

I dried my hands and took out my pocket-book from the inside of my tunic hanging on the wall. Rinaldi took the note, folded it without rising from the bed and slid it in his breeches pocket. He smiled, "I must make on Miss Barkley the impression of a man of sufficient wealth. You are my great and good friend and financial protector."

"Go to hell," I said.

That night at the mess I sat next to the priest and he was disappointed and suddenly hurt that I had not gone to the Abruzzi. He had written to his father that I was coming and they had made preparations. I myself felt as badly as he did and could not understand why I had not gone. It was what I had wanted to do and I tried to explain how one thing had led to another and finally he saw it and understood that I had really wanted to go and it was almost all right. I had drunk much wine and afterward coffee and Strega and I explained, winefully, how we did not do the things we wanted to do; we never did such things.

We two were talking while the others argued. I had wanted to go to Abruzzi. I had gone to no place where the roads were frozen and hard as iron, where it was clear cold and dry and the snow was dry and powdery and hare-tracks in the snow and the peasants took off their hats and called you Lord and there was good hunting.

I had gone to no such place but to the smoke of cafés and nights when the room whirled and you needed to look at the wall to make it stop, nights in bed, drunk, when you knew that that was all there was, and the strange excitement of waking and not knowing who it was with you, and the world all unreal in the dark and so exciting that you must resume again unknowing and not caring in the night, sure that this was all and all and all and not caring. Suddenly to care very much and to sleep to wake with it sometimes morning and all that had been there gone and everything sharp and hard and clear and sometimes a dispute about the cost. Sometimes still pleasant and fond and warm and breakfast and lunch. Sometimes all niceness gone and glad to get out on the street but always another day starting and then another night. I tried to tell about the night and the difference between the night and the day and how the night was better unless the day was very clean and cold and I could not tell it; as I cannot tell it now. But if you have had it you know. He had not had it but he understood that I had really wanted to go to the Abruzzi but had not gone and we were still friends, with many tastes alike, but with the difference between us. He had always known what I did not know and what, when I learned it, I was always able to forget. But I did not know that then, although I learned it later. In the meantime we were all at the mess, the meal was finished, and the argument went on. We two stopped talking and the captain shouted, "Priest not happy. Priest not happy without girls."

"I am happy," said the priest.

"Priest not happy. Priest wants Austrians to win the war," the captain said. The others listened. The priest shook his head.

"No," he said.

"Priest wants us never to attack. Don't you want us never to attack?"

"No. If there is a war I suppose we must attack."

"Must attack. Shall attack!"

The priest nodded.

"Leave him alone," the major said. "He's all right."

"He can't do anything about it anyway," the captain said. We all got up and left the table.

CHAPTER 4

THE BATTERY in the next garden woke me in the morning and I saw the sun coming through the window and got out of the bed. I went to the window and looked out. The gravel paths were moist and the grass was wet with dew. The battery fired twice and the air came each time like a blow and shook the window and made the front of my pajamas flap. I could not see the guns but they were evidently firing directly over us. It was a nuisance to have them there but it was a comfort that they were no bigger. As I looked out at the garden I heard a motor truck starting on the road. I dressed, went downstairs, had some coffee in the kitchen and went out to the garage.

Ten cars were lined up side by side under the long shed. They were top-heavy, blunt-nosed ambulances, painted gray and built like moving-vans. The mechanics were working on one out in the yard. Three others were up in the mountains at dressing stations.

"Do they ever shell that battery?" I asked one of the mechanics.

"No, Signor Tenente. It is protected by the little hill."

"How's everything?"

"Not so bad. This machine is no good but the others march." He stopped working and smiled. "Were you on permission?"

"Yes."

He wiped his hands on his jumper and grinned. "You have a good time?" The others all grinned too.

"Fine," I said. "What's the matter with this machine?"

"It's no good. One thing after another."

"What's the matter now?"

"New rings."

I left them working, the car looking disgraced and empty with the engine open and parts spread on the work bench, and went in under the shed and looked at each of the cars. They were moderately clean, a few freshly washed, the others dusty. I looked at the tires carefully, looking for cuts or stone bruises. Everything seemed in good condition. It evidently made no difference whether I was there to look after things or not. I had imagined that the condition of the cars, whether or not things were obtainable, the smooth functioning of the business of removing wounded and sick from the dressing stations, hauling them back from the mountains to the clearing station and then distributing them to the hospitals named on their papers, depended to a considerable extent on myself. Evidently it did not matter whether I was there or not.

"Has there been any trouble getting parts?" I asked the sergeant mechanic.

"No, Signor Tenente."

"Where is the gasoline park now?"

"At the same place."

"Good," I said and went back to the house and drank another bowl of coffee at the mess table. The coffee was a pale gray and sweet with condensed milk. Outside the window it was a lovely spring morning. There was that beginning of a feeling of dryness in the nose that meant the day would be hot later on. That day I visited the posts in the mountains and was back in town late in the afternoon.

The whole thing seemed to run better while I was away. The offensive was going to start again I heard. The division for which we worked were to attack at a place up the river and the major told me that I would see about the posts for during the attack. The attack would cross the river up above the narrow gorge and spread up the hillside. The posts for the cars would have to be as near the river as they could get and keep covered. They would, of course, be selected by the infantry but we were supposed to work it out. It was one of those things that gave you a false feeling of soldiering.

I was very dusty and dirty and went up to my room to wash. Rinaldi was sitting on the bed with a copy of Hugo's English grammar. He was dressed, wore his black boots, and his hair shone.

"Splendid," he said when he saw me. "You will come with me to see Miss Barkley."

"No."

"Yes. You will please come and make me a good impression on her."

"All right. Wait till I get cleaned up."

"Wash up and come as you are."

I washed, brushed my hair and we started.

"Wait a minute," Rinaldi said. "Perhaps we should have a drink." He opened his trunk and took out a bottle.

"Not Strega," I said.

"No. Grappa."

"All right."

He poured two glasses and we touched them, first fingers extended. The grappa was very strong.

"Another?"

"All right," I said. We drank the second grappa, Rinaldi put away the bottle and we went down the stairs. It was hot walking through the town but the sun was starting to go down and it was very pleasant. The British hospital was a big villa built by Germans before the war. Miss Barkley was in the garden. Another nurse was with her. We saw their white uniforms through the trees and walked toward them. Rinaldi saluted. I saluted too but more moderately.

"How do you do?" Miss Barkley said. "You're not an Italian, are you?"

"Oh, no."

Rinaldi was talking with the other nurse. They were laughing. "What an odd thing—to be in the Italian army."

"It's not really the army. It's only the ambulance."

"It's very odd though. Why did you do it?"

"I don't know," I said. "There isn't always an explanation for everything."

"Oh, isn't there? I was brought up to think there was."

"That's awfully nice."

"Do we have to go on and talk this way?"

"No," I said.

"That's a relief. Isn't it?"

"What is the stick?" I asked. Miss Barkley was quite tall. She wore what seemed to me to be a nurse's uniform, was blonde and had a tawny skin and gray eyes. I thought she was very beautiful. She was carrying a thin rattan stick like a toy riding-crop, bound in leather.

"It belonged to a boy who was killed last year."

"I'm awfully sorry."

"He was a very nice boy. He was going to marry me and he was killed in the Somme."

"It was a ghastly show."

"Were you there?"

"No."

"I've heard about it," she said. "There's not really any war of that sort down here. They sent me the little stick. His mother sent it to me. They returned it with his things."

"Had you been engaged long?"

"Eight years. We grew up together."

"And why didn't you marry?"

"I don't know," she said. "I was a fool not to. I could have given him that anyway.

But I thought it would be bad for him."

"I see."

"Have you ever loved any one?"

"No," I said.

We sat down on a bench and I looked at her.

"You have beautiful hair," I said.

"Do you like it?"

"Very much."

"I was going to cut it all off when he died."

"No."

"I wanted to do something for him. You see I didn't care about the other thing and he could have had it all. He could have had anything he wanted if I would have known. I would have married him or anything. I know all about it now. But then he wanted to go to war and I didn't know."

I did not say anything.

"I didn't know about anything then. I thought it would be worse for him. I thought perhaps he couldn't stand it and then of course he was killed and that was the end of it."

"I don't know."

"Oh, yes," she said. "That's the end of it."

We looked at Rinaldi talking with the other nurse.

"What is her name?"

"Ferguson. Helen Ferguson. Your friend is a doctor, isn't he?"

"Yes. He's very good."

"That's splendid. You rarely find any one any good this close to the front. This is close to the front, isn't it?"

"Quite."

"It's a silly front," she said. "But it's very beautiful. Are they going to have an offensive?"

"Yes."

"Then we'll have to work. There's no work now."

"Have you done nursing long?"

"Since the end of 'fifteen. I started when he did. I remember having a silly idea he might come to the hospital where I was. With a sabre cut, I suppose, and a bandage around his head. Or shot through the shoulder. Something picturesque."

"This is the picturesque front," I said.

"Yes," she said. "People can't realize what France is like. If they did, it couldn't all go on. He didn't have a sabre cut. They blew him all to bits."

I didn't say anything.

"Do you suppose it will always go on?"

"No."

"What's to stop it?"

"It will crack somewhere."

"We'll crack. We'll crack in France. They can't go on doing things like the Somme and not crack."

"They won't crack here," I said.

"You think not?"

"No. They did very well last summer."

"They may crack," she said. "Anybody may crack."

"The Germans too."

"No," she said. "I think not."

We went over toward Rinaldi and Miss Ferguson.

"You love Italy?" Rinaldi asked Miss Ferguson in English.

"Quite well."

"No understand," Rinaldi shook his head.

"Abbastanza bene," I translated. He shook his head.

"That is not good. You love England?"

"Not too well. I'm Scotch, you see."

Rinaldi looked at me blankly.

"She's Scotch, so she loves Scotland better than England," I said in Italian.

"But Scotland is England."

I translated this for Miss Ferguson.

"Pas encore," said Miss Ferguson.

"Not really?"

"Never. We do not like the English."

"Not like the English? Not like Miss Barkley?"

"Oh, that's different. You mustn't take everything so literally."

After a while we said good-night and left. Walking home Rinaldi said, "Miss Barkley prefers you to me. That is very clear. But the little Scotch one is very nice."

"Very," I said. I had not noticed her. "You like her?"

"No," said Rinaldi.

CHAPTER 5

THE NEXT AFTERNOON I went to call on Miss Barkley again. She was not in the garden and I went to the side door of the villa where the ambulances drove up. Inside I saw the head nurse, who said Miss Barkley was on duty– "there's a war on, you know."

I said I knew.

"You're the American in the Italian army?" she asked.

"Yes, ma'am."

"How did you happen to do that? Why didn't you join up with us?"

"I don't know," I said. "Could I join now?"

"I'm afraid not now. Tell me. Why did you join up with the Italians?"

"I was in Italy," I said, "and I spoke Italian."

"Oh," she said. "I'm learning it. It's beautiful language."

"Somebody said you should be able to learn it in two weeks."

"Oh, I'll not learn it in two weeks. I've studied it for months now. You may come and see her after seven o'clock if you wish. She'll be off then. But don't bring a lot of Italians."

"Not even for the beautiful language?"

"No. Nor for the beautiful uniforms."

"Good evening," I said.

"A rivederci, Tenente."

"A rivederla." I saluted and went out. It was impossible to salute foreigners as an Italian, without embarrassment. The Italian salute never seemed made for export.

The day had been hot. I had been up the river to the bridgehead at Plava. It was there that the offensive was to begin. It had been impossible to advance on the far side the year before because there was only one road leading down from the pass to the pontoon bridge and it was under machine-gun and shell fire for nearly a mile. It was not wide enough either to carry all the transport for an offensive and the Austrians could make a shambles out of it. But the Italians had crossed and spread out a little way on the far side to hold about a mile and a half on the Austrian side of the river. It was a nasty place and the Austrians should not have let them hold it. I suppose it was mutual tolerance because the Austrians still kept a bridgehead further down the river. The Austrian trenches were above on the hillside only a few yards from the Italian lines. There had been a little town but it was all rubble. There was what was left of a railway station and a smashed permanent bridge that could not be repaired and used because it was in plain sight.

I went along the narrow road down toward the river, left the car at the dressing station under the hill, crossed the pontoon bridge, which was protected by a shoulder of the mountain, and went through the trenches in the smashed-down town and along the edge of the slope. Everybody was in the dugouts. There were racks of rockets standing to be touched off to call for help from the artillery or to signal with if the telephone wires were cut. It was quiet, hot and dirty. I looked across the wire at the Austrian lines. Nobody was in sight. I had a drink with a captain that I knew in one of the dugouts and went back across the bridge.

A new wide road was being finished that would go over the mountain and zig-zag down to the bridge. When this road was finished the offensive would start. It came down through the forest in sharp turns. The system was to bring everything down the new road and take the empty trucks, carts and loaded ambulances and all returning traffic up the old narrow road. The dressing station was on the Austrian side of the river under the edge of the hill and stretcher-bearers would bring the wounded back across the pontoon bridge. It would be the same when the offensive started. As far as I could make out the last mile or so of the new road where it started to level out would be able to be shelled steadily by the Austrians. It looked as though it might be a mess. But I found a place where the cars would be sheltered after they passed that last bad-looking bit and could wait for the wounded to be brought across the pontoon bridge. I would have liked to drive over the new road but it was not yet finished. It looked wide and well made with a good grade and the turns looked very impressive where you could see them through openings in the forest on the mountain side. The cars would be all right with their good metal-to-metal brakes and anyway, coming down, they would not be loaded. I drove back up the narrow road.

Two carabinieri held the car up. A shell had fallen and while we waited three others fell up the road. They were seventy-sevens and came with a whishing rush of air, a hard bright burst and flash and then gray smoke that blew across the road. The carabinieri waved us to go on. Passing where the shells had landed I avoided the small broken places and smelled the high explosive and the smell of blasted clay and stone and freshly shattered flint. I drove back to Gorizia and our villa and, as I said, went to call on Miss Barkley, who was on duty.

At dinner I ate very quickly and left for the villa where the British had their hospital. It was really very large and beautiful and there were fine trees in the grounds. Miss Barkley was sitting on a bench in the garden. Miss Ferguson was with her. They seemed glad to see me and in a little while Miss Ferguson excused herself and went away.

"I'll leave you two," she said. "You get along very well without me."

"Don't go, Helen," Miss Barkley said.

"I'd really rather. I must write some letters."

"Good-night," I said.

"Good-night, Mr. Henry."

"Don't write anything that will bother the censor."

"Don't worry. I only write about what a beautiful place we live in and how brave the Italians are."

"That way you'll be decorated."

"That will be nice. Good-night, Catherine."

"I'll see you in a little while," Miss Barkley said. Miss Ferguson walked away in the dark.

"She's nice," I said.

"Oh, yes, she's very nice. She's a nurse."

"Aren't you a nurse?"

"Oh, no. I'm something called a V. A. D. We work very hard but no one trusts us."

"Why not?"

"They don't trust us when there's nothing going on. When there is really work they trust us."

"What is the difference?"

"A nurse is like a doctor. It takes a long time to be. A V. A. D. is a short cut."

"I see."

"The Italians didn't want women so near the front. So we're all on very special behavior. We don't go out."

"I can come here though."

"Oh, yes. We're not cloistered."

"Let's drop the war."

"It's very hard. There's no place to drop it."

"Let's drop it anyway."

"All right."

We looked at each other in the dark. I thought she was very beautiful and I took her hand. She let me take it and I held it and put my arm around under her arm.

"No," she said. I kept my arm where it was.

"Why not?"

"No."

"Yes," I said. "Please." I leaned forward in the dark to kiss her and there was a sharp stinging flash. She had slapped my face hard. Her hand had hit my nose and eyes, and tears came in my eyes from the reflex.

"I'm so sorry," she said. I felt I had a certain advantage.

"You were quite right."

"I'm dreadfully sorry," she said. "I just couldn't stand the nurse's-evening-off aspect of it. I didn't mean to hurt you. I did hurt you, didn't I?"

She was looking at me in the dark. I was angry and yet certain, seeing it all ahead like the moves in a chess game.

"You did exactly right," I said. "I don't mind at all."

"Poor man."

"You see I've been leading a sort of a funny life. And I never even talk English. And then you are so very beautiful." I looked at her.

"You don't need to say a lot of nonsense. I said I was sorry. We do get along."

"Yes," I said. "And we have gotten away from the war."

She laughed. It was the first time I had ever heard her laugh. I watched her face.

"You are sweet," she said.

"No, I'm not."

"Yes. You are a dear. I'd be glad to kiss you if you don't mind."

I looked in her eyes and put my arm around her as I had before and kissed her. I kissed her hard and held her tight and tried to open her lips; they were closed tight. I was still angry and as I held her suddenly she shivered. I held her close against me and could feel her heart beating and her lips opened and her head went back against my hand and then she was crying on my shoulder.

"Oh, darling," she said. "You will be good to me, won't you?"

What the hell, I thought. I stroked her hair and patted her shoulder. She was crying.

"You will, won't you?" She looked up at me. "Because we're going to have a strange life."

After a while I walked with her to the door of the villa and she went in and I walked home. Back at the villa I went upstairs to the room. Rinaldi was lying on his bed. He looked at me.

"So you make progress with Miss Barkley?"

"We are friends."

"You have that pleasant air of a dog in heat."

I did not understand the word.

"Of a what?"

He explained.

"You," I said, "have that pleasant air of a dog who—"

"Stop it," he said. "In a little while we would say insulting things." He laughed.

"Good-night," I said.

"Good-night, little puppy."

I knocked over his candle with the pillow and got into bed in the dark.

Rinaldi picked up the candle, lit it and went on reading.

CHAPTER 6

I WAS AWAY for two days at the posts. When I got home it was too late and I did not see Miss Barkley until the next evening. She was not in the garden and I had to wait in the office of the hospital until she came down. There were many marble busts on painted wooden pillars along the walls of the room they used for an office. The hall too, that the office opened on, was lined with them. They had the complete marble quality of all looking alike. Sculpture had always seemed a dull business—still, bronzes looked like something. But marble busts all looked like a cemetery. There was one fine cemetery though—the one at Pisa. Genoa was the place to see the bad marbles. This had been the villa of a very wealthy German and the busts must have cost him plenty. I wondered who had done them and how much he got. I tried to make out whether they were members of the family or what; but they were all uniformly classical. You could not tell anything about them.

I sat on a chair and held my cap. We were supposed to wear steel helmets even in Gorizia but they were uncomfortable and too bloody theatrical in a town where the civilian inhabitants had not been evacuated. I wore one when we went up to the posts and carried an English gas mask. We were just beginning to get some of them. They were a real mask. Also we were required to wear an automatic pistol; even doctors and sanitary officers. I felt it against the back of the chair. You were liable to arrest if you did not have one worn in plain sight. Rinaldi carried a holster stuffed with toilet paper. I wore a real one and felt like a gunman until I practiced firing it. It was an Astra 7.65 caliber with a short barrel and it jumped so sharply when you let it off that there was no question of hitting anything. I practiced with it, holding below the target and trying to master the jerk of the ridiculous short barrel until I could hit within a yard of where I aimed at twenty paces and then the ridiculousness of carrying a pistol at all came over me and I soon forgot it and carried it flopping against the small of my back with no feeling at all except a vague sort of shame when I met English-speaking people. I sat now in the chair and an orderly of some sort looked at me disapprovingly from behind a desk while I looked at the marble floor, the pillars with the marble busts, and the frescoes on the wall and waited for Miss Barkley. The frescoes were not bad. Any frescoes were good when they started to peel and flake off.

I saw Catherine Barkley coming down the hall, and stood up. She did not seem tall walking toward me but she looked very lovely.

"Good-evening, Mr. Henry," she said.

"How do you do?" I said. The orderly was listening behind the desk.

"Shall we sit here or go out in the garden?"

"Let's go out. It's much cooler."

I walked behind her out into the garden, the orderly looking after us. When we were out on the gravel drive she said, "Where have you been?"

"I've been out on post."

"You couldn't have sent me a note?"

"No," I said. "Not very well. I thought I was coming back."

"You ought to have let me know, darling."

We were off the driveway, walking under the trees. I took her hands, then stopped and kissed her.

"Isn't there anywhere we can go?"

"No," she said. "We have to just walk here. You've been away a long time."

"This is the third day. But I'm back now."

She looked at me, "And you do love me?"

"Yes."

"You did say you loved me, didn't you?"

"Yes," I lied. "I love you." I had not said it before.

"And you call me Catherine?"

"Catherine." We walked on a way and were stopped under a tree.

"Say, 'I've come back to Catherine in the night.'"

"I've come back to Catherine in the night."

"Oh, darling, you have come back, haven't you?"

"Yes."

"I love you so and it's been awful. You won't go away?"

"No. I'll always come back."

"Oh, I love you so. Please put your hand there again."

"It's not been away." I turned her so I could see her face when I kissed her and I saw that her eyes were shut. I kissed both her shut eyes. I thought she was probably a little crazy. It was all right if she was. I did not care what I was getting into. This was better than going every evening to the house for officers where the girls climbed all over you and put your cap on backward as a sign of affection between their trips upstairs with brother officers. I knew I did not love Catherine Barkley nor had any idea of loving her. This was a game, like bridge, in which you said things instead of playing cards. Like bridge you had to pretend you were playing for money or playing for some stakes. Nobody had mentioned what the stakes were. It was all right with me.

"I wish there was some place we could go," I said. I was experiencing the masculine difficulty of making love very long standing up.

"There isn't any place," she said. She came back from wherever she had been.

"We might sit there just for a little while."

We sat on the flat stone bench and I held Catherine Barkley's hand. She would not let me put my arm around her.

"Are you very tired?" she asked.

"No."

She looked down at the grass.

"This is a rotten game we play, isn't it?"

"What game?"

"Don't be dull."

"I'm not, on purpose."

"You're a nice boy," she said. "And you play it as well as you know how. But it's a rotten game."

"Do you always know what people think?"

"Not always. But I do with you. You don't have to pretend you love me. That's over for the evening. Is there anything you'd like to talk about?"

"But I do love you."

"Please let's not lie when we don't have to. I had a very fine little show and I'm all right now. You see I'm not mad and I'm not gone off. It's only a little sometimes."

I pressed her hand, "Dear Catherine."

"It sounds very funny now—Catherine. You don't pronounce it very much alike. But you're very nice. You're a very good boy."

"That's what the priest said."

"Yes, you're very good. And you will come and see me?"

"Of course."

"And you don't have to say you love me. That's all over for a while." She stood up and put out her hand. "Good-night."

I wanted to kiss her.

"No," she said. "I'm awfully tired."

"Kiss me, though," I said.

"I'm awfully tired, darling."

"Kiss me."

"Do you want to very much?"

"Yes."

We kissed and she broke away suddenly. "No. Good-night, please, darling." We walked to the door and I saw her go in and down the hall. I liked to watch her move. She went on down the hall. I went on home. It was a hot night and there was a good deal going on up in the mountains. I watched the flashes on San Gabriele.

I stopped in front of the Villa Rossa. The shutters were up but it was still going on inside. Somebody was singing. I went on home. Rinaldi came in while I was undressing.

"Ah, ha!" he said. "It does not go so well. Baby is puzzled."

"Where have you been?"

"At the Villa Rossa. It was very edifying, baby. We all sang. Where have you been?"

"Calling on the British."

"Thank God I did not become involved with the British."

CHAPTER 7

I CAME BACK the next afternoon from our first mountain post and stopped the car at the smistimento where the wounded and sick were sorted by their papers and the papers marked for the different hospitals. I had been driving and I sat in the car and the driver took the papers in. It was a hot day and the sky was very bright and blue and the road was white and dusty. I sat in the high seat of the Fiat and thought about nothing. A regiment went by in the road and I watched them pass. The men were hot and sweating. Some wore their steel helmets but most of them carried them slung from their packs. Most of the helmets were too big and came down almost over the ears of the men who wore them. The officers all wore helmets; better-fitting helmets. It was half of the brigata Basilicata. I identified them by their red and white striped collar mark. There were stragglers going by long after the regiment had passed—men who could not keep up with their platoons. They were sweaty, dusty and tired. Some looked pretty bad. A soldier came along after the last of the stragglers. He was walking with a limp. He stopped and sat down beside the road. I got down and went over.

"What's the matter?"

He looked at me, then stood up.

"I'm going on."

"What's the trouble?"

"—the war."

"What's wrong with your leg?"

"It's not my leg. I got a rupture."

"Why don't you ride with the transport?" I asked. "Why don't you go to the hospital?"

"They won't let me. The lieutenant said I slipped the truss on purpose."

"Let me feel it."

"It's way out."

"Which side is it on?"

"Here."

I felt it.

"Cough," I said.

"I'm afraid it will make it bigger. It's twice as big as it was this morning."

"Sit down," I said. "As soon as I get the papers on these wounded I'll take you along the road and drop you with your medical officers."

"He'll say I did it on purpose."

"They can't do anything," I said. "It's not a wound. You've had it before, haven't you?"

"But I lost the truss."

"They'll send you to a hospital."

"Can't I stay here, Tenente?"

"No, I haven't any papers for you."

The driver came out of the door with the papers for the wounded in the car.

"Four for 105. Two for 132," he said. They were hospitals beyond the river.

"You drive," I said. I helped the soldier with the rupture up on the seat with us.

"You speak English?" he asked.

"Sure."

"How you like this goddam war?"

"Rotten."

"I say it's rotten. Jesus Christ, I say it's rotten."

"Were you in the States?"

"Sure. In Pittsburgh. I knew you was an American."

"Don't I talk Italian good enough?"

"I knew you was an American all right."

"Another American," said the driver in Italian looking at the hernia man.

"Listen, lootenant. Do you have to take me to that regiment?"

"Yes."

"Because the captain doctor knew I had this rupture. I threw away the goddam truss so it would get bad and I wouldn't have to go to the line again."

"I see."

"Couldn't you take me no place else?"

"If it was closer to the front I could take you to a first medical post. But back here you've got to have papers."

"If I go back they'll make me get operated on and then they'll put me in the line all the time."

I thought it over.

"You wouldn't want to go in the line all the time, would you?" he asked.

"No."

"Jesus Christ, ain't this a goddam war?"

"Listen," I said. "You get out and fall down by the road and get a bump on your head and I'll pick you up on our way back and take you to a hospital. We'll stop by the road here, Aldo." We stopped at the side of the road. I helped him down.

"I'll be right here, lieutenant," he said.

"So long," I said. We went on and passed the regiment about a mile ahead, then crossed the river, cloudy with snow-water and running fast through the spiles of the bridge, to ride along the road across the plain and deliver the wounded at the two hospitals. I drove coming back and went fast with the empty car to find the man from Pittsburgh. First we passed the regiment, hotter and slower than ever: then the stragglers. Then we saw a horse ambulance stopped by the road. Two men were lifting the hernia man to put him in. They had come back for him. He shook his head at me. His helmet was off and his forehead was bleeding below the hair line. His nose was skinned and there was dust on the bloody patch and dust in his hair.

"Look at the bump, lieutenant!" he shouted. "Nothing to do. They come back for me."

When I got back to the villa it was five o'clock and I went out where we washed the cars, to take a shower. Then I made out my report in my room, sitting in my trousers and an undershirt in front of the open window. In two days the offensive was to start and I would go with the cars to Plava. It was a long time since I had written to the States and I knew I should write but I had let it go so long that it was almost impossible to write now. There was nothing to write about. I sent a couple of army Zona di Guerra post-cards, crossing out everything except, I am well. That should handle them. Those post-cards would be very fine in America; strange and mysterious. This was a strange and mysterious war zone but I supposed it was quite well run and grim compared to other wars with the Austrians. The Austrian army was created to give Napoleon victories; any Napoleon. I wished we had a Napoleon, but instead we had Il Generale Cadorna, fat and prosperous and Vittorio Emmanuele, the tiny man with the long thin neck and the goat beard. Over on the right they had the Duke of Aosta. Maybe he was too good-looking to be a great general but he looked like a man. Lots of them would have liked him to be king. He looked like a king. He was the King's uncle and commanded the third army. We were in the second army. There were some British batteries up with the third army. I had met two gunners from that lot, in Milan. They were very nice and we had a big evening. They were big and shy and embarrassed and very appreciative together of anything that happened. I wish that I was with the British. It would have been much simpler. Still I would probably have been killed. Not in this ambulance business. Yes, even in the ambulance business. British ambulance drivers were killed sometimes. Well, I knew I would not be killed. Not in this war. It did not have anything to do with me. It seemed no more dangerous to me myself than war in the movies. I wished to God it was over though. Maybe it would finish this summer. Maybe the Austrians would crack. They had always cracked in other wars. What was the matter with this war? Everybody said the French were through. Rinaldi said that the French had mutinied and troops marched on Paris. I asked him what happened and he said, "Oh, they stopped them." I wanted to go to Austria without war. I wanted to go to the Black Forest. I wanted to go to the Hartz Mountains.

Where were the Hartz Mountains anyway? They were fighting in the Carpathians. I did not want to go there anyway. It might be good though. I could go to Spain if there was no war. The sun was going down and the day was cooling off. After supper I would go and see Catherine Barkley. I wish she were here now. I wished I were in Milan with her. I would like to eat at the Cova and then walk down the Via Manzoni in the hot evening and cross over and turn off along the canal and go to the hotel with Catherine Barkley. Maybe she would. Maybe she would pretend that I was her boy that was killed and we would go in the front door and the porter would take off his cap and I would stop at the concierge's desk and ask for the key and she would stand by the elevator and then we would get in the elevator and it would go up very slowly clicking at all the floors and then our floor and the boy would open the door and stand there and she would step out and I would step out and we would walk down the hall and I would put the key in the door and open it and go in and then take down the telephone and ask them to send a bottle of capri bianca in a silver bucket full of ice and you would hear the ice against the pail coming down the corridor and the boy would knock and I would say leave it outside the door please. Because we would not wear any clothes because it was so hot and the window open and the swallows flying over the roofs of the houses and when it was dark afterward and you went to the window very small bats hunting over the houses and close down over the trees and we would drink the capri and the door locked and it hot and only a sheet and the whole night and we would both love each other all night in the hot night in Milan. That was how it ought to be. I would eat quickly and go and see Catherine Barkley.

They talked too much at the mess and I drank wine because tonight we were not all brothers unless I drank a little and talked with the priest about Archbishop Ireland who was, it seemed, a noble man and with whose injustice, the injustices he had received and in which I participated as an American, and of which I had never heard, I feigned acquaintance. It would have been impolite not to have known something of them when I had listened to such a splendid explanation of their causes which were, after all, it seemed, misunderstandings. I thought he had a fine name and he came from Minnesota which made a lovely name: Ireland of Minnesota, Ireland of Wisconsin, Ireland of Michigan. What made it pretty was that it sounded like Island. No that wasn't it. There was more to it than that. Yes, father. That is true, father. Perhaps, father. No, father. Well, maybe yes, father. You know more about it than I do, father. The priest was good but dull. The officers were not good but dull. The King was good but dull. The wine was bad but not dull. It took the enamel off your teeth and left it on the roof of your mouth.

"And the priest was locked up," Rocca said, "because they found the three per cent bonds on his person. It was in France of course. Here they would never have arrested him. He denied all knowledge of the five per cent bonds. This took place at Béziers. I was there and reading of it in the paper, went to the jail and asked to see the priest. It was quite evident he had stolen the bonds."

"I don't believe a word of this," Rinaldi said.

"Just as you like," Rocca said. "But I am telling it for our priest here. It is very informative. He is a priest; he will appreciate it."

The priest smiled. "Go on," he said. "I am listening."

"Of course some of the bonds were not accounted for but the priest had all of the three per cent bonds and several local obligations, I forget exactly what they were. So I went to the jail, now this is the point of the story, and I stood outside his cell and I said as though I were going to confession, 'Bless me, father, for you have sinned.'"

There was great laughter from everybody.

"And what did he say?" asked the priest. Rocca ignored this and went on to explain the joke to me. "You see the point, don't you?" It seemed it was a very funny joke if you understood it properly. They poured me more wine and I told the story about the English private soldier who was placed under the shower bath. Then the major told the story of the eleven Czecho-slovaks and the Hungarian corporal. After some more wine I told the story of the jockey who found the penny. The major said there was an Italian story something like that about the duchess who could not sleep at night. At this point the priest left and I told the story about the travelling salesman who arrived at five o'clock in the morning at Marseilles when the mistral was blowing. The major said he had heard a report that I could drink. I denied this. He said it was true and by the corpse of Bacchus we would test whether it was true or not. Not Bacchus, I said. Not Bacchus. Yes, Bacchus, he said. I should drink cup for cup and glass for glass with Bassi, Fillipo Vincenza. Bassi said no that was no test because he had already drunk twice as much as I. I said that was a foul lie and, Bacchus or no Bacchus, Fillipo Vincenza Bassi or Bassi Fillippo Vicenza had never touched a drop all evening and what was his name anyway? He said was my name Frederico Enrico or Enrico Federico? I said let the best man win, Bacchus barred, and the major started us with red wine in mugs. Half-way through the wine I did not want any more. I remembered where I was going.

"Bassi wins," I said. "He's a better man than I am. I have to go."

"He does really," said Rinaldi. "He has a rendezvous. I know all about it."

"I have to go."

"Another night," said Bassi. "Another night when you feel stronger." He slapped me on the shoulder. There were lighted candles on the table. All the officers were very happy. "Good-night, gentlemen," I said.

Rinaldi went out with me. We stood outside the door on the patch and he said, "You better not go up there drunk."

"I'm not drunk, Rinin. Really."

"You'd better chew some coffee."

"Nonsense."

"I'll get some, baby. You walk up and down." He came back with a handful of roasted coffee beans. "Chew those, baby, and God be with you."

"Bacchus," I said.

"I'll walk down with you."

"I'm perfectly all right."

We walked along together through the town and I chewed the coffee. At the gate of the driveway that led up to the British villa, Rinaldi said good-night.

"Good-night," I said. "Why don't you come in?"

He shook his head. "No," he said. "I like the simpler pleasures."

"Thank you for the coffee beans."

"Nothing, baby. Nothing."

I started down the driveway. The outlines of the cypresses that lined it were sharp and clear. I looked back and saw Rinaldi standing watching me and waved to him.

I sat in the reception hall of the villa, waiting for Catherine Barkley to come down. Some one was coming down the hallway. I stood up, but it was not Catherine. It was Miss Ferguson.

"Hello," she said. "Catherine asked me to tell you she was sorry she couldn't see you this evening."

"I'm so sorry. I hope she's not ill."

"She's not awfully well."

"Will you tell her how sorry I am?"

"Yes, I will."

"Do you think it would be any good to try and see her tomorrow?"

"Yes, I do."

"Thank you very much," I said. "Good-night."

I went out the door and suddenly I felt lonely and empty. I had treated seeing Catherine very lightly, I had gotten somewhat drunk and had nearly forgotten to come but when I could not see her there I was feeling lonely and hollow.

CHAPTER 8

THE NEXT AFTERNOON we heard there was to be an attack up the river that night and that we were to take four cars there. Nobody knew anything about it although they all spoke with great positiveness and strategical knowledge. I was riding in the first car and as we passed the entry to the British hospital I told the driver to stop. The other cars pulled up. I got out and told the driver to go on and that if we had not caught up to them at the junction of the road to Cormons to wait there. I hurried up the driveway and inside the reception hall I asked for Miss Barkley.

"She's on duty."

"Could I see her just for a moment?"

They sent an orderly to see and she came back with him.

"I stopped to ask if you were better. They told me you were on duty, so I asked to see you."

"I'm quite well," she said, "I think the heat knocked me over yesterday."

"I have to go."

"I'll just step out the door a minute."

"And you're all right?" I asked outside.

"Yes, darling. Are you coming to-night?"

"No. I'm leaving now for a show up above Plava."

"A show?"

"I don't think it's anything."

"And you'll be back?"

"To-morrow."

She was unclasping something from her neck. She put it in my hand. "It's a Saint Anthony," she said. "And come to-morrow night."

"You're not a Catholic, are you?"

"No. But they say a Saint Anthony's very useful."

"I'll take care of him for you. Good-by."

"No," she said, "not good-by."

"All right."

"Be a good boy and be careful. No, you can't kiss me here. You can't."

"All right."

I looked back and saw her standing on the steps. She waved and I kissed my hand and held it out. She waved again and then I was out of the driveway and climbing up into the seat of the ambulance and we started. The Saint Anthony was in a little white metal capsule. I opened the capsule and spilled him out into my hand.

"Saint Anthony?" asked the driver.

"Yes."

"I have one." His right hand left the wheel and opened a button on his tunic and pulled it out from under his shirt.

"See?"

I put my Saint Anthony back in the capsule, spilled the thin gold chain together and put it all in my breast pocket.

"You don't wear him?"

"No."

"It's better to wear him. That's what it's for."

"All right," I said. I undid the clasp of the gold chain and put it around my neck and clasped it. The saint hung down on the outside of my uniform and I undid the throat of my tunic, unbuttoned the shirt collar and dropped him in under the shirt. I felt him in his metal box against my chest while we drove. Then I forgot about him. After I was wounded I never found him. Some one probably got it at one of the dressing stations.

We drove fast when we were over the bridge and soon we saw the dust of the other cars ahead down the road. The road curved and we saw the three cars looking quite small, the dust rising from the wheels and going off through the trees. We caught them and passed them and turned off on a road that climbed up into the hills. Driving in convoy is not unpleasant if you are the first car and I settled back in the seat and watched the country. We were in the foothills on the near side of the river and as the road mounted there were the high mountains off to the north with snow still on the tops. I looked back and saw the three cars all climbing, spaced by the interval of their dust. We passed a long column of loaded mules, the drivers walking along beside the mules wearing red fezzes. They were bersaglieri.

Beyond the mule train the road was empty and we climbed through the hills and then went down over the shoulder of a long hill into a river-valley. There were trees along both sides of the road and through the right line of trees I saw the river, the water clear, fast and shallow. The river was low and there were stretches of sand and pebbles with a narrow channel of water and sometimes the water spread like a sheen over the pebbly bed. Close to the bank I saw deep pools, the water blue like the sky. I saw arched stone bridges over the river where tracks turned off from the road and we passed stone farmhouses with pear trees candelabraed against their south walls and low stone walls in the fields. The road went up the valley a long way and then we turned off and commenced to climb into the hills again. The road climbed steeply going up and back and forth through chestnut woods to level finally along a ridge. I could look down through the woods and see, far below, with the sun on it, the line of the river that separated the two armies. We went along the rough new military road that followed the crest of the ridge and I looked to the north at the two ranges of mountains, green and dark to the snow-line and then white and lovely in the sun. Then, as the road mounted along the ridge, I saw a third range of mountains, higher snow mountains, that looked chalky white and furrowed, with strange planes, and then there were mountains far off beyond all these that you could hardly tell if you really saw. Those were all the Austrians' mountains and we had nothing like them. Ahead there was a rounded turn-off in the road to the right and looking down I could see the road dropping through the trees. There were troops on this road and motor trucks and mules with mountain guns and as we went down, keeping to the side, I could see the river far down below, the line of ties and rails running along it, the old bridge where the railway crossed to the other side and across, under a hill beyond the river, the broken houses of the little town that was to be taken.

It was nearly dark when we came down and turned onto the main road that ran beside the river.

CHAPTER 9

THE ROAD WAS crowded and there were screens of corn-stalk and straw matting on both sides and matting over the top so that it was like the entrance at a circus or a native village. We drove slowly in this matting-covered tunnel and came out onto a bare cleared space where the railway station had been. The road here was below the level of the river bank and all along the side of the sunken road there were holes dug in the bank with infantry in them. The sun was going down and looking up along the bank as we drove I saw the Austrian observation balloons above the hills on the other side dark against the sunset. We parked the cars beyond a brickyard. The ovens and some deep holes had been equipped as dressing stations. There were three doctors that I knew. I talked with the major and learned that when it should start and our cars should be loaded we would drive them back along the screened road and up to the main road along the ridge where there would be a post and other cars to clear them. He hoped the road would not jam. It was a one-road show. The road was screened because it was in sight of the Austrians across the river. Here at the brickyard we were sheltered from rifle or machine-gun fire by the river bank. There was one smashed bridge across the river. They were going to put over another bridge when the bombardment started and some troops were to cross at the shallows up above at the bend of the river. The major was a little man with upturned mustaches. He had been in the war in Libya and wore two wound-stripes. He said that if the thing went well he would see that I was decorated. I said I hoped it would go well but that he was too kind. I asked him if there was a big dugout where the drivers could stay and he sent a soldier to show me. I went with him and found the dugout, which was very good. The drivers were pleased with it and I left them there. The major asked me to have a drink with him and two other officers. We drank rum and it was very friendly. Outside it was getting dark. I asked what time the attack was to be and they said as soon as it was dark. I went back to the drivers. They were sitting in the dugout talking and when I came in they stopped. I gave them each a package of cigarettes, Macedonias, loosely packed cigarettes that spilled tobacco and needed to have the ends twisted before you smoked them. Manera lit his lighter and passed it around. The lighter was shaped like a Fiat radiator. I told them what I had heard.

"Why didn't we see the post when we came down?" Passini asked.

"It was just beyond where we turned off."

"That road will be a dirty mess," Manera said.

"They'll shell the—out of us."

"Probably."

"What about eating, lieutenant? We won't get a chance to eat after this thing starts."

"I'll go and see now," I said.

"You want us to stay here or can we look around?"

"Better stay here."

I went back to the major's dugout and he said the field kitchen would be along and the drivers could come and get their stew. He would loan them mess tins if they did not have them. I said I thought they had them. I went back and told the drivers I would get them as soon as the food came. Manera said he hoped it would come before the bombardment started. They were silent until I went out. They were all mechanics and hated the war.

I went out to look at the cars and see what was going on and then came back and sat down in the dugout with the four drivers. We sat on the ground with our backs against the wall and smoked. Outside it was nearly dark. The earth of the dugout was warm and dry and I let my shoulders back against the wall, sitting on the small of my back, and relaxed.

"Who goes to the attack?" asked Gavuzzi.

"Bersaglieri."

"All bersaglieri?"

"I think so."

"There aren't enough troops here for a real attack."

"It is probably to draw attention from where the real attack will be."

"Do the men know that who attack?"

"I don't think so."

"Of course they don't," Manera said. "They wouldn't attack if they did."

"Yes, they would," Passini said. "Bersaglieri are fools."

"They are brave and have good discipline," I said.

"They are big through the chest by measurement, and healthy. But they are still fools."

"The granatieri are tall," Manera said. This was a joke. They all laughed.

"Were you there, Tenente, when they wouldn't attack and they shot every tenth man?"

"No."

"It is true. They lined them up afterward and took every tenth man. Carabinieri shot them."

"Carabinieri," said Passini and spat on the floor. "But those grenadiers; all over six feet. They wouldn't attack."

"If everybody would not attack the war would be over," Manera said.

"It wasn't that way with the granatieri. They were afraid. The officers all came from such good families."

"Some of the officers went alone."

"A sergeant shot two officers who would not get out."

"Some troops went out."

"Those that went out were not lined up when they took the tenth men."

"One of those shot by the carabinieri is from my town," Passini said. "He was a big smart tall boy to be in the granatieri. Always in Rome. Always with the girls. Always with the carabinieri." He laughed. "Now they have a guard outside his house with a bayonet and nobody can come to see his mother and father and sisters and his father loses his civil rights and cannot even vote. They are all without law to protect them. Anybody can take their property."

"If it wasn't that that happens to their families nobody would go to the attack."

"Yes. Alpini would. These V. E. soldiers would. Some bersaglieri."

"Bersaglieri have run too. Now they try to forget it."

"You should not let us talk this way, Tenente. Evviva l'esercito," Passini said sarcastically.

"I know how you talk," I said. "But as long as you drive the cars and behave—"

"—and don't talk so other officers can hear," Manera finished.

"I believe we should get the war over," I said. "It would not finish it if one side stopped fighting. It would only be worse if we stopped fighting."

"It could not be worse," Passini said respectfully. "There is nothing worse than war."

"Defeat is worse."

"I do not believe it," Passini said still respectfully. "What is defeat? You go home."

"They come after you. They take your home. They take your sisters."

"I don't believe it," Passini said. "They can't do that to everybody. Let everybody defend his home. Let them keep their sisters in the house."

"They hang you. They come and make you be a soldier again. Not in the auto-ambulance, in the infantry."

"They can't hang every one."

"An outside nation can't make you be a soldier," Manera said. "At the first battle you all run."

"Like the Tchecos."

"I think you do not know anything about being conquered and so you think it is not bad."

"Tenente," Passini said. "We understand you let us talk. Listen. There is nothing as bad as war. We in the auto-ambulance cannot even realize at all how bad it is. When people realize how bad it is they cannot do anything to stop it because they go crazy. There are some people who never realize. There are people who are afraid of their officers. It is with them the war is made."

"I know it is bad but we must finish it."

"It doesn't finish. There is no finish to a war."

"Yes there is."

Passini shook his head.

"War is not won by victory. What if we take San Gabriele?"

"What if we take the Carso and Monfalcone and Trieste? Where are we then? Did you see all the far mountains to-day? Do you think we could take all them too? Only if the Austrians stop fighting. One side must stop fighting. Why don't we stop fighting? If they come down into Italy they will get tired and go away. They have their own country. But no, instead there is a war."

"You're an orator."

"We think. We read. We are not peasants. We are mechanics. But even the peasants know better than to believe in a war. Everybody hates this war."

"There is a class that controls a country that is stupid and does not realize anything and never can. That is why we have this war."

"Also they make money out of it."

"Most of them don't," said Passini. "They are too stupid. They do it for nothing. For stupidity."

"We must shut up," said Manera. "We talk too much even for the Tenente."

"He likes it," said Passini. "We will convert him."

"But now we will shut up," Manera said.

"Do we eat yet, Tenente?" Gavuzzi asked.

"I will go and see," I said. Gordini stood up and went outside with me.

"Is there anything I can do, Tenente? Can I help in any way?" He was the quietest one of the four. "Come with me if you want," I said, "and we'll see."

It was dark outside and the long light from the search-lights was moving over the mountains. There were big search-lights on that front mounted on camions that you passed sometimes on the roads at night, close behind the lines, the camion stopped a little off the road, an officer directing the light and the crew scared. We crossed the brickyard, and stopped at the main dressing station. There was a little shelter of green branches outside over the entrance and in the dark the night wind rustled the leaves dried by the sun. Inside there was a light. The major was at the telephone sitting on a box. One of the medical captains said the attack had been put forward an hour. He offered me a glass of cognac. I looked at the board tables, the instruments shining in the light, the basins and the stoppered bottles. Gordini stood behind me. The major got up from the telephone.

"It starts now," he said. "It has been put back again."

I looked outside, it was dark and the Austrian search-lights were moving on the mountains behind us. It was quiet for a moment still, then from all the guns behind us the bombardment started.

"Savoia," said the major.

"About the soup, major," I said. He did not hear me. I repeated it.

"It hasn't come up."

A big shell came in and burst outside in the brickyard. Another burst and in the noise you could hear the smaller noise of the brick and dirt raining down.

"What is there to eat?"

"We have a little pasta asciutta," the major said.

"I'll take what you can give me."

The major spoke to an orderly who went out of sight in the back and came back with a metal basin of cold cooked macaroni. I handed it to Gordini.

"Have you any cheese?"

The major spoke grudgingly to the orderly who ducked back into the hole again and came out with a quarter of a white cheese.

"Thank you very much," I said.

"You'd better not go out."

Outside something was set down beside the entrance. One of the two men who had carried it looked in.

"Bring him in," said the major. "What's the matter with you? Do you want us to come outside and get him?"

The two stretcher-bearers picked up the man under the arms and by the legs and brought him in.

"Slit the tunic," the major said.

He held a forceps with some gauze in the end. The two captains took off their coats. "Get out of here," the major said to the two stretcher-bearers.

"Come on," I said to Gordini.

"You better wait until the shelling is over," the major said over his shoulder.

"They want to eat," I said.

"As you wish."

Outside we ran across the brickyard. A shell burst short near the river bank. Then there was one that we did not hear coming until the sudden rush. We both went flat and with the flash and bump of the burst and the smell heard the singing off of the fragments and the rattle of falling brick. Gordini got up and ran for the dugout. I was after him, holding the cheese, its smooth surface covered with brick dust. Inside the dugout were the three drivers sitting against the wall, smoking.

"Here, you patriots," I said.

"How are the cars?" Manera asked.

"All right."

"Did they scare you, Tenente?"

"You're damned right," I said.

I took out my knife, opened it, wiped off the blade and pared off the dirty outside surface of the cheese. Gavuzzi handed me the basin of macaroni.

"Start in to eat, Tenente."

"No," I said. "Put it on the floor. We'll all eat."

"There are no forks."

"What the hell," I said in English.

I cut the cheese into pieces and laid them on the macaroni.

"Sit down to it," I said. They sat down and waited. I put thumb and fingers into the macaroni and lifted. A mass loosened.

"Lift it high, Tenente."

I lifted it to arm's length and the strands cleared. I lowered it into the mouth, sucked and snapped in the ends, and chewed, then took a bite of cheese, chewed, and then a drink of the wine. It tasted of rusty metal. I handed the canteen back to

Passini.

"It's rotten," he said. "It's been in there too long. I had it in the car."

They were all eating, holding their chins close over the basin, tipping their heads back, sucking in the ends. I took another mouthful and some cheese and a rinse of wine. Something landed outside that shook the earth.

"Four hundred twenty or minnenwerfer," Gavuzzi said.

"There aren't any four hundred twenties in the mountains," I said.

"They have big Skoda guns. I've seen the holes."

"Three hundred fives."

We went on eating. There was a cough, a noise like a railway engine starting and then an explosion that shook the earth again.

"This isn't a deep dugout," Passini said.

"That was a big trench mortar."

"Yes, sir."

I ate the end of my piece of cheese and took a swallow of wine. Through the other noise I heard a cough, then came the chuh-chuh-chuh-chuh—then there was a flash, as when a blast-furnace door is swung open, and a roar that started white and went red and on and on in a rushing wind. I tried to breathe but my breath would not come and I felt myself rush bodily out of myself and out and out and out and all the time bodily in the wind. I went out swiftly, all of myself, and I knew I was dead and that it had all been a mistake to think you just died. Then I floated, and instead of going on I felt myself slide back. I breathed and I was back. The ground was torn up and in front of my head there was a splintered beam of wood. In the jolt of my head I heard somebody crying. I thought somebody was screaming. I tried to move but I could not move. I heard the machine-guns and rifles firing across the river and all along the river. There was a great splashing and I saw the star-shells go up and burst and float whitely and rockets going up and heard the bombs, all this in a moment, and then I heard close to me some one saying "Mama Mia! Oh, mama Mia!" I pulled and twisted and got my legs loose finally and turned around and touched him. It was Passini and when I touched him he screamed. His legs were toward me and I saw in the dark and the light that they were both smashed above the knee. One leg was gone and the other was held by tendons and part of the trouser and the stump twitched and jerked as though it were not connected. He bit his arm and moaned, "Oh mama mia, mama Mia," then, "Dio te salve, Maria. Dio te salve, Maria. Oh Jesus shoot me Christ shoot me mama mia mama Mia oh purest lovely Mary shoot me. Stop it. Stop it. Stop it. Oh Jesus lovely Mary stop it. Oh oh oh oh," then choking, "Mama mama mia." Then he was quiet, biting his arm, the stump of his leg twitching.

"Porta feriti!" I shouted holding my hands cupped. "Porta feriti!" I tried to get closer to Passini to try to put a tourniquet on the legs but I could not move. I tried again and my legs moved a little. I could pull backward along with my arms and elbows. Passini was quiet now. I sat beside him, undid my tunic and tried to rip the tail of my shirt. It would not rip and I bit the edge of the cloth to start it. Then I thought of his puttees. I had on wool stockings but Passini wore puttees. All the drivers wore puttees but Passini had only one leg. I unwound the puttee and while I was doing it I saw there was no need to try and make a tourniquet because he was dead already. I made sure he was dead. There were three others to locate. I sat up straight and as I did so something inside my head moved like the weights on a doll's eyes and it hit me inside in back of my eyeballs. My legs felt warm and wet and my shoes were wet and warm inside. I knew that I was hit and leaned over and put my hand on my knee. My knee wasn't there. My hand went in and my knee was down on my shin. I wiped my hand on my shirt and another floating light came very slowly down and I looked at my leg and was very afraid. Oh, God, I said, get me out of here. I knew, however, that there had been three others. There were four drivers. Passini was dead. That left three. Some one took hold of me under the arms and somebody else lifted my legs.

"There are three others," I said. "One is dead."

"It's Manera. We went for a stretcher but there wasn't any. How are you, Tenente?"

"Where is Gordini and Gavuzzi?"

"Gordini's at the post getting bandaged. Gavuzzi has your legs. Hold on to my neck, Tenente. Are you badly hit?"

"In the leg. How is Gordini?"

"He's all right. It was a big trench mortar shell."

"Passini's dead."

"Yes. He's dead."

A shell fell close and they both dropped to the ground and dropped me. "I'm sorry, Tenente," said Manera. "Hang onto my neck."

"If you drop me again."

"It was because we were scared."

"Are you unwounded?"

"We are both wounded a little."

"Can Gordini drive?"

"I don't think so."

They dropped me once more before we reached the post.

"You sons of bitches," I said.

"I am sorry, Tenente," Manera said. "We won't drop you again."

Outside the post a great many of us lay on the ground in the dark. They carried wounded in and brought them out. I could see the light come out from the dressing station when the curtain opened and they brought some one in or out. The dead were off to one side. The doctors were working with their sleeves up to their shoulders and were red as butchers. There were not enough stretchers. Some of the wounded were noisy but most were quiet. The wind blew the leaves in the bower over the door of the dressing station and the night was getting cold. Stretcher-bearers came in all the time, put their stretchers down, unloaded them and went away. As soon as I got to the dressing station Manera brought a medical sergeant out and he put bandages on both my legs. He said there was so much dirt blown into the wound that there had not been much hemorrhage. They would take me as soon as possible. He went back inside. Gordini could not drive, Manera said. His shoulder was smashed and his head was hurt. He had not felt bad but now the shoulder had stiffened. He was sitting up beside one of the brick walls. Manera and Gavuzzi each went off with a load of wounded. They could drive all right. The British had come with three ambulances and they had two men on each ambulance. One of their drivers came over to me, brought by Gordini who looked very white and sick. The Britisher leaned over.

"Are you hit badly?" he asked. He was a tall man and wore steel-rimmed spectacles.

"In the legs."

"It's not serious I hope. Will you have a cigarette?"

"Thanks."

"They tell me you've lost two drivers."

"Yes. One killed and the fellow that brought you."

"What rotten luck. Would you like us to take the cars?"

"That's what I wanted to ask you."

"We'd take quite good care of them and return them to the villa. 206 aren't you?"

"Yes."

"It's a charming place. I've seen you about. They tell me you're an American."

"Yes."

"I'm English."

"No!"

"Yes, English. Did you think I was Italian? There were some Italians with one of our units."

"It would be fine if you would take the cars," I said.

"We'll be most careful of them," he straightened up. "This chap of yours was very anxious for me to see you." He patted Gordini on the shoulder. Gordini winced and smiled. The Englishman broke into voluble and perfect Italian. "Now everything is arranged. I've seen your Tenente. We will take over the two cars. You won't worry now." He broke off, "I must do something about getting you out of here. I'll see the medical wallahs. We'll take you back with us."

He walked across to the dressing station, stepping carefully among the wounded. I saw the blanket open, the light came out and he went in.

"He will look after you, Tenente," Gordini said.

"How are you, Franco?"

"I am all right." He sat down beside me. In a moment the blanket in front of the dressing station opened and two stretcher-bearers came out followed by the tall Englishman. He brought them over to me.

"Here is the American Tenente," he said in Italian.

"I'd rather wait," I said. "There are much worse wounded than me. I'm all right."

"Come, come," he said. "Don't be a bloody hero." Then in Italian: "Lift him very carefully about the legs. His legs are very painful. He is the legitimate son of President Wilson." They picked me up and took me into the dressing room. Inside they were operating on all the tables. The little major looked at us furious. He recognized me and waved a forceps.

"Ça va bien?"

"Ça va."

"I have brought him in," the tall Englishman said in Italian. "The only son of the American Ambassador. He can be here until you are ready to take him. Then I will take him with my first load." He bent over me. "I'll look up their adjutant to do your papers and it will all go much faster." He stooped to go under the doorway and went out. The major was unhooking the forceps now, dropping them in a basin. I followed his hands with my eyes. Now he was bandaging. Then the stretcher-bearers took the man off the table.

"I'll take the American Tenente," one of the captains said. They lifted me onto the table. It was hard and slippery. There were many strong smells, chemical smells and the sweet smell of blood. They took off my trousers and the medical captain commenced dictating to the sergeant-adjutant while he worked, "Multiple superficial wounds of the left and right thigh and left and right knee and right foot. Profound wounds of right knee and foot. Lacerations of the scalp (he probed—Does that hurt?—Christ, yes!) with possible fracture of the skull. Incurred in the line of duty. That's what keeps you from being court-martialled for self-inflicted wounds," he said. "Would you like a drink of brandy? How did you run into this thing anyway? What were you trying to do? Commit suicide? Antitetanus please, and mark a cross on both legs. Thank you. I'll clean this up a little, wash it out, and put on a dressing. Your blood coagulates beautifully."

The adjutant, looking up from the paper, "What inflicted the wounds?"

The medical captain, "What hit you?"

Me, with the eyes shut, "A trench mortar shell."

The captain, doing things that hurt sharply and severing tissue— "Are you sure?"

Me—trying to lie still and feeling my stomach flutter when the flesh was cut, "I think so."

Captain doctor—(interested in something he was finding), "Fragments of enemy trench-mortar shell. Now I'll probe for some of this if you like but it's not necessary. I'll paint all this and—Does that sting? Good, that's nothing to how it will feel later. The pain hasn't started yet. Bring him a glass of brandy. The shock dulls the pain; but this is all right, you have nothing to worry about if it doesn't infect and it rarely does now. How is your head?"

"Good Christ!" I said.

"Better not drink too much brandy then. If you've got a fracture you don't want inflammation. How does that feel?"

Sweat ran all over me.

"Good Christ!" I said.

"I guess you've got a fracture all right. I'll wrap you up and don't bounce your head around." He bandaged, his hands moving very fast and the bandage coming taut and sure. "All right, good luck and Vive la France."

"He's an American," one of the other captains said.

"I thought you said he was a Frenchman. He talks French," the captain said. "I've known him before. I always thought he was French." He drank a half tumbler of cognac. "Bring on something serious. Get some more of that Antitetanus." The captain waved to me. They lifted me and the blanket-flap went across my face as we went out. Outside the sergeant-adjutant knelt down beside me where I lay, "Name?" he asked softly. "Middle name? First name? Rank? Where born? What class? What corps?" and so on. "I'm sorry for your head, Tenente. I hope you feel better. I'm sending you now with the English ambulance."

"I'm all right," I said. "Thank you very much." The pain that the major had spoken about had started and all that was happening was without interest or relation. After a while the English ambulance came up and they put me onto a stretcher and lifted the stretcher up to the ambulance level and shoved it in. There was another stretcher by the side with a man on it whose nose I could see, waxy-looking, out of the bandages. He breathed very heavily. There were stretchers lifted and slid into the slings above. The tall English driver came around and looked in, "I'll take it very easily," he said. "I hope you'll be comfy." I felt the engine start, felt him climb up into the front seat, felt the brake come off and the clutch go in, then we started. I lay still and let the pain ride.

As the ambulance climbed along the road, it was slow in the traffic, sometimes it stopped, sometimes it backed on a turn, then finally it climbed quite fast. I felt something dripping. At first it dropped slowly and regularly, then it pattered into a stream. I shouted to the driver. He stopped the car and looked in through the hole behind his seat.

"What is it?"

"The man on the stretcher over me has a hemorrhage."

"We're not far from the top. I wouldn't be able to get the stretcher out alone." He started the car. The stream kept on. In the dark I could not see where it came from the canvas overhead. I tried to move sideways so that it did not fall on me. Where it had run down under my shirt it was warm and sticky. I was cold and my leg hurt so that it made me sick. After a while the stream from the stretcher above lessened and started to drip again and I heard and felt the canvas above move as the man on the stretcher settled more comfortably.

"How is he?" the Englishman called back. "We're almost up."

"He's dead I think," I said.

The drops fell very slowly, as they fall from an icicle after the sun has gone. It was cold in the car in the night as the road climbed. At the post on the top they took the stretcher out and put another in and we went on.

CHAPTER 10

IN THE WARD at the field hospital they told me a visitor was coming to see me in the afternoon. It was a hot day and there were many flies in the room. My orderly had cut paper into strips and tied the strips to a stick to make a brush that swished the flies away. I watched them settle on the ceiling. When he stopped swishing and fell asleep they came down and I blew them away and finally covered my face with my hands and slept too. It was very hot and when I woke my legs itched. I waked the orderly and he poured mineral water on the dressings. That made the bed damp and cool. Those of us that were awake talked across the ward. The afternoon was a quiet time. In the morning they came to each bed in turn, three men nurses and a doctor and picked you up out of bed and carried you into the dressing room so that the beds could be made while we were having our wounds dressed. It was not a pleasant trip to the dressing room and I did not know until later that beds could be made with men in them. My orderly had finished pouring water and the bed felt cool and lovely and I was telling him where to scratch on the soles of my feet against the itching when one of the doctors brought in Rinaldi. He came in very fast and bent down over the bed and kissed me. I saw he wore gloves.

"How are you, baby? How do you feel? I bring you this—" It was a bottle of cognac. The orderly brought a chair and he sat down, "and good news. You will be decorated. They want to get you the medaglia d'argento but perhaps they can get only the bronze."

"What for?"

"Because you are gravely wounded. They say if you can prove you did any heroic act you can get the silver. Otherwise it will be the bronze. Tell me exactly what happened. Did you do any heroic act?"

"No," I said. "I was blown up while we were eating cheese."

"Be serious. You must have done something heroic either before or after. Remember carefully."

"I did not."

"Didn't you carry anybody on your back? Gordini says you carried several people on your back but the medical major at the first post declares it is impossible. He had to sign the proposition for the citation."

"I didn't carry anybody. I couldn't move."

"That doesn't matter," said Rinaldi.

He took off his gloves.

"I think we can get you the silver. Didn't you refuse to be medically aided before the others?"

"Not very firmly."

"That doesn't matter. Look how you are wounded. Look at your valorous conduct in asking to go always to the first line. Besides, the operation was successful."

"Did they cross the river all right?"

"Enormously. They take nearly a thousand prisoners. It's in the bulletin. Didn't you see it?"

"No."

"I'll bring it to you. It is a successful coup de main."

"How is everything?"

"Splendid. We are all splendid. Everybody is proud of you. Tell me just exactly how it happened. I am positive you will get the silver. Go on tell me. Tell me all about it." He paused and thought. "Maybe you will get an English medal too. There was an English there. I'll go and see him and ask if he will recommend you. He ought to be able to do something. Do you suffer much? Have a drink. Orderly, go get a corkscrew. Oh you should see what I did in the removal of three metres of small intestine and better now than ever. It is one for The Lancet. You do me a translation and I will send it to The Lancet. Every day I am better. Poor dear baby, how do you feel? Where is that damn corkscrew? You are so brave and quiet I forget you are suffering." He slapped his gloves on the edge of the bed.

"Here is the corkscrew, Signor Tenente," the orderly said.

"Open the bottle. Bring a glass. Drink that, baby. How is your poor head? I looked at your papers. You haven't any fracture. That major at the first post was a hog-butcher. I would take you and never hurt you. I never hurt anybody. I learn how to do it. Every day I learn to do things smoother and better. You must forgive me for talking so much, baby. I am very moved to see you badly wounded. There, drink that. It's good. It cost fifteen lire. It ought to be good. Five stars. After I leave here I'll go see that English and he'll get you an English medal."

"They don't give them like that."

"You are so modest. I will send the liaison officer. He can handle the English."

"Have you seen Miss Barkley?"

"I will bring her here. I will go now and bring her here."

"Don't go," I said. "Tell me about Gorizia. How are the girls?"

"There are no girls. For two weeks now they haven't changed them. I don't go there any more. It is disgraceful. They aren't girls; they are old war comrades."

"You don't go at all?"

"I just go to see if there is anything new. I stop by. They all ask for you. It is a disgrace that they should stay so long that they become friends."

"Maybe girls don't want to go to the front any more."

"Of course they do. They have plenty of girls. It is just bad administration. They are keeping them for the pleasure of dugout hiders in the rear."

"Poor Rinaldi," I said. "All alone at the war with no new girls."

Rinaldi poured himself another glass of the cognac.

"I don't think it will hurt you, baby. You take it."

I drank the cognac and felt it warm all the way down. Rinaldi poured another glass. He was quieter now. He held up the glass. "To your valorous wounds. To the silver medal. Tell me, baby, when you lie here all the time in the hot weather don't you get excited?"

"Sometimes."

"I can't imagine lying like that. I would go crazy."

"You are crazy."

"I wish you were back. No one to come in at night from adventures. No one to make fun of. No one to lend me money. No blood brother and roommate. Why do you get yourself wounded?"

"You can make fun of the priest."

"That priest. It isn't me that makes fun of him. It is the captain. I like him. If you must have a priest have that priest. He's coming to see you. He makes big preparations."

"I like him."

"Oh, I knew it. Sometimes I think you and he are a little that way. You know."

"No, you don't."

"Yes, I do sometimes. A little that way like the number of the first regiment of the Brigata Ancona."

"Oh, go to hell."

He stood up and put on his gloves.

"Oh I love to tease you, baby. With your priest and your English girl, and really you are just like me underneath."

"No, I'm not."

"Yes, we are. You are really an Italian. All fire and smoke and nothing inside. You only pretend to be American. We are brothers and we love each other."

"Be good while I'm gone," I said.

"I will send Miss Barkley. You are better with her without me. You are purer and sweeter."

"Oh, go to hell."

"I will send her. Your lovely cool goddess. English goddess. My God what would a man do with a woman like that except worship her? What else is an Englishwoman good for?"

"You are an ignorant foul-mouthed dago."

"A what?"

"An ignorant wop."

"Wop. You are a frozen-faced . . . wop."

"You are ignorant. Stupid." I saw that word pricked him and kept on. "Uninformed. Inexperienced, stupid from inexperience."

"Truly? I tell you something about your good women. Your goddesses. There is only one difference between taking a girl who has always been good and a woman. With a girl it is painful. That's all I know." He slapped the bed with his glove. "And you never know if the girl will really like it."

"Don't get angry."

"I'm not angry. I just tell you, baby, for your own good. To save you trouble."

"That's the only difference?"

"Yes. But millions of fools like you don't know it."

"You were sweet to tell me."

"We won't quarrel, baby. I love you too much. But don't be a fool."

"No. I'll be wise like you."

"Don't be angry, baby. Laugh. Take a drink. I must go, really."

"You're a good old boy."

"Now you see. Underneath we are the same. We are war brothers. Kiss me good-by."

"You're sloppy."

"No. I am just more affectionate."

I felt his breath come toward me. "Good-by. I come to see you again soon." His breath went away. "I won't kiss you if you don't want. I'll send your English girl. Good-by, baby. The cognac is under the bed. Get well soon."

He was gone.

CHAPTER 11

IT WAS DUSK when the priest came. They had brought the soup and afterward taken away the bowls and I was lying looking at the rows of beds and out the window at the tree-top that moved a little in the evening breeze. The breeze came in through the window and it was cooler with the evening. The flies were on the ceiling now and on the electric light bulbs that hung on wires. The lights were only turned on when some one was brought in at night or when something was being done. It made me feel very young to have the dark come after the dusk and then remain. It was like being put to bed after early supper. The orderly came down between the beds and stopped. Some one was with him. It was the priest. He stood there small, brown-faced, and embarrassed.

"How do you do?" he asked. He put some packages down by the bed, on the floor.

"All right, father."

He sat down in the chair that had been brought for Rinaldi and looked out of the window embarrassedly. I noticed his face looked very tired.

"I can only stay a minute," he said. "It is late."

"It's not late. How is the mess?"

He smiled. "I am still a great joke," he sounded tired too. "Thank God they are all well.

"I am so glad you are all right," he said. "I hope you don't suffer." He seemed very tired and I was not used to seeing him tired.

"Not any more."

"I miss you at the mess."

"I wish I were there. I always enjoyed our talking."

"I brought you a few little things," he said. He picked up the packages. "This is mosquito netting. This is a bottle of vermouth. You like vermouth? These are English papers."

"Please open them."

He was pleased and undid them. I held the mosquito netting in my hands. The vermouth he held up for me to see and then put it on the floor beside the bed. I held up one of the sheaf of English papers. I could read the headlines by turning it so the half-light from the window was on it. It was *The News of the World.*

"The others are illustrated," he said.

"It will be a great happiness to read them. Where did you get them?"

"I sent for them to Mestre. I will have more."

"You were very good to come, father. Will you drink a glass of vermouth?"

"Thank you. You keep it. It's for you."

"No, drink a glass."

"All right. I will bring you more then."

The orderly brought the glasses and opened the bottle. He broke off the cork and the end had to be shoved down into the bottle. I could see the priest was disappointed but he said, "That's all right. It's no matter."

"Here's to your health, father."

"To your better health."

Afterward he held the glass in his hand and we looked at one another. Sometimes we talked and were good friends but to-night it was difficult.

"What's the matter, father? You seem very tired."

"I am tired but I have no right to be."

"It's the heat."

"No. This is only the spring. I feel very low."

"You have the war disgust."

"No. But I hate the war."

"I don't enjoy it," I said. He shook his head and looked out of the window.

"You do not mind it. You do not see it. You must forgive me. I know you are wounded."

"That is an accident."

"Still even wounded you do not see it. I can tell. I do not see it myself but I feel it a little."

"When I was wounded we were talking about it. Passini was talking."

The priest put down the glass. He was thinking about something else.

"I know them because I am like they are," he said.

"You are different though."

"But really I am like they are."

"The officers don't see anything."

"Some of them do. Some are very delicate and feel worse than any of us."

"They are mostly different."

"It is not education or money. It is something else. Even if they had education or money men like Passini would not wish to be officers. I would not be an officer."

"You rank as an officer. I am an officer."

"I am not really. You are not even an Italian. You are a foreigner. But you are nearer the officers than you are to the men."

"What is the difference?"

"I cannot say it easily. There are people who would make war. In this country there are many like that. There are other people who would not make war."

"But the first ones make them do it."

"Yes."

"And I help them."

"You are a foreigner. You are a patriot."

"And the ones who would not make war? Can they stop it?"

"I do not know."

He looked out of the window again. I watched his face.

"Have they ever been able to stop it?"

"They are not organized to stop things and when they get organized their leaders sell them out."

"Then it's hopeless?"

"It is never hopeless. But sometimes I cannot hope. I try always to hope but sometimes I cannot."

"Maybe the war will be over."

"I hope so."

"What will you do then?"

"If it is possible I will return to the Abruzzi."

His brown face was suddenly very happy.

"You love the Abruzzi?"

"Yes, I love it very much."

"You ought to go there then."

"I would be too happy. If I could live there and love God and serve Him."

"And be respected," I said.

"Yes and be respected. Why not?"

"No reason not. You should be respected."

"It does not matter. But there in my country it is understood that a man may love God. It is not a dirty joke."

"I understand."

He looked at me and smiled.

"You understand but you do not love God."

"No."

"You do not love Him at all?" he asked.

"I am afraid of Him in the night sometimes."

"You should love Him."

"I don't love much."

"Yes," he said. "You do. What you tell me about in the nights. That is not love. That is only passion and lust. When you love you wish to do things for. You wish to sacrifice for. You wish to serve."

"I don't love."

"You will. I know you will. Then you will be happy."

"I'm happy. I've always been happy."

"It is another thing. You cannot know about it unless you have it."

"Well," I said. "If I ever get it I will tell you."

"I stay too long and talk too much." He was worried that he really did.

"No. Don't go. How about loving women? If I really loved some woman would it be like that?"

"I don't know about that. I never loved any woman."

"What about your mother?"

"Yes, I must have loved my mother."

"Did you always love God?"

"Ever since I was a little boy."

"Well," I said. I did not know what to say. "You are a fine boy," I said.

"I am a boy," he said. "But you call me father."

"That's politeness."

He smiled.

"I must go, really," he said. "You do not want me for anything?" he asked hopefully.

"No. Just to talk."

"I will take your greetings to the mess."

"Thank you for the many fine presents."

"Nothing."

"Come and see me again."

"Yes. Good-by," he patted my hand.

"So long," I said in dialect.

"Ciaou," he repeated.

It was dark in the room and the orderly, who had sat by the foot of the bed, got up and went out with him. I liked him very much and I hoped he would get back to the Abruzzi some time. He had a rotten life in the mess and he was fine about it but I thought how he would be in his own country. At Capracotta, he had told me, there were trout in the stream below the town. It was forbidden to play the flute at night. When the young men serenaded only the flute was forbidden. Why, I had asked. Because it was bad for the girls to hear the flute at night. The peasants all called you "Don" and when you met them they took off their hats. His father hunted every day and stopped to eat at the houses of peasants. They were always honored. For a foreigner to hunt he must present a certificate that he had never been arrested. There were bears on the Gran Sasso D'Italia but it was a long way. Aquila was a fine town. It was cool in the summer at night and the spring in Abruzzi was the most beautiful in Italy. But what was lovely was the fall to go hunting through the chestnut woods. The birds were all good because they fed on grapes and you never took a lunch because the peasants were always honored if you would eat with them at their houses. After a while I went to sleep.

CHAPTER 12

THE ROOM was long with windows on the right-hand side and a door at the far end that went into the dressing room. The row of beds that mine was in faced the windows and another row, under the windows, faced the wall. If you lay on your left side you could see the dressing-room door. There was another door at the far end that people sometimes came in by. If any one were going to die they put a screen around the bed so you could not see them die, but only the shoes and puttees of doctors and men nurses showed under the bottom of the screen and sometimes at the end there would be whispering. Then the priest would come out from behind the screen and afterward the men nurses would go back behind the screen to come out again carrying the one who was dead with a blanket over him down the corridor between the beds and some one folded the screen and took it away.

That morning the major in charge of the ward asked me if I felt that I could travel the next day. I said I could. He said then they would ship me out early in the morning. He said I would be better off making the trip now before it got too hot.

Ernest Hemingway

When they lifted you up out of bed to carry you into the dressing room you could look out of the window and see the new graves in the garden. A soldier sat outside the door that opened onto the garden making crosses and painting on them the names, rank, and regiment of the men who were buried in the garden. He also ran errands for the ward and in his spare time made me a cigarette lighter out of an empty Austrian rifle cartridge. The doctors were very nice and seemed very capable. They were anxious to ship me to Milan where there were better X-ray facilities and where, after the operation, I could take mechanotherapy. I wanted to go to Milan too. They wanted to get us all out and back as far as possible because all the beds were needed for the offensive, when it should start.

The night before I left the field hospital Rinaldi came in to see me with the major from our mess. They said that I would go to an American hospital in Milan that had just been installed. Some American ambulance units were to be sent down and this hospital would look after them and any other Americans on service in Italy. There were many in the Red Cross. The States had declared war on Germany but not on Austria.

The Italians were sure America would declare war on Austria too and they were very excited about any Americans coming down, even the Red Cross. They asked me if I thought President Wilson would declare war on Austria and I said it was only a matter of days. I did not know what we had against Austria but it seemed logical that they should declare war on her if they did on Germany. They asked me if we would declare war on Turkey. I said that was doubtful. Turkey, I said, was our national bird but the joke translated so badly and they were so puzzled and suspicious that I said yes, we would probably declare war on Turkey. And on Bulgaria? We had drunk several glasses of brandy and I said yes by God on Bulgaria too and on Japan. But, they said, Japan is an ally of England. You can't trust the bloody English. The Japanese want Hawaii, I said. Where is Hawaii? It is in the Pacific Ocean. Why do the Japanese want it? They don't really want it, I said. That is all talk. The Japanese are a wonderful little people fond of dancing and light wines. Like the French, said the major. We will get Nice and Savoia from the French. We will get Corsica and all the Adriatic coast-line, Rinaldi said. Italy will return to the splendors of Rome, said the major. I don't like Rome, I said. It is hot and full of fleas. You don't like Rome? Yes, I love Rome. Rome is the mother of nations. I will never forget Romulus suckling the Tiber. What? Nothing. Let's all go to Rome.

Let's go to Rome to-night and never come back. Rome is a beautiful city, said the major. The mother and father of nations, I said. Roma is feminine, said Rinaldi. It cannot be the father. Who is the father, then, the Holy Ghost? Don't blaspheme. I wasn't blaspheming, I was asking for information. You are drunk, baby. Who made me drunk? I made you drunk, said the major. I made you drunk because I love you and because America is in the war. Up to the hilt, I said. You go away in the morning, baby, Rinaldi said. To Rome, I said. No, to Milan. To Milan, said the major, to the Crystal Palace, to the Cova, to Campari's, to Biffi's, to the galleria. You lucky boy. To the Gran Italia, I said, where I will borrow money from George. To the Scala, said Rinaldi. You will go to the Scala. Every night, I said. You won't be able to afford it every night, said the major.

The tickets are very expensive. I will draw a sight draft on my grandfather, I said. A what? A sight draft. He has to pay or I go to jail. Mr. Cunningham at the bank does it. I live by sight drafts. Can a grandfather jail a patriotic grandson who is dying that Italy may live? Live the American Garibaldi, said Rinaldi. Viva the sight drafts, I said. We must be quiet, said the major. Already we have been asked many times to be quiet. Do you go to-morrow really, Federico? He goes to the American hospital I tell you, Rinaldi said. To the beautiful nurses. Not the nurses with beards of the field hospital. Yes, yes, said the major, I know he goes to the American hospital. I don't mind their beards, I said. If any man wants to raise a beard let him. Why don't you raise a beard, Signor Maggiore? It could not go in a gas mask. Yes it could. Anything can go in a gas mask. I've vomited into a gas mask. Don't be so loud, baby, Rinaldi said. We all know you have been at the front. Oh, you fine baby, what will I do while you are gone? We must go, said the major. This becomes sentimental. Listen, I have a surprise for you. Your English. You know? The English you go to see every night at their hospital? She is going to Milan too. She goes with another to be at the American hospital. They had not got nurses yet from America. I talked to-day with the head of their riparto. They have too many women here at the front. They send some back. How do you like that, baby? All right. Yes? You go to live in a big city and have your English there to cuddle you. Why don't I get wounded? Maybe you will, I said. We must go, said the major. We drink and make noise and disturb Federico. Don't go. Yes, we must go. Good-by. Good luck. Many things. Ciaou. Ciaou. Ciaou. Come back quickly, baby. Rinaldi kissed me. You smell of lysol. Good-by, baby. Goodby. Many things. The major patted my shoulder. They tiptoed out. I found I was quite drunk but went to sleep.

The next day in the morning we left for Milan and arrived forty-eight hours later. It was a bad trip. We were sidetracked for a long time this side of Mestre and children came and peeked in. I got a little boy to go for a bottle of cognac but he came back and said he could only get grappa. I told him to get it and when it came I gave him the change and the man beside me and I got drunk and slept until past Vicenza where I woke up and was very sick on the floor. It did not matter because the man on that side had been very sick on the floor several times before. Afterward I thought I could not stand the thirst and in the yards outside of Verona I called to a soldier who was walking up and down beside the train and he got me a drink of water. I woke Georgetti, the other boy who was drunk, and offered him some water. He said to pour it on his shoulder and went back to sleep. The soldier would not take the penny I offered him and brought me a pulpy orange. I sucked on that and spit out the pith and watched the soldier pass up and down past a freight-car outside and after a while the train gave a jerk and started.

BOOK TWO

CHAPTER 13

WE GOT INTO Milan early in the morning and they unloaded us in the freight yard. An ambulance took me to the American hospital. Riding in the ambulance on a stretcher I could not tell what part of town we were passing through but when they unloaded the stretcher I saw a market-place and an open wine shop with a girl sweeping out. They were watering the street and it smelled of the early morning. They put the stretcher down and went in. The porter came out with them. He had gray mustaches, wore a doorman's cap and was in his shirt sleeves. The stretcher would not go into the elevator and they discussed whether it was better to lift me off the stretcher and go up in the elevator or carry the stretcher up the stairs. I listened to them discussing it. They decided on the elevator. They lifted me from the stretcher. "Go easy," I said. "Take it softly."

In the elevator we were crowded and as my legs bent the pain was very bad. "Straighten out the legs," I said.

"We can't, Signor Tenente. There isn't room." The man who said this had his arm around me and my arm was around his neck. His breath came in my face metallic with garlic and red wine.

"Be gentle," the other man said.

"Son of a bitch who isn't gentle!"

"Be gentle I say," the man with my feet repeated.

I saw the doors of the elevator closed, and the grill shut and the fourth-floor button pushed by the porter. The porter looked worried. The elevator rose slowly.

"Heavy?" I asked the man with the garlic.

"Nothing," he said. His face was sweating and he grunted. The elevator rose steadily and stopped. The man holding the feet opened the door and stepped out. We were on a balcony. There were several doors with brass knobs. The man carrying the feet pushed a button that rang a bell. We heard it inside the doors. No one came. Then the porter came up the stairs.

"Where are they?" the stretcher-bearers asked.

"I don't know," said the porter. "They sleep down stairs."

"Get somebody."

The porter rang the bell, then knocked on the door, then he opened the door and went in. When he came back there was an elderly woman wearing glasses with him. Her hair was loose and half-falling and she wore a nurse's dress.

"I can't understand," she said. "I can't understand Italian."

"I can speak English," I said. "They want to put me somewhere."

"None of the rooms are ready. There isn't any patient expected." She tucked at her hair and looked at me near-sightedly.

"Show them any room where they can put me."

"I don't know," she said. "There's no patient expected. I couldn't put you in just any room."

"Any room will do," I said. Then to the porter in Italian, "Find an empty room."

"They are all empty," said the porter. "You are the first patient." He held his cap in his hand and looked at the elderly nurse.

"For Christ's sweet sake take me to some room." The pain had gone on and on with the legs bent and I could feel it going in and out of the bone. The porter went in the door, followed by the gray-haired woman, then came hurrying back. "Follow me," he said. They carried me down a long hallway and into a room with drawn blinds. It smelled of new furniture. There was a bed and a big wardrobe with a mirror. They laid me down on the bed.

"I can't put on sheets," the woman said. "The sheets are locked up."

I did not speak to her. "There is money in my pocket," I said to the porter. "In the buttoned-down pocket." The porter took out the money. The two stretcher-bearers stood beside the bed holding their caps. "Give them five lire apiece and five lire for yourself. My papers are in the other pocket. You may give them to the nurse."

The stretcher-bearers saluted and said thank you. "Good-by," I said. "And many thanks." They saluted again and went out.

"Those papers," I said to the nurse, "describe my case and the treatment already given."

The woman picked them up and looked at them through her glasses. There were three papers and they were folded. "I don't know what to do," she said. "I can't read Italian. I can't do anything without the doctor's orders." She commenced to cry and put the papers in her apron pocket. "Are you an American?" she asked crying.

"Yes. Please put the papers on the table by the bed."

It was dim and cool in the room. As I lay on the bed I could see the big mirror on the other side of the room but could not see what it reflected. The porter stood by the bed. He had a nice face and was very kind.

"You can go," I said to him. "You can go too," I said to the nurse. "What is your name?"

"Mrs. Walker."

"You can go, Mrs. Walker. I think I will go to sleep."

I was alone in the room. It was cool and did not smell like a hospital. The mattress was firm and comfortable and I lay without moving, hardly breathing, happy in feeling the pain lessen. After a while I wanted a drink of water and found the bell on a cord by the bed and rang it but nobody came. I went to sleep.

When I woke I looked around. There was sunlight coming in through the shutters. I saw the big armoire, the bare walls, and two chairs. My legs in the dirty bandages, stuck straight out in the bed. I was careful not to move them. I was thirsty and I reached for the bell and pushed the button. I heard the door open and looked and it was a nurse. She looked young and pretty.

"Good-morning," I said.

"Good-morning," she said and came over to the bed. "We haven't been able to get the doctor. He's gone to Lake Como. No one knew there was a patient coming. What's wrong with you anyway?"

"I'm wounded. In the legs and feet and my head is hurt."

"What's your name?"

"Henry. Frederic Henry."

"I'll wash you up. But we can't do anything to the dressings until the doctor comes."

"Is Miss Barkley here?"

"No. There's no one by that name here."

"Who was the woman who cried when I came in?"

The nurse laughed. "That's Mrs. Walker. She was on night duty and she'd been asleep. She wasn't expecting any one."

While we were talking she was undressing me, and when I was undressed, except for the bandages, she washed me, very gently and smoothly. The washing felt very good. There was a bandage on my head but she washed all around the edge.

"Where were you wounded?"

"On the Isonze north of Plava."

"Where is that?"

"North of Gorizia."

I could see that none of the places meant anything to her.

"Do you have a lot of pain?"

"No. Not much now."

She put a thermometer in my mouth.

"The Italians put it under the arm," I said.

"Don't talk."

When she took the thermometer out she read it and then shook it.

"What's the temperature?"

"You're not supposed to know that."

"Tell me what it is."

"It's almost normal."

"I never have any fever. My legs are full of old iron too."

"What do you mean?"

"They're full of trench-mortar fragments, old screws and bedsprings and things."

She shook her head and smiled.

"If you had any foreign bodies in your legs they would set up an inflammation and you'd have fever."

"All right," I said. "We'll see what comes out."

She went out of the room and came back with the old nurse of the early morning. Together they made the bed with me in it. That was new to me and an admirable proceeding.

"Who is in charge here?"

"Miss Van Campen."

"How many nurses are there?"

"Just us two."

"Won't there be more?"

"Some more are coming."

"When will they get here?"

"I don't know. You ask a great many questions for a sick boy."

"I'm not sick," I said. "I'm wounded."

They had finished making the bed and I lay with a clean smooth sheet under me and another sheet over me. Mrs. Walker went out and came back with a pajama jacket. They put that on me and I felt very clean and dressed.

"You're awfully nice to me," I said. The nurse called Miss Gage giggled. "Could I have a drink of water?" I asked.

"Certainly. Then you can have breakfast."

"I don't want breakfast. Can I have the shutters opened please?"

The light had been dim in the room and when the shutters were opened it was bright sunlight and I looked out on a balcony and beyond were the tile roofs of houses and chimneys. I looked out over the tiled roofs and saw white clouds and the sky very blue.

"Don't you know when the other nurses are coming?"

"Why? Don't we take good care of you?"

"You're very nice."

"Would you like to use the bedpan?"

"I might try."

They helped me and held me up but it was not any use. Afterward I lay and looked out the open doors onto the balcony.

"When does the doctor come?"

"When he gets back. We've tried to telephone to Lake Como for him."

"Aren't there any other doctors?"

"He's the doctor for the hospital."

Miss Gage brought a pitcher of water and a glass. I drank three glasses and then they left me and I looked out the window a while and went back to sleep. I ate some lunch and in the afternoon Miss Van Campen, the superintendent, came up to see me. She did not like me and I did not like her. She was small and neatly suspicious and too good for her position. She asked many questions and seemed to think it was somewhat disgraceful that I was with the Italians.

"Can I have wine with the meals?" I asked her.

"Only if the doctor prescribes it."

"I can't have it until he comes?"

"Absolutely not."

"You plan on having him come eventually?"

"We've telephoned him at Lake Como."

She went out and Miss Gage came back.

"Why were you rude to Miss Van Campen?" she asked after she had done something for me very skilfully.

"I didn't mean to be. But she was snooty."

"She said you were domineering and rude."

"I wasn't. But what's the idea of a hospital without a doctor?"

"He's coming. They've telephoned for him to Lake Como."

"What does he do there? Swim?"

"No. He has a clinic there."

"Why don't they get another doctor?"

"Hush. Hush. Be a good boy and he'll come."

I sent for the porter and when he came I told him in Italian to get me a bottle of Cinzano at the wine shop, a fiasco of chianti and the evening papers. He went away and brought them wrapped in newspaper, unwrapped them and, when I asked him to, drew the corks and put the wine and vermouth under the bed. They left me alone and I lay in bed and read the papers awhile, the news from the front, and the list of dead officers with their decorations and then reached down and brought up the bottle of Cinzano and held it straight up on my stomach, the cool glass against my stomach, and took little drinks making rings on my stomach from holding the bottle there between drinks, and watched it get dark outside over the roofs of the town. The swallows circled around and I watched them and the night-hawks flying above the roofs and drank the Cinzano. Miss Gage brought up a glass with some eggnog in it. I lowered the vermouth bottle to the other side of the bed when she came in.

"Miss Van Campen had some sherry put in this," she said. "You shouldn't be rude to her. She's not young and this hospital is a big responsibility for her. Mrs. Walker's too old and she's no use to her."

"She's a splendid woman," I said. "Thank her very much."

"I'm going to bring your supper right away."

"That's all right," I said. "I'm not hungry."

When she brought the tray and put it on the bed table I thanked her and ate a little of the supper. Afterward it was dark outside and I could see the beams of the search-lights moving in the sky. I watched for a while and then went to sleep. I slept heavily except once I woke sweating and scared and then went back to sleep trying to stay outside of my dream. I woke for good long before it was light and heard roosters crowing and stayed on awake until it began to be light. I was tired and once it was really light I went back to sleep again.

CHAPTER 14

IT WAS BRIGHT sunlight in the room when I woke. I thought I was back at the front and stretched out in bed. My legs hurt me and I looked down at them still in the dirty bandages, and seeing them knew where I was. I reached up for the bell-cord and pushed the button. I heard it buzz down the hall and then some one coming on rubber soles along the hall. It was Miss Gage and she looked a little older in the bright sunlight and not so pretty.

"Good-morning," she said. "Did you have a good night?"

"Yes. Thanks very much," I said. "Can I have a barber?"

"I came in to see you and you were asleep with this in the bed with you."

She opened the armoire door and held up the vermouth bottle. It was nearly empty. "I put the other bottle from under the bed in there too," she said. "Why didn't you ask me for a glass?"

"I thought maybe you wouldn't let me have it."

"I'd have had some with you."

"You're a fine girl."

"It isn't good for you to drink alone," she said. "You mustn't do it."

"All right."

"Your friend Miss Barkley's come," she said.

"Really?"

"Yes. I don't like her."

"You will like her. She's awfully nice."

She shook her head. "I'm sure she's fine. Can you move just a little to this side? That's fine. I'll clean you up for breakfast." She washed me with a cloth and soap and warm water. "Hold your shoulder up," she said. "That's fine."

"Can I have the barber before breakfast?"

"I'll send the porter for him." She went out and came back. "He's gone for him," she said and dipped the cloth she held in the basin of water.

The barber came with the porter. He was a man of about fifty with an upturned mustache. Miss Gage was finished with me and went out and the barber lathered my face and shaved. He was very solemn and refrained from talking.

"What's the matter? Don't you know any news?" I asked.

"What news?"

"Any news. What's happened in the town?"

"It is time of war," he said. "The enemy's ears are everywhere."

I looked up at him. "Please hold your face still," he said and went on shaving. "I will tell nothing."

"What's the matter with you?" I asked.

"I am an Italian. I will not communicate with the enemy."

I let it go at that. If he was crazy, the sooner I could get out from under the razor the better. Once I tried to get a good look at him. "Beware," he said. "The razor is sharp."

I paid him when it was over and tipped him half a lira. He returned the coins.

"I will not. I am not at the front. But I am an Italian."

"Get the hell out of here."

"With your permission," he said and wrapped his razors in newspaper. He went out leaving the five copper coins on the table beside the bed. I rang the bell. Miss Gage came in. "Would you ask the porter to come please?"

"All right."

The porter came in. He was trying to keep from laughing.

"Is that barber crazy?"

"No, signorino. He made a mistake. He doesn't understand very well and he thought I said you were an Austrian officer."

"Oh," I said.

"Ho ho ho," the porter laughed. "He was funny. One move from you he said and he would have—" he drew his forefinger across his throat.

"Ho ho ho," he tried to keep from laughing. "When I tell him you were not an Austrian. Ho ho ho."

"Ho ho ho," I said bitterly. "How funny if he would cut my throat. Ho ho ho."

"No, signorino. No, no. He was so frightened of an Austrian. Ho ho ho."

"Ho ho ho," I said. "Get out of here."

He went out and I heard him laughing in the hall. I heard some one coming down the hallway. I looked toward the door. It was Catherine Barkley.

She came in the room and over to the bed.

"Hello, darling," she said. She looked fresh and young and very beautiful. I thought I had never seen any one so beautiful.

"Hello," I said. When I saw her I was in love with her. Everything turned over inside of me. She looked toward the door, saw there was no one, then she sat on the side of the bed and leaned over and kissed me. I pulled her down and kissed her and felt her heart beating.

"You sweet," I said. "Weren't you wonderful to come here?"

"It wasn't very hard. It may be hard to stay."

"You've got to stay," I said. "Oh, you're wonderful." I was crazy about her. I could not believe she was really there and held her tight to me.

"You mustn't," she said. "You're not well enough."

"Yes, I am. Come on."

"No. You're not strong enough."

"Yes. I am. Yes. Please."

"You do love me?"

"I really love you. I'm crazy about you. Come on please."

"Feel our hearts beating."

"I don't care about our hearts. I want you. I'm just mad about you."

"You really love me?"

"Don't keep on saying that. Come on. Please. Please, Catherine."

"All right but only for a minute."

"All right," I said. "Shut the door."

"You can't. You shouldn't."

"Come on. Don't talk. Please come on."

Catherine sat in a chair by the bed. The door was open into the hall. The wildness was gone and I felt finer than I had ever felt.

She asked, "Now do you believe I love you?"

"Oh, you're lovely," I said. "You've got to stay. They can't send you away. I'm crazy in love with you."

"We'll have to be awfully careful. That was just madness. We can't do that."

"We can at night."

"We'll have to be awfully careful. You'll have to be careful in front of other people."

"I will."

"You'll have to be. You're sweet. You do love me, don't you?"

"Don't say that again. You don't know what that does to me."

"I'll be careful then. I don't want to do anything more to you. I have to go now, darling, really."

"Come back right away."

"I'll come when I can."

"Good-by."

"Good-by, sweet."

She went out. God knows I had not wanted to fall in love with her. I had not wanted to fall in love with any one. But God knows I had and I lay on the bed in the room of the hospital in Milan and all sorts of things went through my head but I felt wonderful and finally Miss Gage came in.

"The doctor's coming," she said. "He telephoned from Lake Como."

"When does he get here?"

"He'll be here this afternoon."

CHAPTER 15

NOTHING HAPPENED until afternoon. The doctor was a thin quiet little man who seemed disturbed by the war. He took out a number of small steel splinters from my thighs with delicate and refined distaste. He used a local anæsthetic called something or other "snow," which froze the tissue and avoided pain until the probe, the scalpel or the forceps got below the frozen portion. The anæsthetized area was clearly defined by the patient and after a time the doctor's fragile delicacy was exhausted and he said it would be better to have an X-ray. Probing was unsatisfactory, he said.

The X-ray was taken at the Ospedale Maggiore and the doctor who did it was excitable, efficient and cheerful. It was arranged by holding up the shoulders, that the patient should see personally some of the larger foreign bodies through the machine. The plates were to be sent over. The doctor requested me to write in his pocket notebook, my name, and regiment and some sentiment. He declared that the foreign bodies were ugly, nasty, brutal. The Austrians were sons of bitches. How many had I killed? I had not killed any but I was anxious to please—and I said I had killed plenty. Miss Gage was with me and the doctor put his arm around her and said she was more beautiful than Cleopatra. Did she understand that? Cleopatra the former queen of Egypt. Yes, by God she was. We returned to the little hospital in the ambulance and after a while and much lifting I was upstairs and in bed again. The plates came that afternoon, the doctor had said by God he would have them that afternoon and he did. Catherine Barkley showed them to me. They were in red envelopes and she took them out of the envelopes and held them up to the light and we both looked.

"That's your right leg," she said, then put the plate back in the envelope. "This is your left."

"Put them away," I said, "and come over to the bed."

"I can't," she said. "I just brought them in for a second to show you."

She went out and I lay there. It was a hot afternoon and I was sick of lying in bed.

I sent the porter for the papers, all the papers he could get.

Before he came back three doctors came into the room. I have noticed that doctors who fail in the practice of medicine have a tendency to seek one another's company and aid in consultation. A doctor who cannot take out your appendix properly will recommend to you a doctor who will be unable to remove your tonsils with success. These were three such doctors.

"This is the young man," said the house doctor with the delicate hands.

"How do you do?" said the tall gaunt doctor with the beard. The third doctor, who carried the X-ray plates in their red envelopes, said nothing.

"Remove the dressings?" questioned the bearded doctor.

"Certainly. Remove the dressings, please, nurse," the house doctor said to Miss Gage. Miss Gage removed the dressings. I looked down at the legs. At the field hospital they had the look of not too freshly ground hamburger steak. Now they were crusted and the knee was swollen and discolored and the calf sunken but there was no pus.

"Very clean," said the house doctor. "Very clean and nice."

"Um," said the doctor with the beard. The third doctor looked over the house doctor's shoulder.

"Please move the knee," said the bearded doctor.

"I can't."

"Test the articulation?" the bearded doctor questioned. He had a stripe beside the three stars on his sleeve. That meant he was a first captain.

"Certainly," the house doctor said. Two of them took hold of my right leg very gingerly and bent it.

"That hurts," I said.

"Yes. Yes. A little further, doctor."

"That's enough. That's as far as it goes," I said.

"Partial articulation," said the first captain. He straightened up. "May I see the plates again, please, doctor?" The third doctor handed him one of the plates. "No. The left leg, please."

"That is the left leg, doctor."

"You are right. I was looking from a different angle." He returned the plate. The other plate he examined for some time. "You see, doctor?" he pointed to one of the foreign bodies which showed spherical and clear against the light. They examined the plate for some time.

"Only one thing I can say," the first captain with the beard said. "It is a question of time. Three months, six months probably."

"Certainly the synovial fluid must re-form."

"Certainly. It is a question of time. I could not conscientiously open a knee like that before the projectile was encysted."

"I agree with you, doctor."

"Six months for what?" I asked.

"Six months for the projectile to encyst before the knee can be opened safely."

"I don't believe it," I said.

"Do you want to keep your knee, young man?"

"No," I said.

"What?"

"I want it cut off," I said, "so I can wear a hook on it."

"What do you mean? A hook?"

"He is joking," said the house doctor. He patted my shoulder very delicately. "He wants to keep his knee. This is a very brave young man. He has been proposed for the silver medal of valor."

"All my felicitations," said the first captain. He shook my hand. "I can only say that to be on the safe side you should wait at least six months before opening such a knee. You are welcome of course to another opinion."

"Thank you very much," I said. "I value your opinion."

The first captain looked at his watch.

"We must go," he said. "All my best wishes."

"All my best wishes and many thanks," I said. I shook hands with the third doctor. "Capitano Varini–Tenente Enry," and they all three went out of the room.

"Miss Gage," I called. She came in. "Please ask the house doctor to come back a minute."

He came in holding his cap and stood by the bed. "Did you wish to see me?"

"Yes. I can't wait six months to be operated on. My God, doctor, did you ever stay in bed six months?"

"You won't be in bed all the time. You must first have the wounds exposed to the sun. Then afterward you can be on crutches."

"For six months and then have an operation?"

"That is the safe way. The foreign bodies must be allowed to encyst and the synovial fluid will re-form. Then it will be safe to open up the knee."

"Do you really think yourself I will have to wait that long?"

"That is the safe way."

"Who is that first captain?"

"He is a very excellent surgeon of Milan."

"He's a first captain, isn't he?"

"Yes, but he is an excellent surgeon."

"I don't want my leg fooled with by a first captain. If he was any good he would be made a major. I know what a first captain is, doctor."

"He is an excellent surgeon and I would rather have his judgment than any surgeon I know."

"Could another surgeon see it?"

"Certainly if you wish. But I would take Dr. Varella's opinion myself."

"Could you ask another surgeon to come and see it?"

"I will ask Valentini to come."

"Who is he?"

"He is a surgeon of the Ospedale Maggiore."

"Good. I appreciate it very much. You understand, doctor, I couldn't stay in bed six months."

"You would not be in bed. You would first take a sun cure. Then you could have light exercise. Then when it was encysted we would operate."

"But I can't wait six months."

The doctor spread his delicate fingers on the cap he held and smiled. "You are in such a hurry to get back to the front?"

"Why not?"

"It is very beautiful," he said. "You are a noble young man." He stooped over and kissed me very delicately on the forehead. "I will send for Valentini. Do not worry and excite yourself. Be a good boy."

"Will you have a drink?" I asked.

"No thank you. I never drink alcohol."

"Just have one." I rang for the porter to bring glasses.

"No. No thank you. They are waiting for me."

"Good-by," I said.

"Good-by."

Two hours later Dr. Valentini came into the room. He was in a great hurry and the points of his mustache stood straight up. He was a major, his face was tanned and he laughed all the time.

"How did you do it, this rotten thing?" he asked. "Let me see the plates. Yes. Yes. That's it. You look healthy as a goat. Who's the pretty girl? Is she your girl? I thought so. Isn't this a bloody war? How does that feel? You are a fine boy. I'll make you better than new. Does that hurt? You bet it hurts. How they love to hurt you, these doctors. What have they done for you so far? Can't that girl talk Italian? She should learn. What a lovely girl. I could teach her. I will be a patient here myself. No, but I will do all your maternity work free. Does she understand that? She will make you a fine boy. A fine blonde like she is. That's fine. That's all right. What a lovely girl. Ask her if she eats supper with me. No I won't take her away from you. Thank you. Thank you very much, Miss. That's all."

"That's all I want to know." He patted me on the shoulder. "Leave the dressings off."

"Will you have a drink, Dr. Valentini?"

"A drink? Certainly. I will have ten drinks. Where are they?"

"In the armoire. Miss Barkley will get the bottle."

"Cheery oh. Cheery oh to you, Miss. What a lovely girl. I will bring you better cognac than that." He wiped his mustache.

"When do you think it can be operated on?"

"To-morrow morning. Not before. Your stomach must be emptied. You must be washed out. I will see the old lady downstairs and leave instructions. Good-by. I see you to-morrow. I'll bring you better cognac than that. You are very comfortable here. Good-by. Until to-morrow. Get a good sleep. I'll see you early." He waved from the doorway, his mustaches went straight up, his brown face was smiling. There was a star in a box on his sleeve because he was a major.

CHAPTER 16

THAT NIGHT a bat flew into the room through the open door that led onto the balcony and through which we watched the night over the roofs of the town. It was dark in our room except for the small light of the night over the town and the bat was not frightened but hunted in the room as though he had been outside. We lay and watched him and I do not think he saw us because we lay so still. After he went out we saw a searchlight come on and watched the beam move across the sky and then go off and it was dark again. A breeze came in the night and we heard the men of the anti-aircraft gun on the next roof talking. It was cool and they were putting on their capes. I worried in the night about some one coming up but Catherine said they were all asleep. Once in the night we went to sleep and when I woke she was not there but I heard her coming along the hall and the door opened and she came back to the bed and said it was all right she had been downstairs and they were all asleep. She had been outside Miss Van Campen's door and heard her breathing in her sleep. She brought crackers and we ate them and drank some vermouth. We were very hungry but she said that would all have to be gotten out of me in the morning. I went to sleep again in the morning when it was light and when I was awake I found she was gone again. She came in looking fresh and lovely and sat on the bed and the sun rose while I had the thermometer in my mouth and we smelled the dew on the roofs and then the coffee of the men at the gun on the next roof.

"I wish we could go for a walk," Catherine said. "I'd wheel you if we had a chair."

"How would I get into the chair?"

"We'd do it."

"We could go out to the park and have breakfast outdoors." I looked out the open doorway.

"What we'll really do," she said, "is get you ready for your friend Dr. Valentini."

"I thought he was grand."

"I didn't like him as much as you did. But I imagine he's very good."

"Come back to bed, Catherine. Please," I said.

"I can't. Didn't we have a lovely night?"

"And can you be on night duty to-night?"

"I probably will. But you won't want me."

"Yes, I will."

"No, you won't. You've never been operated on. You don't know how you'll be."

"I'll be all right."

"You'll be sick and I won't be anything to you."

"Come back then now."

"No," she said. "I have to do the chart, darling, and fix you up."

"You don't really love me or you'd come back again."

"You're such a silly boy." She kissed me. "That's all right for the chart. Your temperature's always normal. You've such a lovely temperature."

"You've got a lovely everything."

"Oh no. You have the lovely temperature. I'm awfully proud of your temperature."

"Maybe all our children will have fine temperatures."

"Our children will probably have beastly temperatures."

"What do you have to do to get me ready for Valentini?"

"Not much. But quite unpleasant."

"I wish you didn't have to do it."

"I don't. I don't want any one else to touch you. I'm silly. I get furious if they touch you."

"Even Ferguson?"

"Especially Ferguson and Gage and the other, what's her name?"

"Walker?"

"That's it. They've too many nurses here now. There must be some more patients or they'll send us away. They have four nurses now."

"Perhaps there'll be some. They need that many nurses. It's quite a big hospital."

"I hope some will come. What would I do if they sent me away? They will unless there are more patients."

"I'd go too."

"Don't be silly. You can't go yet. But get well quickly, darling, and we will go somewhere."

"And then what?"

"Maybe the war will be over. It can't always go on."

"I'll get well," I said. "Valentini will fix me."

"He should with those mustaches. And, darling, when you're going under the ether just think about something else—not us. Because people get very blabby under an anæsthetic."

"What should I think about?"

"Anything. Anything but us. Think about your people. Or even any other girl."

"No."

"Say your prayers then. That ought to create a splendid impression."

"Maybe I won't talk."

"That's true. Often people don't talk."

"I won't talk."

"Don't brag, darling. Please don't brag. You're so sweet and you don't have to brag."

"I won't talk a word."

"Now you're bragging, darling. You know you don't need to brag. Just start your prayers or poetry or something when they tell you to breathe deeply. You'll be lovely that way and I'll be so proud of you. I'm very proud of you anyway. You have such a lovely temperature and you sleep like a little boy with your arm around the pillow and think it's me. Or is it some other girl? Some fine Italian girl?"

"It's you."

"Of course it's me. Oh I do love you and Valentini will make you a fine leg. I'm glad I don't have to watch it."

"And you'll be on night duty to-night."

"Yes. But you won't care."

"You wait and see."

"There, darling. Now you're all clean inside and out. Tell me. How many people have you ever loved?"

"Nobody."

"Not me even?"

"Yes, you."

"How many others really?"

"None."

"How many have you—how do you say it?—stayed with?"

"None."

"You're lying to me."

"Yes."

"It's all right. Keep right on lying to me. That's what I want you to do. Were they pretty?"

"I never stayed with any one."

"That's right. Were they very attractive?"

"I don't know anything about it."

"You're just mine. That's true and you've never belonged to any one else. But I don't care if you have. I'm not afraid of them. But don't tell me about them. When a man stays with a girl when does she say how much it costs?"

"I don't know."

"Of course not. Does she say she loves him? Tell me that. I want to know that."

"Yes. If he wants her to."

"Does he say he loves her? Tell me please. It's important."

"He does if he wants to."

"But you never did? Really?"

"No."

"Not really. Tell me the truth."

"No," I lied.

"You wouldn't," she said. "I knew you wouldn't. Oh, I love you, darling."

Outside the sun was up over the roofs and I could see the points of the cathedral with the sunlight on them. I was clean inside and outside and waiting for the doctor.

"And that's it?" Catherine said. "She says just what he wants her to?"

"Not always."

"But I will. I'll say just what you wish and I'll do what you wish and then you will never want any other girls, will you?" She looked at me very happily. "I'll do what you want and say what you want and then I'll be a great success, won't I?"

"Yes."

"What would you like me to do now that you're all ready?"

"Come to the bed again."

"All right. I'll come."

"Oh, darling, darling, darling," I said.

"You see," she said. "I do anything you want."

"You're so lovely."

"I'm afraid I'm not very good at it yet."

"You're lovely."

"I want what you want. There isn't any me any more. Just what you want."

"You sweet."

"I'm good. Aren't I good? You don't want any other girls, do you?"

"No."

"You see? I'm good. I do what you want."

CHAPTER 17

WHEN I WAS awake after the operation I had not been away. You do not go away. They only choke you. It is not like dying it is just a chemical choking so you do not feel, and afterward you might as well have been drunk except that when you throw up nothing comes but bile and you do not feel better afterward. I saw sandbags at the end of the bed. They were on pipes that came out of the cast. After a while I saw Miss Gage and she said, "How is it now?"

"Better," I said.

"He did a wonderful job on your knee."

"How long did it take?"

"Two hours and a half."

"Did I say anything silly?"

"Not a thing. Don't talk. Just be quiet."

I was sick and Catherine was right. It did not make any difference who was on night duty.

There were three other patients in the hospital now, a thin boy in the Red Cross from Georgia with malaria, a nice boy, also thin, from New York, with malaria and jaundice, and a fine boy who had tried to unscrew the fuse-cap from a combination shrapnel and high explosive shell for a souvenir. This was a shrapnel shell used by the Austrians in the mountains with a nose-cap which went on after the burst and exploded on contact.

Catherine Barkley was greatly liked by the nurses because she would do night duty indefinitely. She had quite a little work with the malaria people, the boy who had unscrewed the nose-cap was a friend of ours and never rang at night, unless it was necessary but between the times of working we were together. I loved her very much and she loved me. I slept in the daytime and we wrote notes during the day when we were awake and sent them by Ferguson. Ferguson was a fine girl. I never learned anything about her except that she had a brother in the Fifty-Second Division and a brother in Mesopotamia and she was very good to Catherine Barkley.

"Will you come to our wedding, Fergy?" I said to her once.

"You'll never get married."

"We will."

"No you won't."

"Why not?"

"You'll fight before you'll marry."

"We never fight."

"You've time yet."

"We don't fight."

"You'll die then. Fight or die. That's what people do. They don't marry."

I reached for her hand. "Don't take hold of me," she said. "I'm not crying. Maybe you'll be all right you two. But watch out you don't get her in trouble. You get her in trouble and I'll kill you."

"I won't get her in trouble."

"Well watch out then. I hope you'll be all right. You have a good time."

"We have a fine time."

"Don't fight then and don't get her into trouble."

"I won't."

"Mind you watch out. I don't want her with any of these war babies."

"You're a fine girl, Fergy."

"I'm not. Don't try to flatter me. How does your leg feel?"

"Fine."

"How is your head?" She touched the top of it with her fingers. It was sensitive like a foot that had gone to sleep. "It's never bothered me."

"A bump like that could make you crazy. It never bothers you?"

"No."

"You're a lucky young man. Have you the letter done? I'm going down."

"It's here," I said.

"You ought to ask her not to do night duty for a while. She's getting very tired."

"All right. I will."

"I want to do it but she won't let me. The others are glad to let her have it. You might give her just a little rest."

"All right."

"Miss Van Campen spoke about you sleeping all the forenoons."

"She would."

"It would be better if you let her stay off nights a little while."

"I want her to."

"You do not. But if you would make her I'd respect you for it."

"I'll make her."

"I don't believe it." She took the note and went out. I rang the bell and in a little while Miss Gage came in.

"What's the matter?"

"I just wanted to talk to you. Don't you think Miss Barkley ought to go off night duty for a while? She looks awfully tired. Why does she stay on so long?"

Miss Gage looked at me.

"I'm a friend of yours," she said. "You don't have to talk to me like that."

"What do you mean?"

"Don't be silly. Was that all you wanted?"

"Do you want a vermouth?"

"All right. Then I have to go." She got out the bottle from the armoire and brought a glass.

"You take the glass," I said. "I'll drink out of the bottle."

"Here's to you," said Miss Gage.

"What did Van Campen say about me sleeping late in the mornings?"

"She just jawed about it. She calls you our privileged patient."

"To hell with her."

"She isn't mean," Miss Gage said. "She's just old and cranky. She never liked you."

"No."

"Well, I do. And I'm your friend. Don't forget that."

"You're awfully damned nice."

"No. I know who you think is nice. But I'm your friend. How does your leg feel?"

"Fine."

"I'll bring some cold mineral water to pour over it. It must itch under the cast. It's hot outside."

"You're awful nice."

"Does it itch much?"

"No. It's fine."

"I'll fix those sandbags better." She leaned over. "I'm your friend."

"I know you are."

"No you don't. But you will some day."

Catherine Barkley took three nights off night duty and then she came back on again. It was as though we met again after each of us had been away on a long journey.

CHAPTER 18

WE HAD a lovely time that summer. When I could go out we rode in a carriage in the park. I remember the carriage, the horse going slowly, and up ahead the back of the driver with his varnished high hat, and Catherine Barkley sitting beside me. If we let our hands touch, just the side of my hand touching hers, we were excited. Afterward when I could get around on crutches we went to dinner at Biffi's or the Gran Italia and sat at the tables outside on the floor of the galleria. The waiters came in and out and there were people going by and candles with shades on the tablecloths and after we decided that we liked the Gran Italia best, George, the headwaiter, saved us a table. He was a fine waiter and we let him order the meal while we looked at the people, and the great galleria in the dusk, and each other. We drank dry white capri iced in a bucket; although we tried many of the other wines, fresa, barbera and the sweet white wines. They had no wine waiter because of the war and George would smile ashamedly when I asked about wines like fresa.

"If you imagine a country that makes a wine because it tastes like strawberries," he said.

"Why shouldn't it?" Catherine asked. "It sounds splendid."

"You try it, lady," said George, "if you want to. But let me bring a little bottle of margaux for the Tenente."

"I'll try it too, George."

"Sir, I can't recommend you to. It doesn't even taste like strawberries."

"It might," said Catherine. "It would be wonderful if it did."

"I'll bring it," said George, "and when the lady is satisfied I'll take it away."

It was not much of a wine. As he said, it did not even taste like strawberries. We went back to capri. One evening I was short of money and George loaned me a hundred lire. "That's all right, Tenente," he said. "I know how it is. I know how a man gets short. If you or the lady need money I've always got money."

After dinner we walked through the galleria, past the other restaurants and the shops with their steel shutters down, and stopped at the little place where they sold sandwiches; ham and lettuce sandwiches and anchovy sandwiches made of very tiny brown glazed rolls and only about as long as your finger. They were to eat in the night when we were hungry. Then we got into an open carriage outside the galleria in front of the cathedral and rode to the hospital. At the door of the hospital the porter came out to help with the crutches. I paid the driver, and then we rode upstairs in the elevator. Catherine got off at the lower floor where the nurses lived and I went on up and went down the hall on crutches to my room; sometimes I undressed and got into bed and sometimes I sat out on the balcony with my leg up on another chair and watched the swallows over the roofs and waited for Catherine. When she came upstairs it was as though she had been away on a long trip and I went along the hall with her on the crutches and carried the basins and waited outside the doors, or went in with her; it depending on whether they were friends of ours or not, and when she had done all there was to be done we sat out on the balcony outside my room. Afterward I went to bed and when they were all asleep and she was sure they would not call she came in. I loved to take her hair down and she sat on the bed and kept very still, except suddenly she would dip down to kiss me while I was doing it, and I would take out the pins and lay them on the sheet and it would be loose and I would watch her while she kept very still and then take out the last two pins and it would all come down and she would drop her head and we would both be inside of it, and it was the feeling of inside a tent or behind a falls.

She had wonderfully beautiful hair and I would lie sometimes and watch her twisting it up in the light that came in the open door and it shone even in the night as water shines sometimes just before it is really daylight. She had a lovely face and body and lovely smooth skin too. We would be lying together and I would touch her cheeks and her forehead and under her eyes and her chin and throat with the tips of my fingers and say, "Smooth as piano keys," and she would stroke my chin with her finger and say, "Smooth as emery paper and very hard on piano keys."

"Is it rough?"

"No, darling. I was just making fun of you."

It was lovely in the nights and if we could only touch each other we were happy. Besides all the big times we had many small ways of making love and we tried putting thoughts in the other one's head while we were in different rooms. It seemed to work sometimes but that was probably because we were thinking the same thing anyway.

We said to each other that we were married the first day she had come to the hospital and we counted months from our wedding day. I wanted to be really married but Catherine said that if we were they would send her away and if we merely started on the formalities they would watch her and would break us up. We would have to be married under Italian law and the formalities were terrific. I wanted us to be married really because I worried about having a child if I thought about it, but we pretended to ourselves we were married and did not worry much and I suppose I enjoyed not being married, really. I know one night we talked about it and Catherine said, "But, darling, they'd send me away."

"Maybe they wouldn't."

"They would. They'd send me home and then we would be apart until after the war."

"I'd come on leave."

"You couldn't get to Scotland and back on a leave. Besides, I won't leave you. What good would it do to marry now? We're really married. I couldn't be any more married."

"I only wanted to for you."

"There isn't any me. I'm you. Don't make up a separate me."

"I thought girls always wanted to be married."

"They do. But, darling, I am married. I'm married to you. Don't I make you a good wife?"

"You're a lovely wife."

"You see, darling, I had one experience of waiting to be married."

"I don't want to hear about it."

"You know I don't love any one but you. You shouldn't mind because some one else loved me."

"I do."

"You shouldn't be jealous of some one who's dead when you have everything."

"No, but I don't want to hear about it."

"Poor darling. And I know you've been with all kinds of girls and it doesn't matter to me."

"Couldn't we be married privately some way? Then if anything happened to me or if you had a child."

"There's no way to be married except by church or state. We are married privately. You see, darling, it would mean everything to me if I had any religion. But I haven't any religion."

"You gave me the Saint Anthony."

"That was for luck. Some one gave it to me."

"Then nothing worries you?"

"Only being sent away from you. You're my religion. You're all I've got."

"All right. But I'll marry you the day you say."

"Don't talk as though you had to make an honest woman of me, darling. I'm a very honest woman. You can't be ashamed of something if you're only happy and proud of it. Aren't you happy?"

"But you won't ever leave me for some one else."

"No, darling. I won't ever leave you for some one else. I suppose all sorts of dreadful things will happen to us. But you don't have to worry about that."

"I don't. But I love you so much and you did love some one else before."

"And what happened to him?"

"He died."

"Yes and if he hadn't I wouldn't have met you. I'm not unfaithful, darling. I've plenty of faults but I'm very faithful. You'll be sick of me I'll be so faithful."

"I'll have to go back to the front pretty soon."

"We won't think about that until you go. You see I'm happy, darling, and we have a lovely time. I haven't been happy for a long time and when I met you perhaps I was nearly crazy. Perhaps I was crazy. But now we're happy and we love each other. Do let's please just be happy. You are happy, aren't you? Is there anything I do you don't like? Can I do anything to please you? Would you like me to take down my hair? Do you want to play?"

"Yes and come to bed."

"All right. I'll go and see the patients first."

CHAPTER 19

THE SUMMER went that way. I do not remember much about the days, except that they were hot and that there were many victories in the papers. I was very healthy and my legs healed quickly so that it was not very long after I was first on crutches before I was through with them and walking with a cane. Then I started treatments at the Ospedale Maggiore for bending the knees, mechanical treatments, baking in a box of mirrors with violet rays, massage, and baths. I went over there afternoons and afterward stopped at the café and had a drink and read the papers. I did not roam around the town; but wanted to get home to the hospital from the café. All I wanted was to see Catherine. The rest of the time I was glad to kill. Mostly I slept in the mornings, and in the afternoons, sometimes, I went to the races, and late to the mechanotherapy treatments. Sometimes I stopped in at the Anglo-American Club and sat in a deep leather-cushioned chair in front of the window and read the magazines. They would not let us go out together when I was off crutches because it was unseemly for a nurse to be seen unchaperoned with a patient who did not look as though he needed attendance, so we were not together much in the afternoons. Although sometimes we could go out to dinner if Ferguson went along. Miss Van Campen had accepted the status that we were great friends because she got a great amount of work out of Catherine. She thought Catherine came from very good people and that prejudiced her in her favor finally. Miss Van Campen admired family very much and came from an excellent family herself. The hospital was quite busy, too, and that kept her occupied. It was a hot summer and I knew many people in Milan but always was anxious to get back home to the hospital as soon as the afternoon was over. At the front they were advancing on the Carso, they had taken Kuk across from Plava and were taking the Bainsizza plateau. The West front did not sound so good. It looked as though the war were going on for a long time. We were in the war now but I thought it would take a year to get any great amount of troops over and train them for combat. Next year would be a bad year, or a good year maybe. The Italians were using up an awful amount of men. I did not see how it could go on. Even if they took all the Bainsizza and Monte San Gabriele there were plenty of mountains beyond for the Austrians. I had seen them. All the highest mountains were beyond. On the Carso they were going forward but there were marshes and swamps down by the sea. Napoleon would have whipped the Austrians on the plains. He never would have fought them in the mountains. He would have let them come down and whipped them around Verona. Still nobody was whipping any one on the Western front. Perhaps wars weren't won any more. Maybe they went on forever. Maybe it was another Hundred Years' War. I put the paper back on the rack and left the club. I went down the steps carefully and walked up the Via Manzoni. Outside the Gran Hotel I met old Meyers and his wife getting out of a carriage. They were coming back from the races. She was a big-busted woman in black satin. He was short and old, with a white mustache and walked flat-footed with a cane.

"How do you do? How do you do?" She shook hands. "Hello," said Meyers.

"How were the races?"

"Fine. They were just lovely. I had three winners."

"How did you do?" I asked Meyers.

"All right. I had a winner."

"I never know how he does," Mrs. Meyers said. "He never tells me."

"I do all right," Meyers said. He was being cordial. "You ought to come out." While he talked you had the impression that he was not looking at you or that he mistook you for some one else.

"I will," I said.

"I'm coming up to the hospital to see you," Mrs. Meyers said. "I have some things for my boys. You're all my boys. You certainly are my dear boys."

"They'll be glad to see you."

"Those dear boys. You too. You're one of my boys."

"I have to get back," I said.

"You give my love to all those dear boys. I've got lots of things to bring. I've some fine marsala and cakes."

"Good-by," I said. "They'll be awfully glad to see you."

"Good-by," said Meyers. "You come around to the galleria. You know where my table is. We're all there every afternoon." I went on up the street. I wanted to buy something at the Cova to take to Catherine. Inside, at the Cova, I bought a box of chocolate and while the girl wrapped it up I walked over to the bar. There were a couple of British and some aviators. I had a martini alone, paid for it, picked up the box of chocolate at the outside counter and walked on home toward the hospital. Outside the little bar up the street from the Scala there were some people I knew, a vice-consul, two fellows who studied singing, and Ettore Moretti, an Italian from San Francisco who was in the Italian army. I had a drink with them. One of the singers was named Ralph Simmons, and he was singing under the name of Enrico DelCredo. I never knew how well he could sing but he was always on the point of something very big happening. He was fat and looked shopworn around the nose and mouth as though he had hayfever. He had come back from singing in Piacenza. He had sung Tosca and it had been wonderful.

"Of course you've never heard me sing," he said.

"When will you sing here?"

"I'll be at the Scala in the fall."

"I'll bet they throw the benches at you," Ettore said. "Did you hear how they threw the benches at him in Modena?"

"It's a damned lie."

"They threw the benches at him," Ettore said. "I was there. I threw six benches myself."

"You're just a wop from Frisco."

"He can't pronounce Italian," Ettore said. "Everywhere he goes they throw the benches at him."

"Piacenza's the toughest house to sing in the north of Italy," the other tenor said. "Believe me that's a tough little house to sing." This tenor's name was Edgar Saunders, and he sang under the name of Edouardo Giovanni.

"I'd like to be there to see them throw the benches at you," Ettore said. "You can't sing Italian."

"He's a nut," said Edgar Saunders. "All he knows how to say is throw benches."

"That's all they know how to do when you two sing," Ettore said. "Then when you go to America you'll tell about your triumphs at the Scala. They wouldn't let you get by the first note at the Scala."

"I'll sing at the Scala," Simmons said. "I'm going to sing Tosca in October."

"We'll go, won't we, Mac?" Ettore said to the vice-consul. "They'll need somebody to protect them."

"Maybe the American army will be there to protect them," the vice-consul said. "Do you want another drink, Simmons? You want a drink, Saunders?"

"All right," said Saunders.

"I hear you're going to get the silver medal," Ettore said to me. "What kind of citation you going to get?"

"I don't know. I don't know I'm going to get it."

"You're going to get it. Oh boy, the girls at the Cova will think you're fine then. They'll all think you killed two hundred Austrians or captured a whole trench by yourself. Believe me, I got to work for my decorations."

"How many have you got, Ettore?" asked the vice-consul.

"He's got everything," Simmons said. "He's the boy they're running the war for."

"I've got the bronze twice and three silver medals," said Ettore. "But the papers on only one have come through."

"What's the matter with the others?" asked Simmons.

"The action wasn't successful," said Ettore. "When the action isn't successful they hold up all the medals."

"How many times have you been wounded, Ettore?"

"Three times bad. I got three wound stripes. See?" He pulled his sleeve around. The stripes were parallel silver lines on a black background sewed to the cloth of the sleeve about eight inches below the shoulder.

"You got one too," Ettore said to me. "Believe me they're fine to have. I'd rather have them than medals. Believe me, boy, when you get three you've got something. You only get one for a wound that puts you three months in the hospital."

"Where were you wounded, Ettore?" asked the vice-consul.

Ettore pulled up his sleeve. "Here," he showed the deep smooth red scar. "Here on my leg. I can't show you that because I got puttees on; and in the foot. There's dead bone in my foot that stinks right now. Every morning I take new little pieces out and it stinks all the time."

"What hit you?" asked Simmons.

"A hand-grenade. One of those potato mashers. It just blew the whole side of my foot off. You know those potato mashers?" He turned to me.

"Sure."

"I saw the son of a bitch throw it," Ettore said. "It knocked me down and I thought I was dead all right but those damn potato mashers haven't got anything in them. I shot the son of a bitch with my rifle. I always carry a rifle so they can't tell I'm an officer."

"How did he look?" asked Simmons.

"That was the only one he had," Ettore said. "I don't know why he threw it. I guess he always wanted to throw one. He never saw any real fighting probably. I shot the son of a bitch all right."

"How did he look when you shot him?" Simmons asked.

"Hell, how should I know?" said Ettore. "I shot him in the belly. I was afraid I'd miss him if I shot him in the head."

"How long have you been an officer, Ettore?" I asked.

"Two years. I'm going to be a captain. How long have you been a lieutenant?"

"Going on three years."

"You can't be a captain because you don't know the Italian language well enough," Ettore said. "You can talk but you can't read and write well enough. You got to have an education to be a captain. Why don't you go in the American army?"

"Maybe I will."

"I wish to God I could. Oh, boy, how much does a captain get, Mac?"

"I don't know exactly. Around two hundred and fifty dollars, I think."

"Jesus Christ what I could do with two hundred and fifty dollars. You better get in the American army quick, Fred. See if you can't get me in."

"All right."

"I can command a company in Italian. I could learn it in English easy."

"You'd be a general," said Simmons.

"No, I don't know enough to be a general. A general's got to know a hell of a lot. You guys think there ain't anything to war. You ain't got brains enough to be a second-class corporal."

"Thank God I don't have to be," Simmons said.

"Maybe you will if they round up all you slackers. Oh, boy, I'd like to have you two in my platoon. Mac too. I'd make you my orderly, Mac."

"You're a great boy, Ettore," Mac said. "But I'm afraid you're a militarist."

"I'll be a colonel before the war's over," Ettore said.

"If they don't kill you."

"They won't kill me." He touched the stars at his collar with his thumb and forefinger. "See me do that? We always touch our stars if anybody mentions getting killed."

"Let's go, Sim," said Saunders standing up.

"All right."

"So long," I said. "I have to go too." It was a quarter to six by the clock inside the bar. "Ciaou, Ettore."

"Ciaou, Fred," said Ettore. "That's pretty fine you're going to get the silver medal."

"I don't know I'll get it."

"You'll get it all right, Fred. I heard you were going to get it all right."

"Well, so long," I said. "Keep out of trouble, Ettore."

"Don't worry about me. I don't drink and I don't run around. I'm no boozer and whorehound. I know what's good for me."

"So long," I said. "I'm glad you're going to be promoted captain."

"I don't have to wait to be promoted. I'm going to be a captain for merit of war. You know. Three stars with the crossed swords and crown above. That's me."

"Good luck."

"Good luck. When you going back to the front?"

"Pretty soon."

"Well, I'll see you around."

"So long."

"So long. Don't take any bad nickels."

I walked on down a back street that led to a cross-cut to the hospital. Ettore was twenty-three. He had been brought up by an uncle in San Francisco and was visiting his father and mother in Torino when war was declared. He had a sister, who had been sent to America with him at the same time to live with the uncle, who would graduate from normal school this year. He was a legitimate hero who bored every one he met. Catherine could not stand him.

"We have heroes too," she said. "But usually, darling, they're much quieter."

"I don't mind him."

"I wouldn't mind him if he wasn't so conceited and didn't bore me, and bore me, and bore me."

"He bores me."

"You're sweet to say so, darling. But you don't need to. You can picture him at the front and you know he's useful but he's so much the type of boy I don't care for."

"I know."

"You're awfully sweet to know, and I try and like him but he's a dreadful, dreadful boy really."

"He said this afternoon he was going to be a captain."

"I'm glad," said Catherine. "That should please him."

"Wouldn't you like me to have some more exalted rank?"

"No, darling. I only want you to have enough rank so that we're admitted to the better restaurants."

"That's just the rank I have."

"You have a splendid rank. I don't want you to have any more rank. It might go to your head. Oh, darling, I'm awfully glad you're not conceited. I'd have married you even if you were conceited but it's very restful to have a husband who's not conceited."

We were talking softly out on the balcony. The moon was supposed to rise but there was a mist over the town and it did not come up and in a little while it started to drizzle and we came in. Outside the mist turned to rain and in a little while it was raining hard and we heard it drumming on the roof. I got up and stood at the door to see if it was raining in but it wasn't, so I left the door open.

"Who else did you see?" Catherine asked.

"Mr. and Mrs. Meyers."

"They're a strange lot."

"He's supposed to have been in the penitentiary at home. They let him out to die."

"And he lived happily in Milan forever after."

"I don't know how happily."

"Happily enough after jail I should think."

"She's bringing some things here."

"She brings splendid things. Were you her dear boy?"

"One of them."

"You are all her dear boys," Catherine said. "She prefers the dear boys. Listen to it rain."

"It's raining hard."

"And you'll always love me, won't you?"

"Yes."

"And the rain won't make any difference?"

"No."

"That's good. Because I'm afraid of the rain."

"Why?" I was sleepy. Outside the rain was falling steadily.

"I don't know, darling. I've always been afraid of the rain."

"I like it."

"I like to walk in it. But it's very hard on loving."

"I'll love you always."

"I'll love you in the rain and in the snow and in the hail and—what else is there?"

"I don't know. I guess I'm sleepy."

"Go to sleep, darling, and I'll love you no matter how it is."

"You're not really afraid of the rain are you?"

"Not when I'm with you."

"Why are you afraid of it?"

"I don't know."

"Tell me."

"Don't make me."

"Tell me."

"No."

"Tell me."

"All right. I'm afraid of the rain because sometimes I see me dead in it."

"No."

"And sometimes I see you dead in it."

"That's more likely."

"No, it's not, darling. Because I can keep you safe. I know I can. But nobody can help themselves."

"Please stop it. I don't want you to get Scotch and crazy tonight. We won't be together much longer."

"No, but I am Scotch and crazy. But I'll stop it. It's all nonsense."

"Yes it's all nonsense."

"It's all nonsense. It's only nonsense. I'm not afraid of the rain. I'm not afraid of the rain. Oh, oh, God, I wish I wasn't." She was crying. I comforted her and she stopped crying. But outside it kept on raining.

CHAPTER 20

ONE DAY in the afternoon we went to the races. Ferguson went too and Crowell Rodgers, the boy who had been wounded in the eyes by the explosion of the shell nose-cap. The girls dressed to go after lunch while Crowell and I sat on the bed in his room and read the past performances of the horses and the predictions in the racing paper. Crowell's head was bandaged and he did not care much about these races but read the racing paper constantly and kept track of all the horses for something to do. He said the horses were a terrible lot but they were all the horses we had. Old Meyers liked him and gave him tips. Meyers won on nearly every race but disliked to give tips because it brought down the prices. The racing was very crooked. Men who had been ruled off the turf everywhere else were racing in Italy. Meyers' information was good but I hated to ask him because sometimes he did not answer, and always you could see it hurt him to tell you, but he felt obligated to tell us for some reason and he hated less to tell Crowell. Crowell's eyes had been hurt, one was hurt badly, and Meyers had trouble with his eyes and so he liked Crowell. Meyers never told his wife what horses he was playing and she won or lost, mostly lost, and talked all the time.

We four drove out to San Siro in an open carriage. It was a lovely day and we drove out through the park and out along the tramway and out of town where the road was dusty. There were villas with iron fences and big overgrown gardens and ditches with water flowing and green vegetable gardens with dust on the leaves. We could look across the plain and see farmhouses and the rich green farms with their irrigation ditches and the mountains to the north. There were many carriages going into the race track and the men at the gate let us in without cards because we were in uniform. We left the carriage, bought programmes, and walked across the infield and then across the smooth thick turf of the course to the paddock. The grandstands were old and made of wood and the betting booths were under the stands and in a row out near the stables. There was a crowd of soldiers along the fence in the infield. The paddock was fairly well filled with people and they were walking the horses around in a ring under the trees behind the grandstand. We saw people we knew and got chairs for Ferguson and Catherine and watched the horses.

They went around, one after the other, their heads down, the grooms leading them. One horse, a purplish black, Crowell swore was dyed that color. We watched him and it seemed possible. He had only come out just before the bell rang to saddle. We looked him up in the programme from the number on the groom's arm and it was listed a black gelding named Japalac. The race was for horses that had never won a race worth one thousand lire or more. Catherine was sure his color had been changed. Ferguson said she could not tell. I thought he looked suspicious. We all agreed we ought to back him and pooled one hundred lire. The odds sheets showed he would pay thirty-five to one. Crowell went over and bought the tickets while we watched the jockeys ride around once more and then go out under the trees to the track and gallop slowly up to the turn where the start was to be.

We went up in the grand-stand to watch the race. They had no elastic barrier at San Siro then and the starter lined up all the horses, they looked very small way up the track, and then sent them off with a crack of his long whip. They came past us with the black horse well in front and on the turn he was running away from the others. I watched them on the far side with the glasses and saw the jockey fighting to hold him in but he could not hold him and when they came around the turn and into the stretch the black horse was fifteen lengths ahead of the others. He went way on up and around the turn after the finish.

"Isn't it wonderful," Catherine said. "We'll have over three thousand lire. He must be a splendid horse."

"I hope his color doesn't run," Crowell said, "before they pay off."

"He was really a lovely horse," Catherine said. "I wonder if Mr. Meyers backed him."

"Did you have the winner?" I called to Meyers. He nodded.

"I didn't," Mrs. Meyers said. "Who did you children bet on?"

"Japalac."

"Really? He's thirty-five to one!"

"We liked his color."

"I didn't. I thought he looked seedy. They told me not to back him."

"He won't pay much," Meyers said.

"He's marked thirty-five to one in the quotes," I said.

"He won't pay much. At the last minute," Meyers said, "they put a lot of money on him."

"Who?"

"Kempton and the boys. You'll see. He won't pay two to one."

"Then we won't get three thousand lire," Catherine said. "I don't like this crooked racing!"

"We'll get two hundred lire."

"That's nothing. That doesn't do us any good. I thought we were going to get three thousand."

"It's crooked and disgusting," Ferguson said.

"Of course," said Catherine, "if it hadn't been crooked we'd never have backed him at all. But I would have liked the three thousand lire."

"Let's go down and get a drink and see what they pay," Crowell said. We went out to where they posted the numbers and the bell rang to pay off and they put up 18.50 after Japalac to win. That meant he paid less than even money on a ten-lira bet.

We went to the bar under the grand-stand and had a whiskey and soda apiece. We ran into a couple of Italians we knew and McAdams, the vice-consul, and they came up with us when we joined the girls. The Italians were full of manners and McAdams talked to Catherine while we went down to bet again. Mr. Meyers was standing near the pari-mutuel.

"Ask him what he played," I said to Crowell.

"What are you on, Mr. Meyers?" Crowell asked. Meyers took out his programme and pointed to the number five with his pencil.

"Do you mind if we play him too?" Crowell asked.

"Go ahead. Go ahead. But don't tell my wife I gave it to you."

"Will you have a drink?" I asked.

"No thanks. I never drink."

We put a hundred lire on number five to win and a hundred to place and then had another whiskey and soda apiece. I was feeling very good and we picked up a couple more Italians, who each had a drink with us, and went back to the girls. These Italians were also very mannered and matched manners with the two we had collected before. In a little while no one could sit down. I gave the tickets to Catherine.

"What horse is it?"

"I don't know. Mr. Meyers' choice."

"Don't you even know the name?"

"No. You can find it on the programme. Number five I think."

"You have touching faith," she said. The number five won but did not pay anything. Mr. Meyers was angry.

"You have to put up two hundred lire to make twenty," he said. "Twelve lire for ten. It's not worth it. My wife lost twenty lire."

"I'll go down with you," Catherine said to me. The Italians all stood up. We went downstairs and out to the paddock.

"Do you like this?" Catherine asked.

"Yes. I guess I do."

"It's all right, I suppose," she said. "But, darling, I can't stand to see so many people."

"We don't see many."

"No. But those Meyers and the man from the bank with his wife and daughters—"

"He cashes my sight drafts," I said.

"Yes but some one else would if he didn't. Those last four boys were awful."

"We can stay out here and watch the race from the fence."

"That will be lovely. And, darling, let's back a horse we've never heard of and that Mr. Meyers won't be backing."

"All right."

We backed a horse named Light For Me that finished fourth in a field of five. We leaned on the fence and watched the horses go by, their hoofs thudding as they went past, and saw the mountains off in the distance and Milan beyond the trees and the fields.

"I feel so much cleaner," Catherine said. The horses were coming back, through the gate, wet and sweating, the jockeys quieting them and riding up to dismount under the trees.

"Wouldn't you like a drink? We could have one out here and see the horses."

"I'll get them," I said.

"The boy will bring them," Catherine said. She put her hand up and the boy came out from the Pagoda bar beside the stables. We sat down at a round iron table.

"Don't you like it better when we're alone?"

"Yes," I said.

"I felt very lonely when they were all there."

"It's grand here," I said.

"Yes. It's really a pretty course."

"It's nice."

"Don't let me spoil your fun, darling. I'll go back whenever you want."

"No," I said. "We'll stay here and have our drink. Then we'll go down and stand at the water jump for the steeplechase."

"You're awfully good to me," she said.

After we had been alone awhile we were glad to see the others again. We had a good time.

CHAPTER 21

IN SEPTEMBER the first cool nights came, then the days were cool and the leaves on the trees in the park began to turn color and we knew the summer was gone. The fighting at the front went very badly and they could not take San Gabriele. The fighting on the Bainsizza plateau was over and by the middle of the month the fighting for San Gabriele was about over too. They could not take it. Ettore was gone back to the front. The horses were gone to Rome and there was no more racing. Crowell had gone to Rome too, to be sent back to America. There were riots twice in the town against the war and bad rioting in Turin. A British major at the club told me the Italians had lost one hundred and fifty thousand men on the Bainsizza plateau and on San Gabriele. He said they had lost forty thousand on the Carso besides. We had a drink and he talked. He said the fighting was over for the year down here and that the Italians had bitten off more than they could chew. He said the offensive in Flanders was going to the bad. If they killed men as they did this fall the Allies would be cooked in another year. He said we were all cooked but we were all right as long as we did not know it. We were all cooked. The thing was not to recognize it. The last country to realize they were cooked would win the war. We had another drink. Was I on somebody's staff? No. He was. It was all balls. We were alone in the club sitting back in one of the big leather sofas. His boots were smoothly polished dull leather. They were beautiful boots. He said it was all balls. They thought only in divisions and man-power. They all squabbled about divisions and only killed them when they got them. They were all cooked. The Germans won the victories. By God they were soldiers. The old Hun was a soldier. But they were cooked too. We were all cooked. I asked about Russia. He said they were cooked already. I'd soon see they were cooked. Then the Austrians were cooked too. If they got some Hun divisions they could do it. Did he think they would attack this fall? Of course they would. The Italians were cooked. Everybody knew they were cooked. The old Hun would come down through the Trentino and cut the railway at Vicenza and then where would the Italians be? They tried that in 'sixteen, I said. Not with Germans. Yes, I said. But they probably wouldn't do that, he said. It was too simple. They'd try something complicated and get royally cooked. I had to go, I said. I had to get back to the hospital. "Good-by," he said. Then cheerily, "Every sort of luck!" There was a great contrast between his world pessimism and personal cheeriness.

I stopped at a barber shop and was shaved and went home to the hospital. My leg was as well as it would get for a long time. I had been up for examination three days before. There were still some treatments to take before my course at the Ospedale.

Maggiore was finished and I walked along the side street practicing not limping. An old man was cutting silhouettes under an arcade. I stopped to watch him. Two girls were posing and he cut their silhouettes together, snipping very fast and looking at them, his head on one side. The girls were giggling. He showed me the silhouettes before he pasted them on white paper and handed them to the girls.

"They're beautiful," he said. "How about you, Tenente?"

The girls went away looking at their silhouettes and laughing. They were nice-looking girls. One of them worked in the wine shop across from the hospital.

"All right," I said.

"Take your cap off."

"No. With it on."

"It will not be so beautiful," the old man said. "But," he brightened, "it will be more military."

He snipped away at the black paper, then separated the two thicknesses and pasted the profiles on a card and handed them to me.

"How much?"

"That's all right." He waved his hand. "I just made them for you."

"Please." I brought out some coppers. "For pleasure."

"No. I did them for a pleasure. Give them to your girl."

"Many thanks until we meet."

"Until I see thee."

I went on to the hospital. There were some letters, an official one, and some others. I was to have three weeks' convalescent leave and then return to the front. I read it over carefully. Well, that was that. The convalescent leave started October fourth when my course was finished. Three weeks was twenty-one days. That made October twenty-fifth. I told them I would not be in and went to the restaurant a little way up the street from the hospital for supper and read my letters and the Corriere Della Sera at the table. There was a letter from my grandfather, containing family news, patriotic encouragement, a draft for two hundred dollars, and a few clippings; a dull letter from the priest at our mess, a letter from a man I knew who was flying with the French and had gotten in with a wild gang and was telling about it, and a note from Rinaldi asking me how long I was going to skulk in Milano and what was all the news? He wanted me to bring him phonograph records and enclosed a list. I drank a small bottle of chianti with the meal, had a coffee afterward with a glass of cognac, finished the paper, put my letters in my pocket, left the paper on the table with the tip and went out. In my room at the hospital I undressed, put on pajamas and a dressing-gown, pulled down the curtains on the door that opened onto the balcony and sitting up in bed read Boston papers from a pile Mrs. Meyers had left for her boys at the hospital. The Chicago White Sox were winning the American League pennant and the New York Giants were leading the National League. Babe Ruth was a pitcher then playing for Boston. The papers were dull, the news was local and stale, and the war news was all old. The American news was all training camps. I was glad I wasn't in a training camp. The baseball news was all I could read and I did not have the slightest interest in it. A number of papers together made it impossible to read with interest. It was not very timely but I read at it for a while. I wondered if America really got into the war, if they would close down the major leagues. They probably wouldn't. There was still racing in Milan and the war could not be much worse. They had stopped racing in France. That was where our horse Japalac came from. Catherine was not due on duty until nine o'clock. I heard her passing along the floor when she first came on duty and once saw her pass in the hall. She went to several other rooms and finally came into mine.

"I'm late, darling," she said. "There was a lot to do. How are you?"

I told her about my papers and the leave.

"That's lovely," she said. "Where do you want to go?"

"Nowhere. I want to stay here."

"That's silly. You pick a place to go and I'll come too."

"How will you work it?"

"I don't know. But I will."

"You're pretty wonderful."

"No I'm not. But life isn't hard to manage when you've nothing to lose."

"How do you mean?"

"Nothing. I was only thinking how small obstacles seemed that once were so big."

"I should think it might be hard to manage."

"No it won't, darling. If necessary I'll simply leave. But it won't come to that."

"Where should we go?"

"I don't care. Anywhere you want. Anywhere we don't know people."

"Don't you care where we go?"

"No. I'll like any place."

She seemed upset and taut.

"What's the matter, Catherine?"

"Nothing. Nothing's the matter."

"Yes there is."

"No nothing. Really nothing."

"I know there is. Tell me, darling. You can tell me."

"It's nothing."

"Tell me."

"I don't want to. I'm afraid I'll make you unhappy or worry you."

"No it won't."

"You're sure? It doesn't worry me but I'm afraid to worry you."

"It won't if it doesn't worry you."

"I don't want to tell."

"Tell it."

"Do I have to?"

"Yes."

"I'm going to have a baby, darling. It's almost three months along. You're not worried, are you? Please please don't. You mustn't worry."

"All right."

"Is it all right?"

"Of course."

"I did everything. I took everything but it didn't make any difference."

"I'm not worried."

"I couldn't help it, darling, and I haven't worried about it. You mustn't worry or feel badly."

"I only worry about you."

"That's it. That's what you mustn't do. People have babies all the time. Everybody has babies. It's a natural thing."

"You're pretty wonderful."

"No I'm not. But you mustn't mind, darling. I'll try and not make trouble for you. I know I've made trouble now. But haven't I been a good girl until now? You never knew it, did you?"

"No."

"It will all be like that. You simply mustn't worry. I can see you're worrying. Stop it. Stop it right away. Wouldn't you like a drink, darling? I know a drink always makes you feel cheerful."

"No. I feel cheerful. And you're pretty wonderful."

"No I'm not. But I'll fix everything to be together if you pick out a place for us to go. It ought to be lovely in October. We'll have a lovely time, darling, and I'll write you every day while you're at the front."

"Where will you be?"

"I don't know yet. But somewhere splendid. I'll look after all that."

We were quiet awhile and did not talk. Catherine was sitting on the bed and I was looking at her but we did not touch each other. We were apart as when some one comes into a room and people are self-conscious. She put out her hand and took mine.

"You aren't angry are you, darling?"

"No."

"And you don't feel trapped?"

"Maybe a little. But not by you."

"I didn't mean by me. You mustn't be stupid. I meant trapped at all."

"You always feel trapped biologically."

She went away a long way without stirring or removing her hand.

"'Always' isn't a pretty word."

"I'm sorry."

"It's all right. But you see I've never had a baby and I've never even loved any one. And I've tried to be the way you wanted and then you talk about 'always.'"

"I could cut off my tongue," I offered.

"Oh, darling!" she came back from wherever she had been. "You mustn't mind me." We were both together again and the self-consciousness was gone. "We really are the same one and we mustn't misunderstand on purpose."

"We won't."

"But people do. They love each other and they misunderstand on purpose and they fight and then suddenly they aren't the same one."

"We won't fight."

"We mustn't. Because there's only us two and in the world there's all the rest of them. If anything comes between us we're gone and then they have us."

"They won't get us," I said. "Because you're too brave. Nothing ever happens to the brave."

"They die of course."

"But only once."

"I don't know. Who said that?"

"The coward dies a thousand deaths, the brave but one?"

"Of course. Who said it?"

"I don't know."

"He was probably a coward," she said. "He knew a great deal about cowards but nothing about the brave. The brave dies perhaps two thousand deaths if he's intelligent. He simply doesn't mention them."

"I don't know. It's hard to see inside the head of the brave."

"Yes. That's how they keep that way."

"You're an authority."

"You're right, darling. That was deserved."

"You're brave."

"No," she said. "But I would like to be."

"I'm not," I said. "I know where I stand. I've been out long enough to know. I'm like a ball-player that bats two hundred and thirty and knows he's no better."

"What is a ball-player that bats two hundred and thirty? It's awfully impressive."

"It's not. It means a mediocre hitter in baseball."

"But still a hitter," she prodded me.

"I guess we're both conceited," I said. "But you are brave."

"No. But I hope to be."

"We're both brave," I said. "And I'm very brave when I've had a drink."

"We're splendid people," Catherine said. She went over to the armoire and brought me the cognac and a glass. "Have a drink, darling," she said. "You've been awfully good."

"I don't really want one."

"Take one."

"All right." I poured the water glass a third full of cognac and drank it off.

"That was very big," she said. "I know brandy is for heroes. But you shouldn't exaggerate."

"Where will we live after the war?"

"In an old people's home probably," she said. "For three years I looked forward very childishly to the war ending at Christmas. But now I look forward till when our son will be a lieutenant commander."

"Maybe he'll be a general."

"If it's an hundred years' war he'll have time to try both of the services."

"Don't you want a drink?"

"No. It always makes you happy, darling, and it only makes me dizzy."

"Didn't you ever drink brandy?"

"No, darling. I'm a very old-fashioned wife."

I reached down to the floor for the bottle and poured another drink.

"I'd better go to have a look at your compatriots," Catherine said. "Perhaps you'll read the papers until I come back."

"Do you have to go?"

"Now or later."

"All right. Now."

"I'll come back later."

"I'll have finished the papers," I said.

CHAPTER 22

IT TURNED cold that night and the next day it was raining. Coming home from the Ospedale Maggiore it rained very hard and I was wet when I came in. Up in my room the rain was coming down heavily outside on the balcony, and the wind blew it against the glass doors. I changed my clothing and drank some brandy but the brandy did not taste good. I felt sick in the night and in the morning after breakfast I was nauseated.

"There is no doubt about it," the house surgeon said. "Look at the whites of his eyes, Miss."

Miss Gage looked. They had me look in a glass. The whites of the eyes were yellow and it was the jaundice. I was sick for two weeks with it. For that reason we did not spend a convalescent leave together. We had planned to go to Pallanza on Lago Maggiore. It is nice there in the fall when the leaves turn. There are walks you can take and you can troll for trout in the lake. It would have been better than Stresa because there are fewer people at Pallanza. Stresa is so easy to get to from Milan that there are always people you know. There is a nice village at Pallanza and you can row out to the islands where the fishermen live and there is a restaurant on the biggest island. But we did not go.

One day while I was in bed with jaundice Miss Van Campen came in the room, opened the door into the armoire and saw the empty bottles there. I had sent a load of them down by the porter and I believe she must have seen them going out and come up to find some more. They were mostly vermouth bottles, marsala bottles, capri bottles, empty chianti flasks and a few cognac bottles. The porter had carried out the large bottles, those that had held vermouth, and the straw-covered chianti flasks, and left the brandy bottles for the last. It was the brandy bottles and a bottle shaped like a bear, which had held kümmel, that Miss Van Campen found. The bear-shaped bottle enraged her particularly. She held it up, the bear was sitting up on his haunches with his paws up, there was a cork in his glass head and a few sticky crystals at the bottom. I laughed.

"It is kümmel," I said. "The best kümmel comes in those bear-shaped bottles. It comes from Russia."

"Those are all brandy bottles, aren't they?" Miss Van Campen asked.

"I can't see them all," I said. "But they probably are."

"How long has this been going on?"

"I bought them and brought them in myself," I said. "I have had Italian officers visit me frequently and I have kept brandy to offer them."

"You haven't been drinking it yourself?" she said.

"I have also drunk it myself."

"Brandy," she said. "Eleven empty bottles of brandy and that bear liquid."

"Kümmel."

"I will send for some one to take them away. Those are all the empty bottles you have?"

"For the moment."

"And I was pitying you having jaundice. Pity is something that is wasted on you."

"Thank you."

"I suppose you can't be blamed for not wanting to go back to the front. But I should think you would try something more intelligent than producing jaundice with alcoholism."

"With what?"

"With alcoholism. You heard me say it." I did not say anything. "Unless you find something else I'm afraid you will have to go back to the front when you are through with your jaundice. I don't believe self-inflicted jaundice entitles you to a convalescent leave."

"You don't?"

"I do not."

"Have you ever had jaundice, Miss Van Campen?"

"No, but I have seen a great deal of it."

"You noticed how the patients enjoyed it?"

"I suppose it is better than the front."

"Miss Van Campen," I said, "did you ever know a man who tried to disable himself by kicking himself in the scrotum?"

Miss Van Campen ignored the actual question. She had to ignore it or leave the room. She was not ready to leave because she had disliked me for a long time and she was now cashing in.

"I have known many men to escape the front through self-inflicted wounds."

"That wasn't the question. I have seen self-inflicted wounds also. I asked you if you had ever known a man who had tried to disable himself by kicking himself in the scrotum. Because that is the nearest sensation to jaundice and it is a sensation that I believe few women have ever experienced. That was why I asked you if you had ever had the jaundice, Miss Van Campen, because—" Miss Van Campen left the room. Later Miss Gage came in.

"What did you say to Van Campen? She was furious."

"We were comparing sensations. I was going to suggest that she had never experienced childbirth—"

"You're a fool," Gage said. "She's after your scalp."

"She has my scalp," I said. "She's lost me my leave and she might try and get me court-martialled. She's mean enough."

"She never liked you," Gage said. "What's it about?"

"She says I've drunk myself into jaundice so as not to go back to the front."

"Pooh," said Gage. "I'll swear you've never taken a drink. Everybody will swear you've never taken a drink."

"She found the bottles."

"I've told you a hundred times to clear out those bottles. Where are they now?"

"In the armoire."

"Have you a suitcase?"

"No. Put them in that rucksack."

Miss Gage packed the bottles in the rucksack. "I'll give them to the porter," she said. She started for the door.

"Just a minute," Miss Van Campen said. "I'll take those bottles." She had the porter with her. "Carry them, please," she said. "I want to show them to the doctor when I make my report."

She went down the hall. The porter carried the sack. He knew what was in it.

Nothing happened except that I lost my leave.

CHAPTER 23

THE NIGHT I was to return to the front I sent the porter down to hold a seat for me on the train when it came from Turin. The train was to leave at midnight. It was made up at Turin and reached Milan about half-past ten at night and lay in the station until time to leave. You had to be there when it came in, to get a seat. The porter took a friend with him, a machine-gunner on leave who worked in a tailor shop, and was sure that between them they could hold a place. I gave them money for platform tickets and had them take my baggage. There was a big rucksack and two musettes.

I said good-by at the hospital at about five o'clock and went out. The porter had my baggage in his lodge and I told him I would be at the station a little before midnight. His wife called me "Signorino" and cried. She wiped her eyes and shook hands and then cried again. I patted her on the back and she cried once more. She had done my mending and was a very short dumpy, happy-faced woman with white hair. When she cried her whole face went to pieces. I went down to the corner where there was a wine shop and waited inside looking out the window. It was dark outside and cold and misty. I paid for my coffee and grappa and I watched the people going by in the light from the window. I saw Catherine and knocked on the window. She looked, saw me and smiled, and I went out to meet her. She was wearing a dark blue cape and a soft felt hat. We walked along together, along the sidewalk past the wine shops, then across the market square and up the street and through the archway to the cathedral square. There were streetcar tracks and beyond them was the cathedral. It was white and wet in the mist. We crossed the tram tracks. On our left were the shops, their windows lighted, and the entrance to the galleria. There was a fog in the square and when we came close to the front of the cathedral it was very big and the stone was wet.

"Would you like to go in?"

"No," Catherine said. We walked along. There was a soldier standing with his girl in the shadow of one of the stone buttresses ahead of us and we passed them. They were standing tight up against the stone and he had put his cape around her.

"They're like us," I said.

"Nobody is like us," Catherine said. She did not mean it happily.

"I wish they had some place to go."

"It mightn't do them any good."

"I don't know. Everybody ought to have some place to go."

"They have the cathedral," Catherine said. We were past it now. We crossed the far end of the square and looked back at the cathedral. It was fine in the mist. We were standing in front of the leather goods shop. There were riding boots, a rucksack and ski boots in the window. Each article was set apart as an exhibit; the rucksack in the centre, the riding boots on one side and the ski boots on the other. The leather was dark and oiled smooth as a used saddle. The electric light made high lights on the dull oiled leather.

"We'll ski some time."

"In two months there will be ski-ing at Mürren," Catherine said.

"Let's go there."

"All right," she said. We went on past other windows and turned down a side street.

"I've never been this way."

"This is the way I go to the hospital," I said. It was a narrow street and we kept on the right-hand side. There were many people passing in the fog. There were shops and all the windows were lighted. We looked in a window at a pile of cheeses. I stopped in front of an armorer's shop.

"Come in a minute. I have to buy a gun."

"What sort of gun?"

"A pistol." We went in and I unbuttoned my belt and laid it with the empty holster on the counter. Two women were behind the counter. The women brought out several pistols.

"It must fit this," I said, opening the holster. It was a gray leather holster and I had bought it second-hand to wear in the town.

"Have they good pistols?" Catherine asked.

"They're all about the same. Can I try this one?" I asked the woman.

"I have no place now to shoot," she said. "But it is very good. You will not make a mistake with it."

I snapped it and pulled back the action. The spring was rather strong but it worked smoothly. I sighted it and snapped it again.

"It is used," the woman said. "It belonged to an officer who was an excellent shot."

"Did you sell it to him?"

"Yes."

"How did you get it back?"

"From his orderly."

"Maybe you have mine," I said. "How much is this?"

"Fifty lire. It is very cheap."

"All right. I want two extra clips and a box of cartridges."

She brought them from under the counter.

"Have you any need for a sword?" she asked. "I have some used swords very cheap."

"I'm going to the front," I said.

"Oh yes, then you won't need a sword," she said.

I paid for the cartridges and the pistol, filled the magazine and put it in place, put the pistol in my empty holster, filled the extra clips with cartridges and put them in the leather slots on the holster and then buckled on my belt. The pistol felt heavy on the belt. Still, I thought, it was better to have a regulation pistol. You could always get shells.

"Now we're fully armed," I said. "That was the one thing I had to remember to do. Some one got my other one going to the hospital."

"I hope it's a good pistol," Catherine said.

"Was there anything else?" the woman asked.

"I don't believe so."

"The pistol has a lanyard," she said.

"So I noticed." The woman wanted to sell something else.

"You don't need a whistle?"

"I don't believe so."

The woman said good-by and we went out onto the sidewalk. Catherine looked in the window. The woman looked out and bowed to us.

"What are those little mirrors set in wood for?"

"They're for attracting birds. They twirl them out in the field and larks see them and come out and the Italians shoot them."

"They are an ingenious people," Catherine said. "You don't shoot larks do you, darling, in America?"

"Not especially."

We crossed the street and started to walk up the other side.

"I feel better now," Catherine said. "I felt terrible when we started."

"We always feel good when we're together."

"We always will be together."

"Yes, except that I'm going away at midnight."

"Don't think about it, darling."

We walked on up the street. The fog made the lights yellow.

"Aren't you tired?" Catherine asked.

"How about you?"

"I'm all right. It's fun to walk."

"But let's not do it too long."

"No."

We turned down a side street where there were no lights and walked in the street. I stopped and kissed Catherine. While I kissed her I felt her hand on my shoulder. She had pulled my cape around her so it covered both of us. We were standing in the street against a high wall.

"Let's go some place," I said.

"Good," said Catherine. We walked on along the street until it came out onto a wider street that was beside a canal. On the other side was a brick wall and buildings. Ahead, down the street, I saw a streetcar cross a bridge.

"We can get a cab up at the bridge," I said. We stood on the bridge in the fog waiting for a carriage. Several streetcars passed, full of people going home. Then a carriage came along but there was some one in it. The fog was turning to rain.

"We could walk or take a tram," Catherine said.

"One will be along," I said. "They go by here."

"Here one comes," she said.

The driver stopped his horse and lowered the metal sign on his meter. The top of the carriage was up and there were drops of water on the driver's coat. His varnished hat was shining in the wet. We sat back in the seat together and the top of the carriage made it dark.

"Where did you tell him to go?"

"To the station. There's a hotel across from the station where we can go."

"We can go the way we are? Without luggage?"

"Yes," I said.

It was a long ride to the station up side streets in the rain.

"Won't we have dinner?" Catherine asked. "I'm afraid I'll be hungry."

"We'll have it in our room."

"I haven't anything to wear. I haven't even a night-gown."

"We'll get one," I said and called to the driver.

"Go to the Via Manzoni and up that." He nodded and turned off to the left at the next corner. On the big street Catherine watched for a shop.

"Here's a place," she said. I stopped the driver and Catherine got out, walked across the sidewalk and went inside. I sat back in the carriage and waited for her. It was raining and I could smell the wet street and the horse steaming in the rain. She came back with a package and got in and we drove on.

"I was very extravagant, darling," she said, "but it's a fine nightgown."

At the hotel I asked Catherine to wait in the carriage while I went in and spoke to the manager. There were plenty of rooms. Then I went out to the carriage, paid the driver, and Catherine and I walked in together. The small boy in buttons carried the package. The manager bowed us toward the elevator. There was much red plush and brass. The manager went up in the elevator with us.

"Monsieur and Madame wish dinner in their rooms?"

"Yes. Will you have the menu brought up?" I said.

"You wish something special for dinner. Some game or a soufflé?"

The elevator passed three floors with a click each time, then clicked and stopped.

"What have you as game?"

"I could get a pheasant, or a woodcock."

"A woodcock," I said. We walked down the corridor. The carpet was worn. There were many doors. The manager stopped and unlocked a door and opened it.

"Here you are. A lovely room."

The small boy in buttons put the package on the table in the centre of the room. The manager opened the curtains.

"It is foggy outside," he said. The room was furnished in red plush. There were many mirrors, two chairs and a large bed with a satin coverlet. A door led to the bathroom.

"I will send up the menu," the manager said. He bowed and went out.

I went to the window and looked out, then pulled a cord that shut the thick plush curtains. Catherine was sitting on the bed, looking at the cut glass chandelier. She had taken her hat off and her hair shone under the light. She saw herself in one of the mirrors and put her hands to her hair. I saw her in three other mirrors. She did not look happy. She let her cape fall on the bed.

"What's the matter, darling?"

"I never felt like a whore before," she said. I went over to the window and pulled the curtain aside and looked out. I had not thought it would be like this.

"You're not a whore."

"I know it, darling. But it isn't nice to feel like one." Her voice was dry and flat.

"This was the best hotel we could get in," I said. I looked out the window. Across the square were the lights of the station. There were carriages going by on the street and I saw the trees in the park. The lights from the hotel shone on the wet pavement. Oh, hell, I thought, do we have to argue now?

"Come over here please," Catherine said. The flatness was all gone out of her voice. "Come over, please. I'm a good girl again." I looked over at the bed. She was smiling.

I went over and sat on the bed beside her and kissed her.

"You're my good girl."

"I'm certainly yours," she said.

After we had eaten we felt fine, and then after, we felt very happy and in a little time the room felt like our own home. My room at the hospital had been our own home and this room was our home too in the same way.

Catherine wore my tunic over her shoulders while we ate. We were very hungry and the meal was good and we drank a bottle of Capri and a bottle of St. Estephe. I drank most of it but Catherine drank some and it made her feel splendid. For dinner we had a woodcock with soufflé potatoes and purée de marron, a salad, and zabaione for dessert.

"It's a fine room," Catherine said. "It's a lovely room. We should have stayed here all the time we've been in Milan."

"It's a funny room. But it's nice."

"Vice is a wonderful thing," Catherine said. "The people who go in for it seem to have good taste about it. The red plush is really fine. It's just the thing. And the mirrors are very attractive."

"You're a lovely girl."

"I don't know how a room like this would be for waking up in the morning. But it's really a splendid room." I poured another glass of St. Estephe.

"I wish we could do something really sinful," Catherine said. "Everything we do seems so innocent and simple. I can't believe we do anything wrong."

"You're a grand girl."

"I only feel hungry. I get terribly hungry."

"You're a fine simple girl," I said.

"I am a simple girl. No one ever understood it except you."

"Once when I first met you I spent an afternoon thinking how we would go to the Hotel Cavour together and how it would be."

"That was awfully cheeky of you. This isn't the Cavour is it?"

"No. They wouldn't have taken us in there."

"They'll take us in some time. But that's how we differ, darling. I never thought about anything."

"Didn't you ever at all?"

"A little," she said.

"Oh you're a lovely girl."

I poured another glass of wine.

"I'm a very simple girl," Catherine said.

"I didn't think so at first. I thought you were a crazy girl."

"I was a little crazy. But I wasn't crazy in any complicated manner. I didn't confuse you did I, darling?"

"Wine is a grand thing," I said. "It makes you forget all the bad."

"It's lovely," said Catherine. "But it's given my father gout very badly."

"Have you a father?"

"Yes," said Catherine. "He has gout. You won't ever have to meet him. Haven't you a father?"

"No," I said. "A step-father."

"Will I like him?"

"You won't have to meet him."

"We have such a fine time," Catherine said. "I don't take any interest in anything else any more. I'm so very happy married to you."

The waiter came and took away the things. After a while we were very still and we could hear the rain. Down below on the street a motor car honked.

"'But at my back I always hear Time's wingèd chariot hurrying near,'" I said.

"I know that poem," Catherine said. "It's by Marvell. But it's about a girl who wouldn't live with a man."

My head felt very clear and cold and I wanted to talk facts.

"Where will you have the baby?"

"I don't know. The best place I can find."

"How will you arrange it?"

"The best way I can. Don't worry, darling. We may have several babies before the war is over."

"It's nearly time to go."

"I know. You can make it time if you want."

"No."

"Then don't worry, darling. You were fine until now and now you're worrying."

"I won't. How often will you write?"

"Every day. Do they read your letters?"

"They can't read English enough to hurt any."

"I'll make them very confusing," Catherine said.

"But not too confusing."

"I'll just make them a little confusing."

"I'm afraid we have to start to go."

"All right, darling."

"I hate to leave our fine house."

"So do I."

"But we have to go."

"All right. But we're never settled in our home very long."

"We will be."

"I'll have a fine home for you when you come back."

"Maybe I'll be back right away."

"Perhaps you'll be hurt just a little in the foot."

"Or the lobe of the ear."

"No I want your ears the way they are."

"And not my feet?"

"Your feet have been hit already."

"We have to go, darling. Really."

"All right. You go first."

CHAPTER 24

WE WALKED down the stairs instead of taking the elevator. The carpet on the stairs was worn. I had paid for the dinner when it came up and the waiter, who had brought it, was sitting on a chair near the door. He jumped up and bowed and I went with him into the side room and paid the bill for the room. The manager had remembered me as a friend and refused payment in advance but when he retired he had remembered to have the waiter stationed at the door so that I should not get out without paying. I suppose that had happened; even with his friends. One had so many friends in a war.

I asked the waiter to get us a carriage and he took Catherine's package that I was carrying and went out with an umbrella. Outside through the window we saw him crossing the street in the rain. We stood in the side room and looked out the window.

"How do you feel, Cat?"

"Sleepy."

"I feel hollow and hungry."

"Have you anything to eat?"

"Yes, in my musette."

I saw the carriage coming. It stopped, the horse's head hanging in the rain, and the waiter stepped out, opened his umbrella, and came toward the hotel. We met him at the door and walked out under the umbrella down the wet walk to the carriage at the curb. Water was running in the gutter.

"There is your package on the seat," the waiter said. He stood with the umbrella until we were in and I had tipped him.

"Many thanks. Pleasant journey," he said. The coachman lifted the reins and the horse started. The waiter turned away under the umbrella and went toward the hotel. We drove down the street and turned to the left, then came around to the right in front of the station. There were two carabinieri standing under the light just out of the rain. The light shone on their hats. The rain was clear and transparent against the light from the station. A porter came out from under the shelter of the station, his shoulders up against the rain.

"No," I said. "Thanks. I don't need thee."

He went back under the shelter of the archway. I turned to Catherine. Her face was in the shadow from the hood of the carriage.

"We might as well say good-by."

"I can't go in?"

"No."

"Good-by, Cat."

"Will you tell him the hospital?"

"Yes."

I told the driver the address to drive to. He nodded.

"Good-by," I said. "Take good care of yourself and young Catherine."

"Good-by, darling."

"Good-by," I said. I stepped out into the rain and the carriage started. Catherine leaned out and I saw her face in the light. She smiled and waved. The carriage went up the street, Catherine pointed in toward the archway. I looked, there were only the two carabinieri and the archway. I realized she meant for me to get in out of the rain. I went in and stood and watched the carriage turn the corner. Then I started through the station and down the runway to the train.

The porter was on the platform looking for me. I followed him into the train, crowding past people and along the aisle and in through a door to where the machine-gunner sat in the corner of a full compartment. My rucksack and musettes were above his head on the luggage rack. There were many men standing in the corridor and the men in the compartment all looked at us when we came in. There were not enough places in the train and every one was hostile. The machine-gunner stood up for me to sit down. Some one tapped me on the shoulder. I looked around. It was a very tall gaunt captain of artillery with a red scar along his jaw. He had looked through the glass on the corridor and then come in.

"What do you say?" I asked. I had turned and faced him. He was taller than I and his face was very thin under the shadow of his cap-visor and the scar was new and shiny. Every one in the compartment was looking at me.

"You can't do that," he said. "You can't have a soldier save you a place."

"I have done it."

He swallowed and I saw his Adam's apple go up and then down. The machine-gunner stood in front of the place. Other men looked in through the glass. No one in the compartment said anything.

"You have no right to do that. I was here two hours before you came."

"What do you want?"

"The seat."

"So do I."

I watched his face and could feel the whole compartment against me. I did not blame them. He was in the right. But I wanted the seat. Still no one said anything.

"Oh, hell," I thought.

"Sit down, Signor Capitano," I said. The machine-gunner moved out of the way and the tall captain sat down. He looked at me. His face seemed hurt. But he had the seat. "Get my things," I said to the machine-gunner. We went out in the corridor. The train was full and I knew there was no chance of a place. I gave the porter and the machine-gunner ten lire apiece. They went down the corridor and outside on the platform looking in the windows but there were no places.

"Maybe some will get off at Brescia," the porter said.

"More will get on at Brescia," said the machine-gunner. I said good-by to them and we shook hands and they left. They both felt badly. Inside the train we were all standing in the corridor when the train started. I watched the lights of the station and the yards as we went out. It was still raining and soon the windows were wet and you could not see out. Later I slept on the floor of the corridor; first putting my pocket-book with my money and papers in it inside my shirt and trousers so that it was inside the leg of my breeches. I slept all night, waking at Brescia and Verona when more men got on the train, but going back to sleep at once. I had my head on one of the musettes and my arms around the other and I could feel the pack and they could all walk over me if they wouldn't step on me. Men were sleeping on the floor all down the corridor. Others stood holding on to the window rods or leaning against the doors. That train was always crowded.

BOOK THREE

CHAPTER 25

NOW IN THE FALL the trees were all bare and the roads were muddy. I rode to Gorizia from Udine on a camion. We passed other camions on the road and I looked at the country. The mulberry trees were bare and the fields were brown. There were wet dead leaves on the road from the rows of bare trees and men were working on the road, tamping stone in the ruts from piles of crushed stone along the side of the road between the trees. We saw the town with a mist over it that cut off the mountains. We crossed the river and I saw that it was running high. It had been raining in the mountains. We came into the town past the factories and then the houses and villas and I saw that many more houses had been hit. On a narrow street we passed a British Red Cross ambulance. The driver wore a cap and his face was thin and very tanned. I did not know him. I got down from the camion in the big square in front of the Town Major's house, the driver handed down my rucksack and I put it on and swung on the two musettes and walked to our villa. It did not feel like a homecoming.

I walked down the damp gravel driveway looking at the villa through the trees. The windows were all shut but the door was open. I went in and found the major sitting at a table in the bare room with maps and typed sheets of paper on the wall.

"Hello," he said. "How are you?" He looked older and drier.

"I'm good," I said. "How is everything?"

"It's all over," he said. "Take off your kit and sit down." I put my pack and the two musettes on the floor and my cap on the pack. I brought the other chair over from the wall and sat down by the desk.

"It's been a bad summer," the major said. "Are you strong now?"

"Yes."

"Did you ever get the decorations?"

"Yes. I got them fine. Thank you very much."

"Let's see them."

I opened my cape so he could see the two ribbons.

"Did you get the boxes with the medals?"

"No. Just the papers."

"The boxes will come later. That takes more time."

"What do you want me to do?"

"The cars are all away. There are six up north at Caporetto. You know Caporetto?"

"Yes," I said. I remembered it as a little white town with a campanile in a valley. It was a clean little town and there was a fine fountain in the square.

"They are working from there. There are many sick now. The fighting is over."

"Where are the others?"

"There are two up in the mountains and four still on the Bainsizza. The other two ambulance sections are in the Carso with the third army."

"What do you wish me to do?"

"You can go and take over the four cars on the Bainsizza if you like. Gino has been up there a long time. You haven't seen it up there, have you?"

"No."

"It was very bad. We lost three cars."

"I heard about it."

"Yes, Rinaldi wrote you."

"Where is Rinaldi?"

"He is here at the hospital. He has had a summer and fall of it."

"I believe it."

"It has been bad," the major said. "You couldn't believe how bad it's been. I've often thought you were lucky to be hit when you were."

"I know I was."

"Next year will be worse," the major said. "Perhaps they will attack now. They say they are to attack but I can't believe it. It is too late. You saw the river?"

"Yes. It's high already."

"I don't believe they will attack now that the rains have started. We will have the snow soon. What about your countrymen? Will there be other Americans besides yourself?"

"They are training an army of ten million."

"I hope we get some of them. But the French will hog them all. We'll never get any down here. All right. You stay here to-night and go out to-morrow with the little car and send Gino back. I'll send somebody with you that knows the road. Gino will tell you everything. They are shelling quite a little still but it is all over. You will want to see the Bainsizza."

"I'm glad to see it. I am glad to be back with you again, Signor Maggiore."

He smiled. "You are very good to say so. I am very tired of this war. If I was away I do not believe I would come back."

"Is it so bad?"

"Yes. It is so bad and worse. Go get cleaned up and find your friend Rinaldi."

I went out and carried my bags up the stairs. Rinaldi was not in the room but his things were there and I sat down on the bed and unwrapped my puttees and took the shoe off my right foot. Then I lay back on the bed. I was tired and my right foot hurt. It seemed silly to lie on the bed with one shoe off, so I sat up and unlaced the other shoe and dropped it on the floor, then lay back on the blanket again. The room was stuffy with the window closed but I was too tired to get up and open it. I saw my things were all in one corner of the room. Outside it was getting dark. I lay on the bed and thought about Catherine and waited for Rinaldi. I was going to try not to think about Catherine except at night before I went to sleep. But now I was tired and there was nothing to do, so I lay and thought about her. I was thinking about her when Rinaldi came in. He looked just the same. Perhaps he was a little thinner.

"Well, baby," he said. I sat up on the bed. He came over, sat down and put his arm around me. "Good old baby." He whacked me on the back and I held both his arms.

"Old baby," he said. "Let me see your knee."

"I'll have to take off my pants."

"Take off your pants, baby. We're all friends here. I want to see what kind of a job they did." I stood up, took off the breeches and pulled off the knee-brace. Rinaldi sat on the floor and bent the knee gently back and forth. He ran his finger along the scar; put his thumbs together over the kneecap and rocked the knee gently with his fingers.

"Is that all the articulation you have?"

"Yes."

"It's a crime to send you back. They ought to get complete articulation."

"It's a lot better than it was. It was stiff as a board."

Rinaldi bent it more. I watched his hands. He had fine surgeon's hands. I looked at the top of his head, his hair shiny and parted smoothly. He bent the knee too far.

"Ouch!" I said.

"You ought to have more treatment on it with the machines," Rinaldi said.

"It's better than it was."

"I see that, baby. This is something I know more about than you." He stood up and sat down on the bed. "The knee itself is a good job." He was through with the knee. "Tell me all about everything."

"There's nothing to tell," I said. "I've led a quiet life."

"You act like a married man," he said. "What's the matter with you?"

"Nothing," I said. "What's the matter with you?"

"This war is killing me," Rinaldi said, "I am very depressed by it." He folded his hands over his knee.

"Oh," I said.

"What's the matter? Can't I even have human impulses?"

"No. I can see you've been having a fine time. Tell me."

"All summer and all fall I've operated. I work all the time. I do everybody's work. All the hard ones they leave to me. By God, baby, I am becoming a lovely surgeon."

"That sounds better."

"I never think. No, by God, I don't think; I operate."

"That's right."

"But now, baby, it's all over. I don't operate now and I feel like hell. This is a terrible war, baby. You believe me when I say it. Now you cheer me up. Did you bring the phonograph records?"

"Yes."

They were wrapped in paper in a cardboard box in my rucksack. I was too tired to get them out.

"Don't you feel good yourself, baby?"

"I feel like hell."

"This war is terrible," Rinaldi said. "Come on. We'll both get drunk and be cheerful. Then we'll go get the ashes dragged. Then we'll feel fine."

"I've had the jaundice," I said, "and I can't get drunk."

"Oh, baby, how you've come back to me. You come back serious and with a liver. I tell you this war is a bad thing. Why did we make it anyway."

"We'll have a drink. I don't want to get drunk but we'll have a drink."

Rinaldi went across the room to the washstand and brought back two glasses and a bottle of cognac.

"It's Austrian cognac," he said. "Seven stars. It's all they captured on San Gabriele."

"Were you up there?"

"No. I haven't been anywhere. I've been here all the time operating. Look, baby, this is your old tooth-brushing glass. I kept it all the time to remind me of you."

"To remind you to brush your teeth."

"No. I have my own too. I kept this to remind me of you trying to brush away the Villa Rossa from your teeth in the morning, swearing and eating aspirin and cursing harlots. Every time I see that glass I think of you trying to clean your conscience with a toothbrush." He came over to the bed. "Kiss me once and tell me you're not serious."

"I never kiss you. You're an ape."

"I know, you are the fine good Anglo-Saxon boy. I know. You are the remorse boy, I know. I will wait till I see the Anglo-Saxon brushing away harlotry with a toothbrush."

"Put some cognac in the glass."

We touched glasses and drank. Rinaldi laughed at me.

"I will get you drunk and take out your liver and put you in a good Italian liver and make you a man again."

I held the glass for some more cognac. It was dark outside now. Holding the glass of cognac, I went over and opened the window. The rain had stopped falling. It was colder outside and there was a mist in the trees.

"Don't throw the cognac out the window," Rinaldi said. "If you can't drink it give it to me."

"Go something yourself," I said. I was glad to see Rinaldi again. He had spent two years teasing me and I had always liked it. We understood each other very well.

"Are you married?" he asked from the bed. I was standing against the wall by the window.

"Not yet."

"Are you in love?"

"Yes."

"With that English girl?"

"Yes."

"Poor baby. Is she good to you?"

"Of course."

"I mean is she good to you practically speaking?"

"Shut up."

"I will. You will see I am a man of extreme delicacy. Does she— ?"

"Rinin," I said. "Please shut up. If you want to be my friend, shut up."

"I don't want to be your friend, baby. I am your friend."

"Then shut up."

"All right."

I went over to the bed and sat down beside Rinaldi. He was holding his glass and looking at the floor.

"You see how it is, Rinin?"

"Oh, yes. All my life I encounter sacred subjects. But very few with you. I suppose you must have them too." He looked at the floor.

"You haven't any?"

"No."

"Not any?"

"No."

"I can say this about your mother and that about your sister?"

"And that about your sister," Rinaldi said swiftly. We both laughed.

"The old superman," I said.

"I am jealous maybe," Rinaldi said.

"No, you're not."

"I don't mean like that. I mean something else. Have you any married friends?"

"Yes," I said.

"I haven't," Rinaldi said. "Not if they love each other."

"Why not?"

"They don't like me."

"Why not?"

"I am the snake. I am the snake of reason."

"You're getting it mixed. The apple was reason."

"No, it was the snake." He was more cheerful.

"You are better when you don't think so deeply," I said.

"I love you, baby," he said. "You puncture me when I become a great Italian thinker. But I know many things I can't say. I know more than you."

"Yes. You do."

"But you will have a better time. Even with remorse you will have a better time."

"I don't think so."

"Oh, yes. That is true. Already I am only happy when I am working." He looked at the floor again.

"You'll get over that."

"No. I only like two other things; one is bad for my work and the other is over in half an hour or fifteen minutes. Sometimes less."

"Sometimes a good deal less."

"Perhaps I have improved, baby. You do not know. But there are only the two things and my work."

"You'll get other things."

"No. We never get anything. We are born with all we have and we never learn. We never get anything new. We all start complete. You should be glad not to be a Latin."

"There's no such thing as a Latin. That is 'Latin' thinking. You are so proud of your defects." Rinaldi looked up and laughed.

"We'll stop, baby. I am tired from thinking so much." He had looked tired when he came in. "It's nearly time to eat. I'm glad you're back. You are my best friend and my war brother."

"When do the war brothers eat?" I asked.

"Right away. We'll drink once more for your liver's sake."

"Like Saint Paul."

"You are inaccurate. That was wine and the stomach. Take a little wine for your stomach's sake."

"Whatever you have in the bottle," I said. "For any sake you mention."

"To your girl," Rinaldi said. He held out his glass.

"All right."

"I'll never say a dirty thing about her."

"Don't strain yourself."

He drank off the cognac. "I am pure," he said. "I am like you, baby. I will get an English girl too. As a matter of fact I knew your girl first but she was a little tall for me. A tall girl for a sister," he quoted.

"You have a lovely pure mind," I said.

"Haven't I? That's why they call me Rinaldo Purissimo."

"Rinaldo Sporchissimo."

"Come on, baby, we'll go down to eat while my mind is still pure."

I washed, combed my hair and we went down the stairs. Rinaldi was a little drunk. In the room where we ate, the meal was not quite ready.

"I'll go get the bottle," Rinaldi said. He went off up the stairs. I sat at the table and he came back with the bottle and poured us each a half tumbler of cognac.

"Too much," I said and held up the glass and sighted at the lamp on the table.

"Not for an empty stomach. It is a wonderful thing. It burns out the stomach completely. Nothing is worse for you."

"All right."

"Self-destruction day by day," Rinaldi said. "It ruins the stomach and makes the hand shake. Just the thing for a surgeon."

"You recommend it?"

"Heartily. I use no other. Drink it down, baby, and look forward to being sick."

I drank half the glass. In the hall I could hear the orderly calling. "Soup! Soup is ready!"

The major came in, nodded to us and sat down. He seemed very small at table.

"Is this all we are?" he asked. The orderly put the soup bowl down and he ladled out a plate full.

"We are all," Rinaldi said. "Unless the priest comes. If he knew Federico was here he would be here."

"Where is he?" I asked.

"He's at 307," the major said. He was busy with his soup. He wiped his mouth, wiping his upturned gray mustache carefully. "He will come I think. I called them and left word to tell him you were here."

"I miss the noise of the mess," I said.

"Yes, it's quiet," the major said.

"I will be noisy," said Rinaldi.

"Drink some wine, Enrico," said the major. He filled my glass. The spaghetti came in and we were all busy. We were finishing the spaghetti when the priest came in. He was the same as ever, small and brown and compact looking. I stood up and we shook hands. He put his hand on my shoulder.

"I came as soon as I heard," he said.

"Sit down," the major said. "You're late."

"Good-evening, priest," Rinaldi said, using the English word. They had taken that up from the priest-baiting captain, who spoke a little English. "Good-evening, Rinaldo," the priest said. The orderly brought him soup but he said he would start with the spaghetti.

"How are you?" he asked me.

"Fine," I said. "How have things been?"

"Drink some wine, priest," Rinaldi said. "Take a little wine for your stomach's sake. That's Saint Paul, you know."

"Yes I know," said the priest politely. Rinaldi filled his glass.

"That Saint Paul," said Rinaldi. "He's the one who makes all the trouble." The priest looked at me and smiled. I could see that the baiting did not touch him now.

"That Saint Paul," Rinaldi said. "He was a rounder and a chaser and then when he was no longer hot he said it was no good. When he was finished he made the rules for us who are still hot. Isn't it true, Federico?"

The major smiled. We were eating meat stew now.

"I never discuss a Saint after dark," I said. The priest looked up from the stew and smiled at me.

"There he is, gone over with the priest," Rinaldi said. "Where are all the good old priest-baiters? Where is Cavalcanti? Where is Brundi? Where is Cesare? Do I have to bait this priest alone without support?"

"He is a good priest," said the major.

"He is a good priest," said Rinaldi. "But still a priest. I try to make the mess like the old days. I want to make Federico happy. To hell with you, priest!"

I saw the major look at him and notice that he was drunk. His thin face was white. The line of his hair was very black against the white of his forehead.

"It's all right, Rinaldo," said the priest. "It's all right."

"To hell with you," said Rinaldi. "To hell with the whole damn business." He sat back in his chair.

"He's been under a strain and he's tired," the major said to me. He finished his meat and wiped up the gravy with a piece of bread.

"I don't give a damn," Rinaldi said to the table. "To hell with the whole business." He looked defiantly around the table, his eyes flat, his face pale.

"All right," I said. "To hell with the whole damn business."

"No, no," said Rinaldi. "You can't do it. You can't do it. I say you can't do it. You're dry and you're empty and there's nothing else. There's nothing else I tell you. Not a damned thing. I know, when I stop working."

The priest shook his head. The orderly took away the stew dish.

"What are you eating meat for?" Rinaldi turned to the priest. "Don't you know it's Friday?"

"It's Thursday," the priest said.

"It's a lie. It's Friday. You're eating the body of our Lord. It's God-meat. I know.

It's dead Austrian. That's what you're eating."

"The white meat is from officers," I said, completing the old joke.

Rinaldi laughed. He filled his glass.

"Don't mind me," he said. "I'm just a little crazy."

"You ought to have a leave," the priest said.

The major shook his head at him. Rinaldi looked at the priest.

"You think I ought to have a leave?"

The major shook his head at the priest. Rinaldi was looking at the priest.

"Just as you like," the priest said. "Not if you don't want."

"To hell with you," Rinaldi said. "They try to get rid of me. Every night they try to get rid of me. I fight them off. What if I have it. Everybody has it. The whole world's got it. First," he went on, assuming the manner of a lecturer, "it's a little pimple. Then we notice a rash between the shoulders. Then we notice nothing at all. We put our faith in mercury."

"Or salvarsan," the major interrupted quietly.

"A mercurial product," Rinaldi said. He acted very elated now. "I know something worth two of that. Good old priest," he said. "You'll never get it. Baby will get it. It's an industrial accident. It's a simple industrial accident."

The orderly brought in the sweet and coffee. The dessert was a sort of black bread pudding with hard sauce. The lamp was smoking; the black smoke going close up inside the chimney.

"Bring two candles and take away the lamp," the major said. The orderly brought two lighted candles each in a saucer, and took out the lamp blowing it out. Rinaldi was quiet now. He seemed all right. We talked and after the coffee we all went out into the hall.

"You want to talk to the priest. I have to go in the town," Rinaldi said. "Good-night, priest."

"Good-night, Rinaldo," the priest said.

"I'll see you, Fredi," Rinaldi said.

"Yes," I said. "Come in early." He made a face and went out the door. The major was standing with us. "He's very tired and overworked," he said. "He thinks too he has syphilis. I don't believe it but he may have. He is treating himself for it. Good-night. You will leave before daylight, Enrico?"

"Yes."

"Good-by then," he said. "Good luck. Peduzzi will wake you and go with you."

"Good-by, Signor Maggiore."

"Good-by. They talk about an Austrian offensive but I don't believe it. I hope not. But anyway it won't be here. Gino will tell you everything. The telephone works well now."

"I'll call regularly."

"Please do. Good-night. Don't let Rinaldi drink so much brandy."

"I'll try not to."

"Good-night, priest."

"Good-night, Signor Maggiore."

He went off into his office.

CHAPTER 26

I WENT TO THE DOOR and looked out. It had stopped raining but there was a mist.

"Should we go upstairs?" I asked the priest.

"I can only stay a little while."

"Come on up."

We climbed the stairs and went into my room. I lay down on Rinaldi's bed. The priest sat on my cot that the orderly had set up. It was dark in the room.

"Well," he said, "how are you really?"

"I'm all right. I'm tired to-night."

"I'm tired too, but from no cause."

"What about the war?"

"I think it will be over soon. I don't know why, but I feel it."

"How do you feel it?"

"You know how your major is? Gentle? Many people are like that now."

"I feel that way myself," I said.

"It has been a terrible summer," said the priest. He was surer of himself now than when I had gone away. "You cannot believe how it has been. Except that you have been there and you know how it can be. Many people have realized the war this summer. Officers whom I thought could never realize it realize it now."

"What will happen?" I stroked the blanket with my hand.

"I do not know but I do not think it can go on much longer."

"What will happen?"

"They will stop fighting."

"Who?"

"Both sides."

"I hope so," I said.

"You don't believe it?"

"I don't believe both sides will stop fighting at once."

"I suppose not. It is too much to expect. But when I see the changes in men I do not think it can go on."

"Who won the fighting this summer?"

"No one."

"The Austrians won," I said. "They kept them from taking San Gabriele. They've won. They won't stop fighting."

"If they feel as we feel they may stop. They have gone through the same thing."

"No one ever stopped when they were winning."

"You discourage me."

"I can only say what I think."

"Then you think it will go on and on? Nothing will ever happen?"

"I don't know. I only think the Austrians will not stop when they have won a victory. It is in defeat that we become Christian."

"The Austrians are Christians–except for the Bosnians."

"I don't mean technically Christian. I mean like Our Lord."

He said nothing.

"We are all gentler now because we are beaten. How would Our Lord have been if Peter had rescued him in the Garden?"

"He would have been just the same."

"I don't think so," I said.

"You discourage me," he said. "I believe and I pray that something will happen. I have felt it very close."

"Something may happen," I said. "But it will happen only to us. If they felt the way we do, it would be all right. But they have beaten us. They feel another way."

"Many of the soldiers have always felt this way. It is not because they were beaten."

"They were beaten to start with. They were beaten when they took them from their farms and put them in the army. That is why the peasant has wisdom, because he is defeated from the start. Put him in power and see how wise he is."

He did not say anything. He was thinking.

"Now I am depressed myself," I said. "That's why I never think about these things. I never think and yet when I begin to talk I say the things I have found out in my mind without thinking."

"I had hoped for something."

"Defeat?"

"No. Something more."

"There isn't anything more. Except victory. It may be worse."

"I hoped for a long time for victory."

"Me too."

"Now I don't know."

"It has to be one or the other."

"I don't believe in victory any more."

"I don't. But I don't believe in defeat. Though it may be better."

"What do you believe in?"

"In sleep," I said. He stood up.

"I am very sorry to have stayed so long. But I like so to talk with you."

"It is very nice to talk again. I said that about sleeping, meaning nothing."

We stood up and shook hands in the dark.

"I sleep at 307 now," he said.

"I go out on post early to-morrow."

"I'll see you when you come back."

"We'll have a walk and talk together." I walked with him to the door.

"Don't go down," he said. "It is very nice that you are back. Though not so nice for you." He put his hand on my shoulder.

"It's all right for me," I said. "Good-night."

"Good-night. Ciaou!"

"Ciaou!" I said. I was deadly sleepy.

CHAPTER 27

I WOKE WHEN Rinaldi came in but he did not talk and I went back to sleep again. In the morning I was dressed and gone before it was light. Rinaldi did not wake when I left.

I had not seen the Bainsizza before and it was strange to go up the slope where the Austrians had been, beyond the place on the river where I had been wounded. There was a steep new road and many trucks. Beyond, the road flattened out and

I saw woods and steep hills in the mist. There were woods that had been taken quickly and not smashed. Then beyond where the road was not protected by the hills it was screened by matting on the sides and over the top. The road ended in a wrecked village. The lines were up beyond. There was much artillery around. The houses were badly smashed but things were very well organized and there were signboards everywhere. We found Gino and he got us some coffee and later I went with him and met various people and saw the posts. Gino said the British cars were working further down the Bainsizza at Ravne. He had great admiration for the British. There was still a certain amount of shelling, he said, but not many wounded. There would be many sick now the rains had started. The Austrians were supposed to attack but he did not believe it. We were supposed to attack too, but they had not brought up any new troops so he thought that was off too. Food was scarce and he would be glad to get a full meal in Gorizia. What kind of supper had I had? I told him and he said that would be wonderful. He was especially impressed by the dolce. I did not describe it in detail, only said it was a dolce, and I think he believed it was something more elaborate than bread pudding.

Did I know where he was going to go? I said I didn't but that some of the other cars were at Caporetto. He hoped he would go up that way. It was a nice little place and he liked the high mountain hauling up beyond. He was a nice boy and every one seemed to like him. He said where it really had been hell was at San Gabriele and the attack beyond Lom that had gone bad. He said the Austrians had a great amount of artillery in the woods along Ternova ridge beyond and above us, and shelled the roads badly at night. There was a battery of naval guns that had gotten on his nerves. I would recognize them because of their flat trajectory. You heard the report and then the shriek commenced almost instantly. They usually fired two guns at once, one right after the other, and the fragments from the burst were enormous. He showed me one, a smoothly jagged piece of metal over a foot long. It looked like babbitting metal.

"I don't suppose they are so effective," Gino said. "But they scare me. They all sound as though they came directly for you. There is the boom, then instantly the shriek and burst. What's the use of not being wounded if they scare you to death?"

He said there were Croats in the lines opposite us now and some Magyars. Our troops were still in the attacking positions. There was no wire to speak of and no place to fall back to if there should be an Austrian attack. There were fine positions for defense along the low mountains that came up out of the plateau but nothing had been done about organizing them for defense. What did I think about the Bainsizza anyway?

I had expected it to be flatter, more like a plateau. I had not realized it was so broken up.

"Alto piano," Gino said, "but no piano."

We went back to the cellar of the house where he lived. I said I thought a ridge that flattened out on top and had a little depth would be easier and more practical to hold than a succession of small mountains. It was no harder to attack up a mountain than on the level, I argued. "That depends on the mountains," he said. "Look at San Gabriele."

"Yes," I said, "but where they had trouble was at the top where it was flat. They got up to the top easy enough."

"Not so easy," he said.

"Yes," I said, "but that was a special case because it was a fortress rather than a mountain, anyway. The Austrians had been fortifying it for years." I meant tactically speaking in a war where there was some movement a succession of mountains were nothing to hold as a line because it was too easy to turn them. You should have possible mobility and a mountain is not very mobile. Also, people always over-shoot downhill. If the flank were turned, the best men would be left on the highest mountains. I did not believe in a war in mountains. I had thought about it a lot, I said. You pinched off one mountain and they pinched off another but when something really started every one had to get down off the mountains.

What were you going to do if you had a mountain frontier? he asked.

I had not worked that out yet, I said, and we both laughed. "But," I said, "in the old days the Austrians were always whipped in the quadrilateral around Verona. They let them come down onto the plain and whipped them there."

"Yes," said Gino. "But those were Frenchmen and you can work out military problems clearly when you are fighting in somebody else's country."

"Yes," I agreed, "when it is your own country you cannot use it so scientifically."

"The Russians did, to trap Napoleon."

"Yes, but they had plenty of country. If you tried to retreat to trap Napoleon in Italy you would find yourself in Brindisi."

"A terrible place," said Gino. "Have you ever been there?"

"Not to stay."

"I am a patriot," Gino said. "But I cannot love Brindisi or Taranto."

"Do you love the Bainsizza?" I asked.

"The soil is sacred," he said. "But I wish it grew more potatoes. You know when we came here we found fields of potatoes the Austrians had planted."

"Has the food really been short?"

"I myself have never had enough to eat but I am a big eater and I have not starved. The mess is average. The regiments in the line get pretty good food but those in support don't get so much. Something is wrong somewhere. There should be plenty of food."

"The dogfish are selling it somewhere else."

"Yes, they give the battalions in the front line as much as they can but the ones in back are very short. They have eaten all the Austrians' potatoes and chestnuts from the woods. They ought to feed them better. We are big eaters. I am sure there is plenty of food. It is very bad for the soldiers to be short of food. Have you ever noticed the difference it makes in the way you think?"

"Yes," I said. "It can't win a war but it can lose one."

"We won't talk about losing. There is enough talk about losing. What has been done this summer cannot have been done in vain."

I did not say anything. I was always embarrassed by the words sacred, glorious, and sacrifice and the expression in vain. We had heard them, sometimes standing in the rain almost out of earshot, so that only the shouted words came through, and had read them, on proclamations that were slapped up by billposters over other proclamations, now for a long time, and I had seen nothing sacred, and the things that were glorious had no glory and the sacrifices were like the stockyards at Chicago if nothing was done with the meat except to bury it. There were many words that you could not stand to hear and finally only the names of places had dignity. Certain numbers were the same way and certain dates and these with the names of the places were all you could say and have them mean anything. Abstract words such as glory, honor, courage, or hallow were obscene beside the concrete names of villages, the numbers of roads, the names of rivers, the numbers of regiments and the dates. Gino was a patriot, so he said things that separated us sometimes, but he was also a fine boy and I understood his being a patriot. He was born one. He left with Peduzzi in the car to go back to Gorizia.

It stormed all that day. The wind drove down the rain and everywhere there was standing water and mud. The plaster of the broken houses was gray and wet. Late in the afternoon the rain stopped and from out number two post I saw the bare wet autumn country with clouds over the tops of the hills and the straw screening over the roads wet and dripping. The sun came out once before it went down and shone on the bare woods beyond the ridge. There were many Austrian guns in the woods on that ridge but only a few fired. I watched the sudden round puffs of shrapnel smoke in the sky above a broken farmhouse near where the line was; soft puffs with a yellow white flash in the centre. You saw the flash, then heard the crack, then saw the smoke ball distort and thin in the wind. There were many iron shrapnel balls in the rubble of the houses and on the road beside the broken house where the post was, but they did not shell near the post that afternoon. We loaded two cars and drove down the road that was screened with wet mats and the last of the sun came through in the breaks between the strips of mattings. Before we were out on the clear road behind the hill the sun was down. We went on down the clear road and as it turned a corner into the open and went into the square arched tunnel of matting the rain started again.

The wind rose in the night and at three o'clock in the morning with the rain coming in sheets there was a bombardment and the Croatians came over across the mountain meadows and through patches of woods and into the front line. They fought in the dark in the rain and a counter-attack of scared men from the second line drove them back. There was much shelling and many rockets in the rain and machine-gun and rifle fire all along the line. They did not come again and it was quieter and between the gusts of wind and rain we could hear the sound of a great bombardment far to the north.

The wounded were coming into the post, some were carried on stretchers, some walking and some were brought on the backs of men that came across the field. They were wet to the skin and all were scared. We filled two cars with stretcher cases as they came up from the cellar of the post and as I shut the door of the second car and fastened it I felt the rain on my face turn to snow. The flakes were coming heavy and fast in the rain.

When daylight came the storm was still blowing but the snow had stopped. It had melted as it fell on the wet ground and now it was raining again. There was another attack just after daylight but it was unsuccessful. We expected an attack all day but it did not come until the sun was going down. The bombardment started to the south below the long wooded ridge where the Austrian guns were concentrated. We expected a bombardment but it did not come. It was getting dark. Guns were firing from the field behind the village and the shells, going away, had a comfortable sound.

We heard that the attack to the south had been unsuccessful. They did not attack that night but we heard that they had broken through to the north. In the night word came that we were to prepare to retreat. The captain at the post told me this. He had it from the Brigade. A little while later he came from the telephone and said it was a lie. The Brigade had received orders that the line of the Bainsizza should be held no matter what happened. I asked about the break through and he said that he had heard at the Brigade that the Austrians had broken through the twenty-seventh army corps up toward Caporetto. There had been a great battle in the north all day.

"If those bastards let them through we are cooked," he said.

"It's Germans that are attacking," one of the medical officers said. The word Germans was something to be frightened of. We did not want to have anything to do with the Germans.

"There are fifteen divisions of Germans," the medical officer said. "They have broken through and we will be cut off."

"At the Brigade, they say this line is to be held. They say they have not broken through badly and that we will hold a line across the mountains from Monte Maggiore."

"Where do they hear this?"

"From the Division."

"The word that we were to retreat came from the Division."

"We work under the Army Corps," I said. "But here I work under you. Naturally when you tell me to go I will go. But get the orders straight."

"The orders are that we stay here. You clear the wounded from here to the clearing station."

"Sometimes we clear from the clearing station to the field hospitals too," I said. "Tell me, I have never seen a retreat–if there is a retreat how are all the wounded evacuated?"

"They are not. They take as many as they can and leave the rest."

"What will I take in the cars?"

"Hospital equipment."

"All right," I said.

The next night the retreat started. We heard that Germans and Austrians had broken through in the north and were coming down the mountain valleys toward

Cividale and Udine. The retreat was orderly, wet and sullen. In the night, going slowly along the crowded roads we passed troops marching under the rain, guns, horses pulling wagons, mules, motor trucks, all moving away from the front. There was no more disorder than in an advance.

That night we helped empty the field hospitals that had been set up in the least ruined villages of the plateau, taking the wounded down to Plava on the river-bed: and the next day hauled all day in the rain to evacuate the hospitals and clearing station at Plava. It rained steadily and the army of the Bainsizza moved down off the plateau in the October rain and across the river where the great victories had commenced in the spring of that year. We came into Gorizia in the middle of the next day. The rain had stopped and the town was nearly empty. As we came up the street they were loading the girls from the soldiers' whorehouse into a truck. There were seven girls and they had on their hats and coats and carried small suitcases. Two of them were crying. Of the others one smiled at us and put out her tongue and fluttered it up and down. She had thick full lips and black eyes.

I stopped the car and went over and spoke to the matron. The girls from the officers' house had left early that morning, she said. Where were they going? To Conegliano, she said. The truck started. The girl with thick lips put out her tongue again at us. The matron waved. The two girls kept on crying. The others looked interestedly out at the town. I got back in the car.

"We ought to go with them," Bonello said. "That would be a good trip."

"We'll have a good trip," I said.

"We'll have a hell of a trip."

"That's what I mean," I said. We came up the drive to the villa.

"I'd like to be there when some of those tough babies climb in and try and hop them."

"You think they will?"

"Sure. Everybody in the Second Army knows that matron."

We were outside the villa.

"They call her the Mother Superior," Bonello said. "The girls are new but everybody knows her. They must have brought them up just before the retreat."

"They'll have a time."

"I'll say they'll have a time. I'd like to have a crack at them for nothing. They charge too much at that house anyway. The government gyps us."

"Take the car out and have the mechanics go over it," I said. "Change the oil and check the differential. Fill it up and then get some sleep."

"Yes, Signor Tenente."

The villa was empty. Rinaldi was gone with the hospital. The major was gone taking hospital personnel in the staff car. There was a note on the window for me to fill the cars with the material piled in the hall and to proceed to Pordenone. The mechanics were gone already. I went out back to the garage. The other two cars came in while I was there and their drivers got down. It was starting to rain again.

"I'm so—sleepy I went to sleep three times coming here from Plava," Piani said. "What are we going to do, Tenente?"

"We'll change the oil, grease them, fill them up, then take them around in front and load up the junk they've left."

"Then do we start?"

"No, we'll sleep for three hours."

"Christ I'm glad to sleep," Bonello said. "I couldn't keep awake driving."

"How's your car, Aymo?" I asked.

"It's all right."

"Get me a monkey suit and I'll help you with the oil."

"Don't you do that, Tenente," Aymo said. "It's nothing to do. You go and pack your things."

"My things are all packed," I said. "I'll go and carry out the stuff that they left for us. Bring the cars around as soon as they're ready."

They brought the cars around to the front of the villa and we loaded them with the hospital equipment which was piled in the hallway. When it was all in, the three cars stood in line down the driveway under the trees in the rain. We went inside.

"Make a fire in the kitchen and dry your things," I said.

"I don't care about dry clothes," Piani said. "I want to sleep."

"I'm going to sleep on the major's bed," Bonello said. "I'm going to sleep where the old man corks off."

"I don't care where I sleep," Piani said.

"There are two beds in here." I opened the door.

"I never knew what was in that room," Bonello said.

"That was old fish-face's room," Piani said.

"You two sleep in there," I said. "I'll wake you."

"The Austrians will wake us if you sleep too long, Tenente," Bonello said.

"I won't oversleep," I said. "Where's Aymo?"

"He went out in the kitchen."

"Get to sleep," I said.

"I'll sleep," Piani said. "I've been asleep sitting up all day. The whole top of my head kept coming down over my eyes."

"Take your boots off," Bonello said. "That's old fish-face's bed."

"Fish-face is nothing to me." Piani lay on the bed, his muddy boots straight out, his head on his arm. I went out to the kitchen. Aymo had a fire in the stove and a kettle of water on.

"I thought I'd start some pasta asciutta," he said. "We'll be hungry when we wake up."

"Aren't you sleepy, Bartolomeo?"

"Not so sleepy. When the water boils I'll leave it. The fire will go down."

"You'd better get some sleep," I said. "We can eat cheese and monkey meat."

"This is better," he said. "Something hot will be good for those two anarchists. You go to sleep, Tenente."

"There's a bed in the major's room."

"You sleep there."

"No, I'm going up to my old room. Do you want a drink, Bartolomeo?"

"When we go, Tenente. Now it wouldn't do me any good."

"If you wake in three hours and I haven't called you, wake me, will you?"

"I haven't any watch, Tenente."

"There's a clock on the wall in the major's room."

"All right."

I went out then through the dining-room and the hall and up the marble stairs to the room where I had lived with Rinaldi. It was raining outside. I went to the window and looked out. It was getting dark and I saw the three cars standing in line under the trees. The trees were dripping in the rain. It was cold and the drops hung to the branches. I went back to Rinaldi's bed and lay down and let sleep take me.

We ate in the kitchen before we started. Aymo had a basin of spaghetti with onions and tinned meat chopped up in it. We sat around the table and drank two bottles of the wine that had been left in the cellar of the villa. It was dark outside and still raining. Piani sat at the table very sleepy.

"I like a retreat better than an advance," Bonello said. "On a retreat we drink barbera."

"We drink it now. To-morrow maybe we drink rainwater," Aymo said.

"To-morrow we'll be in Udine. We'll drink champagne. That's where the slackers live. Wake up, Piani! We'll drink champagne tomorrow in Udine!"

"I'm awake," Piani said. He filled his plate with the spaghetti and meat. "Couldn't you find tomato sauce, Barto?"

"There wasn't any," Aymo said.

"We'll drink champagne in Udine," Bonello said. He filled his glass with the clear red barbera.

"We may drink— before Udine," Piani said.

"Have you eaten enough, Tenente?" Aymo asked.

"I've got plenty. Give me the bottle, Bartolomeo."

"I have a bottle apiece to take in the cars," Aymo said.

"Did you sleep at all?"

"I don't need much sleep. I slept a little."

"To-morrow we'll sleep in the king's bed," Bonello said. He was feeling very good.

"To-morrow maybe we'll sleep in— ," Piani said.

"I'll sleep with the queen," Bonello said. He looked to see how I took the joke.

"You'll sleep with— ," Piani said sleepily.

"That's treason, Tenente," Bonello said. "Isn't that treason?"

"Shut up," I said. "You get too funny with a little wine." Outside it was raining hard. I looked at my watch. It was half-past nine.

"It's time to roll," I said and stood up.

"Who are you going to ride with, Tenente?" Bonello asked.

"With Aymo. Then you come. Then Piani. We'll start out on the road for Cormons."

"I'm afraid I'll go to sleep," Piani said.

"All right. I'll ride with you. Then Bonello. Then Aymo."

"That's the best way," Piani said. "Because I'm so sleepy."

"I'll drive and you sleep awhile."

"No. I can drive just so long as I know somebody will wake me up if I go to sleep."

"I'll wake you up. Put out the lights, Barto."

"You might as well leave them," Bonello said. "We've got no more use for this place."

"I have a small locker trunk in my room," I said. "Will you help take it down, Piani?"

"We'll take it," Piani said. "Come on, Aldo." He went off into the hall with

Bonello. I heard them going upstairs.

"This was a fine place," Bartolomeo Aymo said. He put two bottles of wine and half a cheese into his haversack. "There won't be a place like this again. Where will they retreat to, Tenente?"

"Beyond the Tagliamento, they say. The hospital and the sector are to be at Pordenone."

"This is a better town than Pordenone."

"I don't know Pordenone," I said. "I've just been through there."

"It's not much of a place," Aymo said.

CHAPTER 28

AS WE MOVED out through the town it was empty in the rain and the dark except for columns of troops and guns that were going through the main street. There were many trucks too and some carts going through on other streets and converging on the main road. When we were out past the tanneries onto the main road the troops, the motor trucks, the horse-drawn carts and the guns were in one wide slow-moving column. We moved slowly but steadily in the rain, the radiator cap of our car almost against the tailboard of a truck that was loaded high, the load covered with wet canvas. Then the truck stopped. The whole column was stopped. It started again and we went a little farther, then stopped. I got out and walked ahead, going between the trucks and carts and under the wet necks of the horses. The block was farther ahead. I left the road, crossed the ditch on a footboard and walked along the field beyond the ditch. I could see the stalled column between the trees in the rain as I went forward across from it in the field. I went about a mile. The column did not move, although, on the other side beyond the stalled vehicles I could see the troops moving. I went back to the cars. This block might extend as far as Udine. Piani was asleep over the wheel. I climbed up beside him and went to sleep too. Several hours later I heard the truck ahead of us grinding into gear. I woke Piani and we started, moving a few yards, then stopping, then going on again. It was still raining.

The column stalled again in the night and did not start. I got down and went back to see Aymo and Bonello. Bonello had two sergeants of engineers on the seat of his car with him. They stiffened when I came up.

"They were left to do something to a bridge," Bonello said. "They can't find their unit so I gave them a ride."

"With the Sir Lieutenant's permission."

"With permission," I said.

"The lieutenant is an American," Bonello said. "He'll give anybody a ride."

One of the sergeants smiled. The other asked Bonello if I was an Italian from North or South America.

"He's not an Italian. He's North American English."

The sergeants were polite but did not believe it. I left them and went back to Aymo. He had two girls on the seat with him and was sitting back in the corner and smoking.

"Barto, Barto," I said. He laughed.

"Talk to them, Tenente," he said. "I can't understand them. Hey!" He put his hand on the girl's thigh and squeezed it in a friendly way. The girl drew her shawl tight around her and pushed his hand away. "Hey!" he said. "Tell the Tenente your name and what you're doing here."

The girl looked at me fiercely. The other girl kept her eyes down. The girl who looked at me said something in a dialect I could not understand a word of. She was plump and dark and looked about sixteen.

"Sorella?" I asked and pointed at the other girl.

She nodded her head and smiled.

"All right," I said and patted her knee. I felt her stiffen away when I touched her. The sister never looked up. She looked perhaps a year younger. Aymo put his hand on the elder girl's thigh and she pushed it away. He laughed at her.

"Good man," he pointed at himself. "Good man," he pointed at me. "Don't you worry." The girl looked at him fiercely. The pair of them were like two wild birds.

"What does she ride with me for if she doesn't like me?" Aymo asked. "They got right up in the car the minute I motioned to them." He turned to the girl. "Don't worry," he said. "No danger of— ," using the vulgar word. "No place for— ." I could see she understood the word and that was all. Her eyes looked at him very scared. She pulled the shawl tight. "Car all full," Aymo said. "No danger of— . No place for— ." Every time he said the word the girl stiffened a little. Then sitting stiffly and looking at him she began to cry. I saw her lips working and then tears came down her plump cheeks. Her sister, not looking up, took her hand and they sat there together. The older one, who had been so fierce, began to sob.

"I guess I scared her," Aymo said. "I didn't mean to scare her."

Bartolomeo brought out his knapsack and cut off two pieces of cheese. "Here," he said. "Stop crying."

The older girl shook her head and still cried, but the younger girl took the cheese and commenced to eat. After a while the younger girl gave her sister the second piece of cheese and they both ate. The older sister still sobbed a little.

"She'll be all right after a while," Aymo said.

An idea came to him. "Virgin?" he asked the girl next to him. She nodded her head vigorously. "Virgin too?" he pointed to the sister. Both the girls nodded their heads and the elder said something in dialect.

"That's all right," Bartolomeo said. "That's all right."

Both the girls seemed cheered.

I left them sitting together with Aymo sitting back in the corner and went back to Piani's car. The column of vehicles did not move but the troops kept passing alongside. It was still raining hard and I thought some of the stops in the movement of the column might be from cars with wet wiring. More likely they were from horses or men going to sleep. Still, traffic could tie up in cities when every one was awake. It was the combination of horse and motor vehicles. They did not help each other any. The peasants' carts did not help much either. Those were a couple of fine girls with Barto. A retreat was no place for two virgins. Real virgins. Probably very religious. If there were no war we would probably all be in bed. In bed I lay me down my head. Bed and board. Stiff as a board in bed. Catherine was in bed now between two sheets, over her and under her. Which side did she sleep on? Maybe she wasn't asleep. Maybe she was lying thinking about me. Blow, blow, ye western wind. Well, it blew and it wasn't the small rain but the big rain down that rained. It rained all night. You knew it rained down that rained. Look at it. Christ, that my love were in my arms and I in my bed again. That my love Catherine. That my sweet love Catherine down might rain. Blow her again to me. Well, we were in it. Every one was caught in it and the small rain would not quiet it. "Good-night, Catherine," I said out loud. "I hope you sleep well. If it's too uncomfortable, darling, lie on the other side," I said. "I'll get you some cold water. In a little while it will be morning and then it won't be so bad. I'm sorry he makes you so uncomfortable. Try and go to sleep, sweet."

I was asleep all the time, she said. You've been talking in your sleep. Are you all right?

Are you really there?

Of course I'm here. I wouldn't go away. This doesn't make any difference between us.

You're so lovely and sweet. You wouldn't go away in the night, would you?

Of course I wouldn't go away. I'm always here. I come whenever you want me.

"— ," Piani said. "They've started again."

"I was dopey," I said. I looked at my watch. It was three o'clock in the morning. I reached back behind the seat for a bottle of the barbera.

"You talked out loud," Piani said.

"I was having a dream in English," I said.

The rain was slacking and we were moving along. Before daylight we were stalled again and when it was light we were at a little rise in the ground and I saw the road of the retreat stretched out far ahead, everything stationary except for the infantry filtering through. We started to move again but seeing the rate of progress in the daylight, I knew we were going to have to get off that main road some way and go across country if we ever hoped to reach Udine.

In the night many peasants had joined the column from the roads of the country and in the column there were carts loaded with household goods; there were mirrors projecting up between mattresses, and chickens and ducks tied to carts. There was a sewing machine on the cart ahead of us in the rain. They had saved the most valuable things. On some carts the women sat huddled from the rain and others walked beside the carts keeping as close to them as they could. There were dogs now in the column, keeping under the wagons as they moved along. The road was muddy, the ditches at the side were high with water and beyond the trees that lined the road the fields looked too wet and too soggy to try to cross. I got down from the car and worked up the road a way, looking for a place where I could see ahead to find a side-road we could take across country. I knew there were many side-roads but did not want one that would lead to nothing. I could not remember them because we had always passed them bowling along in the car on the main road and they all looked much alike. Now I knew we must find one if we hoped to get through. No one knew where the Austrians were nor how things were going but I was certain that if the rain should stop and planes come over and get to work on that column that it would be all over. All that was needed was for a few men to leave their trucks or a few horses be killed to tie up completely the movement on the road.

The rain was not falling so heavily now and I thought it might clear. I went ahead along the edge of the road and when there was a small road that led off to the north between two fields with a hedge of trees on both sides, I thought that we had better take it and hurried back to the cars. I told Piani to turn off and went back to tell Bonello and Aymo.

"If it leads nowhere we can turn around and cut back in," I said.

"What about these?" Bonello asked. His two sergeants were beside him on the seat. They were unshaven but still military looking in the early morning.

"They'll be good to push," I said. I went back to Aymo and told him we were going to try it across country.

"What about my virgin family?" Aymo asked. The two girls were asleep.

"They won't be very useful," I said. "You ought to have some one that could push."

"They could go back in the car," Aymo said. "There's room in the car."

"All right if you want them," I said. "Pick up somebody with a wide back to push."

"Bersaglieri," Aymo smiled. "They have the widest backs. They measure them. How do you feel, Tenente?"

"Fine. How are you?"

"Fine. But very hungry."

"There ought to be something up that road and we will stop and eat."

"How's your leg, Tenente?"

"Fine," I said. Standing on the step and looking up ahead I could see Piani's car pulling out onto the little side-road and starting up it, his car showing through the hedge of bare branches. Bonello turned off and followed him and then Piani worked his way out and we followed the two ambulances ahead along the narrow road between hedges. It led to a farmhouse. We found Piani and Bonello stopped in the farmyard. The house was low and long with a trellis with a grape-vine over the door. There was a well in the yard and Piani was getting up water to fill his radiator. So much going in low gear had boiled it out. The farmhouse was deserted. I looked back down the road, the farmhouse was on a slight elevation above the plain, and we could see over the country, and saw the road, the hedges, the fields and the line of trees along the main road where the retreat was passing. The two sergeants were looking through the house. The girls were awake and looking at the courtyard, the well and the two big ambulances in front of the farmhouse, with three drivers at the well. One of the sergeants came out with a clock in his hand.

"Put it back," I said. He looked at me, went in the house and came back without the clock.

"Where's your partner?" I asked.

"He's gone to the latrine." He got up on the seat of the ambulance. He was afraid we would leave him.

"What about breakfast, Tenente?" Bonello asked. "We could eat something. It wouldn't take very long."

"Do you think this road going down on the other side will lead to anything?"

"Sure."

"All right. Let's eat." Piani and Bonello went in the house.

"Come on," Aymo said to the girls. He held his hand to help them down. The older sister shook her head. They were not going into any deserted house. They looked after us.

"They are difficult," Aymo said. We went into the farmhouse together. It was large and dark, an abandoned feeling. Bonello and Piani were in the kitchen.

"There's not much to eat," Piani said. "They've cleaned it out." Bonello sliced a big cheese on the heavy kitchen table.

"Where was the cheese?"

"In the cellar. Piani found wine too and apples."

"That's a good breakfast."

Piani was taking the wooden cork out of a big wicker-covered wine jug. He tipped it and poured a copper pan full.

"It smells all right," he said. "Find some beakers, Barto."

The two sergeants came in.

"Have some cheese, sergeants," Bonello said.

"We should go," one of the sergeants said, eating his cheese and drinking a cup of wine.

"We'll go. Don't worry," Bonello said.

"An army travels on its stomach," I said.

"What?" asked the sergeant.

"It's better to eat."

"Yes. But time is precious."

"I believe the bastards have eaten already," Piani said. The sergeants looked at him. They hated the lot of us.

"You know the road?" one of them asked me.

"No," I said. They looked at each other.

"We would do best to start," the first one said.

"We are starting," I said. I drank another cup of the red wine. It tasted very good after the cheese and apple.

"Bring the cheese," I said and went out. Bonello came out carrying the great jug of wine.

"That's too big," I said. He looked at it regretfully.

"I guess it is," he said. "Give me the canteens to fill." He filled the canteens and some of the wine ran out on the stone paving of the courtyard. Then he picked up the wine jug and put it just inside the door.

"The Austrians can find it without breaking the door down," he said.

"We'll roll," I said. "Piani and I will go ahead." The two engineers were already on the seat beside Bonello. The girls were eating cheese and apples. Aymo was smoking. We started off down the narrow road. I looked back at the two cars coming and the farmhouse. It was a fine, low, solid stone house and the ironwork of the well was very good. Ahead of us the road was narrow and muddy and there was a high hedge on either side. Behind, the cars were following closely.

CHAPTER 29

AT NOON we were stuck in a muddy road about, as nearly as we could figure, ten kilometres from Udine. The rain had stopped during the forenoon and three times we had heard planes coming, seen them pass overhead, watched them go far to the left and heard them bombing on the main highroad. We had worked through a network of secondary roads and had taken many roads that were blind, but had always, by backing up and finding another road, gotten closer to Udine. Now, Aymo's car, in backing so that we might get out of a blind road, had gotten into the soft earth at the side and the wheels, spinning, had dug deeper and deeper until the car rested on its differential. The thing to do now was to dig out in front of the wheels, put in brush so that the chains could grip, and then push until the car was on the road. We were all down on the road around the car. The two sergeants looked at the car and examined the wheels. Then they started off down the road without a word. I went after them.

"Come on," I said. "Cut some brush."

"We have to go," one said.

"Get busy," I said, "and cut brush."

"We have to go," one said. The other said nothing. They were in a hurry to start. They would not look at me.

"I order you to come back to the car and cut brush," I said. The one sergeant turned. "We have to go on. In a little while you will be cut off. You can't order us. You're not our officer."

"I order you to cut brush," I said. They turned and started down the road.

"Halt," I said. They kept on down the muddy road, the hedge on either side. "I order you to halt," I called. They went a little faster. I opened up my holster, took the pistol, aimed at the one who had talked the most, and fired. I missed and they both started to run. I shot three times and dropped one. The other went through the hedge and was out of sight. I fired at him through the hedge as he ran across the field. The pistol clicked empty and I put in another clip. I saw it was too far to shoot at the second sergeant. He was far across the field, running, his head held low. I commenced to reload the empty clip. Bonello came up.

"Let me go finish him," he said. I handed him the pistol and he walked down to where the sergeant of engineers lay face down across the road. Bonello leaned over, put the pistol against the man's head and pulled the trigger. The pistol did not fire.

"You have to cock it," I said. He cocked it and fired twice. He took hold of the sergeant's legs and pulled him to the side of the road so he lay beside the hedge. He came back and handed me the pistol.

"The son of a bitch," he said. He looked toward the sergeant. "You see me shoot him, Tenente?"

"We've got to get the brush quickly," I said. "Did I hit the other one at all?"

"I don't think so," Aymo said. "He was too far away to hit with a pistol."

"The dirty scum," Piani said. We were all cutting twigs and branches. Everything had been taken out of the car. Bonello was digging out in front of the wheels. When we were ready Aymo started the car and put it into gear. The wheels spun round throwing brush and mud. Bonello and I pushed until we could feel our joints crack. The car would not move.

"Rock her back and forth, Barto," I said.

He drove the engine in reverse, then forward. The wheels only dug in deeper. Then the car was resting on the differential again, and the wheels spun freely in the holes they had dug. I straightened up.

"We'll try her with a rope," I said.

"I don't think it's any use, Tenente. You can't get a straight pull."

"We have to try it," I said. "She won't come out any other way."

Piani's and Bonello's cars could only move straight ahead down the narrow road.

We roped both cars together and pulled. The wheels only pulled sideways against the ruts.

"It's no good," I shouted. "Stop it."

Piani and Bonello got down from their cars and came back. Aymo got down. The girls were up the road about forty yards sitting on a stone wall.

"What do you say, Tenente?" Bonello asked.

"We'll dig out and try once more with the brush," I said. I looked down the road. It was my fault. I had led them up here. The sun was almost out from behind the clouds and the body of the sergeant lay beside the hedge.

"We'll put his coat and cape under," I said. Bonello went to get them. I cut brush and Aymo and Piani dug out in front and between the wheels. I cut the cape, then ripped it in two, and laid it under the wheel in the mud, then piled brush for the wheels to catch. We were ready to start and Aymo got up on the seat and started the car. The wheels spun and we pushed and pushed. But it wasn't any use.

"It's—ed," I said. "Is there anything you want in the car, Barto?"

Aymo climbed up with Bonello, carrying the cheese and two bottles of wine and his cape. Bonello, sitting behind the wheel, was looking through the pockets of the sergeant's coat.

"Better throw the coat away," I said. "What about Barto's virgins?"

"They can get in the back," Piani said. "I don't think we are going far."

I opened the back door of the ambulance.

"Come on," I said. "Get in." The two girls climbed in and sat in the corner. They seemed to have taken no notice of the shooting. I looked back up the road. The sergeant lay in his dirty long-sleeved underwear. I got up with Piani and we started. We were going to try to cross the field. When the road entered the field I got down and walked ahead. If we could get across, there was a road on the other side. We could not get across. It was too soft and muddy for the cars. When they were finally and completely stalled, the wheels dug in to the hubs, we left them in the field and started on foot for Udine.

When we came to the road which led back toward the main highway I pointed down it to the two girls.

"Go down there," I said. "You'll meet people." They looked at me. I took out my pocket-book and gave them each a ten-lira note. "Go down there," I said, pointing. "Friends! Family!"

They did not understand but they held the money tightly and started down the road. They looked back as though they were afraid I might take the money back. I watched them go down the road, their shawls close around them, looking back apprehensively at us. The three drivers were laughing.

"How much will you give me to go in that direction, Tenente?" Bonello asked.

"They're better off in a bunch of people than alone if they catch them," I said.

"Give me two hundred lire and I'll walk straight back toward Austria," Bonello said.

"They'd take it away from you," Piani said.

"Maybe the war will be over," Aymo said. We were going up the road as fast as we could. The sun was trying to come through. Beside the road were mulberry trees. Through the trees I could see our two big moving-vans of cars stuck in the field. Piani looked back too.

"They'll have to build a road to get them out," he said.

"I wish to Christ we had bicycles," Bonello said.

"Do they ride bicycles in America?" Aymo asked.

"They used to."

"Here it is a great thing," Aymo said. "A bicycle is a splendid thing."

"I wish to Christ we had bicycles," Bonello said. "I'm no walker."

"Is that firing?" I asked. I thought I could hear firing a long way away.

"I don't know," Aymo said. He listened.

"I think so," I said.

"The first thing we will see will be the cavalry," Piani said.

"I don't think they've got any cavalry."

"I hope to Christ not," Bonello said. "I don't want to be stuck on a lance by any—— cavalry."

"You certainly shot that sergeant, Tenente," Piani said. We were walking fast.

"I killed him," Bonello said. "I never killed anybody in this war, and all my life I've wanted to kill a sergeant."

"You killed him on the sit all right," Piani said. "He wasn't flying very fast when you killed him."

"Never mind. That's one thing I can always remember. I killed that— of a sergeant."

"What will you say in confession?" Aymo asked.

"I'll say, 'Bless me, father, I killed a sergeant.'" They all laughed.

"He's an anarchist," Piani said. "He doesn't go to church."

"Piani's an anarchist too," Bonello said.

"Are you really anarchists?" I asked.

"No, Tenente. We're socialists. We come from Imola."

"Haven't you ever been there?"

"No."

"By Christ it's a fine place, Tenente. You come there after the war and we'll show you something."

"Are you all socialists?"

"Everybody."

"Is it a fine town?"

"Wonderful. You never saw a town like that."

"How did you get to be socialists?"

"We're all socialists. Everybody is a socialist. We've always been socialists."

"You come, Tenente. We'll make you a socialist too."

Ahead the road turned off to the left and there was a little hill and, beyond a stone wall, an apple orchard. As the road went uphill they ceased talking. We walked along together all going fast against time.

CHAPTER 30

LATER WE WERE on a road that led to a river. There was a long line of abandoned trucks and carts on the road leading up to the bridge. No one was in sight. The river was high and the bridge had been blown up in the centre; the stone arch was fallen into the river and the brown water was going over it. We went on up the bank looking for a place to cross. Up ahead I knew there was a railway bridge and I thought we might be able to get across there. The path was wet and muddy. We did not see any troops; only abandoned trucks and stores. Along the river bank there was nothing and no one but the wet brush and muddy ground. We went up to the bank and finally we saw the railway bridge.

"What a beautiful bridge," Aymo said. It was a long plain iron bridge across what was usually a dry river-bed.

"We'd better hurry and get across before they blow it up," I said.

"There's nobody to blow it up," Piani said. "They're all gone."

"It's probably mined," Bonello said. "You cross first, Tenente."

"Listen to the anarchist," Aymo said. "Make him go first."

"I'll go," I said. "It won't be mined to blow up with one man."

"You see," Piani said. "That is brains. Why haven't you brains, anarchist?"

"If I had brains I wouldn't be here," Bonello said.

"That's pretty good, Tenente," Aymo said.

"That's pretty good," I said. We were close to the bridge now. The sky had clouded over again and it was raining a little. The bridge looked long and solid. We climbed up the embankment.

"Come one at a time," I said and started across the bridge. I watched the ties and the rails for any trip-wires or signs of explosive but I saw nothing. Down below the gaps in the ties the river ran muddy and fast. Ahead across the wet countryside I could see Udine in the rain. Across the bridge I looked back. Just up the river was another bridge. As I watched, a yellow mud-colored motor car crossed it. The sides of the bridge were high and the body of the car, once on, was out of sight. But I saw the heads of the driver, the man on the seat with him, and the two men on the rear seat. They all wore German helmets. Then the car was over the bridge and out of sight behind the trees and the abandoned vehicles on the road. I waved to Aymo who was crossing and to the others to come on. I climbed down and crouched beside the railway embankment. Aymo came down with me.

"Did you see the car?" I asked.

"No. We were watching you."

"A German staff car crossed on the upper bridge."

"A staff car?"

"Yes."

"Holy Mary."

The others came and we all crouched in the mud behind the embankment, looking across the rails at the bridge, the line of trees, the ditch and the road.

"Do you think we're cut off then, Tenente?"

"I don't know. All I know is a German staff car went along that road."

"You don't feel funny, Tenente? You haven't got strange feelings in the head?"

"Don't be funny, Bonello."

"What about a drink?" Piani asked. "If we're cut off we might as well have a drink." He unhooked his canteen and uncorked it.

"Look! Look!" Aymo said and pointed toward the road. Along the top of the stone bridge we could see German helmets moving. They were bent forward and moved smoothly, almost supernaturally, along. As they came off the bridge we saw them. They were bicycle troops. I saw the faces of the first two. They were ruddy and healthy-looking. Their helmets came low down over their foreheads and the side of their faces. Their carbines were clipped to the frame of the bicycles. Stick bombs hung handle down from their belts. Their helmets and their gray uniforms were wet and they rode easily, looking ahead and to both sides. There were two—then four in line, then two, then almost a dozen; then another dozen—then one alone. They did not talk but we could not have heard them because of the noise from the river. They were gone out of sight up the road.

"Holy Mary," Aymo said.

"They were Germans," Piani said. "Those weren't Austrians."

"Why isn't there somebody here to stop them?" I said. "Why haven't they blown the bridge up? Why aren't there machine-guns along this embankment?"

"You tell us, Tenente," Bonello said.

I was very angry.

"The whole bloody thing is crazy. Down below they blow up a little bridge. Here they leave a bridge on the main road. Where is everybody? Don't they try and stop them at all?"

"You tell us, Tenente," Bonello said. I shut up. It was none of my business; all I had to do was to get to Pordenone with three ambulances. I had failed at that. All I had to do now was get to Pordenone. I probably could not even get to Udine. The hell I couldn't. The thing to do was to be calm and not get shot or captured.

"Didn't you have a canteen open?" I asked Piani. He handed it to me. I took a long drink. "We might as well start," I said. "There's no hurry though. Do you want to eat something?"

"This is no place to stay," Bonello said.

"All right. We'll start."

"Should we keep on this side—out of sight?"

"We'd be better off on top. They may come along this bridge too. We don't want them on top of us before we see them."

We walked along the railroad track. On both sides of us stretched the wet plain. Ahead across the plain was the hill of Udine. The roofs fell away from the castle on the hill. We could see the campanile and the clock-tower. There were many mulberry trees in the fields. Ahead I saw a place where the rails were torn up. The ties had been dug out too and thrown down the embankment.

"Down! down!" Aymo said. We dropped down beside the embankment. There was another group of bicyclists passing along the road. I looked over the edge and saw them go on.

"They saw us but they went on," Aymo said.

"We'll get killed up there, Tenente," Bonello said.

"They don't want us," I said. "They're after something else. We're in more danger if they should come on us suddenly."

"I'd rather walk here out of sight," Bonello said.

"All right. We'll walk along the tracks."

"Do you think we can get through?" Aymo asked.

"Sure. There aren't very many of them yet. We'll go through in the dark."

"What was that staff car doing?"

"Christ knows," I said. We kept on up the tracks. Bonello tired of walking in the mud of the embankment and came up with the rest of us. The railway moved south away from the highway now and we could not see what passed along the road. A short bridge over a canal was blown up but we climbed across on what was left of the span. We heard firing ahead of us.

We came up on the railway beyond the canal. It went on straight toward the town across the low fields. We could see the line of the other railway ahead of us. To the north was the main road where we had seen the cyclists; to the south there was a small branch-road across the fields with thick trees on each side. I thought we had better cut to the south and work around the town that way and across country toward Campoformio and the main road to the Tagliamento. We could avoid the main line of the retreat by keeping to the secondary roads beyond Udine. I knew there were plenty of side-roads across the plain. I started down the embankment.

"Come on," I said. We would make for the side-road and work to the south of the town. We all started down the embankment. A shot was fired at us from the side-road. The bullet went into the mud of the embankment.

"Go on back," I shouted. I started up the embankment, slipping in the mud. The drivers were ahead of me. I went up the embankment as fast as I could go. Two more shots came from the thick brush and Aymo, as he was crossing the tracks, lurched, tripped and fell face down. We pulled him down on the other side and turned him over. "His head ought to be uphill," I said. Piani moved him around. He lay in the mud on the side of the embankment, his feet pointing downhill, breathing blood irregularly. The three of us squatted over him in the rain. He was hit low in the back of the neck and the bullet had ranged upward and come out under the right eye. He died while I was stopping up the two holes. Piani laid his head down, wiped at his face, with a piece of the emergency dressing, then let it alone.

"The— ," he said.

"They weren't Germans," I said. "There can't be any Germans over there."

"Italians," Piani said, using the word as an epithet, "Italiani!" Bonello said nothing. He was sitting beside Aymo, not looking at him. Piani picked up Aymo's cap where it had rolled down the embankment and put it over his face. He took out his canteen.

"Do you want a drink?" Piani handed Bonello the canteen.

"No," Bonello said. He turned to me. "That might have happened to us any time on the railway tracks."

"No," I said. "It was because we started across the field."

Bonello shook his head. "Aymo's dead," he said. "Who's dead next, Tenente? Where do we go now?"

"Those were Italians that shot," I said. "They weren't Germans."

"I suppose if they were Germans they'd have killed all of us," Bonello said.

"We are in more danger from Italians than Germans," I said. "The rear guard are afraid of everything. The Germans know what they're after."

"You reason it out, Tenente," Bonello said.

"Where do we go now?" Piani asked.

"We better lie up some place till it's dark. If we could get south we'd be all right."

"They'd have to shoot us all to prove they were right the first time," Bonello said. "I'm not going to try them."

"We'll find a place to lie up as near to Udine as we can get and then go through when it's dark."

"Let's go then," Bonello said. We went down the north side of the embankment. I looked back. Aymo lay in the mud with the angle of the embankment. He was quite small and his arms were by his side, his puttee-wrapped legs and muddy boots together, his cap over his face. He looked very dead. It was raining. I had liked him as well as any one I ever knew. I had his papers in my pocket and would write to his family. Ahead across the fields was a farmhouse. There were trees around it and the farm buildings were built against the house. There was a balcony along the second floor held up by columns.

"We better keep a little way apart," I said. "I'll go ahead." I started toward the farmhouse. There was a path across the field.

Crossing the field, I did not know but that some one would fire on us from the trees near the farmhouse or from the farmhouse itself. I walked toward it, seeing it very clearly. The balcony of the second floor merged into the barn and there was hay coming out between the columns. The courtyard was of stone blocks and all the trees were dripping with the rain. There was a big empty two-wheeled cart, the shafts tipped high up in the rain. I came to the courtyard, crossed it, and stood under the shelter of the balcony. The door of the house was open and I went in. Bonello and Piani came in after me. It was dark inside. I went back to the kitchen. There were ashes of a fire on the big open hearth. The pots hung over the ashes, but they were empty. I looked around but I could not find anything to eat.

"We ought to lie up in the barn," I said. "Do you think you could find anything to eat, Piani, and bring it up there?"

"I'll look," Piani said.

"I'll look too," Bonello said.

"All right," I said. "I'll go up and look at the barn." I found a stone stairway that went up from the stable underneath. The stable smelt dry and pleasant in the rain. The cattle were all gone, probably driven off when they left. The barn was half full of hay. There were two windows in the roof, one was blocked with boards, the other was a narrow dormer window on the north side. There was a chute so that hay might be pitched down to the cattle. Beams crossed the opening down into the main floor where the hay-carts drove in when the hay was hauled in to be pitched up. I heard the rain on the roof and smelled the hay and, when I went down, the clean smell of dried dung in the stable. We could pry a board loose and see out of the south window down into the courtyard. The other window looked out on the field toward the north. We could get out of either window onto the roof and down, or go down the hay chute if the stairs were impractical. It was a big barn and we could hide in the hay if we heard any one. It seemed like a good place. I was sure we could have gotten through to the south if they had not fired on us. It was impossible that there were Germans there. They were coming from the north and down the road from Cividale. They could not have come through from the south. The Italians were even more dangerous. They were frightened and firing on anything they saw. Last night on the retreat we had heard that there had been many Germans in Italian uniforms mixing with the retreat in the north. I did not believe it. That was one of those things you always heard in the war. It was one of the things the enemy always did to you. You did not know any one who went over in

German uniform to confuse them. Maybe they did but it sounded difficult. I did not believe the Germans did it.

I did not believe they had to. There was no need to confuse our retreat. The size of the army and the fewness of the roads did that. Nobody gave any orders, let alone Germans. Still, they would shoot us for Germans. They shot Aymo. The hay smelled good and lying in a barn in the hay took away all the years in between. We had lain in hay and talked and shot sparrows with an air-rifle when they perched in the triangle cut high up in the wall of the barn. The barn was gone now and one year they had cut the hemlock woods and there were only stumps, dried tree-tops, branches and fireweed where the woods had been. You could not go back. If you did not go forward what happened? You never got back to Milan. And if you got back to Milan what happened? I listened to the firing to the north toward Udine. I could hear machine-gun firing. There was no shelling. That was something. They must have gotten some troops along the road. I looked down in the half-light of the hay-barn and saw Piani standing on the hauling floor. He had a long sausage, a jar of something and two bottles of wine under his arm.

"Come up," I said. "There is the ladder." Then I realized that I should help him with the things and went down. I was vague in the head from lying in the hay. I had been nearly asleep.

"Where's Bonello?" I asked.

"I'll tell you," Piani said. We went up the ladder. Up on the hay we set the things down. Piani took out his knife with the corkscrew and drew the cork on a wine bottle.

"They have sealing-wax on it," he said. "It must be good." He smiled.

"Where's Bonello?" I asked.

Piani looked at me.

"He went away, Tenente," he said. "He wanted to be a prisoner."

I did not say anything.

"He was afraid we would get killed."

I held the bottle of wine and did not say anything.

"You see we don't believe in the war anyway, Tenente."

"Why didn't you go?" I asked.

"I did not want to leave you."

"Where did he go?"

"I don't know, Tenente. He went away."

"All right," I said. "Will you cut the sausage?"

Piani looked at me in the half-light.

"I cut it while we were talking," he said. We sat in the hay and ate the sausage and drank the wine. It must have been wine they had saved for a wedding. It was so old that it was losing its color.

"You look out of this window, Luigi," I said. "I'll go look out the other window."

We had each been drinking out of one of the bottles and I took my bottle with me and went over and lay flat on the hay and looked out the narrow window at the wet country. I do not know what I expected to see but I did not see anything except the fields and the bare mulberry trees and the rain falling. I drank the wine and it did not make me feel good. They had kept it too long and it had gone to pieces and lost its quality and color. I watched it get dark outside; the darkness came very quickly. It would be a black night with the rain. When it was dark there was no use watching any more, so I went over to Piani. He was lying asleep and I did not wake him but sat down beside him for a while. He was a big man and he slept heavily. After a while I woke him and we started.

That was a very strange night. I do not know what I had expected, death perhaps and shooting in the dark and running, but nothing happened. We waited, lying flat beyond the ditch along the main road while a German battalion passed, then when they were gone we crossed the road and went on to the north. We were very close to Germans twice in the rain but they did not see us. We got past the town to the north without seeing any Italians, then after a while came on the main channels of the retreat and walked all night toward the Tagliamento. I had not realized how gigantic the retreat was. The whole country was moving, as well as the army. We walked all night, making better time than the vehicles. My leg ached and I was tired but we made good time. It seemed so silly for Bonello to have decided to be taken prisoner. There was no danger. We had walked through two armies without incident. If Aymo had not been killed there would never have seemed to be any danger. No one had bothered us when we were in plain sight along the railway. The killing came suddenly and unreasonably. I wondered where Bonello was.

"How do you feel, Tenente?" Piani asked. We were going along the side of a road crowded with vehicles and troops.

"Fine."

"I'm tired of this walking."

"Well, all we have to do is walk now. We don't have to worry."

"Bonello was a fool."

"He was a fool all right."

"What will you do about him, Tenente?"

"I don't know."

"Can't you just put him down as taken prisoner?"

"I don't know."

"You see if the war went on they would make bad trouble for his family."

"The war won't go on," a soldier said. "We're going home. The war is over."

"Everybody's going home."

"We're all going home."

"Come on, Tenente," Piani said. He wanted to get past them.

"Tenente? Who's a Tenente? A basso gli ufficiali! Down with the officers!"

Piani took me by the arm. "I better call you by your name," he said. "They might try and make trouble. They've shot some officers." We worked up past them.

"I won't make a report that will make trouble for his family." I went on with our conversation.

"If the war is over it makes no difference," Piani said. "But I don't believe it's over. It's too good that it should be over."

"We'll know pretty soon," I said.

"I don't believe it's over. They all think it's over but I don't believe it."

"Viva la Pace!" a soldier shouted out. "We're going home!"

"It would be fine if we all went home," Piani said. "Wouldn't you like to go home?"

"Yes."

"We'll never go. I don't think it's over."

"Andiamo a casa!" a soldier shouted.

"They throw away their rifles," Piani said. "They take them off and drop them down while they're marching. Then they shout."

"They ought to keep their rifles."

"They think if they throw away their rifles they can't make them fight."

In the dark and the rain, making our way along the side of the road I could see that many of the troops still had their rifles. They stuck up above the capes.

"What brigade are you?" an officer called out.

"Brigata di Pace," some one shouted. "Peace Brigade!" The officer said nothing.

"What does he say? What does the officer say?"

"Down with the officer. Viva la Pace!"

"Come on," Piani said. We passed two British ambulances, abandoned in the block of vehicles.

"They're from Gorizia," Piani said. "I know the cars."

"They got further than we did."

"They started earlier."

"I wonder where the drivers are?"

"Up ahead probably."

"The Germans have stopped outside Udine," I said. "These people will all get across the river."

"Yes," Piani said. "That's why I think the war will go on."

"The Germans could come on," I said. "I wonder why they don't come on."

"I don't know. I don't know anything about this kind of war."

"They have to wait for their transport I suppose."

"I don't know," Piani said. Alone he was much gentler. When he was with the others he was a very rough talker.

"Are you married, Luigi?"

"You know I am married."

"Is that why you did not want to be a prisoner?"

"That is one reason. Are you married, Tenente?"

"No."

"Neither is Bonello."

"You can't tell anything by a man's being married. But I should think a married man would want to get back to his wife," I said. I would be glad to talk about wives.

"Yes."

"How are your feet?"

"They're sore enough."

Before daylight we reached the bank of the Tagliamento and followed down along the flooded river to the bridge where all the traffic was crossing.

"They ought to be able to hold at this river," Piani said. In the dark the flood looked high. The water swirled and it was wide. The wooden bridge was nearly three-quarters of a mile across, and the river, that usually ran in narrow channels in the wide stony bed far below the bridge, was close under the wooden planking. We went along the bank and then worked our way into the crowd that were crossing the bridge. Crossing slowly in the rain a few feet above the flood, pressed tight in the crowd, the box of an artillery caisson just ahead, I looked over the side and watched the river. Now that we could not go our own pace I felt very tired. There was no exhilaration in crossing the bridge. I wondered what it would be like if a plane bombed it in the daytime.

"Piani," I said.

"Here I am, Tenente." He was a little ahead in the jam. No one was talking. They were all trying to get across as soon as they could: thinking only of that. We were almost across. At the far end of the bridge there were officers and carabinieri standing on both sides flashing lights. I saw them silhouetted against the sky-line. As we came close to them I saw one of the officers point to a man in the column. A carabiniere went in after him and came out holding the man by the arm. He took him away from the road. We came almost opposite them. The officers were scrutinizing every one in the column, sometimes speaking to each other, going forward to flash a light in some one's face. They took some one else out just before we came opposite. I saw the man. He was a lieutenant-colonel. I saw the stars in the box on his sleeve as they flashed a light on him. His hair was gray and he was short and fat. The carabiniere pulled him in behind the line of officers. As we came opposite I saw one or two of them look at me. Then one pointed at me and spoke to a carabiniere. I saw the carabiniere start for me, come through the edge of the column toward me, then felt him take me by the collar.

"What's the matter with you?" I said and hit him in the face. I saw his face under the hat, upturned mustaches and blood coming down his cheek. Another one dove in toward us.

"What's the matter with you?" I said. He did not answer. He was watching a chance to grab me. I put my arm behind me to loosen my pistol.

"Don't you know you can't touch an officer?"

The other one grabbed me from behind and pulled my arm up so that it twisted in the socket. I turned with him and the other one grabbed me around the neck. I kicked his shins and got my left knee into his groin.

"Shoot him if he resists," I heard some one say.

"What's the meaning of this?" I tried to shout but my voice was not very loud. They had me at the side of the road now.

"Shoot him if he resists," an officer said. "Take him over back."

"Who are you?"

"You'll find out."

"Who are you?"

"Battle police," another officer said.

"Why don't you ask me to step over instead of having one of these airplanes grab me?"

They did not answer. They did not have to answer. They were battle police.

"Take him back there with the others," the first officer said. "You see. He speaks Italian with an accent."

"So do you, you— ," I said.

"Take him back with the others," the first officer said. They took me down behind the line of officers below the road toward a group of people in a field by the river bank. As we walked toward them shots were fired. I saw flashes of the rifles and heard the reports. We came up to the group. There were four officers standing together, with a man in front of them with a carabiniere on each side of him. A group of men were standing guarded by carabinieri. Four other carabinieri stood near the questioning officers, leaning on their carbines. They were wide-hatted carabinieri. The two who had me shoved me in with the group waiting to be questioned. I looked at the man the officers were questioning. He was the fat gray-haired little lieutenant-colonel they had taken out of the column. The questioners had all the efficiency, coldness and command of themselves of Italians who are firing and are not being fired on.

"Your brigade?"

He told them.

"Regiment?"

He told them.

"Why are you not with your regiment?"

He told them.

"Do you not know that an officer should be with his troops?" He did.

That was all. Another officer spoke.

"It is you and such as you that have let the barbarians onto the sacred soil of the fatherland."

"I beg your pardon," said the lieutenant-colonel.

"It is because of treachery such as yours that we have lost the fruits of victory."

"Have you ever been in a retreat?" the lieutenant-colonel asked.

"Italy should never retreat."

We stood there in the rain and listened to this. We were facing the officers and the prisoner stood in front and a little to one side of us.

"If you are going to shoot me," the lieutenant-colonel said, "please shoot me at once without further questioning. The questioning is stupid." He made the sign of the cross. The officers spoke together. One wrote something on a pad of paper.

"Abandoned his troops, ordered to be shot," he said.

Two carabinieri took the lieutenant-colonel to the river bank. He walked in the rain, an old man with his hat off, a carabinieri on either side. I did not watch them shoot him but I heard the shots. They were questioning some one else. This officer too was separated from his troops. He was not allowed to make an explanation. He cried when they read the sentence from the pad of paper, and they were questioning another when they shot him. They made a point of being intent on questioning the next man while the man who had been questioned before was being shot. In this way there was obviously nothing they could do about it. I did not know whether I should wait to be questioned or make a break now. I was obviously a German in Italian uniform. I saw how their minds worked; if they had minds and if they worked. They were all young men and they were saving their country. The second army was being re-formed beyond the Tagliamento. They were executing officers of the rank of major and above who were separated from their troops. They were also dealing summarily with German agitators in Italian uniform. They wore steel helmets. Only two of us had steel helmets. Some of the carabinieri had them. The other carabinieri wore the wide hat. Airplanes we called them. We stood in the rain and were taken out one at a time to be questioned and shot. So far they had shot every one they had questioned. The questioners had that beautiful detachment and devotion to stern justice of men dealing in death without being in any danger of it. They were questioning a full colonel of a line regiment. Three more officers had just been put in with us.

"Where was his regiment?"

I looked at the carabinieri. They were looking at the newcomers. The others were looking at the colonel. I ducked down, pushed between two men, and ran for the river, my head down. I tripped at the edge and went in with a splash. The water was very cold and I stayed under as long as I could. I could feel the current swirl me and I stayed under until I thought I could never come up. The minute I came up I took a breath and went down again. It was easy to stay under with so much clothing and my boots. When I came up the second time I saw a piece of timber ahead of me and reached it and held on with one hand. I kept my head behind it and did not even look over it. I did not want to see the bank. There were shots when I ran and shots when I came up the first time. I heard them when I was almost above water. There were no shots now. The piece of timber swung in the current and I held it with one hand. I looked at the bank. It seemed to be going by very fast. There was much wood in the stream. The water was very cold. We passed the brush of an island above the water. I held onto the timber with both hands and let it take me along. The shore was out of sight now.

CHAPTER 31

YOU DO NOT know how long you are in a river when the current moves swiftly. It seems a long time and it may be very short. The water was cold and in flood and many things passed that had been floated off the banks when the river rose. I was lucky to have a heavy timber to hold on to, and I lay in the icy water with my chin on the wood, holding as easily as I could with both hands. I was afraid of cramps and I hoped we would move toward the shore. We went down the river in a long curve. It was beginning to be light enough so I could see the bushes along the shoreline. There was a brush island ahead and the current moved toward the shore. I wondered if I should take off my boots and clothes and try to swim ashore, but decided not to. I had never thought of anything but that I would reach the shore some way, and I would be in a bad position if I landed barefoot. I had to get to Mestre some way.

I watched the shore come close, then swing away, then come closer again. We were floating more slowly. The shore was very close now. I could see twigs on the willow bush. The timber swung slowly so that the bank was behind me and I knew we were in an eddy. We went slowly around. As I saw the bank again, very close now, I tried holding with one arm and kicking and swimming the timber toward the bank with the other, but I did not bring it any closer. I was afraid we would move out of the eddy and, holding with one hand, I drew up my feet so they were against the side of the timber and shoved hard toward the bank. I could see the brush, but even with my momentum and swimming as hard as I could, the current was taking me away. I thought then I would drown because of my boots, but I thrashed and fought through the water, and when I looked up the bank was coming toward me, and I kept thrashing and swimming in a heavy-footed panic until I reached it. I hung to the willow branch and did not have strength to pull myself up but I knew I would not drown now. It had never occurred to me on the timber that

I might drown. I felt hollow and sick in my stomach and chest from the effort, and I held to the branches and waited. When the sick feeling was gone I pulled into the willow bushes and rested again, my arms around some brush, holding tight with my hands to the branches. Then I crawled out, pushed on through the willows and onto the bank. It was half-daylight and I saw no one. I lay flat on the bank and heard the river and the rain.

After a while I got up and started along the bank. I knew there was no bridge across the river until Latisana. I thought I might be opposite San Vito. I began to think out what I should do. Ahead there was a ditch running into the river. I went toward it. So far I had seen no one and I sat down by some bushes along the bank of the ditch and took off my shoes and emptied them of water. I took off my coat, took my wallet with my papers and my money all wet in it out of the inside pocket and then wrung the coat out. I took off my trousers and wrung them too, then my shirt and under clothing. I slapped and rubbed myself and then dressed again. I had lost my cap.

Before I put on my coat I cut the cloth stars off my sleeves and put them in the inside pocket with my money. My money was wet but was all right. I counted it. There were three thousand and some lire. My clothes felt wet and clammy and I slapped my arms to keep the circulation going. I had woven underwear and I did not think I would catch cold if I kept moving. They had taken my pistol at the road and I put the holster under my coat. I had no cape and it was cold in the rain. I started up the bank of the canal. It was daylight and the country was wet, low and dismal looking. The fields were bare and wet; a long way away I could see a campanile rising out of the plain. I came up onto a road. Ahead I saw some troops coming down the road. I limped along the side of the road and they passed me and paid no attention to me. They were a machine-gun detachment going up toward the river. I went on down the road.

That day I crossed the Venetian plain. It is a low level country and under the rain it is even flatter. Toward the sea there are salt marshes and very few roads. The roads all go along the river mouths to the sea and to cross the country you must go along the paths beside the canals. I was working across the country from the north to the south and had crossed two railway lines and many roads and finally I came out at the end of a path onto a railway line where it ran beside a marsh. It was the main line from Venice to Trieste, with a high solid embankment, a solid roadbed and double track. Down the tracks a way was a flag-station and I could see soldiers on guard. Up the line there was a bridge over a stream that flowed into the marsh. I could see a guard too at the bridge. Crossing the fields to the north I had seen a train pass on this railroad, visible a long way across the flat plain, and I thought a train might come from Portogruaro. I watched the guards and lay down on the embankment so that I could see both ways along the track. The guard at the bridge walked a way up the line toward where I lay, then turned and went back toward the bridge. I lay, and was hungry, and waited for the train. The one I had seen was so long that the engine moved it very slowly and I was sure I could get aboard it. After I had almost given up hoping for one I saw a train coming. The engine, coming straight on, grew larger slowly. I looked at the guard at the bridge. He was walking on the near side of the bridge but on the other side of the tracks. That would put him out of sight when the train passed. I watched the engine come nearer. It was working hard. I could see there were many cars. I knew there would be guards on the train, and I tried to see where they were, but, keeping out of sight, I could not. The engine was almost to where I was lying. When it came opposite, working and puffing even on the level, and I saw the engineer pass, I stood up and stepped up close to the passing cars. If the guards were watching I was a less suspicious object standing beside the track. Several closed freight-cars passed. Then I saw a low open car of the sort they call gondolas coming, covered with canvas. I stood until it had almost passed, then jumped and caught the rear hand-rods and pulled up. I crawled down between the gondola and the shelter of the high freight-car behind. I did not think any one had seen me. I was holding to the hand-rods and crouching low, my feet on the coupling. We were almost opposite the bridge. I remembered the guard. As we passed him he looked at me. He was a boy and his helmet was too big for him. I stared at him contemptuously and he looked away. He thought I had something to do with the train.

We were past. I saw him still looking uncomfortable, watching the other cars pass and I stooped to see how the canvas was fastened. It had grummets and was laced down at the edge with cord. I took out my knife, cut the cord and put my arm under. There were hard bulges under the canvas that tightened in the rain. I looked up and ahead. There was a guard on the freight-car ahead but he was looking forward. I let go of the hand-rails and ducked under the canvas. My forehead hit something that gave me a violent bump and I felt blood on my face but I crawled on in and lay flat. Then I turned around and fastened down the canvas.

I was in under the canvas with guns. They smelled cleanly of oil and grease. I lay and listened to the rain on the canvas and the clicking of the car over the rails. There was a little light came through and I lay and looked at the guns. They had their canvas jackets on. I thought they must have been sent ahead from the third army. The bump on my forehead was swollen and I stopped the bleeding by lying still and letting it coagulate, then picked away the dried blood except over the cut. It was nothing. I had no handkerchief, but feeling with my fingers I washed away where the dried blood had been, with rainwater that dripped from the canvas, and wiped it clean with the sleeve of my coat. I did not want to look conspicuous. I knew I would have to get out before they got to Mestre because they would be taking care of these guns. They had no guns to lose or forget about. I was terrifically hungry.

CHAPTER 32

LYING ON the floor of the flat-car with the guns beside me under the canvas I was wet, cold and very hungry. Finally I rolled over and lay flat on my stomach with my head on my arms. My knee was stiff, but it had been very satisfactory. Valentini had done a fine job. I had done half the retreat on foot and swum part of the Tagliamento with his knee. It was his knee all right. The other knee was mine. Doctors did things to you and then it was not your body any more. The head was mine, and the inside of the belly. It was very hungry in there. I could feel it turn over on itself. The head was mine, but not to use, not to think with, only to remember and not too much remember.

I could remember Catherine but I knew I would get crazy if I thought about her when I was not sure yet I would see her, so I would not think about her, only about her a little, only about her with the car going slowly and clickingly, and some light through the canvas and my lying with Catherine on the floor of the car. Hard as the floor of the car to lie not thinking only feeling, having been away too long, the clothes wet and the floor moving only a little each time and lonesome inside and alone with wet clothing and hard floor for a wife.

You did not love the floor of a flat-car nor guns with canvas jackets and the smell of vaselined metal or a canvas that rain leaked through, although it is very fine under a canvas and pleasant with guns; but you loved some one else whom now you knew was not even to be pretended there; you seeing now very clearly and coldly—not so coldly as clearly and emptily. You saw emptily, lying on your stomach, having been present when one army moved back and another came forward. You had lost your cars and your men as a floorwalker loses the stock of his department in a fire. There was, however, no insurance. You were out of it now. You had no more obligation. If they shot floorwalkers after a fire in the department store because they spoke with an accent they had always had, then certainly the floorwalkers would not be expected to return when the store opened again for business. They might seek other employment; if there was any other employment and the police did not get them.

Anger was washed away in the river along with any obligation. Although that ceased when the carabiniere put his hands on my collar. I would like to have had the uniform off although I did not care much about the outward forms. I had taken off the stars, but that was for convenience. It was no point of honor. I was not against them. I was through. I wished them all the luck. There were the good ones, and the brave ones, and the calm ones and the sensible ones, and they deserved it. But it was not my show any more and I wished this bloody train would get to Mestre and I would eat and stop thinking. I would have to stop.

Piani would tell them they had shot me. They went through the pockets and took the papers of the people they shot. They would not have my papers. They might call me drowned. I wondered what they would hear in the States. Dead from wounds and other causes. Good Christ I was hungry. I wondered what had become of the priest at the mess. And Rinaldi. He was probably at Pordenone. If they had not gone further back. Well, I would never see him now. I would never see any of them now. That life was over. I did not think he had syphilis. It was not a serious disease anyway if you took it in time, they said. But he would worry. I would worry too if I had it. Any one would worry.

I was not made to think. I was made to eat. My God, yes. Eat and drink and sleep with Catherine. To-night maybe. No that was impossible. But to-morrow night, and a good meal and sheets and never going away again except together. Probably have to go damned quickly. She would go. I knew she would go. When would we go? That was something to think about. It was getting dark. I lay and thought where we would go. There were many places.

BOOK FOUR

CHAPTER 33

I DROPPED OFF the train in Milan as it slowed to come into the station early in the morning before it was light. I crossed the track and came out between some buildings and down onto the street. A wine shop was open and I went in for some coffee. It smelled of early morning, of swept dust, spoons in coffee-glasses and the wet circles left by wine-glasses. The proprietor was behind the bar. Two soldiers sat at a table. I stood at the bar and drank a glass of coffee and ate a piece of bread. The coffee was gray with milk, and I skimmed the milk scum off the top with a piece of bread. The proprietor looked at me.

"You want a glass of grappa?"

"No thanks."

"On me," he said and poured a small glass and pushed it toward me. "What's happening at the front?"

"I would not know."

"They are drunk," he said, moving his hand toward the two soldiers. I could believe him. They looked drunk.

"Tell me," he said, "what is happening at the front?"

"I would not know about the front."

"I saw you come down the wall. You came off the train."

"There is a big retreat."

"I read the papers. What happens? Is it over?"

"I don't think so."

He filled the glass with grappa from a short bottle. "If you are in trouble," he said, "I can keep you."

"I am not in trouble."

"If you are in trouble stay here with me."

"Where does one stay?"

"In the building. Many stay here. Any who are in trouble stay here."

"Are many in trouble?"

"It depends on the trouble. You are a South American?"

"No."

"Speak Spanish?"

"A little."

He wiped off the bar.

"It is hard now to leave the country but in no way impossible."

"I have no wish to leave."

"You can stay here as long as you want. You will see what sort of man I am."

"I have to go this morning but I will remember the address to return."

He shook his head. "You won't come back if you talk like that. I thought you were in real trouble."

"I am in no trouble. But I value the address of a friend."

I put a ten-lira note on the bar to pay for the coffee.

"Have a grappa with me," I said.

"It is not necessary."

"Have one."

He poured the two glasses.

"Remember," he said. "Come here. Do not let other people take you in. Here you are all right."

"I am sure."

"You are sure?"

"Yes."

He was serious. "Then let me tell you one thing. Do not go about with that coat."

"Why?"

"On the sleeves it shows very plainly where the stars have been cut away. The cloth is a different color."

I did not say anything.

"If you have no papers I can give you papers."

"What papers?"

"Leave-papers."

"I have no need for papers. I have papers."

"All right," he said. "But if you need papers I can get what you wish."

"How much are such papers?"

"It depends on what they are. The price is reasonable."

"I don't need any now."

He shrugged his shoulders.

"I'm all right," I said.

When I went out he said, "Don't forget that I am your friend."

"No."

"I will see you again," he said.

"Good," I said.

Outside I kept away from the station, where there were military police, and picked up a cab at the edge of the little park. I gave the driver the address of the hospital. At the hospital I went to the porter's lodge. His wife embraced me. He shook my hand.

"You are back. You are safe."

"Yes."

"Have you had breakfast?"

"Yes."

"How are you, Tenente? How are you?" the wife asked.

"Fine."

"Won't you have breakfast with us?"

"No, thank you. Tell me is Miss Barkley here at the hospital now?"

"Miss Barkley?"

"The English lady nurse."

"His girl," the wife said. She patted my arm and smiled.

"No," the porter said. "She is away."

My heart went down. "You are sure? I mean the tall blonde English young lady."

"I am sure. She is gone to Stresa."

"When did she go?"

"She went two days ago with the other lady English."

"Good," I said. "I wish you to do something for me. Do not tell any one you have seen me. It is very important."

"I won't tell any one," the porter said. I gave him a ten-lira note. He pushed it away.

"I promise you I will tell no one," he said. "I don't want any money."

"What can we do for you, Signor Tenente?" his wife asked.

"Only that," I said.

"We are dumb," the porter said. "You will let me know anything I can do?"

"Yes," I said. "Good-by. I will see you again."

They stood in the door, looking after me.

I got into the cab and gave the driver the address of Simmons, one of the men I knew who was studying singing.

Simmons lived a long way out in the town toward the Porta Magenta. He was still in bed and sleepy when I went to see him.

"You get up awfully early, Henry," he said.

"I came in on the early train."

"What's all this retreat? Were you at the front? Will you have a cigarette? They're in that box on the table." It was a big room with a bed beside the wall, a piano over on the far side and a dresser and table. I sat on a chair by the bed. Simmons sat propped up by the pillows and smoked.

"I'm in a jam, Sim," I said.

"So am I," he said. "I'm always in a jam. Won't you smoke?"

"No," I said. "What's the procedure in going to Switzerland?"

"For you? The Italians wouldn't let you out of the country."

"Yes. I know that. But the Swiss. What will they do?"

"They intern you."

"I know. But what's the mechanics of it?"

"Nothing. It's very simple. You can go anywhere. I think you just have to report or something. Why? Are you fleeing the police?"

"Nothing definite yet."

"Don't tell me if you don't want. But it would be interesting to hear. Nothing happens here. I was a great flop at Piacenza."

"I'm awfully sorry."

"Oh yes—I went very badly. I sung well too. I'm going to try it again at the Lyrico here."

"I'd like to be there."

"You're awfully polite. You aren't in a bad mess, are you?"

"I don't know."

"Don't tell me if you don't want. How do you happen to be away from the bloody front?"

"I think I'm through with it."

"Good boy. I always knew you had sense. Can I help you any way?"

"You're awfully busy."

"Not a bit of it, my dear Henry. Not a bit of it. I'd be happy to do anything."

"You're about my size. Would you go out and buy me an outfit of civilian clothes? I've clothes but they're all at Rome."

"You did live there, didn't you? It's a filthy place. How did you ever live there?"

"I wanted to be an architect."

"That's no place for that. Don't buy clothes. I'll give you all the clothes you want. I'll fit you out so you'll be a great success. Go in that dressing room. There's a closet. Take anything you want. My dear fellow, you don't want to buy clothes."

"I'd rather buy them, Sim."

"My dear fellow, it's easier for me to let you have them than go out and buy them. Have you got a passport? You won't get far without a passport."

"Yes. I've still got my passport."

"Then get dressed, my dear fellow, and off to old Helvetia."

"It's not that simple. I have to go up to Stresa first."

"Ideal, my dear fellow. You just row a boat across. If I wasn't trying to sing, I'd go with you. I'll go yet."

"You could take up yodelling."

"My dear fellow, I'll take up yodelling yet. I really can sing though. That's the strange part."

"I'll bet you can sing."

He lay back in bed smoking a cigarette.

"Don't bet too much. But I can sing though. It's damned funny, but I can. I like to sing. Listen." He roared into "Africana," his neck swelling, the veins standing out. "I can sing," he said. "Whether they like it or not." I looked out of the window. "I'll go down and let my cab go."

"Come back up, my dear fellow, and we'll have breakfast." He stepped out of bed, stood straight, took a deep breath and commenced doing bending exercises. I went downstairs and paid off the cab.

CHAPTER 34

IN CIVILIAN CLOTHES I felt a masquerader. I had been in uniform a long time and I missed the feeling of being held by your clothes. The trousers felt very floppy. I had bought a ticket at Milan for Stresa. I had also bought a new hat. I could not wear Sim's hat but his clothes were fine. They smelled of tobacco and as I sat in the compartment and looked out the window the new hat felt very new and the clothes very old. I myself felt as sad as the wet Lombard country that was outside through the window. There were some aviators in the compartment who did not think much of me. They avoided looking at me and were very scornful of a civilian my age. I did not feel insulted. In the old days I would have insulted them and picked a fight. They got off at Gallarate and I was glad to be alone. I had the paper but I did not read it because I did not want to read about the war. I was going to forget the war. I had made a separate peace. I felt damned lonely and was glad when the train got to Stresa.

At the station I had expected to see the porters from the hotels but there was no one. The season had been over a long time and no one met the train. I got down from the train with my bag, it was Sim's bag, and very light to carry, being empty except for two shirts, and stood under the roof of the station in the rain while the train went on. I found a man in the station and asked him if he knew what hotels were open. The Grand-Hôtel & des Isles Borromées was open and several small hotels that stayed open all the year. I started in the rain for the Isles Borromées carrying my bag. I saw a carriage coming down the street and signalled to the driver. It was better to arrive in a carriage. We drove up to the carriage entrance of the big hotel and the concierge came out with an umbrella and was very polite.

I took a good room. It was very big and light and looked out on the lake. The clouds were down over the lake but it would be beautiful with the sunlight. I was expecting my wife, I said. There was a big double bed, a *letto matrimoniale* with a satin coverlet. The hotel was very luxurious. I went down the long halls, down the wide stairs, through the rooms to the bar. I knew the barman and sat on a high stool and ate salted almonds and potato chips. The martini felt cool and clean.

"What are you doing here in *borghese*?" the barman asked after he had mixed a second martini.

"I am on leave. Convalescing-leave."

"There is no one here. I don't know why they keep the hotel open."

"Have you been fishing?"

"I've caught some beautiful pieces. Trolling this time of year you catch some beautiful pieces."

"Did you ever get the tobacco I sent?"

"Yes. Didn't you get my card?"

I laughed. I had not been able to get the tobacco. It was American pipe-tobacco that he wanted, but my relatives had stopped sending it or it was being held up. Anyway it never came.

"I'll get some somewhere," I said. "Tell me have you seen two English girls in the town? They came here day before yesterday."

"They are not at the hotel."

"They are nurses."

"I have seen two nurses. Wait a minute, I will find out where they are."

"One of them is my wife," I said. "I have come here to meet her."

"The other is my wife."

"I am not joking."

"Pardon my stupid joke," he said. "I did not understand." He went away and was gone quite a little while. I ate olives, salted almonds and potato chips and looked at myself in civilian clothes in the mirror behind the bar. The bartender came back. "They are at the little hotel near the station," he said.

"How about some sandwiches?"

"I'll ring for some. You understand there is nothing here, now there are no people."

"Isn't there really any one at all?"

"Yes. There are a few people."

The sandwiches came and I ate three and drank a couple more martinis. I had never tasted anything so cool and clean. They made me feel civilized. I had had too much red wine, bread, cheese, bad coffee and grappa. I sat on the high stool before the pleasant mahogany, the brass and the mirrors and did not think at all. The barman asked me some question.

"Don't talk about the war," I said. The war was a long way away. Maybe there wasn't any war. There was no war here. Then I realized it was over for me. But I did not have the feeling that it was really over. I had the feeling of a boy who thinks of what is happening at a certain hour at the schoolhouse from which he has played truant.

Catherine and Helen Ferguson were at supper when I came to their hotel. Standing in the hallway I saw them at table. Catherine's face was away from me and I saw the line of her hair and her cheek and her lovely neck and shoulders. Ferguson was talking. She stopped when I came in.

"My God," she said.

"Hello," I said.

"Why it's you!" Catherine said. Her face lighted up. She looked too happy to believe it. I kissed her. Catherine blushed and I sat down at the table.

"You're a fine mess," Ferguson said. "What are you doing here? Have you eaten?"

"No." The girl who was serving the meal came in and I told her to bring a plate for me. Catherine looked at me all the time, her eyes happy.

"What are you doing in mufti?" Ferguson asked.

"I'm in the Cabinet."

"You're in some mess."

"Cheer up, Fergy. Cheer up just a little."

"I'm not cheered by seeing you. I know the mess you've gotten this girl into. You're no cheerful sight to me."

Catherine smiled at me and touched me with her foot under the table.

"No one got me in a mess, Fergy. I get in my own messes."

"I can't stand him," Ferguson said. "He's done nothing but ruin you with his sneaking Italian tricks. Americans are worse than Italians."

"The Scotch are such a moral people," Catherine said.

"I don't mean that. I mean his Italian sneakiness."

"Am I sneaky, Fergy?"

"You are. You're worse than sneaky. You're like a snake. A snake with an Italian uniform: with a cape around your neck."

"I haven't got an Italian uniform now."

"That's just another example of your sneakiness. You had a love affair all summer and got this girl with child and now I suppose you'll sneak off."

I smiled at Catherine and she smiled at me.

"We'll both sneak off," she said.

"You're two of the same thing," Ferguson said. "I'm ashamed of you, Catherine Barkley. You have no shame and no honor and you're as sneaky as he is."

"Don't, Fergy," Catherine said and patted her hand. "Don't denounce me. You know we like each other."

"Take your hand away," Ferguson said. Her face was red. "If you had any shame it would be different. But you're God knows how many months gone with child and you think it's a joke and are all smiles because your seducer's come back. You've no shame and no feelings." She began to cry. Catherine went over and put her arm around her. As she stood comforting Ferguson, I could see no change in her figure.

"I don't care," Ferguson sobbed. "I think it's dreadful."

"There, there, Fergy," Catherine comforted her. "I'll be ashamed. Don't cry, Fergy. Don't cry, old Fergy."

"I'm not crying," Ferguson sobbed. "I'm not crying. Except for the awful thing you've gotten into." She looked at me. "I hate you," she said. "She can't make me not hate you. You dirty sneaking American Italian." Her eyes and nose were red with crying.

Catherine smiled at me.

"Don't you smile at him with your arm around me."

"You're unreasonable, Fergy."

"I know it," Ferguson sobbed. "You mustn't mind me, either of you. I'm so upset. I'm not reasonable. I know it. I want you both to be happy."

"We're happy," Catherine said. "You're a sweet Fergy."

Ferguson cried again. "I don't want you happy the way you are. Why don't you get married? You haven't got another wife have you?"

"No," I said. Catherine laughed.

"It's nothing to laugh about," Ferguson said. "Plenty of them have other wives."

"We'll be married, Fergy," Catherine said, "if it will please you."

"Not to please me. You should want to be married."

"We've been very busy."

"Yes. I know. Busy making babies." I thought she was going to cry again but she went into bitterness instead. "I suppose you'll go off with him now to-night?"

"Yes," said Catherine. "If he wants me."

"What about me?"

"Are you afraid to stay here alone?"

"Yes, I am."

"Then I'll stay with you."

"No, go on with him. Go with him right away. I'm sick of seeing both of you."

"We'd better finish dinner."

"No. Go right away."

"Fergy, be reasonable."

"I say get out right away. Go away both of you."

"Let's go then," I said. I was sick of Fergy.

"You do want to go. You see you want to leave me even to eat dinner alone. I've always wanted to go to the Italian lakes and this is how it is. Oh, Oh," she sobbed, then looked at Catherine and choked.

"We'll stay till after dinner," Catherine said. "And I'll not leave you alone if you want me to stay. I won't leave you alone, Fergy."

"No. No. I want you to go. I want you to go." She wiped her eyes. "I'm so unreasonable. Please don't mind me."

The girl who served the meal had been upset by all the crying. Now as she brought in the next course she seemed relieved that things were better.

That night at the hotel, in our room with the long empty hall outside and our shoes outside the door, a thick carpet on the floor of the room, outside the windows the rain falling and in the room light and pleasant and cheerful, then the light out and it exciting with smooth sheets and the bed comfortable, feeling that we had come home, feeling no longer alone, waking in the night to find the other one there, and not gone away; all other things were unreal. We slept when we were tired and if we woke the other one woke too so one was not alone. Often a man wishes to be alone and a girl wishes to be alone too and if they love each other they are jealous of that in each other, but I can truly say we never felt that. We could feel alone when we were together, alone against the others. It has only happened to me like that once. I have been alone while I was with many girls and that is the way that you can be most lonely. But we were never lonely and never afraid when we were together. I know that the night is not the same as the day: that all things are different, that the things of the night cannot be explained in the day, because they do not then exist, and the night can be a dreadful time for lonely people once their loneliness has started. But with Catherine there was almost no difference in the night except that it was an even better time. If people bring so much courage to this world the world has to kill them to break them, so of course it kills them. The world breaks every one and afterward many are strong at the broken places. But those that will not break it kills. It kills the very good and the very gentle and the very brave impartially. If you are none of these you can be sure it will kill you too but there will be no special hurry.

I remember waking in the morning. Catherine was asleep and the sunlight was coming in through the window. The rain had stopped and I stepped out of bed and across the floor to the window. Down below were the gardens, bare now but beautifully regular, the gravel paths, the trees, the stone wall by the lake and the lake in the sunlight with the mountains beyond. I stood at the window looking out and when I turned away I saw Catherine was awake and watching me.

"How are you, darling?" she said. "Isn't it a lovely day?"

"How do you feel?"

"I feel very well. We had a lovely night."

"Do you want breakfast?"

She wanted breakfast. So did I and we had it in bed, the November sunlight coming in the window, and the breakfast tray across my lap.

"Don't you want the paper? You always wanted the paper in the hospital."

"No," I said. "I don't want the paper now."

"Was it so bad you don't want even to read about it?"

"I don't want to read about it."

"I wish I had been with you so I would know about it too."

"I'll tell you about it if I ever get it straight in my head."

"But won't they arrest you if they catch you out of uniform?"

"They'll probably shoot me."

"Then we'll not stay here. We'll get out of the country."

"I'd thought something of that."

"We'll get out. Darling, you shouldn't take silly chances. Tell me how did you come from Mestre to Milan?"

"I came on the train. I was in uniform then."

"Weren't you in danger then?"

"Not much. I had an old order of movement. I fixed the dates on it in Mestre."

"Darling, you're liable to be arrested here any time. I won't have it. It's silly to do something like that. Where would we be if they took you off?"

"Let's not think about it. I'm tired of thinking about it."

"What would you do if they came to arrest you?"

"Shoot them."

"You see how silly you are, I won't let you go out of the hotel until we leave here."

"Where are we going to go?"

"Please don't be that way, darling. We'll go wherever you say. But please find some place to go right away."

"Switzerland is down the lake, we can go there."

"That will be lovely."

It was clouding over outside and the lake was darkening.

"I wish we did not always have to live like criminals," I said.

"Darling, don't be that way. You haven't lived like a criminal very long. And we never live like criminals. We're going to have a fine time."

"I feel like a criminal. I've deserted from the army."

"Darling, please be sensible. It's not deserting from the army. It's only the Italian army."

I laughed. "You're a fine girl. Let's get back into bed. I feel fine in bed."

A little while later Catherine said, "You don't feel like a criminal do you?"

"No," I said. "Not when I'm with you."

"You're such a silly boy," she said. "But I'll look after you. Isn't it splendid, darling, that I don't have any morning-sickness?"

"It's grand."

"You don't appreciate what a fine wife you have. But I don't care. I'll get you some place where they can't arrest you and then we'll have a lovely time."

"Let's go there right away."

"We will, darling. I'll go any place any time you wish."

"Let's not think about anything."

"All right."

CHAPTER 35

CATHERINE went along the lake to the little hotel to see Ferguson and I sat in the bar and read the papers. There were comfortable leather chairs in the bar and I sat in one of them and read until the barman came in. The army had not stood at the Tagliamento. They were falling back to the Piave. I remembered the Piave. The railroad crossed it near San Dona going up to the front. It was deep and slow there and quite narrow. Down below there were mosquito marshes and canals. There were some lovely villas. Once, before the war, going up to Cortina D'Ampezzo I had gone along it for several hours in the hills. Up there it looked like a trout stream, flowing swiftly with shallow stretches and pools under the shadow of the rocks. The road turned off from it at Cadore. I wondered how the army that was up there would come down. The barman came in.

"Count Greffi was asking for you," he said.

"Who?"

"Count Greffi. You remember the old man who was here when you were here before."

"Is he here?"

"Yes, he's here with his niece. I told him you were here. He wants you to play billiards."

"Where is he?"

"He's taking a walk."

"How is he?"

"He's younger than ever. He drank three champagne cocktails last night before dinner."

"How's his billiard game?"

"Good. He beat me. When I told him you were here he was very pleased. There's nobody here for him to play with."

Count Greffi was ninety-four years old. He had been a contemporary of Metternich and was an old man with white hair and mustache and beautiful manners. He had been in the diplomatic service of both Austria and Italy and his birthday parties were the great social event of Milan. He was living to be one hundred years old and played a smoothly fluent game of billiards that contrasted with his own ninety-four-year-old brittleness. I had met him when I had been at Stresa once before out of season and while we played billiards we drank champagne. I thought it was a splendid custom and he gave me fifteen points in a hundred and beat me.

"Why didn't you tell me he was here?"

"I forgot it."

"Who else is here?"

"No one you know. There are only six people altogether."

"What are you doing now?"

"Nothing."

"Come on out fishing."

"I could come for an hour."

"Come on. Bring the trolling line."

The barman put on a coat and we went out. We went down and got a boat and I rowed while the barman sat in the stern and let out the line with a spinner and a heavy sinker on the end to troll for lake trout. We rowed along the shore, the barman holding the line in his hand and giving it occasional jerks forward. Stresa looked very deserted from the lake. There were the long rows of bare trees, the big hotels and the closed villas. I rowed across to Isola Bella and went close to the walls, where the water deepened sharply, and you saw the rock wall slanting down in the clear water, and then up and along to the fisherman's island. The sun was under a cloud and the water was dark and smooth and very cold. We did not have a strike though we saw some circles on the water from rising fish.

I rowed up opposite the fisherman's island where there were boats drawn up and men were mending nets.

"Should we get a drink?"

"All right."

I brought the boat up to the stone pier and the barman pulled in the line, coiling it on the bottom of the boat and hooking the spinner on the edge of the gunwale. I stepped out and tied the boat. We went into a little café, sat at a bare wooden table and ordered vermouth.

"Are you tired from rowing?"

"I'll row back," he said.

"I like to row."

"Maybe if you hold the line it will change the luck."

"All right."

"Tell me how goes the war."

"Rotten."

"I don't have to go. I'm too old, like Count Greffi."

"Maybe you'll have to go yet."

"Next year they'll call my class. But I won't go."

"What will you do?"

"Get out of the country. I wouldn't go to war. I was at the war once in Abyssinia. Nix. Why do you go?"

"I don't know. I was a fool."

"Have another vermouth?"

"All right."

The barman rowed back. We trolled up the lake beyond Stresa and then down not far from shore. I held the taut line and felt the faint pulsing of the spinner revolving while I looked at the dark November water of the lake and the deserted shore. The barman rowed with long strokes and on the forward thrust of the boat the line throbbed. Once I had a strike: the line hardened suddenly and jerked back. I pulled and felt the live weight of the trout and then the line throbbed again. I had missed him.

"Did he feel big?"

"Pretty big."

"Once when I was out trolling alone I had the line in my teeth and one struck and nearly took my mouth out."

"The best way is to have it over your leg," I said. "Then you feel it and don't lose your teeth."

I put my hand in the water. It was very cold. We were almost opposite the hotel now.

"I have to go in," the barman said, "to be there for eleven o'clock. L'heure du cocktail."

"All right."

I pulled in the line and wrapped it on a stick notched at each end. The barman put the boat in a little slip in the stone wall and locked it with a chain and padlock.

"Any time you want it," he said, "I'll give you the key."

"Thanks."

We went up to the hotel and into the bar. I did not want another drink so early in the morning so I went up to our room. The maid had just finished doing the room and Catherine was not back yet. I lay down on the bed and tried to keep from thinking.

When Catherine came back it was all right again. Ferguson was downstairs, she said. She was coming to lunch.

"I knew you wouldn't mind," Catherine said.

"No," I said.

"What's the matter, darling?"

"I don't know."

"I know. You haven't anything to do. All you have is me and I go away."

"That's true."

"I'm sorry, darling. I know it must be a dreadful feeling to have nothing at all suddenly."

"My life used to be full of everything," I said. "Now if you aren't with me I haven't a thing in the world."

"But I'll be with you. I was only gone for two hours. Isn't there anything you can do?"

"I went fishing with the barman."

"Wasn't it fun?"

"Yes."

"Don't think about me when I'm not here."

"That's the way I worked it at the front. But there was something to do then."

"Othello with his occupation gone," she teased.

"Othello was a nigger," I said. "Besides, I'm not jealous. I'm just so in love with you that there isn't anything else."

"Will you be a good boy and be nice to Ferguson?"

"I'm always nice to Ferguson unless she curses me."

"Be nice to her. Think how much we have and she hasn't anything."

"I don't think she wants what we have."

"You don't know much, darling, for such a wise boy."

"I'll be nice to her."

"I know you will. You're so sweet."

"She won't stay afterward, will she?"

"No. I'll get rid of her."

"And then we'll come up here."

"Of course. What do you think I want to do?"

We went downstairs to have lunch with Ferguson. She was very impressed by the hotel and the splendor of the dining-room. We had a good lunch with a couple of bottles of white capri. Count Greffi came into the dining-room and bowed to us. His niece, who looked a little like my grandmother, was with him. I told Catherine and Ferguson about him and Ferguson was very impressed. The hotel was very big and grand and empty but the food was good, the wine was very pleasant and finally the wine made us all feel very well. Catherine had no need to feel any better. She was very happy. Ferguson became quite cheerful. I felt very well myself. After lunch Ferguson went back to her hotel. She was going to lie down for a while after lunch she said.

Along late in the afternoon some one knocked on our door.

"Who is it?"

"The Count Greffi wishes to know if you will play billiards with him."

I looked at my watch; I had taken it off and it was under the pillow.

"Do you have to go, darling?" Catherine whispered.

"I think I'd better." The watch was a quarter-past four o'clock. Out loud I said, "Tell the Count Greffi I will be in the billiard-room at five o'clock."

At a quarter to five I kissed Catherine good-by and went into the bathroom to dress. Knotting my tie and looking in the glass I looked strange to myself in the civilian clothes. I must remember to buy some more shirts and socks.

"Will you be away a long time?" Catherine asked. She looked lovely in the bed. "Would you hand me the brush?"

I watched her brushing her hair, holding her head so the weight of her hair all came on one side. It was dark outside and the light over the head of the bed shone on her hair and on her neck and shoulders. I went over and kissed her and held her hand with the brush and her head sunk back on the pillow. I kissed her neck and shoulders. I felt faint with loving her so much.

"I don't want to go away."

"I don't want you to go away."

"I won't go then."

"Yes. Go. It's only for a little while and then you'll come back."

"We'll have dinner up here."

"Hurry and come back."

I found the Count Greffi in the billiard-room. He was practicing strokes, looking very fragile under the light that came down above the billiard table. On a card table a little way beyond the light was a silver icing-bucket with the necks and corks of two champagne bottles showing above the ice. The Count Greffi straightened up when I came toward the table and walked toward me. He put out his hand, "It is such a great pleasure that you are here. You were very kind to come to play with me."

"It was very nice of you to ask me."

"Are you quite well? They told me you were wounded on the Isonzo. I hope you are well again."

"I'm very well. Have you been well?"

"Oh, I am always well. But I am getting old. I detect signs of age now."

"I can't believe it."

"Yes. Do you want to know one? It is easier for me to talk Italian. I discipline myself but I find when I am tired that it is so much easier to talk Italian. So I know I must be getting old."

"We could talk Italian. I am a little tired, too."

"Oh, but when you are tired it will be easier for you to talk English."

"American."

"Yes. American. You will please talk American. It is a delightful language."

"I hardly ever see Americans."

"You must miss them. One misses one's countrymen and especially one's countrywomen. I know that experience. Should we play or are you too tired?"

"I'm not really tired. I said that for a joke. What handicap will you give me?"

"Have you been playing very much?"

"None at all."

"You play very well. Ten points in a hundred?"

"You flatter me."

"Fifteen?"

"That would be fine but you will beat me."

"Should we play for a stake? You always wished to play for a stake."

"I think we'd better."

"All right. I will give you eighteen points and we will play for a franc a point."

He played a lovely game of billiards and with the handicap I was only four ahead at fifty. Count Greffi pushed a button on the wall to ring for the barman.

"Open one bottle please," he said. Then to me, "We will take a little stimulant." The wine was icy cold and very dry and good.

"Should we talk Italian? Would you mind very much? It is my weakness now."

We went on playing, sipping the wine between shots, speaking in Italian, but talking little, concentrated on the game. Count Greffi made his one hundredth point and with the handicap I was only at ninety-four. He smiled and patted me on the shoulder.

"Now we will drink the other bottle and you will tell me about the war." He waited for me to sit down.

"About anything else," I said.

"You don't want to talk about it? Good. What have you been reading?"

"Nothing," I said. "I'm afraid I am very dull."

"No. But you should read."

"What is there written in war-time?"

"There is 'Le Feu' by a Frenchman, Barbusse. There is 'Mr. Britling Sees Through It.'"

"No, he doesn't."

"What?"

"He doesn't see through it. Those books were at the hospital."

"Then you have been reading?"

"Yes, but nothing any good."

"I thought 'Mr. Britling' a very good study of the English middle-class soul."

"I don't know about the soul."

"Poor boy. We none of us know about the soul. Are you Croyant?"

"At night."

Count Greffi smiled and turned the glass with his fingers. "I had expected to become more devout as I grow older but somehow I haven't," he said. "It is a great pity."

"Would you like to live after death?" I asked and instantly felt a fool to mention death. But he did not mind the word.

"It would depend on the life. This life is very pleasant. I would like to live forever," he smiled. "I very nearly have."

We were sitting in the deep leather chairs, the champagne in the ice-bucket and our glasses on the table between us.

"If you ever live to be as old as I am you will find many things strange."

"You never seem old."

"It is the body that is old. Sometimes I am afraid I will break off a finger as one breaks a stick of chalk. And the spirit is no older and not much wiser."

"You are wise."

"No, that is the great fallacy; the wisdom of old men. They do not grow wise. They grow careful."

"Perhaps that is wisdom."

"It is a very unattractive wisdom. What do you value most?"

"Some one I love."

"With me it is the same. That is not wisdom. Do you value life?"

"Yes."

"So do I. Because it is all I have. And to give birthday parties," he laughed. "You are probably wiser than I am. You do not give birthday parties."

We both drank the wine.

"What do you think of the war really?" I asked.

"I think it is stupid."

"Who will win it?"

"Italy."

"Why?"

"They are a younger nation."

"Do younger nations always win wars?"

"They are apt to for a time."

"Then what happens?"

"They become older nations."

"You said you were not wise."

"Dear boy, that is not wisdom. That is cynicism."

"It sounds very wise to me."

"It's not particularly. I could quote you the examples on the other side. But it is not bad. Have we finished the champagne?"

"Almost."

"Should we drink some more? Then I must dress."

"Perhaps we'd better not now."

"You are sure you don't want more?"

"Yes." He stood up.

"I hope you will be very fortunate and very happy and very, very healthy."

"Thank you. And I hope you will live forever."

"Thank you. I have. And if you ever become devout pray for me if I am dead. I am asking several of my friends to do that. I had expected to become devout myself but it has not come." I thought he smiled sadly but I could not tell. He was so old and his face was very wrinkled, so that a smile used so many lines that all gradations were lost.

"I might become very devout," I said. "Anyway, I will pray for you."

"I had always expected to become devout. All my family died very devout. But somehow it does not come."

"It's too early."

"Maybe it is too late. Perhaps I have outlived my religious feeling."

"My own comes only at night."

"Then too you are in love. Do not forget that is a religious feeling."

"You believe so?"

"Of course." He took a step toward the table. "You were very kind to play."

"It was a great pleasure."

"We will walk up stairs together."

CHAPTER 36

THAT NIGHT THERE was a storm and I woke to hear the rain lashing the window-panes. It was coming in the open window. Some one had knocked on the door. I went to the door very softly, not to disturb Catherine, and opened it. The barman stood there. He wore his overcoat and carried his wet hat.

"Can I speak to you, Tenente?"

"What's the matter?"

"It's a very serious matter."

I looked around. The room was dark. I saw the water on the floor from the window. "Come in," I said. I took him by the arm into the bathroom; locked the door and put on the light. I sat down on the edge of the bathtub.

"What's the matter, Emilio? Are you in trouble?"

"No. You are, Tenente."

"Yes?"

"They are going to arrest you in the morning."

"Yes?"

"I came to tell you. I was out in the town and I heard them talking in a café."

"I see."

He stood there, his coat wet, holding his wet hat and said nothing.

"Why are they going to arrest me?"

"For something about the war."

"Do you know what?"

"No. But I know that they know you were here before as an officer and now you are here out of uniform. After this retreat they arrest everybody."

I thought a minute.

"What time do they come to arrest me?"

"In the morning. I don't know the time."

"What do you say to do?"

He put his hat in the washbowl. It was very wet and had been dripping on the floor.

"If you have nothing to fear an arrest is nothing. But it is always bad to be arrested—especially now."

"I don't want to be arrested."

"Then go to Switzerland."

"How?"

"In my boat."

"There is a storm," I said.

"The storm is over. It is rough but you will be all right."

"When should we go?"

"Right away. They might come to arrest you early in the morning."

"What about our bags?"

"Get them packed. Get your lady dressed. I will take care of them."

"Where will you be?"

"I will wait here. I don't want any one to see me outside in the hall."

I opened the door, closed it, and went into the bedroom. Catherine was awake.

"What is it, darling?"

"It's all right, Cat," I said. "Would you like to get dressed right away and go in a boat to Switzerland?"

"Would you?"

"No," I said. "I'd like to go back to bed."

"What is it about?"

"The barman says they are going to arrest me in the morning."

"Is the barman crazy?"

"No."

"Then please hurry, darling, and get dressed so we can start." She sat up on the side of the bed. She was still sleepy. "Is that the barman in the bathroom?"

"Yes."

"Then I won't wash. Please look the other way, darling, and I'll be dressed in just a minute."

I saw her white back as she took off her night-gown and then I looked away because she wanted me to. She was beginning to be a little big with the child and she did not want me to see her. I dressed hearing the rain on the windows. I did not have much to put in my bag.

"There's plenty of room in my bag, Cat, if you need any."

"I'm almost packed," she said. "Darling, I'm awfully stupid, but why is the barman in the bathroom?"

"Sh—he's waiting to take our bags down."

"He's awfully nice."

"He's an old friend," I said. "I nearly sent him some pipe-tobacco once."

I looked out the open window at the dark night. I could not see the lake, only the dark and the rain but the wind was quieter.

"I'm ready, darling," Catherine said.

"All right." I went to the bathroom door. "Here are the bags, Emilio," I said. The barman took the two bags.

"You're very good to help us," Catherine said.

"That's nothing, lady," the barman said. "I'm glad to help you just so I don't get in trouble myself. Listen," he said to me. "I'll take these out the servants' stairs and to the boat. You just go out as though you were going for a walk."

"It's a lovely night for a walk," Catherine said.

"It's a bad night all right."

"I'm glad I've an umbrella," Catherine said.

We walked down the hall and down the wide thickly carpeted stairs. At the foot of the stairs by the door the porter sat behind his desk.

He looked surprised at seeing us.

"You're not going out, sir?" he said.

"Yes," I said. "We're going to see the storm along the lake."

"Haven't you got an umbrella, sir?"

"No," I said. "This coat sheds water."

He looked at it doubtfully. "I'll get you an umbrella, sir," he said. He went away and came back with a big umbrella. "It is a little big, sir," he said. I gave him a ten-lira note. "Oh you are too good, sir. Thank you very much," he said. He held the door open and we went out into the rain. He smiled at Catherine and she smiled at him. "Don't stay out in the storm," he said. "You will get wet, sir and lady." He was only the second porter, and his English was still literally translated.

"We'll be back," I said. We walked down the path under the giant umbrella and out through the dark wet gardens to the road and across the road to the trellised pathway along the lake. The wind was blowing offshore now. It was a cold, wet November wind and I knew it was snowing in the mountains. We came along past the chained boats in the slips along the quay to where the barman's boat should be. The water was dark against the stone. The barman stepped out from beside the row of trees.

"The bags are in the boat," he said.

"I want to pay you for the boat," I said.

"How much money have you?"

"Not so much."

"You send me the money later. That will be all right."

"How much?"

"What you want."

"Tell me how much."

"If you get through send me five hundred francs. You won't mind that if you get through."

"All right."

"Here are sandwiches." He handed me a package. "Everything there was in the bar. It's all here. This is a bottle of brandy and a bottle of wine." I put them in my bag. "Let me pay you for those."

"All right, give me fifty lire."

I gave it to him. "The brandy is good," he said. "You don't need to be afraid to give it to your lady. She better get in the boat." He held the boat, it rising and falling against the stone wall and I helped Catherine in. She sat in the stern and pulled her cape around her.

"You know where to go?"

"Up the lake."

"You know how far?"

"Past Luino."

"Past Luino, Cannero, Cannobio, Tranzano. You aren't in Switzerland until you come to Brissago. You have to pass Monte Tamara."

"What time is it?" Catherine asked.

"It's only eleven o'clock," I said.

"If you row all the time you ought to be there by seven o'clock in the morning."

"Is it that far?"

"It's thirty-five kilometres."

"How should we go? In this rain we need a compass."

"No. Row to Isola Bella. Then on the other side of Isola Madre go with the wind. The wind will take you to Pallanza. You will see the lights. Then go up the shore."

"Maybe the wind will change."

"No," he said. "This wind will blow like this for three days. It comes straight down from the Mattarone. There is a can to bail with."

"Let me pay you something for the boat now."

"No, I'd rather take a chance. If you get through you pay me all you can."

"All right."

"I don't think you'll get drowned."

"That's good."

"Go with the wind up the lake."

"All right." I stepped in the boat.

"Did you leave the money for the hotel?"

"Yes. In an envelope in the room."

"All right. Good luck, Tenente."

"Good luck. We thank you many times."

"You won't thank me if you get drowned."

"What does he say?" Catherine asked.

"He says good luck."

"Good luck," Catherine said. "Thank you very much."

"Are you ready?"

"Yes."

He bent down and shoved us off. I dug at the water with the oars, then waved one hand. The barman waved back deprecatingly. I saw the lights of the hotel and rowed out, rowing straight out until they were out of sight. There was quite a sea running but we were going with the wind.

CHAPTER 37

I ROWED in the dark keeping the wind in my face. The rain had stopped and only came occasionally in gusts. It was very dark, and the wind was cold. I could see Catherine in the stern but I could not see the water where the blades of the oars dipped. The oars were long and there were no leathers to keep them from slipping out. I pulled, raised, leaned forward, found the water, dipped and pulled, rowing as easily as I could. I did not feather the oars because the wind was with us. I knew my hands would blister and I wanted to delay it as long as I could. The boat was light and rowed easily. I pulled it along in the dark water. I could not see, and hoped we would soon come opposite Pallanza.

We never saw Pallanza. The wind was blowing up the lake and we passed the point that hides Pallanza in the dark and never saw the lights. When we finally saw some lights much further up the lake and close to the shore it was Intra. But for a long time we did not see any lights, nor did we see the shore but rowed steadily in the dark riding with the waves. Sometimes I missed the water with the oars in the dark as a wave lifted the boat. It was quite rough; but I kept on rowing, until suddenly we were close ashore against a point of rock that rose beside us; the waves striking against it, rushing high up, then falling back. I pulled hard on the right oar and backed water with the other and we went out into the lake again; the point was out of sight and we were going on up the lake.

"We're across the lake," I said to Catherine.

"Weren't we going to see Pallanza?"

"We've missed it."

"How are you, darling?"

"I'm fine."

"I could take the oars awhile."

"No, I'm fine."

"Poor Ferguson," Catherine said. "In the morning she'll come to the hotel and find we're gone."

"I'm not worrying so much about that," I said, "as about getting into the Swiss part of the lake before it's daylight and the custom guards see us."

"Is it a long way?"

"It's some thirty kilometres from here."

I rowed all night. Finally my hands were so sore I could hardly close them over the oars. We were nearly smashed up on the shore several times. I kept fairly close to the shore because I was afraid of getting lost on the lake and losing time. Sometimes we were so close we could see a row of trees and the road along the shore with the mountains behind. The rain stopped and the wind drove the clouds so that the moon shone through and looking back I could see the long dark point of Castagnola and the lake with white-caps and beyond, the moon on the high snow mountains. Then the clouds came over the moon again and the mountains and the lake were gone, but it was much lighter than it had been before and we could see the shore. I could see it too clearly and pulled out where they would not see the boat if there were custom guards along the Pallanza road. When the moon came out again we could see white villas on the shore on the slopes of the mountain and the white road where it showed through the trees. All the time I was rowing.

The lake widened and across it on the shore at the foot of the mountains on the other side we saw a few lights that should be Luino. I saw a wedgelike gap between the mountains on the other shore and I thought that must be Luino. If it was we were making good time. I pulled in the oars and lay back on the seat. I was very, very tired of rowing. My arms and shoulders and back ached and my hands were sore.

"I could hold the umbrella," Catherine said. "We could sail with that with the wind."

"Can you steer?"

"I think so."

"You take this oar and hold it under your arm close to the side of the boat and steer and I'll hold the umbrella." I went back to the stern and showed her how to hold the oar. I took the big umbrella the porter had given me and sat facing the bow and opened it. It opened with a clap. I held it on both sides, sitting astride the handle hooked over the seat. The wind was full in it and I felt the boat suck forward while I held as hard as I could to the two edges. It pulled hard. The boat was moving fast.

"We're going beautifully," Catherine said. All I could see was umbrella ribs. The umbrella strained and pulled and I felt us driving along with it. I braced my feet and held back on it, then suddenly, it buckled; I felt a rib snap on my forehead, I tried to grab the top that was bending with the wind and the whole thing buckled and went inside out and I was astride the handle of an inside-out, ripped umbrella, where I had been holding a wind-filled pulling sail. I unhooked the handle from the seat, laid the umbrella in the bow and went back to Catherine for the oar. She was laughing. She took my hand and kept on laughing.

"What's the matter?" I took the oar.

"You looked so funny holding that thing."

"I suppose so."

"Don't be cross, darling. It was awfully funny. You looked about twenty feet broad and very affectionate holding the umbrella by the edges—" she choked.

"I'll row."

"Take a rest and a drink. It's a grand night and we've come a long way."

"I have to keep the boat out of the trough of the waves."

"I'll get you a drink. Then rest a little while, darling."

I held the oars up and we sailed with them. Catherine was opening the bag. She handed me the brandy bottle. I pulled the cork with my pocket-knife and took a long drink. It was smooth and hot and the heat went all through me and I felt warmed and cheerful. "It's lovely brandy," I said. The moon was under again but I could see the shore. There seemed to be another point going out a long way ahead into the lake.

"Are you warm enough, Cat?"

"I'm splendid. I'm a little stiff."

"Bail out that water and you can put your feet down."

Then I rowed and listened to the oarlocks and the dip and scrape of the bailing tin under the stern seat.

"Would you give me the bailer?" I said. "I want a drink."

"It's awful dirty."

"That's all right. I'll rinse it."

I heard Catherine rinsing it over the side. Then she handed it to me dipped full of water. I was thirsty after the brandy and the water was icy cold, so cold it made my teeth ache. I looked toward the shore. We were closer to the long point. There were lights in the bay ahead.

"Thanks," I said and handed back the tin pail.

"You're ever so welcome," Catherine said. "There's much more if you want it."

"Don't you want to eat something?"

"No. I'll be hungry in a little while. We'll save it till then."

"All right."

What looked like a point ahead was a long high headland. I went further out in the lake to pass it. The lake was much narrower now. The moon was out again and the guardia di finanza could have seen our boat black on the water if they had been watching.

"How are you, Cat?" I asked.

"I'm all right. Where are we?"

"I don't think we have more than about eight miles more."

"That's a long way to row, you poor sweet. Aren't you dead?"

"No. I'm all right. My hands are sore is all."

We went on up the lake. There was a break in the mountains on the right bank, a flattening-out with a low shore line that I thought must be Cannobio. I stayed a long way out because it was from now on that we ran the most danger of meeting guardia. There was a high dome-capped mountain on the other shore a way ahead. I was tired. It was no great distance to row but when you were out of condition it had been a long way. I knew I had to pass that mountain and go up the lake at least five miles further before we would be in Swiss water. The moon was almost down now but before it went down the sky clouded over again and it was very dark. I stayed well out in the lake, rowing awhile, then resting and holding the oars so that the wind struck the blades.

"Let me row awhile," Catherine said.

"I don't think you ought to."

"Nonsense. It would be good for me. It would keep me from being too stiff."

"I don't think you should, Cat."

"Nonsense. Rowing in moderation is very good for the pregnant lady."

"All right, you row a little moderately. I'll go back, then you come up. Hold on to both gunwales when you come up."

I sat in the stern with my coat on and the collar turned up and watched Catherine row. She rowed very well but the oars were too long and bothered her. I opened the bag and ate a couple of sandwiches and took a drink of the brandy. It made everything much better and I took another drink.

"Tell me when you're tired," I said. Then a little later, "Watch out the oar doesn't pop you in the tummy."

"If it did"—Catherine said between strokes— "life might be much simpler."

I took another drink of the brandy.

"How are you going?"

"All right."

"Tell me when you want to stop."

"All right."

I took another drink of the brandy, then took hold of the two gunwales of the boat and moved forward.

"No. I'm going beautifully."

"Go on back to the stern. I've had a grand rest."

For a while, with the brandy, I rowed easily and steadily. Then I began to catch crabs and soon I was just chopping along again with a thin brown taste of bile from having rowed too hard after the brandy.

"Give me a drink of water, will you?" I said.

"That's easy," Catherine said.

Before daylight it started to drizzle. The wind was down or we were protected by mountains that bounded the curve the lake had made. When I knew daylight was coming I settled down and rowed hard. I did not know where we were and I wanted to get into the Swiss part of the lake. When it was beginning to be daylight we were quite close to the shore. I could see the rocky shore and the trees.

"What's that?" Catherine said. I rested on the oars and listened. It was a motor boat chugging out on the lake. I pulled close up to the shore and lay quiet. The chugging came closer; then we saw the motor boat in the rain a little astern of us. There were four guardia di finanza in the stern, their alpini hats pulled down, their cape collars turned up and their carbines slung across their backs. They all looked sleepy so early in the morning. I could see the yellow on their hats and the yellow marks on their cape collars. The motor boat chugged on and out of sight in the rain.

I pulled out into the lake. If we were that close to the border I did not want to be hailed by a sentry along the road. I stayed out where I could just see the shore and rowed on for three quarters of an hour in the rain. We heard a motor boat once more but I kept quiet until the noise of the engine went away across the lake.

"I think we're in Switzerland, Cat," I said.

"Really?"

"There's no way to know until we see Swiss troops."

"Or the Swiss navy."

"The Swiss navy's no joke for us. That last motor boat we heard was probably the Swiss navy."

"If we're in Switzerland let's have a big breakfast. They have wonderful rolls and butter and jam in Switzerland."

It was clear daylight now and a fine rain was falling. The wind was still blowing outside up the lake and we could see the tops of the white-caps going away from us and up the lake. I was sure we were in Switzerland now. There were many houses back in the trees from the shore and up the shore a way was a village with stone houses, some villas on the hills and a church. I had been looking at the road that skirted the shore for guards but did not see any. The road came quite close to the lake now and I saw a soldier coming out of a café on the road. He wore a gray-green uniform and a helmet like the Germans. He had a healthy-looking face and a little toothbrush mustache. He looked at us.

"Wave to him," I said to Catherine. She waved and the soldier smiled embarrassedly and gave a wave of his hand. I eased up rowing. We were passing the waterfront of the village.

"We must be well inside the border," I said.

"We want to be sure, darling. We don't want them to turn us back at the frontier."

"The frontier is a long way back. I think this is the customs town. I'm pretty sure it's Brissago."

"Won't there be Italians there? There are always both sides at a customs town."

"Not in war-time. I don't think they let the Italians cross the frontier."

It was a nice-looking little town. There were many fishing boats along the quay and nets were spread on racks. There was a fine November rain falling but it looked cheerful and clean even with the rain.

"Should we land then and have breakfast?"

"All right."

I pulled hard on the left oar and came in close, then straightened out when we were close to the quay and brought the boat alongside. I pulled in the oars, took hold of an iron ring, stepped up on the wet stone and was in Switzerland. I tied the boat and held my hand down to Catherine.

"Come on up, Cat. It's a grand feeling."

"What about the bags?"

"Leave them in the boat."

Catherine stepped up and we were in Switzerland together.

"What a lovely country," she said.

"Isn't it grand?"

"Let's go and have breakfast!"

"Isn't it a grand country? I love the way it feels under my shoes."

"I'm so stiff I can't feel it very well. But it feels like a splendid country. Darling, do you realize we're here and out of that bloody place?"

"I do. I really do. I've never realized anything before."

"Look at the houses. Isn't this a fine square? There's a place we can get breakfast."

"Isn't the rain fine? They never had rain like this in Italy. It's cheerful rain."

"And we're here, darling! Do you realize we're here?"

We went inside the café and sat down at a clean wooden table. We were cockeyed excited. A splendid clean-looking woman with an apron came and asked us what we wanted.

"Rolls and jam and coffee," Catherine said.

"I'm sorry, we haven't any rolls in war-time."

"Bread then."

"I can make you some toast."

"All right."

"I want some eggs fried too."

"How many eggs for the gentleman?"

"Three."

"Take four, darling."

"Four eggs."

The woman went away. I kissed Catherine and held her hand very tight. We looked at each other and at the café.

"Darling, darling, isn't it lovely?"

"It's grand," I said.

"I don't mind there not being rolls," Catherine said. "I thought about them all night. But I don't mind it. I don't mind it at all."

"I suppose pretty soon they will arrest us."

"Never mind, darling. We'll have breakfast first. You won't mind being arrested after breakfast. And then there's nothing they can do to us. We're British and American citizens in good standing."

"You have a passport, haven't you?"

"Of course. Oh let's not talk about it. Let's be happy."

"I couldn't be any happier," I said. A fat gray cat with a tail that lifted like a plume crossed the floor to our table and curved against my leg to purr each time she rubbed. I reached down and stroked her. Catherine smiled at me very happily. "Here comes the coffee," she said.

They arrested us after breakfast. We took a little walk through the village then went down to the quay to get our bags. A soldier was standing guard over the boat.

"Is this your boat?"

"Yes."

"Where do you come from?"

"Up the lake."

"Then I have to ask you to come with me."

"How about the bags?"

"You can carry the bags."

I carried the bags and Catherine walked beside me and the soldier walked along behind us to the old custom house. In the custom house a lieutenant, very thin and military, questioned us.

"What nationality are you?"

"American and British."

"Let me see your passports."

I gave him mine and Catherine got hers out of her handbag.

He examined them for a long time.

"Why do you enter Switzerland this way in a boat?"

"I am a sportsman," I said. "Rowing is my great sport. I always row when I get a chance."

"Why do you come here?"

"For the winter sport. We are tourists and we want to do the winter sport."

"This is no place for winter sport."

"We know it. We want to go where they have the winter sport."

"What have you been doing in Italy?"

"I have been studying architecture. My cousin has been studying art."

"Why do you leave there?"

"We want to do the winter sport. With the war going on you cannot study architecture."

"You will please stay where you are," the lieutenant said. He went back into the building with our passports.

"You're splendid, darling," Catherine said. "Keep on the same track. You want to do the winter sport."

"Do you know anything about art?"

"Rubens," said Catherine.

"Large and fat," I said.

"Titian," Catherine said.

"Titian-haired," I said. "How about Mantegna?"

"Don't ask hard ones," Catherine said. "I know him though—very bitter."

"Very bitter," I said. "Lots of nail holes."

"You see I'll make you a fine wife," Catherine said. "I'll be able to talk art with your customers."

"Here he comes," I said. The thin lieutenant came down the length of the custom house, holding our passports.

"I will have to send you into Locarno," he said. "You can get a carriage and a soldier will go in with you."

"All right," I said. "What about the boat?"

"The boat is confiscated. What have you in those bags?"

He went all through the two bags and held up the quarter-bottle of brandy. "Would you join me in a drink?" I asked.

"No thank you." He straightened up. "How much money have you?"

"Twenty-five hundred lire."

He was favorably impressed. "How much has your cousin?"

Catherine had a little over twelve hundred lire. The lieutenant was pleased. His attitude toward us became less haughty.

"If you are going for winter sports," he said, "Wengen is the place. My father has a very fine hotel at Wengen. It is open all the time."

"That's splendid," I said. "Could you give me the name?"

"I will write it on a card." He handed me the card very politely.

"The soldier will take you into Locarno. He will keep your passports. I regret this but it is necessary. I have good hopes they will give you a visa or a police permit at

Locarno."

He handed the two passports to the soldier and carrying the bags we started into the village to order a carriage. "Hi," the lieutenant called to the soldier. He said something in a German dialect to him. The soldier slung his rifle on his back and picked up the bags.

"It's a great country," I said to Catherine.

"It's so practical."

"Thank you very much," I said to the lieutenant. He waved his hand.

"Service!" he said. We followed our guard into the village.

We drove to Locarno in a carriage with the soldier sitting on the front seat with the driver. At Locarno we did not have a bad time. They questioned us but they were polite because we had passports and money. I do not think they believed a word of the story and I thought it was silly but it was like a law-court. You did not want something reasonable, you wanted something technical and then stuck to it without explanations. But we had passports and we would spend the money. So they gave us provisional visas.

At any time this visa might be withdrawn. We were to report to the police wherever we went.

Could we go wherever we wanted? Yes. Where did we want to go?

"Where do you want to go, Cat?"

"Montreux."

"It is a very nice place," the official said. "I think you will like that place."

"Here at Lacarno is a very nice place," another official said. "I am sure you would like it here very much at Locarno. Locarno is a very attractive place."

"We would like some place where there is winter sport."

"There is no winter sport at Montreux."

"I beg your pardon," the other official said. "I come from Montreux. There is very certainly winter sport on the Montreux Oberland Bernois railway. It would be false for you to deny that."

"I do not deny it. I simply said there is no winter sport at Montreux."

"I question that," the other official said. "I question that statement."

"I hold to that statement."

"I question that statement. I myself have *luge-ed* into the streets of Montreux. I have done it not once but several times. Luge-ing is certainly winter sport."

The other official turned to me.

"Is luge-ing your idea of winter sport, sir? I tell you you would be very comfortable here in Locarno. You would find the climate healthy, you would find the environs attractive. You would like it very much."

"The gentleman has expressed a wish to go to Montreux."

"What is luge-ing?" I asked.

"You see he has never even heard of luge-ing!"

That meant a great deal to the second official. He was pleased by that.

"Luge-ing," said the first official, "is tobogganing."

"I beg to differ," the other official shook his head. "I must differ again. The toboggan is very different from the luge. The toboggan is constructed in Canada of flat laths. The luge is a common sled with runners. Accuracy means something."

"Couldn't we toboggan?" I asked.

"Of course you could toboggan," the first official said. "You could toboggan very well. Excellent Canadian toboggans are sold in Montreux. Ochs Brothers sell toboggans. They import their own toboggans."

The second official turned away. "Tobogganing," he said, "requires a special piste. You could not toboggan into the streets of Montreux. Where are you stopping here?"

"We don't know," I said. "We just drove in from Brissago. The carriage is outside."

"You make no mistake in going to Montreux," the first official said. "You will find the climate delightful and beautiful. You will have no distance to go for winter sport."

"If you really want winter sport," the second official said, "you will go to the Engadine or to Mürren. I must protest against your being advised to go to Montreux for the winter sport."

"At Les Avants above Montreux there is excellent winter sport of every sort." The champion of Montreux glared at his colleague.

"Gentlemen," I said, "I am afraid we must go. My cousin is very tired. We will go tentatively to Montreux."

"I congratulate you," the first official shook my hand.

"I believe that you will regret leaving Locarno," the second official said. "At any rate you will report to the police at Montreux."

"There will be no unpleasantness with the police," the first official assured me. "You will find all the inhabitants extremely courteous and friendly."

"Thank you both very much," I said. "We appreciate your advice very much."

"Good-by," Catherine said. "Thank you both very much."

They bowed us to the door, the champion of Locarno a little coldly. We went down the steps and into the carriage.

"My God, darling," Catherine said. "Couldn't we have gotten away any sooner?" I gave the name of a hotel one of the officials had recommended to the driver. He picked up the reins.

"You've forgotten the army," Catherine said. The soldier was standing by the carriage. I gave him a ten-lira note. "I have no Swiss money yet," I said. He thanked me, saluted and went off. The carriage started and we drove to the hotel.

"How did you happen to pick out Montreux?" I asked Catherine. "Do you really want to go there?"

"It was the first place I could think of," she said. "It's not a bad place. We can find some place up in the mountains."

"Are you sleepy?"

"I'm asleep right now."

"We'll get a good sleep. Poor Cat, you had a long bad night."

"I had a lovely time," Catherine said. "Especially when you sailed with the umbrella."

"Can you realize we're in Switzerland?"

"No, I'm afraid I'll wake up and it won't be true."

"I am too."

"It is true, isn't it, darling? I'm not just driving down to the stazione in Milan to see you off."

"I hope not."

"Don't say that. It frightens me. Maybe that's where we're going."

"I'm so groggy I don't know," I said.

"Let me see your hands."

I put them out. They were both blistered raw.

"There's no hole in my side," I said.

"Don't be sacrilegious."

I felt very tired and vague in the head. The exhilaration was all gone. The carriage was going along the street.

"Poor hands," Catherine said.

"Don't touch them," I said. "By God I don't know where we are. Where are we going, driver?" The driver stopped his horse.

"To the Hotel Metropole. Don't you want to go there?"

"Yes," I said. "It's all right, Cat."

"It's all right, darling. Don't be upset. We'll get a good sleep and you won't feel groggy to-morrow."

"I get pretty groggy," I said. "It's like a comic opera to-day. Maybe I'm hungry."

"You're just tired, darling. You'll be fine." The carriage pulled up before the hotel. Some one came out to take our bags.

"I feel all right," I said. We were down on the pavement going into the hotel.

"I know you'll be all right. You're just tired. You've been up a long time."

"Anyhow we're here."

"Yes, we're really here."

We followed the boy with the bags into the hotel.

BOOK FIVE

CHAPTER 38

THAT FALL the snow came very late. We lived in a brown wooden house in the pine trees on the side of the mountain and at night there was frost so that there was thin ice over the water in the two pitchers on the dresser in the morning. Mrs. Guttingen came into the room early in the morning to shut the windows and started a fire in the tall porcelain stove. The pine wood crackled and sparked and then the fire roared in the stove and the second time Mrs. Guttingen came into the room she brought big chunks of wood for the fire and a pitcher of hot water. When the room was warm she brought in breakfast. Sitting up in bed eating breakfast we could see the lake and the mountains across the lake on the French side. There was snow on the tops of the mountains and the lake was a gray steel-blue.

Outside, in front of the chalet a road went up the mountain. The wheel ruts and ridges were iron hard with the frost, and the road climbed steadily through the forest and up and around the mountain to where there were meadows, and barns and cabins in the meadows at the edge of the woods looking across the valley. The valley was deep and there was a stream at the bottom that flowed down into the lake and when the wind blew across the valley you could hear the stream in the rocks.

Sometimes we went off the road and on a path through the pine forest. The floor of the forest was soft to walk on; the frost did not harden it as it did the road. But we did not mind the hardness of the road because we had nails in the soles and heels of our boots and the heel nails bit on the frozen ruts and with nailed boots it was good walking on the road and invigorating. But it was lovely walking in the woods.

In front of the house where we lived the mountain went down steeply to the little plain along the lake and we sat on the porch of the house in the sun and saw the winding of the road down the mountain-side and the terraced vineyards on the side of the lower mountain, the vines all dead now for the winter and the fields divided by stone walls, and below the vineyards the houses of the town on the narrow plain along the lake shore. There was an island with two trees on the lake and the trees looked like the double sails of a fishing-boat. The mountains were sharp and steep on the other side of the lake and down at the end of the lake was the plain of the Rhone Valley flat between the two ranges of mountains; and up the valley where the mountains cut it off was the Dent du Midi. It was a high snowy mountain and it dominated the valley but it was so far away that it did not make a shadow.

When the sun was bright we ate lunch on the porch but the rest of the time we ate upstairs in a small room with plain wooden walls and a big stove in the corner. We bought books and magazines in the town and a copy of "Hoyle" and learned many two-handed card games. The small room with the stove was our living-room. There were two comfortable chairs and a table for books and magazines and we played cards on the dining-table when it was cleared away. Mr. and Mrs. Guttingen lived downstairs and we would hear them talking sometimes in the evening and they were very happy together too. He had been a headwaiter and she had worked as maid in the same hotel and they had saved their money to buy this place. They had a son who was studying to be a headwaiter. He was at a hotel in Zurich. Downstairs there was a parlor where they sold wine and beer, and sometimes in the evening we would hear carts stop outside on the road and men come up the steps to go in the parlor to drink wine.

There was a box of wood in the hall outside the living-room and I kept up the fire from it. But we did not stay up very late. We went to bed in the dark in the big bedroom and when I was undressed I opened the windows and saw the night and the cold stars and the pine trees below the window and then got into bed as fast as I could. It was lovely in bed with the air so cold and clear and the night outside the window. We slept well and if I woke in the night I knew it was from only one cause and I would shift the feather bed over, very softly so that Catherine would not be wakened and then go back to sleep again, warm and with the new lightness of thin covers. The war seemed as far away as the football games of some one else's college. But I knew from the papers that they were still fighting in the mountains because the snow would not come.

Sometimes we walked down the mountain into Montreux. There was a path went down the mountain but it was steep and so usually we took the road and walked down on the wide hard road between fields and then below between the stone walls of the vineyards and on down between the houses of the villages along the way. There were three villages; Chernex, Fontanivent, and the other I forget. Then along the road we passed an old square-built stone château on a ledge on the side of the mountain-side with the terraced fields of vines, each vine tied to a stick to hold it up, the vines dry and brown and the earth ready for the snow and the lake down below flat and gray as steel. The road went down a long grade below the château and then turned to the right and went down very steeply and paved with cobbles, into Montreux.

We did not know any one in Montreux. We walked along beside the lake and saw the swans and the many gulls and terns that flew up when you came close and screamed while they looked down at the water. Out on the lake there were flocks of grebes, small and dark, and leaving trails in the water when they swam.

In the town we walked along the main street and looked in the windows of the shops. There were many big hotels that were closed but most of the shops were open and the people were very glad to see us. There was a fine coiffeur's place where Catherine went to have her hair done. The woman who ran it was very cheerful and the only person we knew in Montreux. While Catherine was there I went up to a beer place and drank dark Munich beer and read the papers. I read the Corriere della Sera and the English and American papers from Paris. All the advertisements were blacked out, supposedly to prevent communication in that way with the enemy. The papers were bad reading. Everything was going very badly every-where. I sat back in the corner with a heavy mug of dark beer and an opened glazed-paper package of pretzels and ate the pretzels for the salty flavor and the good way they made the beer taste and read about disaster. I thought Catherine would come by but she did not come, so I hung the papers back on the rack, paid for my beer and went up the street to look for her. The day was cold and dark and wintry and the stone of the houses looked cold. Catherine was still in the hairdresser's shop. The woman was waving her hair. I sat in the little booth and watched. It was exciting to watch and Catherine smiled and talked to me and my voice was a little thick from being excited. The tongs made a pleasant clicking sound and I could see Catherine in three mirrors and it was pleasant and warm in the booth. Then the woman put up Catherine's hair, and Catherine looked in the mirror and changed it a little, taking out and putting in pins; then stood up. "I'm sorry to have taken such a long time."

"Monsieur was very interested. Were you not, monsieur?" the woman smiled.

"Yes," I said.

We went out and up the street. It was cold and wintry and the wind was blowing. "Oh, darling, I love you so," I said.

"Don't we have a fine time?" Catherine said. "Look. Let's go some place and have beer instead of tea. It's very good for young Catherine. It keeps her small."

"Young Catherine," I said. "That loafer."

"She's been very good," Catherine said. "She makes very little trouble. The doctor says beer will be good for me and keep her small."

"If you keep her small enough and she's a boy, maybe he will be a jockey."

"I suppose if we really have this child we ought to get married," Catherine said. We were in the beer place at the corner table. It was getting dark outside. It was still early but the day was dark and the dusk was coming early.

"Let's get married now," I said.

"No," Catherine said. "It's too embarrassing now. I show too plainly. I won't go before any one and be married in this state."

"I wish we'd gotten married."

"I suppose it would have been better. But when could we, darling?"

"I don't know."

"I know one thing. I'm not going to be married in this splendid matronly state."

"You're not matronly."

"Oh yes, I am, darling. The hairdresser asked me if this was our first. I lied and said no, we had two boys and two girls."

"When will we be married?"

"Any time after I'm thin again. We want to have a splendid wedding with every one thinking what a handsome young couple."

"And you're not worried?"

"Darling, why should I be worried? The only time I ever felt badly was when I felt like a whore in Milan and that only lasted seven minutes and besides it was the room furnishings. Don't I make you a good wife?"

"You're a lovely wife."

"Then don't be too technical, darling. I'll marry you as soon as I'm thin again."

"All right."

"Do you think I ought to drink another beer? The doctor said I was rather narrow in the hips and it's all for the best if we keep young Catherine small."

"What else did he say?" I was worried.

"Nothing. I have a wonderful blood-pressure, darling. He admired my blood-pressure greatly."

"What did he say about you being too narrow in the hips?"

"Nothing. Nothing at all. He said I shouldn't ski."

"Quite right."

"He said it was too late to start if I'd never done it before. He said I could ski if

I wouldn't fall down."

"He's just a big-hearted joker."

"Really he was very nice. We'll have him when the baby comes."

"Did you ask him if you ought to get married?"

"No. I told him we'd been married four years. You see, darling, if I marry you I'll be an American and any time we're married under American law the child is legitimate."

"Where did you find that out?"

"In the New York World Almanac in the library."

"You're a grand girl."

"I'll be very glad to be an American and we'll go to America won't we, darling? I want to see Niagara Falls."

"You're a fine girl."

"There's something else I want to see but I can't remember it."

"The stockyards?"

"No. I can't remember it."

"The Woolworth building?"

"No."

"The Grand Canyon?"

"No. But I'd like to see that."

"What was it?"

"The Golden Gate! That's what I want to see. Where is the Golden Gate?"

"San Francisco."

"Then let's go there. I want to see San Francisco anyway."

"All right. We'll go there."

"Now let's go up the mountain. Should we? Can we get the M.O.B.?"

"There's a train a little after five."

"Let's get that."

"All right. I'll drink one more beer first."

When we went out to go up the street and climb the stairs to the station it was very cold. A cold wind was coming down the Rhone Valley. There were lights in the shop windows and we climbed the steep stone stairway to the upper street, then up another stairs to the station. The electric train was there waiting, all the lights on. There was a dial that showed when it left. The clock hands pointed to ten minutes after five. I looked at the station clock. It was five minutes after. As we got on board

I saw the motorman and conductor coming out of the station wine-shop. We sat down and opened the window. The train was electrically heated and stuffy but fresh cold air came in through the window.

"Are you tired, Cat?" I asked.

"No. I feel splendid."

"It isn't a long ride."

"I like the ride," she said. "Don't worry about me, darling. I feel fine."

Snow did not come until three days before Christmas. We woke one morning and it was snowing. We stayed in bed with the fire roaring in the stove and watched the snow fall. Mrs. Guttingen took away the breakfast trays and put more wood in the stove. It was a big snow storm. She said it had started about midnight. I went to the window and looked out but could not see across the road. It was blowing and snowing wildly. I went back to bed and we lay and talked.

"I wish I could ski," Catherine said. "It's rotten not to be able to ski."

"We'll get a bobsled and come down the road. That's no worse for you than riding in a car."

"Won't it be rough?"

"We can see."

"I hope it won't be too rough."

"After a while we'll take a walk in the snow."

"Before lunch," Catherine said, "so we'll have a good appetite."

"I'm always hungry."

"So am I."

We went out in the snow but it was drifted so that we could not walk far. I went ahead and made a trail down to the station but when we reached there we had gone far enough. The snow was blowing so we could hardly see and we went into the little inn by the station and swept each other off with a broom and sat on a bench and had vermouths.

"It is a big storm," the barmaid said.

"Yes."

"The snow is very late this year."

"Yes."

"Could I eat a chocolate bar?" Catherine asked. "Or is it too close to lunch? I'm always hungry."

"Go on and eat one," I said.

"I'll take one with filberts," Catherine said.

"They are very good," the girl said, "I like them the best."

"I'll have another vermouth," I said.

When we came out to start back up the road our track was filled in by the snow. There were only faint indentations where the holes had been. The snow blew in our faces so we could hardly see. We brushed off and went in to have lunch. Mr. Guttingen served the lunch.

"To-morrow there will be ski-ing," he said. "Do you ski, Mr. Henry?"

"No. But I want to learn."

"You will learn very easily. My boy will be here for Christmas and he will teach you."

"That's fine. When does he come?"

"To-morrow night."

When we were sitting by the stove in the little room after lunch looking out the window at the snow coming down Catherine said, "Wouldn't you like to go on a trip somewhere by yourself, darling, and be with men and ski?"

"No. Why should I?"

"I should think sometimes you would want to see other people besides me."

"Do you want to see other people?"

"No."

"Neither do I."

"I know. But you're different. I'm having a child and that makes me contented not to do anything. I know I'm awfully stupid now and I talk too much and I think you ought to get away so you won't be tired of me."

"Do you want me to go away?"

"No. I want you to stay."

"That's what I'm going to do."

"Come over here," she said. "I want to feel the bump on your head. It's a big bump." She ran her finger over it. "Darling, would you like to grow a beard?"

"Would you like me to?"

"It might be fun. I'd like to see you with a beard."

"All right. I'll grow one. I'll start now this minute. It's a good idea. It will give me something to do."

"Are you worried because you haven't anything to do?"

"No. I like it. I have a fine life. Don't you?"

"I have a lovely life. But I was afraid because I'm big now that maybe I was a bore to you."

"Oh, Cat. You don't know how crazy I am about you."

"This way?"

"Just the way you are. I have a fine time. Don't we have a good life?"

"I do, but I thought maybe you were restless."

"No. Sometimes I wonder about the front and about people I know but I don't worry. I don't think about anything much."

"Who do you wonder about?"

"About Rinaldi and the priest and lots of people I know. But I don't think about them much. I don't want to think about the war. I'm through with it."

"What are you thinking about now?"

"Nothing."

"Yes you were. Tell me."

"I was wondering whether Rinaldi had the syphilis."

"Was that all?"

"Yes."

"Has he the syphilis?"

"I don't know."

"I'm glad you haven't. Did you ever have anything like that?"

"I had gonorrhea."

"I don't want to hear about it. Was it very painful, darling?"

"Very."

"I wish I'd had it."

"No you don't."

"I do. I wish I'd had it to be like you. I wish I'd stayed with all your girls so I could make fun of them to you."

"That's a pretty picture."

"It's not a pretty picture you having gonorrhea."

"I know it. Look at it snow now."

"I'd rather look at you. Darling, why don't you let your hair grow?"

"How grow?"

"Just grow a little longer."

"It's long enough now."

"No, let it grow a little longer and I could cut mine and we'd be just alike only one of us blonde and one of us dark."

"I wouldn't let you cut yours."

"It would be fun. I'm tired of it. It's an awful nuisance in the bed at night."

"I like it."

"Wouldn't you like it short?"

"I might. I like it the way it is."

"It might be nice short. Then we'd both be alike. Oh, darling, I want you so much I want to be you too."

"You are. We're the same one."

"I know it. At night we are."

"The nights are grand."

"I want us to be all mixed up. I don't want you to go away. I just said that. You go if you want to. But hurry right back. Why, darling, I don't live at all when I'm not with you."

"I won't ever go away," I said. "I'm no good when you're not there. I haven't any life at all any more."

"I want you to have a life. I want you to have a fine life. But we'll have it together, won't we?"

"And now do you want me to stop growing my beard or let it go on?"

"Go on. Grow it. It will be exciting. Maybe it will be done for New Year's."

"Now do you want to play chess?"

"I'd rather play with you."

"No. Let's play chess."

"And afterward we'll play?"

"Yes."

"All right."

I got out the chess-board and arranged the pieces. It was still snowing hard outside.

One time in the night I woke up and knew that Catherine was awake too. The moon was shining in the window and made shadows on the bed from the bars on the window-panes.

"Are you awake, sweetheart?"

"Yes. Can't you sleep?"

"I just woke up thinking about how I was nearly crazy when I first met you. Do you remember?"

"You were just a little crazy."

"I'm never that way any more. I'm grand now. You say grand so sweetly. Say grand."

"Grand."

"Oh, you're sweet. And I'm not crazy now. I'm just very, very, very happy."

"Go on to sleep," I said.

"All right. Let's go to sleep at exactly the same moment."

"All right."

But we did not. I was awake for quite a long time thinking about things and watching Catherine sleeping, the moonlight on her face. Then I went to sleep, too.

CHAPTER 39

BY THE MIDDLE of January I had a beard and the winter had settled into bright cold days and hard cold nights. We could walk on the roads again. The snow was packed hard and smooth by the hay-sleds and wood-sledges and the logs that were hauled down the mountain. The snow lay over all the country, down almost to Montreux. The mountains on the other side of the lake were all white and the plain of the Rhone Valley was covered. We took long walks on the other side of the mountain to the Bains de l'Alliaz. Catherine wore hobnailed boots and a cape and carried a stick with a sharp steel point. She did not look big with the cape and we would not walk too fast but stopped and sat on logs by the roadside to rest when she was tired.

There was an inn in the trees at the Bains de l'Alliaz where the woodcutters stopped to drink, and we sat inside warmed by the stove and drank hot red wine with spices and lemon in it. They called it glühwein and it was a good thing to warm you and to celebrate with. The inn was dark and smoky inside and afterward when you went out the cold air came sharply into your lungs and numbed the edge of your nose as you inhaled. We looked back at the inn with light coming from the windows and the woodcutters' horses stamping and jerking their heads outside to keep warm. There was frost on the hairs of their muzzles and their breathing made plumes of frost in the air. Going up the road toward home the road was smooth and slippery for a while and the ice orange from the horses until the wood-hauling track turned off. Then the road was clean-packed snow and led through the woods, and twice coming home in the evening, we saw foxes.

It was a fine country and every time that we went out it was fun.

"You have a splendid beard now," Catherine said. "It looks just like the woodcutters'. Did you see the man with the tiny gold earrings?"

"He's a chamois hunter," I said. "They wear them because they say it makes them hear better."

"Really? I don't believe it. I think they wear them to show they are chamois hunters. Are there chamois near here?"

"Yes, beyond the Dent de Jaman."

"It was fun seeing the fox."

"When he sleeps he wraps that tail around him to keep warm."

"It must be a lovely feeling."

"I always wanted to have a tail like that. Wouldn't it be fun if we had brushes like a fox?"

"It might be very difficult dressing."

"We'd have clothes made, or live in a country where it wouldn't make any difference."

"We live in a country where nothing makes any difference. Isn't it grand how we never see any one? You don't want to see people do you, darling?"

"No."

"Should we sit here just a minute? I'm a little bit tired."

We sat close together on the logs. Ahead the road went down through the forest.

"She won't come between us, will she? The little brat."

"No. We won't let her."

"How are we for money?"

"We have plenty. They honored the last sight draft."

"Won't your family try and get hold of you now they know you're in Switzerland?"

"Probably. I'll write them something."

"Haven't you written them?"

"No. Only the sight draft."

"Thank God I'm not your family."

"I'll send them a cable."

"Don't you care anything about them?"

"I did, but we quarrelled so much it wore itself out."

"I think I'd like them. I'd probably like them very much."

"Let's not talk about them or I'll start to worry about them." After a while I said, "Let's go on if you're rested."

"I'm rested."

We went on down the road. It was dark now and the snow squeaked under our boots. The night was dry and cold and very clear.

"I love your beard," Catherine said. "It's a great success. It looks so stiff and fierce and it's very soft and a great pleasure."

"Do you like it better than without?"

"I think so. You know, darling, I'm not going to cut my hair now until after young Catherine's born. I look too big and matronly now. But after she's born and I'm thin again I'm going to cut it and then I'll be a fine new and different girl for you. We'll go together and get it cut, or I'll go alone and come and surprise you."

I did not say anything.

"You won't say I can't, will you?"

"No. I think it would be exciting."

"Oh, you're so sweet. And maybe I'd look lovely, darling, and be so thin and exciting to you and you'll fall in love with me all over again."

"Hell," I said, "I love you enough now. What do you want to do? Ruin me?"

"Yes. I want to ruin you."

"Good," I said, "that's what I want too."

CHAPTER 40

WE HAD a fine life. We lived through the months of January and February and the winter was very fine and we were very happy. There had been short thaws when the wind blew warm and the snow softened and the air felt like spring, but always the clear hard cold had come again and the winter had returned. In March came the first break in the winter. In the night it started raining. It rained on all morning and turned the snow to slush and made the mountain-side dismal. There were clouds over the lake and over the valley. It was raining high up the mountain. Catherine wore heavy overshoes and I wore Mr. Guttingen's rubber-boots and we walked to the station under an umbrella, through the slush and the running water that was washing the ice of the roads bare, to stop at the pub before lunch for a vermouth. Outside we could hear the rain.

"Do you think we ought to move into town?"

"What do you think?" Catherine asked.

"If the winter is over and the rain keeps up it won't be fun up here. How long is it before young Catherine?"

"About a month. Perhaps a little more."

"We might go down and stay in Montreux."

"Why don't we go to Lausanne? That's where the hospital is."

"All right. But I thought maybe that was too big a town."

"We can be as much alone in a bigger town and Lausanne might be nice."

"When should we go?"

"I don't care. Whenever you want, darling. I don't want to leave here if you don't want."

"Let's see how the weather turns out."

It rained for three days. The snow was all gone now on the mountain-side below the station. The road was a torrent of muddy snow-water. It was too wet and slushy to go out. On the morning of the third day of rain we decided to go down into town.

"That is all right, Mr. Henry," Guttingen said. "You do not have to give me any notice. I did not think you would want to stay now the bad weather is come."

"We have to be near the hospital anyway on account of Madame," I said.

"I understand," he said. "Will you come back some time and stay, with the little one?"

"Yes, if you would have room."

"In the spring when it is nice you could come and enjoy it. We could put the little one and the nurse in the big room that is closed now and you and Madame could have your same room looking out over the lake."

"I'll write about coming," I said. We packed and left on the train that went down after lunch. Mr. and Mrs. Guttingen came down to the station with us and he hauled our baggage down on a sled through the slush. They stood beside the station in the rain waving good-by.

"They were very sweet," Catherine said.

"They were fine to us."

We took the train to Lausanne from Montreux. Looking out the window toward where we had lived you could not see the mountains for the clouds. The train stopped in Vevey, then went on, passing the lake on one side and on the other the wet brown fields and the bare woods and the wet houses. We came into Lausanne and went into a medium-sized hotel to stay. It was still raining as we drove through the streets and into the carriage entrance of the hotel. The concierge with brass keys on his lapels, the elevator, the carpets on the floors, and the white washbowls with shining fixtures, the brass bed and the big comfortable bedroom all seemed very great luxury after the Guttingens. The windows of the room looked out on a wet garden with a wall topped by an iron fence. Across the street, which sloped steeply, was another hotel with a similar wall and garden. I looked out at the rain falling in the fountain of the garden.

Catherine turned on all the lights and commenced unpacking. I ordered a whiskey and soda and lay on the bed and read the papers I had bought at the station. It was March, 1918, and the German offensive had started in France. I drank the whiskey and soda and read while Catherine unpacked and moved around the room.

"You know what I have to get, darling," she said.

"What?"

"Baby clothes. There aren't many people reach my time without baby things."

"You can buy them."

"I know. That's what I'll do to-morrow. I'll find out what is necessary."

"You ought to know. You were a nurse."

"But so few of the soldiers had babies in the hospitals."

"I did."

She hit me with the pillow and spilled the whiskey and soda.

"I'll order you another," she said. "I'm sorry I spilled it."

"There wasn't much left. Come on over to the bed."

"No. I have to try and make this room look like something."

"Like what?"

"Like our home."

"Hang out the Allied flags."

"Oh shut up."

"Say it again."

"Shut up."

"You say it so cautiously," I said. "As though you didn't want to offend any one."

"I don't."

"Then come over to the bed."

"All right." She came and sat on the bed. "I know I'm no fun for you, darling. I'm like a big flour-barrel."

"No you're not. You're beautiful and you're sweet."

"I'm just something very ungainly that you've married."

"No you're not. You're more beautiful all the time."

"But I will be thin again, darling."

"You're thin now."

"You've been drinking."

"Just whiskey and soda."

"There's another one coming," she said. "And then should we order dinner up here?"

"That will be good."

"Then we won't go out, will we? We'll just stay in to-night."

"And play," I said.

"I'll drink some wine," Catherine said. "It won't hurt me. Maybe we can get some of our old white capri."

"I know we can," I said. "They'll have Italian wines at a hotel this size."

The waiter knocked at the door. He brought the whiskey in a glass with ice and beside the glass on a tray a small bottle of soda.

"Thank you," I said. "Put it down there. Will you please have dinner for two brought up here and two bottles of dry white capri in ice."

"Do you wish to commence your dinner with soup?"

"Do you want soup, Cat?"

"Please."

"Bring soup for one."

"Thank you, sir." He went out and shut the door. I went back to the papers and the war in the papers and poured the soda slowly over the ice into the whiskey. I would have to tell them not to put ice in the whiskey. Let them bring the ice separately. That way you could tell how much whiskey there was and it would not suddenly be too thin from the soda. I would get a bottle of whiskey and have them bring ice and soda. That was the sensible way. Good whiskey was very pleasant. It was one of the pleasant parts of life.

"What are you thinking, darling?"

"About whiskey."

"What about whiskey?"

"About how nice it is."

Catherine made a face. "All right," she said.

We stayed at that hotel three weeks. It was not bad; the dining-room was usually empty and very often we ate in our room at night. We walked in the town and took the cogwheel railway down to Ouchy and walked beside the lake. The weather became quite warm and it was like spring. We wished we were back in the mountains but the spring weather lasted only a few days and then the cold rawness of the breaking-up of winter came again.

Catherine bought the things she needed for the baby, up in the town. I went to a gymnasium in the arcade to box for exercise. I usually went up there in the morning while Catherine stayed late in bed. On the days of false spring it was very nice, after boxing and taking a shower, to walk along the streets smelling the spring in the air and stop at a café to sit and watch the people and read the paper and drink a vermouth; then go down to the hotel and have lunch with Catherine. The professor at the boxing gymnasium wore mustaches and was very precise and jerky and went all to pieces if you started after him. But it was pleasant in the gym. There was good air and light and I worked quite hard, skipping rope, shadow-boxing, doing abdominal exercises lying on the floor in a patch of sunlight that came through the open window, and occasionally scaring the professor when we boxed. I could not shadow-box in front of the narrow long mirror at first because it looked so strange to see a man with a beard boxing. But finally I just thought it was funny. I wanted to take off the beard as soon as I started boxing but Catherine did not want me to.

Sometimes Catherine and I went for rides out in the country in a carriage. It was nice to ride when the days were pleasant and we found two good places where we could ride out to eat. Catherine could not walk very far now and I loved to ride out along the country roads with her. When there was a good day we had a splendid time and we never had a bad time. We knew the baby was very close now and it gave us both a feeling as though something were hurrying us and we could not lose any time together.

CHAPTER 41

ONE MORNING I awoke about three o'clock hearing Catherine stirring in the bed.

"Are you all right, Cat?"

"I've been having some pains, darling."

"Regularly?"—

"No, not very."

"If you have them at all regularly we'll go to the hospital."

I was very sleepy and went back to sleep. A little while later I woke again.

"Maybe you'd better call up the doctor," Catherine said. "I think maybe this is it."

I went to the phone and called the doctor. "How often are the pains coming?" he asked.

"How often are they coming, Cat?"

"I should think every quarter of an hour."

"You should go to the hospital, then," the doctor said. "I will dress and go there right away myself."

I hung up and called the garage near the station to send up a taxi. No one answered the phone for a long time. Then I finally got a man who promised to send up a taxi at once. Catherine was dressing. Her bag was all packed with the things she would need at the hospital and the baby things. Outside in the hall I rang for the elevator. There was no answer. I went downstairs. There was no one downstairs except the night-watchman. I brought the elevator up myself, put Catherine's bag in it, she stepped in and we went down. The night-watchman opened the door for us and we sat outside on the stone slabs beside the stairs down to the driveway and waited for the taxi. The night was clear and the stars were out. Catherine was very excited.

"I'm so glad it's started," she said. "Now in a little while it will be all over."

"You're a good brave girl."

"I'm not afraid. I wish the taxi would come, though."

We heard it coming up the street and saw its headlights. It turned into the driveway and I helped Catherine in and the driver put the bag up in front.

"Drive to the hospital," I said.

We went out of the driveway and started up the hill.

At the hospital we went in and I carried the bag. There was a woman at the desk who wrote down Catherine's name, age, address, relatives and religion, in a book. She said she had no religion and the woman drew a line in the space after that word. She gave her name as Catherine Henry.

"I will take you up to your room," she said. We went up in an elevator. The woman stopped it and we stepped out and followed her down a hall. Catherine held tight to my arm.

"This is the room," the woman said. "Will you please undress and get into bed? Here is a night-gown for you to wear."

"I have a night-gown," Catherine said.

"It is better for you to wear this night-gown," the woman said.

I went outside and sat on a chair in the hallway.

"You can come in now," the woman said from the doorway. Catherine was lying in the narrow bed wearing a plain, square-cut night-gown that looked as though it were made of rough sheeting. She smiled at me.

"I'm having fine pains now," she said. The woman was holding her wrist and timing the pains with a watch.

"That was a big one," Catherine said. I saw it on her face.

"Where's the doctor?" I asked the woman.

"He's lying down sleeping. He will be here when he is needed."

"I must do something for Madame, now," the nurse said. "Would you please step out again?"

I went out into the hall. It was a bare hall with two windows and closed doors all down the corridor. It smelled of hospital. I sat on the chair and looked at the floor and prayed for Catherine.

"You can come in," the nurse said. I went in.

"Hello, darling," Catherine said.

"How is it?"

"They are coming quite often now." Her face drew up. Then she smiled.

"That was a real one. Do you want to put your hand on my back again, nurse?"

"If it helps you," the nurse said.

"You go away, darling," Catherine said. "Go out and get something to eat. I may do this for a long time the nurse says."

"The first labor is usually protracted," the nurse said.

"Please go out and get something to eat," Catherine said. "I'm fine, really."

"I'll stay awhile," I said.

The pains came quite regularly, then slackened off. Catherine was very excited. When the pains were bad she called them good ones. When they started to fall off she was disappointed and ashamed.

"You go out, darling," she said. "I think you are just making me self-conscious." Her face tied up. "There. That was better. I so want to be a good wife and have this child without any foolishness. Please go and get some breakfast, darling, and then come back. I won't miss you. Nurse is splendid to me."

"You have plenty of time for breakfast," the nurse said.

"I'll go then. Good-by, sweet."

"Good-by," Catherine said, "and have a fine breakfast for me too."

"Where can I get breakfast?" I asked the nurse.

"There's a café down the street at the square," she said. "It should be open now."

Outside it was getting light. I walked down the empty street to the café. There was a light in the window. I went in and stood at the zinc bar and an old man served me a glass of white wine and a brioche. The brioche was yesterday's. I dipped it in the wine and then drank a glass of coffee.

"What do you do at this hour?" the old man asked.

"My wife is in labor at the hospital."

"So. I wish you good luck."

"Give me another glass of wine."

He poured it from the bottle slopping it over a little so some ran down on the zinc. I drank this glass, paid and went out. Outside along the street were the refuse cans from the houses waiting for the collector. A dog was nosing at one of the cans.

"What do you want?" I asked and looked in the can to see if there was anything I could pull out for him; there was nothing on top but coffee-grounds, dust and some dead flowers.

"There isn't anything, dog," I said. The dog crossed the street. I went up the stairs in the hospital to the floor Catherine was on and down the hall to her room. I knocked on the door. There was no answer. I opened the door; the room was empty, except for Catherine's bag on a chair and her dressing-gown hanging on a hook on the wall. I went out and down the hall, looking for somebody. I found a nurse.

"Where is Madame Henry?"

"A lady has just gone to the delivery room."

"Where is it?"

"I will show you."

She took me down to the end of the hall. The door of the room was partly open. I could see Catherine lying on a table, covered by a sheet. The nurse was on one side and the doctor stood on the other side of the table beside some cylinders. The doctor held a rubber mask attached to a tube in one hand.

"I will give you a gown and you can go in," the nurse said. "Come in here, please."

She put a white gown on me and pinned it at the neck in back with a safety pin.

"Now you can go in," she said. I went into the room.

"Hello, darling," Catherine said in a strained voice. "I'm not doing much."

"You are Mr. Henry?" the doctor asked.

"Yes. How is everything going, doctor?"

"Things are going very well," the doctor said. "We came in here where it is easy to give gas for the pains."

"I want it now," Catherine said. The doctor placed the rubber mask over her face and turned a dial and I watched Catherine breathing deeply and rapidly. Then she pushed the mask away. The doctor shut off the petcock.

"That wasn't a very big one. I had a very big one a while ago. The doctor made me go clear out, didn't you, doctor?" Her voice was strange. It rose on the word doctor.

The doctor smiled.

"I want it again," Catherine said. She held the rubber tight to her face and breathed fast. I heard her moaning a little. Then she pulled the mask away and smiled.

"That was a big one," she said. "That was a very big one. Don't you worry, darling. You go away. Go have another breakfast."

"I'll stay," I said.

We had gone to the hospital about three o'clock in the morning. At noon Catherine was still in the delivery room. The pains had slackened again. She looked very tired and worn now but she was still cheerful.

"I'm not any good, darling," she said. "I'm so sorry. I thought I would do it very easily. Now—there's one—" she reached out her hand for the mask and held it over her face. The doctor moved the dial and watched her. In a little while it was over.

"It wasn't much," Catherine said. She smiled. "I'm a fool about the gas. It's wonderful."

"We'll get some for the home," I said.

"There one comes," Catherine said quickly. The doctor turned the dial and looked at his watch.

"What is the interval now?" I asked.

"About a minute."

"Don't you want lunch?"

"I will have something pretty soon," he said.

"You must have something to eat, doctor," Catherine said. "I'm so sorry I go on so long. Couldn't my husband give me the gas?"

"If you wish," the doctor said. "You turn it to the numeral two."

"I see," I said. There was a marker on a dial that turned with a handle.

"I want it now," Catherine said. She held the mask tight to her face. I turned the dial to number two and when Catherine put down the mask I turned it off. It was very good of the doctor to let me do something.

"Did you do it, darling?" Catherine asked. She stroked my wrist.

"Sure."

"You're so lovely." She was a little drunk from the gas.

"I will eat from a tray in the next room," the doctor said. "You can call me any moment." While the time passed I watched him eat, then, after a while, I saw that he was lying down and smoking a cigarette. Catherine was getting very tired.

"Do you think I'll ever have this baby?" she asked.

"Yes, of course you will."

"I try as hard as I can. I push down but it goes away. There it comes. Give it to me."

At two o'clock I went out and had lunch. There were a few men in the café sitting with coffee and glasses of kirsch or marc on the tables. I sat down at a table. "Can I eat?" I asked the waiter.

"It is past time for lunch."

"Isn't there anything for all hours?"

"You can have choucroute."

"Give me choucroute and beer."

"A demi or a bock?"

"A light demi."

The waiter brought a dish of sauerkraut with a slice of ham over the top and a sausage buried in the hot wine-soaked cabbage. I ate it and drank the beer. I was very hungry. I watched the people at the tables in the café. At one table they were playing cards. Two men at the table next me were talking and smoking. The café was full of smoke. The zinc bar, where I had breakfasted, had three people behind it now; the old man, a plump woman in a black dress who sat behind a counter and kept track of everything served to the tables, and a boy in an apron. I wondered how many children the woman had and what it had been like.

When I was through with the choucroute I went back to the hospital. The street was all clean now. There were no refuse cans out. The day was cloudy but the sun was trying to come through.

I rode upstairs in the elevator, stepped out and went down the hall to Catherine's room, where I had left my white gown. I put it on and pinned it in back at the neck. I looked in the glass and saw myself looking like a fake doctor with a beard. I went down the hall to the delivery room. The door was closed and I knocked. No one answered so I turned the handle and went in. The doctor sat by Catherine. The nurse was doing something at the other end of the room.

"Here is your husband," the doctor said.

"Oh, darling, I have the most wonderful doctor," Catherine said in a very strange voice. "He's been telling me the most wonderful story and when the pain came too badly he put me all the way out. He's wonderful. You're wonderful, doctor."

"You're drunk," I said.

"I know it," Catherine said. "But you shouldn't say it." Then "Give it to me. Give it to me." She clutched hold of the mask and breathed short and deep, pantingly, making the respirator click. Then she gave a long sigh and the doctor reached with his left hand and lifted away the mask.

"That was a very big one," Catherine said. Her voice was very strange. "I'm not going to die now, darling. I'm past where I was going to die. Aren't you glad?"

"Don't you get in that place again."

"I won't. I'm not afraid of it though. I won't die, darling."

"You will not do any such foolishness," the doctor said. "You would not die and leave your husband."

"Oh, no. I won't die. I wouldn't die. It's silly to die. There it comes. Give it to me."

After a while the doctor said, "You will go out, Mr. Henry, for a few moments and I will make an examination."

"He wants to see how I am doing," Catherine said. "You can come back afterward, darling, can't he, doctor?"

"Yes," said the doctor. "I will send word when he can come back."

I went out the door and down the hall to the room where Catherine was to be after the baby came. I sat in a chair there and looked at the room. I had the paper in my coat that I had bought when I went out for lunch and I read it. It was beginning to be dark outside and I turned the light on to read. After a while I stopped reading and turned off the light and watched it get dark outside. I wondered why the doctor did not send for me. Maybe it was better I was away. He probably wanted me away for a while. I looked at my watch. If he did not send for me in ten minutes I would go down anyway.

Poor, poor dear Cat. And this was the price you paid for sleeping together. This was the end of the trap. This was what people got for loving each other. Thank God for gas, anyway. What must it have been like before there were anæsthetics? Once it started, they were in the mill-race. Catherine had a good time in the time of pregnancy. It wasn't bad. She was hardly ever sick. She was not awfully uncomfortable until toward the last. So now they got her in the end. You never got away with anything. Get away hell! It would have been the same if we had been married fifty times. And what if she should die? She won't die. People don't die in childbirth nowadays. That was what all husbands thought. Yes, but what if she should die? She won't die. She's just having a bad time. The initial labor is usually protracted. She's only having a bad time. Afterward we'd say what a bad time and Catherine would say it wasn't really so bad. But what if she should die? She can't die. Yes, but what if she should die? She can't, I tell you. Don't be a fool. It's just a bad time. It's just nature giving her hell. It's only the first labor, which is almost always protracted. Yes, but what if she should die? She can't die. Why would she die? What reason is there for her to die? There's just a child that has to be born, the by-product of good nights in Milan. It makes trouble and is born and then you look after it and get fond of it maybe. But what if she should die? She won't die. But what if she should die? She won't. She's all right. But what if she should die? She can't die. But what if she should die? Hey, what about that? What if she should die?

The doctor came into the room.

"How does it go, doctor?"

"It doesn't go," he said.

"What do you mean?"

"Just that. I made an examination—" He detailed the result of the examination. "Since then I've waited to see. But it doesn't go."

"What do you advise?"

"There are two things. Either a high forceps delivery which can tear and be quite dangerous besides being possibly bad for the child, and a Cæsarean."

"What is the danger of a Cæsarean?" What if she should die!

"It should be no greater than the danger of an ordinary delivery."

"Would you do it yourself?"

"Yes. I would need possibly an hour to get things ready and to get the people I would need. Perhaps a little less."

"What do you think?"

"I would advise a Cæsarean operation. If it were my wife I would do a Cæsarean."

"What are the after effects?"

"There are none. There is only the scar."

"What about infection?"

"The danger is not so great as in a high forceps delivery."

"What if you just went on and did nothing?"

"You would have to do something eventually. Mrs. Henry is already losing much of her strength. The sooner we operate now the safer."

"Operate as soon as you can," I said.

"I will go and give the instructions."

I went into the delivery room. The nurse was with Catherine who lay on the table, big under the sheet, looking very pale and tired.

"Did you tell him he could do it?" she asked.

"Yes."

"Isn't that grand. Now it will be all over in an hour. I'm almost done, darling. I'm going all to pieces. Please give me that. It doesn't work. Oh, it doesn't work!"

"Breathe deeply."

"I am. Oh, it doesn't work any more. It doesn't work!"

"Get another cylinder," I said to the nurse.

"That is a new cylinder."

"I'm just a fool, darling," Catherine said. "But it doesn't work any more." She began to cry. "Oh, I wanted so to have this baby and not make trouble, and now I'm all done and all gone to pieces and it doesn't work. Oh, darling, it doesn't work at all. I don't care if I die if it will only stop. Oh, please, darling, please make it stop. There it comes. Oh Oh Oh!" She breathed sobbingly in the mask. "It doesn't work. It doesn't work. It doesn't work. Don't mind me, darling. Please don't cry. Don't mind me. I'm just gone all to pieces. You poor sweet. I love you so and I'll be good again. I'll be good this time. Can't they give me something? If they could only give me something."

"I'll make it work. I'll turn it all the way."

"Give it to me now."

I turned the dial all the way and as she breathed hard and deep her hand relaxed on the mask. I shut off the gas and lifted the mask. She came back from a long way away.

"That was lovely, darling. Oh, you're so good to me."

"You be brave, because I can't do that all the time. It might kill you."

"I'm not brave any more, darling. I'm all broken. They've broken me. I know it now."

"Everybody is that way."

"But it's awful. They just keep it up till they break you."

"In an hour it will be over."

"Isn't that lovely? Darling, I won't die, will I?"

"No. I promise you won't."

"Because I don't want to die and leave you, but I get so tired of it and I feel I'm going to die."

"Nonsense. Everybody feels that."

"Sometimes I know I'm going to die."

"You won't. You can't."

"But what if I should?"

"I won't let you."

"Give it to me quick. Give it to me!"

Then afterward, "I won't die. I won't let myself die."

"Of course you won't."

"You'll stay with me?"

"Not to watch it."

"No, just to be there."

"Sure. I'll be there all the time."

"You're so good to me. There, give it to me. Give me some more. It's not working!"

I turned the dial to three and then four. I wished the doctor would come back. I was afraid of the numbers above two.

Finally a new doctor came in with two nurses and they lifted Catherine onto a wheeled stretcher and we started down the hall. The stretcher went rapidly down the hall and into the elevator where every one had to crowd against the wall to make room; then up, then an open door and out of the elevator and down the hall on rubber wheels to the operating room. I did not recognize the doctor with his cap and mask on. There was another doctor and more nurses.

"They've got to give me something," Catherine said. "They've got to give me something. Oh please, doctor, give me enough to do some good!"

One of the doctors put a mask over her face and I looked through the door and saw the bright small amphitheatre of the operating room.

"You can go in the other door and sit up there," a nurse said to me. There were benches behind a rail that looked down on the white table and the lights. I looked at Catherine. The mask was over her face and she was quiet now. They wheeled the stretcher forward. I turned away and walked down the hall. Two nurses were hurrying toward the entrance to the gallery.

"It's a Cæsarean," one said. "They're going to do a Cæsarean."

The other one laughed, "We're just in time. Aren't we lucky?" They went in the door that led to the gallery.

Another nurse came along. She was hurrying too.

"You go right in there. Go right in," she said.

"I'm staying outside."

She hurried in. I walked up and down the hall. I was afraid to go in. I looked out the window. It was dark but in the light from the window I could see it was raining. I went into a room at the far end of the hall and looked at the labels on bottles in a glass case. Then I came out and stood in the empty hall and watched the door of the operating room.

A doctor came out followed by a nurse. He held something in his two hands that looked like a freshly skinned rabbit and hurried across the corridor with it and in through another door. I went down to the door he had gone into and found them in the room doing things to a new-born child. The doctor held him up for me to see. He held him by the heels and slapped him.

"Is he all right?"

"He's magnificent. He'll weigh five kilos."

I had no feeling for him. He did not seem to have anything to do with me. I felt no feeling of fatherhood.

"Aren't you proud of your son?" the nurse asked. They were washing him and wrapping him in something. I saw the little dark face and dark hand, but I did not see him move or hear him cry. The doctor was doing something to him again. He looked upset.

"No," I said. "He nearly killed his mother."

"It isn't the little darling's fault. Didn't you want a boy?"

"No," I said. The doctor was busy with him. He held him up by the feet and slapped him. I did not wait to see it. I went out in the hall. I could go in now and see. I went in the door and a little way down the gallery. The nurses who were sitting at the rail motioned for me to come down where they were. I shook my head. I could see enough where I was.

I thought Catherine was dead. She looked dead. Her face was gray, the part of it that I could see. Down below, under the light, the doctor was sewing up the great long, forcep-spread, thick-edged wound. Another doctor in a mask gave the anæsthetic. Two nurses in masks handed things. It looked like a drawing of the Inquisition. I knew as I watched I could have watched it all, but I was glad I hadn't. I do not think I could have watched them cut, but I watched the wound closed into a high welted ridge with quick skilful-looking stitches like a cobbler's, and was glad. When the wound was closed I went out into the hall and walked up and down again. After a while the doctor came out.

"How is she?"

"She is all right. Did you watch?"

He looked tired.

"I saw you sew up. The incision looked very long."

"You thought so?"

"Yes. Will that scar flatten out?"

"Oh, yes."

After a while they brought out the wheeled stretcher and took it very rapidly down the hallway to the elevator. I went along beside it. Catherine was moaning. Downstairs they put her in the bed in her room. I sat in a chair at the foot of the bed. There was a nurse in the room. I got up and stood by the bed. It was dark in the room. Catherine put out her hand. "Hello, darling," she said. Her voice was very weak and tired.

"Hello, you sweet."

"What sort of baby was it?"

"Sh—don't talk," the nurse said.

"A boy. He's long and wide and dark."

"Is he all right?"

"Yes," I said. "He's fine."

I saw the nurse look at me strangely.

"I'm awfully tired," Catherine said. "And I hurt like hell. Are you all right, darling?"

"I'm fine. Don't talk."

"You were lovely to me. Oh, darling, I hurt dreadfully. What does he look like?"

"He looks like a skinned rabbit with a puckered-up old-man's face."

"You must go out," the nurse said. "Madame Henry must not talk."

"I'll be outside."

"Go and get something to eat."

"No. I'll be outside." I kissed Catherine. She was very gray and weak and tired.

"May I speak to you?" I said to the nurse. She came out in the hall with me. I walked a little way down the hall.

"What's the matter with the baby?" I asked.

"Didn't you know?"

"No."

"He wasn't alive."

"He was dead?"

"They couldn't start him breathing. The cord was caught around his neck or something."

"So he's dead."

"Yes. It's such a shame. He was such a fine big boy. I thought you knew."

"No," I said. "You better go back in with Madame."

I sat down on the chair in front of a table where there were nurses' reports hung on clips at the side and looked out of the window. I could see nothing but the dark and the rain falling across the light from the window. So that was it. The baby was dead. That was why the doctor looked so tired. But why had they acted the way they did in the room with him? They supposed he would come around and start breathing probably. I had no religion but I knew he ought to have been baptized. But what if he never breathed at all. He hadn't. He had never been alive. Except in Catherine. I'd felt him kick there often enough. But I hadn't for a week. Maybe he was choked all the time. Poor little kid. I wished the hell I'd been choked like that. No I didn't. Still there would not be all this dying to go through. Now Catherine would die. That was what you did. You died. You did not know what it was about. You never had time to learn. They threw you in and told you the rules and the first time they caught you off base they killed you. Or they killed you gratuitously like Aymo. Or gave you the syphilis like Rinaldi. But they killed you in the end. You could count on that. Stay around and they would kill you.

Once in camp I put a log on top of the fire and it was full of ants. As it commenced to burn, the ants swarmed out and went first toward the centre where the fire was; then turned back and ran toward the end. When there were enough on the end they fell off into the fire. Some got out, their bodies burnt and flattened, and went off not knowing where they were going. But most of them went toward the fire and then back toward the end and swarmed on the cool end and finally fell off into the fire. I remember thinking at the time that it was the end of the world and a splendid chance to be a messiah and lift the log off the fire and throw it out where the ants could get off onto the ground. But I did not do anything but throw a tin cup of water on the log, so that I would have the cup empty to put whiskey in before I added water to it. I think the cup of water on the burning log only steamed the ants.

So now I sat out in the hall and waited to hear how Catherine was. The nurse did not come out, so after a while I went to the door and opened it very softly and looked in. I could not see at first because there was a bright light in the hall and it was dark in the room. Then I saw the nurse sitting by the bed and Catherine's head on a pillow, and she was all flat under the sheet. The nurse put her finger to her lips, then stood up and came to the door.

"How is she?" I asked.

"She's all right," the nurse said. "You should go and have your supper and then come back if you wish."

I went down the hall and then down the stairs and out the door of the hospital and down the dark street in the rain to the café. It was brightly lighted inside and there were many people at the tables. I did not see a place to sit, and a waiter came up to me and took my wet coat and hat and showed me a place at a table across from an elderly man who was drinking beer and reading the evening paper. I sat down and asked the waiter what the plat du jour was.

"Veal stew—but it is finished."

"What can I have to eat?"

"Ham and eggs, eggs with cheese, or choucroute."

"I had choucroute this noon," I said.

"That's true," he said. "That's true. You ate choucroute this noon." He was a middle-aged man with a bald top to his head and his hair slicked over it. He had a kind face.

"What do you want? Ham and eggs or eggs with cheese?"

"Ham and eggs," I said, "and beer."

"A demi-blonde?"

"Yes," I said.

"I remembered," he said. "You took a demi-blonde this noon."

I ate the ham and eggs and drank the beer. The ham and eggs were in a round dish—the ham underneath and the eggs on top. It was very hot and at the first mouthful I had to take a drink of beer to cool my mouth. I was hungry and I asked the waiter for another order. I drank several glasses of beer. I was not thinking at all but read the paper of the man opposite me. It was about the break through on the British front. When he realized I was reading the back of his paper he folded it over. I thought of asking the waiter for a paper, but I could not concentrate. It was hot in the café and the air was bad. Many of the people at the tables knew one another. There were several card games going on. The waiters were busy bringing drinks from the bar to the tables. Two men came in and could find no place to sit. They stood opposite the table where I was. I ordered another beer. I was not ready to leave yet. It was too soon to go back to the hospital. I tried not to think and to be perfectly calm. The men stood around but no one was leaving, so they went out. I drank another beer. There was quite a pile of saucers now on the table in front of me. The man opposite me had taken off his spectacles, put them away in a case, folded his paper and put it in his pocket and now sat holding his liqueur glass and looking out at the room. Suddenly I knew I had to get back. I called the waiter, paid the reckoning, got into my coat, put on my hat and started out the door. I walked through the rain up to the hospital.

Upstairs I met the nurse coming down the hall.

"I just called you at the hotel," she said. Something dropped inside me.

"What is wrong?"

"Mrs. Henry has had a hemorrhage."

"Can I go in?"

"No, not yet. The doctor is with her."

"Is it dangerous?"

"It is very dangerous." The nurse went into the room and shut the door. I sat outside in the hall. Everything was gone inside of me. I did not think. I could not think. I knew she was going to die and I prayed that she would not. Don't let her die. Oh, God, please don't let her die. I'll do anything for you if you won't let her die. Please, please, please, dear God, don't let her die. Dear God, don't let her die. Please, please, please don't let her die. God please make her not die. I'll do anything you say if you don't let her die. You took the baby but don't let her die. That was all right but don't let her die. Please, please, dear God, don't let her die.

The nurse opened the door and motioned with her finger for me to come. I followed her into the room. Catherine did not look up when I came in. I went over to the side of the bed. The doctor was standing by the bed on the opposite side. Catherine looked at me and smiled. I bent down over the bed and started to cry.

"Poor darling," Catherine said very softly. She looked gray.

"You're all right, Cat," I said. "You're going to be all right."

"I'm going to die," she said; then waited and said, "I hate it."

I took her hand.

"Don't touch me," she said. I let go of her hand. She smiled. "Poor darling. You touch me all you want."

"You'll be all right, Cat. I know you'll be all right."

"I meant to write you a letter to have if anything happened, but I didn't do it."

"Do you want me to get a priest or any one to come and see you?"

"Just you," she said. Then a little later, "I'm not afraid. I just hate it."

"You must not talk so much," the doctor said.

"All right," Catherine said.

"Do you want me to do anything, Cat? Can I get you anything?"

Catherine smiled, "No." Then a little later, "You won't do our things with another girl, or say the same things, will you?"

"Never."

"I want you to have girls, though."

"I don't want them."

"You are talking too much," the doctor said. "Mr. Henry must go out. He can come back again later. You are not going to die. You must not be silly."

"All right," Catherine said. "I'll come and stay with you nights," she said. It was very hard for her to talk.

"Please go out of the room," the doctor said. "You cannot talk." Catherine winked at me, her face gray. "I'll be right outside," I said.

"Don't worry, darling," Catherine said. "I'm not a bit afraid. It's just a dirty trick."

"You dear, brave sweet."

I waited outside in the hall. I waited a long time. The nurse came to the door and came over to me. "I'm afraid Mrs. Henry is very ill," she said. "I'm afraid for her."

"Is she dead?"

"No, but she is unconscious."

It seems she had one hemorrhage after another. They couldn't stop it. I went into the room and stayed with Catherine until she died. She was unconscious all the time, and it did not take her very long to die.

Outside the room, in the hall, I spoke to the doctor, "Is there anything I can do to-night?"

"No. There is nothing to do. Can I take you to your hotel?"

"No, thank you. I am going to stay here a while."

"I know there is nothing to say. I cannot tell you—"

"No," I said. "There's nothing to say."

"Good-night," he said. "I cannot take you to your hotel?"

"No, thank you."

"It was the only thing to do," he said. "The operation proved—"

"I do not want to talk about it," I said.

"I would like to take you to your hotel."

"No, thank you."

He went down the hall. I went to the door of the room.

"You can't come in now," one of the nurses said.

"Yes I can," I said.

"You can't come in yet."

"You get out," I said. "The other one too."

But after I had got them out and shut the door and turned off the light it wasn't any good. It was like saying good-by to a statue. After a while I went out and left the hospital and walked back to the hotel in the rain.

Men Without Women

Table of Contents

The Undefeated

MANUEL GARCIA CLIMBED THE STAIRS to Don Miguel Retana's office. He set down his suitcase and knocked on the door. There was no answer. Manuel, standing in the hallway, felt there was someone in the room. He felt it through the door.

"Retana," he said, listening.

There was no answer.

He's there, all right, Manuel thought.

"Retana," he said and banged the door.

"Who's there?" said someone in the office.

"Me, Manolo," Manuel said.

"What do you want?" asked the voice.

"I want to work," Manuel said.

Something in the door clicked several times and it swung open. Manuel went in, carrying his suitcase.

A little man sat behind a desk at the far side of the room. Over his head was a bull's head, stuffed by a Madrid taxidermist; on the walls were framed photographs and bull-fight posters.

The little man sat looking at Manuel.

"I thought they'd killed you," he said.

Manuel knocked with his knuckles on the desk. The little man sat looking at him across the desk.

"How many corridas you had this year?" Retana asked.

"One," he answered.

"Just that one?" the little man asked.

"That's all."

"I read about it in the papers," Retana said. He leaned back in the chair and looked at Manuel.

Manuel looked up at the stuffed bull. He had seen it often before. He felt a certain family interest in it. It had killed his brother, the promising one, about nine years ago. Manuel remembered the day. There was a brass plate on the oak shield the bull's head was mounted on. Manuel could not read it, but he imagined it was in memory of his brother. Well, he had been a good kid.

The plate said: "The Bull 'Mariposa' of the Duke of Veragua, which accepted 9 varas for 7 caballos, and caused the death of Antonio Garcia, Novillero, April 27, 1909."

Retana saw him looking at the stuffed bull's head.

"The lot the Duke sent me for Sunday will make a scandal," he said. "They're all bad in the legs. What do they say about them at the Café?"

"I don't know," Manuel said. "I just got in."

"Yes," Retana said. "You still have your bag."

He looked at Manuel, leaning back behind the big desk.

"Sit down," he said. "Take off your cap."

Manuel sat down; his cap off, his face was changed. He looked pale, and his *coleta* pinned forward on his head, so that it would not show under the cap, gave him a strange look.

"You don't look well," Retana said.

"I just got out of the hospital," Manuel said.

"I heard they'd cut your leg off," Retana said.

"No," said Manuel. "It got all right."

Retana leaned forward across the desk and pushed a wooden box of cigarettes toward Manuel.

"Have a cigarette," he said.

"Thanks."

Manuel lit it.

"Smoke?" he said, offering the match to Retana.

"No," Retana waved his hand, "I never smoke."

Retana watched him smoking.

"Why don't you get a job and go to work?" he said.

"I don't want to work," Manuel said. "I am a bullfighter."

"There aren't any bullfighters any more," Retana said.

"I'm a bullfighter," Manuel said.

"Yes, while you're in there," Retana said.

Manuel laughed.

Retana sat, saying nothing and looking at Manuel.

"I'll put you in a nocturnal if you want," Retana offered.

"When?" Manuel asked.

"Tomorrow night."

"I don't like to substitute for anybody," Manuel said. That was the way they all got killed. That was the way Salvador got killed. He tapped with his knuckles on the table.

"It's all I've got," Retana said.

"Why don't you put me on next week?" Manuel suggested.

"You wouldn't draw," Retana said. "All they want is Litri and Rubito and La Torre. Those kids are good."

"They'd come to see me get it," Manuel said, hopefully.

"No, they wouldn't. They don't know who you are any more."

"I've got a lot of stuff," Manuel said.

"I'm offering to put you on tomorrow night," Retana said. "You can work with young Hernandez and kill two *novillos* after the Charlots."

"Whose *novillos?*" Manuel asked.

"I don't know. Whatever stuff they've got in the corrals. What the veterinaries won't pass in the daytime."

"I don't like to substitute," Manuel said.

"You can take it or leave it," Retana said. He leaned forward over the papers. He was no longer interested. The appeal that Manuel had made to him for a moment when he thought of the old days was gone. He would like to get him to substitute for Larita because he could get him cheaply. He could get others cheaply too. He would like to help him though. Still he had given him the chance. It was up to him.

"How much do I get?" Manuel asked. He was still playing with the idea of refusing. But he knew he could not refuse.

"Two hundred and fifty pesetas," Retana said. He had thought of five hundred, but when he opened his mouth it said two hundred and fifty.

"You pay Villalta seven thousand," Manuel said.

"You're not Villalta," Retana said.

"I know it," Manuel said.

"He draws it, Manolo," Retana said in explanation.

"Sure," said Manuel. He stood up. "Give me three hundred, Retana."

"All right," Retana agreed. He reached in the drawer for a paper.

"Can I have fifty now?" Manuel asked.

"Sure," said Retana. He took a fifty-peseta note out of his pocket-book and laid it, spread out flat, on the table.

Manuel picked it up and put it in his pocket.

"What about a *cuadrilla*?" he asked.

"There's the boys that always work for me nights," Retana said. "They're all right."

"How about picadors?" Manuel asked.

"They're not much," Retana admitted.

"I've got to have one good pic," Manuel said.

"Get him then," Retana said. "Go and get him."

"Not out of this," Manuel said. "I'm not paying for any *cuadrilla* out of sixty duros."

Retana said nothing but looked at Manuel across the big desk.

"You know I've got to have one good pic," Manuel said.

Retana said nothing but looked at Manuel from a long way off.

"It isn't right," Manuel said.

Retana was still considering him, leaning back in his chair, considering him from a long way away.

"There're the regular pics," he offered.

"I know," Manuel said. "I know your regular pics."

Retana did not smile. Manuel knew it was over.

"All I want is an even break," Manuel said reasoningly. "When I go out there I want to be able to call my shots on the bull. It only takes one good picador."

He was talking to a man who was no longer listening.

"If you want something extra," Retana said, "go and get it. There will be a regular *cuadrilla* out there. Bring as many of your own pics as you want.

The *charlotada* is over by 10.30."

"All right," Manuel said. "If that's the way you feel about it."

"That's the way," Retana said.

"I'll see you tomorrow night," Manuel said.

"I'll be out there," Retana said.

Manuel picked up his suitcase and went out.

"Shut the door," Retana called.

Manuel looked back. Retana was sitting forward looking at some papers. Manuel pulled the door tight until it clicked.

He went down the stairs and out of the door into the hot brightness of the street. It was very hot in the street and the light on the white buildings was sudden and hard on his eyes. He walked down the shady side of the steep street toward the Puerta del Sol. The shade felt solid and cool as running water. The heat came suddenly as he crossed the intersecting streets. Manuel saw no one he knew in all the people he passed.

Just before the Puerta del Sol he turned into a café.

It was quiet in the café. There were a few men sitting at tables against the wall. At one table four men played cards. Most of the men sat against the wall smoking, empty coffee-cups and liqueur-glasses before them on the tables. Manuel went through the long room to a small room in back. A man sat at a table in the corner asleep. Manuel sat down at one of the tables.

A waiter came in and stood beside Manuel's table.

"Have you seen Zurito?" Manuel asked him.

"He was in before lunch," the waiter answered. "He won't be back before five o'clock."

"Bring me some coffee and milk and a shot of the ordinary," Manuel said.

The waiter came back into the room carrying a tray with a big coffee-glass and a liqueur-glass on it. In his left hand he held a bottle of brandy. He swung these down to the table and a boy who had followed him poured coffee and milk into the glass from two shiny, spouted pots with long handles.

Manuel took off his cap and the waiter noticed his pigtail pinned forward on his head. He winked at the coffee-boy as he poured out the brandy into the little glass beside Manuel's coffee. The coffee-boy looked at Manuel's pale face curiously.

"You fighting here?" asked the waiter, corking up the bottle.

"Yes," Manuel said. "Tomorrow."

The waiter stood there, holding the bottle on one hip.

"You in the Charlie Chaplins?" he asked.

The coffee-boy looked away, embarrassed.

"No. In the ordinary."

"I thought they were going to have Chaves and Hernandez," the waiter said.

"No. Me and another."

"Who? Chaves or Hernandez?"

"Hernandez, I think."

"What's the matter with Chaves?"

"He got hurt."

"Where did you hear that?"

"Retana."

"Hey, Looie," the waiter called to the next room, "Chaves got *cogida.*"

Manuel had taken the wrapper off the lumps of sugar and dropped them into his coffee. He stirred it and drank it down, sweet, hot, and warming in his empty stomach. He drank off the brandy.

"Give me another shot of that," he said to the waiter.

The waiter uncorked the bottle and poured the glass full, slopping another drink into the saucer. Another waiter had come up in front of the table. The coffee-boy was gone.

"Is Chaves hurt bad?" the second waiter asked Manuel.

"I don't know," Manuel said, "Retana didn't say."

"A hell of a lot he cares," the tall waiter said. Manuel had not seen him before. He must have just come up.

"If you stand in with Retana in this town, you're a made man," the tall waiter said. "If you aren't in with him, you might just as well go out and shoot yourself."

"You said it," the other waiter who had come in said. "You said it then."

"You're right I said it," said the tall waiter. "I know what I'm talking about when I talk about that bird."

"Look what he's done for Villalta," the first waiter said.

"And that ain't all," the tall waiter said. "Look what he's done for Marcial Lalanda. Look what he's done for Nacional."

"You said it, kid," agreed the short waiter.

Manuel looked at them, standing talking in front of his table. He had drunk his second brandy. They had forgotten about him. They were not interested in him.

"Look at that bunch of camels," the tall waiter went on. "Did you ever see this Nacional II?"

"I seen him last Sunday, didn't I?" the original waiter said.

"He's a giraffe," the short waiter said.

"What did I tell you?" the tall waiter said. "Those are Retana's boys."

"Say, give me another shot of that," Manuel said. He had poured the brandy the waiter had slopped over in the saucer into his glass and drank it while they were talking.

The original waiter poured his glass full mechanically, and the three of them went out of the room talking.

In the far corner the man was still asleep, snoring slightly on the intaking breath, his head back against the wall.

Manuel drank his brandy. He felt sleepy himself. It was too hot to go out into the town. Besides there was nothing to do. He wanted to see Zurito. He would go to sleep while he waited. He kicked his suitcase under the table to be sure it was there. Perhaps it would be better to put it back under the seat, against the wall. He leaned down and shoved it under. Then he leaned forward on the table and went to sleep.

When he woke there was someone sitting across the table from him. It was a big man with a heavy brown face like an Indian. He had been sitting there some time. He had waved the waiter away and sat reading the paper and occasionally looking down at Manuel, asleep, his head on the table. He read the paper laboriously, forming the words with his lips as he read. When it tired him he looked at Manuel. He sat heavily in the chair, his black Cordoba hat tipped forward.

Manuel sat up and looked at him.

"Hello, Zurito," he said.

"Hello, kid," the big man said.

"I've been asleep." Manuel rubbed his forehead with the back of his fist.

"I thought maybe you were."

"How's everything?"

"Good. How is everything with you?"

"Not so good."

They were both silent. Zurito, the picador, looked at Manuel's white face. Manuel looked down at the picador's enormous hands folding the paper to put away in his pocket.

"I got a favor to ask you, Manos," Manuel said.

Manosduros was Zurito's nickname. He never heard it without thinking of his huge hands. He put them forward on the table self-consciously.

"Let's have a drink," he said.

"Sure," said Manuel.

The waiter came and went and came again. He went out of the room looking back at the two men at the table.

"What's the matter, Manolo?" Zurito set down his glass.

"Would you pic two bulls for me tomorrow night?" Manuel asked, looking up at Zurito across the table.

"No," said Zurito. "I'm not pic-ing."

Manuel looked down at his glass. He had expected that answer; now he had it. Well, he had it.

"I'm sorry, Manolo, but I'm not pic-ing." Zurito looked at his hands.

"That's all right," Manuel said.

"I'm too old," Zurito said.

"I just asked you," Manuel said.

"Is it the nocturnal tomorrow?"

"That's it. I figured if I had just one good pic, I could get away with it."

"How much are you getting?"

"Three hundred pesetas."

"I get more than that for pic-ing."

"I know," said Manuel. "I didn't have any right to ask you."

"What do you keep on doing it for?" Zurito asked. "Why don't you cut off your *coleta*, Manolo?"

"I don't know," Manuel said.

"You're pretty near as old as I am," Zurito said.

"I don't know," Manuel said. "I got to do it. If I can fix it so that I get an even break, that's all I want. I got to stick with it, Manos."

"No, you don't."

"Yes, I do. I've tried keeping away from it."

"I know how you feel. But it isn't right. You ought to get out and stay out."

"I can't do it. Besides, I've been going good lately."

Zurito looked at his face.

"You've been in the hospital."

"But I was going great when I got hurt."

Zurito said nothing. He tipped the cognac out of his saucer into his glass.

"The papers said they never saw a better *faena*," Manuel said.

Zurito looked at him.

"You know when I get going I'm good," Manuel said.

"You're too old," the picador said.

"No," said Manuel. "You're ten years older than I am."

"With me it's different."

"I'm not too old," Manuel said.

They sat silent, Manuel watching the picador's face.

"I was going great till I got hurt," Manuel offered.

"You ought to have seen me, Manos," Manuel said, reproachfully.

"I don't want to see you," Zurito said. "It makes me nervous."

"You haven't seen me lately."

"I've seen you plenty."

Zurito looked at Manuel, avoiding his eyes.

"You ought to quit it, Manolo."

"I can't," Manuel said. "I'm going good now, I tell you."

Zurito leaned forward, his hands on the table.

"Listen. I'll pic for you and if you don't go big tomorrow night, you'll quit. See? Will you do that?"

"Sure."

Zurito leaned back, relieved.

"You got to quit," he said. "No monkey business. You got to cut the *coleta.*"

"I won't have to quit," Manuel said. "You watch me. I've got the stuff."

Zurito stood up. He felt tired from arguing.

"You got to quit," he said. "I'll cut your *coleta* myself."

"No, you won't," Manuel said. "You won't have a chance."

Zurito called the waiter.

"Come on," said Zurito. "Come on up to the house."

Manuel reached under the seat for his suitcase. He was happy. He knew Zurito would pic for him. He was the best picador living. It was all simple now.

"Come on up to the house and we'll eat," Zurito said.

Manuel stood in the *patio de caballos* waiting for the Charlie Chaplins to be over. Zurito stood beside him. Where they stood it was dark. The high door that led into the bull-ring was shut. Above them they heard a shout, then another shout of laughter. Then there was silence. Manuel liked the smell of the stables about the *patio de caballos*. It smelt good in the dark. There was another roar from the arena and then applause, prolonged applause, going on and on.

"You ever seen these fellows?" Zurito asked, big and looming beside Manuel in the dark.

"No," Manuel said.

"They're pretty funny," Zurito said. He smiled to himself in the dark.

The high, double, tight-fitting door into the bull-ring swung open and

Manuel saw the ring in the hard light of the arc-lights, the plaza, dark all the way around, rising high; around the edge of the ring were running and bowing two men dressed like tramps, followed by a third in the uniform of a hotel bell-boy who stooped and picked up the hats and canes thrown down onto the sand and tossed them back up into the darkness.

The electric light went on in the patio.

"I'll climb onto one of those ponies while you collect the kids," Zurito said.

Behind them came the jingle of the mules, coming out to go into the arena and be hitched onto the dead bull.

The members of the *cuadrilla*, who had been watching the burlesque from the runway between the *barrera* and the seats, came walking back and stood in a group talking, under the electric light in the patio. A good-looking lad in a silver-and-orange suit came up to Manuel and smiled.

"I'm Hernandez," he said and put out his hand.

Manuel shook it.

"They're regular elephants we've got tonight," the boy said cheerfully.

"They're big ones with horns," Manuel agreed.

"You drew the worst lot," the boy said.

"That's all right," Manuel said. "The bigger they are, the more meat for the poor."

"Where did you get that one?" Hernandez grinned.

"That's an old one," Manuel said. "You line up your *cuadrilla*, so I can see what I've got."

"You've got some good kids," Hernandez said. He was very cheerful. He had been on twice before in nocturnals and was beginning to get a following in Madrid. He was happy the fight would start in a few minutes.

"Where are the pics?" Manuel asked.

"They're back in the corrals fighting about who gets the beautiful horses," Hernandez grinned.

The mules came through the gate in a rush, the whips snapping, bells jangling and the young bull ploughing a furrow of sand.

They formed up for the *paseo* as soon as the bull had gone through.

Manuel and Hernandez stood in front. The youths of the *cuadrillas* were behind, their heavy capes furled over their arms. In back, the four picadors, mounted, holding their steel-tipped push-poles erect in the half-dark of the corral.

"It's a wonder Retana wouldn't give us enough light to see the horses by," one picador said.

He knows we'll be happier if we don't get too good a look at these skins," another pic answered.

"This thing I'm on barely keeps me off the ground," the first picador said.

"Well, they're horses."

"Sure, they're horses."

They talked, sitting their gaunt horses in the dark.

Zurito said nothing. He had the only steady horse of the lot. He had tried him, wheeling him in the corrals and he responded to the bit and the spurs. He had taken the bandage off his right eye and cut the strings where they had tied his ears tight shut at the base. He was a good, solid horse, solid on his legs. That was all he needed. He intended to ride him all through the *corrida*. He had already, since he had mounted, sitting in the half-dark in the big, quilted saddle, waiting for the *paseo*, pic-ed through the whole *corrida* in his mind. The other picadors went on talking on both sides of him. He did not hear them.

The two matadors stood together in front of their three *peones*, their capes furled over their left arms in the same fashion. Manuel was thinking about the three lads in back of him. They were all three Madrileños, like Hernandez, boys about nineteen. One of them, a gypsy, serious, aloof, and dark-faced, he liked the look of. He turned.

"What's your name, kid?" he asked the gypsy.

"Fuentes," the gypsy said.

"That's a good name," Manuel said.

The gypsy smiled, showing his teeth.

"You take the bull and give him a little run when he comes out," Manuel said.

"All right," the gypsy said. His face was serious. He began to think about just what he would do.

"Here she goes," Manuel said to Hernandez.

"All right. We'll go."

Heads up, swinging with the music, their right arms swinging free, they stepped out, crossing the sanded arena under the arc-lights, the *cuadrillas* opening out behind, the picadors riding after, behind came the bull-ring servants and the jingling mules. The crowd applauded Hernandez as they marched across the arena. Arrogant, swinging, they looked straight ahead as they marched.

They bowed before the president, and the procession broke up into its component parts. The bull-fighters went over to the *barrera* and changed their heavy mantles for the light fighting capes. The mules went out. The picadors galloped jerkily around the ring, and two rode out the gate they had come in by. The servants swept the sand smooth.

Manuel drank a glass of water poured for him by one of Retana's deputies, who was acting as his manager and sword-handler. Hernandez came over from speaking with his own manager.

"You got a good hand, kid," Manuel complimented him.

"They like me," Hernandez said happily.

"How did the *paseo* go?" Manuel asked Retana's man.

"Like a wedding," said the handler. "Fine. You came out like Joselito and Belmonte."

Zurito rode by, a bulky equestrian statue. He wheeled his horse and faced him toward the *toril* on the far side of the ring where the bull would come out. It was strange under the arc-light. He pic-ed in the hot afternoon sun for big money. He didn't like this arc-light business. He wished they would get started.

Manuel went up to him.

"Pic him, Manos," he said. "Cut him down to size for me."

"I'll pic him, kid," Zurito spat on the sand. "I'll make him jump out of the ring."

"Lean on him, Manos," Manuel said.

"I'll lean on him," Zurito said. "What's holding it up?"

"He's coming now," Manuel said.

Zurito sat there, his feet in the box-stirrups, his great legs in the buckskin-covered armor gripping the horse, the reins in his left hand, the long pic held in his right hand, his broad hat well down over his eyes to shade them from the lights, watching the distant door of the *toril*. His horse's ears quivered. Zurito patted him with his left hand.

The red door of the *toril* swung back and for a moment Zurito looked into the empty passageway far across the arena. Then the bull came out in a rush, skidding on his four legs as he came out under the lights, then charging in a gallop, moving softly in a fast gallop, silent except as he woofed through wide nostrils as he charged, glad to be free after the dark pen.

In the first row of seats, slightly bored, leaning forward to write on the cement wall in front of his knees, the substitute bull-fight critic of *El Heraldo* scribbled: "Campagnero, Negro, 42, came out at 90 miles an hour with plenty of gas — —"

Manuel, leaning against the *barrera*, watching the bull, waved his hand and the gypsy ran out, trailing his cape. The bull, in full gallop, pivoted and charged the cape, his head down, his tail rising. The gypsy moved in a zigzag, and as he passed, the bull caught sight of him and abandoned the cape to charge the man. The gyp sprinted and vaulted the red fence of the *barrera* as the bull struck it with his horns. He tossed into it twice with his horns, banging into the wood blindly.

The critic of *El Heraldo* lit a cigarette and tossed the match at the bull, then wrote in his note-book, "large and with enough horns to satisfy the cash customers, Campagnero showed a tendency to cut into the terrain of the bull-fighters."

Manuel stepped out on the hard sand as the bull banged into the fence. Out of the corner of his eye he saw Zurito sitting the white horse close to the *barrera*, about a quarter of the way around the ring to the left. Manuel held the cape close in front of him, a fold in each hand, and shouted at the bull. "Huh! Huh!" The bull turned, seemed to brace against the fence as he charged in a scramble, driving into the cape as Manuel side-stepped, pivoted on his heels with the charge of the bull, and swung the cape just ahead of the horns. At the end of the swing he was facing the bull again and held the cape in the same position close in front of his body, and pivoted again as the bull recharged. Each time, as he swung, the crowd shouted.

Four times he swung with the bull, lifting the cape so it billowed full, and each time bringing the bull around to charge again. Then, at the end of the fifth swing, he held the cape against his hip and pivoted, so the cape swung out like a ballet dancer's skirt and wound the bull around himself like a belt, to step clear, leaving the bull facing Zurito on the white horse, come up and planted firm, the horse facing the bull, its ears forward, its lips nervous, Zurito, his hat over his eyes, leaning forward, the long pole sticking out before and behind in a sharp angle under his right arm, held half-way down, the triangular iron point facing the bull.

El Heraldo's second-string critic, drawing on his cigarette, his eyes on the bull, wrote: "The veteran Manolo designed a series of acceptable *verónicas*, ending in a very Belmontistic *recorte* that earned applause from the regulars, and we entered the *tercio of the cavalry*."

Zurito sat his horse, measuring the distance between the bull and the end of the pic. As he looked, the bull gathered himself together and charged, his eyes on the horse's chest. As he lowered his head to hook, Zurito sunk the point of the pic in the swelling hump of muscle above the bull's shoulder, leaned all his weight on the shaft, and with his left hand pulled the white horse into the air, front hoofs pawing, and swung him to the right as he pushed the bull under and through so the horns passed safely under the horse's belly and the horse came down, quivering, the bull's tail brushing his chest as he charged the cape Hernandez offered him.

Hernandez ran sideways, taking the bull out and away with the cape, toward the other picador. He fixed him with a swing of the cape, squarely facing the horse and rider, and stepped back. As the bull saw the horse he charged. The picador's lance slid along his back, and as the shock of the charge lifted the horse, the picador was already half-way out of the saddle, lifting his right leg clear as he missed with the lance and falling to the left side to keep the horse between him and the bull. The horse, lifted and gored, crashed over with the bull driving into him, the picador gave a shove with his boots against the horse and lay clear, waiting to be lifted and hauled away and put on his feet.

Manuel let the bull drive into the fallen horse; he was in no hurry, the picador was safe; besides, it did a picador like that good to worry. He'd stay on longer next time. Lousy pics! He looked across the sand at Zurito a little way out from the *barrera*, his horse rigid, waiting.

"Huh!" he called to the bull, "*Tomar*!" holding the cape in both hands so it would catch his eye. The bull detached himself from the horse and charged the cape, and Manuel, running sideways and holding the cape spread wide, stopped, swung on his heels, and brought the bull sharply around facing Zurito.

"Campagnero accepted a pair of *varas* for the death of one *rosinante*, with Hernandez and Manolo at the *quites*," El Heraldo's critic wrote. "He pressed on the iron and clearly showed he was no horse-lover. The veteran Zurito resurrected some of his old stuff with the pike-pole, notably the *suerte* – –"

"*Olé! Olé!*" the man sitting beside him shouted. The shout was lost in the roar of the crowd, and he slapped the critic on the back. The critic looked up to see Zurito, directly below him, leaning far out over his horse, the length of the pic rising in a sharp angle under his armpit, holding the pic almost by the point, bearing down with all his weight, holding the bull off, the bull pushing and driving to get at the horse, and Zurito, far out, on top of him, holding him, holding him, and slowly pivoting the horse against the pressure, so that at last he was clear. Zurito felt the moment when the horse was clear and the bull could come past, and relaxed the absolute steel lock of his resistance, and the triangular steel point of the pic ripped in the bull's hump of shoulder muscle as he tore loose to find Hernandez's cape before his muzzle. He charged blindly into the cape and the boy took him out into the open arena.

Zurito sat patting his horse and looking at the bull charging the cape that Hernandez swung for him out under the bright light while the crowd shouted.

"You see that one?" he said to Manuel.

"It was a wonder," Manuel said.

"I got him that time," Zurito said. "Look at him now."

At the conclusion of a closely turned pass of the cape the bull slid to his knees. He was up at once, but far out across the sand Manuel and Zurito saw the shine of the pumping flow of blood, smooth against the black of the bull's shoulder.

"I got him that time," Zurito said.

"He's a good bull," Manuel said.

"If they gave me another shot at him, I'd kill him," Zurito said.

"They'll change the thirds on us," Manuel said.

"Look at him now," Zurito said.

"I got to go over there," Manuel said, and started on a run for the other side of the ring, where the *monos* were leading a horse out by the bridle toward the bull, whacking him on the legs with rods and all, in a procession, trying to get him toward the bull, who stood, dropping his head, pawing, unable to make up his mind to charge.

Zurito, sitting his horse, walking him toward the scene, not missing any detail, scowled.

Finally the bull charged, the horse leaders ran for the *barrera, the picador* hit too far back, and the bull got under the horse, lifted him, threw him onto his back.

Zurito watched. The *monos*, in their red shirts, running out to drag the picador clear. The picador, now on his feet, swearing and flopping his arms. Manuel and Hernandez standing ready with their capes. And the bull, the great, black bull, with a horse on his back, hooves dangling, the bridle caught in the horns. Black bull with a horse on his back, staggering short-legged, then arching his neck and lifting, thrusting, charging to slide the horse off, horse sliding down. Then the bull into a lunging charge at the cape Manuel spread for him.

The bull was slower now, Manuel felt. He was bleeding badly. There was a sheen of blood all down his flank.

Manuel offered him the cape again. There he came, eyes open, ugly, watching the cape. Manuel stepped to the side and raised his arms, tightening the cape ahead of the bull for the *verónica*.

Now he was facing the bull. Yes, his head was going down a little. He was carrying it lower. That was Zurito.

Manuel flopped the cape; there he comes; he side-stepped and swung in another *verónica*. He's shooting awfully accurately, he thought. He's had enough fight, so he's watching now. He's hunting now. Got his eye on me. But I always give him the cape.

He shook the cape at the bull; there he comes; he side-stepped. Awful close that time. I don't want to work that close to him.

The edge of the cape was wet with blood where it had swept along the bull's back as he went by.

All right, here's the last one.

Manuel, facing the bull, having turned with him each charge, offered the cape with his two hands. The bull looked at him. Eyes watching, horns straight forward, the bull looked at him, watching.

"Huh!" Manuel said, "*Toro!*" and leaning back, swung the cape forward. Here he comes. He side-stepped, swung the cape in back of him, and pivoted, so the bull followed a swirl of cape and then was left with nothing, fixed by the pass, dominated by the cape. Manuel swung the cape under his muzzle with one hand, to show the bull was fixed, and walked away.

There was no applause.

Manuel walked across the sand toward the *barrera*, while Zurito rode out of the ring. The trumpet had blown to change the act to the planting of the *banderillas* while Manuel had been working with the bull. He had not consciously noticed it. The *monos* were spreading canvas over the two dead horses and sprinkling sawdust around them.

Manuel came up to the *barrera* for a drink of water. Retana's man handed him the heavy porous jug.

Fuentes, the tall gypsy, was standing holding a pair of *banderillas*, holding them together, slim, red sticks, fish-hook points out. He looked at Manuel.

"Go on out there," Manuel said.

The gypsy trotted out. Manuel set down the jug and watched. He wiped his face with his handkerchief.

The critic of *El Heraldo* reached for the bottle of warm champagne that stood between his feet, took a drink, and finished his paragraph.

" – the aged Manolo rated no applause for a vulgar series of lances with the cape and we entered the third of the palings."

Alone in the center of the ring the bull stood, still fixed. Fuentes, tall, flat-backed, walking toward him arrogantly, his arms spread out, the two slim, red sticks, one in each hand, held by the fingers, points straight forward. Fuentes walked forward. Back of him and to one side was a peon with a cape. The bull looked at him and was no longer fixed.

His eyes watched Fuentes, now standing still. Now he leaned back, calling to him. Fuentes twitched the two *banderillas* and the light on the steel points caught the bull's eye.

His tail went up and he charged.

He came straight, his eyes on the man. Fuentes stood still, leaning back, the *banderillas* pointing forward. As the bull lowered his head to hook, Fuentes leaned backward, his arms came together and rose, his two hands touching, the *banderillas* two descending red lines, and leaning forward drove the points into the bull's shoulder, leaning far in over the bull's horns and pivoting on the two upright sticks, his legs tight together, his body curving to one side to let the bull pass.

"*Olé!*" from the crowd.

The bull was hooking wildly, jumping like a trout, all four feet off the ground. The red shaft of the *banderillas* tossed as he jumped.

Manuel, standing at the *barrera*, noticed that he looked always to the right.

"Tell him to drop the next pair on the right," he said to the kid who started to run out to Fuentes with the new *banderillas*.

A heavy hand fell on his shoulder. It was Zurito.

"How do you feel, kid?" he asked.

Manuel was watching the bull.

Zurito leaned forward on the *barrera*, leaning the weight of his body on his arms. Manuel turned to him.

"You're going good," Zurito said.

Manuel shook his head. He had nothing to do now until the next third. The gypsy was very good with the *banderillas*. The bull would come to him in the next third in good shape. He was a good bull. It had all been easy up to now. The final stuff with the sword was all he worried over. He did not really worry. He did not even think about it. But standing there he had a heavy sense of apprehension. He looked out at the bull, planning his *faena*, his work with the red cloth that was to reduce the bull, to make him manageable.

The gypsy was walking out toward the bull again, walking heel-and-toe, insultingly, like a ballroom dancer, the red shafts of the *banderillas* twitching with his walk. The bull watched him, not fixed now, hunting him, but waiting to get close enough so he could be sure of getting him, getting the horns into him.

As Fuentes walked forward the bull charged. Fuentes ran across the quarter of a circle as the bull charged and, as he passed running backward, stopped, swung forward, rose on his toes, arms straight out, and sunk the *banderillas* straight down into the tight of the big shoulder muscles as the bull missed him.

The crowd were wild about it.

"That kid won't stay in this night stuff long," Retana's man said to Zurito.

"He's good," Zurito said.

"Watch him now."

They watched.

Fuentes was standing with his back against the *barrera*. Two of the *cuadrilla* were back of him, with their capes ready to flop over the fence to distract the bull.

The bull, with his tongue out, his barrel heaving, was watching the gypsy.

He thought he had him now. Back against the red planks. Only a short charge away. The bull watched him.

The gypsy bent back, drew back his arms, the *banderillas* pointing at the bull. He called to the bull, stamped one foot. The bull was suspicious. He wanted the man. No more barbs in the shoulder.

Fuentes walked a little closer to the bull. Bent back. Called again. Somebody in the crowd shouted a warning.

"He's too damn close," Zurito said.

"Watch him," Retana's man said.

Leaning back, inciting the bull with the *banderillas*, Fuentes jumped, both feet off the ground. As he jumped the bull's tail rose and he charged. Fuentes came down on his toes, arms straight out, whole body arching forward, and drove the shafts straight down as he swung his body clear of the right horn.

The bull crashed into the *barrera* where the flopping capes had attracted his eye as he lost the man.

The gypsy came running along the *barrera* toward Manuel, taking the applause of the crowd. His vest was ripped where he had not quite cleared the point of the horn. He was happy about it, showing it to the spectators. He made the tour of the ring. Zurito saw him go by, smiling, pointing at his vest. He smiled.

Somebody else was planting the last pair of *banderillas*. Nobody was paying any attention.

Retana's man tucked a baton inside the red cloth of a *muleta*, folded the cloth over it, and handed it over the *barrera* to Manuel. He reached in the leather sword-case, took out a sword, and holding it by its leather scabbard, reached it over the fence to Manuel. Manuel pulled the blade out by the red hilt and the scabbard fell limp.

He looked at Zurito. The big man saw he was sweating.

"Now you get him, kid," Zurito said.

Manuel nodded.

"He's in good shape," Zurito said.

"Just like you want him," Retana's man assured him.

Manuel nodded.

The trumpeter, up under the roof, blew for the final act, and Manuel walked across the arena toward where, up in the dark boxes, the president must be.

In the front row of seats the substitute bull-fight critic of *El Heraldo* took a long drink of the warm champagne. He had decided it was not worth while to write a running story and would write up the *corrida* back in the office. What the hell was it anyway? Only a nocturnal. If he missed anything he would get it out of the morning papers. He took another drink of the champagne. He had a date at Maxim's at twelve. Who were these bull-fighters anyway? Kids and bums. A bunch of bums. He put his pad of paper in his pocket and looked over toward Manuel, standing very much alone in the ring, gesturing with his hat in a salute toward a box he could not see high up in the dark plaza. Out in the ring the bull stood quiet, looking at nothing.

"I dedicate this bull to you, Mr. President, and to the public of Madrid, the most intelligent and generous of the world," was what Manuel was saying. It was a formula. He said it all. It was a little long for nocturnal use.

He bowed at the dark, straightened, tossed his hat over his shoulder, and, carrying the *muleta* in his left hand and the sword in his right, walked out toward the bull.

Manuel walked toward the bull. The bull looked at him; his eyes were quick. Manuel noticed the way the *banderillas* hung down on his left shoulder and the steady sheen of blood from Zurito's pic-ing. He noticed the way the bull's feet were. As he walked forward, holding the *muleta* in his left hand and the sword in his right, he watched the bull's feet. The bull could not charge without gathering his feet together. Now he stood square on them, dully.

Manuel walked toward him, watching his feet. This was all right. He could do this. He must work to get the bull's head down, so he could go in past the horns and kill him. He did not think about the sword, not about killing the bull. He thought about one thing at a time. The coming things oppressed him, though. Walking forward, watching the bull's feet, he saw successively his eyes, his wet muzzle, and the wide, forward-pointing spread of his horns. The bull had light circles about his eyes. His eyes watched Manuel. He felt he was going to get this little one with the white face.

Standing still now and spreading the red cloth of the *muleta* with the sword, pricking the point into the cloth so that the sword, now held in his left hand, spread the red flannel like the jib of a boat, Manuel noticed the points of the bull's horns. One of them was splintered from banging against the *barrera*. The other was sharp as a porcupine quill. Manuel noticed while spreading the *muleta* that the white base of the horn was stained red. While he noticed these things he did not lose sight of the bull's feet. The bull watched Manuel steadily.

He's on the defensive now, Manuel thought. He's reserving himself. I've got to bring him out of that and get his head down. Always get his head down. Zurito had his head down once, but he's come back. He'll bleed when I start him going and that will bring it down.

Holding the *muleta*, with the sword in his left hand widening it in front of him, he called to the bull.

The bull looked at him.

He leaned back insultingly and shook the wide-spread flannel.

The bull saw the *muleta*. It was a bright scarlet under the arc-light. The bull's legs tightened.

Here he comes. Whoosh! Manuel turned as the bull came and raised the *muleta* so that it passed over the bull's horns and swept down his broad back from head to tail. The bull had gone clean up in the air with the charge. Manuel had not moved.

At the end of the pass the bull turned like a cat coming around a corner and faced Manuel.

He was on the offensive again. His heaviness was gone. Manuel noted the fresh blood shining down the black shoulder and dripping down the bull's leg. He drew the sword out of the *muleta* and held it in his right hand. The *muleta* held low down in his left hand, leaning toward the left, he called to the bull. The bull's legs tightened, his eyes on the *muleta*. Here he comes,

Manuel thought. Yuh!

He swung with the charge, sweeping the *muleta* ahead of the bull, his feet firm, the sword following the curve, a point of light under the arcs.

The bull recharged as the *pase natural* finished and Manuel raised the *muleta* for a *pase de pecho.* Firmly planted, the bull came by his chest under the raised *muleta.* Manuel leaned his head back to avoid the clattering *banderillo* shafts. The hot, black bull body touched his chest as it passed.

Too damn close, Manuel thought. Zurito, leaning on the *barrera*, spoke rapidly to the gypsy, who trotted out toward Manuel with a cape. Zurito pulled his hat down low and looked out across the arena at Manuel.

Manuel was facing the bull again, the *muleta* held low and to the left. The bull's head was down as he watched the *muleta.*

"If it was Belmonte doing that stuff, they'd go crazy," Retana's man said.

Zurito said nothing. He was watching Manuel out in the center of the arena.

"Where did the boss dig this fellow up?" Retana's man asked.

"Out of the hospital," Zurito said.

"That's where he's going damn quick," Retana's man said.

Zurito turned on him.

"Knock on that," he said, pointing to the *barrera.*

"I was just kidding, man," Retana's man said.

"Knock on the wood."

Retana's man leaned forward and knocked three times on the *barrera.*

"Watch the *faena*," Zurito said.

Out in the center of the ring, under the lights, Manuel was kneeling, facing the bull, and as he raised the *muleta* in both hands the bull charged, tail up.

Manuel swung his body clear and, as the bull recharged, brought around the *muleta* in a half-circle that pulled the bull to his knees.

"Why, that one's a great bull-fighter," Retana's man said.

"No, he's not," said Zurito.

Manuel stood up and, the *muleta* in his left hand, the sword in his right, acknowledged the applause from the dark plaza.

The bull had humped himself up from his knees and stood waiting, his head hung low.

Zurito spoke to two of the other lads of the *cuadrilla* and they ran out to stand back of Manuel with their capes. There were four men back of him now. Hernandez had followed him since he first came out with the *muleta*. Fuentes stood watching, his cape held against his body, tall, in repose, watching lazy-eyed. Now the two came up. Hernandez motioned them to stand one at each side. Manuel stood alone, facing the bull.

Manuel waved back the men with the capes. Stepping back cautiously, they saw his face was white and sweating.

Didn't they know enough to keep back? Did they want to catch the bull's eye with the capes after he was fixed and ready? He had enough to worry about without that kind of thing.

The bull was standing, his four feet square, looking at the *muleta*. Manuel furled the *muleta* in his left hand. The bull's eyes watched it. His body was heavy on his feet. He carried his head low, but not too low.

Manuel lifted the *muleta* at him. The bull did not move. Only his eyes watched.

He's all lead, Manuel thought. He's all square. He's framed right. He'll take it.

He thought in bull-fight terms. Sometimes he had a thought and the particular piece of slang would not come into his mind and he could not realize the thought. His instincts and his knowledge worked automatically, and his brain worked slowly and in words. He knew all about bulls. He did not have to think about them. He just did the right thing. His eyes noted things and his body performed the necessary measures without thought. If he thought about it, he would be gone.

Now, facing the bull, he was conscious of many things at the same time. There were the horns, the one splintered, the other smoothly sharp, the need to profile himself toward the left horn, lance himself short and straight, lower the *muleta* so the bull would follow it, and, going in over the horns, put the sword all the way into a little spot about as big as a five-peseta piece straight in back of the neck, between the sharp pitch of the bull's shoulders. He must do all this and must then come out from between the horns. He was conscious he must do all this, but his only thought was in words: "*Corto y derecho.*"

"*Corto y derecho*," he thought, furling the *muleta*. Short and straight. *Corto y derecho*, he drew the sword out of the *muleta*, profiled on the splintered left horn, dropped the *muleta* across his body, so his right hand with the sword on the level with his eye made the sign of the cross, and, rising on his toes, sighted along the dipping blade of the sword at the spot high up between the bull's shoulders.

Corto y derecho he launched himself on the bull.

There was a shock, and he felt himself go up in the air. He pushed on the sword as he went up and over, and it flew out of his hand. He hit the ground and the bull was on him. Manuel, lying on the ground, kicked at the bull's muzzle with his slippered feet. Kicking, kicking, the bull after him, missing him in his excitement, bumping him with his head, driving the horns into the sand. Kicking like a man keeping a ball in the air, Manuel kept the bull from getting a clean thrust at him.

Manuel felt the wind on his back from the capes flopping at the bull, and then the bull was gone, gone over him in a rush. Dark, as his belly went over. Not even stepped on.

Manuel stood up and picked up the *muleta*. Fuentes handed him the sword. It was bent where it had struck the shoulder-blade. Manuel straightened it on his knee and ran toward the bull, standing now beside one of the dead horses. As he ran, his jacket flopped where it had been ripped under his armpit.

"Get him out of there," Manuel shouted to the gypsy. The bull had smelled the blood of the dead horse and ripped into the canvas-cover with his horns. He charged Fuentes's cape, with the canvas hanging from his splintered horn, and the crowd laughed. Out in the ring, he tossed his head to rid himself of the canvas. Hernandez, running up from behind him, grabbed the end of the canvas and neatly lifted it off the horn.

The bull followed it in a half-charge and stopped still. He was on the defensive again. Manuel was walking toward him with the sword and *muleta.* Manuel swung the *muleta* before him. The bull would not charge.

Manuel profiled toward the bull, sighting along the dipping blade of the sword. The bull was motionless, seemingly dead on his feet, incapable of another charge.

Manuel rose to his toes, sighting along the steel, and charged.

Again there was the shock and he felt himself being borne back in a rush, to strike hard on the sand. There was no chance of kicking this time. The bull was on top of him. Manuel lay as though dead, his head on his arms, and the bull bumped him. Bumped his back, bumped his face in the sand. He felt the horn go into the sand between his folded arms. The bull hit him in the small of the back. His face drove into the sand. The horn drove through one of his sleeves and the bull ripped it off. Manuel was tossed clear and the bull followed the capes.

Manuel got up, found the sword and *muleta*, tried the point of the sword with his thumb, and then ran toward the *barrera* for a new sword.

Retana's man handed him the sword over the edge of the *barrera.*

"Wipe off your face," he said.

Manuel, running again toward the bull, wiped his bloody face with his handkerchief. He had not seen Zurito. Where was Zurito?

The *cuadrilla* had stepped away from the bull and waited with their capes. The bull stood, heavy and dull again after the action.

Manuel walked toward him with the *muleta.* He stopped and shook it. The bull did not respond. He passed it right and left, left and right before the bull's muzzle. The bull's eyes watched it and turned with the swing, but he would not charge. He was waiting for Manuel.

Manuel was worried. There was nothing to do but go in. *Corto y derecho.* He profiled close to the bull, crossed the *muleta* in front of his body and charged. As he pushed in the sword, he jerked his body to the left to clear the horn. The bull passed him and the sword shot up in the air, twinkling under the arc-lights, to fall red-hilted on the sand.

Manuel ran over and picked it up. It was bent and he straightened it over his knee.

As he came running toward the bull, fixed again now, he passed Hernandez standing with his cape.

"He's all bone," the boy said encouragingly.

Manuel nodded, wiping his face. He put the bloody handkerchief in his pocket.

There was the bull. He was close to the *barrera* now. Damn him. Maybe he was all bone. Maybe there was not any place for the sword to go in. The hell there wasn't! He'd show them.

He tried a pass with the *muleta* and the bull did not move. Manuel chopped the *muleta* back and forth in front of the bull. Nothing doing.

He furled the *muleta*, drew the sword out, profiled and drove in on the bull. He felt the sword buckle as he shoved it in, leaning his weight on it, and then it shot high in the air, end-over-ending into the crowd. Manuel had jerked clear as the sword jumped.

The first cushions thrown down out of the dark missed him. Then one hit him in the face, his bloody face looking toward the crowd. They were coming down fast. Spotting the sand. Somebody threw an empty champagne-bottle from close range. It hit Manuel on the foot. He stood there watching the dark, where the things were coming from. Then something whished through the air and struck by him. Manuel leaned over and picked it up. It was his sword. He straightened it over his knee and gestured with it to the crowd.

"Thank you," he said. "Thank you."

Oh, the dirty bastards! Dirty bastards! Oh, the lousy, dirty bastards! He kicked into a cushion as he ran.

There was the bull. The same as ever. All right, you dirty, lousy bastard!

Manuel passed the *muleta* in front of the bull's black muzzle.

Nothing doing.

You won't! All right. He stepped close and jammed the sharp peak of the *muleta* into the bull's damp muzzle.

The bull was on him as he jumped back and as he tripped on a cushion he felt the horn go into him, into his side. He grabbed the horn with his two hands and rode backward, holding tight onto the place. The bull tossed him and he was clear. He lay still. It was all right. The bull was gone.

He got up coughing and feeling broken and gone. The dirty bastards!

"Give me the sword," he shouted. "Give me the stuff."

Fuentes came up with the *muleta* and the sword.

Hernandez put his arm around him.

"Go on to the infirmary, man," he said. "Don't be a damn fool."

"Get away from me," Manuel said. "Get to hell away from me."

He twisted free. Hernandez shrugged his shoulders. Manuel ran toward the bull.

There was the bull standing, heavy, firmly planted.

All right, you bastard! Manuel drew the sword out of the *muleta*, sighted with the same movement, and flung himself onto the bull. He felt the sword go in all the way. Right up to the guard. Four fingers and his thumb into the bull. The blood was hot on his knuckles, and he was on top of the bull.

The bull lurched with him as he lay on, and seemed to sink; then he was standing clear. He looked at the bull going down slowly over on his side, then suddenly four feet in the air.

Then he gestured at the crowd, his hand warm from the bull blood.

All right, you bastards! He wanted to say something, but he started to cough. It was hot and choking. He looked down for the *muleta*. He must go over and salute the president. President hell! He was sitting down looking at something. It was the bull. His four feet up. Thick tongue out. Things crawling around on his belly and under his legs. Crawling where the hair was thin. Dead bull. To hell with the bull! To hell with them all! He started to get to his feet and commenced to cough. He sat down again, coughing. Somebody came and pushed him up.

They carried him across the ring to the infirmary, running with him across the sand, standing blocked at the gate as the mules came in, then around under the dark passageway, men grunting as they took him up the stairway, and then laid him down.

The doctor and two men in white were waiting for him. They laid him out on the table. They were cutting away his shirt. Manuel felt tired. His whole chest felt scalding inside. He started to cough and they held something to his mouth. Everybody was very busy.

There was an electric light in his eyes. He shut his eyes.

He heard someone coming very heavily up the stairs. Then he did not hear it. Then he heard a noise far off. That was the crowd. Well, somebody would have to kill his other bull. They had cut away all his shirt. The doctor smiled at him. There was Retana.

"Hello, Retana!" Manuel said. He could not hear his voice.

Retana smiled at him and said something. Manuel could not hear it.

Zurito stood beside the table, bending over where the doctor was working. He was in his picador clothes, without his hat.

Zurito said something to him. Manuel could not hear it.

Zurito was speaking to Retana. One of the men in white smiled and handed Retana a pair of scissors. Retana gave them to Zurito. Zurito said something to Manuel. He could not hear it.

To hell with this operating-table. He'd been on plenty of operating-tables before. He was not going to die. There would be a priest if he was going to die.

Zurito was saying something to him. Holding up the scissors.

That was it. They were going to cut off his *coleta*. They were going to cut off his pigtail.

Manuel sat up on the operating-table. The doctor stepped back, angry. Someone grabbed him and held him.

"You couldn't do a thing like that, Manos," he said.

He heard suddenly, clearly, Zurito's voice.

"That's all right," Zurito said. "I won't do it. I was joking."

"I was going good," Manuel said. "I didn't have any luck. That was all."

Manuel lay back. They had put something over his face. It was all familiar. He inhaled deeply. He felt very tired. He was very, very tired. They took the thing away from his face.

"I was going good," Manuel said weakly. "I was going great."

Retana looked at Zurito and started for the door.

"I'll stay here with him," Zurito said.

Retana shrugged his shoulders.

Manuel opened his eyes and looked at Zurito.

"Wasn't I going good, Manos?" he asked, for confirmation.

"Sure," said Zurito. "You were going great."

The doctor's assistant put the cone over Manuel's face and he inhaled deeply. Zurito stood awkwardly, watching.

IN ANOTHER COUNTRY

IN THE FALL THE WAR WAS ALWAYS there, but we did not go to it any more. It was cold in the fall in Milan and the dark came very early. Then the electric lights came on, and it was pleasant along the streets looking in the windows. There was much game hanging outside the shops, and the snow powdered in the fur of the foxes and the wind blew their tails. The deer hung stiff and heavy and empty, and small birds blew in the wind and the wind turned their feathers. It was a cold fall and the wind came down from the mountains.

We were all at the hospital every afternoon, and there were different ways of walking across the town through the dusk to the hospital. Two of the ways were alongside canals, but they were long. Always, though, you crossed a bridge across a canal to enter the hospital. There was a choice of three bridges. On one of them a woman sold roasted chestnuts. It was warm, standing in front of her charcoal fire, and the chestnuts were warm afterward in your pocket. The hospital was very old and very beautiful, and you entered through a gate and walked across a courtyard and out a gate on the other side. There were usually funerals starting from the courtyard. Beyond the old hospital were the new brick pavilions, and there we met every afternoon and were all very polite and interested in what was the matter, and sat in the machines that were to make so much difference.

The doctor came up to the machine where I was sitting and said: "What did you like best to do before the war? Did you practice a sport?"

I said: "Yes, football."

"Good" he said. "You will be able to play football again better than ever."

My knee did not bend and the leg dropped straight from the knee to the ankle without a calf, and the machine was to bend the knee and make it move as in riding a tricycle. But it did not bend yet, and instead the machine lurched when it came to the bending part. The doctor said: "That will all pass. You are a fortunate young man. You will play football again like a champion."

In the next machine was a major who had a little hand like a baby's. He winked at me when the doctor examined his hand, which was between two leather straps that bounced up and down and flapped the stiff fingers, and said: "And will I too play football, captain-doctor?" He had been a very great fencer, and before the war the greatest fencer in Italy.

The doctor went to his office in a back room and brought a photograph which showed a hand that had been withered almost as small as the major's, before it had taken a machine course, and after was a little larger. The major held the photograph with his good hand and looked at it very carefully. "A wound?" he asked.

"An industrial accident," the doctor said.

"Very interesting, very interesting," the major said, and handed it back to the doctor.

"You have confidence?"

"No," said the major.

There were three boys who came each day who were about the same age I was. They were all three from Milan, and one of them was to be a lawyer, and one was to be a painter, and one had intended to be a soldier, and after we were finished with the machines, sometimes we walked back together to the Café Cova, which was next door to the Scala. We walked the short way through the communist quarter because we were four together. The people hated us because we were officers, and from a wine-shop some one would call out, "*A basso gli ufficiali!*" as we passed. Another boy who walked with us sometimes and made us five wore a black silk handkerchief across his face because he had no nose then and his face was to be rebuilt. He had gone out to the front from the military academy and been wounded within an hour after he had gone into the front line for the first time. They rebuilt his face, but he came from a very old family and they could never get the nose exactly right. He went to South America and worked in a bank. But this was a long time ago, and then we did not any of us know how it was going to be afterward. We only knew then that there was always the war, but that we were not going to it any more.

We all had the same medals, except the boy with the black silk bandage across his face, and he had not been at the front long enough to get any medals. The tall boy with a very pale face who was to be a lawyer had been a lieutenant of *Arditi* and had three medals of the sort we each had only one of. He had lived a very long time with death and was a little detached. We were all a little detached, and there was nothing that held us together except that we met every afternoon at the hospital. Although, as we walked to the Cova through the tough part of town, walking in the dark, with light and singing coming out of the wine-shops, and sometimes having to walk into the street when the men and women would crowd together on the sidewalk so that we would have had to jostle them to get by, we felt held together by there being something that had happened that they, the people who disliked us, did not understand.

We ourselves all understood the Cova, where it was rich and warm and not too brightly lighted, and noisy and smoky at certain hours, and there were always girls at the tables and the illustrated papers on a rack on the wall. The girls at the Cova were very patriotic, and I found that the most patriotic people in Italy were the café girls – and I believe they are still patriotic.

The boys at first were very polite about my medals and asked me what I had done to get them. I showed them the papers, which were written in very beautiful language and full of *fratellanza* and *abnegazione*, but which really said, with the adjectives removed, that I had been given the medals because I was an American. After that their manner changed a little toward me, although I was their friend against outsiders. I was a friend, but I was never really one of them after they had read the citations, because it had been different with them and they had done very different things to get their medals. I had been wounded, it was true; but we all knew that being wounded, after all, was really an accident. I was never ashamed of the ribbons, though, and sometimes, after the cocktail hour, I would imagine myself having done all the things they had done to get their medals; but walking home at night through the empty streets with the cold wind and all the shops closed, trying to keep near the street lights, I knew that I would never have done such things, and I was very much afraid to die, and often lay in bed at night by myself, afraid to die and wondering how I would be when I went back to the front again.

The three with the medals were like hunting-hawks; and I was not a hawk, although I might seem a hawk to those who had never hunted; they, the three, knew better and so we drifted apart. But I stayed good friends with the boy who had been wounded his first day at the front, because he would never know now how he would have turned out; so he could never be accepted either, and I liked him because I thought perhaps he would not have turned out to be a hawk either.

The major, who had been the great fencer, did not believe in bravery, and spent much time while we sat in the machines correcting my grammar. He had complimented me on how I spoke Italian, and we talked together very easily. One day I had said that Italian seemed such an easy language to me that I could not take a great interest in it; everything was so easy to say. "Ah, yes," the major said. "Why, then, do you not take up the use of grammar?" So we took up the use of grammar, and soon Italian was such a difficult language that I was afraid to talk to him until I had the grammar straight in my mind.

The major came very regularly to the hospital. I do not think he ever missed a day, although I am sure he did not believe in the machines. There was a time when none of us believed in the machines, and one day the major said it was all nonsense. The machines were new then and it was we who were to prove them. It was an idiotic idea, he said, "a theory, like another." I had not learned my grammar, and he said I was a stupid impossible disgrace, and he was a fool to have bothered with me. He was a small man and he sat straight up in his chair with his right hand thrust into the machine and looked straight ahead at the wall while the straps thumped up and down with his fingers in them.

"What will you do when the war is over if it is over?" he asked me. "Speak grammatically!"

"I will go to the States."

"Are you married?"

"No, but I hope to be."

"The more of a fool you are," he said. He seemed very angry. "A man must not marry."

"Why, Signor Maggiore?"

"Don't call me 'Signor Maggiore.'"

"Why must not a man marry?"

"He cannot marry. He cannot marry," he said angrily. "If he is to lose everything, he should not place himself in a position to lose that. He should not place himself in a position to lose. He should find things he cannot lose."

He spoke very angrily and bitterly, and looked straight ahead while he talked.

"But why should he necessarily lose it?"

"He'll lose it," the major said. He was looking at the wall. Then he looked down at the machine and jerked his little hand out from between the straps and slapped it hard against his thigh. "He'll lose it," he almost shouted. "Don't argue with me!" Then he called to the attendant who ran the machines. "Come and turn this damned thing off."

He went back into the other room for the light treatment and the massage. Then I heard him ask the doctor if he might use his telephone and he shut the door. When he came back into the room, I was sitting in another machine. He was wearing his cape and had his cap on, and he came directly toward my machine and put his arm on my shoulder.

"I am so sorry," he said, and patted me on the shoulder with his good hand. "I would not be rude. My wife has just died. You must forgive me."

"Oh—" I said, feeling sick for him. "I am *so* sorry."

He stood there biting his lower lip. "It is very difficult," he said. "I cannot resign myself."

He looked straight past me and out through the window. Then he began to cry. "I am utterly unable to resign myself," he said and choked. And then crying, his head up looking at nothing, carrying himself straight and soldierly, with tears on both his cheeks and biting his lips, he walked past the machines and out the door.

The doctor told me that the major's wife, who was very young and whom he had not married until he was definitely invalided out of the war, had died of pneumonia. She had been sick only a few days. No one expected her to die. The major did not come to the hospital for three days. Then he came at the usual hour, wearing a black band on the sleeve of his uniform. When he came back, there were large framed photographs around the wall, of all sorts of wounds before and after they had been cured by the machines. In front of the machine the major used were three photographs of hands like his that were completely restored. I do not know where the doctor got them. I always understood we were the first to use the machines. The photographs did not make much difference to the major because he only looked out of the window.

HILLS LIKE WHITE ELEPHANTS

THE HILLS ACROSS THE VALLEY OF THE Ebro were long and white. On this side there was no shade and no trees and the station was between two lines of rails in the sun. Close against the side of the station there was the warm shadow of the building and a curtain, made of strings of bamboo beads, hung across the open door into the bar, to keep out flies. The American and the girl with him sat at a table in the shade, outside the building. It was very hot and the express from Barcelona would come in forty minutes. It stopped at this junction for two minutes and went on to Madrid.

"What should we drink?" the girl asked. She had taken off her hat and put it on the table.

"It's pretty hot," the man said.

"Let's drink beer."

"*Dos cervezas*," the man said into the curtain.

"Big ones?" a woman asked from the doorway.

"Yes. Two big ones."

The woman brought two glasses of beer and two felt pads. She put the felt pads and the beer glasses on the table and looked at the man and the girl. The girl was looking off at the line of hills. They were white in the sun and the country was brown and dry.

"They look like white elephants," she said.

"I've never seen one," the man drank his beer.

"No, you wouldn't have."

"I might have," the man said. "Just because you say I wouldn't have doesn't prove anything."

The girl looked at the bead curtain. "They've painted something on it," she said. "What does it say?"

"Anis del Toro. It's a drink."

"Could we try it?"

The man called "Listen" through the curtain. The woman came out from the bar.

"Four reales."

"We want two Anis del Toro."

"With water?"

"Do you want it with water?"

"I don't know," the girl said. "Is it good with water?"

"It's all right."

"You want them with water?" asked the woman.

"Yes, with water."

"It tastes like licorice," the girl said and put the glass down.

"That's the way with everything."

"Yes," said the girl. "Everything tastes of licorice. Especially all the things you've waited so long for, like absinthe."

"Oh, cut it out."

"You started it," the girl said. "I was being amused. I was having a fine time."

"Well, let's try and have a fine time."

"All right. I was trying. I said the mountains looked like white elephants. Wasn't that bright?"

"That was bright."

"I wanted to try this new drink: That's all we do, isn't it – look at things and try new drinks?"

"I guess so."

The girl looked across at the hills.

"They're lovely hills," she said. "They don't really look like white elephants. I just meant the coloring of their skin through the trees."

"Should we have another drink?"

"All right."

The warm wind blew the bead curtain against the table.

"The beer's nice and cool," the man said.

"It's lovely," the girl said.

"It's really an awfully simple operation, Jig," the man said. "It's not really an operation at all."

The girl looked at the ground the table legs rested on.

"I know you wouldn't mind it, Jig. It's really not anything. It's just to let the air in."

The girl did not say anything.

"I'll go with you and I'll stay with you all the time. They just let the air in and then it's all perfectly natural."

"Then what will we do afterward?"

"We'll be fine afterward. Just like we were before."

"What makes you think so?"

"That's the only thing that bothers us. It's the only thing that's made us unhappy."

The girl looked at the bead curtain, put her hand out and took hold of two of the strings of beads.

"And you think then we'll be all right and be happy."

"I know we will. You don't have to be afraid. I've known lots of people that have done it."

"So have I," said the girl. "And afterward they were all so happy."

"Well," the man said, "if you don't want to you don't have to. I wouldn't have you do it if you didn't want to. But I know it's perfectly simple."

"And you really want to?"

"I think it's the best thing to do. But I don't want you to do it if you don't really want to."

"And if I do it you'll be happy and things will be like they were and you'll love me?"

"I love you now. You know I love you."

"I know. But if I do it, then it will be nice again if I say things are like white elephants, and you'll like it?"

"I'll love it. I love it now but I just can't think about it. You know how I get when I worry."

"If I do it you won't ever worry?"

"I won't worry about that because it's perfectly simple."

"Then I'll do it. Because I don't care about me."

"What do you mean?"

"I don't care about me."

"Well, I care about you."

"Oh, yes. But I don't care about me. And I'll do it and then everything will be fine."

"I don't want you to do it if you feel that way."

The girl stood up and walked to the end of the station. Across, on the other side, were fields of grain and trees along the banks of the Ebro. Far away, beyond the river, were mountains. The shadow of a cloud moved across the field of grain and she saw the river through the trees.

"And we could have all this," she said. "And we could have everything and every day we make it more impossible."

"What did you say?"

"I said we could have everything."

"We can have everything."

"No, we can't."

"We can have the whole world."

"No, we can't."

"We can go everywhere."

"No, we can't. It isn't ours any more."

"It's ours."

"No, it isn't. And once they take it away, you never get it back."

"But they haven't taken it away."

"We'll wait and see."

"Come on back in the shade," he said. "You mustn't feel that way."

"I don't feel any way," the girl said. "I just know things."

"I don't want you to do anything that you don't want to do–"

"Nor that isn't good for me," she said. "I know. Could we have another beer?"

"All right. But you've got to realize – –"

"I realize," the girl said. "Can't we maybe stop talking?"

They sat down at the table and the girl looked across at the hills on the dry side of the valley and the man looked at her and at the table.

"You've got to realize," he said, "that I don't want you to do it if you don't want to. I'm perfectly willing to go through with it if it means anything to you."

"Doesn't it mean anything to you? We could get along."

"Of course it does. But I don't want anybody but you. I don't want any one else. And I know it's perfectly simple."

"Yes, you know it's perfectly simple."

"It's all right for you to say that, but I do know it."

"Would you do something for me now?"

"I'd do anything for you."

"Would you please please please please please please please stop talking?"

He did not say anything but looked at the bags against the wall of the station. There were labels on them from all the hotels where they had spent nights.

"But I don't want you to," he said, "I don't care anything about it."

"I'll scream," the girl said.

The woman came out through the curtains with two glasses of beer and put them down on the damp felt pads. "The train comes in five minutes," she said.

"What did she say?" asked the girl.

"That the train is coming in five minutes."

The girl smiled brightly at the woman, to thank her.

"I'd better take the bags over to the other side of the station," the man said. She smiled at him.

"All right. Then come back and we'll finish the beer."

He picked up the two heavy bags and carried them around the station to the other tracks. He looked up the tracks but could not see the train. Coming back, he walked through the barroom, where people waiting for the train were drinking. He drank an Anis at the bar and looked at the people. They were all waiting reasonably for the train. He went out through the bead curtain. She was sitting at the table and smiled at him.

"Do you feel better?" he asked.

"I feel fine," she said. "There's nothing wrong with me. I feel fine."

The Killers

THE DOOR OF HENRY'S LUNCH-ROOM opened and two men came in. They sat down at the counter.

"What's yours?" George asked them.

"I don't know," one of the men said. "What do you want to eat, Al?"

"I don't know," said Al. "I don't know what I want to eat."

Outside it was getting dark. The street-light came on outside the window. The two men at the counter read the menu. From the other end of the counter Nick Adams watched them. He had been talking to George when they came in.

"I'll have a roast pork tenderloin with apple sauce and mashed potatoes," the first man said.

"It isn't ready yet."

"What the hell do you put it on the card for?"

"That's the dinner," George explained. "You can get that at six o'clock."

George looked at the clock on the wall behind the counter.

"It's five o'clock."

"The clock says twenty minutes past five," the second man said.

"It's twenty minutes fast."

"Oh, to hell with the clock," the first man said. "What have you got to eat?"

"I can give you any kind of sandwiches," George said. "You can have ham and eggs, bacon and eggs, liver and bacon, or a steak."

"Give me chicken croquettes with green peas and cream sauce and mashed potatoes."

"That's the dinner."

"Everything we want's the dinner, eh? That's the way you work it."

"I can give you ham and eggs, bacon and eggs, liver — —"

"I'll take ham and eggs," the man called Al said. He wore a derby hat and a black overcoat buttoned across the chest. His face was small and white and he had tight lips. He wore a silk muffler and gloves.

"Give me bacon and eggs," said the other man. He was about the same size as Al. Their faces were different, but they were dressed like twins. Both wore overcoats too tight for them. They sat leaning forward, their elbows on the counter.

"Got anything to drink?" Al asked.

"Silver beer, bevo, ginger-ale," George said.

"I mean you got anything to *drink?*"

"Just those I said."

"This is a hot town," said the other. "What do they call it?"

"Summit."

"Ever hear of it?" Al asked his friend.

"No," said the friend.

"What do you do here nights?" Al asked.

"They eat the dinner," his friend said. "They all come here and eat the big dinner."

"That's right," George said.

"So you think that's right?" Al asked George.

"Sure."

"You're a pretty bright boy, aren't you?"

"Sure," said George.

"Well, you're not," said the other little man. "Is he, Al?"

"He's dumb," said Al. He turned to Nick. "What's your name?"

"Adams."

"Another bright boy," Al said. "Ain't he a bright boy, Max?"

"The town's full of bright boys," Max said.

George put the two platters, one of ham and eggs, the other of bacon and eggs, on the counter. He set down two side-dishes of fried potatoes and closed the wicket into the kitchen.

"Which is yours?" he asked Al.

"Don't you remember?"

"Ham and eggs."

"Just a bright boy," Max said. He leaned forward and took the ham and eggs. Both men ate with their gloves on. George watched them eat.

"What are *you* looking it?" Max looked at George.

"Nothing."

"The hell you were. You were looking at me."

"Maybe the boy meant it for a joke, Max," Al said.

George laughed.

"*You* don't have to laugh," Max said to him. "*You* don't have to laugh at all, see?"

"All right," said George.

"So he thinks it's all right." Max turned to Al. "He thinks it's all right. That's a good one."

"Oh, he's a thinker," Al said. They went on eating.

"What's the bright boy's name down the counter?" Al asked Max.

"Hey, bright boy," Max said to Nick. "You go around on the other side of the counter with your boy friend."

"What's the idea?" Nick asked.

"There isn't any idea."

"You better go around, bright boy," Al said. Nick went around behind the counter.

"What's the idea?" George asked.

"None of your damn business," Al said. "Who's out in the kitchen?"

"The nigger."

"What do you mean the nigger?"

"The nigger that cooks."

"Tell him to come in."

"What's the idea?"

"Tell him to come in."

"Where do you think you are?"

"We know damn well where we are," the man called Max said. "Do we look silly?"

"You talk silly," Al said to him. "What the hell do you argue with this kid for? Listen," he said to George, "tell the nigger to come out here."

"What are you going to do to him?"

"Nothing. Use your head, bright boy. What would we do to a nigger?"

George opened the slit that opened back into the kitchen. "Sam," he called. "Come in here a minute."

The door to the kitchen opened and the nigger came in. "What was it?" he asked. The two men at the counter took a look at him.

"All right, nigger. You stand right there," Al said.

Sam, the nigger, standing in his apron, looked at the two men sitting at the counter. "Yes, sir," he said. Al got down from his stool.

"I'm going back to the kitchen with the nigger and bright boy," he said. "Go on back to the kitchen, nigger. You go with him, bright boy." The little man walked after Nick and Sam, the cook, back into the kitchen. The door shut after them. The man called Max sat at the counter opposite George. He didn't look at George but looked in the mirror that ran along back of the counter. Henry's had been made over from a saloon into a lunch-counter.

"Well, bright boy," Max said, looking into the mirror, "why don't you say something?"

"What's it all about?"

"Hey, Al," Max called, "bright boy wants to know what it's all about."

"Why don't you tell him?" Al's voice came from the kitchen.

"What do you think it's all about?"

"I don't know."

"What do you think?"

Max looked into the mirror all the time he was talking.

"I wouldn't say."

"Hey, Al, bright boy says he wouldn't say what he thinks it's all about."

"I can hear you, all right," Al said from the kitchen. He had propped open the slit that dishes passed through into the kitchen with a catsup bottle. "Listen, bright boy," he said from the kitchen to George. "Stand a little further along the bar. You move a little to the left, Max." He was like a photographer arranging for a group picture.

"Talk to me, bright boy," Max said. "What do you think's going to happen?"

George did not say anything.

"I'll tell you," Max said. "We're going to kill a Swede. Do you know a big Swede named Ole Andreson?"

"Yes."

"He comes here to eat every night, don't he?"

"Sometimes he comes here."

"He comes here at six o'clock, don't he?"

"If he comes."

"We know all that, bright boy," Max said. "Talk about something else. Ever go to the movies?"

"Once in a while."

"You ought to go to the movies more. The movies are fine for a bright boy like you."

"What are you going to kill Ole Andreson for? What did he ever do to you?"

"He never had a chance to do anything to us. He never even seen us."

"And he's only going to see us once," Al said from the kitchen.

"What are you going to kill him for, then?" George asked.

"We're killing him for a friend. Just to oblige a friend, bright boy."

"Shut up," said Al from the kitchen. "You talk too goddam much."

"Well, I got to keep bright boy amused. Don't I, bright boy?"

"You talk too damn much," Al said. "The nigger and my bright boy are amused by themselves. I got them tied up like a couple of girl friends in the convent."

"I suppose you were in a convent?"

"You never know."

"You were in a kosher convent. That's where you were."

George looked up at the clock.

"If anybody comes in you tell them the cook is off, and if they keep after it, you tell them you'll go back and cook yourself. Do you get that, bright boy?"

"All right," George said. "What you going to do with us afterward?"

"That'll depend," Max said. "That's one of those things you never know at the time."

George looked up at the clock. It was a quarter past six. The door from the street opened. A street-car motorman came in.

"Hello, George," he said. "Can I get supper?"

"Sam's gone out," George said. "He'll be back in about half an hour."

"I'd better go up the street," the motorman said. George looked at the clock. It was twenty minutes past six.

"That was nice, bright boy," Max said. "You're a regular little gentleman."

"He knew I'd blow his head off," Al said from the kitchen.

"No," said Max. "It ain't that. Bright boy is nice. He's a nice boy. I like him."

At six-fifty-five George said: "He's not coming."

Two other people had been in the lunch-room. Once George had gone out to the kitchen and made a ham-and-egg sandwich "to go" that a man wanted to take with him. Inside the kitchen he saw Al, his derby hat tipped back, sitting on a stool beside the wicket with the muzzle of a sawed-off shotgun resting on the ledge. Nick and the cook were back to back in the corner, a towel tied in each of their mouths. George had cooked the sandwich, wrapped it up in oiled paper, put it in a bag, brought it in, and the man had paid for it and gone out.

"Bright boy can do everything," Max said. "He can cook and everything. You'd make some girl a nice wife, bright boy."

"Yes?" George said. "Your friend, Ole Andreson, isn't going to come."

"We'll give him ten minutes," Max said.

Max watched the mirror and the clock. The hands of the clock marked seven o'clock, and then five minutes past seven.

"Come on, Al," said Max. "We better go. He's not coming."

"Better give him five minutes," Al said from the kitchen.

In the five minutes a man came in, and George explained that the cook was sick.

"Why the hell don't you get another cook?" the man asked. "Aren't you running a lunch-counter?" He went out.

"Come on, Al," Max said.

"What about the two bright boys and the nigger?"

"They're all right."

"You think so?"

"Sure. We're through with it."

"I don't like it," said Al. "It's sloppy. You talk too much."

"Oh, what the hell," said Max. "We got to keep amused, haven't we?"

"You talk too much, all the same," Al said. He came out from the kitchen. The cutoff barrels of the shotgun made a slight bulge under the waist of his too tight-fitting overcoat. He straightened his coat with his gloved hands.

"So long, bright boy," he said to George. "You got a lot of luck."

"That's the truth," Max said. "You ought to play the races, bright boy."

The two of them went out the door. George watched them, through the window, pass under the arc-light and cross the street. In their tight overcoats and derby hats they looked like a vaudeville team. George went back through the swinging-door into the kitchen and untied Nick and the cook.

"I don't want any more of that," said Sam, the cook. "I don't want any more of that."

Nick stood up. He had never had a towel in his mouth before.

"Say," he said. "What the hell?" He was trying to swagger it off.

"They were going to kill Ole Andreson," George said. "They were going to shoot him when he came in to eat."

"Ole Andreson?"

"Sure."

The cook felt the corners of his mouth with his thumbs.

"They all gone?" he asked.

"Yeah," said George. "They're gone now."

"I don't like it," said the cook. "I don't like any of it at all."

"Listen," George said to Nick. "You better go see Ole Andreson."

"All right."

"You better not have anything to do with it at all," Sam, the cook, said.

"You better stay way out of it."

"Don't go if you don't want to," George said.

"Mixing up in this ain't going to get you anywhere," the cook said. "You stay out of it."

"I'll go see him," Nick said to George. "Where does he live?"

The cook turned away.

"Little boys always know what they want to do," he said.

"He lives up at Hirsch's rooming-house," George said to Nick.

"I'll go up there."

Outside the arc-light shone through the bare branches of a tree. Nick walked up the street beside the car-tracks and turned at the next arc-light down a side-street. Three houses up the street was Hirsch's rooming-house. Nick walked up the two steps and pushed the bell. A woman came to the door.

"Is Ole Andreson here?"

"Do you want to see him?"

"Yes, if he's in."

Nick followed the woman up a flight of stairs and back to the end of a corridor. She knocked on the door.

"Who is it?"

"It's somebody to see you, Mr. Andreson," the woman said.

"It's Nick Adams."

"Come in."

Nick opened the door and went into the room. Ole Andreson was lying on the bed with all his clothes on. He had been a heavyweight prizefighter and he was too long for the bed. He lay with his head on two pillows. He did not look at Nick.

"What was it?" he asked.

"I was up at Henry's," Nick said, "and two fellows came in and tied up me and the cook, and they said they were going to kill you."

It sounded silly when he said it. Ole Andreson said nothing.

"They put us out in the kitchen," Nick went on. "They were going to shoot you when you came in to supper."

Ole Andreson looked at the wall and did not say anything.

"George thought I better come and tell you about it."

"There isn't anything I can do about it," Ole Andreson said.

"I'll tell you what they were like."

"I don't want to know what they were like," Ole Andreson said. He looked at the wall. "Thanks for coming to tell me about it."

"That's all right."

Nick looked at the big man lying on the bed.

"Don't you want me to go and see the police?"

"No," Ole Andreson said. "That wouldn't do any good."

"Isn't there something I could do?"

"No. There ain't anything to do."

"Maybe it was just a bluff."

"No. It ain't just a bluff."

Ole Andreson rolled over toward the wall.

"The only thing is," he said, talking toward the wall, "I just can't make up my mind to go out. I been in here all day."

"Couldn't you get out of town?"

"No," Ole Andreson said. "I'm through with all that running around."

He looked at the wall.

"There ain't anything to do now."

"Couldn't you fix it up some way?"

"No. I got in wrong." He talked in the same flat voice. "There ain't anything to do. After a while I'll make up my mind to go out."

"I better go back and see George," Nick said.

"So long," said Ole Andreson. He did not look toward Nick. "Thanks for coming around."

Nick went out. As he shut the door he saw Ole Andreson with all his clothes on, lying on the bed looking at the wall.

"He's been in his room all day," the landlady said down-stairs. "I guess he don't feel well. I said to him: 'Mr. Andreson, you ought to go out and take a walk on a nice fall day like this,' but he didn't feel like it."

"He doesn't want to go out."

"I'm sorry he don't feel well," the woman said. "He's an awfully nice man. He was in the ring, you know."

"I know it."

"You'd never know it except from the way his face is," the woman said. They stood talking just inside the street door. "He's just as gentle."

"Well, good-night, Mrs. Hirsch," Nick said.

"I'm not Mrs. Hirsch," the woman said. "She owns the place. I just look after it for her. I'm Mrs. Bell."

"Well, good-night, Mrs. Bell," Nick said.

"Good-night," the woman said.

Nick walked up the dark street to the corner under the arc-light, and then along the car-tracks to Henry's eating-house. George was inside, back of the counter.

"Did you see Ole?"

"Yes," said Nick. "He's in his room and he won't go out."

The cook opened the door from the kitchen when he heard Nick's voice.

"I don't even listen to it," he said and shut the door.

"Did you tell him about it?" George asked.

"Sure. I told him but he knows what it's all about."

"What's he going to do?"

"Nothing."

"They'll kill him."

"I guess they will."

"He must have got mixed up in something in Chicago."

"I guess so," said Nick.

"It's a hell of a thing."

"It's an awful thing," Nick said.

They did not say anything. George reached down for a towel and wiped the counter.

"I wonder what he did?" Nick said.

"Double-crossed somebody. That's what they kill them for."

"I'm going to get out of this town," Nick said.

"Yes," said George. "That's a good thing to do."

"I can't stand to think about him waiting in the room and knowing he's going to get it. It's too damned awful."

"Well," said George, "you better not think about it."

Che Ti Dice La Patria?

THE ROAD OF THE PASS WAS HARD AND smooth and not yet dusty in the early morning. Below were the hills with oak and chestnut trees, and far away below was the sea. On the other side were snowy mountains.

We came down from the pass through wooded country. There were bags of charcoal piled beside the road, and through the trees we saw charcoal-burners' huts. It was Sunday and the road, rising and falling, but always dropping away from the altitude of the pass, went through the scrub woods and through villages.

Outside the villages there were fields with vines. The fields were brown and the vines coarse and thick. The houses were white, and in the streets the men, in their Sunday clothes, were playing bowls. Against the walls of some of the houses there were pear trees, their branches candelabraed against the white walls. The pear trees had been sprayed, and the walls of the houses were stained a metallic blue-green by the spray vapor. There were small clearings around the villages where the vines grew, and then the woods.

In a village, twenty kilometres above Spezia, there was a crowd in the square, and a young man carrying a suitcase came up to the car and asked us to take him in to Spezia.

"There are only two places, and they are occupied," I said. We had an old Ford coupé.

"I will ride on the outside."

"You will be uncomfortable."

"That makes nothing. I must go to Spezia."

"Should we take him?" I asked Guy.

"He seems to be going anyway," Guy said. The young man handed in a parcel through the window.

"Look after this," he said. Two men tied his suitcase on the back of the car, above our suitcases. He shook hands with every one, explained that to a Fascist and a man as used to travelling as himself there was no discomfort, and climbed up on the running-board on the left-hand side of the car, holding on inside, his right arm through the open window.

"You can start," he said. The crowd waved. He waved with his free hand.

"What did he say?" Guy asked me.

"That we could start."

"Isn't he nice?" Guy said.

The road followed a river. Across the river were mountains. The sun was taking the frost out of the grass. It was bright and cold and the air came through the open wind-shield.

"How do you think he likes it out there?" Guy was looking up the road. His view out of his side of the car was blocked by our guest. The young man projected from the side of the car like the figurehead of a ship. He had turned his coat collar up and pulled his hat down and his nose looked cold in the wind.

"Maybe he'll get enough of it," Guy said. "That's the side our bum tire's on."

"Oh, he'd leave us if we blew out," I said. "He wouldn't get his travelling-clothes dirty."

"Well, I don't mind him," Guy said– "except the way he leans out on the turns."

The woods were gone; the road had left the river to climb; the radiator was boiling; the young man looked annoyedly and suspiciously at the steam and rusty water; the engine was grinding, with both Guy's feet on the first-speed pedal, up and up, back and forth and up, and, finally, out level. The grinding stopped, and in the new quiet there was a great churning bubbling in the radiator. We were at the top of the last range above Spezia and the sea. The road descended with short, barely rounded turns. Our guest hung out on the turns and nearly pulled the top-heavy car over.

"You can't tell him not to," I said to Guy. "It's his sense of self-preservation."

"The great Italian sense."

"The greatest Italian sense."

We came down around curves, through deep dust, the dust powdering the olive trees. Spezia spread below along the sea. The road flattened outside the town. Our guest put his head in the window.

"I want to stop."

"Stop it," I said to Guy.

We slowed up, at the side of the road. The young man got down, went to the back of the car and untied the suitcase.

"I stop here, so you won't get into trouble carrying passengers," he said. "My package."

I handed him the package. He reached in his pocket.

"How much do I owe you?"

"Nothing."

"Why not?"

"I don't know," I said.

"Then thanks," the young man said, not "thank you," or "thank you very much," or "thank you a thousand times," all of which you formerly said in Italy to a man when he handed you a time-table or explained about a direction. The young man uttered the lowest form of the word "thanks" and looked after us suspiciously as Guy started the car. I waved my hand at him. He was too dignified to reply. We went on into Spezia.

"That's a young man that will go a long way in Italy," I said to Guy.

"Well," said Guy, "he went twenty kilometres with us."

A MEAL IN SPEZIA

We came into Spezia looking for a place to eat. The street was wide and the houses high and yellow. We followed the tram-track into the center of town. On the walls of the houses were stencilled eye-bugging portraits of Mussolini, with hand-painted "*vivas*," the double V in black paint with drippings of paint down the wall. Side-streets went down to the harbor. It was bright and the people were all out for Sunday. The stone paving had been sprinkled and there were damp stretches in the dust. We went close to the curb to avoid a tram.

"Let's eat somewhere simple," Guy said.

We stopped opposite two restaurant signs. We were standing across the street and I was buying the papers. The two restaurants were side by side. A woman standing in the doorway of one smiled at us and we crossed the street and went in.

It was dark inside and at the back of the room three girls were sitting at a table with an old woman. Across from us, at another table, sat a sailor. He sat there neither eating nor drinking. Further back, a young man in a blue suit was writing at a table. His hair was pomaded and shining and he was very smartly dressed and clean-cut looking.

The light came through the doorway, and through the window where vegetables, fruit, steaks, and chops were arranged in a show-case. A girl came and took our order and another girl stood in the doorway. We noticed that she wore nothing under her house dress. The girl who took our order put her arm around Guy's neck while we were looking at the menu. There were three girls in all, and they all took turns going and standing in the doorway. The old woman at the table in the back of the room spoke to them and they sat down again with her.

There was no doorway leading from the room except into the kitchen. A curtain hung over it. The girl who had taken our order came in from the kitchen with spaghetti. She put it on the table and brought a bottle of red wine and sat down at the table.

"Well," I said to Guy, "you wanted to eat some place simple."

"This isn't simple. This is complicated."

"What do you say?" asked the girl. "Are you Germans?"

"South Germans," I said. "The South Germans are a gentle, lovable people."

"Don't understand," she said.

"What's the mechanics of this place?" Guy asked. "Do I have to let her put her arm around my neck?"

"Certainly," I said. "Mussolini has abolished the brothels. This is a restaurant."

The girl wore a one-piece dress. She leaned forward against the table and put her hands on her breasts and smiled. She smiled better on one side than on the other and turned the good side toward us. The charm of the good side had been enhanced by some event which had smoothed the other side of her nose in, as warm wax can be smoothed. Her nose, however, did not look like warm wax. It was very cold and firmed, only smoothed in. "You like me?" she asked Guy.

"He adores you," I said. "But he doesn't speak Italian."

"*Ich spreche Deutsch*", she said, and stroked Guy's hair.

"Speak to the lady in your native tongue, Guy."

"Where do you come from?" asked the lady.

"Potsdam."

"And you will stay here now for a little while?"

"In this so dear Spezia?" I asked.

"Tell her we have to go," said Guy. "Tell her we are very ill, and have no money."

"My friend is a misogynist," I said, "an old German misogynist."

"Tell him I love him."

I told him.

"Will you shut your mouth and get us out of here?" Guy said. The lady had placed another arm around his neck. "Tell him he is mine," she said. I told him.

"Will you get us out of here?"

"You are quarrelling," the lady said. "You do not love one another."

"We are Germans," I said proudly, "old South Germans."

"Tell him he is a beautiful boy," the lady said. Guy is thirty-eight and takes some pride in the fact that he is taken for a travelling salesman in France. "You are a beautiful boy," I said.

"Who says so?" Guy asked, "you or her?"

"She does. I'm just your interpreter. Isn't that what you got me in on this trip for?"

"I'm glad it's her," said Guy. "I didn't want to have to leave you here too."

"I don't know. Spezia's a lovely place."

"Spezia," the lady said. "You are talking about Spezia."

"Lovely place," I said.

"It is my country," she said. "Spezia is my home and Italy is my country."

"She says that Italy is her country."

"Tell her it looks like her country," Guy said.

"What have you for dessert?" I asked.

"Fruit," she said. "We have bananas."

"Bananas are all right," Guy said. "They've got skins on."

"Oh, he takes bananas," the lady said. She embraced Guy.

"What does she say?" he asked, keeping his face out of the way.

"She is pleased because you take bananas."

"Tell her I don't take bananas."

"The Signor does not take bananas."

"Ah," said the lady, crestfallen, "he doesn't take bananas."

"Tell her I take a cold bath every morning," Guy said.

"The Signor takes a cold bath every morning."

"No understand," the lady said.

Across from us, the property sailor had not moved. No one in the place paid any attention to him.

"We want the bill," I said.

"Oh, no. You must stay."

"Listen," the clean-cut young man said from the table where he was writing, "let them go. These two are worth nothing."

The lady took my hand. "You won't stay? You won't ask him to stay?"

"We have to go," I said. "We have to get to Pisa, or if possible, Firenze, tonight. We can amuse ourselves in those cities at the end of the day. It is now the day. In the day we must cover distance."

"To stay a little while is nice."

"To travel is necessary during the light of day."

"Listen," the clean-cut young man said. "Don't bother to talk with these two. I tell you they are worth nothing and I know."

"Bring us the bill," I said. She brought the bill from the old woman and went back and sat at the table. Another girl came in from the kitchen. She walked the length of the room and stood in the doorway.

"Don't bother with these two," the clean-cut young man said in a wearied voice. "Come and eat. They are worth nothing."

We paid the bill and stood up. All the girls, the old woman, and the clean-cut young man sat down at table together. The property sailor sat with his head in his hands. No one had spoken to him all the time we were at lunch. The girl brought us our change that the old woman counted out for her and went back to her place at the table. We left a tip on the table and went out. When we were seated in the car ready to start, the girl came out and stood in the door. We started and I waved to her. She did not wave, but stood there looking after us.

After the Rain

It was raining hard when we passed through the suburbs of Genoa and, even going very slowly behind the tram-cars and the motor trucks, liquid mud splashed on to the sidewalks, so that people stepped into doorways as they saw us coming. In San Pier d'Arena, the industrial suburb outside of Genoa, there is a wide street with two car-tracks and we drove down the center to avoid sending the mud on to the men going home from work. On our left was the Mediterranean. There was a big sea running and waves broke and the wind blew the spray against the car. A river-bed that, when we had passed, going into Italy, had been wide, stony and dry, was running brown, and up to the banks. The brown water discolored the sea and as the waves thinned and cleared in breaking, the light came through the yellow water and the crests, detached by the wind, blew across the road.

A big car passed us, going fast, and a sheet of muddy water rose up and over our wind-shield and radiator. The automatic wind-shield cleaner moved back and forth, spreading the film over the glass. We stopped and ate lunch at Sestri. There was no heat in the restaurant and we kept our hats and coats on. We could see the car outside, through the window. It was covered with mud and was stopped beside some boats that had been pulled up beyond the waves. In the restaurant you could see your breath.

The *pasta asciutta* was good; the wine tasted of alum, and we poured water in it. Afterward the waiter brought beefsteak and fried potatoes. A man and a woman sat at the far end of the restaurant. He was middleaged and she was young and wore black. All during the meal she would blow out her breath in the cold damp air. The man would look at it and shake his head. They ate without talking and the man held her hand under the table. She was good-looking and they seemed very sad. They had a travelling-bag with them.

We had the papers and I read the account of the Shanghai fighting aloud to Guy. After the meal, he left with the waiter in search for a place which did not exist in the restaurant, and I cleaned off the wind-shield, the lights and the license plates with a rag. Guy came back and we backed the car out and started. The waiter had taken him across the road and into an old house. The people in the house were suspicious and the waiter had remained with Guy to see nothing was stolen.

"Although I don't know how, me not being a plumber, they expected me to steal anything," Guy said.

As we came up on a headland beyond the town, the wind struck the car and nearly tipped it over.

"It's good it blows us away from the sea," Guy said.

"Well," I said, "they drowned Shelley somewhere along here."

"That was down by Viareggio," Guy said. "Do you remember what we came to this country for?"

"Yes," I said, "but we didn't get it."

"We'll be out of it tonight."

"If we can get past Ventimiglia."

"We'll see. I don't like to drive this coast at night." It was early afternoon and the sun was out. Below, the sea was blue with whitecaps running toward Savona. Back, beyond the cape, the brown and blue water joined. Out ahead of us, a tramp steamer was going up the coast.

"Can you still see Genoa?" Guy asked.

"Oh, yes."

"That next big cape ought to put it out of sight."

"We'll see it a long time yet. I can still see Portofino Cape behind it."

Finally we could not see Genoa. I looked back as we came out and there was only the sea, and below, in the bay, a line of beach with fishing-boats and above, on the side of the hill, a town and then capes far down the coast.

"It's gone now," I said to Guy.

"Oh, it's been gone a long time now."

"But we couldn't be sure till we got way out."

There was a sign with a picture of an S-turn and *Svolta Pericolosa*. The road curved around the headland and the wind blew through the crack in the wind-shield. Below the cape was a flat stretch beside the sea. The wind had dried the mud and the wheels were beginning to lift dust. On the flat road we passed a Fascist riding a bicycle, a heavy revolver in a holster on his back. He held the middle of the road on his bicycle and we turned out for him. He looked up at us as we passed. Ahead there was a railway crossing, and as we came toward it the gates went down.

As we waited, the Fascist came up on his bicycle. The train went by and Guy started the engine.

"Wait," the bicycle man shouted from behind the car. "Your number's dirty."

I got out with a rag. The number had been cleaned at lunch.

"You can read it," I said.

"You think so?"

"Read it."

"I cannot read it. It is dirty."

I wiped it off with the rag.

"How's that?"

"Twenty-five lire."

"What?" I said. "You could have read it. It's only dirty from the state of the roads."

"You don't like Italian roads?"

"They are dirty."

"Fifty lire." He spat in the road. "Your car is dirty and you are dirty too."

"Good. And give me a receipt with your name."

He took out a receipt book, made in duplicate, and perforated, so one side could be given to the customer, and the other side filled in and kept as a stub. There was no carbon to record what the customer's ticket said.

"Give me fifty lire."

He wrote in indelible pencil, tore out the slip and handed it to me. I read it.

"This is for twenty-five lire."

"A mistake," he said, and changed the twenty-five to fifty.

"And now the other side. Make it fifty in the part you keep."

He smiled a beautiful Italian smile and wrote something on the receipt stub, holding it so I could not see.

"Go on," he said, "before your number gets dirty again."

We drove for two hours after it was dark and slept in Mentone that night. It seemed very cheerful and clean and sane and lovely. We had driven from Ventimiglia to Pisa and Florence, across the Romagna to Rimini, back through Forli, Imola, Bologna, Parma, Piacenza and Genoa, to Ventimiglia again. The whole trip had taken only ten days. Naturally, in such a short trip, we had no opportunity to see how things were with the country or the people.

FIFTY GRAND

"HOW ARE YOU GOING YOURSELF, Jack?" I asked him.

"You seen this Walcott?" he says.

"Just in the gym."

"Well," Jack says, "I'm going to need a lot of luck with that boy."

"He can't hit you, Jack," Soldier said.

"I wish to hell he couldn't."

"He couldn't hit you with a handful of bird-shot."

"Bird-shot'd be all right," Jack says. "I wouldn't mind bird-shot any."

"He looks easy to hit," I said.

"Sure," Jack says, "he ain't going to last long. He ain't going to last like you and me, Jerry. But right now he's got everything."

"You'll left-hand him to death."

"Maybe," Jack says. "Sure. I got a chance to."

"Handle him like you handled Kid Lewis."

"Kid Lewis," Jack said. "That kike!"

The three of us, Jack Brennan, Soldier Bartlett, and I were in Hanley's. There were a couple of broads sitting at the next table to us. They had been drinking.

"What do you mean, kike?" one of the broads says. "What do you mean, kike, you big Irish bum?"

"Sure," Jack says. "That's it."

"Kikes," this broad goes on. "They're always talking about kikes, these big Irishmen. What do you mean, kikes?"

"Come on. Let's get out of here."

"Kikes," this broad goes on. "Whoever saw you ever buy a drink? Your wife sews your pockets up every morning. These Irishmen and their kikes! Ted Lewis could lick you too."

"Sure," Jack says. "And you give away a lot of things free too, don't you?"

We went out. That was Jack. He could say what he wanted to when he wanted to say it.

Jack started training out at Danny Hogan's health farm over in Jersey. It was nice out there but Jack didn't like it much. He didn't like being away from his wife and the kids, and he was sore and grouchy most of the time. He liked me and we got along fine together; and he liked Hogan, but after a while Soldier Bartlett commenced to get on his nerves. A kidder gets to be an awful thing around a camp if his stuff goes sort of sour. Soldier was always kidding Jack, just sort of kidding him all the time. It wasn't very funny and it wasn't very good, and it began to get to Jack. It was sort of stuff like this. Jack would finish up with the weights and the bag and pull on the gloves.

"You want to work?" he'd say to Soldier.

"Sure. How you want me to work?" Soldier would ask. "Want me to treat you rough like Walcott? Want me to knock you down a few times?"

"That's it," Jack would say. He didn't like it any, though.

One morning we were all out on the road. We'd been out quite a way and now we were coming back. We'd go along fast for three minutes and then walk a minute, and then go fast for three minutes again. Jack wasn't ever what you would call a sprinter. He'd move around fast enough in the ring if he had to, but he wasn't any too fast on the road. All the time we were walking Soldier was kidding him. We came up the hill to the farmhouse.

"Well," says Jack, "you better go back to town, Soldier."

"What do you mean?"

"You better go back to town and stay there."

"What's the matter?"

"I'm sick of hearing you talk."

"Yes?" says Soldier.

"Yes," says Jack.

"You'll be a damn sight sicker when Walcott gets through with you."

"Sure," says Jack, "maybe I will. But I know I'm sick of you."

So Soldier went off on the train to town that same morning. I went down with him to the train. He was good and sore.

"I was just kidding him," he said. We were waiting on the platform. "He can't pull that stuff with me, Jerry."

"He's nervous and crabby," I said. "He's a good fellow, Soldier."

"The hell he is. The hell he's ever been a good fellow."

"Well," I said, "so long, Soldier."

The train had come in. He climbed up with his bag.

"So long, Jerry," he says. "You be in town before the fight?"

"I don't think so."

"See you then."

He went in and the conductor swung up and the train went out. I rode back to the farm in the cart. Jack was on the porch writing a letter to his wife. The mail had come and I got the papers and went over on the other side of the porch and sat down to read. Hogan came out the door and walked over to me.

"Did he have a jam with Soldier?"

"Not a jam," I said. "He just told him to go back to town."

"I could see it coming," Hogan said. "He never liked Soldier much."

"No. He don't like many people."

"He's a pretty cold one," Hogan said.

"Well, he's always been fine to me."

"Me too," Hogan said. "I got no kick on him. He's a cold one, though."

Hogan went in through the screen door and I sat there on the porch and read the papers. It was just starting to get fall weather and it's nice country there in Jersey, up in the hills, and after I read the paper through I sat there and looked out at the country and the road down below against the woods with cars going along it, lifting the dust up. It was fine weather and pretty nice-looking country. Hogan came to the door and I said, "Say, Hogan, haven't you got anything to shoot out here?"

"No," Hogan said. "Only sparrows."

"Seen the paper?" I said to Hogan.

"What's in it?"

"Sande booted three of them in yesterday."

"I got that on the telephone last night."

"You follow them pretty close, Hogan?" I asked.

"Oh, I keep in touch with them," Hogan said.

"How about Jack?" I says. "Does he still play them?"

"Him?" said Hogan. "Can you see him doing it?"

Just then Jack came around the corner with the letter in his hand. He's wearing a sweater and an old pair of pants and boxing shoes.

"Got a stamp, Hogan?" he asks.

"Give me the letter," Hogan said. "I'll mail it for you."

"Say, Jack," I said, "didn't you used to play the ponies?"

"Sure."

"I knew you did. I knew I used to see you out at Sheepshead."

"What did you lay off them for?" Hogan asked.

"Lost money."

Jack sat down on the porch by me. He leaned back against a post. He shut his eyes in the sun.

"Want a chair?" Hogan asked.

"No," said Jack. "This is fine."

"It's a nice day," I said. "It's pretty nice out in the country."

"I'd a damn sight rather be in town with the wife."

"Well, you only got another week."

"Yes," Jack says. "That's so."

We sat there on the porch. Hogan was inside at the office.

"What do you think about the shape I'm in?" Jack asked me.

"Well, you can't tell," I said. "You got a week to get around into form."

"Don't stall me."

"Well," I said, "you're not right."

"I'm not sleeping," Jack said.

"You'll be all right in a couple of days."

"No," says Jack, "I got the insomnia."

"What's on your mind?"

"I miss the wife."

"Have her come out."

"No. I'm too old for that."

"We'll take a long walk before you turn in and get you good and tired."

"Tired!" Jack says. "I'm tired all the time."

He was that way all week. He wouldn't sleep at night and he'd get up in the morning feeling that way, you know, when you can't shut your hands. "He's stale as poorhouse cake," Hogan said. "He's nothing."

"I never seen Walcott," I said.

"He'll kill him," said Hogan. "He'll tear him in two."

"Well," I said, "everybody's got to get it sometime."

"Not like this, though," Hogan said. "They'll think he never trained. It gives the farm a black eye."

"You hear what the reporters said about him?"

"Didn't I! They said he was awful. They said they oughtn't to let him fight."

"Well," I said, "they're always wrong, ain't they?"

"Yes," said Hogan. "But this time they're right."

"What the hell do they know about whether a man's right or not?"

"Well," said Hogan, "they're not such fools."

"All they did was pick Willard at Toledo. This Lardner, he's so wise now, ask him about when he picked Willard at Toledo."

"Aw, he wasn't out," Hogan said. "He only writes the big fights."

"I don't care who they are," I said. "What the hell do they know? They can write maybe, but what the hell do they know?"

"You don't think Jack's in any shape, do you?" Hogan asked.

"No. He's through. All he needs is to have Corbett pick him to win for it to be all over."

"Well, Corbett'll pick him," Hogan says.

"Sure. He'll pick him."

That night Jack didn't sleep any either. The next morning was the last day before the fight. After breakfast we were out on the porch again.

"What do you think about, Jack, when you can't sleep?" I said.

"Oh, I worry," Jack says. "I worry about property I got up in the Bronx, I worry about property I got in Florida. I worry about the kids. I worry about the wife. Sometimes I think about fights. I think about that kike Ted Lewis and I get sore. I got some stocks and I worry about them. What the hell don't I think about?"

"Well," I said, "tomorrow night it'll all be over."

"Sure," said Jack. "That always helps a lot, don't it? That just fixes everything all up, I suppose. Sure."

He was sore all day. We didn't do any work. Jack just moved around a little to loosen up. He shadow-boxed a few rounds. He didn't even look good doing that. He skipped the rope a little while. He couldn't sweat.

"He'd be better not to do any work at all," Hogan said. We were standing watching him skip rope. "Don't he ever sweat at all any more?"

"He can't sweat."

"Do you suppose he's got the con? He never had any trouble making weight did he?"

"No, he hasn't got any con. He just hasn't got anything inside any more."

"He ought to sweat," said Hogan.

Jack came over, skipping the rope. He was skipping up and down in front of us, forward and back, crossing his arms every third time.

"Well," he says. "What are you buzzards talking about?"

"I don't think you ought to work any more," Hogan says. "You'll be stale."

"Wouldn't that be awful?" Jack says and skips away down the floor, slapping the rope hard.

That afternoon John Collins showed up out at the farm. Jack was up in his room. John came out in a car from town. He had a couple of friends with him. The car stopped and they all got out.

"Where's Jack?" John asked me.

"Up in his room, lying down."

"Lying down?"

"Yes," I said.

"How is he?"

I looked at the two fellows that were with John.

"They're friends of his," John said.

"He's pretty bad," I said.

"What's the matter with him?"

"He don't sleep."

"Hell," said John. "That Irishman could never sleep."

"He isn't right," I said.

"Hell," John said. "He's never right. I've had him for ten years and he's never been right yet."

The fellows who were with him laughed.

"I want you to shake hands with Mr. Morgan and Mr. Steinfelt," John said. "This is Mr. Doyle. He's been training Jack."

"Glad to meet you," I said.

"Let's go up and see the boy," the fellow called Morgan said.

"Let's have a look at him," Steinfelt said.

We all went upstairs.

"Where's Hogan?" John asked.

"He's out in the barn with a couple of his customers," I said.

"He got many people out here now?" John asked.

"Just two."

"Pretty quiet, ain't it?" Morgan said.

"Yes," I said. "It's pretty quiet."

We were outside Jack's room. John knocked on the door. There wasn't any answer.

"Maybe he's asleep," I said.

"What the hell's he sleeping in the daytime for?"

John turned the handle and we all went in. Jack was lying asleep on the bed. He was face down and his face was in the pillow. Both his arms were around the pillow.

"Hey, Jack!" John said to him.

Jack's head moved a little on the pillow. "Jack!" John says, leaning over him. Jack just dug a little deeper in the pillow. John touched him on the shoulder. Jack sat up and looked at us. He hadn't shaved and he was wearing an old sweater.

"Christ! Why can't you let me sleep?" he says to John.

"Don't be sore," John says. "I didn't mean to wake you up."

"Oh no," Jack says. "Of course not."

"You know Morgan and Steinfelt," John said.

"Glad to see you," Jack says.

"How do you feel, Jack?" Morgan asks him.

"Fine," Jack says. "How the hell would I feel?"

"You look fine," Steinfelt says.

"Yes, don't I," says Jack. "Say," he says to John. "You're my manager. You get a big enough cut. Why the hell don't you come out here when the reporters was out! You want Jerry and me to talk to them?"

"I had Lew fighting in Philadelphia," John said.

"What the hell's that to me?" Jack says. "You're my manager. You get a big enough cut, don't you? You aren't making me any money in Philadelphia, are you? Why the hell aren't you out here when I ought to have you?"

"Hogan was here."

"Hogan," Jack says. "Hogan's as dumb as I am."

"Soldier Bahtlett was out here wukking with you for a while, wasn't he?" Steinfelt said to change the subject.

"Yes, he was out here," Jack says. "He was out here all right."

"Say, Jerry," John said to me. "Would you go and find Hogan and tell him we want to see him in about half an hour?"

"Sure," I said.

"Why the hell can't he stick around?" Jack says. "Stick around, Jerry." Morgan and Steinfelt looked at each other.

"Quiet down, Jack," John said to him.

"I better go find Hogan," I said.

"All right, if you want to go," Jack says. "None of these guys are going to send you away, though."

"I'll go find Hogan," I said.

Hogan was out in the gym in the barn. He had a couple of his health-farm patients with the gloves on. They neither one wanted to hit the other, for fear the other would come back and hit him.

"That'll do," Hogan said when he saw me come in. "You can stop the slaughter. You gentlemen take a shower and Bruce will rub you down."

They climbed out through the ropes and Hogan came over to me.

"John Collins is out with a couple of friends to see Jack," I said.

"I saw them come up in the car."

"Who are the two fellows with John?"

"They're what you call wise boys," Hogan said. "Don't you know them two?"

"No," I said.

"That's Happy Steinfelt and Lew Morgan. They got a pool-room."

"I been away a long time," I said.

"Sure," said Hogan. "That Happy Steinfelt's a big operator."

"I've heard his name," I said.

"He's a pretty smooth boy," Hogan said. "They're a couple of sharpshooters."

"Well," I said. "They want to see us in half an hour."

"You mean they don't want to see us until a half an hour?"

"That's it."

"Come on in the office," Hogan said. "To hell with those sharpshooters."

After about thirty minutes or so Hogan and I went upstairs. We knocked on Jack's door. They were talking inside the room.

"Wait a minute," somebody said.

"To hell with that stuff," Hogan said. "When you want to see me I'm down in the office."

We heard the door unlock. Steinfelt opened it.

"Come on in, Hogan," he says. "We're all going to have a drink."

"Well," says Hogan. "That's something."

We went in. Jack was sitting on the bed. John and Morgan were sitting on a couple of chairs. Steinfelt was standing up.

"You're a pretty mysterious lot of boys," Hogan said.

"Hello, Danny," John says.

"Hello, Danny," Morgan says and shakes hands.

Jack doesn't say anything. He just sits there on the bed. He ain't with the others. He's all by himself. He was wearing an old blue jersey and pants and had on boxing shoes. He needed a shave. Steinfelt and Morgan were dressers. John was quite a dresser too. Jack sat there looking Irish and tough.

Steinfelt brought out a bottle and Hogan brought in some glasses and everybody had a drink. Jack and I took one and the rest of them went on and had two or three each.

"Better save some for your ride back," Hogan said.

"Don't you worry. We got plenty," Morgan said.

Jack hadn't drunk anything since the one drink. He was standing up and looking at them. Morgan was sitting on the bed where Jack had sat.

"Have a drink, Jack," John said and handed him the glass and the bottle.

"No," Jack said, "I never liked to go to these wakes."

They all laughed. Jack didn't laugh.

They were all feeling pretty good when they left. Jack stood on the porch when they got into the car. They waved to him.

"So long," Jack said.

We had supper. Jack didn't say anything all during the meal except, "Will you pass me this?" or "Will you pass me that?" The two health-farm patients ate at the same table with us. They were pretty nice fellows. After we finished eating we went out on the porch. It was dark early.

"Like to take a walk, Jerry?" Jack asked.

"Sure," I said.

We put on our coats and started out. It was quite a way down to the main road and then we walked along the main road about a mile and a half. Cars kept going by and we would pull out to the side until they were past. Jack didn't say anything. After we had stepped out into the bushes to let a big car go by Jack said, "To hell with this walking. Come on back to Hogan's."

We went along a side road that cut up over the hill and cut across the fields back to Hogan's. We could see the lights of the house up on the hill. We came around to the front of the house and there standing in the doorway was

Hogan.

"Have a good walk?" Hogan asked.

"Oh, fine," Jack said. "Listen, Hogan. Have you got any liquor?"

"Sure," says Hogan. "What's the idea?"

"Send it up to the room," Jack says. "I'm going to sleep tonight."

"You're the doctor," Hogan says.

"Come on up to the room, Jerry," Jack says.

Upstairs Jack sat on the bed with his head in his hands.

"Ain't it a life?" Jack says.

Hogan brought in a quart of liquor and two glasses.

"Want some ginger ale?"

"What do you think I want to do, get sick?"

"I just asked you," said Hogan.

"Have a drink?" said Jack.

"No, thanks," said Hogan. He went out.

"How about you, Jerry?"

"I'll have one with you," I said.

Jack poured out a couple of drinks. "Now," he said, "I want to take it slow and easy."

"Put some water in it," I said.

"Yes," Jack said. "I guess that's better."

We had a couple of drinks without saying anything. Jack started to pour me another.

"No," I said, "that's all I want."

"All right," Jack said. He poured himself out another big shot and put water in it. He was lighting up a little.

"That was a fine bunch out here this afternoon," he said. "They don't take any chances, those two."

Then a little later, "Well," he says, "they're right. What the hell's the good in taking chances?"

"Don't you want another, Jerry?" he said. "Come on, drink along with me."

"I don't need it, Jack," I said. "I feel all right."

"Just have one more," Jack said. It was softening him up.

"All right," I said.

Jack poured one for me and another big one for himself.

"You know," he said, "I like liquor pretty well. If I hadn't been boxing I would have drunk quite a lot."

"Sure," I said.

"You know," he said, "I missed a lot, boxing."

"You made plenty of money."

"Sure, that's what I'm after. You know I miss a lot, Jerry."

"How do you mean?"

"Well," he says, "like about the wife. And being away from home so much. It don't do my girls any good. 'Who's your old man?' some of those society kids'll say to them. 'My old man's Jack Brennan.' That don't do them any good."

"Hell," I said, "all that makes a difference is if they got dough."

"Well," says Jack, "I got the dough for them all right."

He poured out another drink. The bottle was about empty.

"Put some water in it," I said. Jack poured in some water.

"You know," he says, "you ain't got any idea how I miss the wife."

"Sure."

"You ain't got any idea. You can't have an idea what it's like."

"It ought to be better out in the country than in town."

"With me now," Jack said, "it don't make any difference where I am. You can't have an idea what it's like."

"Have another drink."

"Am I getting soused? Do I talk funny?"

"You're coming on all right."

"You can't have an idea what it's like. They ain't anybody can have an idea what it's like."

"Except the wife," I said.

"She knows," Jack said. "She knows all right. She knows. You bet she knows."

"Put some water in that," I said.

"Jerry," says Jack, "you can't have an idea what it gets to be like."

He was good and drunk. He was looking at me steady. His eyes were sort of too steady.

"You'll sleep all right," I said.

"Listen Jerry," Jack says. "You want to make some money? Get some money down on Walcott."

"Yes?"

"Listen, Jerry," Jack put down the glass. "I'm not drunk now, see? You know what I'm betting on him? Fifty grand."

"That's a lot of dough."

"Fifty grand," Jack says, "at two to one. I'll get twenty-five thousand bucks. Get some money on him, Jerry."

"It sounds good," I said.

"How can I beat him?" Jack says. "It ain't crooked. How can I beat him? Why not make money on it?"

"Put some water in that," I said.

"I'm through after this fight," Jack says. "I'm through with it. I got to take a beating. Why shouldn't I make money on it?"

"Sure."

"I ain't slept for a week," Jack says. "All night I lay awake and worry my can off. I can't sleep, Jerry. You ain't got an idea what it's like when you can't sleep."

"Sure."

"I can't sleep. That's all. I just can't sleep. What's the use of taking care of yourself all these years when you can't sleep?"

"It's bad."

"You ain't got an idea what it's like, Jerry, when you can't sleep."

"Put some water in that," I said.

Well, about eleven o'clock Jack passes out and I put him to bed. Finally he's so he can't keep from sleeping. I helped him get his clothes off and got him into bed.

"You'll sleep all right, Jack," I said.

"Sure," Jack says, "I'll sleep now."

"Good night, Jack," I said.

"Good night, Jerry," Jack says. "You're the only friend I got."

"Oh, hell," I said.

"You're the only friend I got," Jack says, "the only friend I got."

"Go to sleep," I said.

"I'll sleep," Jack says.

Downstairs Hogan was sitting at the desk in the office reading the papers. He looked up. "Well, you get your boy friend to sleep?" he asks.

"He's off."

"It's better for him than not sleeping," Hogan said.

"Sure."

"You'd have a hell of a time explaining that to these sport writers though," Hogan said.

"Well, I'm going to bed myself," I said.

"Good night," said Hogan.

In the morning I came downstairs about eight o'clock and got some breakfast. Hogan had his two customers out in the barn doing exercises. I went out and watched them.

"One! Two! Three! Four!" Hogan was counting for them. "Hello, Jerry," he said. "Is Jack up yet?"

"No. He's still sleeping."

I went back to my room and packed up to go in to town. About nine-thirty I heard Jack getting up in the next room. When I heard him go downstairs I went down after him. Jack was sitting at the breakfast table. Hogan had come in and was standing beside the table.

"How do you feel, Jack?" I asked him.

"Not so bad."

"Sleep well?" Hogan asked.

"I slept all right," Jack said. "I got a thick tongue but I ain't got a head."

"Good," said Hogan. "That was good liquor."

"Put it on the bill," Jack says.

"What time you want to go into town?" Hogan asked.

"Before lunch," Jack says. "The eleven o'clock train."

"Sit down, Jerry," Jack said. Hogan went out.

I sat down at the table. Jack was eating a grapefruit. When he'd find a seed he'd spit it out in the spoon and dump it on the plate.

"I guess I was pretty stewed last night," he started.

"You drank some liquor."

"I guess I said a lot of fool things."

"You weren't bad."

"Where's Hogan?" he asked. He was through with the grapefruit.

"He's out in front in the office."

"What did I say about betting on the fight?" Jack asked. He was holding the spoon and sort of poking at the grapefruit with it.

The girl came in with some ham and eggs and took away the grapefruit.

"Bring me another glass of milk," Jack said to her. She went out.

"You said you had fifty grand on Walcott," I said.

"That's right," Jack said.

"That's a lot of money."

"I don't feel too good about it," Jack said.

"Something might happen."

"No," Jack said. "He wants the title bad. They'll be shooting with him all right."

"You can't ever tell."

"No. He wants the title. It's worth a lot of money to him."

"Fifty grand is a lot of money," I said.

"It's business," said Jack. "I can't win. You know I can't win anyway."

"As long as you're in there you got a chance."

"No," Jack says. "I'm all through. It's just business."

"How do you feel?"

"Pretty good," Jack said. "The sleep was what I needed."

"You might go good."

"I'll give them a good show," Jack said.

After breakfast Jack called up his wife on the long-distance. He was inside the booth telephoning.

"That's the first time he's called her up since he's out here," Hogan said.

"He writes her every day."

"Sure," Hogan says, "a letter only costs two cents."

Hogan said good-by to us and Bruce, the nigger rubber, drove us down to the train in the cart.

"Good-by, Mr. Brennan," Bruce said at the train, "I sure hope you knock his can off."

"So long," Jack said. He gave Bruce two dollars. Bruce had worked on him a lot. He looked kind of disappointed. Jack saw me looking at Bruce holding the two dollars.

"It's all in the bill," he said. "Hogan charged me for the rubbing."

On the train going into town Jack didn't talk. He sat in the corner of the seat with his ticket in his hat-band and looked out of the window. Once he turned and spoke to me.

"I told the wife I'd take a room at the Shelby tonight," he said. "It's just around the comer from the Garden. I can go up to the house tomorrow morning."

"That's a good idea," I said. "Your wife ever see you fight, Jack?"

"No," Jack says. "She never seen me fight."

I thought he must be figuring on taking an awful beating if he doesn't want to go home afterward. In town we took a taxi up to the Shelby. A boy came out and took our bags and we went in to the desk.

"How much are the rooms?" Jack asked.

"We only have double rooms," the clerk says. "I can give you a nice double room for ten dollars."

"That's too steep."

"I can give you a double room for seven dollars."

"With a bath?"

"Certainly."

"You might as well bunk with me, Jerry," Jack says.

"Oh," I said, "I'll sleep down at my brother-in-law's."

"I don't mean for you to pay it," Jack says. "I just want to get my money's worth."

"Will you register, please?" the clerk says. He looked at the names. "Number 238, Mr. Brennan."

We went up in the elevator. It was a nice big room with two beds and a door opening into a bath-room.

"This is pretty good," Jack says.

The boy who brought us up pulled up the curtains and brought in our bags. Jack didn't make any move, so I gave the boy a quarter. We washed up and Jack said we better go out and get something to eat.

We ate a lunch at Jimmy Hanley's place. Quite a lot of the boys were there. When we were about half through eating, John came in and sat down with us. Jack didn't talk much.

"How are you on the weight, Jack?" John asked him. Jack was putting away a pretty good lunch.

"I could make it with my clothes on," Jack said. He never had to worry about taking off weight. He was a natural welterweight and he'd never gotten fat. He'd lost weight out at Hogan's.

"Well, that's one thing you never had to worry about," John said.

"That's one thing," Jack says.

We went around to the Garden to weigh in after lunch. The match was made at a hundred forty-seven pounds at three o'clock. Jack stepped on the scales with a towel around him. The bar didn't move. Walcott had just weighed and was standing with a lot of people around him.

"Let's see what you weigh, Jack," Freedman, Walcott's manager said.

"All right, weigh *him* then," Jack jerked his head toward Walcott.

"Drop the towel," Freedman said.

"What do you make it?" Jack asked the fellows who were weighing.

"One hundred and forty-three pounds," the fat man who was weighing said.

"You're down fine, Jack," Freedman says.

"Weigh *him*," Jack says.

Walcott came over. He was a blond with wide shoulders and arms like a heavyweight. He didn't have much legs. Jack stood about half a head taller than he did.

"Hello, Jack," he said. His face was plenty marked up.

"Hello," said Jack. "How you feel?"

"Good," Walcott says. He dropped the towel from around his waist and stood on the scales. He had the widest shoulders and back you ever saw.

"One hundred and forty-six pounds and twelve ounces."

Walcott stepped off and grinned at Jack.

"Well," John says to him, "Jack's spotting you about four pounds."

"More than that when I come in, kid," Walcott says. "I'm going to go and eat now."

We went back and Jack got dressed. "He's a pretty tough-looking boy," Jack says to me.

"He looks as though he'd been hit plenty of times."

"Oh, yes," Jack says. "He ain't hard to hit."

"Where are you going?" John asked when Jack was dressed.

"Back to the hotel," Jack says. "You looked after everything?"

"Yes," John says. "It's all looked after."

"I'm going to lie down a while," Jack says.

"I'll come around for you about a quarter to seven and we'll go and eat."

"All right."

Up at the hotel Jack took off his shoes and his coat and lay down for a while. I wrote a letter. I looked over a couple of times and Jack wasn't sleeping. He was lying perfectly still but every once in a while his eyes would open. Finally he sits up.

"Want to play some cribbage, Jerry?" he says.

"Sure," I said.

He went over to his suitcase and got out the cards and the cribbage board. We played cribbage and he won three dollars off me. John knocked at the door and came in.

"Want to play some cribbage, John?" Jack asked him.

John put his hat down on the table. It was all wet. His coat was wet too.

"Is it raining?" Jack asks.

"It's pouring," John says. "The taxi I had got tied up in the traffic and I got out and walked."

"Come on, play some cribbage," Jack says.

"You ought to go and eat."

"No," says Jack. "I don't want to eat yet."

So they played cribbage for about half an hour and Jack won a dollar and a half off him.

"Well, I suppose we got to go eat," Jack says. He went to the window and looked out.

"Is it still raining?"

"Yes."

"Let's eat in the hotel," John says.

"All right," Jack says, "I'll play you once more to see who pays for the meal."

After a little while Jack gets up and says, "You buy the meal, John," and we went downstairs and ate in the big dining-room.

After we ate we went upstairs and Jack played cribbage with John again and won two dollars and a half off him. Jack was feeling pretty good. John had a bag with him with all his stuff in it. Jack took off his shirt and collar and put on a jersey and a sweater, so he wouldn't catch cold when he came out, and put his ring clothes and his bathrobe in a bag.

"You all ready?" John asks him. "I'll call up and have them get a taxi."

Pretty soon the telephone rang and they said the taxi was waiting.

We rode down in the elevator and went out through the lobby, and got in a taxi and rode around to the Garden. It was raining hard but there was a lot of people outside on the streets. The Garden was sold out. As we came in on our way to the dressing-room I saw how full it was. It looked like half a mile down to the ring. It was all dark. Just the lights over the ring.

"It's a good thing, with this rain, they didn't try and pull this fight in the ball park," John said.

"They got a good crowd," Jack says.

"This is a fight that would draw a lot more than the Garden could hold."

"You can't tell about the weather," Jack says.

John came to the door of the dressing-room and poked his head in. Jack was sitting there with his bathrobe on, he had his arms folded and was looking at the floor. John had a couple of handlers with him. They looked over his shoulder. Jack looked up.

"Is he in?" he asked.

"He's just gone down," John said.

We started down. Walcott was just getting into the ring. The crowd gave him a big hand. He climbed through between the ropes and put his two fists together and smiled, and shook them at the crowd, first at one side of the ring, then at the other, and then sat down. Jack got a good hand coming down through the crowd. Jack is Irish and the Irish always get a pretty good hand. An Irishman don't draw in New York like a Jew or an Italian but they always get a good hand. Jack climbed up and bent down to go through the ropes and Walcott came over from his corner and pushed the rope down for Jack to go through. The crowd thought that was wonderful. Walcott put his hand on Jack's shoulder and they stood there just for a second.

"So you're going to be one of these popular champions," Jack says to him. "Take your goddam hand off my shoulder."

"Be yourself," Walcott says.

This is all great for the crowd. How gentlemanly the boys are before the fight. How they wish each other luck.

Solly Freedman came over to our corner while Jack is bandaging his hands and John is over in Walcott's corner. Jack puts his thumb through the slit in the bandage and then wrapped his hand nice and smooth. I taped it around the wrist and twice across the knuckles.

"Hey," Freedman says. "Where do you get all that tape?"

"Feel of it," Jack says. "It's soft, ain't it? Don't be a hick."

Freedman stands there all the time while Jack bandages the other hand,

and one of the boys that's going to handle him brings the gloves and I pull them on and work them around.

"Say, Freedman," Jack asks, "what nationality is this Walcott?"

"I don't know," Solly says. "He's some sort of a Dane."

"He's a Bohemian," the lad who brought the gloves said.

The referee called them out to the center of the ring and Jack walks out. Walcott comes out smiling. They met and the referee put his arm on each of their shoulders.

"Hello, popularity," Jack says to Walcott.

"Be yourself."

"What do you call yourself 'Walcott' for?" Jack says. "Didn't you know he was a nigger?"

"Listen—" says the referee, and he gives them the same old line. Once Walcott interrupts him. He grabs Jack's arm and says, "Can I hit when he's got me like this?"

"Keep your hands off me," Jack says. "There ain't no moving-pictures of this."

They went back to their comers. I lifted the bathrobe off Jack and he leaned on the ropes and flexed his knees a couple of times and scuffed his shoes in the rosin. The gong rang and Jack turned quick and went out. Walcott came toward him and they touched gloves and as soon as Walcott dropped his hands Jack jumped his left into his face twice. There wasn't anybody ever boxed better than Jack. Walcott was after him, going forward all the time with his chin on his chest. He's a hooker and he carries his hands pretty low. All he knows is to get in there and sock. But every time he gets in there close, Jack has the left hand in his face. It's just as though it's automatic. Jack just raises the left hand up and it's in Walcott's face. Three or four times Jack brings the right over but Walcott gets it on the shoulder or high up on the head. He's just like all these hookers. The only thing he's afraid of is another one of the same kind. He's covered everywhere you can hurt him. He don't care about a left hand in his face.

After about four rounds Jack has him bleeding bad and his face all cut up, but every time Walcott's got in close he's socked so hard he's got two big red patches on both sides just below Jack's ribs. Every time he gets in close, Jack ties him up, then gets one hand loose and uppercuts him, but when Walcott gets his hands loose he socks Jack in the body so they can hear it outside in the street. He's a socker.

It goes along like that for three rounds more. They don't talk any. They're working all the time. We worked over Jack plenty too, in between the rounds. He don't look good at all but he never does much work in the ring. He don't move around much and that left hand is just automatic. It's just like it was connected with Walcott's face and Jack just had to wish it in every time. Jack is always calm in close and he doesn't waste any juice. He knows everything about working in close too and he's getting away with a lot of stuff. While they were in our corner I watched him tie Walcott up, get his right hand loose, turn it and come up with an uppercut that got Walcott's nose with the heel of the glove. Walcott was bleeding bad and leaned his nose on Jack's shoulder so as to give Jack some of it too, and Jack sort of lifted his shoulder sharp and caught him against the nose, and then brought down the right hand and did the same thing again.

Walcott was sore as hell. By the time they'd gone five rounds he hated Jack's guts. Jack wasn't sore; that is, he wasn't any sorer than he always was. He certainly did used to make the fellows he fought hate boxing. That was why he hated Kid Lewis so. He never got the Kid's goat. Kid Lewis always had about three new dirty things Jack couldn't do. Jack was as safe as a church all the time he was in there, as long as he was strong. He certainly was treating Walcott rough. The funny thing was it looked as though Jack was an open classic boxer. That was because he had all that stuff too.

After the seventh round Jack says, "My left's getting heavy."

From then he started to take a beating. It didn't show at first. But instead of him running the fight it was Walcott was running it, instead of being safe all the time now he was in trouble. He couldn't keep him out with the left hand now. It looked as though it was the same as ever, only now instead of Walcott's punches just missing him they were just hitting him. He took an awful beating in the body.

"What's the round?" Jack asked.

"The eleventh."

"I can't stay," Jack says. "My legs are going bad."

Walcott had been just hitting him for a long time. It was like a baseball catcher pulls the ball and takes some of the shock off. From now on Walcott commenced to land solid. He certainly was a socking-machine. Jack was just trying to block everything now. It didn't show what an awful beating he was taking. In between the rounds I worked on his legs. The muscles would flutter under my hands all the time I was rubbing them. He was sick as hell.

"How's it go?" he asked John, turning around, his face all swollen.

"It's his fight."

"I think I can last," Jack says. "I don't want this bohunk to stop me."

It was going just the way he thought it would. He knew he couldn't beat Walcott. He wasn't strong any more. He was all right though. His money was all right and now he wanted to finish it off right to please himself. He didn't want to be knocked out.

The gong rang and we pushed him out. He went out slow. Walcott came right out after him. Jack put the left in his face and Walcott took it, came in under it and started working on Jack's body. Jack tried to tie him up and it was just like trying to hold on to a buzz-saw. Jack broke away from it and missed with the right. Walcott clipped him with a left hook and Jack went down. He went down on his hands and knees and looked at us. The referee started counting. Jack was watching us and shaking his head. At eight John motioned to him. You couldn't hear on account of the crowd. Jack got up. The referee had been holding Walcott back with one arm while he counted.

When Jack was on his feet Walcott started toward him.

"Watch yourself, Jimmy," I heard Solly Freedman yell to him.

Walcott came up to Jack looking at him. Jack stuck the left hand at him. Walcott just shook his head. He backed Jack up against the ropes, measured him and then hooked the left very light to the side of Jack's head and socked the right into the body as hard as he could sock, just as low as he could get it. He must have hit him five inches below the belt. I thought the eyes would come out of Jack's head. They stuck way out. His mouth come open.

The referee grabbed Walcott. Jack stepped forward. If he went down there went fifty thousand bucks. He walked as though all his insides were going to fall out.

"It wasn't low," he said. "It was a accident."

The crowd were yelling so you couldn't hear anything.

"I'm all right," Jack says. They were right in front of us. The referee looks at John and then he shakes his head.

"Come on, you polak son-of-a-bitch," Jack says to Walcott.

John was hanging onto the ropes. He had the towel ready to chuck in. Jack was standing just a little way out from the ropes. He took a step forward. I saw the sweat come out on his face like somebody had squeezed it and a big drop went down his nose.

"Come on and fight," Jack says to Walcott.

The referee looked at John and waved Walcott on.

"Go in there, you slob," he says.

Walcott went in. He didn't know what to do either. He never thought Jack could have stood it. Jack put the left in his face. There was such a hell of a lot of yelling going on. They were right in front of us. Walcott hit him twice. Jack's face was the worst thing I ever saw – the look on it! He was holding himself and all his body together and it all showed on his face. All the time he was thinking and holding his body in where it was busted.

Then he started to sock. His face looked awful all the time. He started to sock with his hands low down by his side, swinging at Walcott. Walcott covered up and Jack was swinging wild at Walcott's head. Then he swung the left and it hit Walcott in the groin and the right hit Walcott right bang where he'd hit Jack. Way low below the belt. Walcott went down and grabbed himself there and rolled and twisted around.

The referee grabbed Jack and pushed him toward his corner. John jumps into the ring. There was all this yelling going on. The referee was talking with the judges and then the announcer got into the ring with the megaphone and says, "Walcott on a foul."

The referee is talking to John and he says, "What could I do? Jack wouldn't take the foul. Then when he's groggy he fouls him."

"He'd lost it anyway," John says.

Jack's sitting on the chair. I've got his gloves off and he's holding himself in down there with both hands. When he's got something supporting it his face doesn't look so bad.

"Go over and say you're sorry," John says into his ear. "It'll look good."

Jack stands up and the sweat comes out all over his face. I put the bathrobe around him and he holds himself in with one hand under the bathrobe and goes across the ring. They've picked Walcott up and they're working on him. There're a lot of people in Walcott's corner. Nobody speaks to Jack. He leans over Walcott.

"I'm sorry," Jack says. "I didn't mean to foul you."

Walcott doesn't say anything. He looks too damned sick.

"Well, you're the champion now," Jack says to him. "I hope you get a hell of a lot of fun out of it."

"Leave the kid alone," Solly Freedman says.

"Hello, Solly," Jack says. "I'm sorry I fouled your boy."

Freedman just looks at him.

Jack went to his corner walking that funny jerky way and we got him down through the ropes and through the reporters' tables and out down the aisle. A lot of people want to slap Jack on the back. He goes out through all that mob in his bathrobe to the dressing-room. It's a popular win for Walcott. That's the way the money was bet in the Garden.

Once we got inside the dressing-room Jack lay down and shut his eyes.

"We want to get to the hotel and get a doctor," John says.

"I'm all busted inside," Jack says.

"I'm sorry as hell, Jack," John says.

"It's all right," Jack says.

He lies there with his eyes shut.

"They certainly tried a nice double-cross," John said.

"Your friends Morgan and Steinfelt," Jack said. "You got nice friends."

He lies there, his eyes are open now. His face has still got that awful drawn look.

"It's funny how fast you can think when it means that much money," Jack says.

"You're some boy, Jack," John says.

"No," Jack says. "It was nothing."

A Simple Enquiry

OUTSIDE, THE SNOW WAS HIGHER THAN the window. The sunlight came in through the window and shone on a map on the pineboard wall of the hut. The sun was high and the light came in over the top of the snow. A trench had been cut along the open side of the hut, and each clear day the sun, shining on the wall, reflected heat against the snow and widened the trench. It was late March. The major sat at a table against the wall. His adjutant sat at another table.

Around the major's eyes were two white circles where his snow-glasses had protected his face from the sun on the snow. The rest of his face had been burned and then tanned and then burned through the tan. His nose was swollen and there were edges of loose skin where blisters had been. While he worked at the papers he put the fingers of his left hand into a saucer of oil and then spread the oil over his face, touching it very gently with the tips of his fingers. He was very careful to drain his fingers on the edge of the saucer so there was only a film of oil on them, and after he had stroked his forehead and his cheeks, he stroked his nose very delicately between his fingers. When he had finished he stood up, took the saucer of oil and went into the small room of the hut where he slept. "I'm going to take a little sleep," he said to the adjutant. In that army an adjutant is not a commissioned officer. "You will finish up."

"Yes, *signor maggiore*," the adjutant answered. He leaned back in his chair and yawned. He took a paper-covered book out of the pocket of his coat and opened it; then laid it down on the table and lit his pipe. He leaned forward on the table to read and puffed at his pipe. Then he closed the book and put it back in his pocket. He had too much paper-work to get through. He could not enjoy reading until it was done. Outside, the sun went behind a mountain and there was no more light on the wall of the hut. A soldier came in and put some pine branches, chopped into irregular lengths, into the stove. "Be soft, Pinin," the adjutant said to him. "The major is sleeping."

Pinin was the major's orderly. He was a dark-faced boy, and he fixed the stove, putting the pine wood in carefully, shut the door, and went into the back of the hut again. The adjutant went on with his papers.

"Tonani," the major called.

"*Signor maggiore?*"

"Send Pinin in to me."

"Pinin!" the adjutant called. Pinin came into the room. "The major wants you," the adjutant said.

Pinin walked across the main room of the hut toward the major's door. He knocked on the half-opened door. "*Signor maggiore?*"

"Come in," the adjutant heard the major say, "and shut the door."

Inside the room the major lay on his bunk. Pinin stood beside the bunk. The major lay with his head on the rucksack that he had stuffed with spare clothing to make a pillow. His long, burned, oiled face looked at Pinin. His hands lay on the blankets.

"You are nineteen?" he asked.

"Yes, *signor maggiore.*"

"You have ever been in love?"

"How do you mean, *signor maggiore?*"

"In love – with a girl?"

"I have been with girls."

"I did not ask that. I asked if you had been in love – with a girl."

"Yes, *signor maggiore.*"

"You are in love with this girl now? You don't write her. I read all your letters."

"I am in love with her," Pinin said, "but I do not write her."

"You are sure of this?"

"I am sure."

"Tonani," the major said in the same tone of voice, "can you hear me talking?"

There was no answer from the next room.

"He can not hear," the major said. "And you are quite sure that you love a girl?"

"I am sure."

"And," the major looked at him quickly, "that you are not corrupt?"

"I don't know what you mean, corrupt."

"All right," the major said. "You needn't be superior."

Pinin looked at the floor. The major looked at his brown face, down and up him, and at his hands. Then he went on, not smiling, "And you don't really want—" the major paused. Pinin looked at the floor. "That your great desire isn't really—" Pinin looked at the floor. The major leaned his head back on the rucksack and smiled. He was really relieved: life in the army was too complicated. "You're a good boy," he said. "You're a good boy, Pinin. But don't be superior and be careful some one else doesn't come along and take you."

Pinin stood still beside the bunk.

"Don't be afraid," the major said. His hands were folded on the blankets. "I won't touch you. You can go back to your platoon if you like. But you had better stay on as my servant. You've less chance of being killed."

"Do you want anything of me, *signor maggiore?*'

"No," the major said. "Go on and get on with whatever you were doing. Leave the door open when you go out."

Pinin went out, leaving the door open. The adjutant looked up at him as he walked awkwardly across the room and out the door. Pinin was flushed and moved differently than he had moved when he brought in the wood for the fire. The adjutant looked after him and smiled. Pinin came in with more wood for the stove. The major, lying on his bunk, looking at his cloth-covered helmet and his snow-glasses that hung from a nail on the wall, heard him walk across the floor. The little devil, he thought, I wonder if he lied to me.

Ten Indians

AFTER ONE FOURTH OF JULY, NICK, DRIVING home late from town in the big wagon with Joe Garner and his family, passed nine drunken Indians along the road. He remembered there were nine because Joe Garner, driving along in the dusk, pulled up the horses, jumped down into the road and dragged an Indian out of the wheel rut. The Indian had been asleep, face down in the sand. Joe dragged him into bushes and got back up on the wagon-box.

"That makes nine of them," Joe said, "just between here and the edge of town."

"Them Indians," said Mrs. Garner.

Nick was on the back seat with the two Garner boys. He was looking out from the back seat to see the Indian where Joe had dragged him alongside of the road.

"Was it Billy Tabeshaw?" Carl asked.

"No."

"His pants looked mighty like Billy."

"All Indians wear the same kind of pants."

"I didn't see him at all," Frank said. "Pa was down into the road and back up again before I seen a thing. I thought he was killing a snake."

"Plenty of Indians'll kill snakes tonight, I guess," Joe Garner said.

"Them Indians," said Mrs. Garner.

They drove along. The road turned off from the main highway and went up into the hills. It was hard pulling for the horses and the boys got down and walked. The road was sandy. Nick looked back from the top of the hill by the schoolhouse. He saw the lights of Petoskey and, off across Little Traverse Bay, the lights of Harbour Springs. They climbed back in the wagon again.

"They ought to put some gravel on that stretch," Joe Garner said. The wagon went along the road through the woods. Joe and Mrs. Garner sat close together on the front seat. Nick sat between the two boys. The road came out into a clearing.

"Right here was where Pa ran over the skunk."

"It was further on."

"It don't make no difference where it was," Joe said without turning his head. "One place is just as good as another to run over a skunk."

"I saw two skunks last night," Nick said.

"Where?"

"Down by the lake. They were looking for dead fish along the beach."

"They were coons probably," Carl said.

"They were skunks. I guess I know skunks."

"You ought to," Carl said. "You got an Indian girl."

"Stop talking that way, Carl," said Mrs. Garner.

"Well, they smell about the same."

Joe Garner laughed.

"You stop laughing, Joe," Mrs. Garner said. "I won't have Carl talk that way."

"Have you got an Indian girl, Nickie?" Joe asked.

"No."

"He has too, Pa," Frank said. "Prudence Mitchell's his girl."

"She's not."

"He goes to see her every day."

"I don't." Nick, sitting between the two boys in the dark, felt hollow and happy inside himself to be teased about Prudence Mitchell. "She ain't my girl," he said.

"Listen to him," said Carl. "I see them together every day."

"Carl can't get a girl," his mother said, "not even a squaw."

Carl was quiet.

"Carl ain't no good with girls," Frank said.

"You shut up."

"You're all right, Carl," Joe Garner said. "Girls never got a man anywhere. Look at your pa."

"Yes, that's what you would say," Mrs. Garner moved close to Joe as the wagon jolted. "Well, you had plenty of girls in your time."

"I'll bet Pa wouldn't ever have had a squaw for a girl."

"Don't you think it," Joe said. "You better watch out to keep Prudie, Nick."

His wife whispered to him and Joe laughed.

"What you laughing at?" asked Frank.

"Don't you say it, Garner," his wife warned. Joe laughed again.

"Nickie can have Prudence," Joe Garner said. "I got a good girl."

"That's the way to talk," Mrs. Garner said.

The horses were pulling heavily in the sand. Joe reached out in the dark with the whip.

"Come on, pull into it. You'll have to pull harder than this tomorrow."

They trotted down the long hill, the wagon jolting. At the farmhouse everybody got down. Mrs. Garner unlocked the door, went inside, and came out with a lamp in her hand. Carl and Nick unloaded the things from the back of the wagon. Frank sat on the front seat to drive to the barn and put up the horses. Nick went up the steps and opened the kitchen door. Mrs. Garner was building a fire in the stove. She turned from pouring kerosene on the wood.

"Good-by, Mrs. Garner," Nick said. "Thanks for taking me."

"Oh shucks, Nickie."

"I had a wonderful time."

"We like to have you. Won't you stay and eat some supper?"

"I better go. I think Dad probably waited for me."

"Well, get along then. Send Carl up to the house, will you?"

"All right."

"Good-night, Nickie."

"Good-night, Mrs. Garner."

Nick went out the farmyard and down to the barn. Joe and Frank were milking.

"Good-night," Nick said. "I had a swell time."

"Good-night, Nick," Joe Garner called. "Aren't you going to stay and eat?"

"No, I can't. Will you tell Carl his mother wants him?"

"All right. Good-night, Nickie."

Nick walked barefoot along the path through the meadow below the barn. The path was smooth and the dew was cool on his bare feet. He climbed a fence at the end of the meadow, went down through a ravine, his feet wet in the swamp mud, and then climbed up through the dry beech woods until he saw the lights of the cottage. He climbed over the fence and walked around to the front porch. Through the window he saw his father sitting by the table, reading in the light from the big lamp. Nick opened the door and went in.

"Well, Nickie," his father said, "was it a good day?"

"I had a swell time, Dad. It was a swell Fourth of July."

"Are you hungry?"

"You bet."

"What did you do with your shoes?"

"I left them in the wagon at Garner's."

"Come on out to the kitchen."

Nick's father went ahead with the lamp. He stopped and lifted the lid of the ice-box. Nick went on into the kitchen. His father brought in a piece of cold chicken on a plate and a pitcher of milk and put them on the table before Nick. He put down the lamp.

"There's some pie too," he said. "Will that hold you?"

"It's grand."

His father sat down in a chair beside the oil-cloth-covered table. He made a big shadow on the kitchen wall.

"Who won the ball game?"

"Petoskey. Five to three."

His father sat watching him eat and filled his glass from the milk-pitcher. Nick drank and wiped his mouth on his napkin. His father reached over to the shelf for the pie. He cut Nick a big piece. It was huckleberry pie.

"What did you do, Dad?"

"I went out fishing in the morning."

"What did you get?"

"Only perch."

His father sat watching Nick eat the pie.

"What did you do this afternoon?" Nick asked.

"I went for a walk up by the Indian camp."

"Did you see anybody?"

"The Indians were all in town getting drunk."

"Didn't you see anybody at all?"

"I saw your friend, Prudie."

"Where was she?"

"She was in the woods with Frank Washburn. I ran onto them. They were having quite a time."

His father was not looking at him.

"What were they doing?"

"I didn't stay to find out."

"Tell me what they were doing."

"I don't know," his father said. "I just heard them threshing around."

"How did you know it was them?"

"I saw them."

"I thought you said you didn't see them."

"Oh, yes, I saw them."

"Who was it with her?" Nick asked.

"Frank Washburn."

"Were they – were they – –"

"Were they what?"

"Were they happy?"

"I guess so."

His father got up from the table and went out the kitchen screen door. When he came back Nick was looking at his plate. He had been crying.

"Have some more?" His father picked up the knife to cut the pie.

"No," said Nick.

"You better have another piece."

"No, I don't want any."

His father cleared off the table.

"Where were they in the woods?" Nick asked.

"Up back of the camp." Nick looked at his plate. His father said, "You better go to bed, Nick."

"All right."

Nick went into his room, undressed, and got into bed. He heard his father moving around in the living room. Nick lay in the bed with his face in the pillow.

"My heart's broken," he thought. "If I feel this way my heart must be broken."

After a while he heard his father blow out the lamp and go into his own room. He heard a wind come up in the trees outside and felt it come in cool through the screen. He lay for a long time with his face in the pillow, and after a while he forgot to think about Prudence and finally he went to sleep. When he awoke in the night he heard the wind in the hemlock trees outside the cottage and the waves of the lake coming in on the shore, and he went back to sleep. In the morning there was a big wind blowing and the waves were running high up on the beach and he was awake a long time before he remembered that his heart was broken.

A Canary for One

THE TRAIN PASSED VERY QUICKLY A LONG, red stone house with a garden and four thick palm-trees with tables under them in the shade. On the other side was the sea. Then there was a cutting through red stone and clay, and the sea was only occasionally and far below against rocks.

"I bought him in Palermo," the American lady said. "We only had an hour ashore and it was Sunday morning. The man wanted to be paid in dollars and I gave him a dollar and a half. He really sings very beautifully."

It was very hot in the train and it was very hot in the *lit salon* compartment. There was no breeze came through the open window. The American lady pulled the window-blind down and there was no more sea, even occasionally. On the other side there was glass, then the corridor, then an open window, and outside the window were dusty trees and an oiled road and flat fields of grapes, with gray-stone hills behind them.

There was smoke from many tall chimneys – coming into Marseilles, and the train slowed down and followed one track through many others into the station. The train stayed twenty-five minutes in the station at Marseilles and the American lady bought a copy of *The Daily Mail* and a half-bottle of Evian water. She walked a little way along the station platform, but she stayed near the steps of the car because at Cannes, where it stopped for twelve minutes, the train had left with no signal of departure and she had gotten on only just in time. The American lady was a little deaf and she was afraid that perhaps signals of departure were given and that she did not hear them.

The train left the station in Marseilles and there was not only the switchyards and the factory smoke but, looking back, the town of Marseilles and the harbor with stone hills behind it and the last of the sun on the water. As it was getting dark the train passed a farmhouse burning in a field. Motor-cars were stopped along the road and bedding and things from inside the farmhouse were spread in the field. Many people were watching the house burn. After it was dark the train was in Avignon. People got on and off. At the news-stand Frenchmen, returning to Paris, bought that day's French papers. On the station platform were negro soldiers. They wore brown uniforms and were tall and their faces shone, close under the electric light. Their faces were very black and they were too tall to stare. The train left Avignon station with the negroes standing there. A short white sergeant was with them.

Inside the *lit salon* compartment the porter had pulled down the three beds from inside the wall and prepared them for sleeping. In the night the American lady lay without sleeping because the train was a *rapide* and went very fast and she was afraid of the speed in the night. The American lady's bed was the one next to the window. The canary from Palermo, a cloth spread over his cage, was out of the draft in the corridor that went into the compartment wash-room. There was a blue light outside the compartment, and all night the train went very fast and the American lady lay awake and waited for a wreck.

In the morning the train was near Paris, and after the American lady had come out from the wash-room, looking very wholesome and middle-aged and American in spite of not having slept, and had taken the cloth off the birdcage and hung the cage in the sun, she went back to the restaurant-car for breakfast. When she came back to the *lit salon* compartment again, the beds had been pushed back into the wall and made into seats, the canary was shaking his feathers in the sunlight that came through the open window, and the train was much nearer Paris.

"He loves the sun," the American lady said. "He'll sing now in a little while."

The canary shook his feathers and pecked into them. "I've always loved birds," the American lady said. "I'm taking him home to my little girl. There – he's singing now."

The canary chirped and the feathers on his throats stood out, then he dropped his bill and pecked into his feathers again. The train crossed a river and passed through a very carefully tended forest. The train passed through many outside of Paris towns. There were tram-cars in the towns and big advertisements for the Belle Jardinière and Dubonnet and Pernod on the walls toward the train. All that the train passed through looked as though it were before breakfast. For several minutes I had not listened to the American lady, who was talking to my wife.

"Is your husband American too?" asked the lady.

"Yes," said my wife. "We're both Americans."

"I thought you were English."

"Oh, no."

"Perhaps that was because I wore braces," I said. I had started to say suspenders and changed it to braces in the mouth, to keep my English character. The American lady did not hear. She was really quite deaf; she read lips, and I had not looked toward her. I had looked out of the window. She went on talking to my wife.

"I'm so glad you're Americans. American men make the best husbands," the American lady was saying. "That was why we left the Continent, you know. My daughter fell in love with a man in Vevey." She stopped. "They were simply madly in love." She stopped again. "I took her away, of course."

"Did she get over it?" asked my wife.

"I don't think so," said the American lady. "She wouldn't eat anything and she wouldn't sleep at all. I've tried so very hard, but she doesn't seem to take an interest in anything. She doesn't care about things. I couldn't have her marrying a foreigner." She paused. "Some one, a very good friend, told me once, 'No foreigner can make an American girl a good husband.'"

"No," said my wife, "I suppose not."

The American lady admired my wife's travelling-coat, and it turned out that the American lady had bought her own clothes for twenty years now from the same *maison de couture* in the Rue Saint Honoré. They had her measurements, and a *vendeuse* who knew her and her tastes picked the dresses out for her and they were sent to America. They came to the post-office near where she lived up-town in New York, and the duty was never exorbitant because they opened the dresses there in the post-office to appraise them and they were always very simple-looking and with no gold lace nor ornaments that would make the dresses look expensive. Before the present *vendeuse*, named Thérèse, there had been another *vendeuse*, named Amélie. Altogether there had only been these two in the twenty years. It had always been the same couturier. Prices, however, had gone up. The exchange, though, equalized that. They had her daughter's measurements now too. She was grown up and there was not much chance of their changing now.

The train was now coming into Paris. The fortifications were levelled but grass had not grown. There were many cars standing on tracks – brown wooden restaurant-cars and brown wooden sleeping-cars that would go to Italy at five o'clock that night, if that train still left at five; the cars were marked Paris-Rome, and cars, with seats on the roofs, that went back and forth to the suburbs with, at certain hours, people in all the seats and on the roofs, if that were the way it were still done, and passing were the white walls and many windows of houses. Nothing had eaten any breakfast.

"Americans make the best husbands," the American lady said to my wife. I was getting down the bags. "American men are the only men in the world to marry."

"How long ago did you leave Vevey?" asked my wife.

"Two years ago this fall. It's her, you know, that I'm taking the canary to."

"Was the man your daughter was in love with a Swiss?"

"Yes," said the American lady. "He was from a very good family in Vevey. He was going to be an engineer. They met there in Vevey. They used to go on long walks together."

"I know Vevey," said my wife. "We were there on our honeymoon."

"Were you really? That must have been lovely. I had no idea, of course, that she'd fall in love with him."

"It was a very lovely place," said my wife.

"Yes," said the American lady. "Isn't it lovely? Where did you stop there?"

"We stayed at the Trois Couronnes," said my wife.

"It's such a fine old hotel," said the American lady.

"Yes," said my wife. "We had a very fine room and in the fall the country was lovely."

"Were you there in the fall?"

"Yes," said my wife.

We were passing three cars that had been in a wreck. They were splintered open and the roofs sagged in.

"Look," I said. "There's been a wreck."

The American lady looked and saw the last car. "I was afraid of just that all night," she said. "I have terrific presentiments about things sometimes. I'll never travel on a *rapide* again at night. There must be other comfortable trains that don't go so fast."

Then the train was in the dark of the Gare de Lyons, and then stopped and porters came up to the windows. I handed bags through the windows, and we were out on the dim longness of the platform, and the American lady put herself in charge of one of three men from Cook's who said: "Just a moment, madame, and I'll look for your name."

The porter brought a truck and piled on the baggage, and my wife said good-by and I said good-by to the American lady, whose name had been found by the man from Cook's on a typewritten page in a sheaf of typewritten pages which he replaced in his pocket.

We followed the porter with the truck down the long cement platform beside the train. At the end was a gate and a man took the tickets.

We were returning to Paris to set up separate residences.

An Alpine Idyll

IT WAS HOT COMING DOWN INTO THE VALLEY even in the early morning. The sun melted the snow from the skis we were carrying and dried the wood. It was spring in the valley but the sun was very hot. We came along the road into Galtur carrying our skis and rucksacks. As we passed the churchyard a burial was just over. I said, "Grüss Gott", *to the priest as he walked past us coming out of the churchyard. The priest bowed.*

"It's funny a priest never speaks to you," John said.

"You'd think they'd like to say 'Grüss Gott.'"

"They never answer," John said.

We stopped in the road and watched the sexton shovelling in the new earth. A peasant with a black beard and high leather boots stood beside the grave. The sexton stopped shovelling and straightened his back. The peasant in the high boots took the spade from the sexton and went on filling in the grave – spreading the earth evenly as a man spreading manure in a garden. In the bright May morning the grave-filling looked unreal. I could not imagine any one being dead.

"Imagine being buried on a day like this," I said to John.

"I wouldn't like it."

"Well," I said, "we don't have to do it."

We went on up the road past the houses of the town to the inn. We had been skiing in the Silvretta for a month, and it was good to be down in the valley. In the Silvretta the skiing had been all right, but it was spring skiing, the snow was good only in the early morning and again in the evening. The rest of the time it was spoiled by the sun. We were both tired of the sun. You could not get away from the sun. The only shadows were made by rocks or by the hut that was built under the protection of a rock beside a glacier, and in the shade the sweat froze in your underclothing. You could not sit outside the hut without dark glasses. It was pleasant to be burned black but the sun had been very tiring. You could not rest in it. I was glad to be down away from snow. It was too late in the spring to be up in the Silvretta. I was a little tired of skiing. We had stayed too long. I could taste the snow water we had been drinking melted off the tin roof of the hut. The taste was a part of the way I felt about skiing. I was glad there were other things beside skiing, and I was glad to be down, away from the unnatural high mountain spring, into this May morning in the valley.

The innkeeper sat on the porch of the inn, his chair tipped back against the wall. Beside him sat the cook.

"*Ski-hell!*" said the innkeeper.

"*Heil!*" we said and leaned the skis against the wall and took off our packs.

"How was it up above?" asked the innkeeper.

"*Schön.* A little too much sun."

"Yes. There's too much sun this time of year."

The cook sat on in his chair. The innkeeper went in with us and unlocked his office and brought out our mail. There was a bundle of letters and some papers.

"Let's get some beer," John said.

"Good. We'll drink it inside."

The proprietor brought two bottles and we drank them while we read the letters.

"We better have some more beer," John said. A girl brought it this time. She smiled as she opened the bottles.

"Many letters," she said.

"Yes. Many."

"*Prosit,*" she said and went out, taking the empty bottles.

"I'd forgotten what beer tasted like."

"I hadn't," John said. "Up in the hut I used to think about it a lot."

"Well," I said, "we've got it now."

"You oughtn't to ever do anything too long."

"No. We were up there too long."

"Too damn long," John said. "It's no good doing a thing too long."

The sun came through the open window and shone through the beer bottles on the table. The bottles were half full. There was a little froth on the beer in the bottles, not much because it was very cold. It collared up when you poured it into the tall glasses. I looked out of the open window at the white road. The trees beside the road were dusty. Beyond was a green field and a stream. There were trees along the stream and a mill with a water wheel. Through the open side of the mill I saw a long log and a saw in it rising and falling. No one seemed to be tending it. There were four crows walking in the green field. One crow sat in a tree watching. Outside on the porch the cook got off his chair and passed into the hall that led back into the kitchen. Inside, the sunlight shone through the empty glasses on the table. John was leaning forward with his head on his arms.

Through the window I saw two men come up the front steps. They came into the drinking room. One was the bearded peasant in the high boots. The other was the sexton. They sat down at the table under the window. The girl came in and stood by their table. The peasant did not seem to see her. He sat with his hands on the table. He wore his old army clothes. There were patches on the elbows.

"What will it be?" asked the sexton. The peasant did not pay any attention.

"What will you drink?"

"Schnapps," the peasant said.

"And a quarter litre of red wine," the sexton told the girl.

The girl brought the drinks and the peasant drank the schnapps. He looked out of the window. The sexton watched him. John had his head forward on the table. He was asleep.

The innkeeper came in and went over to the table. He spoke in dialect and the sexton answered him. The peasant looked out of the window. The innkeeper went out of the room. The peasant stood up. He took a folded ten-thousand kronen note out of a leather pocketbook and unfolded it. The girl came up.

"*Alles?*" she asked.

"*Alles*," he said.

"Let me buy the wine," the sexton said.

"*Alles*," the peasant repeated to the girl. She put her hand in the pocket of her apron, brought it out full of coins and counted out the change. The peasant went out the door. As soon as he was gone the innkeeper came into the room again and spoke to the sexton. He sat down at the table. They talked in dialect. The sexton was amused. The innkeeper was disgusted. The sexton stood up from the table. He was a little man with a mustache. He leaned out of the window and looked up the road.

"There he goes in," he said.

"In the Löwen?"

"*Ja.*"

They talked again and then the innkeeper came over to our table. The innkeeper was a tall man and old. He looked at John asleep.

"He's pretty tired."

"Yes, we were up early."

"Will you want to eat soon?"

"Any time," I said. "What is there to eat?"

"Anything you want. The girl will bring the eating-card."

The girl brought the menu. John woke up. The menu was written in ink on a card and the card slipped into a wooden paddle.

"There's the *Speisekarte*," I said to John. He looked at it. He was still sleepy.

"Won't you have a drink with us?" I asked the innkeeper. He sat down. "Those peasants are beasts," said the innkeeper.

"We saw that one at a funeral coming into town."

"That was his wife."

"Oh."

"He's a beast. All these peasants are beasts."

"How do you mean?"

"You wouldn't believe it. You wouldn't believe what just happened about that one."

"Tell me."

"You wouldn't believe it." The innkeeper spoke to the sexton. "Franz, come over here." The sexton came, bringing his little bottle of wine and his glass.

"The gentlemen are just come down from the Wiesbadenerhütte," the innkeeper said. We shook hands.

"What will you drink?" I asked.

"Nothing," Franz shook his finger.

"Another quarter litre?"

"All right."

"Do you understand dialect?" the innkeeper asked.

"No."

"What's it all about?" John asked.

"He's going to tell us about the peasant we saw filling the grave, coming into town."

"I can't understand it, anyway," John said. "It goes too fast for me."

"That peasant," the innkeeper said, "today he brought his wife in to be buried. She died last November."

"December," said the sexton.

"That makes nothing. She died last December then, and he notified the commune."

"December eighteenth," said the sexton.

"Anyway, he couldn't bring her over to be buried until the snow was gone."

"He lives on the other side of the Paznaun," said the sexton. "But he belongs to this parish."

"He couldn't bring her out at all?" I asked.

"No. He can only come, from where he lives, on skis until the snow melts. So today he brought her in to be buried and the priest, when he looked at her face, didn't want to bury her. You go on and tell it," he said to the sexton. "Speak German, not dialect."

"It was very funny with the priest," said the sexton. "In the report to the commune she died of heart trouble. We knew she had heart trouble here. She used to faint in church sometimes. She did not come for a long time. She wasn't strong to climb. When the priest uncovered her face he asked Olz, 'Did your wife suffer much?' 'No,' said Olz. 'When I came in the house she was dead across the bed.'

"The priest looked at her again. He didn't like it.

"'How did her face get that way?'

"I don't know,' Olz said.

"'You'd better find out,' the priest said, and put the blanket back. Olz didn't say anything. The priest looked at him. Olz looked back at the priest. 'You want to know?'

"'I must know,' the priest said."

"This is where it's good," the innkeeper said. "Listen to this. Go on Franz."

"'Well,' said Olz, 'when she died I made the report to the commune and I put her in the shed across the top of the big wood. When I started to use the big wood she was stiff and I put her up against the wall. Her mouth was open and when I came into the shed at night to cut up the big wood, I hung the lantern from it.'

"'Why did you do that?' asked the priest.

"'I don't know,' said Olz.

"'Did you do that many times?'

"'Every time I went to work in the shed at night.'

"'It was very wrong,' said the priest. 'Did you love your wife?'

"'*Ja*, I loved her,' Olz said. 'I loved her fine.'"

"Did you understand it all?" asked the innkeeper. "You understand it all about his wife?"

"I heard it."

"How about eating?" John asked.

"You order," I said. "Do you think it's true?" I asked the innkeeper.

"Sure it's true," he said. "These peasants are beasts."

"Where did he go now?"

"He's gone to drink at my colleague's, the Löwen."

"He didn't want to drink with me," said the sexton.

"He didn't want to drink with me, after *he* knew about his wife," said the innkeeper.

"Say," said John. "How about eating?"

"All right," I said.

A Pursuit Race

WILLIAM CAMPBELL HAD BEEN IN A PURSUIT race with a burlesque show ever since Pittsburgh. In a pursuit race, in bicycle racing, riders start at equal intervals to ride after one another. They ride very fast because the race is usually limited to a short distance and if they slow their riding another rider who maintains his pace will make up the space that separated them equally at the start. As soon as a rider is caught and passed he is out of the race and must get down from his bicycle and leave the track. If none of the riders are caught the winner of the race is the one who has gained the most distance. In most pursuit races, if there are only two riders, one of the riders is caught inside of six miles. The burlesque show caught William Campbell at Kansas City.

William Campbell had hoped to hold a slight lead over the burlesque show until they reached the Pacific coast. As long as he preceded the burlesque show as advance man he was being paid. When the burlesque show caught up with him he was in bed. He was in bed when the manager of the burlesque troupe came into his room and after the manager had gone out he decided that he might as well stay in bed. It was very cold in Kansas City and he was in no hurry to go out. He did not like Kansas City. He reached under the bed for a bottle and drank. It made his stomach feel better. Mr. Turner, the manager of the burlesque show, had refused a drink.

William Campbell's interview with Mr. Turner had been a little strange. Mr. Turner had knocked on the door. Campbell had said: "Come in!" When Mr. Turner came into the room he saw clothing on a chair, an open suitcase, the bottle on a chair beside the bed, and some one lying in the bed completely covered by the bed-clothes.

"Mister Campbell," Mr. Turner said.

"You can't fire me," William Campbell said from underneath the covers. It was warm and white and close under the covers. "You can't fire me because I've got down off my bicycle."

"You're drunk," Mr. Turner said.

"Oh, yes," William Campbell said, speaking directly against the sheet and feeling the texture with his lips.

"You're a fool," Mr. Turner said. He turned off the electric light. The electric light had been burning all night. It was now ten o'clock in the morning. "You're a drunken fool. When did you get into this town?"

"I got into this town last night," William Campbell said, speaking against the sheet. He found he liked to talk through a sheet. "Did you ever talk through a sheet?"

"Don't try to be funny. You aren't funny."

"I'm not being funny. I'm just talking through a sheet."

"You're talking through a sheet all right."

"You can go now, Mr. Turner," Campbell said. "I don't work for you any more."

"You know that anyway."

"I know a lot," William Campbell said. He pulled down the sheet and looked at Mr. Turner. "I know enough so I don't mind looking at you at all. Do you want to hear what I know?"

"No."

"Good," said William Campbell. "Because really I don't know anything at all. I was just talking." He pulled the sheet up over his face again. "I love it under a sheet," he said. Mr. Turner stood beside the bed. He was a middle-aged man with a large stomach and a bald head and he had many things to do. "You ought to stop off here, Billy, and take a cure," he said. "I'll fix it up if you want to do it."

"I don't want to take a cure," William Campbell said. "I don't want to take a cure at all. I am perfectly happy. All my life I have been perfectly happy."

"How long have you been this way?"

"What a question!" William Campbell breathed in and out through the sheet.

"How long have you been stewed, Billy?"

"Haven't I done my work?"

"Sure. I just asked you how long you've been stewed, Billy."

"I don't know. But I've got my wolf back," he touched the sheet with his tongue. "I've had him for a week."

"The hell you have."

"Oh, yes. My dear wolf. Every time I take a drink he goes outside the room. He can't stand alcohol. The poor little fellow." He moved his tongue round and round on the sheet. "He's a lovely wolf. He's just like he always was." William Campbell shut his eyes and took a deep breath.

"You got to take a cure, Billy," Mr. Turner said. "You won't mind the Keeley. It isn't bad."

"The Keeley," William Campbell said. "It isn't far from London." He shut his eyes and opened them, moving the eyelashes against the sheet. "I just love sheets," he said. He looked at Mr. Turner.

"Listen, you think I'm drunk."

"You *are* drunk."

"No, I'm not."

"You're drunk and you've had D.T.'s."

"No." William Campbell held the sheet around his head. "Dear sheet," he said. He breathed against it gently. "Pretty sheet. You love me, don't you, sheet? It's all in the price of the room. Just like in Japan. No," he said. "Listen Billy, dear Sliding Billy, I have a surprise for you. I'm not drunk. I'm hopped to the eyes."

"No," said Mr. Turner.

"Take a look." William Campbell pulled up the right sleeve of his pyjama jacket under the sheet, then shoved the right forearm out. "Look at that." On the forearm, from just above the wrist to the elbow, were small blue circles around tiny dark blue punctures. The circles almost touched one another. "That's the new development," William Campbell said. "I drink a little now once in a while, just to drive the wolf out of the room."

"They got a cure for that," "Sliding Billy" Turner said.

"No," William Campbell said. "They haven't got a cure for anything."

"You can't just quit like that, Billy," Turner said. He sat on the bed.

"Be careful of my sheet," William Campbell said.

"You can't just quit at your age and take to pumping yourself full of that stuff just because you got in a jam."

"There's a law against it. If that's what you mean."

"No, I mean you got to fight it out."

Billy Campbell caressed the sheet with his lips and his tongue. "Dear sheet," he said. "I can kiss this sheet and see right through it at the same time."

"Cut it out about the sheet. You can't just take to that stuff, Billy."

William Campbell shut his eyes. He was beginning to feel a slight nausea. He knew that this nausea would increase steadily, without there ever being the relief of sickness, until something were done against it. It was at this point that he suggested that Mr. Turner have a drink. Mr. Turner declined. William Campbell took a drink from the bottle. It was a temporary measure. Mr. Turner watched him. Mr. Turner had been in this room much longer than he should have been, he had many things to do; although living in daily association with people who used drugs, he had a horror of drugs, and he was very fond of William Campbell; he did not wish to leave him. He was very sorry for him and he felt a cure might help. He knew there were good cures in Kansas City. But he had to go. He stood up.

"Listen, Billy," William Campbell said, "I want to tell you something. You're called 'Sliding Billy.' That's because you can slide. I'm called just Billy. That's because I never could slide at all. I can't slide, Billy. I can't slide. It just catches. Every time I try it, it catches." He shut his eyes. "I can't slide, Billy. It's awful when you can't slide."

"Yes," said "Sliding Billy" Turner.

"Yes, what?" William Campbell looked at him.

"You were saying."

"No," said William Campbell. "I wasn't saying. It must have been a mistake."

"You were saying about sliding."

"No. It couldn't have been about sliding. But listen, Billy, and I'll tell you a secret. Stick to sheets, Billy. Keep away from women and horses and, and—" he stopped " — eagles, Billy. If you love horses you'll get horse-shit, and if you love eagles you'll get eagle-shit." He stopped and put his head under the sheet.

"I got to go," said "Sliding Billy" Turner.

"If you love women you'll get a dose," William Campbell said. "If you love horses—"

"Yes, you said that."

"Said what?"

"About horses and eagles."

"Oh, yes. And if you love sheets." He breathed on the sheet and stroked his nose against it. "I don't know about sheets," he said. "I just started to love this sheet."

"I have to go," Mr. Turner said. "I got a lot to do."

"That's all right," William Campbell said. "Everybody's got to go."

"I better go."

"All right, you go."

"Are you all right, Billy?"

"I was never so happy in my life."

"And you're all right?"

"I'm fine. You go along. I'll just lie here for a little while. Around noon I'll get up."

But when Mr. Turner came up to William Campbell's room at noon William Campbell was sleeping and as Mr. Turner was a man who knew what things in life were very valuable he did not wake him.

TODAY IS FRIDAY

Three Roman soldiers are in a drinking-place at eleven o'clock at night. There are barrels around the wall. Behind the wooden counter is a Hebrew wine-seller. The three Roman soldiers are a little cock-eyed.

1st Roman Soldier — You tried the red?

2d Soldier — No, I ain't tried it.

1st Soldier — You better try it.

2d Soldier — All right, George, we'll have a round of the red.

Hebrew Wine-seller — Here you are, gentlemen. You'll like that. *[He sets down an earthenware pitcher that he has filled from one of the casks.]* That's a nice little wine.

1st Soldier — Have a drink of it yourself. *[He turns to the third Roman soldier who is leaning on a barrel.]* What's the matter with you?

3d Roman Soldier — I got a gut-ache.

2d Soldier — You've been drinking water.

1st Soldier — Try some of the red.

3d Soldier — I can't drink the damn stuff. It makes my gut sour.

1st Soldier — You been out here too long.

3d Soldier — Hell don't I know it?

1st Soldier — Say, George, can't you give this gentleman something to fix up his stomach?

Hebrew Wine-seller — I got it right here.

[The third Roman soldier tastes the cup that the wine-seller has mixed for him.]

3d Soldier — Hey, what you put in that, camel chips?

Wine-seller — You drink that right down, Lootenant. That'll fix you up right.

3d Soldier — Well, I couldn't feel any worse.

1st Soldier — Take a chance on it. George fixed me up fine the other day.

Wine-seller — You were in bad shape, Lootenant. I know what fixes up a bad stomach.

[The third Roman soldier drinks the cup down.]

3d Roman Soldier — Jesus Christ. *[He makes a face.]*

2d Soldier — That false alarm!

1st Soldier — Oh, I don't know. He was pretty good in there today.

2d Soldier — Why didn't he come down off the cross?

1st Soldier — He didn't want to come down off the cross. That's not his play.

2d Soldier — Show me a guy that doesn't want to come down off the cross.

1st Soldier — Aw, hell, you don't know anything about it. Ask George there. Did he want to come down off the cross, George?

Wine-seller — I'll tell you, gentlemen, I wasn't out there. It's a thing I haven't taken any interest in.

2d Soldier — Listen, I seen a lot of them — here and plenty of other places. Any time you show me one that doesn't want to get down off the cross when the time comes — when the time comes, I mean — I'll climb right up with him.

1st Soldier — I thought he was pretty good in there today.

3d Soldier — He was all right.

2d Roman Soldier — You guys don't know what I'm talking about. I'm not saying whether he was good or not. What I mean is, when the time comes. When they first start nailing him, there isn't none of them wouldn't stop it if they could.

1st Soldier — Didn't you follow it, George?

Wine-seller — No, I didn't take any interest in it, Lootenant.

1st Soldier — I was surprised how he acted.

3d Soldier — The part I don't like is the nailing them on. You know, that must get to you pretty bad.

2d Soldier — It isn't that that's so bad, as when they first lift 'em up. *[He makes a lifting gesture with his two palms together.]* When the weight starts to pull on 'em. That's when it gets 'em.

3d Roman Soldier — It take some of them pretty bad.

1st Soldier — Ain't I seen 'em? I seen plenty of them. I tell you, he was pretty good in there today.

[The second Roman soldier smiles at the Hebrew wine-seller.]

2d Soldier – You're a regular Christer, big boy.

1st Soldier – Sure, go on and kid him. But listen while I tell you something. He was pretty good in there today.

2d Soldier – What about some more wine?

[The wine-seller looks up expectantly. The third Roman soldier is sitting with his head down. He does not look well]

3d Soldier – I don't want any more.

2d Soldier – Just for two, George.

[The wine-seller puts out a pitcher of wine, a size smaller than the last one. He leans forward on the wooden counter.]

1st Roman Soldier – You see his girl?

2d Soldier – Wasn't I standing right by her?

1st Soldier – She's a nice-looker.

2d Soldier – I knew her before he did. *[He winks at the wine-seller.]*

1st Soldier – I used to see her around the town.

2d Soldier – She used to have a lot of stuff. He never brought *her* no good luck.

1st Soldier – Oh, he ain't lucky. But he looked pretty good to me in there today.

2d Soldier – What become of his gang?

1st Soldier – Oh, they faded out. Just the women stuck by him.

2d Roman Soldier – They were a pretty yellow crowd. When they seen him go up there they didn't want any of it.

1st Soldier – The women stuck all right.

2d Soldier – Sure, they stuck all right.

1st Roman Soldier – You see me slip the old spear into him?

2d Roman Soldier – You'll get into trouble doing that some day.

1st Soldier – It was the least I could do for him. I'll tell you he looked pretty good to me in there today.

Hebrew Wine-seller – Gentlemen, you know I got to close.

1st Roman Soldier – We'll have one more round.

2d Roman Soldier – What's the use? This stuff don't get you anywhere. Come on, let's go.

1st Soldier – Just another round.

3d Roman Soldier – *[Getting up from the barrel.]* No, come on. Let's go. I feel like hell tonight.

1st Soldier – Just one more.

2d Soldier – No, come on. We're going to go. Good-night, George. Put it on the bill.

Wine-seller – Good-night, gentlemen. *[He looks a little worried.]* You couldn't let me have a little something on account, Lootenant?

2d Roman Soldier – What the hell, George! Wednesday's payday.

Wineseller – It's all right, Lootenant. Good-night, gentlemen.

[The three Roman soldiers go out the door into the street.]

[Outside in the street.]

2d Roman Soldier – George is a kike just like all the rest of them.

1st Roman Soldier – Oh, George is a nice fella.

2d Soldier – Everybody's a nice fella to you tonight.

3d Roman Soldier – Come on, let's go up to the barracks. I feel like hell tonight.

2d Soldier – You been out here too long.

3d Roman Soldier – No, it ain't just that. I feel like hell.

2d Soldier – You been out here too long. That's all.

CURTAIN

BANAL STORY

SO HE ATE AN ORANGE, SLOWLY SPITTING out the seeds. Outside, the snow was turning to rain. Inside, the electric stove seemed to give no heat and rising from his writing-table, he sat down upon the stove. How good it felt! Here, at last, was life.

He reached for another orange. Far away in Paris, Mascart had knocked Danny Frush cuckoo in the second round. Far off in Mesopotamia, twenty-one feet of snow had fallen. Across the world in distant Australia, the English cricketers were sharpening up their wickets. *There* was Romance.

Patrons of the arts and letters have discovered *The Forum*, he read. It is the guide, philosopher, and friend of the thinking minority. Prize short-stories – will their authors write our best-sellers of tomorrow?

You will enjoy these warm, homespun, American tales, bits of real life on the open ranch, in crowded tenement or comfortable home, and all with a healthy undercurrent of humor.

I must read them, he thought.

He read on. Our children's children – what of them? Who of them? New means must be discovered to find room for us under the sun. Shall this be done by war or can it be done by peaceful methods?

Or will we all have to move to Canada?

Our deepest convictions – will Science upset them? Our civilization – is it inferior to older orders of things?

And meanwhile, in the far-off dripping jungles of Yucatan, sounded the chopping of the axes of the gum-choppers.

Do we want big men – or do we want them cultured? Take Joyce. Take President Coolidge. What star must our college students aim at? There is Jack Britton. There is Doctor Henry Van Dyke. Can we reconcile the two? Take the case of Young Stribling.

And what of our daughters who must make their own Soundings? Nancy Hawthorne is obliged to make her own Soundings in the sea of life. Bravely and sensibly she faces the problems which come to every girl of eighteen.

It was a splendid booklet.

Are you a girl of eighteen? Take the case of Joan of Arc. Take the case of Bernard Shaw. Take the case of Betsy Ross.

Think of these things in 1925 – Was there a risqué page in Puritan history? Were there two sides to Pocahontas? Did she have a fourth dimension?

Are modem paintings – and poetry – Art? Yes and No. Take Picasso.

Have tramps codes of conduct? Send your mind adventuring.

There is Romance everywhere. *Forum* writers talk to the point, are possessed of humor and wit. But they do not try to be smart and are never long-winded.

Live the full life of the mind, exhilarated by new ideas, intoxicated by the Romance of the unusual. He laid down the booklet.

And meanwhile, stretched flat on a bed in a darkened room in his house in Triana, Manuel Garcia Maera lay with a tube in each lung, drowning with the pneumonia. All the papers in Andalucia devoted special supplements to his death, which had been expected for some days. Men and boys bought full-length colored pictures of him to remember him by, and lost the picture they had of him in their memories by looking at the lithographs. Bull-fighters were very relieved he was dead, because he did always in the bull-ring the things they could only do sometimes. They all marched in the rain behind his coffin and there were one hundred and forty-seven bull-fighters followed him out to the cemetery, where they buried him in the tomb next to Joselito. After the funeral every one sat in the cafés out of the rain, and many colored pictures of Maera were sold to men who rolled them up and put them away in their pockets.

Now I Lay Me

THAT NIGHT WE LAY ON THE FLOOR IN the room and I listened to the silk-worms eating. The silk-worms fed in racks of mulberry leaves and all night you could hear them eating and a dropping sound in the leaves. I myself did not want to sleep because I had been living for a long time with the knowledge that if I ever shut my eyes in the dark and let myself go, my soul would go out of my body. I had been that way for a long time, ever since I had been blown up at night and felt it go out of me and go off and then come back. I tried never to think about it, but it had started to go since, in the nights, just at the moment of going off to sleep, and I could only stop it by a very great effort. So while now I am fairly sure that it would not really have gone out, yet then, that summer, I was unwilling to make the experiment.

I had different ways of occupying myself while I lay awake. I would think of a trout stream I had fished along when I was a boy and fish its whole length very carefully in my mind; fishing very carefully under all the logs, all the turns of the bank, the deep holes and the clear shallow stretches, sometimes catching trout and sometimes losing them. I would stop fishing at noon to eat my lunch; sometimes on a log over the stream; sometimes on a high bank under a tree, and I always ate my lunch very slowly and watched the stream below me while I ate. Often I ran out of bait because I would take only ten worms with me in a tobacco tin when I started. When I had used them all I had to find more worms, and sometimes it was very difficult digging in the bank of the stream where the cedar trees kept out the sun and there was no grass but only the bare moist earth and often I could find no worms. Always though I found some kind of bait, but one time in the swamp I could find no bait at all and had to cut up one of the trout I had caught and use him for bait.

Sometimes I found insects in the swamp meadows, in the grass or under ferns, and used them. There were beetles and insects with legs like grass stems, and grubs in old rotten logs; white grubs with brown pinching heads that would not stay on the hook and emptied into nothing in the cold water, and wood ticks under logs where sometimes I found angle-worms that slipped into the ground as soon as the log was raised. Once I used a salamander from under an old log. The salamander was very small and neat and agile and a lovely color. He had tiny feet that tried to hold on to the hook, and after that one time I never used a salamander, although I found them very often. Nor did I use crickets, because of the way they acted about the hook.

Sometimes the stream ran through an open meadow, and in the dry grass I would catch grasshoppers and use them for bait and sometimes I would catch grasshoppers and toss them into the stream and watch them float along swimming on the stream and circling on the surface as the current took them and then disappear as a trout rose. Sometimes I would fish four or five different streams in the night; starting as near as I could get to their source and fishing them down stream. When I had finished too quickly and the time did not go, I would fish the stream over again, starting where it emptied into the lake and fishing back up stream, trying for all the trout I had missed coming down. Some nights too I made up streams, and some of them were very exciting, and it was like being awake and dreaming. Some of those streams I still remember and think that I have fished in them, and they are confused with streams I really know. I gave them all names and went to them on the train and sometimes walked for miles to get to them.

But some nights I could not fish, and on those nights I was cold-awake and said my prayers over and over and tried to pray for all the people I had ever known. That took up a great amount of time, for if you try to remember all the people you have ever known, going back to the earliest thing you remember – which was, with me, the attic of the house where I was born and my mother and father's wedding-cake in a tin box hanging from one of the rafters, and, in the attic, jars of snakes and other specimens that my father had collected as a boy and preserved in alcohol, the alcohol sunken in the jars so the backs of some of the snakes and specimens were exposed and had turned white – if you thought back that far, you remembered a great many people. If you prayed for all of them, saying a Hail Mary and an Our Father for each one, it took a long time and finally it would be light, and then you could go to sleep, if you were in a place where you could sleep in the daylight.

On those nights I tried to remember everything that had ever happened to me, starting with just before I went to the war and remembering back from one thing to another. I found I could only remember back to that attic in my grandfather's house. Then I would start there and remember this way again, until I reached the war.

I remember, after my grandfather died we moved away from that house and to a new house designed and built by my mother. Many things that were not to be moved were burned in the back-yard and I remember those jars from the attic being thrown in the fire, and how they popped in the heat and the fire flamed up from the alcohol. I remember the snakes burning in the fire in the back-yard. But there were no people in that, only things. I could not remember who burned the things even, and I would go on until I came to people and then stop and pray for them.

About the new house I remember how my mother was always cleaning things out and making a good clearance. One time when my father was away on a hunting trip she made a good thorough cleaning out in the basement and burned everything that should not have been there. When my father came home and got down from his buggy and hitched the horse, the fire was still burning in the road beside the house. I went out to meet him. He handed me his shotgun and looked at the fire. "What's this?" he asked.

"I've been cleaning out the basement, dear," my mother said from the porch. She was standing there smiling, to meet him. My father looked at the fire and kicked at something. Then he leaned over and picked something out of the ashes. "Get a rake, Nick," he said to me. I went to the basement and brought a rake and my father raked very carefully in the ashes. He raked out stone axes and stone skinning knives and tools for making arrow-heads and pieces of pottery and many arrow-heads. They had all been blackened and chipped by the fire. My father raked them all out very carefully and spread them on the grass by the road. His shotgun in its leather case and his game-bags were on the grass where he had left them when he stepped down from the buggy.

"Take the gun and the bags in the house, Nick, and bring me a paper," he said. My mother had gone inside the house. I took the shotgun, which was heavy to carry and banged against my legs, and the two game-bags and started toward the house. "Take them one at a time," my father said. "Don't try and carry too much at once." I put down the game-bags and took in the shotgun and brought out a newspaper from the pile in my father's office. My father spread all the blackened, chipped stone implements on the paper and then wrapped them up. "The best arrow-heads went all to pieces," he said. He walked into the house with the paper package and I stayed outside on the grass with the two game-bags. After a while I took them in. In remembering that, there were only two people, so I would pray for them both.

Some nights, though, I could not remember my prayers even. I could only get as far as "On earth as it is in heaven" and then have to start all over and be absolutely unable to get past that. Then I would have to recognize that I could not remember and give up saying my prayers that night and try something else. So on some nights I would try to remember all the animals in the world by name and then the birds and then fishes and then countries and cities and then kinds of food and the names of all the streets I could remember in Chicago, and when I could not remember anything at all any more I would just listen. And I do not remember a night on which you could not hear things. If I could have a light I was not afraid to sleep, because I knew my soul would only go out of me if it were dark. So, of course, many nights I was where I could have a light and then I slept because I was nearly always tired and often very sleepy. And I am sure many times too that I slept without knowing it – but I never slept knowing it, and on this night I listened to the silk-worms. You can hear silk-worms eating very clearly in the night and I lay with my eyes open and listened to them.

There was only one other person in the room and he was awake too. I listened to him being awake, for a long time. He could not lie as quietly as I could because, perhaps, he had not had as much practice being awake. We were lying on blankets spread over straw and when he moved the straw was noisy, but the silk-worms were not frightened by any noise we made and ate on steadily. There were the noises of night seven kilometres behind the lines outside but they were different from the small noises inside the room in the dark. The other man in the room tried lying quietly. Then he moved again. I moved too, so he would know I was awake. He had lived ten years in Chicago. They had taken him for a soldier in nineteen fourteen when he had come back to visit his family, and they had given him me for an orderly because he spoke English. I heard him listening, so I moved again in the blankets.

"Can't you sleep, Signor Tenente?" he asked.

"No."

"I can't sleep, either."

"What's the matter?"

"I don't know. I can't sleep."

"You feel all right?"

"Sure. I feel good. I just can't sleep."

"You want to talk a while?" I asked.

"Sure. What can you talk about in this damn place."

"This place is pretty good," I said.

"Sure," he said. "It's all right."

"Tell me about out in Chicago," I said.

"Oh," he said, "I told you all that once."

"Tell me about how you got married."

"I told you that."

"Was the letter you got Monday – from her?"

"Sure. She writes me all the time. She's making good money with the place."

"You'll have a nice place when you go back."

"Sure. She runs it fine. She's making a lot of money."

"Don't you think we'll wake them up, talking?" I asked.

"No. They can't hear. Anyway, they sleep like pigs. I'm different," he said.

"I'm nervous."

"Talk quiet," I said. "Want a smoke?"

We smoked skilfully in the dark.

"You don't smoke much, Signor Tenente."

"No. I've just about cut it out."

"Well," he said, "it don't do you any good and I suppose you get so you don't miss it. Did you ever hear a blind man won't smoke because he can't see the smoke come out?"

"I don't believe it."

"I think it's all bull, myself," he said. "I just heard it somewhere. You know how you hear things."

We were both quiet and I listened to the silk-worms.

"You hear those damn silk-worms?" he asked. "You can hear them chew."

"It's funny," I said.

"Say, Signor Tenente, is there something really the matter that you can't sleep? I never see you sleep. You haven't slept nights ever since I been with you."

"I don't know, John," I said. "I got in pretty bad shape along early last spring and at night it bothers me."

"Just like I am," he said. "I shouldn't have ever got in this war. I'm too nervous."

"Maybe it will get better."

"Say, Signor Tenente, what did you get in this war for, anyway?"

"I don't know, John. I wanted to, then."

"Wanted to," he said. "That's a hell of a reason."

"We oughtn't to talk out loud," I said.

"They sleep just like pigs," he said. "They can't understand the English language, anyway. They don't know a damn thing. What are you going to do when it's over and we go back to the States?"

"I'll get a job on a paper."

"In Chicago?"

"Maybe."

"Do you ever read what this fellow Brisbane writes? My wife cuts it out for me and sends it to me."

"Sure."

"Did you ever meet him?"

"No, but I've seen him."

"I'd like to meet that fellow. He's a fine writer. My wife don't read English but she takes the paper just like when I was home and she cuts out the editorials and the sport page and sends them to me."

"How are your kids?"

"They're fine. One of the girls is in the fourth grade now. You know, Signor Tenente, if I didn't have the kids I wouldn't be your orderly now. They'd have made me stay in the line all the time."

"I'm glad you've got them."

"So am I. They're fine kids but I want a boy. Three girls and no boy. That's a hell of a note."

"Why don't you try and go to sleep?"

"No, I can't sleep now. I'm wide awake now, Signor Tenente. Say, I'm worried about you not sleeping though."

"It'll be all right, John."

"Imagine a young fellow like you not to sleep."

"I'll get all right. It just takes a while."

"You got to get all right. A man can't get along that don't sleep. Do you worry about anything? You got anything on your mind?"

"No, John, I don't think so."

"You ought to get married, Signor Tenente. Then you wouldn't worry."

"I don't know."

"You ought to get married. Why don't you pick out some nice Italian girl with plenty of money? You could get any one you want. You're young and you got good decorations and you look nice. You been wounded a couple of times."

"I can't talk the language well enough."

"You talk it fine. To hell with talking the language. You don't have to talk to them. Marry them."

"I'll think about it."

"You know some girls, don't you?"

"Sure."

"Well, you marry the one with the most money. Over here, the way they're brought up, they'll all make you a good wife."

"I'll think about it."

"Don't think about it, Signor Tenente. Do it."

"All right."

"A man ought to be married. You'll never regret it. Every man ought to be married."

"All right," I said. "Let's try and sleep a while."

"All right, Signor Tenente. I'll try it again. But you remember what I said."

"I'll remember it," I said. "Now let's sleep a while, John."

"All right," he said. "I hope you sleep, Signor Tenente."

I heard him roll in his blankets on the straw and then he was very quiet and I listened to him breathing regularly. Then he started to snore. I listened to him snore for a long time and then I stopped listening to him snore and listened to the silk-worms eating. They ate steadily, making a dropping in the leaves. I had a new thing to think about and I lay in the dark with my eyes open and thought of all the girls I had ever known and what kind of wives they would make. It was a very interesting thing to think about and for a while it killed off trout-fishing and interfered with my prayers. Finally, though, I went back to trout-fishing, because I found that I could remember all the streams and there was always something new about them, while the girls, after I had thought about them a few times, blurred and I could not call them into my mind and finally they all blurred and all became rather the same and I gave up thinking about them almost altogether. But I kept on with my prayers and I prayed very often for John in the nights and his class was removed from active service before the October offensive. I was glad he was not there, because he would have been a great worry to me. He came to the hospital in Milan to see me several months after and was very disappointed that I had not yet married, and I know he would feel very badly if he knew that, so far, I have never married. He was going back to America and he was very certain about marriage and knew it would fix up everything.

A FAREWELL TO ARMS

BOOK ONE

CHAPTER 1

IN THE LATE SUMMER of that year we lived in a house in a village that looked across the river and the plain to the mountains. In the bed of the river there were pebbles and boulders, dry and white in the sun, and the water was clear and swiftly moving and blue in the channels. Troops went by the house and down the road and the dust they raised powdered the leaves of the trees. The trunks of the trees too were dusty and the leaves fell early that year and we saw the troops marching along the road and the dust rising and leaves, stirred by the breeze, falling and the soldiers marching and afterward the road bare and white except for the leaves.

The plain was rich with crops; there were many orchards of fruit trees and beyond the plain the mountains were brown and bare. There was fighting in the mountains and at night we could see the flashes from the artillery. In the dark it was like summer lightning, but the nights were cool and there was not the feeling of a storm coming.

Sometimes in the dark we heard the troops marching under the window and guns going past pulled by motor-tractors. There was much traffic at night and many mules on the roads with boxes of ammunition on each side of their pack-saddles and gray motor trucks that carried men, and other trucks with loads covered with canvas that moved slower in the traffic. There were big guns too that passed in the day drawn by tractors, the long barrels of the guns covered with green branches and green leafy branches and vines laid over the tractors. To the north we could look across a valley and see a forest of chestnut trees and behind it another mountain on this side of the river. There was fighting for that mountain too, but it was not successful, and in the fall when the rains came the leaves all fell from the chestnut trees and the branches were bare and the trunks black with rain. The vineyards were thin and bare-branched too and all the country wet and brown and dead with the autumn. There were mists over the river and clouds on the mountain and the trucks splashed mud on the road and the troops were muddy and wet in their capes; their rifles were wet and under their capes the two leather cartridge-boxes on the front of the belts, gray leather boxes heavy with the packs of clips of thin, long 6.5 mm. cartridges, bulged forward under the capes so that the men, passing on the road, marched as though they were six months gone with child.

There were small gray motor cars that passed going very fast; usually there was an officer on the seat with the driver and more officers in the back seat. They splashed more mud than the camions even and if one of the officers in the back was very small and sitting between two generals, he himself so small that you could not see his face but only the top of his cap and his narrow back, and if the car went especially fast it was probably the King. He lived in Udine and came out in this way nearly every day to see how things were going, and things went very badly.

At the start of the winter came the permanent rain and with the rain came the cholera. But it was checked and in the end only seven thousand died of it in the army.

CHAPTER 2

THE NEXT YEAR there were many victories. The mountain that was beyond the valley and the hillside where the chestnut forest grew was captured and there were victories beyond the plain on the plateau to the south and we crossed the river in August and lived in a house in Gorizia that had a fountain and many thick shady trees in a walled garden and a wistaria vine purple on the side of the house. Now the fighting was in the next mountains beyond and was not a mile away. The town was very nice and our house was very fine. The river ran behind us and the town had been captured very handsomely but the mountains beyond it could not be taken and I was very glad the Austrians seemed to want to come back to the town some time, if the war should end, because they did not bombard it to destroy it but only a little in a military way. People lived on in it and there were hospitals and cafés and artillery up side streets and two bawdy houses, one for troops and one for officers, and with the end of the summer, the cool nights, the fighting in the mountains beyond the town, the shell-marked iron of the railway bridge, the smashed tunnel by the river where the fighting had been, the trees around the square and the long avenue of trees that led to the square; these with there being girls in the town, the King passing in his motor car, sometimes now seeing his face and little long necked body and gray beard like a goat's chin tuft; all these with the sudden interiors of houses that had lost a wall through shelling, with plaster and rubble in their gardens and sometimes in the street, and the whole thing going well on the Carso made the fall very different from the last fall when we had been in the country. The war was changed too.

The forest of oak trees on the mountain beyond the town was gone. The forest had been green in the summer when we had come into the town but now there were the stumps and the broken trunks and the ground torn up, and one day at the end of the fall when I was out where the oak forest had been I saw a cloud coming over the mountain. It came very fast and the sun went a dull yellow and then everything was gray and the sky was covered and the cloud came on down the mountain and suddenly we were in it and it was snow. The snow slanted across the wind, the bare ground was covered, the stumps of trees projected, there was snow on the guns and there were paths in the snow going back to the latrines behind trenches.

Later, below in the town, I watched the snow falling, looking out of the window of the bawdy house, the house for officers, where I sat with a friend and two glasses drinking a bottle of Asti, and, looking out at the snow falling slowly and heavily, we knew it was all over for that year. Up the river the mountains had not been taken; none of the mountains beyond the river had been taken. That was all left for next year. My friend saw the priest from our mess going by in the street, walking carefully in the slush, and pounded on the window to attract his attention. The priest looked up. He saw us and smiled. My friend motioned for him to come in. The priest shook his head and went on. That night in the mess after the spaghetti course, which every one ate very quickly and seriously, lifting the spaghetti on the fork until the loose strands hung clear then lowering it into the mouth, or else using a continuous lift and sucking into the mouth, helping ourselves to wine from the grass-covered gallon flask; it swung in a metal cradle and you pulled the neck of the flask down with the forefinger and the wine, clear red, tannic and lovely, poured out into the glass held with the same hand; after this course, the captain commenced picking on the priest.

The priest was young and blushed easily and wore a uniform like the rest of us but with a cross in dark red velvet above the left breast pocket of his gray tunic. The captain spoke pidgin Italian for my doubtful benefit, in order that I might understand perfectly, that nothing should be lost.

"Priest to-day with girls," the captain said looking at the priest and at me. The priest smiled and blushed and shook his head. This captain baited him often.

"Not true?" asked the captain. "To-day I see priest with girls."

"No," said the priest. The other officers were amused at the baiting.

"Priest not with girls," went on the captain. "Priest never with girls," he explained to me. He took my glass and filled it, looking at my eyes all the time, but not losing sight of the priest.

"Priest every night five against one." Every one at the table laughed. "You understand? Priest every night five against one." He made a gesture and laughed loudly. The priest accepted it as a joke.

"The Pope wants the Austrians to win the war," the major said. "He loves Franz Joseph. That's where the money comes from. I am an atheist."

"Did you ever read the 'Black Pig'?" asked the lieutenant. "I will get you a copy. It was that which shook my faith."

"It is a filthy and vile book," said the priest. "You do not really like it."

"It is very valuable," said the lieutenant. "It tells you about those priests. You will like it," he said to me. I smiled at the priest and he smiled back across the candle-light. "Don't you read it," he said.

"I will get it for you," said the lieutenant.

"All thinking men are atheists," the major said. "I do not believe in the Free Masons however."

"I believe in the Free Masons," the lieutenant said. "It is a noble organization." Some one came in and as the door opened I could see the snow falling.

"There will be no more offensive now that the snow has come," I said.

"Certainly not," said the major. "You should go on leave. You should go to Rome, Naples, Sicily — —"

"He should visit Amalfi," said the lieutenant. "I will write you cards to my family in Amalfi. They will love you like a son."

"He should go to Palermo."

"He ought to go to Capri."

"I would like you to see Abruzzi and visit my family at Capracotta," said the priest.

"Listen to him talk about the Abruzzi. There's more snow there than here. He doesn't want to see peasants. Let him go to centres of culture and civilization."

"He should have fine girls. I will give you the addresses of places in Naples. Beautiful young girls — accompanied by their mothers. Ha! Ha! Ha!" The captain spread his hand open, the thumb up and fingers outspread as when you make shadow pictures. There was a shadow from his hand on the wall. He spoke again in pidgin Italian. "You go away like this," he pointed to the thumb, "and come back like this," he touched the little finger. Every one laughed.

"Look," said the captain. He spread the hand again. Again the candle-light made its shadows on the wall. He started with the upright thumb and named in their order the thumb and four fingers, "soto-tenente (the thumb), tenente (first finger), capitano (next finger), maggiore (next to the little finger), and tenente-colonello (the little finger). You go away soto-tenente! You come back sotocolonello!" They all laughed. The captain was having a great success with finger games. He looked at the priest and shouted, "Every night priest five against one!" They all laughed again.

"You must go on leave at once," the major said.

"I would like to go with you and show you things," the lieutenant said.

"When you come back bring a phonograph."

"Bring good opera disks."

"Bring Caruso."

"Don't bring Caruso. He bellows."

"Don't you wish you could bellow like him?"

"He bellows. I say he bellows!"

"I would like you to go to Abruzzi," the priest said. The others were shouting. "There is good hunting. You would like the people and though it is cold it is clear and dry. You could stay with my family. My father is a famous hunter."

"Come on," said the captain. "We go whorehouse before it shuts."

"Good-night," I said to the priest.

"Good-night," he said.

CHAPTER 3

WHEN I CAME BACK to the front we still lived in that town. There were many more guns in the country around and the spring had come. The fields were green and there were small green shoots on the vines, the trees along the road had small leaves and a breeze came from the sea. I saw the town with the hill and the old castle above it in a cup in the hills with the mountains beyond, brown mountains with a little green on their slopes. In the town there were more guns, there were some new hospitals, you met British men and sometimes women, on the street, and a few more houses had been hit by shell fire. It was warm and like the spring and I walked down the alleyway of trees, warmed from the sun on the wall, and found we still lived in the same house and that it all looked the same as when I had left it. The door was open, there was a soldier sitting on a bench outside in the sun, an ambulance was waiting by the side door and inside the door, as I went in, there was the smell of marble floors and hospital. It was all as I had left it except that now it was spring. I looked in the door of the big room and saw the major sitting at his desk, the window open and the sunlight coming into the room. He did not see me and I did not know whether to go in and report or go upstairs first and clean up. I decided to go on upstairs.

The room I shared with the lieutenant Rinaldi looked out on the courtyard. The window was open, my bed was made up with blankets and my things hung on the wall, the gas mask in an oblong tin can, the steel helmet on the same peg. At the foot of the bed was my flat trunk, and my winter boots, the leather shiny with oil, were on the trunk. My Austrian sniper's rifle with its blued octagon barrel and the lovely dark walnut, cheek-fitted, schutzen stock, hung over the two beds. The telescope that fitted it was, I remembered, locked in the trunk. The lieutenant, Rinaldi, lay asleep on the other bed. He woke when he heard me in the room and sat up.

"Ciaou!" he said. "What kind of time did you have?"

"Magnificent."

We shook hands and he put his arm around my neck and kissed me.

"Oughf," I said.

"You're dirty," he said. "You ought to wash. Where did you go and what did you do? Tell me everything at once."

"I went everywhere. Milan, Florence, Rome, Naples, Villa San Giovanni, Messina, Taormina — —"

"You talk like a time-table. Did you have any beautiful adventures?"

"Yes."

"Where?"

"Milano, Firenze, Roma, Napoli — —"

"That's enough. Tell me really what was the best."

"In Milano."

"That was because it was first. Where did you meet her? In the Cova? Where did you go? How did you feel? Tell me everything at once. Did you stay all night?"

"Yes."

"That's nothing. Here now we have beautiful girls. New girls never been to the front before."

"Wonderful."

"You don't believe me? We will go now this afternoon and see. And in the town we have beautiful English girls. I am now in love with Miss Barkley. I will take you to call. I will probably marry Miss Barkley."

"I have to get washed and report. Doesn't anybody work now?"

"Since you are gone we have nothing but frostbites, chilblains, jaundice, gonorrhea, self-inflicted wounds, pneumonia and hard and soft chancres. Every week some one gets wounded by rock fragments. There are a few real wounded. Next week the war starts again. Perhaps it start again. They say so. Do you think I would do right to marry Miss Barkley — after the war of course?"

"Absolutely," I said and poured the basin full of water.

"To-night you will tell me everything," said Rinaldi. "Now I must go back to sleep to be fresh and beautiful for Miss Barkley."

I took off my tunic and shirt and washed in the cold water in the basin. While I rubbed myself with a towel I looked around the room and out the window and at Rinaldi lying with his eyes closed on the bed. He was good-looking, was my age, and he came from Amalfi. He loved being a surgeon and we were great friends. While I was looking at him he opened his eyes.

"Have you any money?"

"Yes."

"Loan me fifty lire."

I dried my hands and took out my pocket-book from the inside of my tunic hanging on the wall. Rinaldi took the note, folded it without rising from the bed and slid it in his breeches pocket. He smiled, "I must make on Miss Barkley the impression of a man of sufficient wealth. You are my great and good friend and financial protector."

"Go to hell," I said.

That night at the mess I sat next to the priest and he was disappointed and suddenly hurt that I had not gone to the Abruzzi. He had written to his father that I was coming and they had made preparations. I myself felt as badly as he did and could not understand why I had not gone. It was what I had wanted to do and I tried to explain how one thing had led to another and finally he saw it and understood that I had really wanted to go and it was almost all right. I had drunk much wine and afterward coffee and Strega and I explained, winefully, how we did not do the things we wanted to do; we never did such things.

We two were talking while the others argued. I had wanted to go to Abruzzi. I had gone to no place where the roads were frozen and hard as iron, where it was clear cold and dry and the snow was dry and powdery and hare-tracks in the snow and the peasants took off their hats and called you Lord and there was good hunting. I had gone to no such place but to the smoke of cafés and nights when the room whirled and you needed to look at the wall to make it stop, nights in bed, drunk, when you knew that that was all there was, and the strange excitement of waking and not knowing who it was with you, and the world all unreal in the dark and so exciting that you must resume again unknowing and not caring in the night, sure that this was all and all and all and not caring. Suddenly to care very much and to sleep to wake with it sometimes morning and all that had been there gone and everything sharp and hard and clear and sometimes a dispute about the cost. Sometimes still pleasant and fond and warm and breakfast and lunch. Sometimes all niceness gone and glad to get out on the street but always another day starting and then another night. I tried to tell about the night and the difference between the night and the day and how the night was better unless the day was very clean and cold and I could not tell it; as I cannot tell it now. But if you have had it you know. He had not had it but he understood that I had really wanted to go to the Abruzzi but had not gone and we were still friends, with many tastes alike, but with the difference between us. He had always known what I did not know and what, when I learned it, I was always able to forget. But I did not know that then, although I learned it later. In the meantime we were all at the mess, the meal was finished, and the argument went on. We two stopped talking and the captain shouted, "Priest not happy. Priest not happy without girls."

"I am happy," said the priest.

"Priest not happy. Priest wants Austrians to win the war," the captain said. The others listened. The priest shook his head.

"No," he said.

"Priest wants us never to attack. Don't you want us never to attack?"

"No. If there is a war I suppose we must attack."

"Must attack. Shall attack!"

The priest nodded.

"Leave him alone," the major said. "He's all right."

"He can't do anything about it anyway," the captain said. We all got up and left the table.

CHAPTER 4

THE BATTERY in the next garden woke me in the morning and I saw the sun coming through the window and got out of the bed. I went to the window and looked out. The gravel paths were moist and the grass was wet with dew. The battery fired twice and the air came each time like a blow and shook the window and made the front of my pajamas flap. I could not see the guns but they were evidently firing directly over us. It was a nuisance to have them there but it was a comfort that they were no bigger. As I looked out at the garden I heard a motor truck starting on the road. I dressed, went downstairs, had some coffee in the kitchen and went out to the garage.

Ten cars were lined up side by side under the long shed. They were top-heavy, blunt-nosed ambulances, painted gray and built like moving-vans. The mechanics were working on one out in the yard. Three others were up in the mountains at dressing stations.

"Do they ever shell that battery?" I asked one of the mechanics.

"No, Signor Tenente. It is protected by the little hill."

"How's everything?"

"Not so bad. This machine is no good but the others march." He stopped working and smiled. "Were you on permission?"

"Yes."

He wiped his hands on his jumper and grinned. "You have a good time?" The others all grinned too.

"Fine," I said. "What's the matter with this machine?"

"It's no good. One thing after another."

"What's the matter now?"

"New rings."

I left them working, the car looking disgraced and empty with the engine open and parts spread on the work bench, and went in under the shed and looked at each of the cars. They were moderately clean, a few freshly washed, the others dusty. I looked at the tires carefully, looking for cuts or stone bruises. Everything seemed in good condition. It evidently made no difference whether I was there to look after things or not. I had imagined that the condition of the cars, whether or not things were obtainable, the smooth functioning of the business of removing wounded and sick from the dressing stations, hauling them back from the mountains to the clearing station and then distributing them to the hospitals named on their papers, depended to a considerable extent on myself. Evidently it did not matter whether I was there or not.

"Has there been any trouble getting parts?" I asked the sergeant mechanic.

"No, Signor Tenente."

"Where is the gasoline park now?"

"At the same place."

"Good," I said and went back to the house and drank another bowl of coffee at the mess table. The coffee was a pale gray and sweet with condensed milk. Outside the window it was a lovely spring morning. There was that beginning of a feeling of dryness in the nose that meant the day would be hot later on. That day I visited the posts in the mountains and was back in town late in the afternoon.

The whole thing seemed to run better while I was away. The offensive was going to start again I heard. The division for which we worked were to attack at a place up the river and the major told me that I would see about the posts for during the attack. The attack would cross the river up above the narrow gorge and spread up the hillside. The posts for the cars would have to be as near the river as they could get and keep covered. They would, of course, be selected by the infantry but we were supposed to work it out. It was one of those things that gave you a false feeling of soldiering.

I was very dusty and dirty and went up to my room to wash. Rinaldi was sitting on the bed with a copy of Hugo's English grammar. He was dressed, wore his black boots, and his hair shone.

"Splendid," he said when he saw me. "You will come with me to see Miss Barkley."

"No."

"Yes. You will please come and make me a good impression on her."

"All right. Wait till I get cleaned up."

"Wash up and come as you are."

I washed, brushed my hair and we started.

"Wait a minute," Rinaldi said. "Perhaps we should have a drink." He opened his trunk and took out a bottle.

"Not Strega," I said.

"No. Grappa."

"All right."

He poured two glasses and we touched them, first fingers extended. The grappa was very strong.

"Another?"

"All right," I said. We drank the second grappa, Rinaldi put away the bottle and we went down the stairs. It was hot walking through the town but the sun was starting to go down and it was very pleasant. The British hospital was a big villa built by Germans before the war. Miss Barkley was in the garden. Another nurse was with her. We saw their white uniforms through the trees and walked toward them. Rinaldi saluted. I saluted too but more moderately.

"How do you do?" Miss Barkley said. "You're not an Italian, are you?"

"Oh, no."

Rinaldi was talking with the other nurse. They were laughing. "What an odd thing – to be in the Italian army."

"It's not really the army. It's only the ambulance."

"It's very odd though. Why did you do it?"

"I don't know," I said. "There isn't always an explanation for everything."

"Oh, isn't there? I was brought up to think there was."

"That's awfully nice."

"Do we have to go on and talk this way?"

"No," I said.

"That's a relief. Isn't it?"

"What is the stick?" I asked. Miss Barkley was quite tall. She wore what seemed to me to be a nurse's uniform, was blonde and had a tawny skin and gray eyes. I thought she was very beautiful. She was carrying a thin rattan stick like a toy riding-crop, bound in leather.

"It belonged to a boy who was killed last year."

"I'm awfully sorry."

"He was a very nice boy. He was going to marry me and he was killed in the Somme."

"It was a ghastly show."

"Were you there?"

"No."

"I've heard about it," she said. "There's not really any war of that sort down here. They sent me the little stick. His mother sent it to me. They returned it with his things."

"Had you been engaged long?"

"Eight years. We grew up together."

"And why didn't you marry?"

"I don't know," she said. "I was a fool not to. I could have given him that anyway. But I thought it would be bad for him."

"I see."

"Have you ever loved any one?"

"No," I said.

We sat down on a bench and I looked at her.

"You have beautiful hair," I said.

"Do you like it?"

"Very much."

"I was going to cut it all off when he died."

"No."

"I wanted to do something for him. You see I didn't care about the other thing and he could have had it all. He could have had anything he wanted if I would have known. I would have married him or anything. I know all about it now. But then he wanted to go to war and I didn't know."

I did not say anything.

"I didn't know about anything then. I thought it would be worse for him. I thought perhaps he couldn't stand it and then of course he was killed and that was the end of it."

"I don't know."

"Oh, yes," she said. "That's the end of it."

We looked at Rinaldi talking with the other nurse.

"What is her name?"

"Ferguson. Helen Ferguson. Your friend is a doctor, isn't he?"

"Yes. He's very good."

"That's splendid. You rarely find any one any good this close to the front. This is close to the front, isn't it?"

"Quite."

"It's a silly front," she said. "But it's very beautiful. Are they going to have an offensive?"

"Yes."

"Then we'll have to work. There's no work now."

"Have you done nursing long?"

"Since the end of 'fifteen. I started when he did. I remember having a silly idea he might come to the hospital where I was. With a sabre cut, I suppose, and a bandage around his head. Or shot through the shoulder. Something picturesque."

"This is the picturesque front," I said.

"Yes," she said. "People can't realize what France is like. If they did, it couldn't all go on. He didn't have a sabre cut. They blew him all to bits."

I didn't say anything.

"Do you suppose it will always go on?"

"No."

"What's to stop it?"

"It will crack somewhere."

"We'll crack. We'll crack in France. They can't go on doing things like the Somme and not crack."

"They won't crack here," I said.

"You think not?"

"No. They did very well last summer."

"They may crack," she said. "Anybody may crack."

"The Germans too."

"No," she said. "I think not."

We went over toward Rinaldi and Miss Ferguson.

"You love Italy?" Rinaldi asked Miss Ferguson in English.

"Quite well."

"No understand," Rinaldi shook his head.

"Abbastanza bene," I translated. He shook his head.

"That is not good. You love England?"

"Not too well. I'm Scotch, you see."

Rinaldi looked at me blankly.

"She's Scotch, so she loves Scotland better than England," I said in Italian.

"But Scotland is England."

I translated this for Miss Ferguson.

"Pas encore," said Miss Ferguson.

"Not really?"

"Never. We do not like the English."

"Not like the English? Not like Miss Barkley?"

"Oh, that's different. You mustn't take everything so literally."

After a while we said good-night and left. Walking home Rinaldi said, "Miss Barkley prefers you to me. That is very clear. But the little Scotch one is very nice."

"Very," I said. I had not noticed her. "You like her?"

"No," said Rinaldi.

CHAPTER 5

THE NEXT AFTERNOON I went to call on Miss Barkley again. She was not in the garden and I went to the side door of the villa where the ambulances drove up. Inside I saw the head nurse, who said Miss Barkley was on duty– "there's a war on, you know."

I said I knew.

"You're the American in the Italian army?" she asked.

"Yes, ma'am."

"How did you happen to do that? Why didn't you join up with us?"

"I don't know," I said. "Could I join now?"

"I'm afraid not now. Tell me. Why did you join up with the Italians?"

"I was in Italy," I said, "and I spoke Italian."

"Oh," she said. "I'm learning it. It's beautiful language."

"Somebody said you should be able to learn it in two weeks."

"Oh, I'll not learn it in two weeks. I've studied it for months now. You may come and see her after seven o'clock if you wish. She'll be off then. But don't bring a lot of Italians."

"Not even for the beautiful language?"

"No. Nor for the beautiful uniforms."

"Good evening," I said.

"A rivederci, Tenente."

"A rivederla." I saluted and went out. It was impossible to salute foreigners as an Italian, without embarrassment. The Italian salute never seemed made for export.

The day had been hot. I had been up the river to the bridgehead at Plava. It was there that the offensive was to begin. It had been impossible to advance on the far side the year before because there was only one road leading down from the pass to the pontoon bridge and it was under machine-gun and shell fire for nearly a mile. It was not wide enough either to carry all the transport for an offensive and the Austrians could make a shambles out of it. But the Italians had crossed and spread out a little way on the far side to hold about a mile and a half on the Austrian side of the river. It was a nasty place and the Austrians should not have let them hold it. I suppose it was mutual tolerance because the Austrians still kept a bridgehead further down the river. The Austrian trenches were above on the hillside only a few yards from the Italian lines. There had been a little town but it was all rubble. There was what was left of a railway station and a smashed permanent bridge that could not be repaired and used because it was in plain sight.

I went along the narrow road down toward the river, left the car at the dressing station under the hill, crossed the pontoon bridge, which was protected by a shoulder of the mountain, and went through the trenches in the smashed-down town and along the edge of the slope. Everybody was in the dugouts. There were racks of rockets standing to be touched off to call for help from the artillery or to signal with if the telephone wires were cut. It was quiet, hot and dirty. I looked across the wire at the Austrian lines. Nobody was in sight. I had a drink with a captain that I knew in one of the dugouts and went back across the bridge.

A new wide road was being finished that would go over the mountain and zig-zag down to the bridge. When this road was finished the offensive would start. It came down through the forest in sharp turns. The system was to bring everything down the new road and take the empty trucks, carts and loaded ambulances and all returning traffic up the old narrow road. The dressing station was on the Austrian side of the river under the edge of the hill and stretcher-bearers would bring the wounded back across the pontoon bridge. It would be the same when the offensive started. As far as I could make out the last mile or so of the new road where it started to level out would be able to be shelled steadily by the Austrians. It looked as though it might be a mess. But I found a place where the cars would be sheltered after they passed that last bad-looking bit and could wait for the wounded to be brought across the pontoon bridge. I would have liked to drive over the new road but it was not yet finished. It looked wide and well made with a good grade and the turns looked very impressive where you could see them through openings in the forest on the mountain side. The cars would be all right with their good metal-to-metal brakes and anyway, coming down, they would not be loaded. I drove back up the narrow road.

Two carabinieri held the car up. A shell had fallen and while we waited three others fell up the road. They were seventy-sevens and came with a whishing rush of air, a hard bright burst and flash and then gray smoke that blew across the road. The carabinieri waved us to go on. Passing where the shells had landed I avoided the small broken places and smelled the high explosive and the smell of blasted clay and stone and freshly shattered flint. I drove back to Gorizia and our villa and, as I said, went to call on Miss Barkley, who was on duty.

At dinner I ate very quickly and left for the villa where the British had their hospital. It was really very large and beautiful and there were fine trees in the grounds. Miss Barkley was sitting on a bench in the garden. Miss Ferguson was with her. They seemed glad to see me and in a little while Miss Ferguson excused herself and went away.

"I'll leave you two," she said. "You get along very well without me."

"Don't go, Helen," Miss Barkley said.

"I'd really rather. I must write some letters."

"Good-night," I said.

"Good-night, Mr. Henry."

"Don't write anything that will bother the censor."

"Don't worry. I only write about what a beautiful place we live in and how brave the Italians are."

"That way you'll be decorated."

"That will be nice. Good-night, Catherine."

"I'll see you in a little while," Miss Barkley said. Miss Ferguson walked away in the dark.

"She's nice," I said.

"Oh, yes, she's very nice. She's a nurse."

"Aren't you a nurse?"

"Oh, no. I'm something called a V. A. D. We work very hard but no one trusts us."

"Why not?"

"They don't trust us when there's nothing going on. When there is really work they trust us."

"What is the difference?"

"A nurse is like a doctor. It takes a long time to be. A V. A. D. is a short cut."

"I see."

"The Italians didn't want women so near the front. So we're all on very special behavior. We don't go out."

"I can come here though."

"Oh, yes. We're not cloistered."

"Let's drop the war."

"It's very hard. There's no place to drop it."

"Let's drop it anyway."

"All right."

We looked at each other in the dark. I thought she was very beautiful and I took her hand. She let me take it and I held it and put my arm around under her arm.

"No," she said. I kept my arm where it was.

"Why not?"

"No."

"Yes," I said. "Please." I leaned forward in the dark to kiss her and there was a sharp stinging flash. She had slapped my face hard. Her hand had hit my nose and eyes, and tears came in my eyes from the reflex.

"I'm so sorry," she said. I felt I had a certain advantage.

"You were quite right."

"I'm dreadfully sorry," she said. "I just couldn't stand the nurse's-evening-off aspect of it. I didn't mean to hurt you. I did hurt you, didn't I?"

She was looking at me in the dark. I was angry and yet certain, seeing it all ahead like the moves in a chess game.

"You did exactly right," I said. "I don't mind at all."

"Poor man."

"You see I've been leading a sort of a funny life. And I never even talk English. And then you are so very beautiful." I looked at her.

"You don't need to say a lot of nonsense. I said I was sorry. We do get along."

"Yes," I said. "And we have gotten away from the war."

She laughed. It was the first time I had ever heard her laugh. I watched her face.

"You are sweet," she said.

"No, I'm not."

"Yes. You are a dear. I'd be glad to kiss you if you don't mind."

I looked in her eyes and put my arm around her as I had before and kissed her. I kissed her hard and held her tight and tried to open her lips; they were closed tight. I was still angry and as I held her suddenly she shivered. I held her close against me and could feel her heart beating and her lips opened and her head went back against my hand and then she was crying on my shoulder.

"Oh, darling," she said. "You will be good to me, won't you?"

What the hell, I thought. I stroked her hair and patted her shoulder. She was crying.

"You will, won't you?" She looked up at me. "Because we're going to have a strange life."

After a while I walked with her to the door of the villa and she went in and I walked home. Back at the villa I went upstairs to the room. Rinaldi was lying on his bed. He looked at me.

"So you make progress with Miss Barkley?"

"We are friends."

"You have that pleasant air of a dog in heat."

I did not understand the word.

"Of a what?"

He explained.

"You," I said, "have that pleasant air of a dog who – –"

"Stop it," he said. "In a little while we would say insulting things." He laughed.

"Good-night," I said.

"Good-night, little puppy."

I knocked over his candle with the pillow and got into bed in the dark.

Rinaldi picked up the candle, lit it and went on reading.

CHAPTER 6

I WAS AWAY for two days at the posts. When I got home it was too late and I did not see Miss Barkley until the next evening. She was not in the garden and I had to wait in the office of the hospital until she came down. There were many marble busts on painted wooden pillars along the walls of the room they used for an office. The hall too, that the office opened on, was lined with them. They had the complete marble quality of all looking alike. Sculpture had always seemed a dull business – still, bronzes looked like something. But marble busts all looked like a cemetery. There was one fine cemetery though – the one at Pisa. Genoa was the place to see the bad marbles. This had been the villa of a very wealthy German and the busts must have cost him plenty. I wondered who had done them and how much he got. I tried to make out whether they were members of the family or what; but they were all uniformly classical. You could not tell anything about them.

I sat on a chair and held my cap. We were supposed to wear steel helmets even in Gorizia but they were uncomfortable and too bloody theatrical in a town where the civilian inhabitants had not been evacuated. I wore one when we went up to the posts and carried an English gas mask. We were just beginning to get some of them. They were a real mask. Also we were required to wear an automatic pistol; even doctors and sanitary officers. I felt it against the back of the chair. You were liable to arrest if you did not have one worn in plain sight. Rinaldi carried a holster stuffed with toilet paper. I wore a real one and felt like a gunman until I practiced firing it. It was an Astra 7.65 caliber with a short barrel and it jumped so sharply when you let it off that there was no question of hitting anything. I practiced with it, holding below the target and trying to master the jerk of the ridiculous short barrel until I could hit within a yard of where I aimed at twenty paces and then the ridiculousness of carrying a pistol at all came over me and I soon forgot it and carried it flopping against the small of my back with no feeling at all except a vague sort of shame when I met English-speaking people. I sat now in the chair and an orderly of some sort looked at me disapprovingly from behind a desk while I looked at the marble floor, the pillars with the marble busts, and the frescoes on the wall and waited for Miss Barkley. The frescoes were not bad. Any frescoes were good when they started to peel and flake off.

I saw Catherine Barkley coming down the hall, and stood up. She did not seem tall walking toward me but she looked very lovely.

"Good-evening, Mr. Henry," she said.

"How do you do?" I said. The orderly was listening behind the desk.

"Shall we sit here or go out in the garden?"

"Let's go out. It's much cooler."

I walked behind her out into the garden, the orderly looking after us. When we were out on the gravel drive she said, "Where have you been?"

"I've been out on post."

"You couldn't have sent me a note?"

"No," I said. "Not very well. I thought I was coming back."

"You ought to have let me know, darling."

We were off the driveway, walking under the trees. I took her hands, then stopped and kissed her.

"Isn't there anywhere we can go?"

"No," she said. "We have to just walk here. You've been away a long time."

"This is the third day. But I'm back now."

She looked at me, "And you do love me?"

"Yes."

"You did say you loved me, didn't you?"

"Yes," I lied. "I love you." I had not said it before.

"And you call me Catherine?"

"Catherine." We walked on a way and were stopped under a tree.

"Say, 'I've come back to Catherine in the night.'"

"I've come back to Catherine in the night."

"Oh, darling, you have come back, haven't you?"

"Yes."

"I love you so and it's been awful. You won't go away?"

"No. I'll always come back."

"Oh, I love you so. Please put your hand there again."

"It's not been away." I turned her so I could see her face when I kissed her and I saw that her eyes were shut. I kissed both her shut eyes. I thought she was probably a little crazy. It was all right if she was. I did not care what I was getting into. This was better than going every evening to the house for officers where the girls climbed all over you and put your cap on backward as a sign of affection between their trips upstairs with brother officers. I knew I did not love Catherine Barkley nor had any idea of loving her. This was a game, like bridge, in which you said things instead of playing cards. Like bridge you had to pretend you were playing for money or playing for some stakes. Nobody had mentioned what the stakes were. It was all right with me.

"I wish there was some place we could go," I said. I was experiencing the masculine difficulty of making love very long standing up.

"There isn't any place," she said. She came back from wherever she had been.

"We might sit there just for a little while."

We sat on the flat stone bench and I held Catherine Barkley's hand. She would not let me put my arm around her.

"Are you very tired?" she asked.

"No."

She looked down at the grass.

"This is a rotten game we play, isn't it?"

"What game?"

"Don't be dull."

"I'm not, on purpose."

"You're a nice boy," she said. "And you play it as well as you know how. But it's a rotten game."

"Do you always know what people think?"

"Not always. But I do with you. You don't have to pretend you love me. That's over for the evening. Is there anything you'd like to talk about?"

"But I do love you."

"Please let's not lie when we don't have to. I had a very fine little show and I'm all right now. You see I'm not mad and I'm not gone off. It's only a little sometimes."

I pressed her hand, "Dear Catherine."

"It sounds very funny now—Catherine. You don't pronounce it very much alike. But you're very nice. You're a very good boy."

"That's what the priest said."

"Yes, you're very good. And you will come and see me?"

"Of course."

"And you don't have to say you love me. That's all over for a while." She stood up and put out her hand. "Good-night."

I wanted to kiss her.

"No," she said. "I'm awfully tired."

"Kiss me, though," I said.

"I'm awfully tired, darling."

"Kiss me."

"Do you want to very much?"

"Yes."

We kissed and she broke away suddenly. "No. Good-night, please, darling." We walked to the door and I saw her go in and down the hall. I liked to watch her move. She went on down the hall. I went on home. It was a hot night and there was a good deal going on up in the mountains. I watched the flashes on San Gabriele.

I stopped in front of the Villa Rossa. The shutters were up but it was still going on inside. Somebody was singing. I went on home. Rinaldi came in while I was undressing.

"Ah, ha!" he said. "It does not go so well. Baby is puzzled."

"Where have you been?"

"At the Villa Rossa. It was very edifying, baby. We all sang. Where have you been?"

"Calling on the British."

"Thank God I did not become involved with the British."

CHAPTER 7

I CAME BACK the next afternoon from our first mountain post and stopped the car at the smistimento where the wounded and sick were sorted by their papers and the papers marked for the different hospitals. I had been driving and I sat in the car and the driver took the papers in. It was a hot day and the sky was very bright and blue and the road was white and dusty. I sat in the high seat of the Fiat and thought about nothing. A regiment went by in the road and I watched them pass. The men were hot and sweating. Some wore their steel helmets but most of them carried them slung from their packs. Most of the helmets were too big and came down almost over the ears of the men who wore them. The officers all wore helmets; better-fitting helmets. It was half of the brigata Basilicata. I identified them by their red and white striped collar mark. There were stragglers going by long after the regiment had passed — men who could not keep up with their platoons. They were sweaty, dusty and tired. Some looked pretty bad. A soldier came along after the last of the stragglers. He was walking with a limp. He stopped and sat down beside the road. I got down and went over.

"What's the matter?"

He looked at me, then stood up.

"I'm going on."

"What's the trouble?"

" — the war."

"What's wrong with your leg?"

"It's not my leg. I got a rupture."

"Why don't you ride with the transport?" I asked. "Why don't you go to the hospital?"

"They won't let me. The lieutenant said I slipped the truss on purpose."

"Let me feel it."

"It's way out."

"Which side is it on?"

"Here."

I felt it.

"Cough," I said.

"I'm afraid it will make it bigger. It's twice as big as it was this morning."

"Sit down," I said. "As soon as I get the papers on these wounded I'll take you along the road and drop you with your medical officers."

"He'll say I did it on purpose."

"They can't do anything," I said. "It's not a wound. You've had it before, haven't you?"

"But I lost the truss."

"They'll send you to a hospital."

"Can't I stay here, Tenente?"

"No, I haven't any papers for you."

The driver came out of the door with the papers for the wounded in the car.

"Four for 105. Two for 132," he said. They were hospitals beyond the river.

"You drive," I said. I helped the soldier with the rupture up on the seat with us.

"You speak English?" he asked.

"Sure."

"How you like this goddam war?"

"Rotten."

"I say it's rotten. Jesus Christ, I say it's rotten."

"Were you in the States?"

"Sure. In Pittsburgh. I knew you was an American."

"Don't I talk Italian good enough?"

"I knew you was an American all right."

"Another American," said the driver in Italian looking at the hernia man.

"Listen, lootenant. Do you have to take me to that regiment?"

"Yes."

"Because the captain doctor knew I had this rupture. I threw away the goddam truss so it would get bad and I wouldn't have to go to the line again."

"I see."

"Couldn't you take me no place else?"

"If it was closer to the front I could take you to a first medical post. But back here you've got to have papers."

"If I go back they'll make me get operated on and then they'll put me in the line all the time."

I thought it over.

"You wouldn't want to go in the line all the time, would you?" he asked.

"No."

"Jesus Christ, ain't this a goddam war?"

"Listen," I said. "You get out and fall down by the road and get a bump on your head and I'll pick you up on our way back and take you to a hospital. We'll stop by the road here, Aldo." We stopped at the side of the road. I helped him down.

"I'll be right here, lieutenant," he said.

"So long," I said. We went on and passed the regiment about a mile ahead, then crossed the river, cloudy with snow-water and running fast through the spiles of the bridge, to ride along the road across the plain and deliver the wounded at the two hospitals. I drove coming back and went fast with the empty car to find the man from Pittsburgh. First we passed the regiment, hotter and slower than ever: then the stragglers. Then we saw a horse ambulance stopped by the road. Two men were lifting the hernia man to put him in. They had come back for him. He shook his head at me. His helmet was off and his forehead was bleeding below the hair line. His nose was skinned and there was dust on the bloody patch and dust in his hair.

"Look at the bump, lieutenant!" he shouted. "Nothing to do. They come back for me."

When I got back to the villa it was five o'clock and I went out where we washed the cars, to take a shower. Then I made out my report in my room, sitting in my trousers and an undershirt in front of the open window. In two days the offensive was to start and I would go with the cars to Plava. It was a long time since I had written to the States and I knew I should write but I had let it go so long that it was almost impossible to write now. There was nothing to write about. I sent a couple of army Zona di Guerra post-cards, crossing out everything except, I am well. That should handle them. Those post-cards would be very fine in America; strange and mysterious. This was a strange and mysterious war zone but I supposed it was quite well run and grim compared to other wars with the Austrians. The Austrian army was created to give Napoleon victories; any Napoleon. I wished we had a Napoleon, but instead we had Il Generale Cadorna, fat and prosperous and Vittorio Emmanuele, the tiny man with the long thin neck and the goat beard. Over on the right they had the Duke of Aosta. Maybe he was too good-looking to be a great general but he looked like a man. Lots of them would have liked him to be king. He looked like a king. He was the King's uncle and commanded the third army. We were in the second army. There were some British batteries up with the third army. I had met two gunners from that lot, in Milan. They were very nice and we had a big evening. They were big and shy and embarrassed and very appreciative together of anything that happened. I wish that I was with the British. It would have been much simpler. Still I would probably have been killed. Not in this ambulance business. Yes, even in the ambulance business. British ambulance drivers were killed sometimes. Well, I knew I would not be killed. Not in this war. It did not have anything to do with me. It seemed no more dangerous to me myself than war in the movies. I wished to God it was over though. Maybe it would finish this summer. Maybe the Austrians would crack. They had always cracked in other wars. What was the matter with this war? Everybody said the French were through. Rinaldi said that the French had mutinied and troops marched on Paris. I asked him what happened and he said, "Oh, they stopped them." I wanted to go to Austria without war. I wanted to go to the Black Forest. I wanted to go to the Hartz Mountains.

Where were the Hartz Mountains anyway? They were fighting in the Carpathians. I did not want to go there anyway. It might be good though. I could go to Spain if there was no war. The sun was going down and the day was cooling off. After supper I would go and see Catherine Barkley. I wish she were here now. I wished I were in Milan with her. I would like to eat at the Cova and then walk down the Via Manzoni in the hot evening and cross over and turn off along the canal and go to the hotel with Catherine Barkley. Maybe she would. Maybe she would pretend that I was her boy that was killed and we would go in the front door and the porter would take off his cap and I would stop at the concierge's desk and ask for the key and she would stand by the elevator and then we would get in the elevator and it would go up very slowly clicking at all the floors and then our floor and the boy would open the door and stand there and she would step out and I would step out and we would walk down the hall and I would put the key in the door and open it and go in and then take down the telephone and ask them to send a bottle of capri bianca in a silver bucket full of ice and you would hear the ice against the pail coming down the corridor and the boy would knock and I would say leave it outside the door please. Because we would not wear any clothes because it was so hot and the window open and the swallows flying over the roofs of the houses and when it was dark afterward and you went to the window very small bats hunting over the houses and close down over the trees and we would drink the capri and the door locked and it hot and only a sheet and the whole night and we would both love each other all night in the hot night in Milan. That was how it ought to be. I would eat quickly and go and see Catherine Barkley.

They talked too much at the mess and I drank wine because tonight we were not all brothers unless I drank a little and talked with the priest about Archbishop Ireland who was, it seemed, a noble man and with whose injustice, the injustices he had received and in which I participated as an American, and of which I had never heard, I feigned acquaintance. It would have been impolite not to have known something of them when I had listened to such a splendid explanation of their causes which were, after all, it seemed, misunderstandings. I thought he had a fine name and he came from Minnesota which made a lovely name: Ireland of Minnesota, Ireland of Wisconsin, Ireland of Michigan. What made it pretty was that it sounded like Island. No that wasn't it. There was more to it than that. Yes, father. That is true, father. Perhaps, father. No, father. Well, maybe yes, father. You know more about it than I do, father. The priest was good but dull. The officers were not good but dull. The King was good but dull. The wine was bad but not dull. It took the enamel off your teeth and left it on the roof of your mouth.

"And the priest was locked up," Rocca said, "because they found the three per cent bonds on his person. It was in France of course. Here they would never have arrested him. He denied all knowledge of the five per cent bonds. This took place at Béziers. I was there and reading of it in the paper, went to the jail and asked to see the priest. It was quite evident he had stolen the bonds."

"I don't believe a word of this," Rinaldi said.

"Just as you like," Rocca said. "But I am telling it for our priest here. It is very informative. He is a priest; he will appreciate it."

The priest smiled. "Go on," he said. "I am listening."

"Of course some of the bonds were not accounted for but the priest had all of the three per cent bonds and several local obligations, I forget exactly what they were. So I went to the jail, now this is the point of the story, and I stood outside his cell and I said as though I were going to confession, 'Bless me, father, for you have sinned.'"

There was great laughter from everybody.

"And what did he say?" asked the priest. Rocca ignored this and went on to explain the joke to me. "You see the point, don't you?" It seemed it was a very funny joke if you understood it properly. They poured me more wine and I told the story about the English private soldier who was placed under the shower bath. Then the major told the story of the eleven Czecho-slovaks and the Hungarian corporal. After some more wine I told the story of the jockey who found the penny. The major said there was an Italian story something like that about the duchess who could not sleep at night. At this point the priest left and I told the story about the travelling salesman who arrived at five o'clock in the morning at Marseilles when the mistral was blowing. The major said he had heard a report that I could drink. I denied this. He said it was true and by the corpse of Bacchus we would test whether it was true or not. Not Bacchus, I said. Not Bacchus. Yes, Bacchus, he said. I should drink cup for cup and glass for glass with Bassi, Fillipo Vincenza. Bassi said no that was no test because he had already drunk twice as much as I. I said that was a foul lie and, Bacchus or no Bacchus, Fillipo Vincenza Bassi or Bassi Fillippo Vicenza had never touched a drop all evening and what was his name anyway? He said was my name Frederico Enrico or Enrico Federico? I said let the best man win, Bacchus barred, and the major started us with red wine in mugs. Half-way through the wine I did not want any more. I remembered where I was going.

"Bassi wins," I said. "He's a better man than I am. I have to go."

"He does really," said Rinaldi. "He has a rendezvous. I know all about it."

"I have to go."

"Another night," said Bassi. "Another night when you feel stronger." He slapped me on the shoulder. There were lighted candles on the table. All the officers were very happy. "Good-night, gentlemen," I said.

Rinaldi went out with me. We stood outside the door on the patch and he said, "You better not go up there drunk."

"I'm not drunk, Rinin. Really."

"You'd better chew some coffee."

"Nonsense."

"I'll get some, baby. You walk up and down." He came back with a handful of roasted coffee beans. "Chew those, baby, and God be with you."

"Bacchus," I said.

"I'll walk down with you."

"I'm perfectly all right."

We walked along together through the town and I chewed the coffee. At the gate of the driveway that led up to the British villa, Rinaldi said good-night.

"Good-night," I said. "Why don't you come in?"

He shook his head. "No," he said. "I like the simpler pleasures."

"Thank you for the coffee beans."

"Nothing, baby. Nothing."

I started down the driveway. The outlines of the cypresses that lined it were sharp and clear. I looked back and saw Rinaldi standing watching me and waved to him.

I sat in the reception hall of the villa, waiting for Catherine Barkley to come down. Some one was coming down the hallway. I stood up, but it was not Catherine. It was Miss Ferguson.

"Hello," she said. "Catherine asked me to tell you she was sorry she couldn't see you this evening."

"I'm so sorry. I hope she's not ill."

"She's not awfully well."

"Will you tell her how sorry I am?"

"Yes, I will."

"Do you think it would be any good to try and see her tomorrow?"

"Yes, I do."

"Thank you very much," I said. "Good-night."

I went out the door and suddenly I felt lonely and empty. I had treated seeing Catherine very lightly, I had gotten somewhat drunk and had nearly forgotten to come but when I could not see her there I was feeling lonely and hollow.

CHAPTER 8

THE NEXT AFTERNOON we heard there was to be an attack up the river that night and that we were to take four cars there. Nobody knew anything about it although they all spoke with great positiveness and strategical knowledge. I was riding in the first car and as we passed the entry to the British hospital I told the driver to stop. The other cars pulled up. I got out and told the driver to go on and that if we had not caught up to them at the junction of the road to Cormons to wait there. I hurried up the driveway and inside the reception hall I asked for Miss Barkley.

"She's on duty."

"Could I see her just for a moment?"

They sent an orderly to see and she came back with him.

"I stopped to ask if you were better. They told me you were on duty, so I asked to see you."

"I'm quite well," she said, "I think the heat knocked me over yesterday."

"I have to go."

"I'll just step out the door a minute."

"And you're all right?" I asked outside.

"Yes, darling. Are you coming to-night?"

"No. I'm leaving now for a show up above Plava."

"A show?"

"I don't think it's anything."

"And you'll be back?"

"To-morrow."

She was unclasping something from her neck. She put it in my hand. "It's a Saint Anthony," she said. "And come to-morrow night."

"You're not a Catholic, are you?"

"No. But they say a Saint Anthony's very useful."

"I'll take care of him for you. Good-by."

"No," she said, "not good-by."

"All right."

"Be a good boy and be careful. No, you can't kiss me here. You can't."

"All right."

I looked back and saw her standing on the steps. She waved and I kissed my hand and held it out. She waved again and then I was out of the driveway and climbing up into the seat of the ambulance and we started. The Saint Anthony was in a little white metal capsule. I opened the capsule and spilled him out into my hand.

"Saint Anthony?" asked the driver.

"Yes."

"I have one." His right hand left the wheel and opened a button on his tunic and pulled it out from under his shirt.

"See?"

I put my Saint Anthony back in the capsule, spilled the thin gold chain together and put it all in my breast pocket.

"You don't wear him?"

"No."

"It's better to wear him. That's what it's for."

"All right," I said. I undid the clasp of the gold chain and put it around my neck and clasped it. The saint hung down on the outside of my uniform and I undid the throat of my tunic, unbuttoned the shirt collar and dropped him in under the shirt. I felt him in his metal box against my chest while we drove. Then I forgot about him. After I was wounded I never found him. Some one probably got it at one of the dressing stations.

We drove fast when we were over the bridge and soon we saw the dust of the other cars ahead down the road. The road curved and we saw the three cars looking quite small, the dust rising from the wheels and going off through the trees. We caught them and passed them and turned off on a road that climbed up into the hills. Driving in convoy is not unpleasant if you are the first car and I settled back in the seat and watched the country. We were in the foothills on the near side of the river and as the road mounted there were the high mountains off to the north with snow still on the tops. I looked back and saw the three cars all climbing, spaced by the interval of their dust. We passed a long column of loaded mules, the drivers walking along beside the mules wearing red fezzes. They were bersaglieri.

Beyond the mule train the road was empty and we climbed through the hills and then went down over the shoulder of a long hill into a river-valley. There were trees along both sides of the road and through the right line of trees I saw the river, the water clear, fast and shallow. The river was low and there were stretches of sand and pebbles with a narrow channel of water and sometimes the water spread like a sheen over the pebbly bed. Close to the bank I saw deep pools, the water blue like the sky. I saw arched stone bridges over the river where tracks turned off from the road and we passed stone farmhouses with pear trees candelabraed against their south walls and low stone walls in the fields. The road went up the valley a long way and then we turned off and commenced to climb into the hills again. The road climbed steeply going up and back and forth through chestnut woods to level finally along a ridge. I could look down through the woods and see, far below, with the sun on it, the line of the river that separated the two armies. We went along the rough new military road that followed the crest of the ridge and I looked to the north at the two ranges of mountains, green and dark to the snow-line and then white and lovely in the sun. Then, as the road mounted along the ridge, I saw a third range of mountains, higher snow mountains, that looked chalky white and furrowed, with strange planes, and then there were mountains far off beyond all these that you could hardly tell if you really saw. Those were all the Austrians' mountains and we had nothing like them. Ahead there was a rounded turn-off in the road to the right and looking down I could see the road dropping through the trees. There were troops on this road and motor trucks and mules with mountain guns and as we went down, keeping to the side, I could see the river far down below, the line of ties and rails running along it, the old bridge where the railway crossed to the other side and across, under a hill beyond the river, the broken houses of the little town that was to be taken.

It was nearly dark when we came down and turned onto the main road that ran beside the river.

CHAPTER 9

THE ROAD WAS crowded and there were screens of corn-stalk and straw matting on both sides and matting over the top so that it was like the entrance at a circus or a native village. We drove slowly in this matting-covered tunnel and came out onto a bare cleared space where the railway station had been. The road here was below the level of the river bank and all along the side of the sunken road there were holes dug in the bank with infantry in them. The sun was going down and looking up along the bank as we drove I saw the Austrian observation balloons above the hills on the other side dark against the sunset. We parked the cars beyond a brickyard. The ovens and some deep holes had been equipped as dressing stations. There were three doctors that I knew. I talked with the major and learned that when it should start and our cars should be loaded we would drive them back along the screened road and up to the main road along the ridge where there would be a post and other cars to clear them. He hoped the road would not jam. It was a one-road show. The road was screened because it was in sight of the Austrians across the river. Here at the brickyard we were sheltered from rifle or machine-gun fire by the river bank. There was one smashed bridge across the river. They were going to put over another bridge when the bombardment started and some troops were to cross at the shallows up above at the bend of the river. The major was a little man with upturned mustaches. He had been in the war in Libya and wore two wound-stripes. He said that if the thing went well he would see that I was decorated. I said I hoped it would go well but that he was too kind. I asked him if there was a big dugout where the drivers could stay and he sent a soldier to show me. I went with him and found the dugout, which was very good. The drivers were pleased with it and I left them there. The major asked me to have a drink with him and two other officers. We drank rum and it was very friendly. Outside it was getting dark. I asked what time the attack was to be and they said as soon as it was dark. I went back to the drivers. They were sitting in the dugout talking and when I came in they stopped. I gave them each a package of cigarettes, Macedonias, loosely packed cigarettes that spilled tobacco and needed to have the ends twisted before you smoked them. Manera lit his lighter and passed it around. The lighter was shaped like a Fiat radiator. I told them what I had heard.

"Why didn't we see the post when we came down?" Passini asked.

"It was just beyond where we turned off."

"That road will be a dirty mess," Manera said.

"They'll shell the – out of us."

"Probably."

"What about eating, lieutenant? We won't get a chance to eat after this thing starts."

"I'll go and see now," I said.

"You want us to stay here or can we look around?"

"Better stay here."

I went back to the major's dugout and he said the field kitchen would be along and the drivers could come and get their stew. He would loan them mess tins if they did not have them. I said I thought they had them. I went back and told the drivers I would get them as soon as the food came. Manera said he hoped it would come before the bombardment started. They were silent until I went out. They were all mechanics and hated the war.

I went out to look at the cars and see what was going on and then came back and sat down in the dugout with the four drivers. We sat on the ground with our backs against the wall and smoked. Outside it was nearly dark. The earth of the dugout was warm and dry and I let my shoulders back against the wall, sitting on the small of my back, and relaxed.

"Who goes to the attack?" asked Gavuzzi.

"Bersaglieri."

"All bersaglieri?"

"I think so."

"There aren't enough troops here for a real attack."

"It is probably to draw attention from where the real attack will be."

"Do the men know that who attack?"

"I don't think so."

"Of course they don't," Manera said. "They wouldn't attack if they did."

"Yes, they would," Passini said. "Bersaglieri are fools."

"They are brave and have good discipline," I said.

"They are big through the chest by measurement, and healthy. But they are still fools."

"The granatieri are tall," Manera said. This was a joke. They all laughed.

"Were you there, Tenente, when they wouldn't attack and they shot every tenth man?"

"No."

"It is true. They lined them up afterward and took every tenth man. Carabinieri shot them."

"Carabinieri," said Passini and spat on the floor. "But those grenadiers; all over six feet. They wouldn't attack."

"If everybody would not attack the war would be over," Manera said.

"It wasn't that way with the granatieri. They were afraid. The officers all came from such good families."

"Some of the officers went alone."

"A sergeant shot two officers who would not get out."

"Some troops went out."

"Those that went out were not lined up when they took the tenth men."

"One of those shot by the carabinieri is from my town," Passini said. "He was a big smart tall boy to be in the granatieri. Always in Rome. Always with the girls. Always with the carabinieri." He laughed. "Now they have a guard outside his house with a bayonet and nobody can come to see his mother and father and sisters and his father loses his civil rights and cannot even vote. They are all without law to protect them. Anybody can take their property."

"If it wasn't that that happens to their families nobody would go to the attack."

"Yes. Alpini would. These V. E. soldiers would. Some bersaglieri."

"Bersaglieri have run too. Now they try to forget it."

"You should not let us talk this way, Tenente. Evviva l'esercito," Passini said sarcastically.

"I know how you talk," I said. "But as long as you drive the cars and behave—"

" — and don't talk so other officers can hear," Manera finished.

"I believe we should get the war over," I said. "It would not finish it if one side stopped fighting. It would only be worse if we stopped fighting."

"It could not be worse," Passini said respectfully. "There is nothing worse than war."

"Defeat is worse."

"I do not believe it," Passini said still respectfully. "What is defeat? You go home."

"They come after you. They take your home. They take your sisters."

"I don't believe it," Passini said. "They can't do that to everybody. Let everybody defend his home. Let them keep their sisters in the house."

"They hang you. They come and make you be a soldier again. Not in the auto-ambulance, in the infantry."

"They can't hang every one."

"An outside nation can't make you be a soldier," Manera said. "At the first battle you all run."

"Like the Tchecos."

"I think you do not know anything about being conquered and so you think it is not bad."

"Tenente," Passini said. "We understand you let us talk. Listen. There is nothing as bad as war. We in the auto-ambulance cannot even realize at all how bad it is. When people realize how bad it is they cannot do anything to stop it because they go crazy. There are some people who never realize. There are people who are afraid of their officers. It is with them the war is made."

"I know it is bad but we must finish it."

"It doesn't finish. There is no finish to a war."

"Yes there is."

Passini shook his head.

"War is not won by victory. What if we take San Gabriele?"

"What if we take the Carso and Monfalcone and Trieste? Where are we then? Did you see all the far mountains to-day? Do you think we could take all them too? Only if the Austrians stop fighting. One side must stop fighting. Why don't we stop fighting? If they come down into Italy they will get tired and go away. They have their own country. But no, instead there is a war."

"You're an orator."

"We think. We read. We are not peasants. We are mechanics. But even the peasants know better than to believe in a war. Everybody hates this war."

"There is a class that controls a country that is stupid and does not realize anything and never can. That is why we have this war."

"Also they make money out of it."

"Most of them don't," said Passini. "They are too stupid. They do it for nothing. For stupidity."

"We must shut up," said Manera. "We talk too much even for the Tenente."

"He likes it," said Passini. "We will convert him."

"But now we will shut up," Manera said.

"Do we eat yet, Tenente?" Gavuzzi asked.

"I will go and see," I said. Gordini stood up and went outside with me.

"Is there anything I can do, Tenente? Can I help in any way?" He was the quietest one of the four. "Come with me if you want," I said, "and we'll see."

It was dark outside and the long light from the search-lights was moving over the mountains. There were big search-lights on that front mounted on camions that you passed sometimes on the roads at night, close behind the lines, the camion stopped a little off the road, an officer directing the light and the crew scared. We crossed the brickyard, and stopped at the main dressing station. There was a little shelter of green branches outside over the entrance and in the dark the night wind rustled the leaves dried by the sun. Inside there was a light. The major was at the telephone sitting on a box. One of the medical captains said the attack had been put forward an hour. He offered me a glass of cognac. I looked at the board tables, the instruments shining in the light, the basins and the stoppered bottles. Gordini stood behind me. The major got up from the telephone.

"It starts now," he said. "It has been put back again."

I looked outside, it was dark and the Austrian search-lights were moving on the mountains behind us. It was quiet for a moment still, then from all the guns behind us the bombardment started.

"Savoia," said the major.

"About the soup, major," I said. He did not hear me. I repeated it.

"It hasn't come up."

A big shell came in and burst outside in the brickyard. Another burst and in the noise you could hear the smaller noise of the brick and dirt raining down.

"What is there to eat?"

"We have a little pasta asciutta," the major said.

"I'll take what you can give me."

The major spoke to an orderly who went out of sight in the back and came back with a metal basin of cold cooked macaroni. I handed it to Gordini.

"Have you any cheese?"

The major spoke grudgingly to the orderly who ducked back into the hole again and came out with a quarter of a white cheese.

"Thank you very much," I said.

"You'd better not go out."

Outside something was set down beside the entrance. One of the two men who had carried it looked in.

"Bring him in," said the major. "What's the matter with you? Do you want us to come outside and get him?"

The two stretcher-bearers picked up the man under the arms and by the legs and brought him in.

"Slit the tunic," the major said.

He held a forceps with some gauze in the end. The two captains took off their coats. "Get out of here," the major said to the two stretcher-bearers.

"Come on," I said to Gordini.

"You better wait until the shelling is over," the major said over his shoulder.

"They want to eat," I said.

"As you wish."

Outside we ran across the brickyard. A shell burst short near the river bank. Then there was one that we did not hear coming until the sudden rush. We both went flat and with the flash and bump of the burst and the smell heard the singing off of the fragments and the rattle of falling brick. Gordini got up and ran for the dugout. I was after him, holding the cheese, its smooth surface covered with brick dust. Inside the dugout were the three drivers sitting against the wall, smoking.

"Here, you patriots," I said.

"How are the cars?" Manera asked.

"All right."

"Did they scare you, Tenente?"

"You're damned right," I said.

I took out my knife, opened it, wiped off the blade and pared off the dirty outside surface of the cheese. Gavuzzi handed me the basin of macaroni.

"Start in to eat, Tenente."

"No," I said. "Put it on the floor. We'll all eat."

"There are no forks."

"What the hell," I said in English.

I cut the cheese into pieces and laid them on the macaroni.

"Sit down to it," I said. They sat down and waited. I put thumb and fingers into the macaroni and lifted. A mass loosened.

"Lift it high, Tenente."

I lifted it to arm's length and the strands cleared. I lowered it into the mouth, sucked and snapped in the ends, and chewed, then took a bite of cheese, chewed, and then a drink of the wine. It tasted of rusty metal. I handed the canteen back to Passini.

"It's rotten," he said. "It's been in there too long. I had it in the car."

They were all eating, holding their chins close over the basin, tipping their heads back, sucking in the ends. I took another mouthful and some cheese and a rinse of wine. Something landed outside that shook the earth.

"Four hundred twenty or minnenwerfer," Gavuzzi said.

"There aren't any four hundred twenties in the mountains," I said.

"They have big Skoda guns. I've seen the holes."

"Three hundred fives."

We went on eating. There was a cough, a noise like a railway engine starting and then an explosion that shook the earth again.

"This isn't a deep dugout," Passini said.

"That was a big trench mortar."

"Yes, sir."

I ate the end of my piece of cheese and took a swallow of wine. Through the other noise I heard a cough, then came the chuh-chuh-chuh-chuh – then there was a flash, as when a blast-furnace door is swung open, and a roar that started white and went red and on and on in a rushing wind. I tried to breathe but my breath would not come and I felt myself rush bodily out of myself and out and out and out and all the time bodily in the wind. I went out swiftly, all of myself, and I knew I was dead and that it had all been a mistake to think you just died. Then I floated, and instead of going on I felt myself slide back. I breathed and I was back. The ground was torn up and in front of my head there was a splintered beam of wood. In the jolt of my head I heard somebody crying. I thought somebody was screaming. I tried to move but I could not move. I heard the machine-guns and rifles firing across the river and all along the river. There was a great splashing and I saw the star-shells go up and burst and float whitely and rockets going up and heard the bombs, all this in a moment, and then I heard close to me some one saying "Mama Mia! Oh, mama Mia!" I pulled and twisted and got my legs loose finally and turned around and touched him. It was Passini and when I touched him he screamed. His legs were toward me and I saw in the dark and the light that they were both smashed above the knee. One leg was gone and the other was held by tendons and part of the trouser and the stump twitched and jerked as though it were not connected. He bit his arm and moaned, "Oh mama mia, mama Mia," then, "Dio te salve, Maria. Dio te salve, Maria. Oh Jesus shoot me Christ shoot me mama mia mama Mia oh purest lovely Mary shoot me. Stop it. Stop it. Stop it. Oh Jesus lovely Mary stop it. Oh oh oh oh," then choking, "Mama mama mia." Then he was quiet, biting his arm, the stump of his leg twitching.

"Porta feriti!" I shouted holding my hands cupped. "Porta feriti!" I tried to get closer to Passini to try to put a tourniquet on the legs but I could not move. I tried again and my legs moved a little. I could pull backward along with my arms and elbows. Passini was quiet now. I sat beside him, undid my tunic and tried to rip the tail of my shirt. It would not rip and I bit the edge of the cloth to start it. Then I thought of his puttees. I had on wool stockings but Passini wore puttees. All the drivers wore puttees but Passini had only one leg. I unwound the puttee and while I was doing it I saw there was no need to try and make a tourniquet because he was dead already. I made sure he was dead. There were three others to locate. I sat up straight and as I did so something inside my head moved like the weights on a doll's eyes and it hit me inside in back of my eyeballs. My legs felt warm and wet and my shoes were wet and warm inside. I knew that I was hit and leaned over and put my hand on my knee. My knee wasn't there. My hand went in and my knee was down on my shin. I wiped my hand on my shirt and another floating light came very slowly down and I looked at my leg and was very afraid. Oh, God, I said, get me out of here. I knew, however, that there had been three others. There were four drivers. Passini was dead. That left three. Some one took hold of me under the arms and somebody else lifted my legs.

"There are three others," I said. "One is dead."

"It's Manera. We went for a stretcher but there wasn't any. How are you, Tenente?"

"Where is Gordini and Gavuzzi?"

"Gordini's at the post getting bandaged. Gavuzzi has your legs. Hold on to my neck, Tenente. Are you badly hit?"

"In the leg. How is Gordini?"

"He's all right. It was a big trench mortar shell."

"Passini's dead."

"Yes. He's dead."

A shell fell close and they both dropped to the ground and dropped me. "I'm sorry, Tenente," said Manera. "Hang onto my neck."

"If you drop me again."

"It was because we were scared."

"Are you unwounded?"

"We are both wounded a little."

"Can Gordini drive?"

"I don't think so."

They dropped me once more before we reached the post.

"You sons of bitches," I said.

"I am sorry, Tenente," Manera said. "We won't drop you again."

Outside the post a great many of us lay on the ground in the dark. They carried wounded in and brought them out. I could see the light come out from the dressing station when the curtain opened and they brought some one in or out. The dead were off to one side. The doctors were working with their sleeves up to their shoulders and were red as butchers. There were not enough stretchers. Some of the wounded were noisy but most were quiet. The wind blew the leaves in the bower over the door of the dressing station and the night was getting cold. Stretcher-bearers came in all the time, put their stretchers down, unloaded them and went away. As soon as I got to the dressing station Manera brought a medical sergeant out and he put bandages on both my legs. He said there was so much dirt blown into the wound that there had not been much hemorrhage. They would take me as soon as possible. He went back inside. Gordini could not drive, Manera said. His shoulder was smashed and his head was hurt. He had not felt bad but now the shoulder had stiffened. He was sitting up beside one of the brick walls. Manera and Gavuzzi each went off with a load of wounded. They could drive all right. The British had come with three ambulances and they had two men on each ambulance. One of their drivers came over to me, brought by Gordini who looked very white and sick. The Britisher leaned over.

"Are you hit badly?" he asked. He was a tall man and wore steel-rimmed spectacles.

"In the legs."

"It's not serious I hope. Will you have a cigarette?"

"Thanks."

"They tell me you've lost two drivers."

"Yes. One killed and the fellow that brought you."

"What rotten luck. Would you like us to take the cars?"

"That's what I wanted to ask you."

"We'd take quite good care of them and return them to the villa. 206 aren't you?"

"Yes."

"It's a charming place. I've seen you about. They tell me you're an American."

"Yes."

"I'm English."

"No!"

"Yes, English. Did you think I was Italian? There were some Italians with one of our units."

"It would be fine if you would take the cars," I said.

"We'll be most careful of them," he straightened up. "This chap of yours was very anxious for me to see you." He patted Gordini on the shoulder. Gordini winced and smiled. The Englishman broke into voluble and perfect Italian. "Now everything is arranged. I've seen your Tenente. We will take over the two cars. You won't worry now." He broke off, "I must do something about getting you out of here. I'll see the medical wallahs. We'll take you back with us."

He walked across to the dressing station, stepping carefully among the wounded. I saw the blanket open, the light came out and he went in.

"He will look after you, Tenente," Gordini said.

"How are you, Franco?"

"I am all right." He sat down beside me. In a moment the blanket in front of the dressing station opened and two stretcher-bearers came out followed by the tall Englishman. He brought them over to me.

"Here is the American Tenente," he said in Italian.

"I'd rather wait," I said. "There are much worse wounded than me. I'm all right."

"Come, come," he said. "Don't be a bloody hero." Then in Italian: "Lift him very carefully about the legs. His legs are very painful. He is the legitimate son of President Wilson." They picked me up and took me into the dressing room. Inside they were operating on all the tables. The little major looked at us furious. He recognized me and waved a forceps.

"Ça va bien?"

"Ça va."

"I have brought him in," the tall Englishman said in Italian. "The only son of the American Ambassador. He can be here until you are ready to take him. Then I will take him with my first load." He bent over me. "I'll look up their adjutant to do your papers and it will all go much faster." He stooped to go under the doorway and went out. The major was unhooking the forceps now, dropping them in a basin. I followed his hands with my eyes. Now he was bandaging. Then the stretcher-bearers took the man off the table.

"I'll take the American Tenente," one of the captains said. They lifted me onto the table. It was hard and slippery. There were many strong smells, chemical smells and the sweet smell of blood. They took off my trousers and the medical captain commenced dictating to the sergeant-adjutant while he worked, "Multiple superficial wounds of the left and right thigh and left and right knee and right foot. Profound wounds of right knee and foot. Lacerations of the scalp (he probed – Does that hurt? – Christ, yes!) with possible fracture of the skull. Incurred in the line of duty. That's what keeps you from being court-martialled for self-inflicted wounds," he said. "Would you like a drink of brandy? How did you run into this thing anyway? What were you trying to do? Commit suicide? Antitetanus please, and mark a cross on both legs. Thank you. I'll clean this up a little, wash it out, and put on a dressing. Your blood coagulates beautifully."

The adjutant, looking up from the paper, "What inflicted the wounds?"

The medical captain, "What hit you?"

Me, with the eyes shut, "A trench mortar shell."

The captain, doing things that hurt sharply and severing tissue– "Are you sure?"

Me – trying to lie still and feeling my stomach flutter when the flesh was cut, "I think so."

Captain doctor – (interested in something he was finding), "Fragments of enemy trench-mortar shell. Now I'll probe for some of this if you like but it's not necessary. I'll paint all this and – Does that sting? Good, that's nothing to how it will feel later. The pain hasn't started yet. Bring him a glass of brandy. The shock dulls the pain; but this is all right, you have nothing to worry about if it doesn't infect and it rarely does now. How is your head?"

"Good Christ!" I said.

"Better not drink too much brandy then. If you've got a fracture you don't want inflammation. How does that feel?"

Sweat ran all over me.

"Good Christ!" I said.

"I guess you've got a fracture all right. I'll wrap you up and don't bounce your head around." He bandaged, his hands moving very fast and the bandage coming taut and sure. "All right, good luck and Vive la France."

"He's an American," one of the other captains said.

"I thought you said he was a Frenchman. He talks French," the captain said. "I've known him before. I always thought he was French." He drank a half tumbler of cognac. "Bring on something serious. Get some more of that Antitetanus." The captain waved to me. They lifted me and the blanket-flap went across my face as we went out. Outside the sergeant-adjutant knelt down beside me where I lay, "Name?" he asked softly. "Middle name? First name? Rank? Where born? What class? What corps?" and so on. "I'm sorry for your head, Tenente. I hope you feel better. I'm sending you now with the English ambulance."

"I'm all right," I said. "Thank you very much." The pain that the major had spoken about had started and all that was happening was without interest or relation. After a while the English ambulance came up and they put me onto a stretcher and lifted the stretcher up to the ambulance level and shoved it in. There was another stretcher by the side with a man on it whose nose I could see, waxy-looking, out of the bandages. He breathed very heavily. There were stretchers lifted and slid into the slings above. The tall English driver came around and looked in, "I'll take it very easily," he said. "I hope you'll be comfy." I felt the engine start, felt him climb up into the front seat, felt the brake come off and the clutch go in, then we started. I lay still and let the pain ride.

As the ambulance climbed along the road, it was slow in the traffic, sometimes it stopped, sometimes it backed on a turn, then finally it climbed quite fast. I felt something dripping. At first it dropped slowly and regularly, then it pattered into a stream. I shouted to the driver. He stopped the car and looked in through the hole behind his seat.

"What is it?"

"The man on the stretcher over me has a hemorrhage."

"We're not far from the top. I wouldn't be able to get the stretcher out alone." He started the car. The stream kept on. In the dark I could not see where it came from the canvas overhead. I tried to move sideways so that it did not fall on me. Where it had run down under my shirt it was warm and sticky. I was cold and my leg hurt so that it made me sick. After a while the stream from the stretcher above lessened and started to drip again and I heard and felt the canvas above move as the man on the stretcher settled more comfortably.

"How is he?" the Englishman called back. "We're almost up."

"He's dead I think," I said.

The drops fell very slowly, as they fall from an icicle after the sun has gone. It was cold in the car in the night as the road climbed. At the post on the top they took the stretcher out and put another in and we went on.

CHAPTER 10

IN THE WARD at the field hospital they told me a visitor was coming to see me in the afternoon. It was a hot day and there were many flies in the room. My orderly had cut paper into strips and tied the strips to a stick to make a brush that swished the flies away. I watched them settle on the ceiling. When he stopped swishing and fell asleep they came down and I blew them away and finally covered my face with my hands and slept too. It was very hot and when I woke my legs itched. I waked the orderly and he poured mineral water on the dressings. That made the bed damp and cool. Those of us that were awake talked across the ward. The afternoon was a quiet time. In the morning they came to each bed in turn, three men nurses and a doctor and picked you up out of bed and carried you into the dressing room so that the beds could be made while we were having our wounds dressed. It was not a pleasant trip to the dressing room and I did not know until later that beds could be made with men in them. My orderly had finished pouring water and the bed felt cool and lovely and I was telling him where to scratch on the soles of my feet against the itching when one of the doctors brought in Rinaldi. He came in very fast and bent down over the bed and kissed me. I saw he wore gloves.

"How are you, baby? How do you feel? I bring you this—" It was a bottle of cognac. The orderly brought a chair and he sat down, "and good news. You will be decorated. They want to get you the medaglia d'argento but perhaps they can get only the bronze."

"What for?"

"Because you are gravely wounded. They say if you can prove you did any heroic act you can get the silver. Otherwise it will be the bronze. Tell me exactly what happened. Did you do any heroic act?"

"No," I said. "I was blown up while we were eating cheese."

"Be serious. You must have done something heroic either before or after. Remember carefully."

"I did not."

"Didn't you carry anybody on your back? Gordini says you carried several people on your back but the medical major at the first post declares it is impossible. He had to sign the proposition for the citation."

"I didn't carry anybody. I couldn't move."

"That doesn't matter," said Rinaldi.

He took off his gloves.

"I think we can get you the silver. Didn't you refuse to be medically aided before the others?"

"Not very firmly."

"That doesn't matter. Look how you are wounded. Look at your valorous conduct in asking to go always to the first line. Besides, the operation was successful."

"Did they cross the river all right?"

"Enormously. They take nearly a thousand prisoners. It's in the bulletin. Didn't you see it?"

"No."

"I'll bring it to you. It is a successful coup de main."

"How is everything?"

"Splendid. We are all splendid. Everybody is proud of you. Tell me just exactly how it happened. I am positive you will get the silver. Go on tell me. Tell me all about it." He paused and thought. "Maybe you will get an English medal too. There was an English there. I'll go and see him and ask if he will recommend you. He ought to be able to do something. Do you suffer much? Have a drink. Orderly, go get a corkscrew. Oh you should see what I did in the removal of three metres of small intestine and better now than ever. It is one for The Lancet. You do me a translation and I will send it to The Lancet. Every day I am better. Poor dear baby, how do you feel? Where is that damn corkscrew? You are so brave and quiet I forget you are suffering." He slapped his gloves on the edge of the bed.

"Here is the corkscrew, Signor Tenente," the orderly said.

"Open the bottle. Bring a glass. Drink that, baby. How is your poor head? I looked at your papers. You haven't any fracture. That major at the first post was a hog-butcher. I would take you and never hurt you. I never hurt anybody. I learn how to do it. Every day I learn to do things smoother and better. You must forgive me for talking so much, baby. I am very moved to see you badly wounded. There, drink that. It's good. It cost fifteen lire. It ought to be good. Five stars. After I leave here I'll go see that English and he'll get you an English medal."

"They don't give them like that."

"You are so modest. I will send the liaison officer. He can handle the English."

"Have you seen Miss Barkley?"

"I will bring her here. I will go now and bring her here."

"Don't go," I said. "Tell me about Gorizia. How are the girls?"

"There are no girls. For two weeks now they haven't changed them. I don't go there any more. It is disgraceful. They aren't girls; they are old war comrades."

"You don't go at all?"

"I just go to see if there is anything new. I stop by. They all ask for you. It is a disgrace that they should stay so long that they become friends."

"Maybe girls don't want to go to the front any more."

"Of course they do. They have plenty of girls. It is just bad administration. They are keeping them for the pleasure of dugout hiders in the rear."

"Poor Rinaldi," I said. "All alone at the war with no new girls."

Rinaldi poured himself another glass of the cognac.

"I don't think it will hurt you, baby. You take it."

I drank the cognac and felt it warm all the way down. Rinaldi poured another glass. He was quieter now. He held up the glass. "To your valorous wounds. To the silver medal. Tell me, baby, when you lie here all the time in the hot weather don't you get excited?"

"Sometimes."

"I can't imagine lying like that. I would go crazy."

"You are crazy."

"I wish you were back. No one to come in at night from adventures. No one to make fun of. No one to lend me money. No blood brother and roommate. Why do you get yourself wounded?"

"You can make fun of the priest."

"That priest. It isn't me that makes fun of him. It is the captain. I like him. If you must have a priest have that priest. He's coming to see you. He makes big preparations."

"I like him."

"Oh, I knew it. Sometimes I think you and he are a little that way. You know."

"No, you don't."

"Yes, I do sometimes. A little that way like the number of the first regiment of the Brigata Ancona."

"Oh, go to hell."

He stood up and put on his gloves.

"Oh I love to tease you, baby. With your priest and your English girl, and really you are just like me underneath."

"No, I'm not."

"Yes, we are. You are really an Italian. All fire and smoke and nothing inside. You only pretend to be American. We are brothers and we love each other."

"Be good while I'm gone," I said.

"I will send Miss Barkley. You are better with her without me. You are purer and sweeter."

"Oh, go to hell."

"I will send her. Your lovely cool goddess. English goddess. My God what would a man do with a woman like that except worship her? What else is an Englishwoman good for?"

"You are an ignorant foul-mouthed dago."

"A what?"

"An ignorant wop."

"Wop. You are a frozen-faced . . . wop."

"You are ignorant. Stupid." I saw that word pricked him and kept on. "Uninformed. Inexperienced, stupid from inexperience."

"Truly? I tell you something about your good women. Your goddesses. There is only one difference between taking a girl who has always been good and a woman. With a girl it is painful. That's all I know." He slapped the bed with his glove. "And you never know if the girl will really like it."

"Don't get angry."

"I'm not angry. I just tell you, baby, for your own good. To save you trouble."

"That's the only difference?"

"Yes. But millions of fools like you don't know it."

"You were sweet to tell me."

"We won't quarrel, baby. I love you too much. But don't be a fool."

"No. I'll be wise like you."

"Don't be angry, baby. Laugh. Take a drink. I must go, really."

"You're a good old boy."

"Now you see. Underneath we are the same. We are war brothers. Kiss me goodby."

"You're sloppy."

"No. I am just more affectionate."

I felt his breath come toward me. "Good-by. I come to see you again soon." His breath went away. "I won't kiss you if you don't want. I'll send your English girl. Good-by, baby. The cognac is under the bed. Get well soon."

He was gone.

CHAPTER 11

IT WAS DUSK when the priest came. They had brought the soup and afterward taken away the bowls and I was lying looking at the rows of beds and out the window at the tree-top that moved a little in the evening breeze. The breeze came in through the window and it was cooler with the evening. The flies were on the ceiling now and on the electric light bulbs that hung on wires. The lights were only turned on when some one was brought in at night or when something was being done. It made me feel very young to have the dark come after the dusk and then remain. It was like being put to bed after early supper. The orderly came down between the beds and stopped. Some one was with him. It was the priest. He stood there small, brown-faced, and embarrassed.

"How do you do?" he asked. He put some packages down by the bed, on the floor.

"All right, father."

He sat down in the chair that had been brought for Rinaldi and looked out of the window embarrassedly. I noticed his face looked very tired.

"I can only stay a minute," he said. "It is late."

"It's not late. How is the mess?"

He smiled. "I am still a great joke," he sounded tired too. "Thank God they are all well.

"I am so glad you are all right," he said. "I hope you don't suffer." He seemed very tired and I was not used to seeing him tired.

"Not any more."

"I miss you at the mess."

"I wish I were there. I always enjoyed our talking."

"I brought you a few little things," he said. He picked up the packages. "This is mosquito netting. This is a bottle of vermouth. You like vermouth? These are English papers."

"Please open them."

He was pleased and undid them. I held the mosquito netting in my hands. The vermouth he held up for me to see and then put it on the floor beside the bed. I held up one of the sheaf of English papers. I could read the headlines by turning it so the half-light from the window was on it. It was *The News of the World*.

"The others are illustrated," he said.

"It will be a great happiness to read them. Where did you get them?"

"I sent for them to Mestre. I will have more."

"You were very good to come, father. Will you drink a glass of vermouth?"

"Thank you. You keep it. It's for you."

"No, drink a glass."

"All right. I will bring you more then."

The orderly brought the glasses and opened the bottle. He broke off the cork and the end had to be shoved down into the bottle. I could see the priest was disappointed but he said, "That's all right. It's no matter."

"Here's to your health, father."

"To your better health."

Afterward he held the glass in his hand and we looked at one another. Sometimes we talked and were good friends but to-night it was difficult.

"What's the matter, father? You seem very tired."

"I am tired but I have no right to be."

"It's the heat."

"No. This is only the spring. I feel very low."

"You have the war disgust."

"No. But I hate the war."

"I don't enjoy it," I said. He shook his head and looked out of the window.

"You do not mind it. You do not see it. You must forgive me. I know you are wounded."

"That is an accident."

"Still even wounded you do not see it. I can tell. I do not see it myself but I feel it a little."

"When I was wounded we were talking about it. Passini was talking."

The priest put down the glass. He was thinking about something else.

"I know them because I am like they are," he said.

"You are different though."

"But really I am like they are."

"The officers don't see anything."

"Some of them do. Some are very delicate and feel worse than any of us."

"They are mostly different."

"It is not education or money. It is something else. Even if they had education or money men like Passini would not wish to be officers. I would not be an officer."

"You rank as an officer. I am an officer."

"I am not really. You are not even an Italian. You are a foreigner. But you are nearer the officers than you are to the men."

"What is the difference?"

"I cannot say it easily. There are people who would make war. In this country there are many like that. There are other people who would not make war."

"But the first ones make them do it."

"Yes."

"And I help them."

"You are a foreigner. You are a patriot."

"And the ones who would not make war? Can they stop it?"

"I do not know."

He looked out of the window again. I watched his face.

"Have they ever been able to stop it?"

"They are not organized to stop things and when they get organized their leaders sell them out."

"Then it's hopeless?"

"It is never hopeless. But sometimes I cannot hope. I try always to hope but sometimes I cannot."

"Maybe the war will be over."

"I hope so."

"What will you do then?"

"If it is possible I will return to the Abruzzi."

His brown face was suddenly very happy.

"You love the Abruzzi?"

"Yes, I love it very much."

"You ought to go there then."

"I would be too happy. If I could live there and love God and serve Him."

"And be respected," I said.

"Yes and be respected. Why not?"

"No reason not. You should be respected."

"It does not matter. But there in my country it is understood that a man may love God. It is not a dirty joke."

"I understand."

He looked at me and smiled.

"You understand but you do not love God."

"No."

"You do not love Him at all?" he asked.

"I am afraid of Him in the night sometimes."

"You should love Him."

"I don't love much."

"Yes," he said. "You do. What you tell me about in the nights. That is not love. That is only passion and lust. When you love you wish to do things for. You wish to sacrifice for. You wish to serve."

"I don't love."

"You will. I know you will. Then you will be happy."

"I'm happy. I've always been happy."

"It is another thing. You cannot know about it unless you have it."

"Well," I said. "If I ever get it I will tell you."

"I stay too long and talk too much." He was worried that he really did.

"No. Don't go. How about loving women? If I really loved some woman would it be like that?"

"I don't know about that. I never loved any woman."

"What about your mother?"

"Yes, I must have loved my mother."

"Did you always love God?"

"Ever since I was a little boy."

"Well," I said. I did not know what to say. "You are a fine boy," I said.

"I am a boy," he said. "But you call me father."

"That's politeness."

He smiled.

"I must go, really," he said. "You do not want me for anything?" he asked hopefully.

"No. Just to talk."

"I will take your greetings to the mess."

"Thank you for the many fine presents."

"Nothing."

"Come and see me again."

"Yes. Good-by," he patted my hand.

"So long," I said in dialect.

"Ciaou," he repeated.

It was dark in the room and the orderly, who had sat by the foot of the bed, got up and went out with him. I liked him very much and I hoped he would get back to the Abruzzi some time. He had a rotten life in the mess and he was fine about it but I thought how he would be in his own country. At Capracotta, he had told me, there were trout in the stream below the town. It was forbidden to play the flute at night. When the young men serenaded only the flute was forbidden. Why, I had asked. Because it was bad for the girls to hear the flute at night. The peasants all called you "Don" and when you met them they took off their hats. His father hunted every day and stopped to eat at the houses of peasants. They were always honored. For a foreigner to hunt he must present a certificate that he had never been arrested. There were bears on the Gran Sasso D'Italia but it was a long way. Aquila was a fine town. It was cool in the summer at night and the spring in Abruzzi was the most beautiful in Italy. But what was lovely was the fall to go hunting through the chestnut woods. The birds were all good because they fed on grapes and you never took a lunch because the peasants were always honored if you would eat with them at their houses. After a while I went to sleep.

CHAPTER 12

THE ROOM was long with windows on the right-hand side and a door at the far end that went into the dressing room. The row of beds that mine was in faced the windows and another row, under the windows, faced the wall. If you lay on your left side you could see the dressing-room door. There was another door at the far end that people sometimes came in by. If any one were going to die they put a screen around the bed so you could not see them die, but only the shoes and puttees of doctors and men nurses showed under the bottom of the screen and sometimes at the end there would be whispering. Then the priest would come out from behind the screen and afterward the men nurses would go back behind the screen to come out again carrying the one who was dead with a blanket over him down the corridor between the beds and some one folded the screen and took it away.

That morning the major in charge of the ward asked me if I felt that I could travel the next day. I said I could. He said then they would ship me out early in the morning. He said I would be better off making the trip now before it got too hot.

When they lifted you up out of bed to carry you into the dressing room you could look out of the window and see the new graves in the garden. A soldier sat outside the door that opened onto the garden making crosses and painting on them the names, rank, and regiment of the men who were buried in the garden. He also ran errands for the ward and in his spare time made me a cigarette lighter out of an empty Austrian rifle cartridge. The doctors were very nice and seemed very capable. They were anxious to ship me to Milan where there were better X-ray facilities and where, after the operation, I could take mechanotherapy. I wanted to go to Milan too. They wanted to get us all out and back as far as possible because all the beds were needed for the offensive, when it should start.

The night before I left the field hospital Rinaldi came in to see me with the major from our mess. They said that I would go to an American hospital in Milan that had just been installed. Some American ambulance units were to be sent down and this hospital would look after them and any other Americans on service in Italy. There were many in the Red Cross. The States had declared war on Germany but not on Austria.

The Italians were sure America would declare war on Austria too and they were very excited about any Americans coming down, even the Red Cross. They asked me if I thought President Wilson would declare war on Austria and I said it was only a matter of days. I did not know what we had against Austria but it seemed logical that they should declare war on her if they did on Germany. They asked me if we would declare war on Turkey. I said that was doubtful. Turkey, I said, was our national bird but the joke translated so badly and they were so puzzled and suspicious that I said yes, we would probably declare war on Turkey. And on Bulgaria? We had drunk several glasses of brandy and I said yes by God on Bulgaria too and on Japan. But, they said, Japan is an ally of England. You can't trust the bloody English. The Japanese want Hawaii, I said. Where is Hawaii? It is in the Pacific Ocean. Why do the Japanese want it? They don't really want it, I said. That is all talk. The Japanese are a wonderful little people fond of dancing and light wines. Like the French, said the major. We will get Nice and Savoia from the French. We will get Corsica and all the Adriatic coast-line, Rinaldi said. Italy will return to the splendors of Rome, said the major. I don't like Rome, I said. It is hot and full of fleas. You don't like Rome? Yes, I love Rome. Rome is the mother of nations. I will never forget Romulus suckling the Tiber. What? Nothing. Let's all go to Rome.

Let's go to Rome to-night and never come back. Rome is a beautiful city, said the major. The mother and father of nations, I said. Roma is feminine, said Rinaldi. It cannot be the father. Who is the father, then, the Holy Ghost? Don't blaspheme. I wasn't blaspheming, I was asking for information. You are drunk, baby. Who made me drunk? I made you drunk, said the major. I made you drunk because I love you and because America is in the war. Up to the hilt, I said. You go away in the morning, baby, Rinaldi said. To Rome, I said. No, to Milan. To Milan, said the major, to the Crystal Palace, to the Cova, to Campari's, to Biffi's, to the galleria. You lucky boy. To the Gran Italia, I said, where I will borrow money from George. To the Scala, said Rinaldi. You will go to the Scala. Every night, I said. You won't be able to afford it every night, said the major.

The tickets are very expensive. I will draw a sight draft on my grandfather, I said. A what? A sight draft. He has to pay or I go to jail. Mr. Cunningham at the bank does it. I live by sight drafts. Can a grandfather jail a patriotic grandson who is dying that Italy may live? Live the American Garibaldi, said Rinaldi. Viva the sight drafts, I said. We must be quiet, said the major. Already we have been asked many times to be quiet. Do you go to-morrow really, Federico? He goes to the American hospital I tell you, Rinaldi said. To the beautiful nurses. Not the nurses with beards of the field hospital. Yes, yes, said the major, I know he goes to the American hospital. I don't mind their beards, I said. If any man wants to raise a beard let him. Why don't you raise a beard, Signor Maggiore? It could not go in a gas mask. Yes it could. Anything can go in a gas mask. I've vomited into a gas mask. Don't be so loud, baby, Rinaldi said. We all know you have been at the front. Oh, you fine baby, what will I do while you are gone? We must go, said the major. This becomes sentimental. Listen, I have a surprise for you. Your English. You know? The English you go to see every night at their hospital? She is going to Milan too. She goes with another to be at the American hospital. They had not got nurses yet from America. I talked to-day with the head of their riparto. They have too many women here at the front. They send some back. How do you like that, baby? All right. Yes? You go to live in a big city and have your English there to cuddle you. Why don't I get wounded? Maybe you will, I said. We must go, said the major. We drink and make noise and disturb Federico. Don't go. Yes, we must go. Good-by. Good luck. Many things. Ciaou. Ciaou. Ciaou. Come back quickly, baby. Rinaldi kissed me. You smell of lysol. Good-by, baby. Goodby. Many things. The major patted my shoulder. They tiptoed out. I found I was quite drunk but went to sleep.

The next day in the morning we left for Milan and arrived forty-eight hours later. It was a bad trip. We were sidetracked for a long time this side of Mestre and children came and peeked in. I got a little boy to go for a bottle of cognac but he came back and said he could only get grappa. I told him to get it and when it came I gave him the change and the man beside me and I got drunk and slept until past Vicenza where I woke up and was very sick on the floor. It did not matter because the man on that side had been very sick on the floor several times before. Afterward I thought I could not stand the thirst and in the yards outside of Verona I called to a soldier who was walking up and down beside the train and he got me a drink of water. I woke Georgetti, the other boy who was drunk, and offered him some water. He said to pour it on his shoulder and went back to sleep. The soldier would not take the penny I offered him and brought me a pulpy orange. I sucked on that and spit out the pith and watched the soldier pass up and down past a freight-car outside and after a while the train gave a jerk and started.

BOOK TWO

CHAPTER 13

WE GOT INTO Milan early in the morning and they unloaded us in the freight yard. An ambulance took me to the American hospital. Riding in the ambulance on a stretcher I could not tell what part of town we were passing through but when they unloaded the stretcher I saw a market-place and an open wine shop with a girl sweeping out. They were watering the street and it smelled of the early morning. They put the stretcher down and went in. The porter came out with them. He had gray mustaches, wore a doorman's cap and was in his shirt sleeves. The stretcher would not go into the elevator and they discussed whether it was better to lift me off the stretcher and go up in the elevator or carry the stretcher up the stairs. I listened to them discussing it. They decided on the elevator. They lifted me from the stretcher. "Go easy," I said. "Take it softly."

In the elevator we were crowded and as my legs bent the pain was very bad. "Straighten out the legs," I said.

"We can't, Signor Tenente. There isn't room." The man who said this had his arm around me and my arm was around his neck. His breath came in my face metallic with garlic and red wine.

"Be gentle," the other man said.

"Son of a bitch who isn't gentle!"

"Be gentle I say," the man with my feet repeated.

I saw the doors of the elevator closed, and the grill shut and the fourth-floor button pushed by the porter. The porter looked worried. The elevator rose slowly.

"Heavy?" I asked the man with the garlic.

"Nothing," he said. His face was sweating and he grunted. The elevator rose steadily and stopped. The man holding the feet opened the door and stepped out. We were on a balcony. There were several doors with brass knobs. The man carrying the feet pushed a button that rang a bell. We heard it inside the doors. No one came. Then the porter came up the stairs.

"Where are they?" the stretcher-bearers asked.

"I don't know," said the porter. "They sleep down stairs."

"Get somebody."

The porter rang the bell, then knocked on the door, then he opened the door and went in. When he came back there was an elderly woman wearing glasses with him. Her hair was loose and half-falling and she wore a nurse's dress.

"I can't understand," she said. "I can't understand Italian."

"I can speak English," I said. "They want to put me somewhere."

"None of the rooms are ready. There isn't any patient expected." She tucked at her hair and looked at me near-sightedly.

"Show them any room where they can put me."

"I don't know," she said. "There's no patient expected. I couldn't put you in just any room."

"Any room will do," I said. Then to the porter in Italian, "Find an empty room."

"They are all empty," said the porter. "You are the first patient." He held his cap in his hand and looked at the elderly nurse.

"For Christ's sweet sake take me to some room." The pain had gone on and on with the legs bent and I could feel it going in and out of the bone. The porter went in the door, followed by the gray-haired woman, then came hurrying back. "Follow me," he said. They carried me down a long hallway and into a room with drawn blinds. It smelled of new furniture. There was a bed and a big wardrobe with a mirror. They laid me down on the bed.

"I can't put on sheets," the woman said. "The sheets are locked up."

I did not speak to her. "There is money in my pocket," I said to the porter. "In the buttoned-down pocket." The porter took out the money. The two stretcher-bearers stood beside the bed holding their caps. "Give them five lire apiece and five lire for yourself. My papers are in the other pocket. You may give them to the nurse."

The stretcher-bearers saluted and said thank you. "Good-by," I said. "And many thanks." They saluted again and went out.

"Those papers," I said to the nurse, "describe my case and the treatment already given."

The woman picked them up and looked at them through her glasses. There were three papers and they were folded. "I don't know what to do," she said. "I can't read Italian. I can't do anything without the doctor's orders." She commenced to cry and put the papers in her apron pocket. "Are you an American?" she asked crying.

"Yes. Please put the papers on the table by the bed."

It was dim and cool in the room. As I lay on the bed I could see the big mirror on the other side of the room but could not see what it reflected. The porter stood by the bed. He had a nice face and was very kind.

"You can go," I said to him. "You can go too," I said to the nurse. "What is your name?"

"Mrs. Walker."

"You can go, Mrs. Walker. I think I will go to sleep."

I was alone in the room. It was cool and did not smell like a hospital. The mattress was firm and comfortable and I lay without moving, hardly breathing, happy in feeling the pain lessen. After a while I wanted a drink of water and found the bell on a cord by the bed and rang it but nobody came. I went to sleep.

When I woke I looked around. There was sunlight coming in through the shutters. I saw the big armoire, the bare walls, and two chairs. My legs in the dirty bandages, stuck straight out in the bed. I was careful not to move them. I was thirsty and I reached for the bell and pushed the button. I heard the door open and looked and it was a nurse. She looked young and pretty.

"Good-morning," I said.

"Good-morning," she said and came over to the bed. "We haven't been able to get the doctor. He's gone to Lake Como. No one knew there was a patient coming. What's wrong with you anyway?"

"I'm wounded. In the legs and feet and my head is hurt."

"What's your name?"

"Henry. Frederic Henry."

"I'll wash you up. But we can't do anything to the dressings until the doctor comes."

"Is Miss Barkley here?"

"No. There's no one by that name here."

"Who was the woman who cried when I came in?"

The nurse laughed. "That's Mrs. Walker. She was on night duty and she'd been asleep. She wasn't expecting any one."

While we were talking she was undressing me, and when I was undressed, except for the bandages, she washed me, very gently and smoothly. The washing felt very good. There was a bandage on my head but she washed all around the edge.

"Where were you wounded?"

"On the Isonze north of Plava."

"Where is that?"

"North of Gorizia."

I could see that none of the places meant anything to her.

"Do you have a lot of pain?"

"No. Not much now."

She put a thermometer in my mouth.

"The Italians put it under the arm," I said.

"Don't talk."

When she took the thermometer out she read it and then shook it.

"What's the temperature?"

"You're not supposed to know that."

"Tell me what it is."

"It's almost normal."

"I never have any fever. My legs are full of old iron too."

"What do you mean?"

"They're full of trench-mortar fragments, old screws and bedsprings and things."

She shook her head and smiled.

"If you had any foreign bodies in your legs they would set up an inflammation and you'd have fever."

"All right," I said. "We'll see what comes out."

She went out of the room and came back with the old nurse of the early morning. Together they made the bed with me in it. That was new to me and an admirable proceeding.

"Who is in charge here?"

"Miss Van Campen."

"How many nurses are there?"

"Just us two."

"Won't there be more?"

"Some more are coming."

"When will they get here?"

"I don't know. You ask a great many questions for a sick boy."

"I'm not sick," I said. "I'm wounded."

They had finished making the bed and I lay with a clean smooth sheet under me and another sheet over me. Mrs. Walker went out and came back with a pajama jacket. They put that on me and I felt very clean and dressed.

"You're awfully nice to me," I said. The nurse called Miss Gage giggled. "Could I have a drink of water?" I asked.

"Certainly. Then you can have breakfast."

"I don't want breakfast. Can I have the shutters opened please?"

The light had been dim in the room and when the shutters were opened it was bright sunlight and I looked out on a balcony and beyond were the tile roofs of houses and chimneys. I looked out over the tiled roofs and saw white clouds and the sky very blue.

"Don't you know when the other nurses are coming?"

"Why? Don't we take good care of you?"

"You're very nice."

"Would you like to use the bedpan?"

"I might try."

They helped me and held me up but it was not any use. Afterward I lay and looked out the open doors onto the balcony.

"When does the doctor come?"

"When he gets back. We've tried to telephone to Lake Como for him."

"Aren't there any other doctors?"

"He's the doctor for the hospital."

Miss Gage brought a pitcher of water and a glass. I drank three glasses and then they left me and I looked out the window a while and went back to sleep. I ate some lunch and in the afternoon Miss Van Campen, the superintendent, came up to see me. She did not like me and I did not like her. She was small and neatly suspicious and too good for her position. She asked many questions and seemed to think it was somewhat disgraceful that I was with the Italians.

"Can I have wine with the meals?" I asked her.

"Only if the doctor prescribes it."

"I can't have it until he comes?"

"Absolutely not."

"You plan on having him come eventually?"

"We've telephoned him at Lake Como."

She went out and Miss Gage came back.

"Why were you rude to Miss Van Campen?" she asked after she had done something for me very skilfully.

"I didn't mean to be. But she was snooty."

"She said you were domineering and rude."

"I wasn't. But what's the idea of a hospital without a doctor?"

"He's coming. They've telephoned for him to Lake Como."

"What does he do there? Swim?"

"No. He has a clinic there."

"Why don't they get another doctor?"

"Hush. Hush. Be a good boy and he'll come."

I sent for the porter and when he came I told him in Italian to get me a bottle of Cinzano at the wine shop, a fiasco of chianti and the evening papers. He went away and brought them wrapped in newspaper, unwrapped them and, when I asked him to, drew the corks and put the wine and vermouth under the bed. They left me alone and I lay in bed and read the papers awhile, the news from the front, and the list of dead officers with their decorations and then reached down and brought up the bottle of Cinzano and held it straight up on my stomach, the cool glass against my stomach, and took little drinks making rings on my stomach from holding the bottle there between drinks, and watched it get dark outside over the roofs of the town. The swallows circled around and I watched them and the night-hawks flying above the roofs and drank the Cinzano. Miss Gage brought up a glass with some eggnog in it. I lowered the vermouth bottle to the other side of the bed when she came in.

"Miss Van Campen had some sherry put in this," she said. "You shouldn't be rude to her. She's not young and this hospital is a big responsibility for her. Mrs. Walker's too old and she's no use to her."

"She's a splendid woman," I said. "Thank her very much."

"I'm going to bring your supper right away."

"That's all right," I said. "I'm not hungry."

When she brought the tray and put it on the bed table I thanked her and ate a little of the supper. Afterward it was dark outside and I could see the beams of the search-lights moving in the sky. I watched for a while and then went to sleep. I slept heavily except once I woke sweating and scared and then went back to sleep trying to stay outside of my dream. I woke for good long before it was light and heard roosters crowing and stayed on awake until it began to be light. I was tired and once it was really light I went back to sleep again.

CHAPTER 14

IT WAS BRIGHT sunlight in the room when I woke. I thought I was back at the front and stretched out in bed. My legs hurt me and I looked down at them still in the dirty bandages, and seeing them knew where I was. I reached up for the bell-cord and pushed the button. I heard it buzz down the hall and then some one coming on rubber soles along the hall. It was Miss Gage and she looked a little older in the bright sunlight and not so pretty.

"Good-morning," she said. "Did you have a good night?"

"Yes. Thanks very much," I said. "Can I have a barber?"

"I came in to see you and you were asleep with this in the bed with you."

She opened the armoire door and held up the vermouth bottle. It was nearly empty. "I put the other bottle from under the bed in there too," she said. "Why didn't you ask me for a glass?"

"I thought maybe you wouldn't let me have it."

"I'd have had some with you."

"You're a fine girl."

"It isn't good for you to drink alone," she said. "You mustn't do it."

"All right."

"Your friend Miss Barkley's come," she said.

"Really?"

"Yes. I don't like her."

"You will like her. She's awfully nice."

She shook her head. "I'm sure she's fine. Can you move just a little to this side? That's fine. I'll clean you up for breakfast." She washed me with a cloth and soap and warm water. "Hold your shoulder up," she said. "That's fine."

"Can I have the barber before breakfast?"

"I'll send the porter for him." She went out and came back. "He's gone for him," she said and dipped the cloth she held in the basin of water.

The barber came with the porter. He was a man of about fifty with an upturned mustache. Miss Gage was finished with me and went out and the barber lathered my face and shaved. He was very solemn and refrained from talking.

"What's the matter? Don't you know any news?" I asked.

"What news?"

"Any news. What's happened in the town?"

"It is time of war," he said. "The enemy's ears are everywhere."

I looked up at him. "Please hold your face still," he said and went on shaving. "I will tell nothing."

"What's the matter with you?" I asked.

"I am an Italian. I will not communicate with the enemy."

I let it go at that. If he was crazy, the sooner I could get out from under the razor the better. Once I tried to get a good look at him. "Beware," he said. "The razor is sharp."

I paid him when it was over and tipped him half a lira. He returned the coins.

"I will not. I am not at the front. But I am an Italian."

"Get the hell out of here."

"With your permission," he said and wrapped his razors in newspaper. He went out leaving the five copper coins on the table beside the bed. I rang the bell. Miss Gage came in. "Would you ask the porter to come please?"

"All right."

The porter came in. He was trying to keep from laughing.

"Is that barber crazy?"

"No, signorino. He made a mistake. He doesn't understand very well and he thought I said you were an Austrian officer."

"Oh," I said.

"Ho ho ho," the porter laughed. "He was funny. One move from you he said and he would have—" he drew his forefinger across his throat.

"Ho ho ho," he tried to keep from laughing. "When I tell him you were not an Austrian. Ho ho ho."

"Ho ho ho," I said bitterly. "How funny if he would cut my throat. Ho ho ho."

"No, signorino. No, no. He was so frightened of an Austrian. Ho ho ho."

"Ho ho ho," I said. "Get out of here."

He went out and I heard him laughing in the hall. I heard some one coming down the hallway. I looked toward the door. It was Catherine Barkley.

She came in the room and over to the bed.

"Hello, darling," she said. She looked fresh and young and very beautiful. I thought I had never seen any one so beautiful.

"Hello," I said. When I saw her I was in love with her. Everything turned over inside of me. She looked toward the door, saw there was no one, then she sat on the side of the bed and leaned over and kissed me. I pulled her down and kissed her and felt her heart beating.

"You sweet," I said. "Weren't you wonderful to come here?"

"It wasn't very hard. It may be hard to stay."

"You've got to stay," I said. "Oh, you're wonderful." I was crazy about her. I could not believe she was really there and held her tight to me.

"You mustn't," she said. "You're not well enough."

"Yes, I am. Come on."

"No. You're not strong enough."

"Yes. I am. Yes. Please."

"You do love me?"

"I really love you. I'm crazy about you. Come on please."

"Feel our hearts beating."

"I don't care about our hearts. I want you. I'm just mad about you."

"You really love me?"

"Don't keep on saying that. Come on. Please. Please, Catherine."

"All right but only for a minute."

"All right," I said. "Shut the door."

"You can't. You shouldn't."

"Come on. Don't talk. Please come on."

Catherine sat in a chair by the bed. The door was open into the hall. The wildness was gone and I felt finer than I had ever felt.

She asked, "Now do you believe I love you?"

"Oh, you're lovely," I said. "You've got to stay. They can't send you away. I'm crazy in love with you."

"We'll have to be awfully careful. That was just madness. We can't do that."

"We can at night."

"We'll have to be awfully careful. You'll have to be careful in front of other people."

"I will."

"You'll have to be. You're sweet. You do love me, don't you?"

"Don't say that again. You don't know what that does to me."

"I'll be careful then. I don't want to do anything more to you. I have to go now, darling, really."

"Come back right away."

"I'll come when I can."

"Good-by."

"Good-by, sweet."

She went out. God knows I had not wanted to fall in love with her. I had not wanted to fall in love with any one. But God knows I had and I lay on the bed in the room of the hospital in Milan and all sorts of things went through my head but I felt wonderful and finally Miss Gage came in.

"The doctor's coming," she said. "He telephoned from Lake Como."

"When does he get here?"

"He'll be here this afternoon."

CHAPTER 15

NOTHING HAPPENED until afternoon. The doctor was a thin quiet little man who seemed disturbed by the war. He took out a number of small steel splinters from my thighs with delicate and refined distaste. He used a local anæsthetic called something or other "snow," which froze the tissue and avoided pain until the probe, the scalpel or the forceps got below the frozen portion. The anæsthetized area was clearly defined by the patient and after a time the doctor's fragile delicacy was exhausted and he said it would be better to have an X-ray. Probing was unsatisfactory, he said.

The X-ray was taken at the Ospedale Maggiore and the doctor who did it was excitable, efficient and cheerful. It was arranged by holding up the shoulders, that the patient should see personally some of the larger foreign bodies through the machine. The plates were to be sent over. The doctor requested me to write in his pocket notebook, my name, and regiment and some sentiment. He declared that the foreign bodies were ugly, nasty, brutal. The Austrians were sons of bitches. How many had I killed? I had not killed any but I was anxious to please – and I said I had killed plenty. Miss Gage was with me and the doctor put his arm around her and said she was more beautiful than Cleopatra. Did she understand that? Cleopatra the former queen of Egypt. Yes, by God she was. We returned to the little hospital in the ambulance and after a while and much lifting I was upstairs and in bed again. The plates came that afternoon, the doctor had said by God he would have them that afternoon and he did. Catherine Barkley showed them to me. They were in red envelopes and she took them out of the envelopes and held them up to the light and we both looked.

"That's your right leg," she said, then put the plate back in the envelope. "This is your left."

"Put them away," I said, "and come over to the bed."

"I can't," she said. "I just brought them in for a second to show you."

She went out and I lay there. It was a hot afternoon and I was sick of lying in bed.

I sent the porter for the papers, all the papers he could get.

Before he came back three doctors came into the room. I have noticed that doctors who fail in the practice of medicine have a tendency to seek one another's company and aid in consultation. A doctor who cannot take out your appendix properly will recommend to you a doctor who will be unable to remove your tonsils with success. These were three such doctors.

"This is the young man," said the house doctor with the delicate hands.

"How do you do?" said the tall gaunt doctor with the beard. The third doctor, who carried the X-ray plates in their red envelopes, said nothing.

"Remove the dressings?" questioned the bearded doctor.

"Certainly. Remove the dressings, please, nurse," the house doctor said to Miss Gage. Miss Gage removed the dressings. I looked down at the legs. At the field hospital they had the look of not too freshly ground hamburger steak. Now they were crusted and the knee was swollen and discolored and the calf sunken but there was no pus.

"Very clean," said the house doctor. "Very clean and nice."

"Um," said the doctor with the beard. The third doctor looked over the house doctor's shoulder.

"Please move the knee," said the bearded doctor.

"I can't."

"Test the articulation?" the bearded doctor questioned. He had a stripe beside the three stars on his sleeve. That meant he was a first captain.

"Certainly," the house doctor said. Two of them took hold of my right leg very gingerly and bent it.

"That hurts," I said.

"Yes. Yes. A little further, doctor."

"That's enough. That's as far as it goes," I said.

"Partial articulation," said the first captain. He straightened up. "May I see the plates again, please, doctor?" The third doctor handed him one of the plates. "No. The left leg, please."

"That is the left leg, doctor."

"You are right. I was looking from a different angle." He returned the plate. The other plate he examined for some time. "You see, doctor?" he pointed to one of the foreign bodies which showed spherical and clear against the light. They examined the plate for some time.

"Only one thing I can say," the first captain with the beard said. "It is a question of time. Three months, six months probably."

"Certainly the synovial fluid must re-form."

"Certainly. It is a question of time. I could not conscientiously open a knee like that before the projectile was encysted."

"I agree with you, doctor."

"Six months for what?" I asked.

"Six months for the projectile to encyst before the knee can be opened safely."

"I don't believe it," I said.

"Do you want to keep your knee, young man?"

"No," I said.

"What?"

"I want it cut off," I said, "so I can wear a hook on it."

"What do you mean? A hook?"

"He is joking," said the house doctor. He patted my shoulder very delicately. "He wants to keep his knee. This is a very brave young man. He has been proposed for the silver medal of valor."

"All my felicitations," said the first captain. He shook my hand. "I can only say that to be on the safe side you should wait at least six months before opening such a knee. You are welcome of course to another opinion."

"Thank you very much," I said. "I value your opinion."

The first captain looked at his watch.

"We must go," he said. "All my best wishes."

"All my best wishes and many thanks," I said. I shook hands with the third doctor. "Capitano Varini—Tenente Enry," and they all three went out of the room.

"Miss Gage," I called. She came in. "Please ask the house doctor to come back a minute."

He came in holding his cap and stood by the bed. "Did you wish to see me?"

"Yes. I can't wait six months to be operated on. My God, doctor, did you ever stay in bed six months?"

"You won't be in bed all the time. You must first have the wounds exposed to the sun. Then afterward you can be on crutches."

"For six months and then have an operation?"

"That is the safe way. The foreign bodies must be allowed to encyst and the synovial fluid will re-form. Then it will be safe to open up the knee."

"Do you really think yourself I will have to wait that long?"

"That is the safe way."

"Who is that first captain?"

"He is a very excellent surgeon of Milan."

"He's a first captain, isn't he?"

"Yes, but he is an excellent surgeon."

"I don't want my leg fooled with by a first captain. If he was any good he would be made a major. I know what a first captain is, doctor."

"He is an excellent surgeon and I would rather have his judgment than any surgeon I know."

"Could another surgeon see it?"

"Certainly if you wish. But I would take Dr. Varella's opinion myself."

"Could you ask another surgeon to come and see it?"

"I will ask Valentini to come."

"Who is he?"

"He is a surgeon of the Ospedale Maggiore."

"Good. I appreciate it very much. You understand, doctor, I couldn't stay in bed six months."

"You would not be in bed. You would first take a sun cure. Then you could have light exercise. Then when it was encysted we would operate."

"But I can't wait six months."

The doctor spread his delicate fingers on the cap he held and smiled. "You are in such a hurry to get back to the front?"

"Why not?"

"It is very beautiful," he said. "You are a noble young man." He stooped over and kissed me very delicately on the forehead. "I will send for Valentini. Do not worry and excite yourself. Be a good boy."

"Will you have a drink?" I asked.

"No thank you. I never drink alcohol."

"Just have one." I rang for the porter to bring glasses.

"No. No thank you. They are waiting for me."

"Good-by," I said.

"Good-by."

Two hours later Dr. Valentini came into the room. He was in a great hurry and the points of his mustache stood straight up. He was a major, his face was tanned and he laughed all the time.

"How did you do it, this rotten thing?" he asked. "Let me see the plates. Yes. Yes. That's it. You look healthy as a goat. Who's the pretty girl? Is she your girl? I thought so. Isn't this a bloody war? How does that feel? You are a fine boy. I'll make you better than new. Does that hurt? You bet it hurts. How they love to hurt you, these doctors. What have they done for you so far? Can't that girl talk Italian? She should learn. What a lovely girl. I could teach her. I will be a patient here myself. No, but I will do all your maternity work free. Does she understand that? She will make you a fine boy. A fine blonde like she is. That's fine. That's all right. What a lovely girl. Ask her if she eats supper with me. No I won't take her away from you. Thank you. Thank you very much, Miss. That's all."

"That's all I want to know." He patted me on the shoulder. "Leave the dressings off."

"Will you have a drink, Dr. Valentini?"

"A drink? Certainly. I will have ten drinks. Where are they?"

"In the armoire. Miss Barkley will get the bottle."

"Cheery oh. Cheery oh to you, Miss. What a lovely girl. I will bring you better cognac than that." He wiped his mustache.

"When do you think it can be operated on?"

"To-morrow morning. Not before. Your stomach must be emptied. You must be washed out. I will see the old lady downstairs and leave instructions. Good-by. I see you to-morrow. I'll bring you better cognac than that. You are very comfortable here. Good-by. Until to-morrow. Get a good sleep. I'll see you early." He waved from the doorway, his mustaches went straight up, his brown face was smiling. There was a star in a box on his sleeve because he was a major.

CHAPTER 16

THAT NIGHT a bat flew into the room through the open door that led onto the balcony and through which we watched the night over the roofs of the town. It was dark in our room except for the small light of the night over the town and the bat was not frightened but hunted in the room as though he had been outside. We lay and watched him and I do not think he saw us because we lay so still. After he went out we saw a searchlight come on and watched the beam move across the sky and then go off and it was dark again. A breeze came in the night and we heard the men of the anti-aircraft gun on the next roof talking. It was cool and they were putting on their capes. I worried in the night about some one coming up but Catherine said they were all asleep. Once in the night we went to sleep and when I woke she was not there but I heard her coming along the hall and the door opened and she came back to the bed and said it was all right she had been downstairs and they were all asleep. She had been outside Miss Van Campen's door and heard her breathing in her sleep. She brought crackers and we ate them and drank some vermouth. We were very hungry but she said that would all have to be gotten out of me in the morning. I went to sleep again in the morning when it was light and when I was awake I found she was gone again. She came in looking fresh and lovely and sat on the bed and the sun rose while I had the thermometer in my mouth and we smelled the dew on the roofs and then the coffee of the men at the gun on the next roof.

"I wish we could go for a walk," Catherine said. "I'd wheel you if we had a chair."

"How would I get into the chair?"

"We'd do it."

"We could go out to the park and have breakfast outdoors." I looked out the open doorway.

"What we'll really do," she said, "is get you ready for your friend Dr. Valentini."

"I thought he was grand."

"I didn't like him as much as you did. But I imagine he's very good."

"Come back to bed, Catherine. Please," I said.

"I can't. Didn't we have a lovely night?"

"And can you be on night duty to-night?"

"I probably will. But you won't want me."

"Yes, I will."

"No, you won't. You've never been operated on. You don't know how you'll be."

"I'll be all right."

"You'll be sick and I won't be anything to you."

"Come back then now."

"No," she said. "I have to do the chart, darling, and fix you up."

"You don't really love me or you'd come back again."

"You're such a silly boy." She kissed me. "That's all right for the chart. Your temperature's always normal. You've such a lovely temperature."

"You've got a lovely everything."

"Oh no. You have the lovely temperature. I'm awfully proud of your temperature."

"Maybe all our children will have fine temperatures."

"Our children will probably have beastly temperatures."

"What do you have to do to get me ready for Valentini?"

"Not much. But quite unpleasant."

"I wish you didn't have to do it."

"I don't. I don't want any one else to touch you. I'm silly. I get furious if they touch you."

"Even Ferguson?"

"Especially Ferguson and Gage and the other, what's her name?"

"Walker?"

"That's it. They've too many nurses here now. There must be some more patients or they'll send us away. They have four nurses now."

"Perhaps there'll be some. They need that many nurses. It's quite a big hospital."

"I hope some will come. What would I do if they sent me away? They will unless there are more patients."

"I'd go too."

"Don't be silly. You can't go yet. But get well quickly, darling, and we will go somewhere."

"And then what?"

"Maybe the war will be over. It can't always go on."

"I'll get well," I said. "Valentini will fix me."

"He should with those mustaches. And, darling, when you're going under the ether just think about something else – not us. Because people get very blabby under an anæsthetic."

"What should I think about?"

"Anything. Anything but us. Think about your people. Or even any other girl."

"No."

"Say your prayers then. That ought to create a splendid impression."

"Maybe I won't talk."

"That's true. Often people don't talk."

"I won't talk."

"Don't brag, darling. Please don't brag. You're so sweet and you don't have to brag."

"I won't talk a word."

"Now you're bragging, darling. You know you don't need to brag. Just start your prayers or poetry or something when they tell you to breathe deeply. You'll be lovely that way and I'll be so proud of you. I'm very proud of you anyway. You have such a lovely temperature and you sleep like a little boy with your arm around the pillow and think it's me. Or is it some other girl? Some fine Italian girl?"

"It's you."

"Of course it's me. Oh I do love you and Valentini will make you a fine leg. I'm glad I don't have to watch it."

"And you'll be on night duty to-night."

"Yes. But you won't care."

"You wait and see."

"There, darling. Now you're all clean inside and out. Tell me. How many people have you ever loved?"

"Nobody."

"Not me even?"

"Yes, you."

"How many others really?"

"None."

"How many have you – how do you say it? – stayed with?"

"None."

"You're lying to me."

"Yes."

"It's all right. Keep right on lying to me. That's what I want you to do. Were they pretty?"

"I never stayed with any one."

"That's right. Were they very attractive?"

"I don't know anything about it."

"You're just mine. That's true and you've never belonged to any one else. But I don't care if you have. I'm not afraid of them. But don't tell me about them. When a man stays with a girl when does she say how much it costs?"

"I don't know."

"Of course not. Does she say she loves him? Tell me that. I want to know that."

"Yes. If he wants her to."

"Does he say he loves her? Tell me please. It's important."

"He does if he wants to."

"But you never did? Really?"

"No."

"Not really. Tell me the truth."

"No," I lied.

"You wouldn't," she said. "I knew you wouldn't. Oh, I love you, darling."

Outside the sun was up over the roofs and I could see the points of the cathedral with the sunlight on them. I was clean inside and outside and waiting for the doctor.

"And that's it?" Catherine said. "She says just what he wants her to?"

"Not always."

"But I will. I'll say just what you wish and I'll do what you wish and then you will never want any other girls, will you?" She looked at me very happily. "I'll do what you want and say what you want and then I'll be a great success, won't I?"

"Yes."

"What would you like me to do now that you're all ready?"

"Come to the bed again."

"All right. I'll come."

"Oh, darling, darling, darling," I said.

"You see," she said. "I do anything you want."

"You're so lovely."

"I'm afraid I'm not very good at it yet."

"You're lovely."

"I want what you want. There isn't any me any more. Just what you want."

"You sweet."

"I'm good. Aren't I good? You don't want any other girls, do you?"

"No."

"You see? I'm good. I do what you want."

CHAPTER 17

WHEN I WAS awake after the operation I had not been away. You do not go away. They only choke you. It is not like dying it is just a chemical choking so you do not feel, and afterward you might as well have been drunk except that when you throw up nothing comes but bile and you do not feel better afterward. I saw sandbags at the end of the bed. They were on pipes that came out of the cast. After a while I saw Miss Gage and she said, "How is it now?"

"Better," I said.

"He did a wonderful job on your knee."

"How long did it take?"

"Two hours and a half."

"Did I say anything silly?"

"Not a thing. Don't talk. Just be quiet."

I was sick and Catherine was right. It did not make any difference who was on night duty.

There were three other patients in the hospital now, a thin boy in the Red Cross from Georgia with malaria, a nice boy, also thin, from New York, with malaria and jaundice, and a fine boy who had tried to unscrew the fuse-cap from a combination shrapnel and high explosive shell for a souvenir. This was a shrapnel shell used by the Austrians in the mountains with a nose-cap which went on after the burst and exploded on contact.

Catherine Barkley was greatly liked by the nurses because she would do night duty indefinitely. She had quite a little work with the malaria people, the boy who had unscrewed the nose-cap was a friend of ours and never rang at night, unless it was necessary but between the times of working we were together. I loved her very much and she loved me. I slept in the daytime and we wrote notes during the day when we were awake and sent them by Ferguson. Ferguson was a fine girl. I never learned anything about her except that she had a brother in the Fifty-Second Division and a brother in Mesopotamia and she was very good to Catherine Barkley.

"Will you come to our wedding, Fergy?" I said to her once.

"You'll never get married."

"We will."

"No you won't."

"Why not?"

"You'll fight before you'll marry."

"We never fight."

"You've time yet."

"We don't fight."

"You'll die then. Fight or die. That's what people do. They don't marry."

I reached for her hand. "Don't take hold of me," she said. "I'm not crying. Maybe you'll be all right you two. But watch out you don't get her in trouble. You get her in trouble and I'll kill you."

"I won't get her in trouble."

"Well watch out then. I hope you'll be all right. You have a good time."

"We have a fine time."

"Don't fight then and don't get her into trouble."

"I won't."

"Mind you watch out. I don't want her with any of these war babies."

"You're a fine girl, Fergy."

"I'm not. Don't try to flatter me. How does your leg feel?"

"Fine."

"How is your head?" She touched the top of it with her fingers. It was sensitive like a foot that had gone to sleep. "It's never bothered me."

"A bump like that could make you crazy. It never bothers you?"

"No."

"You're a lucky young man. Have you the letter done? I'm going down."

"It's here," I said.

"You ought to ask her not to do night duty for a while. She's getting very tired."

"All right. I will."

"I want to do it but she won't let me. The others are glad to let her have it. You might give her just a little rest."

"All right."

"Miss Van Campen spoke about you sleeping all the forenoons."

"She would."

"It would be better if you let her stay off nights a little while."

"I want her to."

"You do not. But if you would make her I'd respect you for it."

"I'll make her."

"I don't believe it." She took the note and went out. I rang the bell and in a little while Miss Gage came in.

"What's the matter?"

"I just wanted to talk to you. Don't you think Miss Barkley ought to go off night duty for a while? She looks awfully tired. Why does she stay on so long?"

Miss Gage looked at me.

"I'm a friend of yours," she said. "You don't have to talk to me like that."

"What do you mean?"

"Don't be silly. Was that all you wanted?"

"Do you want a vermouth?"

"All right. Then I have to go." She got out the bottle from the armoire and brought a glass.

"You take the glass," I said. "I'll drink out of the bottle."

"Here's to you," said Miss Gage.

"What did Van Campen say about me sleeping late in the mornings?"

"She just jawed about it. She calls you our privileged patient."

"To hell with her."

"She isn't mean," Miss Gage said. "She's just old and cranky. She never liked you."

"No."

"Well, I do. And I'm your friend. Don't forget that."

"You're awfully damned nice."

"No. I know who you think is nice. But I'm your friend. How does your leg feel?"

"Fine."

"I'll bring some cold mineral water to pour over it. It must itch under the cast. It's hot outside."

"You're awful nice."

"Does it itch much?"

"No. It's fine."

"I'll fix those sandbags better." She leaned over. "I'm your friend."

"I know you are."

"No you don't. But you will some day."

Catherine Barkley took three nights off night duty and then she came back on again. It was as though we met again after each of us had been away on a long journey.

CHAPTER 18

WE HAD a lovely time that summer. When I could go out we rode in a carriage in the park. I remember the carriage, the horse going slowly, and up ahead the back of the driver with his varnished high hat, and Catherine Barkley sitting beside me. If we let our hands touch, just the side of my hand touching hers, we were excited. Afterward when I could get around on crutches we went to dinner at Biffi's or the Gran Italia and sat at the tables outside on the floor of the galleria. The waiters came in and out and there were people going by and candles with shades on the tablecloths and after we decided that we liked the Gran Italia best, George, the headwaiter, saved us a table. He was a fine waiter and we let him order the meal while we looked at the people, and the great galleria in the dusk, and each other. We drank dry white capri iced in a bucket; although we tried many of the other wines, fresa, barbera and the sweet white wines. They had no wine waiter because of the war and George would smile ashamedly when I asked about wines like fresa.

"If you imagine a country that makes a wine because it tastes like strawberries," he said.

"Why shouldn't it?" Catherine asked. "It sounds splendid."

"You try it, lady," said George, "if you want to. But let me bring a little bottle of margaux for the Tenente."

"I'll try it too, George."

"Sir, I can't recommend you to. It doesn't even taste like strawberries."

"It might," said Catherine. "It would be wonderful if it did."

"I'll bring it," said George, "and when the lady is satisfied I'll take it away."

It was not much of a wine. As he said, it did not even taste like strawberries. We went back to capri. One evening I was short of money and George loaned me a hundred lire. "That's all right, Tenente," he said. "I know how it is. I know how a man gets short. If you or the lady need money I've always got money."

After dinner we walked through the galleria, past the other restaurants and the shops with their steel shutters down, and stopped at the little place where they sold sandwiches; ham and lettuce sandwiches and anchovy sandwiches made of very tiny brown glazed rolls and only about as long as your finger. They were to eat in the night when we were hungry. Then we got into an open carriage outside the galleria in front of the cathedral and rode to the hospital. At the door of the hospital the porter came out to help with the crutches. I paid the driver, and then we rode upstairs in the elevator. Catherine got off at the lower floor where the nurses lived and I went on up and went down the hall on crutches to my room; sometimes I undressed and got into bed and sometimes I sat out on the balcony with my leg up on another chair and watched the swallows over the roofs and waited for Catherine. When she came upstairs it was as though she had been away on a long trip and I went along the hall with her on the crutches and carried the basins and waited outside the doors, or went in with her; it depending on whether they were friends of ours or not, and when she had done all there was to be done we sat out on the balcony outside my room. Afterward I went to bed and when they were all asleep and she was sure they would not call she came in. I loved to take her hair down and she sat on the bed and kept very still, except suddenly she would dip down to kiss me while I was doing it, and I would take out the pins and lay them on the sheet and it would be loose and I would watch her while she kept very still and then take out the last two pins and it would all come down and she would drop her head and we would both be inside of it, and it was the feeling of inside a tent or behind a falls.

She had wonderfully beautiful hair and I would lie sometimes and watch her twisting it up in the light that came in the open door and it shone even in the night as water shines sometimes just before it is really daylight. She had a lovely face and body and lovely smooth skin too. We would be lying together and I would touch her cheeks and her forehead and under her eyes and her chin and throat with the tips of my fingers and say, "Smooth as piano keys," and she would stroke my chin with her finger and say, "Smooth as emery paper and very hard on piano keys."

"Is it rough?"

"No, darling. I was just making fun of you."

It was lovely in the nights and if we could only touch each other we were happy. Besides all the big times we had many small ways of making love and we tried putting thoughts in the other one's head while we were in different rooms. It seemed to work sometimes but that was probably because we were thinking the same thing anyway.

We said to each other that we were married the first day she had come to the hospital and we counted months from our wedding day. I wanted to be really married but Catherine said that if we were they would send her away and if we merely started on the formalities they would watch her and would break us up. We would have to be married under Italian law and the formalities were terrific. I wanted us to be married really because I worried about having a child if I thought about it, but we pretended to ourselves we were married and did not worry much and I suppose I enjoyed not being married, really. I know one night we talked about it and Catherine said, "But, darling, they'd send me away."

"Maybe they wouldn't."

"They would. They'd send me home and then we would be apart until after the war."

"I'd come on leave."

"You couldn't get to Scotland and back on a leave. Besides, I won't leave you. What good would it do to marry now? We're really married. I couldn't be any more married."

"I only wanted to for you."

"There isn't any me. I'm you. Don't make up a separate me."

"I thought girls always wanted to be married."

"They do. But, darling, I am married. I'm married to you. Don't I make you a good wife?"

"You're a lovely wife."

"You see, darling, I had one experience of waiting to be married."

"I don't want to hear about it."

"You know I don't love any one but you. You shouldn't mind because some one else loved me."

"I do."

"You shouldn't be jealous of some one who's dead when you have everything."

"No, but I don't want to hear about it."

"Poor darling. And I know you've been with all kinds of girls and it doesn't matter to me."

"Couldn't we be married privately some way? Then if anything happened to me or if you had a child."

"There's no way to be married except by church or state. We are married privately. You see, darling, it would mean everything to me if I had any religion. But I haven't any religion."

"You gave me the Saint Anthony."

"That was for luck. Some one gave it to me."

"Then nothing worries you?"

"Only being sent away from you. You're my religion. You're all I've got."

"All right. But I'll marry you the day you say."

"Don't talk as though you had to make an honest woman of me, darling. I'm a very honest woman. You can't be ashamed of something if you're only happy and proud of it. Aren't you happy?"

"But you won't ever leave me for some one else."

"No, darling. I won't ever leave you for some one else. I suppose all sorts of dreadful things will happen to us. But you don't have to worry about that."

"I don't. But I love you so much and you did love some one else before."

"And what happened to him?"

"He died."

"Yes and if he hadn't I wouldn't have met you. I'm not unfaithful, darling. I've plenty of faults but I'm very faithful. You'll be sick of me I'll be so faithful."

"I'll have to go back to the front pretty soon."

"We won't think about that until you go. You see I'm happy, darling, and we have a lovely time. I haven't been happy for a long time and when I met you perhaps I was nearly crazy. Perhaps I was crazy. But now we're happy and we love each other. Do let's please just be happy. You are happy, aren't you? Is there anything I do you don't like? Can I do anything to please you? Would you like me to take down my hair? Do you want to play?"

"Yes and come to bed."

"All right. I'll go and see the patients first."

CHAPTER 19

THE SUMMER went that way. I do not remember much about the days, except that they were hot and that there were many victories in the papers. I was very healthy and my legs healed quickly so that it was not very long after I was first on crutches before I was through with them and walking with a cane. Then I started treatments at the Ospedale Maggiore for bending the knees, mechanical treatments, baking in a box of mirrors with violet rays, massage, and baths. I went over there afternoons and afterward stopped at the café and had a drink and read the papers. I did not roam around the town; but wanted to get home to the hospital from the café. All I wanted was to see Catherine. The rest of the time I was glad to kill. Mostly I slept in the mornings, and in the afternoons, sometimes, I went to the races, and late to the mechanotherapy treatments. Sometimes I stopped in at the Anglo-American Club and sat in a deep leather-cushioned chair in front of the window and read the magazines. They would not let us go out together when I was off crutches because it was unseemly for a nurse to be seen unchaperoned with a patient who did not look as though he needed attendance, so we were not together much in the afternoons. Although sometimes we could go out to dinner if Ferguson went along. Miss Van Campen had accepted the status that we were great friends because she got a great amount of work out of Catherine. She thought Catherine came from very good people and that prejudiced her in her favor finally. Miss Van Campen admired family very much and came from an excellent family herself. The hospital was quite busy, too, and that kept her occupied. It was a hot summer and I knew many people in Milan but always was anxious to get back home to the hospital as soon as the afternoon was over. At the front they were advancing on the Carso, they had taken Kuk across from Plava and were taking the Bainsizza plateau. The West front did not sound so good. It looked as though the war were going on for a long time. We were in the war now but I thought it would take a year to get any great amount of troops over and train them for combat. Next year would be a bad year, or a good year maybe. The Italians were using up an awful amount of men. I did not see how it could go on. Even if they took all the Bainsizza and Monte San Gabriele there were plenty of mountains beyond for the Austrians. I had seen them. All the highest mountains were beyond. On the Carso they were going forward but there were marshes and swamps down by the sea. Napoleon would have whipped the Austrians on the plains. He never would have fought them in the mountains. He would have let them come down and whipped them around Verona. Still nobody was whipping any one on the Western front. Perhaps wars weren't won any more. Maybe they went on forever. Maybe it was another Hundred Years' War. I put the paper back on the rack and left the club. I went down the steps carefully and walked up the Via Manzoni. Outside the Gran Hotel I met old Meyers and his wife getting out of a carriage. They were coming back from the races. She was a big-busted woman in black satin. He was short and old, with a white mustache and walked flat-footed with a cane.

"How do you do? How do you do?" She shook hands. "Hello," said Meyers.

"How were the races?"

"Fine. They were just lovely. I had three winners."

"How did you do?" I asked Meyers.

"All right. I had a winner."

"I never know how he does," Mrs. Meyers said. "He never tells me."

"I do all right," Meyers said. He was being cordial. "You ought to come out." While he talked you had the impression that he was not looking at you or that he mistook you for some one else.

"I will," I said.

"I'm coming up to the hospital to see you," Mrs. Meyers said. "I have some things for my boys. You're all my boys. You certainly are my dear boys."

"They'll be glad to see you."

"Those dear boys. You too. You're one of my boys."

"I have to get back," I said.

"You give my love to all those dear boys. I've got lots of things to bring. I've some fine marsala and cakes."

"Good-by," I said. "They'll be awfully glad to see you."

"Good-by," said Meyers. "You come around to the galleria. You know where my table is. We're all there every afternoon." I went on up the street. I wanted to buy something at the Cova to take to Catherine. Inside, at the Cova, I bought a box of chocolate and while the girl wrapped it up I walked over to the bar. There were a couple of British and some aviators. I had a martini alone, paid for it, picked up the box of chocolate at the outside counter and walked on home toward the hospital. Outside the little bar up the street from the Scala there were some people I knew, a vice-consul, two fellows who studied singing, and Ettore Moretti, an Italian from San Francisco who was in the Italian army. I had a drink with them. One of the singers was named Ralph Simmons, and he was singing under the name of Enrico DelCredo. I never knew how well he could sing but he was always on the point of something very big happening. He was fat and looked shopworn around the nose and mouth as though he had hayfever. He had come back from singing in Piacenza. He had sung Tosca and it had been wonderful.

"Of course you've never heard me sing," he said.

"When will you sing here?"

"I'll be at the Scala in the fall."

"I'll bet they throw the benches at you," Ettore said. "Did you hear how they threw the benches at him in Modena?"

"It's a damned lie."

"They threw the benches at him," Ettore said. "I was there. I threw six benches myself."

"You're just a wop from Frisco."

"He can't pronounce Italian," Ettore said. "Everywhere he goes they throw the benches at him."

"Piacenza's the toughest house to sing in the north of Italy," the other tenor said. "Believe me that's a tough little house to sing." This tenor's name was Edgar Saunders, and he sang under the name of Edouardo Giovanni.

"I'd like to be there to see them throw the benches at you," Ettore said. "You can't sing Italian."

"He's a nut," said Edgar Saunders. "All he knows how to say is throw benches."

"That's all they know how to do when you two sing," Ettore said. "Then when you go to America you'll tell about your triumphs at the Scala. They wouldn't let you get by the first note at the Scala."

"I'll sing at the Scala," Simmons said. "I'm going to sing Tosca in October."

"We'll go, won't we, Mac?" Ettore said to the vice-consul. "They'll need somebody to protect them."

"Maybe the American army will be there to protect them," the vice-consul said. "Do you want another drink, Simmons? You want a drink, Saunders?"

"All right," said Saunders.

"I hear you're going to get the silver medal," Ettore said to me. "What kind of citation you going to get?"

"I don't know. I don't know I'm going to get it."

"You're going to get it. Oh boy, the girls at the Cova will think you're fine then. They'll all think you killed two hundred Austrians or captured a whole trench by yourself. Believe me, I got to work for my decorations."

"How many have you got, Ettore?" asked the vice-consul.

"He's got everything," Simmons said. "He's the boy they're running the war for."

"I've got the bronze twice and three silver medals," said Ettore. "But the papers on only one have come through."

"What's the matter with the others?" asked Simmons.

"The action wasn't successful," said Ettore. "When the action isn't successful they hold up all the medals."

"How many times have you been wounded, Ettore?"

"Three times bad. I got three wound stripes. See?" He pulled his sleeve around. The stripes were parallel silver lines on a black background sewed to the cloth of the sleeve about eight inches below the shoulder.

"You got one too," Ettore said to me. "Believe me they're fine to have. I'd rather have them than medals. Believe me, boy, when you get three you've got something. You only get one for a wound that puts you three months in the hospital."

"Where were you wounded, Ettore?" asked the vice-consul.

Ettore pulled up his sleeve. "Here," he showed the deep smooth red scar. "Here on my leg. I can't show you that because I got puttees on; and in the foot. There's dead bone in my foot that stinks right now. Every morning I take new little pieces out and it stinks all the time."

"What hit you?" asked Simmons.

"A hand-grenade. One of those potato mashers. It just blew the whole side of my foot off. You know those potato mashers?" He turned to me.

"Sure."

"I saw the son of a bitch throw it," Ettore said. "It knocked me down and I thought I was dead all right but those damn potato mashers haven't got anything in them. I shot the son of a bitch with my rifle. I always carry a rifle so they can't tell I'm an officer."

"How did he look?" asked Simmons.

"That was the only one he had," Ettore said. "I don't know why he threw it. I guess he always wanted to throw one. He never saw any real fighting probably. I shot the son of a bitch all right."

"How did he look when you shot him?" Simmons asked.

"Hell, how should I know?" said Ettore. "I shot him in the belly. I was afraid I'd miss him if I shot him in the head."

"How long have you been an officer, Ettore?" I asked.

"Two years. I'm going to be a captain. How long have you been a lieutenant?"

"Going on three years."

"You can't be a captain because you don't know the Italian language well enough," Ettore said. "You can talk but you can't read and write well enough. You got to have an education to be a captain. Why don't you go in the American army?"

"Maybe I will."

"I wish to God I could. Oh, boy, how much does a captain get, Mac?"

"I don't know exactly. Around two hundred and fifty dollars, I think."

"Jesus Christ what I could do with two hundred and fifty dollars. You better get in the American army quick, Fred. See if you can't get me in."

"All right."

"I can command a company in Italian. I could learn it in English easy."

"You'd be a general," said Simmons.

"No, I don't know enough to be a general. A general's got to know a hell of a lot. You guys think there ain't anything to war. You ain't got brains enough to be a second-class corporal."

"Thank God I don't have to be," Simmons said.

"Maybe you will if they round up all you slackers. Oh, boy, I'd like to have you two in my platoon. Mac too. I'd make you my orderly, Mac."

"You're a great boy, Ettore," Mac said. "But I'm afraid you're a militarist."

"I'll be a colonel before the war's over," Ettore said.

"If they don't kill you."

"They won't kill me." He touched the stars at his collar with his thumb and forefinger. "See me do that? We always touch our stars if anybody mentions getting killed."

"Let's go, Sim," said Saunders standing up.

"All right."

"So long," I said. "I have to go too." It was a quarter to six by the clock inside the bar. "Ciaou, Ettore."

"Ciaou, Fred," said Ettore. "That's pretty fine you're going to get the silver medal."

"I don't know I'll get it."

"You'll get it all right, Fred. I heard you were going to get it all right."

"Well, so long," I said. "Keep out of trouble, Ettore."

"Don't worry about me. I don't drink and I don't run around. I'm no boozer and whorehound. I know what's good for me."

"So long," I said. "I'm glad you're going to be promoted captain."

"I don't have to wait to be promoted. I'm going to be a captain for merit of war. You know. Three stars with the crossed swords and crown above. That's me."

"Good luck."

"Good luck. When you going back to the front?"

"Pretty soon."

"Well, I'll see you around."

"So long."

"So long. Don't take any bad nickels."

I walked on down a back street that led to a cross-cut to the hospital. Ettore was twenty-three. He had been brought up by an uncle in San Francisco and was visiting his father and mother in Torino when war was declared. He had a sister, who had been sent to America with him at the same time to live with the uncle, who would graduate from normal school this year. He was a legitimate hero who bored every one he met. Catherine could not stand him.

"We have heroes too," she said. "But usually, darling, they're much quieter."

"I don't mind him."

"I wouldn't mind him if he wasn't so conceited and didn't bore me, and bore me, and bore me."

"He bores me."

"You're sweet to say so, darling. But you don't need to. You can picture him at the front and you know he's useful but he's so much the type of boy I don't care for."

"I know."

"You're awfully sweet to know, and I try and like him but he's a dreadful, dreadful boy really."

"He said this afternoon he was going to be a captain."

"I'm glad," said Catherine. "That should please him."

"Wouldn't you like me to have some more exalted rank?"

"No, darling. I only want you to have enough rank so that we're admitted to the better restaurants."

"That's just the rank I have."

"You have a splendid rank. I don't want you to have any more rank. It might go to your head. Oh, darling, I'm awfully glad you're not conceited. I'd have married you even if you were conceited but it's very restful to have a husband who's not conceited."

We were talking softly out on the balcony. The moon was supposed to rise but there was a mist over the town and it did not come up and in a little while it started to drizzle and we came in. Outside the mist turned to rain and in a little while it was raining hard and we heard it drumming on the roof. I got up and stood at the door to see if it was raining in but it wasn't, so I left the door open.

"Who else did you see?" Catherine asked.

"Mr. and Mrs. Meyers."

"They're a strange lot."

"He's supposed to have been in the penitentiary at home. They let him out to die."

"And he lived happily in Milan forever after."

"I don't know how happily."

"Happily enough after jail I should think."

"She's bringing some things here."

"She brings splendid things. Were you her dear boy?"

"One of them."

"You are all her dear boys," Catherine said. "She prefers the dear boys. Listen to it rain."

"It's raining hard."

"And you'll always love me, won't you?"

"Yes."

"And the rain won't make any difference?"

"No."

"That's good. Because I'm afraid of the rain."

"Why?" I was sleepy. Outside the rain was falling steadily.

"I don't know, darling. I've always been afraid of the rain."

"I like it."

"I like to walk in it. But it's very hard on loving."

"I'll love you always."

"I'll love you in the rain and in the snow and in the hail and – what else is there?"

"I don't know. I guess I'm sleepy."

"Go to sleep, darling, and I'll love you no matter how it is."

"You're not really afraid of the rain are you?"

"Not when I'm with you."

"Why are you afraid of it?"

"I don't know."

"Tell me."

"Don't make me."

"Tell me."

"No."

"Tell me."

"All right. I'm afraid of the rain because sometimes I see me dead in it."

"No."

"And sometimes I see you dead in it."

"That's more likely."

"No, it's not, darling. Because I can keep you safe. I know I can. But nobody can help themselves."

"Please stop it. I don't want you to get Scotch and crazy tonight. We won't be together much longer."

"No, but I am Scotch and crazy. But I'll stop it. It's all nonsense."

"Yes it's all nonsense."

"It's all nonsense. It's only nonsense. I'm not afraid of the rain. I'm not afraid of the rain. Oh, oh, God, I wish I wasn't." She was crying. I comforted her and she stopped crying. But outside it kept on raining.

CHAPTER 20

ONE DAY in the afternoon we went to the races. Ferguson went too and Crowell Rodgers, the boy who had been wounded in the eyes by the explosion of the shell nose-cap. The girls dressed to go after lunch while Crowell and I sat on the bed in his room and read the past performances of the horses and the predictions in the racing paper. Crowell's head was bandaged and he did not care much about these races but read the racing paper constantly and kept track of all the horses for something to do. He said the horses were a terrible lot but they were all the horses we had. Old Meyers liked him and gave him tips. Meyers won on nearly every race but disliked to give tips because it brought down the prices. The racing was very crooked. Men who had been ruled off the turf everywhere else were racing in Italy. Meyers' information was good but I hated to ask him because sometimes he did not answer, and always you could see it hurt him to tell you, but he felt obligated to tell us for some reason and he hated less to tell Crowell. Crowell's eyes had been hurt, one was hurt badly, and Meyers had trouble with his eyes and so he liked Crowell. Meyers never told his wife what horses he was playing and she won or lost, mostly lost, and talked all the time.

We four drove out to San Siro in an open carriage. It was a lovely day and we drove out through the park and out along the tramway and out of town where the road was dusty. There were villas with iron fences and big overgrown gardens and ditches with water flowing and green vegetable gardens with dust on the leaves. We could look across the plain and see farmhouses and the rich green farms with their irrigation ditches and the mountains to the north. There were many carriages going into the race track and the men at the gate let us in without cards because we were in uniform. We left the carriage, bought programmes, and walked across the infield and then across the smooth thick turf of the course to the paddock. The grandstands were old and made of wood and the betting booths were under the stands and in a row out near the stables. There was a crowd of soldiers along the fence in the infield. The paddock was fairly well filled with people and they were walking the horses around in a ring under the trees behind the grandstand. We saw people we knew and got chairs for Ferguson and Catherine and watched the horses.

They went around, one after the other, their heads down, the grooms leading them. One horse, a purplish black, Crowell swore was dyed that color. We watched him and it seemed possible. He had only come out just before the bell rang to saddle. We looked him up in the programme from the number on the groom's arm and it was listed a black gelding named Japalac. The race was for horses that had never won a race worth one thousand lire or more. Catherine was sure his color had been changed. Ferguson said she could not tell. I thought he looked suspicious. We all agreed we ought to back him and pooled one hundred lire. The odds sheets showed he would pay thirty-five to one. Crowell went over and bought the tickets while we watched the jockeys ride around once more and then go out under the trees to the track and gallop slowly up to the turn where the start was to be.

We went up in the grand-stand to watch the race. They had no elastic barrier at San Siro then and the starter lined up all the horses, they looked very small way up the track, and then sent them off with a crack of his long whip. They came past us with the black horse well in front and on the turn he was running away from the others. I watched them on the far side with the glasses and saw the jockey fighting to hold him in but he could not hold him and when they came around the turn and into the stretch the black horse was fifteen lengths ahead of the others. He went way on up and around the turn after the finish.

"Isn't it wonderful," Catherine said. "We'll have over three thousand lire. He must be a splendid horse."

"I hope his color doesn't run," Crowell said, "before they pay off."

"He was really a lovely horse," Catherine said. "I wonder if Mr. Meyers backed him."

"Did you have the winner?" I called to Meyers. He nodded.

"I didn't," Mrs. Meyers said. "Who did you children bet on?"

"Japalac."

"Really? He's thirty-five to one!"

"We liked his color."

"I didn't. I thought he looked seedy. They told me not to back him."

"He won't pay much," Meyers said.

"He's marked thirty-five to one in the quotes," I said.

"He won't pay much. At the last minute," Meyers said, "they put a lot of money on him."

"Who?"

"Kempton and the boys. You'll see. He won't pay two to one."

"Then we won't get three thousand lire," Catherine said. "I don't like this crooked racing!"

"We'll get two hundred lire."

"That's nothing. That doesn't do us any good. I thought we were going to get three thousand."

"It's crooked and disgusting," Ferguson said.

"Of course," said Catherine, "if it hadn't been crooked we'd never have backed him at all. But I would have liked the three thousand lire."

"Let's go down and get a drink and see what they pay," Crowell said. We went out to where they posted the numbers and the bell rang to pay off and they put up 18.50 after Japalac to win. That meant he paid less than even money on a ten-lira bet.

We went to the bar under the grand-stand and had a whiskey and soda apiece. We ran into a couple of Italians we knew and McAdams, the vice-consul, and they came up with us when we joined the girls. The Italians were full of manners and McAdams talked to Catherine while we went down to bet again. Mr. Meyers was standing near the pari-mutuel.

"Ask him what he played," I said to Crowell.

"What are you on, Mr. Meyers?" Crowell asked. Meyers took out his programme and pointed to the number five with his pencil.

"Do you mind if we play him too?" Crowell asked.

"Go ahead. Go ahead. But don't tell my wife I gave it to you."

"Will you have a drink?" I asked.

"No thanks. I never drink."

We put a hundred lire on number five to win and a hundred to place and then had another whiskey and soda apiece. I was feeling very good and we picked up a couple more Italians, who each had a drink with us, and went back to the girls. These Italians were also very mannered and matched manners with the two we had collected before. In a little while no one could sit down. I gave the tickets to Catherine.

"What horse is it?"

"I don't know. Mr. Meyers' choice."

"Don't you even know the name?"

"No. You can find it on the programme. Number five I think."

"You have touching faith," she said. The number five won but did not pay anything. Mr. Meyers was angry.

"You have to put up two hundred lire to make twenty," he said. "Twelve lire for ten. It's not worth it. My wife lost twenty lire."

"I'll go down with you," Catherine said to me. The Italians all stood up. We went downstairs and out to the paddock.

"Do you like this?" Catherine asked.

"Yes. I guess I do."

"It's all right, I suppose," she said. "But, darling, I can't stand to see so many people."

"We don't see many."

"No. But those Meyers and the man from the bank with his wife and daughters — —"

"He cashes my sight drafts," I said.

"Yes but some one else would if he didn't. Those last four boys were awful."

"We can stay out here and watch the race from the fence."

"That will be lovely. And, darling, let's back a horse we've never heard of and that Mr. Meyers won't be backing."

"All right."

We backed a horse named Light For Me that finished fourth in a field of five. We leaned on the fence and watched the horses go by, their hoofs thudding as they went past, and saw the mountains off in the distance and Milan beyond the trees and the fields.

"I feel so much cleaner," Catherine said. The horses were coming back, through the gate, wet and sweating, the jockeys quieting them and riding up to dismount under the trees.

"Wouldn't you like a drink? We could have one out here and see the horses."

"I'll get them," I said.

"The boy will bring them," Catherine said. She put her hand up and the boy came out from the Pagoda bar beside the stables. We sat down at a round iron table.

"Don't you like it better when we're alone?"

"Yes," I said.

"I felt very lonely when they were all there."

"It's grand here," I said.

"Yes. It's really a pretty course."

"It's nice."

"Don't let me spoil your fun, darling. I'll go back whenever you want."

"No," I said. "We'll stay here and have our drink. Then we'll go down and stand at the water jump for the steeplechase."

"You're awfully good to me," she said.

After we had been alone awhile we were glad to see the others again. We had a good time.

CHAPTER 21

IN SEPTEMBER the first cool nights came, then the days were cool and the leaves on the trees in the park began to turn color and we knew the summer was gone. The fighting at the front went very badly and they could not take San Gabriele. The fighting on the Bainsizza plateau was over and by the middle of the month the fighting for San Gabriele was about over too. They could not take it. Ettore was gone back to the front. The horses were gone to Rome and there was no more racing. Crowell had gone to Rome too, to be sent back to America. There were riots twice in the town against the war and bad rioting in Turin. A British major at the club told me the Italians had lost one hundred and fifty thousand men on the Bainsizza plateau and on San Gabriele. He said they had lost forty thousand on the Carso besides. We had a drink and he talked. He said the fighting was over for the year down here and that the Italians had bitten off more than they could chew. He said the offensive in Flanders was going to the bad. If they killed men as they did this fall the Allies would be cooked in another year. He said we were all cooked but we were all right as long as we did not know it. We were all cooked. The thing was not to recognize it. The last country to realize they were cooked would win the war. We had another drink. Was I on somebody's staff? No. He was. It was all balls. We were alone in the club sitting back in one of the big leather sofas. His boots were smoothly polished dull leather. They were beautiful boots. He said it was all balls. They thought only in divisions and man-power. They all squabbled about divisions and only killed them when they got them. They were all cooked. The Germans won the victories. By God they were soldiers. The old Hun was a soldier. But they were cooked too. We were all cooked. I asked about Russia. He said they were cooked already. I'd soon see they were cooked. Then the Austrians were cooked too. If they got some Hun divisions they could do it. Did he think they would attack this fall? Of course they would. The Italians were cooked. Everybody knew they were cooked. The old Hun would come down through the Trentino and cut the railway at Vicenza and then where would the Italians be? They tried that in 'sixteen, I said. Not with Germans. Yes, I said. But they probably wouldn't do that, he said. It was too simple. They'd try something complicated and get royally cooked. I had to go, I said. I had to get back to the hospital. "Good-by," he said. Then cheerily, "Every sort of luck!" There was a great contrast between his world pessimism and personal cheeriness.

I stopped at a barber shop and was shaved and went home to the hospital. My leg was as well as it would get for a long time. I had been up for examination three days before. There were still some treatments to take before my course at the Ospedale.

Maggiore was finished and I walked along the side street practicing not limping. An old man was cutting silhouettes under an arcade. I stopped to watch him. Two girls were posing and he cut their silhouettes together, snipping very fast and looking at them, his head on one side. The girls were giggling. He showed me the silhouettes before he pasted them on white paper and handed them to the girls.

"They're beautiful," he said. "How about you, Tenente?"

The girls went away looking at their silhouettes and laughing. They were nice-looking girls. One of them worked in the wine shop across from the hospital.

"All right," I said.

"Take your cap off."

"No. With it on."

"It will not be so beautiful," the old man said. "But," he brightened, "it will be more military."

He snipped away at the black paper, then separated the two thicknesses and pasted the profiles on a card and handed them to me.

"How much?"

"That's all right." He waved his hand. "I just made them for you."

"Please." I brought out some coppers. "For pleasure."

"No. I did them for a pleasure. Give them to your girl."

"Many thanks until we meet."

"Until I see thee."

I went on to the hospital. There were some letters, an official one, and some others. I was to have three weeks' convalescent leave and then return to the front. I read it over carefully. Well, that was that. The convalescent leave started October fourth when my course was finished. Three weeks was twenty-one days. That made October twenty-fifth. I told them I would not be in and went to the restaurant a little way up the street from the hospital for supper and read my letters and the

Corriere Della Sera at the table. There was a letter from my grandfather, containing family news, patriotic encouragement, a draft for two hundred dollars, and a few clippings; a dull letter from the priest at our mess, a letter from a man I knew who was flying with the French and had gotten in with a wild gang and was telling about it, and a note from Rinaldi asking me how long I was going to skulk in Milano and what was all the news? He wanted me to bring him phonograph records and enclosed a list. I drank a small bottle of chianti with the meal, had a coffee afterward with a glass of cognac, finished the paper, put my letters in my pocket, left the paper on the table with the tip and went out. In my room at the hospital I undressed, put on pajamas and a dressing-gown, pulled down the curtains on the door that opened onto the balcony and sitting up in bed read Boston papers from a pile Mrs. Meyers had left for her boys at the hospital. The Chicago White Sox were winning the American League pennant and the New York Giants were leading the National League. Babe Ruth was a pitcher then playing for Boston. The papers were dull, the news was local and stale, and the war news was all old. The American news was all training camps. I was glad I wasn't in a training camp. The baseball news was all I could read and I did not have the slightest interest in it. A number of papers together made it impossible to read with interest. It was not very timely but I read at it for a while. I wondered if America really got into the war, if they would close down the major leagues. They probably wouldn't. There was still racing in Milan and the war could not be much worse. They had stopped racing in France. That was where our horse Japalac came from. Catherine was not due on duty until nine o'clock. I heard her passing along the floor when she first came on duty and once saw her pass in the hall. She went to several other rooms and finally came into mine.

"I'm late, darling," she said. "There was a lot to do. How are you?"

I told her about my papers and the leave.

"That's lovely," she said. "Where do you want to go?"

"Nowhere. I want to stay here."

"That's silly. You pick a place to go and I'll come too."

"How will you work it?"

"I don't know. But I will."

"You're pretty wonderful."

"No I'm not. But life isn't hard to manage when you've nothing to lose."

"How do you mean?"

"Nothing. I was only thinking how small obstacles seemed that once were so big."

"I should think it might be hard to manage."

"No it won't, darling. If necessary I'll simply leave. But it won't come to that."

"Where should we go?"

"I don't care. Anywhere you want. Anywhere we don't know people."

"Don't you care where we go?"

"No. I'll like any place."

She seemed upset and taut.

"What's the matter, Catherine?"

"Nothing. Nothing's the matter."

"Yes there is."

"No nothing. Really nothing."

"I know there is. Tell me, darling. You can tell me."

"It's nothing."

"Tell me."

"I don't want to. I'm afraid I'll make you unhappy or worry you."

"No it won't."

"You're sure? It doesn't worry me but I'm afraid to worry you."

"It won't if it doesn't worry you."

"I don't want to tell."

"Tell it."

"Do I have to?"

"Yes."

"I'm going to have a baby, darling. It's almost three months along. You're not worried, are you? Please please don't. You mustn't worry."

"All right."

"Is it all right?"

"Of course."

"I did everything. I took everything but it didn't make any difference."

"I'm not worried."

"I couldn't help it, darling, and I haven't worried about it. You mustn't worry or feel badly."

"I only worry about you."

"That's it. That's what you mustn't do. People have babies all the time. Everybody has babies. It's a natural thing."

"You're pretty wonderful."

"No I'm not. But you mustn't mind, darling. I'll try and not make trouble for you. I know I've made trouble now. But haven't I been a good girl until now? You never knew it, did you?"

"No."

"It will all be like that. You simply mustn't worry. I can see you're worrying. Stop it. Stop it right away. Wouldn't you like a drink, darling? I know a drink always makes you feel cheerful."

"No. I feel cheerful. And you're pretty wonderful."

"No I'm not. But I'll fix everything to be together if you pick out a place for us to go. It ought to be lovely in October. We'll have a lovely time, darling, and I'll write you every day while you're at the front."

"Where will you be?"

"I don't know yet. But somewhere splendid. I'll look after all that."

We were quiet awhile and did not talk. Catherine was sitting on the bed and I was looking at her but we did not touch each other. We were apart as when some one comes into a room and people are self-conscious. She put out her hand and took mine.

"You aren't angry are you, darling?"

"No."

"And you don't feel trapped?"

"Maybe a little. But not by you."

"I didn't mean by me. You mustn't be stupid. I meant trapped at all."

"You always feel trapped biologically."

She went away a long way without stirring or removing her hand.

"'Always' isn't a pretty word."

"I'm sorry."

"It's all right. But you see I've never had a baby and I've never even loved any one. And I've tried to be the way you wanted and then you talk about 'always.'"

"I could cut off my tongue," I offered.

"Oh, darling!" she came back from wherever she had been. "You mustn't mind me." We were both together again and the self-consciousness was gone. "We really are the same one and we mustn't misunderstand on purpose."

"We won't."

"But people do. They love each other and they misunderstand on purpose and they fight and then suddenly they aren't the same one."

"We won't fight."

"We mustn't. Because there's only us two and in the world there's all the rest of them. If anything comes between us we're gone and then they have us."

"They won't get us," I said. "Because you're too brave. Nothing ever happens to the brave."

"They die of course."

"But only once."

"I don't know. Who said that?"

"The coward dies a thousand deaths, the brave but one?"

"Of course. Who said it?"

"I don't know."

"He was probably a coward," she said. "He knew a great deal about cowards but nothing about the brave. The brave dies perhaps two thousand deaths if he's intelligent. He simply doesn't mention them."

"I don't know. It's hard to see inside the head of the brave."

"Yes. That's how they keep that way."

"You're an authority."

"You're right, darling. That was deserved."

"You're brave."

"No," she said. "But I would like to be."

"I'm not," I said. "I know where I stand. I've been out long enough to know. I'm like a ball-player that bats two hundred and thirty and knows he's no better."

"What is a ball-player that bats two hundred and thirty? It's awfully impressive."

"It's not. It means a mediocre hitter in baseball."

"But still a hitter," she prodded me.

"I guess we're both conceited," I said. "But you are brave."

"No. But I hope to be."

"We're both brave," I said. "And I'm very brave when I've had a drink."

"We're splendid people," Catherine said. She went over to the armoire and brought me the cognac and a glass. "Have a drink, darling," she said. "You've been awfully good."

"I don't really want one."

"Take one."

"All right." I poured the water glass a third full of cognac and drank it off.

"That was very big," she said. "I know brandy is for heroes. But you shouldn't exaggerate."

"Where will we live after the war?"

"In an old people's home probably," she said. "For three years I looked forward very childishly to the war ending at Christmas. But now I look forward till when our son will be a lieutenant commander."

"Maybe he'll be a general."

"If it's an hundred years' war he'll have time to try both of the services."

"Don't you want a drink?"

"No. It always makes you happy, darling, and it only makes me dizzy."

"Didn't you ever drink brandy?"

"No, darling. I'm a very old-fashioned wife."

I reached down to the floor for the bottle and poured another drink.

"I'd better go to have a look at your compatriots," Catherine said. "Perhaps you'll read the papers until I come back."

"Do you have to go?"

"Now or later."

"All right. Now."

"I'll come back later."

"I'll have finished the papers," I said.

CHAPTER 22

IT TURNED cold that night and the next day it was raining. Coming home from the Ospedale Maggiore it rained very hard and I was wet when I came in. Up in my room the rain was coming down heavily outside on the balcony, and the wind blew it against the glass doors. I changed my clothing and drank some brandy but the brandy did not taste good. I felt sick in the night and in the morning after breakfast I was nauseated.

"There is no doubt about it," the house surgeon said. "Look at the whites of his eyes, Miss."

Miss Gage looked. They had me look in a glass. The whites of the eyes were yellow and it was the jaundice. I was sick for two weeks with it. For that reason we did not spend a convalescent leave together. We had planned to go to Pallanza on Lago Maggiore. It is nice there in the fall when the leaves turn. There are walks you can take and you can troll for trout in the lake. It would have been better than Stresa because there are fewer people at Pallanza. Stresa is so easy to get to from Milan that there are always people you know. There is a nice village at Pallanza and you can row out to the islands where the fishermen live and there is a restaurant on the biggest island. But we did not go.

One day while I was in bed with jaundice Miss Van Campen came in the room, opened the door into the armoire and saw the empty bottles there. I had sent a load of them down by the porter and I believe she must have seen them going out and come up to find some more. They were mostly vermouth bottles, marsala bottles, capri bottles, empty chianti flasks and a few cognac bottles. The porter had carried out the large bottles, those that had held vermouth, and the straw-covered chianti flasks, and left the brandy bottles for the last. It was the brandy bottles and a bottle shaped like a bear, which had held kümmel, that Miss Van Campen found. The bear-shaped bottle enraged her particularly. She held it up, the bear was sitting up on his haunches with his paws up, there was a cork in his glass head and a few sticky crystals at the bottom. I laughed.

"It is kümmel," I said. "The best kümmel comes in those bear-shaped bottles. It comes from Russia."

"Those are all brandy bottles, aren't they?" Miss Van Campen asked.

"I can't see them all," I said. "But they probably are."

"How long has this been going on?"

"I bought them and brought them in myself," I said. "I have had Italian officers visit me frequently and I have kept brandy to offer them."

"You haven't been drinking it yourself?" she said.

"I have also drunk it myself."

"Brandy," she said. "Eleven empty bottles of brandy and that bear liquid."

"Kümmel."

"I will send for some one to take them away. Those are all the empty bottles you have?"

"For the moment."

"And I was pitying you having jaundice. Pity is something that is wasted on you."

"Thank you."

"I suppose you can't be blamed for not wanting to go back to the front. But I should think you would try something more intelligent than producing jaundice with alcoholism."

"With what?"

"With alcoholism. You heard me say it." I did not say anything. "Unless you find something else I'm afraid you will have to go back to the front when you are through with your jaundice. I don't believe self-inflicted jaundice entitles you to a convalescent leave."

"You don't?"

"I do not."

"Have you ever had jaundice, Miss Van Campen?"

"No, but I have seen a great deal of it."

"You noticed how the patients enjoyed it?"

"I suppose it is better than the front."

"Miss Van Campen," I said, "did you ever know a man who tried to disable himself by kicking himself in the scrotum?"

Miss Van Campen ignored the actual question. She had to ignore it or leave the room. She was not ready to leave because she had disliked me for a long time and she was now cashing in.

"I have known many men to escape the front through self-inflicted wounds."

"That wasn't the question. I have seen self-inflicted wounds also. I asked you if you had ever known a man who had tried to disable himself by kicking himself in the scrotum. Because that is the nearest sensation to jaundice and it is a sensation that I believe few women have ever experienced. That was why I asked you if you had ever had the jaundice, Miss Van Campen, because—" Miss Van Campen left the room. Later Miss Gage came in.

"What did you say to Van Campen? She was furious."

"We were comparing sensations. I was going to suggest that she had never experienced childbirth — —"

"You're a fool," Gage said. "She's after your scalp."

"She has my scalp," I said. "She's lost me my leave and she might try and get me court-martialled. She's mean enough."

"She never liked you," Gage said. "What's it about?"

"She says I've drunk myself into jaundice so as not to go back to the front."

"Pooh," said Gage. "I'll swear you've never taken a drink. Everybody will swear you've never taken a drink."

"She found the bottles."

"I've told you a hundred times to clear out those bottles. Where are they now?"

"In the armoire."

"Have you a suitcase?"

"No. Put them in that rucksack."

Miss Gage packed the bottles in the rucksack. "I'll give them to the porter," she said. She started for the door.

"Just a minute," Miss Van Campen said. "I'll take those bottles." She had the porter with her. "Carry them, please," she said. "I want to show them to the doctor when I make my report."

She went down the hall. The porter carried the sack. He knew what was in it.

Nothing happened except that I lost my leave.

CHAPTER 23

THE NIGHT I was to return to the front I sent the porter down to hold a seat for me on the train when it came from Turin. The train was to leave at midnight. It was made up at Turin and reached Milan about half-past ten at night and lay in the station until time to leave. You had to be there when it came in, to get a seat. The porter took a friend with him, a machine-gunner on leave who worked in a tailor shop, and was sure that between them they could hold a place. I gave them money for platform tickets and had them take my baggage. There was a big rucksack and two musettes.

I said good-by at the hospital at about five o'clock and went out. The porter had my baggage in his lodge and I told him I would be at the station a little before midnight. His wife called me "Signorino" and cried. She wiped her eyes and shook hands and then cried again. I patted her on the back and she cried once more. She had done my mending and was a very short dumpy, happy-faced woman with white hair. When she cried her whole face went to pieces. I went down to the corner where there was a wine shop and waited inside looking out the window. It was dark outside and cold and misty. I paid for my coffee and grappa and I watched the people going by in the light from the window. I saw Catherine and knocked on the window. She looked, saw me and smiled, and I went out to meet her. She was wearing a dark blue cape and a soft felt hat. We walked along together, along the sidewalk past the wine shops, then across the market square and up the street and through the archway to the cathedral square. There were streetcar tracks and beyond them was the cathedral. It was white and wet in the mist. We crossed the tram tracks. On our left were the shops, their windows lighted, and the entrance to the galleria. There was a fog in the square and when we came close to the front of the cathedral it was very big and the stone was wet.

"Would you like to go in?"

"No," Catherine said. We walked along. There was a soldier standing with his girl in the shadow of one of the stone buttresses ahead of us and we passed them. They were standing tight up against the stone and he had put his cape around her.

"They're like us," I said.

"Nobody is like us," Catherine said. She did not mean it happily.

"I wish they had some place to go."

"It mightn't do them any good."

"I don't know. Everybody ought to have some place to go."

"They have the cathedral," Catherine said. We were past it now. We crossed the far end of the square and looked back at the cathedral. It was fine in the mist. We were standing in front of the leather goods shop. There were riding boots, a rucksack and ski boots in the window. Each article was set apart as an exhibit; the rucksack in the centre, the riding boots on one side and the ski boots on the other. The leather was dark and oiled smooth as a used saddle. The electric light made high lights on the dull oiled leather.

"We'll ski some time."

"In two months there will be ski-ing at Mürren," Catherine said.

"Let's go there."

"All right," she said. We went on past other windows and turned down a side street.

"I've never been this way."

"This is the way I go to the hospital," I said. It was a narrow street and we kept on the right-hand side. There were many people passing in the fog. There were shops and all the windows were lighted. We looked in a window at a pile of cheeses. I stopped in front of an armorer's shop.

"Come in a minute. I have to buy a gun."

"What sort of gun?"

"A pistol." We went in and I unbuttoned my belt and laid it with the empty holster on the counter. Two women were behind the counter. The women brought out several pistols.

"It must fit this," I said, opening the holster. It was a gray leather holster and I had bought it second-hand to wear in the town.

"Have they good pistols?" Catherine asked.

"They're all about the same. Can I try this one?" I asked the woman.

"I have no place now to shoot," she said. "But it is very good. You will not make a mistake with it."

I snapped it and pulled back the action. The spring was rather strong but it worked smoothly. I sighted it and snapped it again.

"It is used," the woman said. "It belonged to an officer who was an excellent shot."

"Did you sell it to him?"

"Yes."

"How did you get it back?"

"From his orderly."

"Maybe you have mine," I said. "How much is this?"

"Fifty lire. It is very cheap."

"All right. I want two extra clips and a box of cartridges."

She brought them from under the counter.

"Have you any need for a sword?" she asked. "I have some used swords very cheap."

"I'm going to the front," I said.

"Oh yes, then you won't need a sword," she said.

I paid for the cartridges and the pistol, filled the magazine and put it in place, put the pistol in my empty holster, filled the extra clips with cartridges and put them in the leather slots on the holster and then buckled on my belt. The pistol felt heavy on the belt. Still, I thought, it was better to have a regulation pistol. You could always get shells.

"Now we're fully armed," I said. "That was the one thing I had to remember to do. Some one got my other one going to the hospital."

"I hope it's a good pistol," Catherine said.

"Was there anything else?" the woman asked.

"I don't believe so."

"The pistol has a lanyard," she said.

"So I noticed." The woman wanted to sell something else.

"You don't need a whistle?"

"I don't believe so."

The woman said good-by and we went out onto the sidewalk. Catherine looked in the window. The woman looked out and bowed to us.

"What are those little mirrors set in wood for?"

"They're for attracting birds. They twirl them out in the field and larks see them and come out and the Italians shoot them."

"They are an ingenious people," Catherine said. "You don't shoot larks do you, darling, in America?"

"Not especially."

We crossed the street and started to walk up the other side.

"I feel better now," Catherine said. "I felt terrible when we started."

"We always feel good when we're together."

"We always will be together."

"Yes, except that I'm going away at midnight."

"Don't think about it, darling."

We walked on up the street. The fog made the lights yellow.

"Aren't you tired?" Catherine asked.

"How about you?"

"I'm all right. It's fun to walk."

"But let's not do it too long."

"No."

We turned down a side street where there were no lights and walked in the street. I stopped and kissed Catherine. While I kissed her I felt her hand on my shoulder. She had pulled my cape around her so it covered both of us. We were standing in the street against a high wall.

"Let's go some place," I said.

"Good," said Catherine. We walked on along the street until it came out onto a wider street that was beside a canal. On the other side was a brick wall and buildings. Ahead, down the street, I saw a streetcar cross a bridge.

"We can get a cab up at the bridge," I said. We stood on the bridge in the fog waiting for a carriage. Several streetcars passed, full of people going home. Then a carriage came along but there was some one in it. The fog was turning to rain.

"We could walk or take a tram," Catherine said.

"One will be along," I said. "They go by here."

"Here one comes," she said.

The driver stopped his horse and lowered the metal sign on his meter. The top of the carriage was up and there were drops of water on the driver's coat. His varnished hat was shining in the wet. We sat back in the seat together and the top of the carriage made it dark.

"Where did you tell him to go?"

"To the station. There's a hotel across from the station where we can go."

"We can go the way we are? Without luggage?"

"Yes," I said.

It was a long ride to the station up side streets in the rain.

"Won't we have dinner?" Catherine asked. "I'm afraid I'll be hungry."

"We'll have it in our room."

"I haven't anything to wear. I haven't even a night-gown."

"We'll get one," I said and called to the driver.

"Go to the Via Manzoni and up that." He nodded and turned off to the left at the next corner. On the big street Catherine watched for a shop.

"Here's a place," she said. I stopped the driver and Catherine got out, walked across the sidewalk and went inside. I sat back in the carriage and waited for her. It was raining and I could smell the wet street and the horse steaming in the rain. She came back with a package and got in and we drove on.

"I was very extravagant, darling," she said, "but it's a fine nightgown."

At the hotel I asked Catherine to wait in the carriage while I went in and spoke to the manager. There were plenty of rooms. Then I went out to the carriage, paid the driver, and Catherine and I walked in together. The small boy in buttons carried the package. The manager bowed us toward the elevator. There was much red plush and brass. The manager went up in the elevator with us.

"Monsieur and Madame wish dinner in their rooms?"

"Yes. Will you have the menu brought up?" I said.

"You wish something special for dinner. Some game or a soufflé?"

The elevator passed three floors with a click each time, then clicked and stopped.

"What have you as game?"

"I could get a pheasant, or a woodcock."

"A woodcock," I said. We walked down the corridor. The carpet was worn. There were many doors. The manager stopped and unlocked a door and opened it.

"Here you are. A lovely room."

The small boy in buttons put the package on the table in the centre of the room. The manager opened the curtains.

"It is foggy outside," he said. The room was furnished in red plush. There were many mirrors, two chairs and a large bed with a satin coverlet. A door led to the bathroom.

"I will send up the menu," the manager said. He bowed and went out.

I went to the window and looked out, then pulled a cord that shut the thick plush curtains. Catherine was sitting on the bed, looking at the cut glass chandelier. She had taken her hat off and her hair shone under the light. She saw herself in one of the mirrors and put her hands to her hair. I saw her in three other mirrors. She did not look happy. She let her cape fall on the bed.

"What's the matter, darling?"

"I never felt like a whore before," she said. I went over to the window and pulled the curtain aside and looked out. I had not thought it would be like this.

"You're not a whore."

"I know it, darling. But it isn't nice to feel like one." Her voice was dry and flat.

"This was the best hotel we could get in," I said. I looked out the window. Across the square were the lights of the station. There were carriages going by on the street and I saw the trees in the park. The lights from the hotel shone on the wet pavement. Oh, hell, I thought, do we have to argue now?

"Come over here please," Catherine said. The flatness was all gone out of her voice. "Come over, please. I'm a good girl again." I looked over at the bed. She was smiling.

I went over and sat on the bed beside her and kissed her.

"You're my good girl."

"I'm certainly yours," she said.

After we had eaten we felt fine, and then after, we felt very happy and in a little time the room felt like our own home. My room at the hospital had been our own home and this room was our home too in the same way.

Catherine wore my tunic over her shoulders while we ate. We were very hungry and the meal was good and we drank a bottle of Capri and a bottle of St. Estephe. I drank most of it but Catherine drank some and it made her feel splendid. For dinner we had a woodcock with soufflé potatoes and purée de marron, a salad, and zabaione for dessert.

"It's a fine room," Catherine said. "It's a lovely room. We should have stayed here all the time we've been in Milan."

"It's a funny room. But it's nice."

"Vice is a wonderful thing," Catherine said. "The people who go in for it seem to have good taste about it. The red plush is really fine. It's just the thing. And the mirrors are very attractive."

"You're a lovely girl."

"I don't know how a room like this would be for waking up in the morning. But it's really a splendid room." I poured another glass of St. Estephe.

"I wish we could do something really sinful," Catherine said. "Everything we do seems so innocent and simple. I can't believe we do anything wrong."

"You're a grand girl."

"I only feel hungry. I get terribly hungry."

"You're a fine simple girl," I said.

"I am a simple girl. No one ever understood it except you."

"Once when I first met you I spent an afternoon thinking how we would go to the Hotel Cavour together and how it would be."

"That was awfully cheeky of you. This isn't the Cavour is it?"

"No. They wouldn't have taken us in there."

"They'll take us in some time. But that's how we differ, darling. I never thought about anything."

"Didn't you ever at all?"

"A little," she said.

"Oh you're a lovely girl."

I poured another glass of wine.

"I'm a very simple girl," Catherine said.

"I didn't think so at first. I thought you were a crazy girl."

"I was a little crazy. But I wasn't crazy in any complicated manner. I didn't confuse you did I, darling?"

"Wine is a grand thing," I said. "It makes you forget all the bad."

"It's lovely," said Catherine. "But it's given my father gout very badly."

"Have you a father?"

"Yes," said Catherine. "He has gout. You won't ever have to meet him. Haven't you a father?"

"No," I said. "A step-father."

"Will I like him?"

"You won't have to meet him."

"We have such a fine time," Catherine said. "I don't take any interest in anything else any more. I'm so very happy married to you."

The waiter came and took away the things. After a while we were very still and we could hear the rain. Down below on the street a motor car honked.

"'But at my back I always hear Time's wingèd chariot hurrying near,'" I said.

"I know that poem," Catherine said. "It's by Marvell. But it's about a girl who wouldn't live with a man."

My head felt very clear and cold and I wanted to talk facts.

"Where will you have the baby?"

"I don't know. The best place I can find."

"How will you arrange it?"

"The best way I can. Don't worry, darling. We may have several babies before the war is over."

"It's nearly time to go."

"I know. You can make it time if you want."

"No."

"Then don't worry, darling. You were fine until now and now you're worrying."

"I won't. How often will you write?"

"Every day. Do they read your letters?"

"They can't read English enough to hurt any."

"I'll make them very confusing," Catherine said.

"But not too confusing."

"I'll just make them a little confusing."

"I'm afraid we have to start to go."

"All right, darling."

"I hate to leave our fine house."

"So do I."

"But we have to go."

"All right. But we're never settled in our home very long."

"We will be."

"I'll have a fine home for you when you come back."

"Maybe I'll be back right away."

"Perhaps you'll be hurt just a little in the foot."

"Or the lobe of the ear."

"No I want your ears the way they are."

"And not my feet?"

"Your feet have been hit already."

"We have to go, darling. Really."

"All right. You go first."

CHAPTER 24

WE WALKED down the stairs instead of taking the elevator. The carpet on the stairs was worn. I had paid for the dinner when it came up and the waiter, who had brought it, was sitting on a chair near the door. He jumped up and bowed and I went with him into the side room and paid the bill for the room. The manager had remembered me as a friend and refused payment in advance but when he retired he had remembered to have the waiter stationed at the door so that I should not get out without paying. I suppose that had happened; even with his friends. One had so many friends in a war.

I asked the waiter to get us a carriage and he took Catherine's package that I was carrying and went out with an umbrella. Outside through the window we saw him crossing the street in the rain. We stood in the side room and looked out the window.

"How do you feel, Cat?"

"Sleepy."

"I feel hollow and hungry."

"Have you anything to eat?"

"Yes, in my musette."

I saw the carriage coming. It stopped, the horse's head hanging in the rain, and the waiter stepped out, opened his umbrella, and came toward the hotel. We met him at the door and walked out under the umbrella down the wet walk to the carriage at the curb. Water was running in the gutter.

"There is your package on the seat," the waiter said. He stood with the umbrella until we were in and I had tipped him.

"Many thanks. Pleasant journey," he said. The coachman lifted the reins and the horse started. The waiter turned away under the umbrella and went toward the hotel. We drove down the street and turned to the left, then came around to the right in front of the station. There were two carabinieri standing under the light just out of the rain. The light shone on their hats. The rain was clear and transparent against the light from the station. A porter came out from under the shelter of the station, his shoulders up against the rain.

"No," I said. "Thanks. I don't need thee."

He went back under the shelter of the archway. I turned to Catherine. Her face was in the shadow from the hood of the carriage.

"We might as well say good-by."

"I can't go in?"

"No."

"Good-by, Cat."

"Will you tell him the hospital?"

"Yes."

I told the driver the address to drive to. He nodded.

"Good-by," I said. "Take good care of yourself and young Catherine."

"Good-by, darling."

"Good-by," I said. I stepped out into the rain and the carriage started. Catherine leaned out and I saw her face in the light. She smiled and waved. The carriage went up the street, Catherine pointed in toward the archway. I looked, there were only the two carabinieri and the archway. I realized she meant for me to get in out of the rain. I went in and stood and watched the carriage turn the corner. Then I started through the station and down the runway to the train.

The porter was on the platform looking for me. I followed him into the train, crowding past people and along the aisle and in through a door to where the machine-gunner sat in the corner of a full compartment. My rucksack and musettes were above his head on the luggage rack. There were many men standing in the corridor and the men in the compartment all looked at us when we came in. There were not enough places in the train and every one was hostile. The machine-gunner stood up for me to sit down. Some one tapped me on the shoulder. I looked around. It was a very tall gaunt captain of artillery with a red scar along his jaw. He had looked through the glass on the corridor and then come in.

"What do you say?" I asked. I had turned and faced him. He was taller than I and his face was very thin under the shadow of his cap-visor and the scar was new and shiny. Every one in the compartment was looking at me.

"You can't do that," he said. "You can't have a soldier save you a place."

"I have done it."

He swallowed and I saw his Adam's apple go up and then down. The machine-gunner stood in front of the place. Other men looked in through the glass. No one in the compartment said anything.

"You have no right to do that. I was here two hours before you came."

"What do you want?"

"The seat."

"So do I."

I watched his face and could feel the whole compartment against me. I did not blame them. He was in the right. But I wanted the seat. Still no one said anything.

"Oh, hell," I thought.

"Sit down, Signor Capitano," I said. The machine-gunner moved out of the way and the tall captain sat down. He looked at me. His face seemed hurt. But he had the seat. "Get my things," I said to the machine-gunner. We went out in the corridor. The train was full and I knew there was no chance of a place. I gave the porter and the machine-gunner ten lire apiece. They went down the corridor and outside on the platform looking in the windows but there were no places.

"Maybe some will get off at Brescia," the porter said.

"More will get on at Brescia," said the machine-gunner. I said good-by to them and we shook hands and they left. They both felt badly. Inside the train we were all standing in the corridor when the train started. I watched the lights of the station and the yards as we went out. It was still raining and soon the windows were wet and you could not see out. Later I slept on the floor of the corridor; first putting my pocket-book with my money and papers in it inside my shirt and trousers so that it was inside the leg of my breeches. I slept all night, waking at Brescia and Verona when more men got on the train, but going back to sleep at once. I had my head on one of the musettes and my arms around the other and I could feel the pack and they could all walk over me if they wouldn't step on me. Men were sleeping on the floor all down the corridor. Others stood holding on to the window rods or leaning against the doors. That train was always crowded.

BOOK THREE

CHAPTER 25

NOW IN THE FALL the trees were all bare and the roads were muddy. I rode to Gorizia from Udine on a camion. We passed other camions on the road and I looked at the country. The mulberry trees were bare and the fields were brown. There were wet dead leaves on the road from the rows of bare trees and men were working on the road, tamping stone in the ruts from piles of crushed stone along the side of the road between the trees. We saw the town with a mist over it that cut off the mountains. We crossed the river and I saw that it was running high. It had been raining in the mountains. We came into the town past the factories and then the houses and villas and I saw that many more houses had been hit. On a narrow street we passed a British Red Cross ambulance. The driver wore a cap and his face was thin and very tanned. I did not know him. I got down from the camion in the big square in front of the Town Major's house, the driver handed down my rucksack and I put it on and swung on the two musettes and walked to our villa. It did not feel like a homecoming.

I walked down the damp gravel driveway looking at the villa through the trees. The windows were all shut but the door was open. I went in and found the major sitting at a table in the bare room with maps and typed sheets of paper on the wall.

"Hello," he said. "How are you?" He looked older and drier.

"I'm good," I said. "How is everything?"

"It's all over," he said. "Take off your kit and sit down." I put my pack and the two musettes on the floor and my cap on the pack. I brought the other chair over from the wall and sat down by the desk.

"It's been a bad summer," the major said. "Are you strong now?"

"Yes."

"Did you ever get the decorations?"

"Yes. I got them fine. Thank you very much."

"Let's see them."

I opened my cape so he could see the two ribbons.

"Did you get the boxes with the medals?"

"No. Just the papers."

"The boxes will come later. That takes more time."

"What do you want me to do?"

"The cars are all away. There are six up north at Caporetto. You know Caporetto?"

"Yes," I said. I remembered it as a little white town with a campanile in a valley. It was a clean little town and there was a fine fountain in the square.

"They are working from there. There are many sick now. The fighting is over."

"Where are the others?"

"There are two up in the mountains and four still on the Bainsizza. The other two ambulance sections are in the Carso with the third army."

"What do you wish me to do?"

"You can go and take over the four cars on the Bainsizza if you like. Gino has been up there a long time. You haven't seen it up there, have you?"

"No."

"It was very bad. We lost three cars."

"I heard about it."

"Yes, Rinaldi wrote you."

"Where is Rinaldi?"

"He is here at the hospital. He has had a summer and fall of it."

"I believe it."

"It has been bad," the major said. "You couldn't believe how bad it's been. I've often thought you were lucky to be hit when you were."

"I know I was."

"Next year will be worse," the major said. "Perhaps they will attack now. They say they are to attack but I can't believe it. It is too late. You saw the river?"

"Yes. It's high already."

"I don't believe they will attack now that the rains have started. We will have the snow soon. What about your countrymen? Will there be other Americans besides yourself?"

"They are training an army of ten million."

"I hope we get some of them. But the French will hog them all. We'll never get any down here. All right. You stay here to-night and go out to-morrow with the little car and send Gino back. I'll send somebody with you that knows the road. Gino will tell you everything. They are shelling quite a little still but it is all over. You will want to see the Bainsizza."

"I'm glad to see it. I am glad to be back with you again, Signor Maggiore."

He smiled. "You are very good to say so. I am very tired of this war. If I was away

I do not believe I would come back."

"Is it so bad?"

"Yes. It is so bad and worse. Go get cleaned up and find your friend Rinaldi."

I went out and carried my bags up the stairs. Rinaldi was not in the room but his things were there and I sat down on the bed and unwrapped my puttees and took the shoe off my right foot. Then I lay back on the bed. I was tired and my right foot hurt. It seemed silly to lie on the bed with one shoe off, so I sat up and unlaced the other shoe and dropped it on the floor, then lay back on the blanket again. The room was stuffy with the window closed but I was too tired to get up and open it. I saw my things were all in one corner of the room. Outside it was getting dark. I lay on the bed and thought about Catherine and waited for Rinaldi. I was going to try not to think about Catherine except at night before I went to sleep. But now I was tired and there was nothing to do, so I lay and thought about her. I was thinking about her when Rinaldi came in. He looked just the same. Perhaps he was a little thinner.

"Well, baby," he said. I sat up on the bed. He came over, sat down and put his arm around me. "Good old baby." He whacked me on the back and I held both his arms.

"Old baby," he said. "Let me see your knee."

"I'll have to take off my pants."

"Take off your pants, baby. We're all friends here. I want to see what kind of a job they did." I stood up, took off the breeches and pulled off the knee-brace. Rinaldi sat on the floor and bent the knee gently back and forth. He ran his finger along the scar; put his thumbs together over the kneecap and rocked the knee gently with his fingers.

"Is that all the articulation you have?"

"Yes."

"It's a crime to send you back. They ought to get complete articulation."

"It's a lot better than it was. It was stiff as a board."

Rinaldi bent it more. I watched his hands. He had fine surgeon's hands. I looked at the top of his head, his hair shiny and parted smoothly. He bent the knee too far.

"Ouch!" I said.

"You ought to have more treatment on it with the machines," Rinaldi said.

"It's better than it was."

"I see that, baby. This is something I know more about than you." He stood up and sat down on the bed. "The knee itself is a good job." He was through with the knee. "Tell me all about everything."

"There's nothing to tell," I said. "I've led a quiet life."

"You act like a married man," he said. "What's the matter with you?"

"Nothing," I said. "What's the matter with you?"

"This war is killing me," Rinaldi said, "I am very depressed by it." He folded his hands over his knee.

"Oh," I said.

"What's the matter? Can't I even have human impulses?"

"No. I can see you've been having a fine time. Tell me."

"All summer and all fall I've operated. I work all the time. I do everybody's work. All the hard ones they leave to me. By God, baby, I am becoming a lovely surgeon."

"That sounds better."

"I never think. No, by God, I don't think; I operate."

"That's right."

"But now, baby, it's all over. I don't operate now and I feel like hell. This is a terrible war, baby. You believe me when I say it. Now you cheer me up. Did you bring the phonograph records?"

"Yes."

They were wrapped in paper in a cardboard box in my rucksack. I was too tired to get them out.

"Don't you feel good yourself, baby?"

"I feel like hell."

"This war is terrible," Rinaldi said. "Come on. We'll both get drunk and be cheerful. Then we'll go get the ashes dragged. Then we'll feel fine."

"I've had the jaundice," I said, "and I can't get drunk."

"Oh, baby, how you've come back to me. You come back serious and with a liver. I tell you this war is a bad thing. Why did we make it anyway."

"We'll have a drink. I don't want to get drunk but we'll have a drink."

Rinaldi went across the room to the washstand and brought back two glasses and a bottle of cognac.

"It's Austrian cognac," he said. "Seven stars. It's all they captured on San Gabriele."

"Were you up there?"

"No. I haven't been anywhere. I've been here all the time operating. Look, baby, this is your old tooth-brushing glass. I kept it all the time to remind me of you."

"To remind you to brush your teeth."

"No. I have my own too. I kept this to remind me of you trying to brush away the Villa Rossa from your teeth in the morning, swearing and eating aspirin and cursing harlots. Every time I see that glass I think of you trying to clean your conscience with a toothbrush." He came over to the bed. "Kiss me once and tell me you're not serious."

"I never kiss you. You're an ape."

"I know, you are the fine good Anglo-Saxon boy. I know. You are the remorse boy, I know. I will wait till I see the Anglo-Saxon brushing away harlotry with a toothbrush."

"Put some cognac in the glass."

We touched glasses and drank. Rinaldi laughed at me.

"I will get you drunk and take out your liver and put you in a good Italian liver and make you a man again."

I held the glass for some more cognac. It was dark outside now. Holding the glass of cognac, I went over and opened the window. The rain had stopped falling. It was colder outside and there was a mist in the trees.

"Don't throw the cognac out the window," Rinaldi said. "If you can't drink it give it to me."

"Go something yourself," I said. I was glad to see Rinaldi again. He had spent two years teasing me and I had always liked it. We understood each other very well.

"Are you married?" he asked from the bed. I was standing against the wall by the window.

"Not yet."

"Are you in love?"

"Yes."

"With that English girl?"

"Yes."

"Poor baby. Is she good to you?"

"Of course."

"I mean is she good to you practically speaking?"

"Shut up."

"I will. You will see I am a man of extreme delicacy. Does she — ?"

"Rinin," I said. "Please shut up. If you want to be my friend, shut up."

"I don't want to be your friend, baby. I am your friend."

"Then shut up."

"All right."

I went over to the bed and sat down beside Rinaldi. He was holding his glass and looking at the floor.

"You see how it is, Rinin?"

"Oh, yes. All my life I encounter sacred subjects. But very few with you. I suppose you must have them too." He looked at the floor.

"You haven't any?"

"No."

"Not any?"

"No."

"I can say this about your mother and that about your sister?"

"And that about your sister," Rinaldi said swiftly. We both laughed.

"The old superman," I said.

"I am jealous maybe," Rinaldi said.

"No, you're not."

"I don't mean like that. I mean something else. Have you any married friends?"

"Yes," I said.

"I haven't," Rinaldi said. "Not if they love each other."

"Why not?"

"They don't like me."

"Why not?"

"I am the snake. I am the snake of reason."

"You're getting it mixed. The apple was reason."

"No, it was the snake." He was more cheerful.

"You are better when you don't think so deeply," I said.

"I love you, baby," he said. "You puncture me when I become a great Italian thinker. But I know many things I can't say. I know more than you."

"Yes. You do."

"But you will have a better time. Even with remorse you will have a better time."

"I don't think so."

"Oh, yes. That is true. Already I am only happy when I am working." He looked at the floor again.

"You'll get over that."

"No. I only like two other things; one is bad for my work and the other is over in half an hour or fifteen minutes. Sometimes less."

"Sometimes a good deal less."

"Perhaps I have improved, baby. You do not know. But there are only the two things and my work."

"You'll get other things."

"No. We never get anything. We are born with all we have and we never learn. We never get anything new. We all start complete. You should be glad not to be a Latin."

"There's no such thing as a Latin. That is 'Latin' thinking. You are so proud of your defects." Rinaldi looked up and laughed.

"We'll stop, baby. I am tired from thinking so much." He had looked tired when he came in. "It's nearly time to eat. I'm glad you're back. You are my best friend and my war brother."

"When do the war brothers eat?" I asked.

"Right away. We'll drink once more for your liver's sake."

"Like Saint Paul."

"You are inaccurate. That was wine and the stomach. Take a little wine for your stomach's sake."

"Whatever you have in the bottle," I said. "For any sake you mention."

"To your girl," Rinaldi said. He held out his glass.

"All right."

"I'll never say a dirty thing about her."

"Don't strain yourself."

He drank off the cognac. "I am pure," he said. "I am like you, baby. I will get an English girl too. As a matter of fact I knew your girl first but she was a little tall for me. A tall girl for a sister," he quoted.

"You have a lovely pure mind," I said.

"Haven't I? That's why they call me Rinaldo Purissimo."

"Rinaldo Sporchissimo."

"Come on, baby, we'll go down to eat while my mind is still pure."

I washed, combed my hair and we went down the stairs. Rinaldi was a little drunk. In the room where we ate, the meal was not quite ready.

"I'll go get the bottle," Rinaldi said. He went off up the stairs. I sat at the table and he came back with the bottle and poured us each a half tumbler of cognac.

"Too much," I said and held up the glass and sighted at the lamp on the table.

"Not for an empty stomach. It is a wonderful thing. It burns out the stomach completely. Nothing is worse for you."

"All right."

"Self-destruction day by day," Rinaldi said. "It ruins the stomach and makes the hand shake. Just the thing for a surgeon."

"You recommend it?"

"Heartily. I use no other. Drink it down, baby, and look forward to being sick."

I drank half the glass. In the hall I could hear the orderly calling. "Soup! Soup is ready!"

The major came in, nodded to us and sat down. He seemed very small at table.

"Is this all we are?" he asked. The orderly put the soup bowl down and he ladled out a plate full.

"We are all," Rinaldi said. "Unless the priest comes. If he knew Federico was here he would be here."

"Where is he?" I asked.

"He's at 307," the major said. He was busy with his soup. He wiped his mouth, wiping his upturned gray mustache carefully. "He will come I think. I called them and left word to tell him you were here."

"I miss the noise of the mess," I said.

"Yes, it's quiet," the major said.

"I will be noisy," said Rinaldi.

"Drink some wine, Enrico," said the major. He filled my glass. The spaghetti came in and we were all busy. We were finishing the spaghetti when the priest came in. He was the same as ever, small and brown and compact looking. I stood up and we shook hands. He put his hand on my shoulder.

"I came as soon as I heard," he said.

"Sit down," the major said. "You're late."

"Good-evening, priest," Rinaldi said, using the English word. They had taken that up from the priest-baiting captain, who spoke a little English. "Good-evening, Rinaldo," the priest said. The orderly brought him soup but he said he would start with the spaghetti.

"How are you?" he asked me.

"Fine," I said. "How have things been?"

"Drink some wine, priest," Rinaldi said. "Take a little wine for your stomach's sake. That's Saint Paul, you know."

"Yes I know," said the priest politely. Rinaldi filled his glass.

"That Saint Paul," said Rinaldi. "He's the one who makes all the trouble." The priest looked at me and smiled. I could see that the baiting did not touch him now.

"That Saint Paul," Rinaldi said. "He was a rounder and a chaser and then when he was no longer hot he said it was no good. When he was finished he made the rules for us who are still hot. Isn't it true, Federico?"

The major smiled. We were eating meat stew now.

"I never discuss a Saint after dark," I said. The priest looked up from the stew and smiled at me.

"There he is, gone over with the priest," Rinaldi said. "Where are all the good old priest-baiters? Where is Cavalcanti? Where is Brundi? Where is Cesare? Do I have to bait this priest alone without support?"

"He is a good priest," said the major.

"He is a good priest," said Rinaldi. "But still a priest. I try to make the mess like the old days. I want to make Federico happy. To hell with you, priest!"

I saw the major look at him and notice that he was drunk. His thin face was white. The line of his hair was very black against the white of his forehead.

"It's all right, Rinaldo," said the priest. "It's all right."

"To hell with you," said Rinaldi. "To hell with the whole damn business." He sat back in his chair.

"He's been under a strain and he's tired," the major said to me. He finished his meat and wiped up the gravy with a piece of bread.

"I don't give a damn," Rinaldi said to the table. "To hell with the whole business." He looked defiantly around the table, his eyes flat, his face pale.

"All right," I said. "To hell with the whole damn business."

"No, no," said Rinaldi. "You can't do it. You can't do it. I say you can't do it. You're dry and you're empty and there's nothing else. There's nothing else I tell you. Not a damned thing. I know, when I stop working."

The priest shook his head. The orderly took away the stew dish.

"What are you eating meat for?" Rinaldi turned to the priest. "Don't you know it's Friday?"

"It's Thursday," the priest said.

"It's a lie. It's Friday. You're eating the body of our Lord. It's God-meat. I know. It's dead Austrian. That's what you're eating."

"The white meat is from officers," I said, completing the old joke.

Rinaldi laughed. He filled his glass.

"Don't mind me," he said. "I'm just a little crazy."

"You ought to have a leave," the priest said.

The major shook his head at him. Rinaldi looked at the priest.

"You think I ought to have a leave?"

The major shook his head at the priest. Rinaldi was looking at the priest.

"Just as you like," the priest said. "Not if you don't want."

"To hell with you," Rinaldi said. "They try to get rid of me. Every night they try to get rid of me. I fight them off. What if I have it. Everybody has it. The whole world's got it. First," he went on, assuming the manner of a lecturer, "it's a little pimple. Then we notice a rash between the shoulders. Then we notice nothing at all. We put our faith in mercury."

"Or salvarsan," the major interrupted quietly.

"A mercurial product," Rinaldi said. He acted very elated now. "I know something worth two of that. Good old priest," he said. "You'll never get it. Baby will get it. It's an industrial accident. It's a simple industrial accident."

The orderly brought in the sweet and coffee. The dessert was a sort of black bread pudding with hard sauce. The lamp was smoking; the black smoke going close up inside the chimney.

"Bring two candles and take away the lamp," the major said. The orderly brought two lighted candles each in a saucer, and took out the lamp blowing it out. Rinaldi was quiet now. He seemed all right. We talked and after the coffee we all went out into the hall.

"You want to talk to the priest. I have to go in the town," Rinaldi said. "Good-night, priest."

"Good-night, Rinaldo," the priest said.

"I'll see you, Fredi," Rinaldi said.

"Yes," I said. "Come in early." He made a face and went out the door. The major was standing with us. "He's very tired and overworked," he said. "He thinks too he has syphilis. I don't believe it but he may have. He is treating himself for it. Good-night. You will leave before daylight, Enrico?"

"Yes."

"Good-by then," he said. "Good luck. Peduzzi will wake you and go with you."

"Good-by, Signor Maggiore."

"Good-by. They talk about an Austrian offensive but I don't believe it. I hope not. But anyway it won't be here. Gino will tell you everything. The telephone works well now."

"I'll call regularly."

"Please do. Good-night. Don't let Rinaldi drink so much brandy."

"I'll try not to."

"Good-night, priest."

"Good-night, Signor Maggiore."

He went off into his office.

CHAPTER 26

I WENT TO THE DOOR and looked out. It had stopped raining but there was a mist.

"Should we go upstairs?" I asked the priest.

"I can only stay a little while."

"Come on up."

We climbed the stairs and went into my room. I lay down on Rinaldi's bed. The priest sat on my cot that the orderly had set up. It was dark in the room.

"Well," he said, "how are you really?"

"I'm all right. I'm tired to-night."

"I'm tired too, but from no cause."

"What about the war?"

"I think it will be over soon. I don't know why, but I feel it."

"How do you feel it?"

"You know how your major is? Gentle? Many people are like that now."

"I feel that way myself," I said.

"It has been a terrible summer," said the priest. He was surer of himself now than when I had gone away. "You cannot believe how it has been. Except that you have been there and you know how it can be. Many people have realized the war this summer. Officers whom I thought could never realize it realize it now."

"What will happen?" I stroked the blanket with my hand.

"I do not know but I do not think it can go on much longer."

"What will happen?"

"They will stop fighting."

"Who?"

"Both sides."

"I hope so," I said.

"You don't believe it?"

"I don't believe both sides will stop fighting at once."

"I suppose not. It is too much to expect. But when I see the changes in men I do not think it can go on."

"Who won the fighting this summer?"

"No one."

"The Austrians won," I said. "They kept them from taking San Gabriele. They've won. They won't stop fighting."

"If they feel as we feel they may stop. They have gone through the same thing."

"No one ever stopped when they were winning."

"You discourage me."

"I can only say what I think."

"Then you think it will go on and on? Nothing will ever happen?"

"I don't know. I only think the Austrians will not stop when they have won a victory. It is in defeat that we become Christian."

"The Austrians are Christians – except for the Bosnians."

"I don't mean technically Christian. I mean like Our Lord."

He said nothing.

"We are all gentler now because we are beaten. How would Our Lord have been if Peter had rescued him in the Garden?"

"He would have been just the same."

"I don't think so," I said.

"You discourage me," he said. "I believe and I pray that something will happen. I have felt it very close."

"Something may happen," I said. "But it will happen only to us. If they felt the way we do, it would be all right. But they have beaten us. They feel another way."

"Many of the soldiers have always felt this way. It is not because they were beaten."

"They were beaten to start with. They were beaten when they took them from their farms and put them in the army. That is why the peasant has wisdom, because he is defeated from the start. Put him in power and see how wise he is."

He did not say anything. He was thinking.

"Now I am depressed myself," I said. "That's why I never think about these things.

I never think and yet when I begin to talk I say the things I have found out in my mind without thinking."

"I had hoped for something."

"Defeat?"

"No. Something more."

"There isn't anything more. Except victory. It may be worse."

"I hoped for a long time for victory."

"Me too."

"Now I don't know."

"It has to be one or the other."

"I don't believe in victory any more."

"I don't. But I don't believe in defeat. Though it may be better."

"What do you believe in?"

"In sleep," I said. He stood up.

"I am very sorry to have stayed so long. But I like so to talk with you."

"It is very nice to talk again. I said that about sleeping, meaning nothing."

We stood up and shook hands in the dark.

"I sleep at 307 now," he said.

"I go out on post early to-morrow."

"I'll see you when you come back."

"We'll have a walk and talk together." I walked with him to the door.

"Don't go down," he said. "It is very nice that you are back. Though not so nice for you." He put his hand on my shoulder.

"It's all right for me," I said. "Good-night."

"Good-night. Ciaou!"

"Ciaou!" I said. I was deadly sleepy.

CHAPTER 27

I WOKE WHEN Rinaldi came in but he did not talk and I went back to sleep again. In the morning I was dressed and gone before it was light. Rinaldi did not wake when I left.

I had not seen the Bainsizza before and it was strange to go up the slope where the Austrians had been, beyond the place on the river where I had been wounded. There was a steep new road and many trucks. Beyond, the road flattened out and I saw woods and steep hills in the mist. There were woods that had been taken quickly and not smashed. Then beyond where the road was not protected by the hills it was screened by matting on the sides and over the top. The road ended in a wrecked village. The lines were up beyond. There was much artillery around. The houses were badly smashed but things were very well organized and there were signboards everywhere. We found Gino and he got us some coffee and later I went with him and met various people and saw the posts. Gino said the British cars were working further down the Bainsizza at Ravne. He had great admiration for the British. There was still a certain amount of shelling, he said, but not many wounded. There would be many sick now the rains had started. The Austrians were supposed to attack but he did not believe it. We were supposed to attack too, but they had not brought up any new troops so he thought that was off too. Food was scarce and he would be glad to get a full meal in Gorizia. What kind of supper had I had? I told him and he said that would be wonderful. He was especially impressed by the dolce. I did not describe it in detail, only said it was a dolce, and I think he believed it was something more elaborate than bread pudding.

Did I know where he was going to go? I said I didn't but that some of the other cars were at Caporetto. He hoped he would go up that way. It was a nice little place and he liked the high mountain hauling up beyond. He was a nice boy and every one seemed to like him. He said where it really had been hell was at San Gabriele and the attack beyond Lom that had gone bad. He said the Austrians had a great amount of artillery in the woods along Ternova ridge beyond and above us, and shelled the roads badly at night. There was a battery of naval guns that had gotten on his nerves. I would recognize them because of their flat trajectory. You heard the report and then the shriek commenced almost instantly. They usually fired two guns at once, one right after the other, and the fragments from the burst were enormous. He showed me one, a smoothly jagged piece of metal over a foot long. It looked like babbitting metal.

"I don't suppose they are so effective," Gino said. "But they scare me. They all sound as though they came directly for you. There is the boom, then instantly the shriek and burst. What's the use of not being wounded if they scare you to death?"

He said there were Croats in the lines opposite us now and some Magyars. Our troops were still in the attacking positions. There was no wire to speak of and no place to fall back to if there should be an Austrian attack. There were fine positions for defense along the low mountains that came up out of the plateau but nothing had been done about organizing them for defense. What did I think about the

Bainsizza anyway?

I had expected it to be flatter, more like a plateau. I had not realized it was so broken up.

"Alto piano," Gino said, "but no piano."

We went back to the cellar of the house where he lived. I said I thought a ridge that flattened out on top and had a little depth would be easier and more practical to hold than a succession of small mountains. It was no harder to attack up a mountain than on the level, I argued. "That depends on the mountains," he said. "Look at San Gabriele."

"Yes," I said, "but where they had trouble was at the top where it was flat. They got up to the top easy enough."

"Not so easy," he said.

"Yes," I said, "but that was a special case because it was a fortress rather than a mountain, anyway. The Austrians had been fortifying it for years." I meant tactically speaking in a war where there was some movement a succession of mountains were nothing to hold as a line because it was too easy to turn them. You should have possible mobility and a mountain is not very mobile. Also, people always over-shoot downhill. If the flank were turned, the best men would be left on the highest mountains. I did not believe in a war in mountains. I had thought about it a lot, I said. You pinched off one mountain and they pinched off another but when something really started every one had to get down off the mountains.

What were you going to do if you had a mountain frontier? he asked.

I had not worked that out yet, I said, and we both laughed. "But," I said, "in the old days the Austrians were always whipped in the quadrilateral around Verona. They let them come down onto the plain and whipped them there."

"Yes," said Gino. "But those were Frenchmen and you can work out military problems clearly when you are fighting in somebody else's country."

"Yes," I agreed, "when it is your own country you cannot use it so scientifically."

"The Russians did, to trap Napoleon."

"Yes, but they had plenty of country. If you tried to retreat to trap Napoleon in Italy you would find yourself in Brindisi."

"A terrible place," said Gino. "Have you ever been there?"

"Not to stay."

"I am a patriot," Gino said. "But I cannot love Brindisi or Taranto."

"Do you love the Bainsizza?" I asked.

"The soil is sacred," he said. "But I wish it grew more potatoes. You know when we came here we found fields of potatoes the Austrians had planted."

"Has the food really been short?"

"I myself have never had enough to eat but I am a big eater and I have not starved. The mess is average. The regiments in the line get pretty good food but those in support don't get so much. Something is wrong somewhere. There should be plenty of food."

"The dogfish are selling it somewhere else."

"Yes, they give the battalions in the front line as much as they can but the ones in back are very short. They have eaten all the Austrians' potatoes and chestnuts from the woods. They ought to feed them better. We are big eaters. I am sure there is plenty of food. It is very bad for the soldiers to be short of food. Have you ever noticed the difference it makes in the way you think?"

"Yes," I said. "It can't win a war but it can lose one."

"We won't talk about losing. There is enough talk about losing. What has been done this summer cannot have been done in vain."

I did not say anything. I was always embarrassed by the words sacred, glorious, and sacrifice and the expression in vain. We had heard them, sometimes standing in the rain almost out of earshot, so that only the shouted words came through, and had read them, on proclamations that were slapped up by billposters over other proclamations, now for a long time, and I had seen nothing sacred, and the things that were glorious had no glory and the sacrifices were like the stockyards at Chicago if nothing was done with the meat except to bury it. There were many words that you could not stand to hear and finally only the names of places had dignity. Certain numbers were the same way and certain dates and these with the names of the places were all you could say and have them mean anything. Abstract words such as glory, honor, courage, or hallow were obscene beside the concrete names of villages, the numbers of roads, the names of rivers, the numbers of regiments and the dates. Gino was a patriot, so he said things that separated us sometimes, but he was also a fine boy and I understood his being a patriot. He was born one. He left with Peduzzi in the car to go back to Gorizia.

It stormed all that day. The wind drove down the rain and everywhere there was standing water and mud. The plaster of the broken houses was gray and wet. Late in the afternoon the rain stopped and from out number two post I saw the bare wet autumn country with clouds over the tops of the hills and the straw screening over the roads wet and dripping. The sun came out once before it went down and shone on the bare woods beyond the ridge. There were many Austrian guns in the woods on that ridge but only a few fired. I watched the sudden round puffs of shrapnel smoke in the sky above a broken farmhouse near where the line was; soft puffs with a yellow white flash in the centre. You saw the flash, then heard the crack, then saw the smoke ball distort and thin in the wind. There were many iron shrapnel balls in the rubble of the houses and on the road beside the broken house where the post was, but they did not shell near the post that afternoon. We loaded two cars and drove down the road that was screened with wet mats and the last of the sun came through in the breaks between the strips of mattings. Before we were out on the clear road behind the hill the sun was down. We went on down the clear road and as it turned a corner into the open and went into the square arched tunnel of matting the rain started again.

The wind rose in the night and at three o'clock in the morning with the rain coming in sheets there was a bombardment and the Croatians came over across the mountain meadows and through patches of woods and into the front line. They fought in the dark in the rain and a counter-attack of scared men from the second line drove them back. There was much shelling and many rockets in the rain and machine-gun and rifle fire all along the line. They did not come again and it was quieter and between the gusts of wind and rain we could hear the sound of a great bombardment far to the north.

The wounded were coming into the post, some were carried on stretchers, some walking and some were brought on the backs of men that came across the field. They were wet to the skin and all were scared. We filled two cars with stretcher cases as they came up from the cellar of the post and as I shut the door of the second car and fastened it I felt the rain on my face turn to snow. The flakes were coming heavy and fast in the rain.

When daylight came the storm was still blowing but the snow had stopped. It had melted as it fell on the wet ground and now it was raining again. There was another attack just after daylight but it was unsuccessful. We expected an attack all day but it did not come until the sun was going down. The bombardment started to the south below the long wooded ridge where the Austrian guns were concentrated. We expected a bombardment but it did not come. It was getting dark. Guns were firing from the field behind the village and the shells, going away, had a comfortable sound.

We heard that the attack to the south had been unsuccessful. They did not attack that night but we heard that they had broken through to the north. In the night word came that we were to prepare to retreat. The captain at the post told me this. He had it from the Brigade. A little while later he came from the telephone and said it was a lie. The Brigade had received orders that the line of the Bainsizza should be held no matter what happened. I asked about the break through and he said that he had heard at the Brigade that the Austrians had broken through the twenty-seventh army corps up toward Caporetto. There had been a great battle in the north all day.

"If those bastards let them through we are cooked," he said.

"It's Germans that are attacking," one of the medical officers said. The word Germans was something to be frightened of. We did not want to have anything to do with the Germans.

"There are fifteen divisions of Germans," the medical officer said. "They have broken through and we will be cut off."

"At the Brigade, they say this line is to be held. They say they have not broken through badly and that we will hold a line across the mountains from Monte Maggiore."

"Where do they hear this?"

"From the Division."

"The word that we were to retreat came from the Division."

"We work under the Army Corps," I said. "But here I work under you. Naturally when you tell me to go I will go. But get the orders straight."

"The orders are that we stay here. You clear the wounded from here to the clearing station."

"Sometimes we clear from the clearing station to the field hospitals too," I said. "Tell me, I have never seen a retreat – if there is a retreat how are all the wounded evacuated?"

"They are not. They take as many as they can and leave the rest."

"What will I take in the cars?"

"Hospital equipment."

"All right," I said.

The next night the retreat started. We heard that Germans and Austrians had broken through in the north and were coming down the mountain valleys toward Cividale and Udine. The retreat was orderly, wet and sullen. In the night, going slowly along the crowded roads we passed troops marching under the rain, guns, horses pulling wagons, mules, motor trucks, all moving away from the front. There was no more disorder than in an advance.

That night we helped empty the field hospitals that had been set up in the least ruined villages of the plateau, taking the wounded down to Plava on the river-bed: and the next day hauled all day in the rain to evacuate the hospitals and clearing station at Plava. It rained steadily and the army of the Bainsizza moved down off the plateau in the October rain and across the river where the great victories had commenced in the spring of that year. We came into Gorizia in the middle of the next day. The rain had stopped and the town was nearly empty. As we came up the street they were loading the girls from the soldiers' whorehouse into a truck. There were seven girls and they had on their hats and coats and carried small suitcases. Two of them were crying. Of the others one smiled at us and put out her tongue and fluttered it up and down. She had thick full lips and black eyes.

I stopped the car and went over and spoke to the matron. The girls from the officers' house had left early that morning, she said. Where were they going? To Conegliano, she said. The truck started. The girl with thick lips put out her tongue again at us. The matron waved. The two girls kept on crying. The others looked interestedly out at the town. I got back in the car.

"We ought to go with them," Bonello said. "That would be a good trip."

"We'll have a good trip," I said.

"We'll have a hell of a trip."

"That's what I mean," I said. We came up the drive to the villa.

"I'd like to be there when some of those tough babies climb in and try and hop them."

"You think they will?"

"Sure. Everybody in the Second Army knows that matron."

We were outside the villa.

"They call her the Mother Superior," Bonello said. "The girls are new but everybody knows her. They must have brought them up just before the retreat."

"They'll have a time."

"I'll say they'll have a time. I'd like to have a crack at them for nothing. They charge too much at that house anyway. The government gyps us."

"Take the car out and have the mechanics go over it," I said. "Change the oil and check the differential. Fill it up and then get some sleep."

"Yes, Signor Tenente."

The villa was empty. Rinaldi was gone with the hospital. The major was gone taking hospital personnel in the staff car. There was a note on the window for me to fill the cars with the material piled in the hall and to proceed to Pordenone. The mechanics were gone already. I went out back to the garage. The other two cars came in while I was there and their drivers got down. It was starting to rain again.

"I'm so — sleepy I went to sleep three times coming here from Plava," Piani said. "What are we going to do, Tenente?"

"We'll change the oil, grease them, fill them up, then take them around in front and load up the junk they've left."

"Then do we start?"

"No, we'll sleep for three hours."

"Christ I'm glad to sleep," Bonello said. "I couldn't keep awake driving."

"How's your car, Aymo?" I asked.

"It's all right."

"Get me a monkey suit and I'll help you with the oil."

"Don't you do that, Tenente," Aymo said. "It's nothing to do. You go and pack your things."

"My things are all packed," I said. "I'll go and carry out the stuff that they left for us. Bring the cars around as soon as they're ready."

They brought the cars around to the front of the villa and we loaded them with the hospital equipment which was piled in the hallway. When it was all in, the three cars stood in line down the driveway under the trees in the rain. We went inside.

"Make a fire in the kitchen and dry your things," I said.

"I don't care about dry clothes," Piani said. "I want to sleep."

"I'm going to sleep on the major's bed," Bonello said. "I'm going to sleep where the old man corks off."

"I don't care where I sleep," Piani said.

"There are two beds in here." I opened the door.

"I never knew what was in that room," Bonello said.

"That was old fish-face's room," Piani said.

"You two sleep in there," I said. "I'll wake you."

"The Austrians will wake us if you sleep too long, Tenente," Bonello said.

"I won't oversleep," I said. "Where's Aymo?"

"He went out in the kitchen."

"Get to sleep," I said.

"I'll sleep," Piani said. "I've been asleep sitting up all day. The whole top of my head kept coming down over my eyes."

"Take your boots off," Bonello said. "That's old fish-face's bed."

"Fish-face is nothing to me." Piani lay on the bed, his muddy boots straight out, his head on his arm. I went out to the kitchen. Aymo had a fire in the stove and a kettle of water on.

"I thought I'd start some pasta asciutta," he said. "We'll be hungry when we wake up."

"Aren't you sleepy, Bartolomeo?"

"Not so sleepy. When the water boils I'll leave it. The fire will go down."

"You'd better get some sleep," I said. "We can eat cheese and monkey meat."

"This is better," he said. "Something hot will be good for those two anarchists. You go to sleep, Tenente."

"There's a bed in the major's room."

"You sleep there."

"No, I'm going up to my old room. Do you want a drink, Bartolomeo?"

"When we go, Tenente. Now it wouldn't do me any good."

"If you wake in three hours and I haven't called you, wake me, will you?"

"I haven't any watch, Tenente."

"There's a clock on the wall in the major's room."

"All right."

I went out then through the dining-room and the hall and up the marble stairs to the room where I had lived with Rinaldi. It was raining outside. I went to the window and looked out. It was getting dark and I saw the three cars standing in line under the trees. The trees were dripping in the rain. It was cold and the drops hung to the branches. I went back to Rinaldi's bed and lay down and let sleep take me.

We ate in the kitchen before we started. Aymo had a basin of spaghetti with onions and tinned meat chopped up in it. We sat around the table and drank two bottles of the wine that had been left in the cellar of the villa. It was dark outside and still raining. Piani sat at the table very sleepy.

"I like a retreat better than an advance," Bonello said. "On a retreat we drink barbera."

"We drink it now. To-morrow maybe we drink rainwater," Aymo said.

"To-morrow we'll be in Udine. We'll drink champagne. That's where the slackers live. Wake up, Piani! We'll drink champagne tomorrow in Udine!"

"I'm awake," Piani said. He filled his plate with the spaghetti and meat. "Couldn't you find tomato sauce, Barto?"

"There wasn't any," Aymo said.

"We'll drink champagne in Udine," Bonello said. He filled his glass with the clear red barbera.

"We may drink — before Udine," Piani said.

"Have you eaten enough, Tenente?" Aymo asked.

"I've got plenty. Give me the bottle, Bartolomeo."

"I have a bottle apiece to take in the cars," Aymo said.

"Did you sleep at all?"

"I don't need much sleep. I slept a little."

"To-morrow we'll sleep in the king's bed," Bonello said. He was feeling very good.

"To-morrow maybe we'll sleep in — ," Piani said.

"I'll sleep with the queen," Bonello said. He looked to see how I took the joke.

"You'll sleep with — ," Piani said sleepily.

"That's treason, Tenente," Bonello said. "Isn't that treason?"

"Shut up," I said. "You get too funny with a little wine." Outside it was raining hard. I looked at my watch. It was half-past nine.

"It's time to roll," I said and stood up.

"Who are you going to ride with, Tenente?" Bonello asked.

"With Aymo. Then you come. Then Piani. We'll start out on the road for Cormons."

"I'm afraid I'll go to sleep," Piani said.

"All right. I'll ride with you. Then Bonello. Then Aymo."

"That's the best way," Piani said. "Because I'm so sleepy."

"I'll drive and you sleep awhile."

"No. I can drive just so long as I know somebody will wake me up if I go to sleep."

"I'll wake you up. Put out the lights, Barto."

"You might as well leave them," Bonello said. "We've got no more use for this place."

"I have a small locker trunk in my room," I said. "Will you help take it down, Piani?"

"We'll take it," Piani said. "Come on, Aldo." He went off into the hall with Bonello. I heard them going upstairs.

"This was a fine place," Bartolomeo Aymo said. He put two bottles of wine and half a cheese into his haversack. "There won't be a place like this again. Where will they retreat to, Tenente?"

"Beyond the Tagliamento, they say. The hospital and the sector are to be at Pordenone."

"This is a better town than Pordenone."

"I don't know Pordenone," I said. "I've just been through there."

"It's not much of a place," Aymo said.

CHAPTER 28

AS WE MOVED out through the town it was empty in the rain and the dark except for columns of troops and guns that were going through the main street. There were many trucks too and some carts going through on other streets and converging on the main road. When we were out past the tanneries onto the main road the troops, the motor trucks, the horse-drawn carts and the guns were in one wide slow-moving column. We moved slowly but steadily in the rain, the radiator cap of our car almost against the tailboard of a truck that was loaded high, the load covered with wet canvas. Then the truck stopped. The whole column was stopped. It started again and we went a little farther, then stopped. I got out and walked ahead, going between the trucks and carts and under the wet necks of the horses. The block was farther ahead. I left the road, crossed the ditch on a footboard and walked along the field beyond the ditch. I could see the stalled column between the trees in the rain as I went forward across from it in the field. I went about a mile. The column did not move, although, on the other side beyond the stalled vehicles I could see the troops moving. I went back to the cars. This block might extend as far as Udine. Piani was asleep over the wheel. I climbed up beside him and went to sleep too. Several hours later I heard the truck ahead of us grinding into gear. I woke Piani and we started, moving a few yards, then stopping, then going on again. It was still raining.

The column stalled again in the night and did not start. I got down and went back to see Aymo and Bonello. Bonello had two sergeants of engineers on the seat of his car with him. They stiffened when I came up.

"They were left to do something to a bridge," Bonello said. "They can't find their unit so I gave them a ride."

"With the Sir Lieutenant's permission."

"With permission," I said.

"The lieutenant is an American," Bonello said. "He'll give anybody a ride."

One of the sergeants smiled. The other asked Bonello if I was an Italian from North or South America.

"He's not an Italian. He's North American English."

The sergeants were polite but did not believe it. I left them and went back to Aymo. He had two girls on the seat with him and was sitting back in the corner and smoking.

"Barto, Barto," I said. He laughed.

"Talk to them, Tenente," he said. "I can't understand them. Hey!" He put his hand on the girl's thigh and squeezed it in a friendly way. The girl drew her shawl tight around her and pushed his hand away. "Hey!" he said. "Tell the Tenente your name and what you're doing here."

The girl looked at me fiercely. The other girl kept her eyes down. The girl who looked at me said something in a dialect I could not understand a word of. She was plump and dark and looked about sixteen.

"Sorella?" I asked and pointed at the other girl.

She nodded her head and smiled.

"All right," I said and patted her knee. I felt her stiffen away when I touched her. The sister never looked up. She looked perhaps a year younger. Aymo put his hand on the elder girl's thigh and she pushed it away. He laughed at her.

"Good man," he pointed at himself. "Good man," he pointed at me. "Don't you worry." The girl looked at him fiercely. The pair of them were like two wild birds.

"What does she ride with me for if she doesn't like me?" Aymo asked. "They got right up in the car the minute I motioned to them." He turned to the girl. "Don't worry," he said. "No danger of — ," using the vulgar word. "No place for — ." I could see she understood the word and that was all. Her eyes looked at him very scared. She pulled the shawl tight. "Car all full," Aymo said. "No danger of — . No place for — ." Every time he said the word the girl stiffened a little. Then sitting stiffly and looking at him she began to cry. I saw her lips working and then tears came down her plump cheeks. Her sister, not looking up, took her hand and they sat there together. The older one, who had been so fierce, began to sob.

"I guess I scared her," Aymo said. "I didn't mean to scare her."

Bartolomeo brought out his knapsack and cut off two pieces of cheese. "Here," he said. "Stop crying."

The older girl shook her head and still cried, but the younger girl took the cheese and commenced to eat. After a while the younger girl gave her sister the second piece of cheese and they both ate. The older sister still sobbed a little.

"She'll be all right after a while," Aymo said.

An idea came to him. "Virgin?" he asked the girl next to him. She nodded her head vigorously. "Virgin too?" he pointed to the sister. Both the girls nodded their heads and the elder said something in dialect.

"That's all right," Bartolomeo said. "That's all right."

Both the girls seemed cheered.

I left them sitting together with Aymo sitting back in the corner and went back to Piani's car. The column of vehicles did not move but the troops kept passing alongside. It was still raining hard and I thought some of the stops in the movement of the column might be from cars with wet wiring. More likely they were from horses or men going to sleep. Still, traffic could tie up in cities when every one was awake. It was the combination of horse and motor vehicles. They did not help each other any. The peasants' carts did not help much either. Those were a couple of fine girls with Barto. A retreat was no place for two virgins. Real virgins. Probably very religious. If there were no war we would probably all be in bed. In bed I lay me down my head. Bed and board. Stiff as a board in bed. Catherine was in bed now between two sheets, over her and under her. Which side did she sleep on? Maybe she wasn't asleep. Maybe she was lying thinking about me. Blow, blow, ye western wind. Well, it blew and it wasn't the small rain but the big rain down that rained. It rained all night. You knew it rained down that rained. Look at it. Christ, that my love were in my arms and I in my bed again. That my love Catherine. That my sweet love Catherine down might rain. Blow her again to me. Well, we were in it. Every one was caught in it and the small rain would not quiet it. "Good-night, Catherine," I said out loud. "I hope you sleep well. If it's too uncomfortable, darling, lie on the other side," I said. "I'll get you some cold water. In a little while it will be morning and then it won't be so bad. I'm sorry he makes you so uncomfortable. Try and go to sleep, sweet."

I was asleep all the time, she said. You've been talking in your sleep. Are you all right?

Are you really there?

Of course I'm here. I wouldn't go away. This doesn't make any difference between us.

You're so lovely and sweet. You wouldn't go away in the night, would you?

Of course I wouldn't go away. I'm always here. I come whenever you want me.

" — ," Piani said. "They've started again."

"I was dopey," I said. I looked at my watch. It was three o'clock in the morning. I reached back behind the seat for a bottle of the barbera.

"You talked out loud," Piani said.

"I was having a dream in English," I said.

The rain was slacking and we were moving along. Before daylight we were stalled again and when it was light we were at a little rise in the ground and I saw the road of the retreat stretched out far ahead, everything stationary except for the infantry filtering through. We started to move again but seeing the rate of progress in the daylight, I knew we were going to have to get off that main road some way and go across country if we ever hoped to reach Udine.

In the night many peasants had joined the column from the roads of the country and in the column there were carts loaded with household goods; there were mirrors projecting up between mattresses, and chickens and ducks tied to carts. There was a sewing machine on the cart ahead of us in the rain. They had saved the most valuable things. On some carts the women sat huddled from the rain and others walked beside the carts keeping as close to them as they could. There were dogs now in the column, keeping under the wagons as they moved along. The road was muddy, the ditches at the side were high with water and beyond the trees that lined the road the fields looked too wet and too soggy to try to cross. I got down from the car and worked up the road a way, looking for a place where I could see ahead to find a side-road we could take across country. I knew there were many side-roads but did not want one that would lead to nothing. I could not remember them because we had always passed them bowling along in the car on the main road and they all looked much alike. Now I knew we must find one if we hoped to get through. No one knew where the Austrians were nor how things were going but I was certain that if the rain should stop and planes come over and get to work on that column that it would be all over. All that was needed was for a few men to leave their trucks or a few horses be killed to tie up completely the movement on the road.

The rain was not falling so heavily now and I thought it might clear. I went ahead along the edge of the road and when there was a small road that led off to the north between two fields with a hedge of trees on both sides, I thought that we had better take it and hurried back to the cars. I told Piani to turn off and went back to tell Bonello and Aymo.

"If it leads nowhere we can turn around and cut back in," I said.

"What about these?" Bonello asked. His two sergeants were beside him on the seat. They were unshaven but still military looking in the early morning.

"They'll be good to push," I said. I went back to Aymo and told him we were going to try it across country.

"What about my virgin family?" Aymo asked. The two girls were asleep.

"They won't be very useful," I said. "You ought to have some one that could push."

"They could go back in the car," Aymo said. "There's room in the car."

"All right if you want them," I said. "Pick up somebody with a wide back to push."

"Bersaglieri," Aymo smiled. "They have the widest backs. They measure them. How do you feel, Tenente?"

"Fine. How are you?"

"Fine. But very hungry."

"There ought to be something up that road and we will stop and eat."

"How's your leg, Tenente?"

"Fine," I said. Standing on the step and looking up ahead I could see Piani's car pulling out onto the little side-road and starting up it, his car showing through the hedge of bare branches. Bonello turned off and followed him and then Piani worked his way out and we followed the two ambulances ahead along the narrow road between hedges. It led to a farmhouse. We found Piani and Bonello stopped in the farmyard. The house was low and long with a trellis with a grape-vine over the door. There was a well in the yard and Piani was getting up water to fill his radiator. So much going in low gear had boiled it out. The farmhouse was deserted. I looked back down the road, the farmhouse was on a slight elevation above the plain, and we could see over the country, and saw the road, the hedges, the fields and the line of trees along the main road where the retreat was passing. The two sergeants were looking through the house. The girls were awake and looking at the courtyard, the well and the two big ambulances in front of the farmhouse, with three drivers at the well. One of the sergeants came out with a clock in his hand.

"Put it back," I said. He looked at me, went in the house and camc back without the clock.

"Where's your partner?" I asked.

"He's gone to the latrine." He got up on the seat of the ambulance. He was afraid we would leave him.

"What about breakfast, Tenente?" Bonello asked. "We could eat something. It wouldn't take very long."

"Do you think this road going down on the other side will lead to anything?"

"Sure."

"All right. Let's eat." Piani and Bonello went in the house.

"Come on," Aymo said to the girls. He held his hand to help them down. The older sister shook her head. They were not going into any deserted house. They looked after us.

"They are difficult," Aymo said. We went into the farmhouse together. It was large and dark, an abandoned feeling. Bonello and Piani were in the kitchen.

"There's not much to eat," Piani said. "They've cleaned it out." Bonello sliced a big cheese on the heavy kitchen table.

"Where was the cheese?"

"In the cellar. Piani found wine too and apples."

"That's a good breakfast."

Piani was taking the wooden cork out of a big wicker-covered wine jug. He tipped it and poured a copper pan full.

"It smells all right," he said. "Find some beakers, Barto."

The two sergeants came in.

"Have some cheese, sergeants," Bonello said.

"We should go," one of the sergeants said, eating his cheese and drinking a cup of wine.

"We'll go. Don't worry," Bonello said.

"An army travels on its stomach," I said.

"What?" asked the sergeant.

"It's better to eat."

"Yes. But time is precious."

"I believe the bastards have eaten already," Piani said. The sergeants looked at him. They hated the lot of us.

"You know the road?" one of them asked me.

"No," I said. They looked at each other.

"We would do best to start," the first one said.

"We are starting," I said. I drank another cup of the red wine. It tasted very good after the cheese and apple.

"Bring the cheese," I said and went out. Bonello came out carrying the great jug of wine.

"That's too big," I said. He looked at it regretfully.

"I guess it is," he said. "Give me the canteens to fill." He filled the canteens and some of the wine ran out on the stone paving of the courtyard. Then he picked up the wine jug and put it just inside the door.

"The Austrians can find it without breaking the door down," he said.

"We'll roll," I said. "Piani and I will go ahead." The two engineers were already on the seat beside Bonello. The girls were eating cheese and apples. Aymo was smoking. We started off down the narrow road. I looked back at the two cars coming and the farmhouse. It was a fine, low, solid stone house and the ironwork of the well was very good. Ahead of us the road was narrow and muddy and there was a high hedge on either side. Behind, the cars were following closely.

CHAPTER 29

AT NOON we were stuck in a muddy road about, as nearly as we could figure, ten kilometres from Udine. The rain had stopped during the forenoon and three times we had heard planes coming, seen them pass overhead, watched them go far to the left and heard them bombing on the main highroad. We had worked through a network of secondary roads and had taken many roads that were blind, but had always, by backing up and finding another road, gotten closer to Udine. Now, Aymo's car, in backing so that we might get out of a blind road, had gotten into the soft earth at the side and the wheels, spinning, had dug deeper and deeper until the car rested on its differential. The thing to do now was to dig out in front of the wheels, put in brush so that the chains could grip, and then push until the car was on the road. We were all down on the road around the car. The two sergeants looked at the car and examined the wheels. Then they started off down the road without a word. I went after them.

"Come on," I said. "Cut some brush."

"We have to go," one said.

"Get busy," I said, "and cut brush."

"We have to go," one said. The other said nothing. They were in a hurry to start. They would not look at me.

"I order you to come back to the car and cut brush," I said. The one sergeant turned. "We have to go on. In a little while you will be cut off. You can't order us. You're not our officer."

"I order you to cut brush," I said. They turned and started down the road.

"Halt," I said. They kept on down the muddy road, the hedge on either side. "I order you to halt," I called. They went a little faster. I opened up my holster, took the pistol, aimed at the one who had talked the most, and fired. I missed and they both started to run. I shot three times and dropped one. The other went through the hedge and was out of sight. I fired at him through the hedge as he ran across the field. The pistol clicked empty and I put in another clip. I saw it was too far to shoot at the second sergeant. He was far across the field, running, his head held low. I commenced to reload the empty clip. Bonello came up.

"Let me go finish him," he said. I handed him the pistol and he walked down to where the sergeant of engineers lay face down across the road. Bonello leaned over, put the pistol against the man's head and pulled the trigger. The pistol did not fire.

"You have to cock it," I said. He cocked it and fired twice. He took hold of the sergeant's legs and pulled him to the side of the road so he lay beside the hedge. He came back and handed me the pistol.

"The son of a bitch," he said. He looked toward the sergeant. "You see me shoot him, Tenente?"

"We've got to get the brush quickly," I said. "Did I hit the other one at all?"

"I don't think so," Aymo said. "He was too far away to hit with a pistol."

"The dirty scum," Piani said. We were all cutting twigs and branches. Everything had been taken out of the car. Bonello was digging out in front of the wheels. When we were ready Aymo started the car and put it into gear. The wheels spun round throwing brush and mud. Bonello and I pushed until we could feel our joints crack. The car would not move.

"Rock her back and forth, Barto," I said.

He drove the engine in reverse, then forward. The wheels only dug in deeper. Then the car was resting on the differential again, and the wheels spun freely in the holes they had dug. I straightened up.

"We'll try her with a rope," I said.

"I don't think it's any use, Tenente. You can't get a straight pull."

"We have to try it," I said. "She won't come out any other way."

Piani's and Bonello's cars could only move straight ahead down the narrow road. We roped both cars together and pulled. The wheels only pulled sideways against the ruts.

"It's no good," I shouted. "Stop it."

Piani and Bonello got down from their cars and came back. Aymo got down. The girls were up the road about forty yards sitting on a stone wall.

"What do you say, Tenente?" Bonello asked.

"We'll dig out and try once more with the brush," I said. I looked down the road. It was my fault. I had led them up here. The sun was almost out from behind the clouds and the body of the sergeant lay beside the hedge.

"We'll put his coat and cape under," I said. Bonello went to get them. I cut brush and Aymo and Piani dug out in front and between the wheels. I cut the cape, then ripped it in two, and laid it under the wheel in the mud, then piled brush for the wheels to catch. We were ready to start and Aymo got up on the seat and started the car. The wheels spun and we pushed and pushed. But it wasn't any use.

"It's – ed," I said. "Is there anything you want in the car, Barto?"

Aymo climbed up with Bonello, carrying the cheese and two bottles of wine and his cape. Bonello, sitting behind the wheel, was looking through the pockets of the sergeant's coat.

"Better throw the coat away," I said. "What about Barto's virgins?"

"They can get in the back," Piani said. "I don't think we are going far."

I opened the back door of the ambulance.

"Come on," I said. "Get in." The two girls climbed in and sat in the corner. They seemed to have taken no notice of the shooting. I looked back up the road. The sergeant lay in his dirty long-sleeved underwear. I got up with Piani and we started. We were going to try to cross the field. When the road entered the field I got down and walked ahead. If we could get across, there was a road on the other side. We could not get across. It was too soft and muddy for the cars. When they were finally and completely stalled, the wheels dug in to the hubs, we left them in the field and started on foot for Udine.

When we came to the road which led back toward the main highway I pointed down it to the two girls.

"Go down there," I said. "You'll meet people." They looked at me. I took out my pocket-book and gave them each a ten-lira note. "Go down there," I said, pointing. "Friends! Family!"

They did not understand but they held the money tightly and started down the road. They looked back as though they were afraid I might take the money back. I watched them go down the road, their shawls close around them, looking back apprehensively at us. The three drivers were laughing.

"How much will you give me to go in that direction, Tenente?" Bonello asked.

"They're better off in a bunch of people than alone if they catch them," I said.

"Give me two hundred lire and I'll walk straight back toward Austria," Bonello said.

"They'd take it away from you," Piani said.

"Maybe the war will be over," Aymo said. We were going up the road as fast as we could. The sun was trying to come through. Beside the road were mulberry trees. Through the trees I could see our two big moving-vans of cars stuck in the field. Piani looked back too.

"They'll have to build a road to get them out," he said.

"I wish to Christ we had bicycles," Bonello said.

"Do they ride bicycles in America?" Aymo asked.

"They used to."

"Here it is a great thing," Aymo said. "A bicycle is a splendid thing."

"I wish to Christ we had bicycles," Bonello said. "I'm no walker."

"Is that firing?" I asked. I thought I could hear firing a long way away.

"I don't know," Aymo said. He listened.

"I think so," I said.

"The first thing we will see will be the cavalry," Piani said.

"I don't think they've got any cavalry."

"I hope to Christ not," Bonello said. "I don't want to be stuck on a lance by any — cavalry."

"You certainly shot that sergeant, Tenente," Piani said. We were walking fast.

"I killed him," Bonello said. "I never killed anybody in this war, and all my life I've wanted to kill a sergeant."

"You killed him on the sit all right," Piani said. "He wasn't flying very fast when you killed him."

"Never mind. That's one thing I can always remember. I killed that — of a sergeant."

"What will you say in confession?" Aymo asked.

"I'll say, 'Bless me, father, I killed a sergeant.'" They all laughed.

"He's an anarchist," Piani said. "He doesn't go to church."

"Piani's an anarchist too," Bonello said.

"Are you really anarchists?" I asked.

"No, Tenente. We're socialists. We come from Imola."

"Haven't you ever been there?"

"No."

"By Christ it's a fine place, Tenente. You come there after the war and we'll show you something."

"Are you all socialists?"

"Everybody."

"Is it a fine town?"

"Wonderful. You never saw a town like that."

"How did you get to be socialists?"

"We're all socialists. Everybody is a socialist. We've always been socialists."

"You come, Tenente. We'll make you a socialist too."

Ahead the road turned off to the left and there was a little hill and, beyond a stone wall, an apple orchard. As the road went uphill they ceased talking. We walked along together all going fast against time.

CHAPTER 30

LATER WE WERE on a road that led to a river. There was a long line of abandoned trucks and carts on the road leading up to the bridge. No one was in sight. The river was high and the bridge had been blown up in the centre; the stone arch was fallen into the river and the brown water was going over it. We went on up the bank looking for a place to cross. Up ahead I knew there was a railway bridge and I thought we might be able to get across there. The path was wet and muddy. We did not see any troops; only abandoned trucks and stores. Along the river bank there was nothing and no one but the wet brush and muddy ground. We went up to the bank and finally we saw the railway bridge.

"What a beautiful bridge," Aymo said. It was a long plain iron bridge across what was usually a dry river-bed.

"We'd better hurry and get across before they blow it up," I said.

"There's nobody to blow it up," Piani said. "They're all gone."

"It's probably mined," Bonello said. "You cross first, Tenente."

"Listen to the anarchist," Aymo said. "Make him go first."

"I'll go," I said. "It won't be mined to blow up with one man."

"You see," Piani said. "That is brains. Why haven't you brains, anarchist?"

"If I had brains I wouldn't be here," Bonello said.

"That's pretty good, Tenente," Aymo said.

"That's pretty good," I said. We were close to the bridge now. The sky had clouded over again and it was raining a little. The bridge looked long and solid. We climbed up the embankment.

"Come one at a time," I said and started across the bridge. I watched the ties and the rails for any trip-wires or signs of explosive but I saw nothing. Down below the gaps in the ties the river ran muddy and fast. Ahead across the wet countryside I could see Udine in the rain. Across the bridge I looked back. Just up the river was another bridge. As I watched, a yellow mud-colored motor car crossed it. The sides of the bridge were high and the body of the car, once on, was out of sight. But I saw the heads of the driver, the man on the seat with him, and the two men on the rear seat. They all wore German helmets. Then the car was over the bridge and out of sight behind the trees and the abandoned vehicles on the road. I waved to Aymo who was crossing and to the others to come on. I climbed down and crouched beside the railway embankment. Aymo came down with me.

"Did you see the car?" I asked.

"No. We were watching you."

"A German staff car crossed on the upper bridge."

"A staff car?"

"Yes."

"Holy Mary."

The others came and we all crouched in the mud behind the embankment, looking across the rails at the bridge, the line of trees, the ditch and the road.

"Do you think we're cut off then, Tenente?"

"I don't know. All I know is a German staff car went along that road."

"You don't feel funny, Tenente? You haven't got strange feelings in the head?"

"Don't be funny, Bonello."

"What about a drink?" Piani asked. "If we're cut off we might as well have a drink." He unhooked his canteen and uncorked it.

"Look! Look!" Aymo said and pointed toward the road. Along the top of the stone bridge we could see German helmets moving. They were bent forward and moved smoothly, almost supernaturally, along. As they came off the bridge we saw them. They were bicycle troops. I saw the faces of the first two. They were ruddy and healthy-looking. Their helmets came low down over their foreheads and the side of their faces. Their carbines were clipped to the frame of the bicycles. Stick bombs hung handle down from their belts. Their helmets and their gray uniforms were wet and they rode easily, looking ahead and to both sides. There were two – then four in line, then two, then almost a dozen; then another dozen – then one alone. They did not talk but we could not have heard them because of the noise from the river. They were gone out of sight up the road.

"Holy Mary," Aymo said.

"They were Germans," Piani said. "Those weren't Austrians."

"Why isn't there somebody here to stop them?" I said. "Why haven't they blown the bridge up? Why aren't there machine-guns along this embankment?"

"You tell us, Tenente," Bonello said.

I was very angry.

"The whole bloody thing is crazy. Down below they blow up a little bridge. Here they leave a bridge on the main road. Where is everybody? Don't they try and stop them at all?"

"You tell us, Tenente," Bonello said. I shut up. It was none of my business; all I had to do was to get to Pordenone with three ambulances. I had failed at that. All I had to do now was get to Pordenone. I probably could not even get to Udine. The hell I couldn't. The thing to do was to be calm and not get shot or captured.

"Didn't you have a canteen open?" I asked Piani. He handed it to me. I took a long drink. "We might as well start," I said. "There's no hurry though. Do you want to eat something?"

"This is no place to stay," Bonello said.

"All right. We'll start."

"Should we keep on this side – out of sight?"

"We'd be better off on top. They may come along this bridge too. We don't want them on top of us before we see them."

We walked along the railroad track. On both sides of us stretched the wet plain. Ahead across the plain was the hill of Udine. The roofs fell away from the castle on the hill. We could see the campanile and the clock-tower. There were many mulberry trees in the fields. Ahead I saw a place where the rails were torn up. The ties had been dug out too and thrown down the embankment.

"Down! down!" Aymo said. We dropped down beside the embankment. There was another group of bicyclists passing along the road. I looked over the edge and saw them go on.

"They saw us but they went on," Aymo said.

"We'll get killed up there, Tenente," Bonello said.

"They don't want us," I said. "They're after something else. We're in more danger if they should come on us suddenly."

"I'd rather walk here out of sight," Bonello said.

"All right. We'll walk along the tracks."

"Do you think we can get through?" Aymo asked.

"Sure. There aren't very many of them yet. We'll go through in the dark."

"What was that staff car doing?"

"Christ knows," I said. We kept on up the tracks. Bonello tired of walking in the mud of the embankment and came up with the rest of us. The railway moved south away from the highway now and we could not see what passed along the road. A short bridge over a canal was blown up but we climbed across on what was left of the span. We heard firing ahead of us.

We came up on the railway beyond the canal. It went on straight toward the town across the low fields. We could see the line of the other railway ahead of us. To the north was the main road where we had seen the cyclists; to the south there was a small branch-road across the fields with thick trees on each side. I thought we had better cut to the south and work around the town that way and across country toward Campoformio and the main road to the Tagliamento. We could avoid the main line of the retreat by keeping to the secondary roads beyond Udine. I knew there were plenty of side-roads across the plain. I started down the embankment.

"Come on," I said. We would make for the side-road and work to the south of the town. We all started down the embankment. A shot was fired at us from the side-road. The bullet went into the mud of the embankment.

"Go on back," I shouted. I started up the embankment, slipping in the mud. The drivers were ahead of me. I went up the embankment as fast as I could go. Two more shots came from the thick brush and Aymo, as he was crossing the tracks, lurched, tripped and fell face down. We pulled him down on the other side and turned him over. "His head ought to be uphill," I said. Piani moved him around. He lay in the mud on the side of the embankment, his feet pointing downhill, breathing blood irregularly. The three of us squatted over him in the rain. He was hit low in the back of the neck and the bullet had ranged upward and come out under the right eye. He died while I was stopping up the two holes. Piani laid his head down, wiped at his face, with a piece of the emergency dressing, then let it alone.

"The — ," he said.

"They weren't Germans," I said. "There can't be any Germans over there."

"Italians," Piani said, using the word as an epithet, "Italiani!" Bonello said nothing. He was sitting beside Aymo, not looking at him. Piani picked up Aymo's cap where it had rolled down the embankment and put it over his face. He took out his canteen.

"Do you want a drink?" Piani handed Bonello the canteen.

"No," Bonello said. He turned to me. "That might have happened to us any time on the railway tracks."

"No," I said. "It was because we started across the field."

Bonello shook his head. "Aymo's dead," he said. "Who's dead next, Tenente? Where do we go now?"

"Those were Italians that shot," I said. "They weren't Germans."

"I suppose if they were Germans they'd have killed all of us," Bonello said.

"We are in more danger from Italians than Germans," I said. "The rear guard are afraid of everything. The Germans know what they're after."

"You reason it out, Tenente," Bonello said.

"Where do we go now?" Piani asked.

"We better lie up some place till it's dark. If we could get south we'd be all right."

"They'd have to shoot us all to prove they were right the first time," Bonello said. "I'm not going to try them."

"We'll find a place to lie up as near to Udine as we can get and then go through when it's dark."

"Let's go then," Bonello said. We went down the north side of the embankment. I looked back. Aymo lay in the mud with the angle of the embankment. He was quite small and his arms were by his side, his puttee-wrapped legs and muddy boots together, his cap over his face. He looked very dead. It was raining. I had liked him as well as any one I ever knew. I had his papers in my pocket and would write to his family. Ahead across the fields was a farmhouse. There were trees around it and the farm buildings were built against the house. There was a balcony along the second floor held up by columns.

"We better keep a little way apart," I said. "I'll go ahead." I started toward the farmhouse. There was a path across the field.

Crossing the field, I did not know but that some one would fire on us from the trees near the farmhouse or from the farmhouse itself. I walked toward it, seeing it very clearly. The balcony of the second floor merged into the barn and there was hay coming out between the columns. The courtyard was of stone blocks and all the trees were dripping with the rain. There was a big empty two-wheeled cart, the shafts tipped high up in the rain. I came to the courtyard, crossed it, and stood under the shelter of the balcony. The door of the house was open and I went in. Bonello and Piani came in after me. It was dark inside. I went back to the kitchen. There were ashes of a fire on the big open hearth. The pots hung over the ashes, but they were empty. I looked around but I could not find anything to eat.

"We ought to lie up in the barn," I said. "Do you think you could find anything to eat, Piani, and bring it up there?"

"I'll look," Piani said.

"I'll look too," Bonello said.

"All right," I said. "I'll go up and look at the barn." I found a stone stairway that went up from the stable underneath. The stable smelt dry and pleasant in the rain. The cattle were all gone, probably driven off when they left. The barn was half full of hay. There were two windows in the roof, one was blocked with boards, the other was a narrow dormer window on the north side. There was a chute so that hay might be pitched down to the cattle. Beams crossed the opening down into the main floor where the hay-carts drove in when the hay was hauled in to be pitched up. I heard the rain on the roof and smelled the hay and, when I went down, the clean smell of dried dung in the stable. We could pry a board loose and see out of the south window down into the courtyard. The other window looked out on the field toward the north. We could get out of either window onto the roof and down, or go down the hay chute if the stairs were impractical. It was a big barn and we could hide in the hay if we heard any one. It seemed like a good place. I was sure we could have gotten through to the south if they had not fired on us. It was impossible that there were Germans there. They were coming from the north and down the road from Cividale. They could not have come through from the south. The Italians were even more dangerous. They were frightened and firing on anything they saw. Last night on the retreat we had heard that there had been many Germans in Italian uniforms mixing with the retreat in the north. I did not believe it. That was one of those things you always heard in the war. It was one of the things the enemy always did to you. You did not know any one who went over in German uniform to confuse them. Maybe they did but it sounded difficult. I did not believe the Germans did it.

I did not believe they had to. There was no need to confuse our retreat. The size of the army and the fewness of the roads did that. Nobody gave any orders, let alone Germans. Still, they would shoot us for Germans. They shot Aymo. The hay smelled good and lying in a barn in the hay took away all the years in between. We had lain in hay and talked and shot sparrows with an air-rifle when they perched in the triangle cut high up in the wall of the barn. The barn was gone now and one year they had cut the hemlock woods and there were only stumps, dried tree-tops, branches and fireweed where the woods had been. You could not go back. If you did not go forward what happened? You never got back to Milan. And if you got back to Milan what happened? I listened to the firing to the north toward Udine. I could hear machine-gun firing. There was no shelling. That was something. They must have gotten some troops along the road. I looked down in the half-light of the hay-barn and saw Piani standing on the hauling floor. He had a long sausage, a jar of something and two bottles of wine under his arm.

"Come up," I said. "There is the ladder." Then I realized that I should help him with the things and went down. I was vague in the head from lying in the hay. I had been nearly asleep.

"Where's Bonello?" I asked.

"I'll tell you," Piani said. We went up the ladder. Up on the hay we set the things down. Piani took out his knife with the corkscrew and drew the cork on a wine bottle.

"They have sealing-wax on it," he said. "It must be good." He smiled.

"Where's Bonello?" I asked.

Piani looked at me.

"He went away, Tenente," he said. "He wanted to be a prisoner."

I did not say anything.

"He was afraid we would get killed."

I held the bottle of wine and did not say anything.

"You see we don't believe in the war anyway, Tenente."

"Why didn't you go?" I asked.

"I did not want to leave you."

"Where did he go?"

"I don't know, Tenente. He went away."

"All right," I said. "Will you cut the sausage?"

Piani looked at me in the half-light.

"I cut it while we were talking," he said. We sat in the hay and ate the sausage and drank the wine. It must have been wine they had saved for a wedding. It was so old that it was losing its color.

"You look out of this window, Luigi," I said. "I'll go look out the other window."

We had each been drinking out of one of the bottles and I took my bottle with me and went over and lay flat on the hay and looked out the narrow window at the wet country. I do not know what I expected to see but I did not see anything except the fields and the bare mulberry trees and the rain falling. I drank the wine and it did not make me feel good. They had kept it too long and it had gone to pieces and lost its quality and color. I watched it get dark outside; the darkness came very quickly. It would be a black night with the rain. When it was dark there was no use watching any more, so I went over to Piani. He was lying asleep and I did not wake him but sat down beside him for a while. He was a big man and he slept heavily. After a while I woke him and we started.

That was a very strange night. I do not know what I had expected, death perhaps and shooting in the dark and running, but nothing happened. We waited, lying flat beyond the ditch along the main road while a German battalion passed, then when they were gone we crossed the road and went on to the north. We were very close to Germans twice in the rain but they did not see us. We got past the town to the north without seeing any Italians, then after a while came on the main channels of the retreat and walked all night toward the Tagliamento. I had not realized how gigantic the retreat was. The whole country was moving, as well as the army. We walked all night, making better time than the vehicles. My leg ached and I was tired but we made good time. It seemed so silly for Bonello to have decided to be taken prisoner. There was no danger. We had walked through two armies without incident. If Aymo had not been killed there would never have seemed to be any danger. No one had bothered us when we were in plain sight along the railway. The killing came suddenly and unreasonably. I wondered where Bonello was.

"How do you feel, Tenente?" Piani asked. We were going along the side of a road crowded with vehicles and troops.

"Fine."

"I'm tired of this walking."

"Well, all we have to do is walk now. We don't have to worry."

"Bonello was a fool."

"He was a fool all right."

"What will you do about him, Tenente?"

"I don't know."

"Can't you just put him down as taken prisoner?"

"I don't know."

"You see if the war went on they would make bad trouble for his family."

"The war won't go on," a soldier said. "We're going home. The war is over."

"Everybody's going home."

"We're all going home."

"Come on, Tenente," Piani said. He wanted to get past them.

"Tenente? Who's a Tenente? A basso gli ufficiali! Down with the officers!"

Piani took me by the arm. "I better call you by your name," he said. "They might try and make trouble. They've shot some officers." We worked up past them.

"I won't make a report that will make trouble for his family." I went on with our conversation.

"If the war is over it makes no difference," Piani said. "But I don't believe it's over. It's too good that it should be over."

"We'll know pretty soon," I said.

"I don't believe it's over. They all think it's over but I don't believe it."

"Viva la Pace!" a soldier shouted out. "We're going home!"

"It would be fine if we all went home," Piani said. "Wouldn't you like to go home?"

"Yes."

"We'll never go. I don't think it's over."

"Andiamo a casa!" a soldier shouted.

"They throw away their rifles," Piani said. "They take them off and drop them down while they're marching. Then they shout."

"They ought to keep their rifles."

"They think if they throw away their rifles they can't make them fight."

In the dark and the rain, making our way along the side of the road I could see that many of the troops still had their rifles. They stuck up above the capes.

"What brigade are you?" an officer called out.

"Brigata di Pace," some one shouted. "Peace Brigade!" The officer said nothing.

"What does he say? What does the officer say?"

"Down with the officer. Viva la Pace!"

"Come on," Piani said. We passed two British ambulances, abandoned in the block of vehicles.

"They're from Gorizia," Piani said. "I know the cars."

"They got further than we did."

"They started earlier."

"I wonder where the drivers are?"

"Up ahead probably."

"The Germans have stopped outside Udine," I said. "These people will all get across the river."

"Yes," Piani said. "That's why I think the war will go on."

"The Germans could come on," I said. "I wonder why they don't come on."

"I don't know. I don't know anything about this kind of war."

"They have to wait for their transport I suppose."

"I don't know," Piani said. Alone he was much gentler. When he was with the others he was a very rough talker.

"Are you married, Luigi?"

"You know I am married."

"Is that why you did not want to be a prisoner?"

"That is one reason. Are you married, Tenente?"

"No."

"Neither is Bonello."

"You can't tell anything by a man's being married. But I should think a married man would want to get back to his wife," I said. I would be glad to talk about wives.

"Yes."

"How are your feet?"

"They're sore enough."

Before daylight we reached the bank of the Tagliamento and followed down along the flooded river to the bridge where all the traffic was crossing.

"They ought to be able to hold at this river," Piani said. In the dark the flood looked high. The water swirled and it was wide. The wooden bridge was nearly three-quarters of a mile across, and the river, that usually ran in narrow channels in the wide stony bed far below the bridge, was close under the wooden planking. We went along the bank and then worked our way into the crowd that were crossing the bridge. Crossing slowly in the rain a few feet above the flood, pressed tight in the crowd, the box of an artillery caisson just ahead, I looked over the side and watched the river. Now that we could not go our own pace I felt very tired. There was no exhilaration in crossing the bridge. I wondered what it would be like if a plane bombed it in the daytime.

"Piani," I said.

"Here I am, Tenente." He was a little ahead in the jam. No one was talking. They were all trying to get across as soon as they could: thinking only of that. We were almost across. At the far end of the bridge there were officers and carabinieri standing on both sides flashing lights. I saw them silhouetted against the sky-line. As we came close to them I saw one of the officers point to a man in the column. A carabiniere went in after him and came out holding the man by the arm. He took him away from the road. We came almost opposite them. The officers were scrutinizing every one in the column, sometimes speaking to each other, going forward to flash a light in some one's face. They took some one else out just before we came opposite. I saw the man. He was a lieutenant-colonel. I saw the stars in the box on his sleeve as they flashed a light on him. His hair was gray and he was short and fat. The carabiniere pulled him in behind the line of officers. As we came opposite I saw one or two of them look at me. Then one pointed at me and spoke to a carabiniere. I saw the carabiniere start for me, come through the edge of the column toward me, then felt him take me by the collar.

"What's the matter with you?" I said and hit him in the face. I saw his face under the hat, upturned mustaches and blood coming down his cheek. Another one dove in toward us.

"What's the matter with you?" I said. He did not answer. He was watching a chance to grab me. I put my arm behind me to loosen my pistol.

"Don't you know you can't touch an officer?"

The other one grabbed me from behind and pulled my arm up so that it twisted in the socket. I turned with him and the other one grabbed me around the neck. I kicked his shins and got my left knee into his groin.

"Shoot him if he resists," I heard some one say.

"What's the meaning of this?" I tried to shout but my voice was not very loud. They had me at the side of the road now.

"Shoot him if he resists," an officer said. "Take him over back."

"Who are you?"

"You'll find out."

"Who are you?"

"Battle police," another officer said.

"Why don't you ask me to step over instead of having one of these airplanes grab me?"

They did not answer. They did not have to answer. They were battle police.

"Take him back there with the others," the first officer said. "You see. He speaks Italian with an accent."

"So do you, you — ," I said.

"Take him back with the others," the first officer said. They took me down behind the line of officers below the road toward a group of people in a field by the river bank. As we walked toward them shots were fired. I saw flashes of the rifles and heard the reports. We came up to the group. There were four officers standing together, with a man in front of them with a carabiniere on each side of him. A group of men were standing guarded by carabinieri. Four other carabinieri stood near the questioning officers, leaning on their carbines. They were wide-hatted carabinieri. The two who had me shoved me in with the group waiting to be questioned. I looked at the man the officers were questioning. He was the fat gray-haired little lieutenant-colonel they had taken out of the column. The questioners had all the efficiency, coldness and command of themselves of Italians who are firing and are not being fired on.

"Your brigade?"

He told them.

"Regiment?"

He told them.

"Why are you not with your regiment?"

He told them.

"Do you not know that an officer should be with his troops?" He did.

That was all. Another officer spoke.

"It is you and such as you that have let the barbarians onto the sacred soil of the fatherland."

"I beg your pardon," said the lieutenant-colonel.

"It is because of treachery such as yours that we have lost the fruits of victory."

"Have you ever been in a retreat?" the lieutenant-colonel asked.

"Italy should never retreat."

We stood there in the rain and listened to this. We were facing the officers and the prisoner stood in front and a little to one side of us.

"If you are going to shoot me," the lieutenant-colonel said, "please shoot me at once without further questioning. The questioning is stupid." He made the sign of the cross. The officers spoke together. One wrote something on a pad of paper.

"Abandoned his troops, ordered to be shot," he said.

Two carabinieri took the lieutenant-colonel to the river bank. He walked in the rain, an old man with his hat off, a carabinieri on either side. I did not watch them shoot him but I heard the shots. They were questioning some one else. This officer too was separated from his troops. He was not allowed to make an explanation. He cried when they read the sentence from the pad of paper, and they were questioning another when they shot him. They made a point of being intent on questioning the next man while the man who had been questioned before was being shot. In this way there was obviously nothing they could do about it. I did not know whether I should wait to be questioned or make a break now. I was obviously a German in Italian uniform. I saw how their minds worked; if they had minds and if they worked. They were all young men and they were saving their country. The second army was being re-formed beyond the Tagliamento. They were executing officers of the rank of major and above who were separated from their troops. They were also dealing summarily with German agitators in Italian uniform. They wore steel helmets. Only two of us had steel helmets. Some of the carabinieri had them. The other carabinieri wore the wide hat. Airplanes we called them. We stood in the rain and were taken out one at a time to be questioned and shot. So far they had shot every one they had questioned. The questioners had that beautiful detachment and devotion to stern justice of men dealing in death without being in any danger of it. They were questioning a full colonel of a line regiment. Three more officers had just been put in with us.

"Where was his regiment?"

I looked at the carabinieri. They were looking at the newcomers. The others were looking at the colonel. I ducked down, pushed between two men, and ran for the river, my head down. I tripped at the edge and went in with a splash. The water was very cold and I stayed under as long as I could. I could feel the current swirl me and I stayed under until I thought I could never come up. The minute I came up I took a breath and went down again. It was easy to stay under with so much clothing and my boots. When I came up the second time I saw a piece of timber ahead of me and reached it and held on with one hand. I kept my head behind it and did not even look over it. I did not want to see the bank. There were shots when I ran and shots when I came up the first time. I heard them when I was almost above water. There were no shots now. The piece of timber swung in the current and I held it with one hand. I looked at the bank. It seemed to be going by very fast. There was much wood in the stream. The water was very cold. We passed the brush of an island above the water. I held onto the timber with both hands and let it take me along. The shore was out of sight now.

CHAPTER 31

YOU DO NOT know how long you are in a river when the current moves swiftly. It seems a long time and it may be very short. The water was cold and in flood and many things passed that had been floated off the banks when the river rose. I was lucky to have a heavy timber to hold on to, and I lay in the icy water with my chin on the wood, holding as easily as I could with both hands. I was afraid of cramps and I hoped we would move toward the shore. We went down the river in a long curve. It was beginning to be light enough so I could see the bushes along the shoreline. There was a brush island ahead and the current moved toward the shore. I wondered if I should take off my boots and clothes and try to swim ashore, but decided not to. I had never thought of anything but that I would reach the shore some way, and I would be in a bad position if I landed barefoot. I had to get to Mestre some way.

I watched the shore come close, then swing away, then come closer again. We were floating more slowly. The shore was very close now. I could see twigs on the willow bush. The timber swung slowly so that the bank was behind me and I knew we were in an eddy. We went slowly around. As I saw the bank again, very close now, I tried holding with one arm and kicking and swimming the timber toward the bank with the other, but I did not bring it any closer. I was afraid we would move out of the eddy and, holding with one hand, I drew up my feet so they were against the side of the timber and shoved hard toward the bank. I could see the brush, but even with my momentum and swimming as hard as I could, the current was taking me away. I thought then I would drown because of my boots, but I thrashed and fought through the water, and when I looked up the bank was coming toward me, and I kept thrashing and swimming in a heavy-footed panic until I reached it. I hung to the willow branch and did not have strength to pull myself up but I knew I would not drown now. It had never occurred to me on the timber that I might drown. I felt hollow and sick in my stomach and chest from the effort, and

I held to the branches and waited. When the sick feeling was gone I pulled into the willow bushes and rested again, my arms around some brush, holding tight with my hands to the branches. Then I crawled out, pushed on through the willows and onto the bank. It was half-daylight and I saw no one. I lay flat on the bank and heard the river and the rain.

After a while I got up and started along the bank. I knew there was no bridge across the river until Latisana. I thought I might be opposite San Vito. I began to think out what I should do. Ahead there was a ditch running into the river. I went toward it. So far I had seen no one and I sat down by some bushes along the bank of the ditch and took off my shoes and emptied them of water. I took off my coat, took my wallet with my papers and my money all wet in it out of the inside pocket and then wrung the coat out. I took off my trousers and wrung them too, then my shirt and under clothing. I slapped and rubbed myself and then dressed again. I had lost my cap.

Before I put on my coat I cut the cloth stars off my sleeves and put them in the inside pocket with my money. My money was wet but was all right. I counted it. There were three thousand and some lire. My clothes felt wet and clammy and I slapped my arms to keep the circulation going. I had woven underwear and I did not think I would catch cold if I kept moving. They had taken my pistol at the road and I put the holster under my coat. I had no cape and it was cold in the rain. I started up the bank of the canal. It was daylight and the country was wet, low and dismal looking. The fields were bare and wet; a long way away I could see a campanile rising out of the plain. I came up onto a road. Ahead I saw some troops coming down the road. I limped along the side of the road and they passed me and paid no attention to me. They were a machine-gun detachment going up toward the river. I went on down the road.

That day I crossed the Venetian plain. It is a low level country and under the rain it is even flatter. Toward the sea there are salt marshes and very few roads. The roads all go along the river mouths to the sea and to cross the country you must go along the paths beside the canals. I was working across the country from the north to the south and had crossed two railway lines and many roads and finally I came out at the end of a path onto a railway line where it ran beside a marsh. It was the main line from Venice to Trieste, with a high solid embankment, a solid roadbed and double track. Down the tracks a way was a flag-station and I could see soldiers on guard. Up the line there was a bridge over a stream that flowed into the marsh.

I could see a guard too at the bridge. Crossing the fields to the north I had seen a train pass on this railroad, visible a long way across the flat plain, and I thought a train might come from Portogruaro. I watched the guards and lay down on the embankment so that I could see both ways along the track. The guard at the bridge walked a way up the line toward where I lay, then turned and went back toward the bridge. I lay, and was hungry, and waited for the train. The one I had seen was so long that the engine moved it very slowly and I was sure I could get aboard it. After I had almost given up hoping for one I saw a train coming. The engine, coming straight on, grew larger slowly. I looked at the guard at the bridge. He was walking on the near side of the bridge but on the other side of the tracks. That would put him out of sight when the train passed. I watched the engine come nearer. It was working hard. I could see there were many cars. I knew there would be guards on the train, and I tried to see where they were, but, keeping out of sight, I could not. The engine was almost to where I was lying. When it came opposite, working and puffing even on the level, and I saw the engineer pass, I stood up and stepped up close to the passing cars. If the guards were watching I was a less suspicious object standing beside the track. Several closed freight-cars passed. Then I saw a low open car of the sort they call gondolas coming, covered with canvas. I stood until it had almost passed, then jumped and caught the rear hand-rods and pulled up. I crawled down between the gondola and the shelter of the high freight-car behind. I did not think any one had seen me. I was holding to the hand-rods and crouching low, my feet on the coupling. We were almost opposite the bridge. I remembered the guard. As we passed him he looked at me. He was a boy and his helmet was too big for him. I stared at him contemptuously and he looked away. He thought I had something to do with the train.

We were past. I saw him still looking uncomfortable, watching the other cars pass and I stooped to see how the canvas was fastened. It had grummets and was laced down at the edge with cord. I took out my knife, cut the cord and put my arm under. There were hard bulges under the canvas that tightened in the rain. I looked up and ahead. There was a guard on the freight-car ahead but he was looking forward. I let go of the hand-rails and ducked under the canvas. My forehead hit something that gave me a violent bump and I felt blood on my face but I crawled on in and lay flat. Then I turned around and fastened down the canvas.

I was in under the canvas with guns. They smelled cleanly of oil and grease. I lay and listened to the rain on the canvas and the clicking of the car over the rails.

There was a little light came through and I lay and looked at the guns. They had their canvas jackets on. I thought they must have been sent ahead from the third army. The bump on my forehead was swollen and I stopped the bleeding by lying still and letting it coagulate, then picked away the dried blood except over the cut. It was nothing. I had no handkerchief, but feeling with my fingers I washed away where the dried blood had been, with rainwater that dripped from the canvas, and wiped it clean with the sleeve of my coat. I did not want to look conspicuous. I knew I would have to get out before they got to Mestre because they would be taking care of these guns. They had no guns to lose or forget about. I was terrifically hungry.

CHAPTER 32

LYING ON the floor of the flat-car with the guns beside me under the canvas I was wet, cold and very hungry. Finally I rolled over and lay flat on my stomach with my head on my arms. My knee was stiff, but it had been very satisfactory. Valentini had done a fine job. I had done half the retreat on foot and swum part of the Tagliamento with his knee. It was his knee all right. The other knee was mine. Doctors did things to you and then it was not your body any more. The head was mine, and the inside of the belly. It was very hungry in there. I could feel it turn over on itself. The head was mine, but not to use, not to think with, only to remember and not too much remember.

I could remember Catherine but I knew I would get crazy if I thought about her when I was not sure yet I would see her, so I would not think about her, only about her a little, only about her with the car going slowly and clickingly, and some light through the canvas and my lying with Catherine on the floor of the car. Hard as the floor of the car to lie not thinking only feeling, having been away too long, the clothes wet and the floor moving only a little each time and lonesome inside and alone with wet clothing and hard floor for a wife.

You did not love the floor of a flat-car nor guns with canvas jackets and the smell of vaselined metal or a canvas that rain leaked through, although it is very fine under a canvas and pleasant with guns; but you loved some one else whom now you knew was not even to be pretended there; you seeing now very clearly and coldly – not so coldly as clearly and emptily. You saw emptily, lying on your stomach, having been present when one army moved back and another came forward. You had lost your cars and your men as a floorwalker loses the stock of his department in a fire.

There was, however, no insurance. You were out of it now. You had no more obligation. If they shot floorwalkers after a fire in the department store because they spoke with an accent they had always had, then certainly the floorwalkers would not be expected to return when the store opened again for business. They might seek other employment; if there was any other employment and the police did not get them.

Anger was washed away in the river along with any obligation. Although that ceased when the carabiniere put his hands on my collar. I would like to have had the uniform off although I did not care much about the outward forms. I had taken off the stars, but that was for convenience. It was no point of honor. I was not against them. I was through. I wished them all the luck. There were the good ones, and the brave ones, and the calm ones and the sensible ones, and they deserved it. But it was not my show any more and I wished this bloody train would get to Mestre and I would eat and stop thinking. I would have to stop.

Piani would tell them they had shot me. They went through the pockets and took the papers of the people they shot. They would not have my papers. They might call me drowned. I wondered what they would hear in the States. Dead from wounds and other causes. Good Christ I was hungry. I wondered what had become of the priest at the mess. And Rinaldi. He was probably at Pordenone. If they had not gone further back. Well, I would never see him now. I would never see any of them now. That life was over. I did not think he had syphilis. It was not a serious disease anyway if you took it in time, they said. But he would worry. I would worry too if I had it. Any one would worry.

I was not made to think. I was made to eat. My God, yes. Eat and drink and sleep with Catherine. To-night maybe. No that was impossible. But to-morrow night, and a good meal and sheets and never going away again except together. Probably have to go damned quickly. She would go. I knew she would go. When would we go? That was something to think about. It was getting dark. I lay and thought where we would go. There were many places.

BOOK FOUR

CHAPTER 33

I DROPPED OFF the train in Milan as it slowed to come into the station early in the morning before it was light. I crossed the track and came out between some buildings and down onto the street. A wine shop was open and I went in for some coffee. It smelled of early morning, of swept dust, spoons in coffee-glasses and the wet circles left by wine-glasses. The proprietor was behind the bar. Two soldiers sat at a table. I stood at the bar and drank a glass of coffee and ate a piece of bread. The coffee was gray with milk, and I skimmed the milk scum off the top with a piece of bread. The proprietor looked at me.

"You want a glass of grappa?"

"No thanks."

"On me," he said and poured a small glass and pushed it toward me. "What's happening at the front?"

"I would not know."

"They are drunk," he said, moving his hand toward the two soldiers. I could believe him. They looked drunk.

"Tell me," he said, "what is happening at the front?"

"I would not know about the front."

"I saw you come down the wall. You came off the train."

"There is a big retreat."

"I read the papers. What happens? Is it over?"

"I don't think so."

He filled the glass with grappa from a short bottle. "If you are in trouble," he said, "I can keep you."

"I am not in trouble."

"If you are in trouble stay here with me."

"Where does one stay?"

"In the building. Many stay here. Any who are in trouble stay here."

"Are many in trouble?"

"It depends on the trouble. You are a South American?"

"No."

"Speak Spanish?"

"A little."

He wiped off the bar.

"It is hard now to leave the country but in no way impossible."

"I have no wish to leave."

"You can stay here as long as you want. You will see what sort of man I am."

"I have to go this morning but I will remember the address to return."

He shook his head. "You won't come back if you talk like that. I thought you were in real trouble."

"I am in no trouble. But I value the address of a friend."

I put a ten-lira note on the bar to pay for the coffee.

"Have a grappa with me," I said.

"It is not necessary."

"Have one."

He poured the two glasses.

"Remember," he said. "Come here. Do not let other people take you in. Here you are all right."

"I am sure."

"You are sure?"

"Yes."

He was serious. "Then let me tell you one thing. Do not go about with that coat."

"Why?"

"On the sleeves it shows very plainly where the stars have been cut away. The cloth is a different color."

I did not say anything.

"If you have no papers I can give you papers."

"What papers?"

"Leave-papers."

"I have no need for papers. I have papers."

"All right," he said. "But if you need papers I can get what you wish."

"How much are such papers?"

"It depends on what they are. The price is reasonable."

"I don't need any now."

He shrugged his shoulders.

"I'm all right," I said.

When I went out he said, "Don't forget that I am your friend."

"No."

"I will see you again," he said.

"Good," I said.

Outside I kept away from the station, where there were military police, and picked up a cab at the edge of the little park. I gave the driver the address of the hospital. At the hospital I went to the porter's lodge. His wife embraced me. He shook my hand.

"You are back. You are safe."

"Yes."

"Have you had breakfast?"

"Yes."

"How are you, Tenente? How are you?" the wife asked.

"Fine."

"Won't you have breakfast with us?"

"No, thank you. Tell me is Miss Barkley here at the hospital now?"

"Miss Barkley?"

"The English lady nurse."

"His girl," the wife said. She patted my arm and smiled.

"No," the porter said. "She is away."

My heart went down. "You are sure? I mean the tall blonde English young lady."

"I am sure. She is gone to Stresa."

"When did she go?"

"She went two days ago with the other lady English."

"Good," I said. "I wish you to do something for me. Do not tell any one you have seen me. It is very important."

"I won't tell any one," the porter said. I gave him a ten-lira note. He pushed it away.

"I promise you I will tell no one," he said. "I don't want any money."

"What can we do for you, Signor Tenente?" his wife asked.

"Only that," I said.

"We are dumb," the porter said. "You will let me know anything I can do?"

"Yes," I said. "Good-by. I will see you again."

They stood in the door, looking after me.

I got into the cab and gave the driver the address of Simmons, one of the men I knew who was studying singing.

Simmons lived a long way out in the town toward the Porta Magenta. He was still in bed and sleepy when I went to see him.

"You get up awfully early, Henry," he said.

"I came in on the early train."

"What's all this retreat? Were you at the front? Will you have a cigarette? They're in that box on the table." It was a big room with a bed beside the wall, a piano over on the far side and a dresser and table. I sat on a chair by the bed. Simmons sat propped up by the pillows and smoked.

"I'm in a jam, Sim," I said.

"So am I," he said. "I'm always in a jam. Won't you smoke?"

"No," I said. "What's the procedure in going to Switzerland?"

"For you? The Italians wouldn't let you out of the country."

"Yes. I know that. But the Swiss. What will they do?"

"They intern you."

"I know. But what's the mechanics of it?"

"Nothing. It's very simple. You can go anywhere. I think you just have to report or something. Why? Are you fleeing the police?"

"Nothing definite yet."

"Don't tell me if you don't want. But it would be interesting to hear. Nothing happens here. I was a great flop at Piacenza."

"I'm awfully sorry."

"Oh yes – I went very badly. I sung well too. I'm going to try it again at the Lyrico here."

"I'd like to be there."

"You're awfully polite. You aren't in a bad mess, are you?"

"I don't know."

"Don't tell me if you don't want. How do you happen to be away from the bloody front?"

"I think I'm through with it."

"Good boy. I always knew you had sense. Can I help you any way?"

"You're awfully busy."

"Not a bit of it, my dear Henry. Not a bit of it. I'd be happy to do anything."

"You're about my size. Would you go out and buy me an outfit of civilian clothes? I've clothes but they're all at Rome."

"You did live there, didn't you? It's a filthy place. How did you ever live there?"

"I wanted to be an architect."

"That's no place for that. Don't buy clothes. I'll give you all the clothes you want. I'll fit you out so you'll be a great success. Go in that dressing room. There's a closet. Take anything you want. My dear fellow, you don't want to buy clothes."

"I'd rather buy them, Sim."

"My dear fellow, it's easier for me to let you have them than go out and buy them. Have you got a passport? You won't get far without a passport."

"Yes. I've still got my passport."

"Then get dressed, my dear fellow, and off to old Helvetia."

"It's not that simple. I have to go up to Stresa first."

"Ideal, my dear fellow. You just row a boat across. If I wasn't trying to sing, I'd go with you. I'll go yet."

"You could take up yodelling."

"My dear fellow, I'll take up yodelling yet. I really can sing though. That's the strange part."

"I'll bet you can sing."

He lay back in bed smoking a cigarette.

"Don't bet too much. But I can sing though. It's damned funny, but I can. I like to sing. Listen." He roared into "Africana," his neck swelling, the veins standing out. "I can sing," he said. "Whether they like it or not." I looked out of the window. "I'll go down and let my cab go."

"Come back up, my dear fellow, and we'll have breakfast." He stepped out of bed, stood straight, took a deep breath and commenced doing bending exercises. I went downstairs and paid off the cab.

CHAPTER 34

IN CIVILIAN CLOTHES I felt a masquerader. I had been in uniform a long time and I missed the feeling of being held by your clothes. The trousers felt very floppy. I had bought a ticket at Milan for Stresa. I had also bought a new hat. I could not wear Sim's hat but his clothes were fine. They smelled of tobacco and as I sat in the compartment and looked out the window the new hat felt very new and the clothes very old. I myself felt as sad as the wet Lombard country that was outside through the window. There were some aviators in the compartment who did not think much of me. They avoided looking at me and were very scornful of a civilian my age. I did not feel insulted. In the old days I would have insulted them and picked a fight. They got off at Gallarate and I was glad to be alone. I had the paper but I did not read it because I did not want to read about the war. I was going to forget the war. I had made a separate peace. I felt damned lonely and was glad when the train got to Stresa.

At the station I had expected to see the porters from the hotels but there was no one. The season had been over a long time and no one met the train. I got down from the train with my bag, it was Sim's bag, and very light to carry, being empty except for two shirts, and stood under the roof of the station in the rain while the train went on. I found a man in the station and asked him if he knew what hotels were open. The Grand-Hôtel & des Isles Borromées was open and several small hotels that stayed open all the year. I started in the rain for the Isles Borromées carrying my bag. I saw a carriage coming down the street and signalled to the driver. It was better to arrive in a carriage. We drove up to the carriage entrance of the big hotel and the concierge came out with an umbrella and was very polite.

I took a good room. It was very big and light and looked out on the lake. The clouds were down over the lake but it would be beautiful with the sunlight. I was expecting my wife, I said. There was a big double bed, a *letto matrimoniale* with a satin coverlet. The hotel was very luxurious. I went down the long halls, down the wide stairs, through the rooms to the bar. I knew the barman and sat on a high stool and ate salted almonds and potato chips. The martini felt cool and clean.

"What are you doing here in *borghese*?" the barman asked after he had mixed a second martini.

"I am on leave. Convalescing-leave."

"There is no one here. I don't know why they keep the hotel open."

"Have you been fishing?"

"I've caught some beautiful pieces. Trolling this time of year you catch some beautiful pieces."

"Did you ever get the tobacco I sent?"

"Yes. Didn't you get my card?"

I laughed. I had not been able to get the tobacco. It was American pipe-tobacco that he wanted, but my relatives had stopped sending it or it was being held up. Anyway it never came.

"I'll get some somewhere," I said. "Tell me have you seen two English girls in the town? They came here day before yesterday."

"They are not at the hotel."

"They are nurses."

"I have seen two nurses. Wait a minute, I will find out where they are."

"One of them is my wife," I said. "I have come here to meet her."

"The other is my wife."

"I am not joking."

"Pardon my stupid joke," he said. "I did not understand." He went away and was gone quite a little while. I ate olives, salted almonds and potato chips and looked at myself in civilian clothes in the mirror behind the bar. The bartender came back. "They are at the little hotel near the station," he said.

"How about some sandwiches?"

"I'll ring for some. You understand there is nothing here, now there are no people."

"Isn't there really any one at all?"

"Yes. There are a few people."

The sandwiches came and I ate three and drank a couple more martinis. I had never tasted anything so cool and clean. They made me feel civilized. I had had too much red wine, bread, cheese, bad coffee and grappa. I sat on the high stool before the pleasant mahogany, the brass and the mirrors and did not think at all. The barman asked me some question.

"Don't talk about the war," I said. The war was a long way away. Maybe there wasn't any war. There was no war here. Then I realized it was over for me. But I did not have the feeling that it was really over. I had the feeling of a boy who thinks of what is happening at a certain hour at the schoolhouse from which he has played truant.

Catherine and Helen Ferguson were at supper when I came to their hotel. Standing in the hallway I saw them at table. Catherine's face was away from me and I saw the line of her hair and her cheek and her lovely neck and shoulders. Ferguson was talking. She stopped when I came in.

"My God," she said.

"Hello," I said.

"Why it's you!" Catherine said. Her face lighted up. She looked too happy to believe it. I kissed her. Catherine blushed and I sat down at the table.

"You're a fine mess," Ferguson said. "What are you doing here? Have you eaten?"

"No." The girl who was serving the meal came in and I told her to bring a plate for me. Catherine looked at me all the time, her eyes happy.

"What are you doing in mufti?" Ferguson asked.

"I'm in the Cabinet."

"You're in some mess."

"Cheer up, Fergy. Cheer up just a little."

"I'm not cheered by seeing you. I know the mess you've gotten this girl into. You're no cheerful sight to me."

Catherine smiled at me and touched me with her foot under the table.

"No one got me in a mess, Fergy. I get in my own messes."

"I can't stand him," Ferguson said. "He's done nothing but ruin you with his sneaking Italian tricks. Americans are worse than Italians."

"The Scotch are such a moral people," Catherine said.

"I don't mean that. I mean his Italian sneakiness."

"Am I sneaky, Fergy?"

"You are. You're worse than sneaky. You're like a snake. A snake with an Italian uniform: with a cape around your neck."

"I haven't got an Italian uniform now."

"That's just another example of your sneakiness. You had a love affair all summer and got this girl with child and now I suppose you'll sneak off."

I smiled at Catherine and she smiled at me.

"We'll both sneak off," she said.

"You're two of the same thing," Ferguson said. "I'm ashamed of you, Catherine Barkley. You have no shame and no honor and you're as sneaky as he is."

"Don't, Fergy," Catherine said and patted her hand. "Don't denounce me. You know we like each other."

"Take your hand away," Ferguson said. Her face was red. "If you had any shame it would be different. But you're God knows how many months gone with child and you think it's a joke and are all smiles because your seducer's come back. You've no shame and no feelings." She began to cry. Catherine went over and put her arm around her. As she stood comforting Ferguson, I could see no change in her figure.

"I don't care," Ferguson sobbed. "I think it's dreadful."

"There, there, Fergy," Catherine comforted her. "I'll be ashamed. Don't cry, Fergy. Don't cry, old Fergy."

"I'm not crying," Ferguson sobbed. "I'm not crying. Except for the awful thing you've gotten into." She looked at me. "I hate you," she said. "She can't make me not hate you. You dirty sneaking American Italian." Her eyes and nose were red with crying.

Catherine smiled at me.

"Don't you smile at him with your arm around me."

"You're unreasonable, Fergy."

"I know it," Ferguson sobbed. "You mustn't mind me, either of you. I'm so upset. I'm not reasonable. I know it. I want you both to be happy."

"We're happy," Catherine said. "You're a sweet Fergy."

Ferguson cried again. "I don't want you happy the way you are. Why don't you get married? You haven't got another wife have you?"

"No," I said. Catherine laughed.

"It's nothing to laugh about," Ferguson said. "Plenty of them have other wives."

"We'll be married, Fergy," Catherine said, "if it will please you."

"Not to please me. You should want to be married."

"We've been very busy."

"Yes. I know. Busy making babies." I thought she was going to cry again but she went into bitterness instead. "I suppose you'll go off with him now to-night?"

"Yes," said Catherine. "If he wants me."

"What about me?"

"Are you afraid to stay here alone?"

"Yes, I am."

"Then I'll stay with you."

"No, go on with him. Go with him right away. I'm sick of seeing both of you."

"We'd better finish dinner."

"No. Go right away."

"Fergy, be reasonable."

"I say get out right away. Go away both of you."

"Let's go then," I said. I was sick of Fergy.

"You do want to go. You see you want to leave me even to eat dinner alone. I've always wanted to go to the Italian lakes and this is how it is. Oh, Oh," she sobbed, then looked at Catherine and choked.

"We'll stay till after dinner," Catherine said. "And I'll not leave you alone if you want me to stay. I won't leave you alone, Fergy."

"No. No. I want you to go. I want you to go." She wiped her eyes. "I'm so unreasonable. Please don't mind me."

The girl who served the meal had been upset by all the crying. Now as she brought in the next course she seemed relieved that things were better.

That night at the hotel, in our room with the long empty hall outside and our shoes outside the door, a thick carpet on the floor of the room, outside the windows the rain falling and in the room light and pleasant and cheerful, then the light out and it exciting with smooth sheets and the bed comfortable, feeling that we had come home, feeling no longer alone, waking in the night to find the other one there, and not gone away; all other things were unreal. We slept when we were tired and if we woke the other one woke too so one was not alone. Often a man wishes to be alone and a girl wishes to be alone too and if they love each other they are jealous of that in each other, but I can truly say we never felt that. We could feel alone when we were together, alone against the others. It has only happened to me like that once. I have been alone while I was with many girls and that is the way that you can be most lonely. But we were never lonely and never afraid when we were together. I know that the night is not the same as the day: that all things are different, that the things of the night cannot be explained in the day, because they do not then exist, and the night can be a dreadful time for lonely people once their loneliness has started. But with Catherine there was almost no difference in the night except that it was an even better time. If people bring so much courage to this world the world has to kill them to break them, so of course it kills them. The world breaks every one and afterward many are strong at the broken places. But those that will not break it kills. It kills the very good and the very gentle and the very brave impartially. If you are none of these you can be sure it will kill you too but there will be no special hurry.

I remember waking in the morning. Catherine was asleep and the sunlight was coming in through the window. The rain had stopped and I stepped out of bed and across the floor to the window. Down below were the gardens, bare now but beautifully regular, the gravel paths, the trees, the stone wall by the lake and the lake in the sunlight with the mountains beyond. I stood at the window looking out and when I turned away I saw Catherine was awake and watching me.

"How are you, darling?" she said. "Isn't it a lovely day?"

"How do you feel?"

"I feel very well. We had a lovely night."

"Do you want breakfast?"

She wanted breakfast. So did I and we had it in bed, the November sunlight coming in the window, and the breakfast tray across my lap.

"Don't you want the paper? You always wanted the paper in the hospital."

"No," I said. "I don't want the paper now."

"Was it so bad you don't want even to read about it?"

"I don't want to read about it."

"I wish I had been with you so I would know about it too."

"I'll tell you about it if I ever get it straight in my head."

"But won't they arrest you if they catch you out of uniform?"

"They'll probably shoot me."

"Then we'll not stay here. We'll get out of the country."

"I'd thought something of that."

"We'll get out. Darling, you shouldn't take silly chances. Tell me how did you come from Mestre to Milan?"

"I came on the train. I was in uniform then."

"Weren't you in danger then?"

"Not much. I had an old order of movement. I fixed the dates on it in Mestre."

"Darling, you're liable to be arrested here any time. I won't have it. It's silly to do something like that. Where would we be if they took you off?"

"Let's not think about it. I'm tired of thinking about it."

"What would you do if they came to arrest you?"

"Shoot them."

"You see how silly you are, I won't let you go out of the hotel until we leave here."

"Where are we going to go?"

"Please don't be that way, darling. We'll go wherever you say. But please find some place to go right away."

"Switzerland is down the lake, we can go there."

"That will be lovely."

It was clouding over outside and the lake was darkening.

"I wish we did not always have to live like criminals," I said.

"Darling, don't be that way. You haven't lived like a criminal very long. And we never live like criminals. We're going to have a fine time."

"I feel like a criminal. I've deserted from the army."

"Darling, please be sensible. It's not deserting from the army. It's only the Italian army."

I laughed. "You're a fine girl. Let's get back into bed. I feel fine in bed."

A little while later Catherine said, "You don't feel like a criminal do you?"

"No," I said. "Not when I'm with you."

"You're such a silly boy," she said. "But I'll look after you. Isn't it splendid, darling, that I don't have any morning-sickness?"

"It's grand."

"You don't appreciate what a fine wife you have. But I don't care. I'll get you some place where they can't arrest you and then we'll have a lovely time."

"Let's go there right away."

"We will, darling. I'll go any place any time you wish."

"Let's not think about anything."

"All right."

CHAPTER 35

CATHERINE went along the lake to the little hotel to see Ferguson and I sat in the bar and read the papers. There were comfortable leather chairs in the bar and I sat in one of them and read until the barman came in. The army had not stood at the Tagliamento. They were falling back to the Piave. I remembered the Piave. The railroad crossed it near San Dona going up to the front. It was deep and slow there and quite narrow. Down below there were mosquito marshes and canals. There were some lovely villas. Once, before the war, going up to Cortina D'Ampezzo I had gone along it for several hours in the hills. Up there it looked like a trout stream, flowing swiftly with shallow stretches and pools under the shadow of the rocks. The road turned off from it at Cadore. I wondered how the army that was up there would come down. The barman came in.

"Count Greffi was asking for you," he said.

"Who?"

"Count Greffi. You remember the old man who was here when you were here before."

"Is he here?"

"Yes, he's here with his niece. I told him you were here. He wants you to play billiards."

"Where is he?"

"He's taking a walk."

"How is he?"

"He's younger than ever. He drank three champagne cocktails last night before dinner."

"How's his billiard game?"

"Good. He beat me. When I told him you were here he was very pleased. There's nobody here for him to play with."

Count Greffi was ninety-four years old. He had been a contemporary of Metternich and was an old man with white hair and mustache and beautiful manners. He had been in the diplomatic service of both Austria and Italy and his birthday parties were the great social event of Milan. He was living to be one hundred years old and played a smoothly fluent game of billiards that contrasted with his own ninety-four-year-old brittleness. I had met him when I had been at Stresa once before out of season and while we played billiards we drank champagne. I thought it was a splendid custom and he gave me fifteen points in a hundred and beat me.

"Why didn't you tell me he was here?"

"I forgot it."

"Who else is here?"

"No one you know. There are only six people altogether."

"What are you doing now?"

"Nothing."

"Come on out fishing."

"I could come for an hour."

"Come on. Bring the trolling line."

The barman put on a coat and we went out. We went down and got a boat and I rowed while the barman sat in the stern and let out the line with a spinner and a heavy sinker on the end to troll for lake trout. We rowed along the shore, the barman holding the line in his hand and giving it occasional jerks forward. Stresa looked very deserted from the lake. There were the long rows of bare trees, the big hotels and the closed villas. I rowed across to Isola Bella and went close to the walls, where the water deepened sharply, and you saw the rock wall slanting down in the clear water, and then up and along to the fisherman's island. The sun was under a cloud and the water was dark and smooth and very cold. We did not have a strike though we saw some circles on the water from rising fish.

I rowed up opposite the fisherman's island where there were boats drawn up and men were mending nets.

"Should we get a drink?"

"All right."

I brought the boat up to the stone pier and the barman pulled in the line, coiling it on the bottom of the boat and hooking the spinner on the edge of the gunwale. I stepped out and tied the boat. We went into a little café, sat at a bare wooden table and ordered vermouth.

"Are you tired from rowing?"

"I'll row back," he said.

"I like to row."

"Maybe if you hold the line it will change the luck."

"All right."

"Tell me how goes the war."

"Rotten."

"I don't have to go. I'm too old, like Count Greffi."

"Maybe you'll have to go yet."

"Next year they'll call my class. But I won't go."

"What will you do?"

"Get out of the country. I wouldn't go to war. I was at the war once in Abyssinia. Nix. Why do you go?"

"I don't know. I was a fool."

"Have another vermouth?"

"All right."

The barman rowed back. We trolled up the lake beyond Stresa and then down not far from shore. I held the taut line and felt the faint pulsing of the spinner revolving while I looked at the dark November water of the lake and the deserted shore. The barman rowed with long strokes and on the forward thrust of the boat the line throbbed. Once I had a strike: the line hardened suddenly and jerked back. I pulled and felt the live weight of the trout and then the line throbbed again. I had missed him.

"Did he feel big?"

"Pretty big."

"Once when I was out trolling alone I had the line in my teeth and one struck and nearly took my mouth out."

"The best way is to have it over your leg," I said. "Then you feel it and don't lose your teeth."

I put my hand in the water. It was very cold. We were almost opposite the hotel now.

"I have to go in," the barman said, "to be there for eleven o'clock. L'heure du cocktail."

"All right."

I pulled in the line and wrapped it on a stick notched at each end. The barman put the boat in a little slip in the stone wall and locked it with a chain and padlock.

"Any time you want it," he said, "I'll give you the key."

"Thanks."

We went up to the hotel and into the bar. I did not want another drink so early in the morning so I went up to our room. The maid had just finished doing the room and Catherine was not back yet. I lay down on the bed and tried to keep from thinking.

When Catherine came back it was all right again. Ferguson was downstairs, she said. She was coming to lunch.

"I knew you wouldn't mind," Catherine said.

"No," I said.

"What's the matter, darling?"

"I don't know."

"I know. You haven't anything to do. All you have is me and I go away."

"That's true."

"I'm sorry, darling. I know it must be a dreadful feeling to have nothing at all suddenly."

"My life used to be full of everything," I said. "Now if you aren't with me I haven't a thing in the world."

"But I'll be with you. I was only gone for two hours. Isn't there anything you can do?"

"I went fishing with the barman."

"Wasn't it fun?"

"Yes."

"Don't think about me when I'm not here."

"That's the way I worked it at the front. But there was something to do then."

"Othello with his occupation gone," she teased.

"Othello was a nigger," I said. "Besides, I'm not jealous. I'm just so in love with you that there isn't anything else."

"Will you be a good boy and be nice to Ferguson?"

"I'm always nice to Ferguson unless she curses me."

"Be nice to her. Think how much we have and she hasn't anything."

"I don't think she wants what we have."

"You don't know much, darling, for such a wise boy."

"I'll be nice to her."

"I know you will. You're so sweet."

"She won't stay afterward, will she?"

"No. I'll get rid of her."

"And then we'll come up here."

"Of course. What do you think I want to do?"

We went downstairs to have lunch with Ferguson. She was very impressed by the hotel and the splendor of the dining-room. We had a good lunch with a couple of bottles of white capri. Count Greffi came into the dining-room and bowed to us. His niece, who looked a little like my grandmother, was with him. I told Catherine and Ferguson about him and Ferguson was very impressed. The hotel was very big and grand and empty but the food was good, the wine was very pleasant and finally the wine made us all feel very well. Catherine had no need to feel any better. She was very happy. Ferguson became quite cheerful. I felt very well myself. After lunch Ferguson went back to her hotel. She was going to lie down for a while after lunch she said.

Along late in the afternoon some one knocked on our door.

"Who is it?"

"The Count Greffi wishes to know if you will play billiards with him."

I looked at my watch; I had taken it off and it was under the pillow.

"Do you have to go, darling?" Catherine whispered.

"I think I'd better." The watch was a quarter-past four o'clock. Out loud I said, "Tell the Count Greffi I will be in the billiard-room at five o'clock."

At a quarter to five I kissed Catherine good-by and went into the bathroom to dress. Knotting my tie and looking in the glass I looked strange to myself in the civilian clothes. I must remember to buy some more shirts and socks.

"Will you be away a long time?" Catherine asked. She looked lovely in the bed. "Would you hand me the brush?"

I watched her brushing her hair, holding her head so the weight of her hair all came on one side. It was dark outside and the light over the head of the bed shone on her hair and on her neck and shoulders. I went over and kissed her and held her hand with the brush and her head sunk back on the pillow. I kissed her neck and shoulders. I felt faint with loving her so much.

"I don't want to go away."

"I don't want you to go away."

"I won't go then."

"Yes. Go. It's only for a little while and then you'll come back."

"We'll have dinner up here."

"Hurry and come back."

I found the Count Greffi in the billiard-room. He was practicing strokes, looking very fragile under the light that came down above the billiard table. On a card table a little way beyond the light was a silver icing-bucket with the necks and corks of two champagne bottles showing above the ice. The Count Greffi straightened up when I came toward the table and walked toward me. He put out his hand, "It is such a great pleasure that you are here. You were very kind to come to play with me."

"It was very nice of you to ask me."

"Are you quite well? They told me you were wounded on the Isonzo. I hope you are well again."

"I'm very well. Have you been well?"

"Oh, I am always well. But I am getting old. I detect signs of age now."

"I can't believe it."

"Yes. Do you want to know one? It is easier for me to talk Italian. I discipline myself but I find when I am tired that it is so much easier to talk Italian. So I know I must be getting old."

"We could talk Italian. I am a little tired, too."

"Oh, but when you are tired it will be easier for you to talk English."

"American."

"Yes. American. You will please talk American. It is a delightful language."

"I hardly ever see Americans."

"You must miss them. One misses one's countrymen and especially one's countrywomen. I know that experience. Should we play or are you too tired?"

"I'm not really tired. I said that for a joke. What handicap will you give me?"

"Have you been playing very much?"

"None at all."

"You play very well. Ten points in a hundred?"

"You flatter me."

"Fifteen?"

"That would be fine but you will beat me."

"Should we play for a stake? You always wished to play for a stake."

"I think we'd better."

"All right. I will give you eighteen points and we will play for a franc a point."

He played a lovely game of billiards and with the handicap I was only four ahead at fifty. Count Greffi pushed a button on the wall to ring for the barman.

"Open one bottle please," he said. Then to me, "We will take a little stimulant." The wine was icy cold and very dry and good.

"Should we talk Italian? Would you mind very much? It is my weakness now."

We went on playing, sipping the wine between shots, speaking in Italian, but talking little, concentrated on the game. Count Greffi made his one hundredth point and with the handicap I was only at ninety-four. He smiled and patted me on the shoulder.

"Now we will drink the other bottle and you will tell me about the war." He waited for me to sit down.

"About anything else," I said.

"You don't want to talk about it? Good. What have you been reading?"

"Nothing," I said. "I'm afraid I am very dull."

"No. But you should read."

"What is there written in war-time?"

"There is 'Le Feu' by a Frenchman, Barbusse. There is 'Mr. Britling Sees Through It.'"

"No, he doesn't."

"What?"

"He doesn't see through it. Those books were at the hospital."

"Then you have been reading?"

"Yes, but nothing any good."

"I thought 'Mr. Britling' a very good study of the English middle-class soul."

"I don't know about the soul."

"Poor boy. We none of us know about the soul. Are you Croyant?"

"At night."

Count Greffi smiled and turned the glass with his fingers. "I had expected to become more devout as I grow older but somehow I haven't," he said. "It is a great pity."

"Would you like to live after death?" I asked and instantly felt a fool to mention death. But he did not mind the word.

"It would depend on the life. This life is very pleasant. I would like to live forever," he smiled. "I very nearly have."

We were sitting in the deep leather chairs, the champagne in the ice-bucket and our glasses on the table between us.

"If you ever live to be as old as I am you will find many things strange."

"You never seem old."

"It is the body that is old. Sometimes I am afraid I will break off a finger as one breaks a stick of chalk. And the spirit is no older and not much wiser."

"You are wise."

"No, that is the great fallacy; the wisdom of old men. They do not grow wise. They grow careful."

"Perhaps that is wisdom."

"It is a very unattractive wisdom. What do you value most?"

"Some one I love."

"With me it is the same. That is not wisdom. Do you value life?"

"Yes."

"So do I. Because it is all I have. And to give birthday parties," he laughed. "You are probably wiser than I am. You do not give birthday parties."

We both drank the wine.

"What do you think of the war really?" I asked.

"I think it is stupid."

"Who will win it?"

"Italy."

"Why?"

"They are a younger nation."

"Do younger nations always win wars?"

"They are apt to for a time."

"Then what happens?"

"They become older nations."

"You said you were not wise."

"Dear boy, that is not wisdom. That is cynicism."

"It sounds very wise to me."

"It's not particularly. I could quote you the examples on the other side. But it is not bad. Have we finished the champagne?"

"Almost."

"Should we drink some more? Then I must dress."

"Perhaps we'd better not now."

"You are sure you don't want more?"

"Yes." He stood up.

"I hope you will be very fortunate and very happy and very, very healthy."

"Thank you. And I hope you will live forever."

"Thank you. I have. And if you ever become devout pray for me if I am dead. I am asking several of my friends to do that. I had expected to become devout myself but it has not come." I thought he smiled sadly but I could not tell. He was so old and his face was very wrinkled, so that a smile used so many lines that all gradations were lost.

"I might become very devout," I said. "Anyway, I will pray for you."

"I had always expected to become devout. All my family died very devout. But somehow it does not come."

"It's too early."

"Maybe it is too late. Perhaps I have outlived my religious feeling."

"My own comes only at night."

"Then too you are in love. Do not forget that is a religious feeling."

"You believe so?"

"Of course." He took a step toward the table. "You were very kind to play."

"It was a great pleasure."

"We will walk up stairs together."

CHAPTER 36

THAT NIGHT THERE was a storm and I woke to hear the rain lashing the window-panes. It was coming in the open window. Some one had knocked on the door. I went to the door very softly, not to disturb Catherine, and opened it. The barman stood there. He wore his overcoat and carried his wet hat.

"Can I speak to you, Tenente?"

"What's the matter?"

"It's a very serious matter."

I looked around. The room was dark. I saw the water on the floor from the window. "Come in," I said. I took him by the arm into the bathroom; locked the door and put on the light. I sat down on the edge of the bathtub.

"What's the matter, Emilio? Are you in trouble?"

"No. You are, Tenente."

"Yes?"

"They are going to arrest you in the morning."

"Yes?"

"I came to tell you. I was out in the town and I heard them talking in a café."

"I see."

He stood there, his coat wet, holding his wet hat and said nothing.

"Why are they going to arrest me?"

"For something about the war."

"Do you know what?"

"No. But I know that they know you were here before as an officer and now you are here out of uniform. After this retreat they arrest everybody."

I thought a minute.

"What time do they come to arrest me?"

"In the morning. I don't know the time."

"What do you say to do?"

He put his hat in the washbowl. It was very wet and had been dripping on the floor.

"If you have nothing to fear an arrest is nothing. But it is always bad to be arrested – especially now."

"I don't want to be arrested."

"Then go to Switzerland."

"How?"

"In my boat."

"There is a storm," I said.

"The storm is over. It is rough but you will be all right."

"When should we go?"

"Right away. They might come to arrest you early in the morning."

"What about our bags?"

"Get them packed. Get your lady dressed. I will take care of them."

"Where will you be?"

"I will wait here. I don't want any one to see me outside in the hall."

I opened the door, closed it, and went into the bedroom. Catherine was awake.

"What is it, darling?"

"It's all right, Cat," I said. "Would you like to get dressed right away and go in a boat to Switzerland?"

"Would you?"

"No," I said. "I'd like to go back to bed."

"What is it about?"

"The barman says they are going to arrest me in the morning."

"Is the barman crazy?"

"No."

"Then please hurry, darling, and get dressed so we can start." She sat up on the side of the bed. She was still sleepy. "Is that the barman in the bathroom?"

"Yes."

"Then I won't wash. Please look the other way, darling, and I'll be dressed in just a minute."

I saw her white back as she took off her night-gown and then I looked away because she wanted me to. She was beginning to be a little big with the child and she did not want me to see her. I dressed hearing the rain on the windows. I did not have much to put in my bag.

"There's plenty of room in my bag, Cat, if you need any."

"I'm almost packed," she said. "Darling, I'm awfully stupid, but why is the barman in the bathroom?"

"Sh — he's waiting to take our bags down."

"He's awfully nice."

"He's an old friend," I said. "I nearly sent him some pipe-tobacco once."

I looked out the open window at the dark night. I could not see the lake, only the dark and the rain but the wind was quieter.

"I'm ready, darling," Catherine said.

"All right." I went to the bathroom door. "Here are the bags, Emilio," I said. The barman took the two bags.

"You're very good to help us," Catherine said.

"That's nothing, lady," the barman said. "I'm glad to help you just so I don't get in trouble myself. Listen," he said to me. "I'll take these out the servants' stairs and to the boat. You just go out as though you were going for a walk."

"It's a lovely night for a walk," Catherine said.

"It's a bad night all right."

"I'm glad I've an umbrella," Catherine said.

We walked down the hall and down the wide thickly carpeted stairs. At the foot of the stairs by the door the porter sat behind his desk.

He looked surprised at seeing us.

"You're not going out, sir?" he said.

"Yes," I said. "We're going to see the storm along the lake."

"Haven't you got an umbrella, sir?"

"No," I said. "This coat sheds water."

He looked at it doubtfully. "I'll get you an umbrella, sir," he said. He went away and came back with a big umbrella. "It is a little big, sir," he said. I gave him a ten-lira note. "Oh you are too good, sir. Thank you very much," he said. He held the door open and we went out into the rain. He smiled at Catherine and she smiled at him. "Don't stay out in the storm," he said. "You will get wet, sir and lady." He was only the second porter, and his English was still literally translated.

"We'll be back," I said. We walked down the path under the giant umbrella and out through the dark wet gardens to the road and across the road to the trellised pathway along the lake. The wind was blowing offshore now. It was a cold, wet November wind and I knew it was snowing in the mountains. We came along past the chained boats in the slips along the quay to where the barman's boat should be. The water was dark against the stone. The barman stepped out from beside the row of trees.

"The bags are in the boat," he said.

"I want to pay you for the boat," I said.

"How much money have you?"

"Not so much."

"You send me the money later. That will be all right."

"How much?"

"What you want."

"Tell me how much."

"If you get through send me five hundred francs. You won't mind that if you get through."

"All right."

"Here are sandwiches." He handed me a package. "Everything there was in the bar. It's all here. This is a bottle of brandy and a bottle of wine." I put them in my bag. "Let me pay you for those."

"All right, give me fifty lire."

I gave it to him. "The brandy is good," he said. "You don't need to be afraid to give it to your lady. She better get in the boat." He held the boat, it rising and falling against the stone wall and I helped Catherine in. She sat in the stern and pulled her cape around her.

"You know where to go?"

"Up the lake."

"You know how far?"

"Past Luino."

"Past Luino, Cannero, Cannobio, Tranzano. You aren't in Switzerland until you come to Brissago. You have to pass Monte Tamara."

"What time is it?" Catherine asked.

"It's only eleven o'clock," I said.

"If you row all the time you ought to be there by seven o'clock in the morning."

"Is it that far?"

"It's thirty-five kilometres."

"How should we go? In this rain we need a compass."

"No. Row to Isola Bella. Then on the other side of Isola Madre go with the wind. The wind will take you to Pallanza. You will see the lights. Then go up the shore."

"Maybe the wind will change."

"No," he said. "This wind will blow like this for three days. It comes straight down from the Mattarone. There is a can to bail with."

"Let me pay you something for the boat now."

"No, I'd rather take a chance. If you get through you pay me all you can."

"All right."

"I don't think you'll get drowned."

"That's good."

"Go with the wind up the lake."

"All right." I stepped in the boat.

"Did you leave the money for the hotel?"

"Yes. In an envelope in the room."

"All right. Good luck, Tenente."

"Good luck. We thank you many times."

"You won't thank me if you get drowned."

"What does he say?" Catherine asked.

"He says good luck."

"Good luck," Catherine said. "Thank you very much."

"Are you ready?"

"Yes."

He bent down and shoved us off. I dug at the water with the oars, then waved one hand. The barman waved back deprecatingly. I saw the lights of the hotel and rowed out, rowing straight out until they were out of sight. There was quite a sea running but we were going with the wind.

CHAPTER 37

I ROWED in the dark keeping the wind in my face. The rain had stopped and only came occasionally in gusts. It was very dark, and the wind was cold. I could see Catherine in the stern but I could not see the water where the blades of the oars dipped. The oars were long and there were no leathers to keep them from slipping out. I pulled, raised, leaned forward, found the water, dipped and pulled, rowing as easily as I could. I did not feather the oars because the wind was with us. I knew my hands would blister and I wanted to delay it as long as I could. The boat was light and rowed easily. I pulled it along in the dark water. I could not see, and hoped we would soon come opposite Pallanza.

We never saw Pallanza. The wind was blowing up the lake and we passed the point that hides Pallanza in the dark and never saw the lights. When we finally saw some lights much further up the lake and close to the shore it was Intra. But for a long time we did not see any lights, nor did we see the shore but rowed steadily in the dark riding with the waves. Sometimes I missed the water with the oars in the dark as a wave lifted the boat. It was quite rough; but I kept on rowing, until suddenly we were close ashore against a point of rock that rose beside us; the waves striking against it, rushing high up, then falling back. I pulled hard on the right oar and backed water with the other and we went out into the lake again; the point was out of sight and we were going on up the lake.

"We're across the lake," I said to Catherine.

"Weren't we going to see Pallanza?"

"We've missed it."

"How are you, darling?"

"I'm fine."

"I could take the oars awhile."

"No, I'm fine."

"Poor Ferguson," Catherine said. "In the morning she'll come to the hotel and find we're gone."

"I'm not worrying so much about that," I said, "as about getting into the Swiss part of the lake before it's daylight and the custom guards see us."

"Is it a long way?"

"It's some thirty kilometres from here."

I rowed all night. Finally my hands were so sore I could hardly close them over the oars. We were nearly smashed up on the shore several times. I kept fairly close to the shore because I was afraid of getting lost on the lake and losing time. Sometimes we were so close we could see a row of trees and the road along the shore with the mountains behind. The rain stopped and the wind drove the clouds so that the moon shone through and looking back I could see the long dark point of Castagnola and the lake with white-caps and beyond, the moon on the high snow mountains. Then the clouds came over the moon again and the mountains and the lake were gone, but it was much lighter than it had been before and we could see the shore. I could see it too clearly and pulled out where they would not see the boat if there were custom guards along the Pallanza road. When the moon came out again we could see white villas on the shore on the slopes of the mountain and the white road where it showed through the trees. All the time I was rowing.

The lake widened and across it on the shore at the foot of the mountains on the other side we saw a few lights that should be Luino. I saw a wedgelike gap between the mountains on the other shore and I thought that must be Luino. If it was we were making good time. I pulled in the oars and lay back on the seat. I was very, very tired of rowing. My arms and shoulders and back ached and my hands were sore.

"I could hold the umbrella," Catherine said. "We could sail with that with the wind."

"Can you steer?"

"I think so."

"You take this oar and hold it under your arm close to the side of the boat and steer and I'll hold the umbrella." I went back to the stern and showed her how to hold the oar. I took the big umbrella the porter had given me and sat facing the bow and opened it. It opened with a clap. I held it on both sides, sitting astride the handle hooked over the seat. The wind was full in it and I felt the boat suck forward while I held as hard as I could to the two edges. It pulled hard. The boat was moving fast.

"We're going beautifully," Catherine said. All I could see was umbrella ribs. The umbrella strained and pulled and I felt us driving along with it. I braced my feet and held back on it, then suddenly, it buckled; I felt a rib snap on my forehead, I tried to grab the top that was bending with the wind and the whole thing buckled and went inside out and I was astride the handle of an inside-out, ripped umbrella, where I had been holding a wind-filled pulling sail. I unhooked the handle from the seat, laid the umbrella in the bow and went back to Catherine for the oar. She was laughing. She took my hand and kept on laughing.

"What's the matter?" I took the oar.

"You looked so funny holding that thing."

"I suppose so."

"Don't be cross, darling. It was awfully funny. You looked about twenty feet broad and very affectionate holding the umbrella by the edges—" she choked.

"I'll row."

"Take a rest and a drink. It's a grand night and we've come a long way."

"I have to keep the boat out of the trough of the waves."

"I'll get you a drink. Then rest a little while, darling."

I held the oars up and we sailed with them. Catherine was opening the bag. She handed me the brandy bottle. I pulled the cork with my pocket-knife and took a long drink. It was smooth and hot and the heat went all through me and I felt warmed and cheerful. "It's lovely brandy," I said. The moon was under again but I could see the shore. There seemed to be another point going out a long way ahead into the lake.

"Are you warm enough, Cat?"

"I'm splendid. I'm a little stiff."

"Bail out that water and you can put your feet down."

Then I rowed and listened to the oarlocks and the dip and scrape of the bailing tin under the stern seat.

"Would you give me the bailer?" I said. "I want a drink."

"It's awful dirty."

"That's all right. I'll rinse it."

I heard Catherine rinsing it over the side. Then she handed it to me dipped full of water. I was thirsty after the brandy and the water was icy cold, so cold it made my teeth ache. I looked toward the shore. We were closer to the long point. There were lights in the bay ahead.

"Thanks," I said and handed back the tin pail.

"You're ever so welcome," Catherine said. "There's much more if you want it."

"Don't you want to eat something?"

"No. I'll be hungry in a little while. We'll save it till then."

"All right."

What looked like a point ahead was a long high headland. I went further out in the lake to pass it. The lake was much narrower now. The moon was out again and the guardia di finanza could have seen our boat black on the water if they had been watching.

"How are you, Cat?" I asked.

"I'm all right. Where are we?"

"I don't think we have more than about eight miles more."

"That's a long way to row, you poor sweet. Aren't you dead?"

"No. I'm all right. My hands are sore is all."

We went on up the lake. There was a break in the mountains on the right bank, a flattening-out with a low shore line that I thought must be Cannobio. I stayed a long way out because it was from now on that we ran the most danger of meeting guardia. There was a high dome-capped mountain on the other shore a way ahead. I was tired. It was no great distance to row but when you were out of condition it had been a long way. I knew I had to pass that mountain and go up the lake at least five miles further before we would be in Swiss water. The moon was almost down now but before it went down the sky clouded over again and it was very dark. I stayed well out in the lake, rowing awhile, then resting and holding the oars so that the wind struck the blades.

"Let me row awhile," Catherine said.

"I don't think you ought to."

"Nonsense. It would be good for me. It would keep me from being too stiff."

"I don't think you should, Cat."

"Nonsense. Rowing in moderation is very good for the pregnant lady."

"All right, you row a little moderately. I'll go back, then you come up. Hold on to both gunwales when you come up."

I sat in the stern with my coat on and the collar turned up and watched Catherine row. She rowed very well but the oars were too long and bothered her. I opened the bag and ate a couple of sandwiches and took a drink of the brandy. It made everything much better and I took another drink.

"Tell me when you're tired," I said. Then a little later, "Watch out the oar doesn't pop you in the tummy."

"If it did" – Catherine said between strokes– "life might be much simpler."

I took another drink of the brandy.

"How are you going?"

"All right."

"Tell me when you want to stop."

"All right."

I took another drink of the brandy, then took hold of the two gunwales of the boat and moved forward.

"No. I'm going beautifully."

"Go on back to the stern. I've had a grand rest."

For a while, with the brandy, I rowed easily and steadily. Then I began to catch crabs and soon I was just chopping along again with a thin brown taste of bile from having rowed too hard after the brandy.

"Give me a drink of water, will you?" I said.

"That's easy," Catherine said.

Before daylight it started to drizzle. The wind was down or we were protected by mountains that bounded the curve the lake had made. When I knew daylight was coming I settled down and rowed hard. I did not know where we were and I wanted to get into the Swiss part of the lake. When it was beginning to be daylight we were quite close to the shore. I could see the rocky shore and the trees.

"What's that?" Catherine said. I rested on the oars and listened. It was a motor boat chugging out on the lake. I pulled close up to the shore and lay quiet. The chugging came closer; then we saw the motor boat in the rain a little astern of us. There were four guardia di finanza in the stern, their alpini hats pulled down, their cape collars turned up and their carbines slung across their backs. They all looked sleepy so early in the morning. I could see the yellow on their hats and the yellow marks on their cape collars. The motor boat chugged on and out of sight in the rain.

I pulled out into the lake. If we were that close to the border I did not want to be hailed by a sentry along the road. I stayed out where I could just see the shore and rowed on for three quarters of an hour in the rain. We heard a motor boat once more but I kept quiet until the noise of the engine went away across the lake.

"I think we're in Switzerland, Cat," I said.

"Really?"

"There's no way to know until we see Swiss troops."

"Or the Swiss navy."

"The Swiss navy's no joke for us. That last motor boat we heard was probably the Swiss navy."

"If we're in Switzerland let's have a big breakfast. They have wonderful rolls and butter and jam in Switzerland."

It was clear daylight now and a fine rain was falling. The wind was still blowing outside up the lake and we could see the tops of the white-caps going away from us and up the lake. I was sure we were in Switzerland now. There were many houses back in the trees from the shore and up the shore a way was a village with stone houses, some villas on the hills and a church. I had been looking at the road that skirted the shore for guards but did not see any. The road came quite close to the lake now and I saw a soldier coming out of a café on the road. He wore a gray-green uniform and a helmet like the Germans. He had a healthy-looking face and a little toothbrush mustache. He looked at us.

"Wave to him," I said to Catherine. She waved and the soldier smiled embarrassedly and gave a wave of his hand. I eased up rowing. We were passing the waterfront of the village.

"We must be well inside the border," I said.

"We want to be sure, darling. We don't want them to turn us back at the frontier."

"The frontier is a long way back. I think this is the customs town. I'm pretty sure it's Brissago."

"Won't there be Italians there? There are always both sides at a customs town."

"Not in war-time. I don't think they let the Italians cross the frontier."

It was a nice-looking little town. There were many fishing boats along the quay and nets were spread on racks. There was a fine November rain falling but it looked cheerful and clean even with the rain.

"Should we land then and have breakfast?"

"All right."

I pulled hard on the left oar and came in close, then straightened out when we were close to the quay and brought the boat alongside. I pulled in the oars, took hold of an iron ring, stepped up on the wet stone and was in Switzerland. I tied the boat and held my hand down to Catherine.

"Come on up, Cat. It's a grand feeling."

"What about the bags?"

"Leave them in the boat."

Catherine stepped up and we were in Switzerland together.

"What a lovely country," she said.

"Isn't it grand?"

"Let's go and have breakfast!"

"Isn't it a grand country? I love the way it feels under my shoes."

"I'm so stiff I can't feel it very well. But it feels like a splendid country. Darling, do you realize we're here and out of that bloody place?"

"I do. I really do. I've never realized anything before."

"Look at the houses. Isn't this a fine square? There's a place we can get breakfast."

"Isn't the rain fine? They never had rain like this in Italy. It's cheerful rain."

"And we're here, darling! Do you realize we're here?"

We went inside the café and sat down at a clean wooden table. We were cockeyed excited. A splendid clean-looking woman with an apron came and asked us what we wanted.

"Rolls and jam and coffee," Catherine said.

"I'm sorry, we haven't any rolls in war-time."

"Bread then."

"I can make you some toast."

"All right."

"I want some eggs fried too."

"How many eggs for the gentleman?"

"Three."

"Take four, darling."

"Four eggs."

The woman went away. I kissed Catherine and held her hand very tight. We looked at each other and at the café.

"Darling, darling, isn't it lovely?"

"It's grand," I said.

"I don't mind there not being rolls," Catherine said. "I thought about them all night. But I don't mind it. I don't mind it at all."

"I suppose pretty soon they will arrest us."

"Never mind, darling. We'll have breakfast first. You won't mind being arrested after breakfast. And then there's nothing they can do to us. We're British and American citizens in good standing."

"You have a passport, haven't you?"

"Of course. Oh let's not talk about it. Let's be happy."

"I couldn't be any happier," I said. A fat gray cat with a tail that lifted like a plume crossed the floor to our table and curved against my leg to purr each time she rubbed. I reached down and stroked her. Catherine smiled at me very happily. "Here comes the coffee," she said.

They arrested us after breakfast. We took a little walk through the village then went down to the quay to get our bags. A soldier was standing guard over the boat.

"Is this your boat?"

"Yes."

"Where do you come from?"

"Up the lake."

"Then I have to ask you to come with me."

"How about the bags?"

"You can carry the bags."

I carried the bags and Catherine walked beside me and the soldier walked along behind us to the old custom house. In the custom house a lieutenant, very thin and military, questioned us.

"What nationality are you?"

"American and British."

"Let me see your passports."

I gave him mine and Catherine got hers out of her handbag.

He examined them for a long time.

"Why do you enter Switzerland this way in a boat?"

"I am a sportsman," I said. "Rowing is my great sport. I always row when I get a chance."

"Why do you come here?"

"For the winter sport. We are tourists and we want to do the winter sport."

"This is no place for winter sport."

"We know it. We want to go where they have the winter sport."

"What have you been doing in Italy?"

"I have been studying architecture. My cousin has been studying art."

"Why do you leave there?"

"We want to do the winter sport. With the war going on you cannot study architecture."

"You will please stay where you are," the lieutenant said. He went back into the building with our passports.

"You're splendid, darling," Catherine said. "Keep on the same track. You want to do the winter sport."

"Do you know anything about art?"

"Rubens," said Catherine.

"Large and fat," I said.

"Titian," Catherine said.

"Titian-haired," I said. "How about Mantegna?"

"Don't ask hard ones," Catherine said. "I know him though – very bitter."

"Very bitter," I said. "Lots of nail holes."

"You see I'll make you a fine wife," Catherine said. "I'll be able to talk art with your customers."

"Here he comes," I said. The thin lieutenant came down the length of the custom house, holding our passports.

"I will have to send you into Locarno," he said. "You can get a carriage and a soldier will go in with you."

"All right," I said. "What about the boat?"

"The boat is confiscated. What have you in those bags?"

He went all through the two bags and held up the quarter-bottle of brandy. "Would you join me in a drink?" I asked.

"No thank you." He straightened up. "How much money have you?"

"Twenty-five hundred lire."

He was favorably impressed. "How much has your cousin?"

Catherine had a little over twelve hundred lire. The lieutenant was pleased. His attitude toward us became less haughty.

"If you are going for winter sports," he said, "Wengen is the place. My father has a very fine hotel at Wengen. It is open all the time."

"That's splendid," I said. "Could you give me the name?"

"I will write it on a card." He handed me the card very politely.

"The soldier will take you into Locarno. He will keep your passports. I regret this but it is necessary. I have good hopes they will give you a visa or a police permit at Locarno."

He handed the two passports to the soldier and carrying the bags we started into the village to order a carriage. "Hi," the lieutenant called to the soldier. He said something in a German dialect to him. The soldier slung his rifle on his back and picked up the bags.

"It's a great country," I said to Catherine.

"It's so practical."

"Thank you very much," I said to the lieutenant. He waved his hand.

"Service!" he said. We followed our guard into the village.

We drove to Locarno in a carriage with the soldier sitting on the front seat with the driver. At Locarno we did not have a bad time. They questioned us but they were polite because we had passports and money. I do not think they believed a word of the story and I thought it was silly but it was like a law-court. You did not want something reasonable, you wanted something technical and then stuck to it without explanations. But we had passports and we would spend the money. So they gave us provisional visas.

At any time this visa might be withdrawn. We were to report to the police wherever we went.

Could we go wherever we wanted? Yes. Where did we want to go?

"Where do you want to go, Cat?"

"Montreux."

"It is a very nice place," the official said. "I think you will like that place."

"Here at Lacarno is a very nice place," another official said. "I am sure you would like it here very much at Locarno. Locarno is a very attractive place."

"We would like some place where there is winter sport."

"There is no winter sport at Montreux."

"I beg your pardon," the other official said. "I come from Montreux. There is very certainly winter sport on the Montreux Oberland Bernois railway. It would be false for you to deny that."

"I do not deny it. I simply said there is no winter sport at Montreux."

"I question that," the other official said. "I question that statement."

"I hold to that statement."

"I question that statement. I myself have *luge-ed* into the streets of Montreux. I have done it not once but several times. Luge-ing is certainly winter sport."

The other official turned to me.

"Is luge-ing your idea of winter sport, sir? I tell you you would be very comfortable here in Locarno. You would find the climate healthy, you would find the environs attractive. You would like it very much."

"The gentleman has expressed a wish to go to Montreux."

"What is luge-ing?" I asked.

"You see he has never even heard of luge-ing!"

That meant a great deal to the second official. He was pleased by that.

"Luge-ing," said the first official, "is tobogganing."

"I beg to differ," the other official shook his head. "I must differ again. The toboggan is very different from the luge. The toboggan is constructed in Canada of flat laths. The luge is a common sled with runners. Accuracy means something."

"Couldn't we toboggan?" I asked.

"Of course you could toboggan," the first official said. "You could toboggan very well. Excellent Canadian toboggans are sold in Montreux. Ochs Brothers sell toboggans. They import their own toboggans."

The second official turned away. "Tobogganing," he said, "requires a special piste. You could not toboggan into the streets of Montreux. Where are you stopping here?"

"We don't know," I said. "We just drove in from Brissago. The carriage is outside."

"You make no mistake in going to Montreux," the first official said. "You will find the climate delightful and beautiful. You will have no distance to go for winter sport."

"If you really want winter sport," the second official said, "you will go to the Engadine or to Mürren. I must protest against your being advised to go to Montreux for the winter sport."

"At Les Avants above Montreux there is excellent winter sport of every sort." The champion of Montreux glared at his colleague.

"Gentlemen," I said, "I am afraid we must go. My cousin is very tired. We will go tentatively to Montreux."

"I congratulate you," the first official shook my hand.

"I believe that you will regret leaving Locarno," the second official said. "At any rate you will report to the police at Montreux."

"There will be no unpleasantness with the police," the first official assured me. "You will find all the inhabitants extremely courteous and friendly."

"Thank you both very much," I said. "We appreciate your advice very much."

"Good-by," Catherine said. "Thank you both very much."

They bowed us to the door, the champion of Locarno a little coldly. We went down the steps and into the carriage.

"My God, darling," Catherine said. "Couldn't we have gotten away any sooner?" I gave the name of a hotel one of the officials had recommended to the driver. He picked up the reins.

"You've forgotten the army," Catherine said. The soldier was standing by the carriage. I gave him a ten-lira note. "I have no Swiss money yet," I said. He thanked me, saluted and went off. The carriage started and we drove to the hotel.

"How did you happen to pick out Montreux?" I asked Catherine. "Do you really want to go there?"

"It was the first place I could think of," she said. "It's not a bad place. We can find some place up in the mountains."

"Are you sleepy?"

"I'm asleep right now."

"We'll get a good sleep. Poor Cat, you had a long bad night."

"I had a lovely time," Catherine said. "Especially when you sailed with the umbrella."

"Can you realize we're in Switzerland?"

"No, I'm afraid I'll wake up and it won't be true."

"I am too."

"It is true, isn't it, darling? I'm not just driving down to the stazione in Milan to see you off."

"I hope not."

"Don't say that. It frightens me. Maybe that's where we're going."

"I'm so groggy I don't know," I said.

"Let me see your hands."

I put them out. They were both blistered raw.

"There's no hole in my side," I said.

"Don't be sacrilegious."

I felt very tired and vague in the head. The exhilaration was all gone. The carriage was going along the street.

"Poor hands," Catherine said.

"Don't touch them," I said. "By God I don't know where we are. Where are we going, driver?" The driver stopped his horse.

"To the Hotel Metropole. Don't you want to go there?"

"Yes," I said. "It's all right, Cat."

"It's all right, darling. Don't be upset. We'll get a good sleep and you won't feel groggy to-morrow."

"I get pretty groggy," I said. "It's like a comic opera to-day. Maybe I'm hungry."

"You're just tired, darling. You'll be fine." The carriage pulled up before the hotel. Some one came out to take our bags.

"I feel all right," I said. We were down on the pavement going into the hotel.

"I know you'll be all right. You're just tired. You've been up a long time."

"Anyhow we're here."

"Yes, we're really here."

We followed the boy with the bags into the hotel.

BOOK FIVE

CHAPTER 38

THAT FALL the snow came very late. We lived in a brown wooden house in the pine trees on the side of the mountain and at night there was frost so that there was thin ice over the water in the two pitchers on the dresser in the morning. Mrs. Guttingen came into the room early in the morning to shut the windows and started a fire in the tall porcelain stove. The pine wood crackled and sparked and then the fire roared in the stove and the second time Mrs. Guttingen came into the room she brought big chunks of wood for the fire and a pitcher of hot water. When the room was warm she brought in breakfast. Sitting up in bed eating breakfast we could see the lake and the mountains across the lake on the French side. There was snow on the tops of the mountains and the lake was a gray steel-blue.

Outside, in front of the chalet a road went up the mountain. The wheel ruts and ridges were iron hard with the frost, and the road climbed steadily through the forest and up and around the mountain to where there were meadows, and barns and cabins in the meadows at the edge of the woods looking across the valley. The valley was deep and there was a stream at the bottom that flowed down into the lake and when the wind blew across the valley you could hear the stream in the rocks.

Sometimes we went off the road and on a path through the pine forest. The floor of the forest was soft to walk on; the frost did not harden it as it did the road. But we did not mind the hardness of the road because we had nails in the soles and heels of our boots and the heel nails bit on the frozen ruts and with nailed boots it was good walking on the road and invigorating. But it was lovely walking in the woods.

In front of the house where we lived the mountain went down steeply to the little plain along the lake and we sat on the porch of the house in the sun and saw the winding of the road down the mountain-side and the terraced vineyards on the side of the lower mountain, the vines all dead now for the winter and the fields divided by stone walls, and below the vineyards the houses of the town on the narrow plain along the lake shore. There was an island with two trees on the lake and the trees looked like the double sails of a fishing-boat. The mountains were sharp and steep on the other side of the lake and down at the end of the lake was the plain of the Rhone Valley flat between the two ranges of mountains; and up the valley where the mountains cut it off was the Dent du Midi. It was a high snowy mountain and it dominated the valley but it was so far away that it did not make a shadow.

When the sun was bright we ate lunch on the porch but the rest of the time we ate upstairs in a small room with plain wooden walls and a big stove in the corner. We bought books and magazines in the town and a copy of "Hoyle" and learned many two-handed card games. The small room with the stove was our living-room. There were two comfortable chairs and a table for books and magazines and we played cards on the dining-table when it was cleared away. Mr. and Mrs. Guttingen lived downstairs and we would hear them talking sometimes in the evening and they were very happy together too. He had been a headwaiter and she had worked as maid in the same hotel and they had saved their money to buy this place. They had a son who was studying to be a headwaiter. He was at a hotel in Zurich. Downstairs there was a parlor where they sold wine and beer, and sometimes in the evening we would hear carts stop outside on the road and men come up the steps to go in the parlor to drink wine.

There was a box of wood in the hall outside the living-room and I kept up the fire from it. But we did not stay up very late. We went to bed in the dark in the big bedroom and when I was undressed I opened the windows and saw the night and the cold stars and the pine trees below the window and then got into bed as fast as I could. It was lovely in bed with the air so cold and clear and the night outside the window. We slept well and if I woke in the night I knew it was from only one cause and I would shift the feather bed over, very softly so that Catherine would not be wakened and then go back to sleep again, warm and with the new lightness of thin covers. The war seemed as far away as the football games of some one else's college. But I knew from the papers that they were still fighting in the mountains because the snow would not come.

Sometimes we walked down the mountain into Montreux. There was a path went down the mountain but it was steep and so usually we took the road and walked down on the wide hard road between fields and then below between the stone walls of the vineyards and on down between the houses of the villages along the way. There were three villages; Chernex, Fontanivent, and the other I forget. Then along the road we passed an old square-built stone château on a ledge on the side of the mountain-side with the terraced fields of vines, each vine tied to a stick to hold it up, the vines dry and brown and the earth ready for the snow and the lake down below flat and gray as steel. The road went down a long grade below the château and then turned to the right and went down very steeply and paved with cobbles, into Montreux.

We did not know any one in Montreux. We walked along beside the lake and saw the swans and the many gulls and terns that flew up when you came close and screamed while they looked down at the water. Out on the lake there were flocks of grebes, small and dark, and leaving trails in the water when they swam.

In the town we walked along the main street and looked in the windows of the shops. There were many big hotels that were closed but most of the shops were open and the people were very glad to see us. There was a fine coiffeur's place where Catherine went to have her hair done. The woman who ran it was very cheerful and the only person we knew in Montreux. While Catherine was there I went up to a beer place and drank dark Munich beer and read the papers. I read the Corriere della Sera and the English and American papers from Paris. All the advertisements were blacked out, supposedly to prevent communication in that way with the enemy. The papers were bad reading. Everything was going very badly every-where. I sat back in the corner with a heavy mug of dark beer and an opened glazed-paper package of pretzels and ate the pretzels for the salty flavor and the good way they made the beer taste and read about disaster. I thought Catherine would come by but she did not come, so I hung the papers back on the rack, paid for my beer and went up the street to look for her. The day was cold and dark and wintry and the stone of the houses looked cold. Catherine was still in the hairdresser's shop. The woman was waving her hair. I sat in the little booth and watched. It was exciting to watch and Catherine smiled and talked to me and my voice was a little thick from being excited. The tongs made a pleasant clicking sound and I could see Catherine in three mirrors and it was pleasant and warm in the booth. Then the woman put up Catherine's hair, and Catherine looked in the mirror and changed it a little, taking out and putting in pins; then stood up. "I'm sorry to have taken such a long time."

"Monsieur was very interested. Were you not, monsieur?" the woman smiled.

"Yes," I said.

We went out and up the street. It was cold and wintry and the wind was blowing. "Oh, darling, I love you so," I said.

"Don't we have a fine time?" Catherine said. "Look. Let's go some place and have beer instead of tea. It's very good for young Catherine. It keeps her small."

"Young Catherine," I said. "That loafer."

"She's been very good," Catherine said. "She makes very little trouble. The doctor says beer will be good for me and keep her small."

"If you keep her small enough and she's a boy, maybe he will be a jockey."

"I suppose if we really have this child we ought to get married," Catherine said. We were in the beer place at the corner table. It was getting dark outside. It was still early but the day was dark and the dusk was coming early.

"Let's get married now," I said.

"No," Catherine said. "It's too embarrassing now. I show too plainly. I won't go before any one and be married in this state."

"I wish we'd gotten married."

"I suppose it would have been better. But when could we, darling?"

"I don't know."

"I know one thing. I'm not going to be married in this splendid matronly state."

"You're not matronly."

"Oh yes, I am, darling. The hairdresser asked me if this was our first. I lied and said no, we had two boys and two girls."

"When will we be married?"

"Any time after I'm thin again. We want to have a splendid wedding with every one thinking what a handsome young couple."

"And you're not worried?"

"Darling, why should I be worried? The only time I ever felt badly was when I felt like a whore in Milan and that only lasted seven minutes and besides it was the room furnishings. Don't I make you a good wife?"

"You're a lovely wife."

"Then don't be too technical, darling. I'll marry you as soon as I'm thin again."

"All right."

"Do you think I ought to drink another beer? The doctor said I was rather narrow in the hips and it's all for the best if we keep young Catherine small."

"What else did he say?" I was worried.

"Nothing. I have a wonderful blood-pressure, darling. He admired my blood-pressure greatly."

"What did he say about you being too narrow in the hips?"

"Nothing. Nothing at all. He said I shouldn't ski."

"Quite right."

"He said it was too late to start if I'd never done it before. He said I could ski if I wouldn't fall down."

"He's just a big-hearted joker."

"Really he was very nice. We'll have him when the baby comes."

"Did you ask him if you ought to get married?"

"No. I told him we'd been married four years. You see, darling, if I marry you I'll be an American and any time we're married under American law the child is legitimate."

"Where did you find that out?"

"In the New York World Almanac in the library."

"You're a grand girl."

"I'll be very glad to be an American and we'll go to America won't we, darling? I want to see Niagara Falls."

"You're a fine girl."

"There's something else I want to see but I can't remember it."

"The stockyards?"

"No. I can't remember it."

"The Woolworth building?"

"No."

"The Grand Canyon?"

"No. But I'd like to see that."

"What was it?"

"The Golden Gate! That's what I want to see. Where is the Golden Gate?"

"San Francisco."

"Then let's go there. I want to see San Francisco anyway."

"All right. We'll go there."

"Now let's go up the mountain. Should we? Can we get the M.O.B.?"

"There's a train a little after five."

"Let's get that."

"All right. I'll drink one more beer first."

When we went out to go up the street and climb the stairs to the station it was very cold. A cold wind was coming down the Rhone Valley. There were lights in the shop windows and we climbed the steep stone stairway to the upper street, then up another stairs to the station. The electric train was there waiting, all the lights on. There was a dial that showed when it left. The clock hands pointed to ten minutes after five. I looked at the station clock. It was five minutes after. As we got on board I saw the motorman and conductor coming out of the station wine-shop. We sat down and opened the window. The train was electrically heated and stuffy but fresh cold air came in through the window.

"Are you tired, Cat?" I asked.

"No. I feel splendid."

"It isn't a long ride."

"I like the ride," she said. "Don't worry about me, darling. I feel fine."

Snow did not come until three days before Christmas. We woke one morning and it was snowing. We stayed in bed with the fire roaring in the stove and watched the snow fall. Mrs. Guttingen took away the breakfast trays and put more wood in the stove. It was a big snow storm. She said it had started about midnight. I went to the window and looked out but could not see across the road. It was blowing and snowing wildly. I went back to bed and we lay and talked.

"I wish I could ski," Catherine said. "It's rotten not to be able to ski."

"We'll get a bobsled and come down the road. That's no worse for you than riding in a car."

"Won't it be rough?"

"We can see."

"I hope it won't be too rough."

"After a while we'll take a walk in the snow."

"Before lunch," Catherine said, "so we'll have a good appetite."

"I'm always hungry."

"So am I."

We went out in the snow but it was drifted so that we could not walk far. I went ahead and made a trail down to the station but when we reached there we had gone far enough. The snow was blowing so we could hardly see and we went into the little inn by the station and swept each other off with a broom and sat on a bench and had vermouths.

"It is a big storm," the barmaid said.

"Yes."

"The snow is very late this year."

"Yes."

"Could I eat a chocolate bar?" Catherine asked. "Or is it too close to lunch? I'm always hungry."

"Go on and eat one," I said.

"I'll take one with filberts," Catherine said.

"They are very good," the girl said, "I like them the best."

"I'll have another vermouth," I said.

When we came out to start back up the road our track was filled in by the snow. There were only faint indentations where the holes had been. The snow blew in our faces so we could hardly see. We brushed off and went in to have lunch. Mr. Guttingen served the lunch.

"To-morrow there will be ski-ing," he said. "Do you ski, Mr. Henry?"

"No. But I want to learn."

"You will learn very easily. My boy will be here for Christmas and he will teach you."

"That's fine. When does he come?"

"To-morrow night."

When we were sitting by the stove in the little room after lunch looking out the window at the snow coming down Catherine said, "Wouldn't you like to go on a trip somewhere by yourself, darling, and be with men and ski?"

"No. Why should I?"

"I should think sometimes you would want to see other people besides me."

"Do you want to see other people?"

"No."

"Neither do I."

"I know. But you're different. I'm having a child and that makes me contented not to do anything. I know I'm awfully stupid now and I talk too much and I think you ought to get away so you won't be tired of me."

"Do you want me to go away?"

"No. I want you to stay."

"That's what I'm going to do."

"Come over here," she said. "I want to feel the bump on your head. It's a big bump." She ran her finger over it. "Darling, would you like to grow a beard?"

"Would you like me to?"

"It might be fun. I'd like to see you with a beard."

"All right. I'll grow one. I'll start now this minute. It's a good idea. It will give me something to do."

"Are you worried because you haven't anything to do?"

"No. I like it. I have a fine life. Don't you?"

"I have a lovely life. But I was afraid because I'm big now that maybe I was a bore to you."

"Oh, Cat. You don't know how crazy I am about you."

"This way?"

"Just the way you are. I have a fine time. Don't we have a good life?"

"I do, but I thought maybe you were restless."

"No. Sometimes I wonder about the front and about people I know but I don't worry. I don't think about anything much."

"Who do you wonder about?"

"About Rinaldi and the priest and lots of people I know. But I don't think about them much. I don't want to think about the war. I'm through with it."

"What are you thinking about now?"

"Nothing."

"Yes you were. Tell me."

"I was wondering whether Rinaldi had the syphilis."

"Was that all?"

"Yes."

"Has he the syphilis?"

"I don't know."

"I'm glad you haven't. Did you ever have anything like that?"

"I had gonorrhea."

"I don't want to hear about it. Was it very painful, darling?"

"Very."

"I wish I'd had it."

"No you don't."

"I do. I wish I'd had it to be like you. I wish I'd stayed with all your girls so I could make fun of them to you."

"That's a pretty picture."

"It's not a pretty picture you having gonorrhea."

"I know it. Look at it snow now."

"I'd rather look at you. Darling, why don't you let your hair grow?"

"How grow?"

"Just grow a little longer."

"It's long enough now."

"No, let it grow a little longer and I could cut mine and we'd be just alike only one of us blonde and one of us dark."

"I wouldn't let you cut yours."

"It would be fun. I'm tired of it. It's an awful nuisance in the bed at night."

"I like it."

"Wouldn't you like it short?"

"I might. I like it the way it is."

"It might be nice short. Then we'd both be alike. Oh, darling, I want you so much I want to be you too."

"You are. We're the same one."

"I know it. At night we are."

"The nights are grand."

"I want us to be all mixed up. I don't want you to go away. I just said that. You go if you want to. But hurry right back. Why, darling, I don't live at all when I'm not with you."

"I won't ever go away," I said. "I'm no good when you're not there. I haven't any life at all any more."

"I want you to have a life. I want you to have a fine life. But we'll have it together, won't we?"

"And now do you want me to stop growing my beard or let it go on?"

"Go on. Grow it. It will be exciting. Maybe it will be done for New Year's."

"Now do you want to play chess?"

"I'd rather play with you."

"No. Let's play chess."

"And afterward we'll play?"

"Yes."

"All right."

I got out the chess-board and arranged the pieces. It was still snowing hard outside.

One time in the night I woke up and knew that Catherine was awake too. The moon was shining in the window and made shadows on the bed from the bars on the window-panes.

"Are you awake, sweetheart?"

"Yes. Can't you sleep?"

"I just woke up thinking about how I was nearly crazy when I first met you. Do you remember?"

"You were just a little crazy."

"I'm never that way any more. I'm grand now. You say grand so sweetly. Say grand."

"Grand."

"Oh, you're sweet. And I'm not crazy now. I'm just very, very, very happy."

"Go on to sleep," I said.

"All right. Let's go to sleep at exactly the same moment."

"All right."

But we did not. I was awake for quite a long time thinking about things and watching Catherine sleeping, the moonlight on her face. Then I went to sleep, too.

CHAPTER 39

BY THE MIDDLE of January I had a beard and the winter had settled into bright cold days and hard cold nights. We could walk on the roads again. The snow was packed hard and smooth by the hay-sleds and wood-sledges and the logs that were hauled down the mountain. The snow lay over all the country, down almost to Montreux. The mountains on the other side of the lake were all white and the plain of the Rhone Valley was covered. We took long walks on the other side of the mountain to the Bains de l'Alliaz. Catherine wore hobnailed boots and a cape and carried a stick with a sharp steel point. She did not look big with the cape and we would not walk too fast but stopped and sat on logs by the roadside to rest when she was tired.

There was an inn in the trees at the Bains de l'Alliaz where the woodcutters stopped to drink, and we sat inside warmed by the stove and drank hot red wine with spices and lemon in it. They called it glühwein and it was a good thing to warm you and to celebrate with. The inn was dark and smoky inside and afterward when you went out the cold air came sharply into your lungs and numbed the edge of your nose as you inhaled. We looked back at the inn with light coming from the windows and the woodcutters' horses stamping and jerking their heads outside to keep warm. There was frost on the hairs of their muzzles and their breathing made plumes of frost in the air. Going up the road toward home the road was smooth and slippery for a while and the ice orange from the horses until the wood-hauling track turned off. Then the road was clean-packed snow and led through the woods, and twice coming home in the evening, we saw foxes.

It was a fine country and every time that we went out it was fun.

"You have a splendid beard now," Catherine said. "It looks just like the woodcutters'. Did you see the man with the tiny gold earrings?"

"He's a chamois hunter," I said. "They wear them because they say it makes them hear better."

"Really? I don't believe it. I think they wear them to show they are chamois hunters. Are there chamois near here?"

"Yes, beyond the Dent de Jaman."

"It was fun seeing the fox."

"When he sleeps he wraps that tail around him to keep warm."

"It must be a lovely feeling."

"I always wanted to have a tail like that. Wouldn't it be fun if we had brushes like a fox?"

"It might be very difficult dressing."

"We'd have clothes made, or live in a country where it wouldn't make any difference."

"We live in a country where nothing makes any difference. Isn't it grand how we never see any one? You don't want to see people do you, darling?"

"No."

"Should we sit here just a minute? I'm a little bit tired."

We sat close together on the logs. Ahead the road went down through the forest.

"She won't come between us, will she? The little brat."

"No. We won't let her."

"How are we for money?"

"We have plenty. They honored the last sight draft."

"Won't your family try and get hold of you now they know you're in Switzerland?"

"Probably. I'll write them something."

"Haven't you written them?"

"No. Only the sight draft."

"Thank God I'm not your family."

"I'll send them a cable."

"Don't you care anything about them?"

"I did, but we quarrelled so much it wore itself out."

"I think I'd like them. I'd probably like them very much."

"Let's not talk about them or I'll start to worry about them." After a while I said, "Let's go on if you're rested."

"I'm rested."

We went on down the road. It was dark now and the snow squeaked under our boots. The night was dry and cold and very clear.

"I love your beard," Catherine said. "It's a great success. It looks so stiff and fierce and it's very soft and a great pleasure."

"Do you like it better than without?"

"I think so. You know, darling, I'm not going to cut my hair now until after young Catherine's born. I look too big and matronly now. But after she's born and I'm thin again I'm going to cut it and then I'll be a fine new and different girl for you. We'll go together and get it cut, or I'll go alone and come and surprise you."

I did not say anything.

"You won't say I can't, will you?"

"No. I think it would be exciting."

"Oh, you're so sweet. And maybe I'd look lovely, darling, and be so thin and exciting to you and you'll fall in love with me all over again."

"Hell," I said, "I love you enough now. What do you want to do? Ruin me?"

"Yes. I want to ruin you."

"Good," I said, "that's what I want too."

CHAPTER 40

WE HAD a fine life. We lived through the months of January and February and the winter was very fine and we were very happy. There had been short thaws when the wind blew warm and the snow softened and the air felt like spring, but always the clear hard cold had come again and the winter had returned. In March came the first break in the winter. In the night it started raining. It rained on all morning and turned the snow to slush and made the mountain-side dismal. There were clouds over the lake and over the valley. It was raining high up the mountain. Catherine wore heavy overshoes and I wore Mr. Guttingen's rubber-boots and we walked to the station under an umbrella, through the slush and the running water that was washing the ice of the roads bare, to stop at the pub before lunch for a vermouth. Outside we could hear the rain.

"Do you think we ought to move into town?"

"What do you think?" Catherine asked.

"If the winter is over and the rain keeps up it won't be fun up here. How long is it before young Catherine?"

"About a month. Perhaps a little more."

"We might go down and stay in Montreux."

"Why don't we go to Lausanne? That's where the hospital is."

"All right. But I thought maybe that was too big a town."

"We can be as much alone in a bigger town and Lausanne might be nice."

"When should we go?"

"I don't care. Whenever you want, darling. I don't want to leave here if you don't want."

"Let's see how the weather turns out."

It rained for three days. The snow was all gone now on the mountain-side below the station. The road was a torrent of muddy snow-water. It was too wet and slushy to go out. On the morning of the third day of rain we decided to go down into town.

"That is all right, Mr. Henry," Guttingen said. "You do not have to give me any notice. I did not think you would want to stay now the bad weather is come."

"We have to be near the hospital anyway on account of Madame," I said.

"I understand," he said. "Will you come back some time and stay, with the little one?"

"Yes, if you would have room."

"In the spring when it is nice you could come and enjoy it. We could put the little one and the nurse in the big room that is closed now and you and Madame could have your same room looking out over the lake."

"I'll write about coming," I said. We packed and left on the train that went down after lunch. Mr. and Mrs. Guttingen came down to the station with us and he hauled our baggage down on a sled through the slush. They stood beside the station in the rain waving good-by.

"They were very sweet," Catherine said.

"They were fine to us."

We took the train to Lausanne from Montreux. Looking out the window toward where we had lived you could not see the mountains for the clouds. The train stopped in Vevey, then went on, passing the lake on one side and on the other the wet brown fields and the bare woods and the wet houses. We came into Lausanne and went into a medium-sized hotel to stay. It was still raining as we drove through the streets and into the carriage entrance of the hotel. The concierge with brass keys on his lapels, the elevator, the carpets on the floors, and the white washbowls with shining fixtures, the brass bed and the big comfortable bedroom all seemed very great luxury after the Guttingens. The windows of the room looked out on a wet garden with a wall topped by an iron fence. Across the street, which sloped steeply, was another hotel with a similar wall and garden. I looked out at the rain falling in the fountain of the garden.

Catherine turned on all the lights and commenced unpacking. I ordered a whiskey and soda and lay on the bed and read the papers I had bought at the station. It was March, 1918, and the German offensive had started in France. I drank the whiskey and soda and read while Catherine unpacked and moved around the room.

"You know what I have to get, darling," she said.

"What?"

"Baby clothes. There aren't many people reach my time without baby things."

"You can buy them."

"I know. That's what I'll do to-morrow. I'll find out what is necessary."

"You ought to know. You were a nurse."

"But so few of the soldiers had babies in the hospitals."

"I did."

She hit me with the pillow and spilled the whiskey and soda.

"I'll order you another," she said. "I'm sorry I spilled it."

"There wasn't much left. Come on over to the bed."

"No. I have to try and make this room look like something."

"Like what?"

"Like our home."

"Hang out the Allied flags."

"Oh shut up."

"Say it again."

"Shut up."

"You say it so cautiously," I said. "As though you didn't want to offend any one."

"I don't."

"Then come over to the bed."

"All right." She came and sat on the bed. "I know I'm no fun for you, darling. I'm like a big flour-barrel."

"No you're not. You're beautiful and you're sweet."

"I'm just something very ungainly that you've married."

"No you're not. You're more beautiful all the time."

"But I will be thin again, darling."

"You're thin now."

"You've been drinking."

"Just whiskey and soda."

"There's another one coming," she said. "And then should we order dinner up here?"

"That will be good."

"Then we won't go out, will we? We'll just stay in to-night."

"And play," I said.

"I'll drink some wine," Catherine said. "It won't hurt me. Maybe we can get some of our old white capri."

"I know we can," I said. "They'll have Italian wines at a hotel this size."

The waiter knocked at the door. He brought the whiskey in a glass with ice and beside the glass on a tray a small bottle of soda.

"Thank you," I said. "Put it down there. Will you please have dinner for two brought up here and two bottles of dry white capri in ice."

"Do you wish to commence your dinner with soup?"

"Do you want soup, Cat?"

"Please."

"Bring soup for one."

"Thank you, sir." He went out and shut the door. I went back to the papers and the war in the papers and poured the soda slowly over the ice into the whiskey. I would have to tell them not to put ice in the whiskey. Let them bring the ice separately. That way you could tell how much whiskey there was and it would not suddenly be too thin from the soda. I would get a bottle of whiskey and have them bring ice and soda. That was the sensible way. Good whiskey was very pleasant. It was one of the pleasant parts of life.

"What are you thinking, darling?"

"About whiskey."

"What about whiskey?"

"About how nice it is."

Catherine made a face. "All right," she said.

We stayed at that hotel three weeks. It was not bad; the dining-room was usually empty and very often we ate in our room at night. We walked in the town and took the cogwheel railway down to Ouchy and walked beside the lake. The weather became quite warm and it was like spring. We wished we were back in the mountains but the spring weather lasted only a few days and then the cold rawness of the breaking-up of winter came again.

Catherine bought the things she needed for the baby, up in the town. I went to a gymnasium in the arcade to box for exercise. I usually went up there in the morning while Catherine stayed late in bed. On the days of false spring it was very nice, after boxing and taking a shower, to walk along the streets smelling the spring in the air and stop at a café to sit and watch the people and read the paper and drink a vermouth; then go down to the hotel and have lunch with Catherine. The professor at the boxing gymnasium wore mustaches and was very precise and jerky and went all to pieces if you started after him. But it was pleasant in the gym. There was good air and light and I worked quite hard, skipping rope, shadow-boxing, doing abdominal exercises lying on the floor in a patch of sunlight that came through the open window, and occasionally scaring the professor when we boxed. I could not shadow-box in front of the narrow long mirror at first because it looked so strange to see a man with a beard boxing. But finally I just thought it was funny. I wanted to take off the beard as soon as I started boxing but Catherine did not want me to.

Sometimes Catherine and I went for rides out in the country in a carriage. It was nice to ride when the days were pleasant and we found two good places where we could ride out to eat. Catherine could not walk very far now and I loved to ride out along the country roads with her. When there was a good day we had a splendid time and we never had a bad time. We knew the baby was very close now and it gave us both a feeling as though something were hurrying us and we could not lose any time together.

CHAPTER 41

ONE MORNING I awoke about three o'clock hearing Catherine stirring in the bed.

"Are you all right, Cat?"

"I've been having some pains, darling."

"Regularly?" –

"No, not very."

"If you have them at all regularly we'll go to the hospital."

I was very sleepy and went back to sleep. A little while later I woke again.

"Maybe you'd better call up the doctor," Catherine said. "I think maybe this is it."

I went to the phone and called the doctor. "How often are the pains coming?" he asked.

"How often are they coming, Cat?"

"I should think every quarter of an hour."

"You should go to the hospital, then," the doctor said. "I will dress and go there right away myself."

I hung up and called the garage near the station to send up a taxi. No one answered the phone for a long time. Then I finally got a man who promised to send up a taxi at once. Catherine was dressing. Her bag was all packed with the things she would need at the hospital and the baby things. Outside in the hall I rang for the elevator. There was no answer. I went downstairs. There was no one downstairs except the night-watchman. I brought the elevator up myself, put Catherine's bag in it, she stepped in and we went down. The night-watchman opened the door for us and we sat outside on the stone slabs beside the stairs down to the driveway and waited for the taxi. The night was clear and the stars were out. Catherine was very excited.

"I'm so glad it's started," she said. "Now in a little while it will be all over."

"You're a good brave girl."

"I'm not afraid. I wish the taxi would come, though."

We heard it coming up the street and saw its headlights. It turned into the driveway and I helped Catherine in and the driver put the bag up in front.

"Drive to the hospital," I said.

We went out of the driveway and started up the hill.

At the hospital we went in and I carried the bag. There was a woman at the desk who wrote down Catherine's name, age, address, relatives and religion, in a book. She said she had no religion and the woman drew a line in the space after that word. She gave her name as Catherine Henry.

"I will take you up to your room," she said. We went up in an elevator. The woman stopped it and we stepped out and followed her down a hall. Catherine held tight to my arm.

"This is the room," the woman said. "Will you please undress and get into bed? Here is a night-gown for you to wear."

"I have a night-gown," Catherine said.

"It is better for you to wear this night-gown," the woman said.

I went outside and sat on a chair in the hallway.

"You can come in now," the woman said from the doorway. Catherine was lying in the narrow bed wearing a plain, square-cut night-gown that looked as though it were made of rough sheeting. She smiled at me.

"I'm having fine pains now," she said. The woman was holding her wrist and timing the pains with a watch.

"That was a big one," Catherine said. I saw it on her face.

"Where's the doctor?" I asked the woman.

"He's lying down sleeping. He will be here when he is needed."

"I must do something for Madame, now," the nurse said. "Would you please step out again?"

I went out into the hall. It was a bare hall with two windows and closed doors all down the corridor. It smelled of hospital. I sat on the chair and looked at the floor and prayed for Catherine.

"You can come in," the nurse said. I went in.

"Hello, darling," Catherine said.

"How is it?"

"They are coming quite often now." Her face drew up. Then she smiled.

"That was a real one. Do you want to put your hand on my back again, nurse?"

"If it helps you," the nurse said.

"You go away, darling," Catherine said. "Go out and get something to eat. I may do this for a long time the nurse says."

"The first labor is usually protracted," the nurse said.

"Please go out and get something to eat," Catherine said. "I'm fine, really."

"I'll stay awhile," I said.

The pains came quite regularly, then slackened off. Catherine was very excited. When the pains were bad she called them good ones. When they started to fall off she was disappointed and ashamed.

"You go out, darling," she said. "I think you are just making me self-conscious." Her face tied up. "There. That was better. I so want to be a good wife and have this child without any foolishness. Please go and get some breakfast, darling, and then come back. I won't miss you. Nurse is splendid to me."

"You have plenty of time for breakfast," the nurse said.

"I'll go then. Good-by, sweet."

"Good-by," Catherine said, "and have a fine breakfast for me too."

"Where can I get breakfast?" I asked the nurse.

"There's a café down the street at the square," she said. "It should be open now."

Outside it was getting light. I walked down the empty street to the café. There was a light in the window. I went in and stood at the zinc bar and an old man served me a glass of white wine and a brioche. The brioche was yesterday's. I dipped it in the wine and then drank a glass of coffee.

"What do you do at this hour?" the old man asked.

"My wife is in labor at the hospital."

"So. I wish you good luck."

"Give me another glass of wine."

He poured it from the bottle slopping it over a little so some ran down on the zinc. I drank this glass, paid and went out. Outside along the street were the refuse cans from the houses waiting for the collector. A dog was nosing at one of the cans.

"What do you want?" I asked and looked in the can to see if there was anything I could pull out for him; there was nothing on top but coffee-grounds, dust and some dead flowers.

"There isn't anything, dog," I said. The dog crossed the street. I went up the stairs in the hospital to the floor Catherine was on and down the hall to her room. I knocked on the door. There was no answer. I opened the door; the room was empty, except for Catherine's bag on a chair and her dressing-gown hanging on a hook on the wall. I went out and down the hall, looking for somebody. I found a nurse.

"Where is Madame Henry?"

"A lady has just gone to the delivery room."

"Where is it?"

"I will show you."

She took me down to the end of the hall. The door of the room was partly open. I could see Catherine lying on a table, covered by a sheet. The nurse was on one side and the doctor stood on the other side of the table beside some cylinders. The doctor held a rubber mask attached to a tube in one hand.

"I will give you a gown and you can go in," the nurse said. "Come in here, please."

She put a white gown on me and pinned it at the neck in back with a safety pin.

"Now you can go in," she said. I went into the room.

"Hello, darling," Catherine said in a strained voice. "I'm not doing much."

"You are Mr. Henry?" the doctor asked.

"Yes. How is everything going, doctor?"

"Things are going very well," the doctor said. "We came in here where it is easy to give gas for the pains."

"I want it now," Catherine said. The doctor placed the rubber mask over her face and turned a dial and I watched Catherine breathing deeply and rapidly. Then she pushed the mask away. The doctor shut off the petcock.

"That wasn't a very big one. I had a very big one a while ago. The doctor made me go clear out, didn't you, doctor?" Her voice was strange. It rose on the word doctor.

The doctor smiled.

"I want it again," Catherine said. She held the rubber tight to her face and breathed fast. I heard her moaning a little. Then she pulled the mask away and smiled.

"That was a big one," she said. "That was a very big one. Don't you worry, darling. You go away. Go have another breakfast."

"I'll stay," I said.

We had gone to the hospital about three o'clock in the morning. At noon Catherine was still in the delivery room. The pains had slackened again. She looked very tired and worn now but she was still cheerful.

"I'm not any good, darling," she said. "I'm so sorry. I thought I would do it very easily. Now – there's one–" she reached out her hand for the mask and held it over her face. The doctor moved the dial and watched her. In a little while it was over.

"It wasn't much," Catherine said. She smiled. "I'm a fool about the gas. It's wonderful."

"We'll get some for the home," I said.

"There one comes," Catherine said quickly. The doctor turned the dial and looked at his watch.

"What is the interval now?" I asked.

"About a minute."

"Don't you want lunch?"

"I will have something pretty soon," he said.

"You must have something to eat, doctor," Catherine said. "I'm so sorry I go on so long. Couldn't my husband give me the gas?"

"If you wish," the doctor said. "You turn it to the numeral two."

"I see," I said. There was a marker on a dial that turned with a handle.

"I want it now," Catherine said. She held the mask tight to her face. I turned the dial to number two and when Catherine put down the mask I turned it off. It was very good of the doctor to let me do something.

"Did you do it, darling?" Catherine asked. She stroked my wrist.

"Sure."

"You're so lovely." She was a little drunk from the gas.

"I will eat from a tray in the next room," the doctor said. "You can call me any moment." While the time passed I watched him eat, then, after a while, I saw that he was lying down and smoking a cigarette. Catherine was getting very tired.

"Do you think I'll ever have this baby?" she asked.

"Yes, of course you will."

"I try as hard as I can. I push down but it goes away. There it comes. Give it to me."

At two o'clock I went out and had lunch. There were a few men in the café sitting with coffee and glasses of kirsch or marc on the tables. I sat down at a table. "Can I eat?" I asked the waiter.

"It is past time for lunch."

"Isn't there anything for all hours?"

"You can have choucroute."

"Give me choucroute and beer."

"A demi or a bock?"

"A light demi."

The waiter brought a dish of sauerkraut with a slice of ham over the top and a sausage buried in the hot wine-soaked cabbage. I ate it and drank the beer. I was very hungry. I watched the people at the tables in the café. At one table they were playing cards. Two men at the table next me were talking and smoking. The café was full of smoke. The zinc bar, where I had breakfasted, had three people behind it now; the old man, a plump woman in a black dress who sat behind a counter and kept track of everything served to the tables, and a boy in an apron. I wondered how many children the woman had and what it had been like.

When I was through with the choucroute I went back to the hospital. The street was all clean now. There were no refuse cans out. The day was cloudy but the sun was trying to come through.

I rode upstairs in the elevator, stepped out and went down the hall to Catherine's room, where I had left my white gown. I put it on and pinned it in back at the neck. I looked in the glass and saw myself looking like a fake doctor with a beard. I went down the hall to the delivery room. The door was closed and I knocked. No one answered so I turned the handle and went in. The doctor sat by Catherine. The nurse was doing something at the other end of the room.

"Here is your husband," the doctor said.

"Oh, darling, I have the most wonderful doctor," Catherine said in a very strange voice. "He's been telling me the most wonderful story and when the pain came too badly he put me all the way out. He's wonderful. You're wonderful, doctor."

"You're drunk," I said.

"I know it," Catherine said. "But you shouldn't say it." Then "Give it to me. Give it to me." She clutched hold of the mask and breathed short and deep, pantingly, making the respirator click. Then she gave a long sigh and the doctor reached with his left hand and lifted away the mask.

"That was a very big one," Catherine said. Her voice was very strange. "I'm not going to die now, darling. I'm past where I was going to die. Aren't you glad?"

"Don't you get in that place again."

"I won't. I'm not afraid of it though. I won't die, darling."

"You will not do any such foolishness," the doctor said. "You would not die and leave your husband."

"Oh, no. I won't die. I wouldn't die. It's silly to die. There it comes. Give it to me."

After a while the doctor said, "You will go out, Mr. Henry, for a few moments and I will make an examination."

"He wants to see how I am doing," Catherine said. "You can come back afterward, darling, can't he, doctor?"

"Yes," said the doctor. "I will send word when he can come back."

I went out the door and down the hall to the room where Catherine was to be after the baby came. I sat in a chair there and looked at the room. I had the paper in my coat that I had bought when I went out for lunch and I read it. It was beginning to be dark outside and I turned the light on to read. After a while I stopped reading and turned off the light and watched it get dark outside. I wondered why the doctor did not send for me. Maybe it was better I was away. He probably wanted me away for a while. I looked at my watch. If he did not send for me in ten minutes I would go down anyway.

Poor, poor dear Cat. And this was the price you paid for sleeping together. This was the end of the trap. This was what people got for loving each other. Thank God for gas, anyway. What must it have been like before there were anæsthetics? Once it started, they were in the mill-race. Catherine had a good time in the time of pregnancy. It wasn't bad. She was hardly ever sick. She was not awfully uncomfortable until toward the last. So now they got her in the end. You never got away with anything. Get away hell! It would have been the same if we had been married fifty times. And what if she should die? She won't die. People don't die in childbirth nowadays. That was what all husbands thought. Yes, but what if she should die? She won't die. She's just having a bad time. The initial labor is usually protracted. She's only having a bad time. Afterward we'd say what a bad time and Catherine would say it wasn't really so bad. But what if she should die? She can't die. Yes, but what if she should die? She can't, I tell you. Don't be a fool. It's just a bad time. It's just nature giving her hell. It's only the first labor, which is almost always protracted. Yes, but what if she should die? She can't die. Why would she die? What reason is there for her to die? There's just a child that has to be born, the by-product of good nights in Milan. It makes trouble and is born and then you look after it and get fond of it maybe. But what if she should die? She won't die. But what if she should die? She won't. She's all right. But what if she should die? She can't die. But what if she should die? Hey, what about that? What if she should die?

The doctor came into the room.

"How does it go, doctor?"

"It doesn't go," he said.

"What do you mean?"

"Just that. I made an examination—" He detailed the result of the examination. "Since then I've waited to see. But it doesn't go."

"What do you advise?"

"There are two things. Either a high forceps delivery which can tear and be quite dangerous besides being possibly bad for the child, and a Cæsarean."

"What is the danger of a Cæsarean?" What if she should die!

"It should be no greater than the danger of an ordinary delivery."

"Would you do it yourself?"

"Yes. I would need possibly an hour to get things ready and to get the people I would need. Perhaps a little less."

"What do you think?"

"I would advise a Cæsarean operation. If it were my wife I would do a Cæsarean."

"What are the after effects?"

"There are none. There is only the scar."

"What about infection?"

"The danger is not so great as in a high forceps delivery."

"What if you just went on and did nothing?"

"You would have to do something eventually. Mrs. Henry is already losing much of her strength. The sooner we operate now the safer."

"Operate as soon as you can," I said.

"I will go and give the instructions."

I went into the delivery room. The nurse was with Catherine who lay on the table, big under the sheet, looking very pale and tired.

"Did you tell him he could do it?" she asked.

"Yes."

"Isn't that grand. Now it will be all over in an hour. I'm almost done, darling. I'm going all to pieces. Please give me that. It doesn't work. Oh, it doesn't work!"

"Breathe deeply."

"I am. Oh, it doesn't work any more. It doesn't work!"

"Get another cylinder," I said to the nurse.

"That is a new cylinder."

"I'm just a fool, darling," Catherine said. "But it doesn't work any more." She began to cry. "Oh, I wanted so to have this baby and not make trouble, and now I'm all done and all gone to pieces and it doesn't work. Oh, darling, it doesn't work at all. I don't care if I die if it will only stop. Oh, please, darling, please make it stop. There it comes. Oh Oh Oh!" She breathed sobbingly in the mask. "It doesn't work. It doesn't work. It doesn't work. Don't mind me, darling. Please don't cry. Don't mind me. I'm just gone all to pieces. You poor sweet. I love you so and I'll be good again. I'll be good this time. Can't they give me something? If they could only give me something."

"I'll make it work. I'll turn it all the way."

"Give it to me now."

I turned the dial all the way and as she breathed hard and deep her hand relaxed on the mask. I shut off the gas and lifted the mask. She came back from a long way away.

"That was lovely, darling. Oh, you're so good to me."

"You be brave, because I can't do that all the time. It might kill you."

"I'm not brave any more, darling. I'm all broken. They've broken me. I know it now."

"Everybody is that way."

"But it's awful. They just keep it up till they break you."

"In an hour it will be over."

"Isn't that lovely? Darling, I won't die, will I?"

"No. I promise you won't."

"Because I don't want to die and leave you, but I get so tired of it and I feel I'm going to die."

"Nonsense. Everybody feels that."

"Sometimes I know I'm going to die."

"You won't. You can't."

"But what if I should?"

"I won't let you."

"Give it to me quick. Give it to me!"

Then afterward, "I won't die. I won't let myself die."

"Of course you won't."

"You'll stay with me?"

"Not to watch it."

"No, just to be there."

"Sure. I'll be there all the time."

"You're so good to me. There, give it to me. Give me some more. It's not working!"

I turned the dial to three and then four. I wished the doctor would come back. I was afraid of the numbers above two.

Finally a new doctor came in with two nurses and they lifted Catherine onto a wheeled stretcher and we started down the hall. The stretcher went rapidly down the hall and into the elevator where every one had to crowd against the wall to make room; then up, then an open door and out of the elevator and down the hall on rubber wheels to the operating room. I did not recognize the doctor with his cap and mask on. There was another doctor and more nurses.

"They've got to give me something," Catherine said. "They've got to give me something. Oh please, doctor, give me enough to do some good!"

One of the doctors put a mask over her face and I looked through the door and saw the bright small amphitheatre of the operating room.

"You can go in the other door and sit up there," a nurse said to me. There were benches behind a rail that looked down on the white table and the lights. I looked at Catherine. The mask was over her face and she was quiet now. They wheeled the stretcher forward. I turned away and walked down the hall. Two nurses were hurrying toward the entrance to the gallery.

"It's a Cæsarean," one said. "They're going to do a Cæsarean."

The other one laughed, "We're just in time. Aren't we lucky?" They went in the door that led to the gallery.

Another nurse came along. She was hurrying too.

"You go right in there. Go right in," she said.

"I'm staying outside."

She hurried in. I walked up and down the hall. I was afraid to go in. I looked out the window. It was dark but in the light from the window I could see it was raining. I went into a room at the far end of the hall and looked at the labels on bottles in a glass case. Then I came out and stood in the empty hall and watched the door of the operating room.

A doctor came out followed by a nurse. He held something in his two hands that looked like a freshly skinned rabbit and hurried across the corridor with it and in through another door. I went down to the door he had gone into and found them in the room doing things to a new-born child. The doctor held him up for me to see. He held him by the heels and slapped him.

"Is he all right?"

"He's magnificent. He'll weigh five kilos."

I had no feeling for him. He did not seem to have anything to do with me. I felt no feeling of fatherhood.

"Aren't you proud of your son?" the nurse asked. They were washing him and wrapping him in something. I saw the little dark face and dark hand, but I did not see him move or hear him cry. The doctor was doing something to him again. He looked upset.

"No," I said. "He nearly killed his mother."

"It isn't the little darling's fault. Didn't you want a boy?"

"No," I said. The doctor was busy with him. He held him up by the feet and slapped him. I did not wait to see it. I went out in the hall. I could go in now and see. I went in the door and a little way down the gallery. The nurses who were sitting at the rail motioned for me to come down where they were. I shook my head. I could see enough where I was.

I thought Catherine was dead. She looked dead. Her face was gray, the part of it that I could see. Down below, under the light, the doctor was sewing up the great long, forcep-spread, thick-edged wound. Another doctor in a mask gave the anæsthetic. Two nurses in masks handed things. It looked like a drawing of the Inquisition. I knew as I watched I could have watched it all, but I was glad I hadn't. I do not think I could have watched them cut, but I watched the wound closed into a high welted ridge with quick skilful-looking stitches like a cobbler's, and was glad. When the wound was closed I went out into the hall and walked up and down again. After a while the doctor came out.

"How is she?"

"She is all right. Did you watch?"

He looked tired.

"I saw you sew up. The incision looked very long."

"You thought so?"

"Yes. Will that scar flatten out?"

"Oh, yes."

After a while they brought out the wheeled stretcher and took it very rapidly down the hallway to the elevator. I went along beside it. Catherine was moaning. Downstairs they put her in the bed in her room. I sat in a chair at the foot of the bed. There was a nurse in the room. I got up and stood by the bed. It was dark in the room. Catherine put out her hand. "Hello, darling," she said. Her voice was very weak and tired.

"Hello, you sweet."

"What sort of baby was it?"

"Sh – don't talk," the nurse said.

"A boy. He's long and wide and dark."

"Is he all right?"

"Yes," I said. "He's fine."

I saw the nurse look at me strangely.

"I'm awfully tired," Catherine said. "And I hurt like hell. Are you all right, darling?"

"I'm fine. Don't talk."

"You were lovely to me. Oh, darling, I hurt dreadfully. What does he look like?"

"He looks like a skinned rabbit with a puckered-up old-man's face."

"You must go out," the nurse said. "Madame Henry must not talk."

"I'll be outside."

"Go and get something to eat."

"No. I'll be outside." I kissed Catherine. She was very gray and weak and tired.

"May I speak to you?" I said to the nurse. She came out in the hall with me. I walked a little way down the hall.

"What's the matter with the baby?" I asked.

"Didn't you know?"

"No."

"He wasn't alive."

"He was dead?"

"They couldn't start him breathing. The cord was caught around his neck or something."

"So he's dead."

"Yes. It's such a shame. He was such a fine big boy. I thought you knew."

"No," I said. "You better go back in with Madame."

I sat down on the chair in front of a table where there were nurses' reports hung on clips at the side and looked out of the window. I could see nothing but the dark and the rain falling across the light from the window. So that was it. The baby was dead. That was why the doctor looked so tired. But why had they acted the way they did in the room with him? They supposed he would come around and start breathing probably. I had no religion but I knew he ought to have been baptized. But what if he never breathed at all. He hadn't. He had never been alive. Except in Catherine. I'd felt him kick there often enough. But I hadn't for a week. Maybe he was choked all the time. Poor little kid. I wished the hell I'd been choked like that. No I didn't. Still there would not be all this dying to go through. Now Catherine would die. That was what you did. You died. You did not know what it was about. You never had time to learn. They threw you in and told you the rules and the first time they caught you off base they killed you. Or they killed you gratuitously like Aymo. Or gave you the syphilis like Rinaldi. But they killed you in the end. You could count on that. Stay around and they would kill you.

Once in camp I put a log on top of the fire and it was full of ants. As it commenced to burn, the ants swarmed out and went first toward the centre where the fire was; then turned back and ran toward the end. When there were enough on the end they fell off into the fire. Some got out, their bodies burnt and flattened, and went off not knowing where they were going. But most of them went toward the fire and then back toward the end and swarmed on the cool end and finally fell off into the fire. I remember thinking at the time that it was the end of the world and a splendid chance to be a messiah and lift the log off the fire and throw it out where the ants could get off onto the ground. But I did not do anything but throw a tin cup of water on the log, so that I would have the cup empty to put whiskey in before I added water to it. I think the cup of water on the burning log only steamed the ants.

So now I sat out in the hall and waited to hear how Catherine was. The nurse did not come out, so after a while I went to the door and opened it very softly and looked in. I could not see at first because there was a bright light in the hall and it was dark in the room. Then I saw the nurse sitting by the bed and Catherine's head on a pillow, and she was all flat under the sheet. The nurse put her finger to her lips, then stood up and came to the door.

"How is she?" I asked.

"She's all right," the nurse said. "You should go and have your supper and then come back if you wish."

I went down the hall and then down the stairs and out the door of the hospital and down the dark street in the rain to the café. It was brightly lighted inside and there were many people at the tables. I did not see a place to sit, and a waiter came up to me and took my wet coat and hat and showed me a place at a table across from an elderly man who was drinking beer and reading the evening paper. I sat down and asked the waiter what the plat du jour was.

"Veal stew – but it is finished."

"What can I have to eat?"

"Ham and eggs, eggs with cheese, or choucroute."

"I had choucroute this noon," I said.

"That's true," he said. "That's true. You ate choucroute this noon." He was a middle-aged man with a bald top to his head and his hair slicked over it. He had a kind face.

"What do you want? Ham and eggs or eggs with cheese?"

"Ham and eggs," I said, "and beer."

"A demi-blonde?"

"Yes," I said.

"I remembered," he said. "You took a demi-blonde this noon."

I ate the ham and eggs and drank the beer. The ham and eggs were in a round dish – the ham underneath and the eggs on top. It was very hot and at the first mouthful I had to take a drink of beer to cool my mouth. I was hungry and I asked the waiter for another order. I drank several glasses of beer. I was not thinking at all but read the paper of the man opposite me. It was about the break through on the British front. When he realized I was reading the back of his paper he folded it over. I thought of asking the waiter for a paper, but I could not concentrate. It was hot in the café and the air was bad. Many of the people at the tables knew one another. There were several card games going on. The waiters were busy bringing drinks from the bar to the tables. Two men came in and could find no place to sit. They stood opposite the table where I was. I ordered another beer. I was not ready to leave yet. It was too soon to go back to the hospital. I tried not to think and to be perfectly calm. The men stood around but no one was leaving, so they went out. I drank another beer. There was quite a pile of saucers now on the table in front of me. The man opposite me had taken off his spectacles, put them away in a case, folded his paper and put it in his pocket and now sat holding his liqueur glass and looking out at the room. Suddenly I knew I had to get back. I called the waiter, paid the reckoning, got into my coat, put on my hat and started out the door. I walked through the rain up to the hospital.

Upstairs I met the nurse coming down the hall.

"I just called you at the hotel," she said. Something dropped inside me.

"What is wrong?"

"Mrs. Henry has had a hemorrhage."

"Can I go in?"

"No, not yet. The doctor is with her."

"Is it dangerous?"

"It is very dangerous." The nurse went into the room and shut the door. I sat outside in the hall. Everything was gone inside of me. I did not think. I could not think. I knew she was going to die and I prayed that she would not. Don't let her die. Oh, God, please don't let her die. I'll do anything for you if you won't let her die. Please, please, please, dear God, don't let her die. Dear God, don't let her die. Please, please, please don't let her die. God please make her not die. I'll do anything you say if you don't let her die. You took the baby but don't let her die. That was all right but don't let her die. Please, please, dear God, don't let her die.

The nurse opened the door and motioned with her finger for me to come. I followed her into the room. Catherine did not look up when I came in. I went over to the side of the bed. The doctor was standing by the bed on the opposite side. Catherine looked at me and smiled. I bent down over the bed and started to cry.

"Poor darling," Catherine said very softly. She looked gray.

"You're all right, Cat," I said. "You're going to be all right."

"I'm going to die," she said; then waited and said, "I hate it."

I took her hand.

"Don't touch me," she said. I let go of her hand. She smiled. "Poor darling. You touch me all you want."

"You'll be all right, Cat. I know you'll be all right."

"I meant to write you a letter to have if anything happened, but I didn't do it."

"Do you want me to get a priest or any one to come and see you?"

"Just you," she said. Then a little later, "I'm not afraid. I just hate it."

"You must not talk so much," the doctor said.

"All right," Catherine said.

"Do you want me to do anything, Cat? Can I get you anything?"

Catherine smiled, "No." Then a little later, "You won't do our things with another girl, or say the same things, will you?"

"Never."

"I want you to have girls, though."

"I don't want them."

"You are talking too much," the doctor said. "Mr. Henry must go out. He can come back again later. You are not going to die. You must not be silly."

"All right," Catherine said. "I'll come and stay with you nights," she said. It was very hard for her to talk.

"Please go out of the room," the doctor said. "You cannot talk." Catherine winked at me, her face gray. "I'll be right outside," I said.

"Don't worry, darling," Catherine said. "I'm not a bit afraid. It's just a dirty trick."

"You dear, brave sweet."

I waited outside in the hall. I waited a long time. The nurse came to the door and came over to me. "I'm afraid Mrs. Henry is very ill," she said. "I'm afraid for her."

"Is she dead?"

"No, but she is unconscious."

It seems she had one hemorrhage after another. They couldn't stop it. I went into the room and stayed with Catherine until she died. She was unconscious all the time, and it did not take her very long to die.

Outside the room, in the hall, I spoke to the doctor, "Is there anything I can do to-night?"

"No. There is nothing to do. Can I take you to your hotel?"

"No, thank you. I am going to stay here a while."

"I know there is nothing to say. I cannot tell you – –"

"No," I said. "There's nothing to say."

"Good-night," he said. "I cannot take you to your hotel?"

"No, thank you."

"It was the only thing to do," he said. "The operation proved – –"

"I do not want to talk about it," I said.

"I would like to take you to your hotel."

"No, thank you."

He went down the hall. I went to the door of the room.

"You can't come in now," one of the nurses said.

"Yes I can," I said.

"You can't come in yet."

"You get out," I said. "The other one too."

But after I had got them out and shut the door and turned off the light it wasn't any good. It was like saying good-by to a statue. After a while I went out and left the hospital and walked back to the hotel in the rain.

THE END

www.ingramcontent.com/pod-product-compliance
Ingram Content Group UK Ltd.
Pitfield, Milton Keynes, MK11 3LW, UK
UKHW021608050125
453025UK00008B/124

9 781515 463085